CU00647460

THE
MILAN
BRIEFCASE

THE
MILAN
BRIEFCASE

Graham Fulbright

Copyright © 2017 Graham Fulbright

The moral right of the author has been asserted.

Apart from any fair dealing for the purposes of research or private study,
or criticism or review, as permitted under the Copyright, Designs and Patents
Act 1988, this publication may only be reproduced, stored or transmitted, in
any form or by any means, with the prior permission in writing of the
publishers, or in the case of reprographic reproduction in accordance with
the terms of licences issued by the Copyright Licensing Agency. Enquiries
concerning reproduction outside those terms should be sent to the publishers.

This is a work of fiction. Names, characters, businesses, places, events
and incidents are either the products of the author's imagination
or used in a fictitious manner. Any resemblance to actual persons,
living or dead, or actual events is purely coincidental.

Matador
9 Priory Business Park,
Wistow Road, Kibworth Beauchamp,
Leicestershire. LE8 0RX
Tel: 0116 279 2299
Email: books@troubador.co.uk
Web: www.troubador.co.uk/matador
Twitter: @matadorbooks

ISBN 978 1785898 686

British Library Cataloguing in Publication Data.
A catalogue record for this book is available from the British Library.

Printed and bound by CPI Group (UK) Ltd, Croydon, CR0 4YY
Typeset in 10pt Aldine401 BT by Troubador Publishing Ltd, Leicester, UK

Matador is an imprint of Troubador Publishing Ltd

'Three things cannot hide for long: the Moon, the Sun and the Truth.' Gautama Buddha

For Tamara and Guy

E vents would have taken a different turn, had Justin not hailed that London minicab. But let's not get ahead of things, because, despite the fashion for shuttling the reader in and out between past, present and future corridors, it makes more sense to begin at the beginning in a corner of north-western Europe familiarly known as Luritania.

They started out as a quartet: three men (Tich – the group's founder and doyen – Justin and Craig) and one woman (Vanessa). The habit of meeting for Sunday morning breakfast in Luritania's Lenfindi Airport passenger terminal was Tich's idea. Why there of all places? Perhaps, suggested Justin, because of the contradictory pull of escapism and rootedness: while others thronged to board aircraft to distant places, the quartet dropped anchor in a breakfast island remote from acquaintances for whom eight o'clock on a Sunday morning was an ungodly hour to be up and about.

On this particular Sunday, the advent of Rashid Jabour, a young development finance banker, brought the group to the desired complement of five, prompting Craig, once everybody had settled down, to make a recommendation.

'I propose celebrating Rashid's arrival by giving our club a name.'

Humphrey Robert Hobart aka Tich, a broad-shouldered, forty-year-old bear of a man with a well-tended auburn beard, reacted to Craig's idea by ruffling demurral from his thatch of red hair.

'Is that really necessary? I trust you're not thinking of The Famous Five. Atrocious and somebody else's intellectual property.'

'Apart from which,' said Vanessa Curtis, stirring powdered cinnamon into her cappuccino, 'who gives a fuck about fame?'

If Rashid, the newcomer, was taken aback by this bluntness from the mouth of the raven-haired young woman to whose charms he felt far from insensitive, Tich and the others failed to bat an eyelid. It was a further element for the young banker to digest in his character reading of the female time-study engineer recruited by the European Executive Committee to spearhead its rationalisation drive. Before Vanessa and Justin arrived at their breakfast table, Craig had imparted three other nuggets to Rashid: Vanessa was a gifted amateur theatrical director; the only person in present company entitled to call her Van was Tich, owner of Luritania's sole secondhand bookshop; she and Justin had been and probably still were more than close friends.

'A jest, Van,' said Tich, raising his stentorian voice above the ceaseless chatter of a nearby group of South Koreans competing with the din of the latest flight departure announcement. 'Your tender generation will not, I suppose, have heard of a children's writer by the name of Enid Blyton, who incorporated that title into a number of her tales. Another reason why it wouldn't suit us is that Blyton's group comprised two lads, two girls and a dog.'

1

'Enid. Not quite in the same category as *The Aeneid?*'

Tich cut himself a slice of almond croissant.' 'No, epic poems were not Miss Blyton's forte.'

Justin broke away from his fixation on the logo on the tail wing of a *Dragonair* Boeing taxiing prior to take off for Hong Kong. 'What was the dog called?'

For once, the book buff looked as if he might have been stumped, but it took only a moment's hesitation to correct that impression. 'Timmy. Rhymes with your ferret, Pliny.'

Rashid expressed surprise. 'A ferret?'

'Yes,' said Craig. 'A likeable creature. Justin occasionally brings it along to our meetings – draped around his neck.'

Justin eased himself back in his seat. 'But, Rashid, I spare people the spectacle of feeding time. Pliny's preferred diet consists of live mice and young rabbits. They keep him healthy. And sociable. When awake. Ferrets spend a good part of the day sleeping. Not as long as a Koala bear but a respectable second.'

'Talking about down under,' said Tich, 'I had a couple of Sheilas in my shop yesterday. Upbraided them for never having heard of Patrick White. Got paid back by being told I'd have more customers if I sold BLTs and milk shakes.'

Craig looked up from his green tea. 'You never thought of doing that?'

'To be honest, yes. But as it would mean employing a full-time help, which I am not prepared to do, and cutting back on space better given over to books, I prefer attracting into my emporium solely those hungering and thirsting after literature.'

Vanessa turned to Rashid. 'Tich lures customers into his dusty realm with the occasional themed window display. Last month, it was Indian literature. Salman Rushdie, V.S. Naipul, Arundhati Roy – joss sticks all over the place, four Kamasutra-rated statuettes – unnoticed by the decency commission – , posters of Vishnu and Shiva …'

Tich dusted icing sugar from his fingers. 'No one can accuse me of not trying. Perhaps my next move should be to teach punters to discriminate between a BLT and BLM.'

Justin leant forward. 'Don't tell me. Mayonnaise?'

'You disappoint me, my friend. Yet another untutored hick more familiar with bacon – I am, of course not referring to the philosopher and essayist but to the offcuts of a farmyard quadruped – than with Byatt, Lessing and Murdoch, that trio of giants among Britain's female literary luminaries.'

Vanessa rolled her eyes. 'I doubt whether Antonia, Doris or Iris would thank you for calling them giants.'

Craig tugged at both ear lobes. 'We've drifted off course. No naming suggestions?'

Vanessa brushed crumbs from her skirt. 'Please not *Solidarity*, already accounted for. And not *Ocean's Five*. Unless we're planning on robbing the casino down by the river. I don't think we are, are we?'

'Wouldn't one of you,' said Rashid, 'have to be called Ocean?'

Tich smoothed down a crumpled shirt front. 'Van's taking a dig at me. My grandfather's first name was Sinbad.'

'Seafaring blood in your veins?'

'Not the Samuel Taylor Coleridge variety. The nearest the old boy got to salt water was competing in sand yachting. As for me, the moment the sea turned choppy on a cross Channel ferry trip, my parents had one sick parrot on their hands. I'm a Eurotunnel shareholder.'

Craig looked across to Justin. 'Any ideas?'

'Not off the top of my head. But since you raised the matter, you've obviously thought of something.'

'Right, but I wanted to give the rest of you the chance to have a say first.'

Vanessa set down her coffee cup in order to add butter to a madeleine.

'Nonsense, Craig. Come on. Out with it.'

Before Craig could answer, Tich intervened. 'Hold on, Van. Your Proustian moment. Unless you've killed those memories stone dead with cow paste.'

'Memories? Fuck all in my case. Seeing as how I was raised on rock cakes and lemon meringue pie.'

'Good on you. Mind you, to be fair to Marcel, whose parents were no less miserly with Christian names than was their son with words, he got carried away by more than unbuttered sponge cake.'

'The Groundbreakers.'

Craig's sudden suggestion froze Vanessa's butter knife hand. 'Seriously, Craig? You see us as groundbreakers? Let's keep it unpretentious. The Sunday Quintet.'

'Sounds too much,' said Tich, 'as if we're into chamber music.'

'All right,' said Rashid. 'Since I seem to be responsible for upsetting the applecart, how about the Quondam Quartet?'

'Now,' said Vanessa in rapt admiration of Rashid's dense head of hair, which had something of the plushness of moleskin about it, 'that's real abnegation. Which is to say it stinks.'

'And what,' said Justin, 'would you suggest?'

'The Quarrelsome or bloody Quibbling Quintet.'

'I think,' said Tich, 'that the Quicksilver Quintet would be kinder for a club aiming to pull the rug from under the feet of civilisation as we know it. How about you, Justin?'

'The Quintessential Quintet? No, too much of a mouthful. Something simple – the Spoilers.'

'I agree,' said Craig. 'Groundbreakers is over the top. As we always meet here, why not the Lenfindi Quintet?'

'Well, hardly mind-shatteringly original,' said Tich. 'But closer to my idea, which was the Sunday Club.'

'And both,' said Vanessa, 'avoid the fucking grandiose. I mean, who are you kidding, Tich? Civilisation's got nothing to worry about from us.'

'I fear you are right, Van. Allowed the occasion to go to my head. If we're all agreed, let it be the Lenfindi Quintet.'

In fact, despite his concession to Craig's proposal, stubbornness would not permit Tich, the group's founder, to think of the five as anything other than the Sunday Club.

'Fine,' said Rashid. 'But, tell me, why did you advertise for additional members in Justin's newsletter?'

'We may have made it sound like that,' said Justin. 'But we wanted only one. To help break the decision-making deadlock we find ourselves up against whenever we're two for, two against a new idea.'

'Yes,' said Tich, 'perhaps I ought to explain the ground rules. We alternate on a monthly basis between matters of levity and enterprises of great pith and moment. You have joined us, you will be glad or upset to learn, at the beginning of a month of levity. Last month we started out by debating whether the Council of Europe was a waste of taxpayers' money. Motion carried three to one. Then we moved on to considering whether, if we had a vote, we would cast it in favour of America's answer to Golda Meir. Motion failed – all four against. That was followed by Brexit. Two for, two against. Abstentions, you will have understood, are taboo. And finally, one of us tabled the motion that neither Ukraine nor Turkey should be let anywhere near the European Union until they had radically cleaned up their acts. Motion carried unanimously.'

'I see. And how many responses did you get to your ad?'

'Eight.'

'Wow. And what, pray, caused you to choose me?'

'We're sorely lacking in advanced IT skills for enterprises of great pith and moment.'

'Come again?'

'Another of my jests. No, we welcomed the idea of widening our horizons with a Lebanese graduate of Caius College Cambridge.'

'And how did you come to form your club in the first place?'

'Tich's idea,' said Craig. 'I was a latecomer after bumping into Justin in the football stadium, where we were watching Luritania getting thrashed by France.'

'And Van and I first met,' said Tich, 'years ago, when she wandered into my shop one morning to ask my late wife if we had anything on Gurdjieff. That alone, aside from her rough-hewn vocabulary, convinced us that here was a woman after our own hearts.'

'Yes,' said Vanessa. 'But not to the extent of drooling over *Beelzebub's Tales to his Grandson*.'

'Justin and I,' continued Tich, 'were already friends. When Craig arrived here to manage running of a fitness centre, I made the mistake of agreeing to play him at squash. The bastard ran rings around me. After that, I retreated into the weightlifting room. My more comfortable arena. Anyway, it was upon learning about Craig's refreshingly anti-establishment views over a free yoghurt and honey that I hit on the idea of our club, bringing together a quartet of likeminded, unattached individuals opposed to the status quo.'

'With an action plan?'

4

'It's early days for that, Rashid. But perhaps your arrival will get the revolutionary juices flowing in the right direction. Next month. Since all work and no play makes Jack a dull boy, this month is, as I said, reserved for levity.'

'And what does that mean?'

Vanessa looked up from inspecting a damaged mother-of-pearl finger nail. 'When we're lost for ideas, Tich sets us homework. For instance, today Justin agreed to entertain us with howlers picked up over the past week in the press, on the net and elsewhere, with each of us offering a side contribution. Very little in my case, I'm afraid, since I've had my hands full.'

'That's a relief. The thought of having to produce a remedy for society's ills on my first appearance was starting to give me the jitters.'

'Yes, let's lighten the Lenfindi Quintet's mood,' said Craig. 'What have you managed to unearth, Justin?'

Justin pulled a sheet of paper from his breast pocket, unfolded it and cast his eyes over the list of quotations.

'I quite liked the story about a C E R E A L killer brought up during a Google search. It suggested a *modus operandi* a tad more novel than poisoning. Such as using a double-barrelled shotgun loaded with grape nuts.

'Then there was this web news item about a poor fellow who tried to immolate himself, according to which by the time the paramedics got to him "he was conscience and barely breathing".

'Ah, here's something from a murder mystery: *While learning to light campfires on the thirteenth green, the Horowitz's chauffeured limousine would be waiting outside the scout hut*. A remarkable feat for a limo.

'Another one here: *His speech was compounded of equal parts conjecture and speculation*. Bertie Russell would probably have passed that on for untangling to A.J. Ayer.

'On a slightly different note, how does the idea of a Filipino prelate named Cardinal Sin grab you?

'But my two nicest pieces come from a pen friend in Saint Petersburg, where she has been attending a Shakespeare festival. Apparently, all the advertisements on roadside lamp posts and in the underground were quoting Hamlet's exhortation to the players to hold the mirror up to nature. The Russian versions rendered this as holding the mirror up to the environment. They made the bard of Avon out to be paving the way for Greenpeace rather than an acute observer of human nature.

'My friend's second contribution let me know that in her Russian version of Shakespeare's Richard III, the king left defenceless on Bosworth field cries out, "A horse! A horse! Half my kingdom for a horse!" It begs the question, was the translator a Jew?'

Tich's expression altered from restrained approbation to pained disbelief. 'A pen friend, Justin. Are you telling me that in this day and age there are still good people who prefer quill to keyboard?'

'Yes, Tich. One thing on which Poe's raven failed to put the kibosh. Our correspondence helps brush up my Russian cursive. But perhaps you have something for us? I sense you straining at the leash.'

'Indeed, it would be remiss of me to let this opportunity pass without drawing on the cornucopia provided by a lesser, present-day William. As it happens, a charitable donor dropped by last week with a load of books, including a guide for writers and editors compiled by this popular scribe. In flicking through this, it occurred to me that the author had fallen prey to the temptation of teaching his grandmother to suck eggs.'

Tich cleared his throat, before reading from a notebook that had seen better days. 'Let me explain. Our Bill gives "*Quod est demonstrandum*" for "What was to be demonstrated". He talks about the infinite mood. Might this be the mood of preference for verbs intended to perpetuate, immortalise or filibuster? He clarifies pronunciation of names some might find baffling, but omits Castlereagh. He socks the reader with a plethora of geographical proper nouns, forgetting to mention that we English refer to Vlissingen as Flushing. He likes shooting his linguistic cuffs, but trips over the turn-ups of literalness in informing us that *objet trouvé* means found object and *noblesse oblige* nobility obligates. He's choosy with etymology, so gives no explanation of the origin of the verb to mesmerise. He offers us ROM but not RAM. The list is longer than your arm. Finally, he uses that atrocious semi-Teutonic adverb *respectively* to single out for praise his proofreading daughters. They would appear to have nodded off on the job.

'How about you, Van? If I understand correctly, not sweet F.A.'

'A close second, because I've been working on pruning the cast list of *Camino Real* by lumping together secondary roles.

'So, all I had time to note on the side was a bit of adverbial bombast and a linguistic *non sequitur*.

'The bombast came from a Westminster MP following the fashion for Russian bashing: "The Russian Federation," he announced, "brazenly flouted international law in annexing Crimea, whereby it brought down upon its head widespread international condemnation". Whereby? Instead of saying goodbye to whereby, it looks as if Harrow and Eton still encourage their progeny to lard their waffling with wherebys.

'And the *non sequitur* is not unrelated to Crimea, home to close on one and a half million Russians but fewer than half a million Ukrainians. It struck me as ironic that, when Ukraine's national netball team came to play our side in Luritania last week, their women were heard speaking to each other exclusively in Russian. So much for insistence on purifying Ukrainian tongues of a barbaric language.'

Tich ruffled his hair. 'Well, thereby hangs a political tale, Van. Material methinks better suited to next month's debates. But if that's all you could manage, let us be grateful. A case of something from Van being better than nothing, whereas nothing is indubitably better than something from that MP of hers. Now Craig, perhaps you can go one better?'

'Not with only two mentions from the Internet. The first from Eurosport's betting commercial: "Life is a game". And here I'll join Vanessa by straying into politics. Try telling "Life is a game" to countless refugees and those left behind under bombardment in Syria.

'My only other Internet video sound borrowing has to do with fruity English pronunciation of Peugeot, the carmakers sponsoring Roland Garros. Lady and gents, I give you Pewgo.'

Tich inclined his head. 'Not quite as rich a crop as usual, I'm sorry to say, Rashid. Obviously, a busier week for some than for others. Never mind. Another bit of nonsense we get up to when the well runs dry is to take a word and, by association, match it to, say, a book and its author and keep going round the table until, horror of horrors, we reach a dead end and call it a day or, praised be the Lord, come full circle.

'To give you an idea of what I mean, let me start the ball rolling by taking as our trigger Justin's *conscience,* but as in "thus conscience does make cowards of us all".

'*Hamlet.* Shakespeare. Your turn Craig.'

'*L'homme est un roseau pensant.* Pascal.'

Vanessa: *Death in the Afternoon.* Hemingway.

Justin: For heaven's sake, Vanessa. Challenge.

Whereas Craig, as much in the dark as Justin, seconded the objection, Tich, trusting to Vanessa's fecund imagination, remained silent, convinced that both men stood to lose out on their challenge.

Vanessa: Bulrushes.

Justin: Shit. Okay. *In Cold Blood.* Truman Capote.

Tich: *Gorky Park.* Martin Cruz Smith.

Craig: *Ice Station Zebra.* Alistair MacLean.

Vanessa: *Green Hills of Africa.* Hemingway. Twins.

Justin: *Roots.* Alex Hayley.

Tich: *The Tree of Life.* Patrick White.

Craig: *East of Eden.* John Steinbeck.

Vanessa: *Genesis.* Cain and Abel. Holy Moses.

Justin: *Crime and Punishment.* Dostoyevsky.

Tich: *Hamlet.* Will Shakespeare. Twins. That was quick. It's not often that neat, ending up with the originator, but Justin handed it to me on a plate.

Rashid scratched the back of his head. 'What was "twins" all about?'

'Something Tich forgot to explain,' said Justin. 'Don't imagine for one moment that the scribbling he's been doing there with that chewed up pencil represent the makings of his long promised Ode to Luritania. He's been keeping the score. The starter is worth one point. Thereafter, every correct follow-on earns the contributor two points. Author repeats – twins, triplets and so on – are worth ten points. Repeats of the same work are penalised by four points. Tich will have docked Craig and me two points each for faulty challenges. And the reward for coming full circle is fifteen points, which royally offsets the starting singleton.'

'And the purpose of all this?'

'The holder of the highest score at the end of the month pockets five euros from each of the rest of us.'

Alert to Tich's devouring glances at her plate, Vanessa offloaded her second pat of butter onto the man whose doctor regularly cautioned him against abusing cholesterol intake, then turned to Rashid.

'How do you think you would have taken this little pastime of ours forward, Rashid? It would have been your turn after my *Genesis*.'

'Maxim Gorky. *The Lower Depths*.'

'Smart operator. Almost twins.'

'It would also,' added Justin, 'have been the perfect prompt for *Crime and Punishment*, again allowing Tich to come full circle. But you would have done better, Vanessa, to ask him the lead-on from *Death in the Afternoon*.'

'No problem,' responded Rashid. *Chronicle of a Death Foretold*. Gabriel García Márquez. If I remember correctly, that would have helped you with *In Cold Blood*.'

Vanessa decided to change tack. 'Truth to tell, I'm more interested in learning a thing or two about our new friend. I understand you work for Europe's latest banking brainwave, MEDRIMCOMB? Not, I take it, selling toxic paper to the Libyans and Egyptians?'

'No, not with a title as portentous as Mediterranean Rim Countries Modernisation Bank. Our remit is to mobilise private and public-sector finance to shore up the Med's southern and eastern rim economies. Primarily with infrastructure loans generating work for the vast number of young unemployed.'

Craig turned away from eying the well-turned calves of a bevy of air stewardesses trundling their roll-ons towards the departure gates. 'You mean deter them from migrating from the southern to the northern rim?'

'That as well.'

'Does the Lebanese connection explain your involvement?'

'Only to the extent that I speak Arabic. My job as loan officer has the potential to take me all over the region.'

'That's a shame,' said Tich. 'Does that mean here today gone tomorrow?'

'Not for the first six months. I'm a new boy, learning the ropes.'

'That's good,' said Justin. 'Six months should give the Lenfindi Quintet enough time to set the world to rights.'

'Couldn't agree more,' said Tich, clapping Rashid on the shoulder. 'Out of the lower depths, Rashid, into the light of a new dawn.'

~᠅~

Craig Roberts had just finished towelling down in his club's shower room following the departure of the last of his spin cycling class. It was one o'clock and most members had headed off for a snack lunch prior to resuming work behind their desks. His few pensioners, one of whom never tired of telling Craig that his days were fuller now they had ever been before, had also peeled off, some for a vegetarian sandwich and juice in the downstairs health bar, others for more serious sustenance in the form of the three-course *menu du jour* on the garden patio of the neighbouring restaurant.

Craig opened his locker and reached for the Swatch given him as an unbirthday present by an old flame. Just time to dress, verify that his new training software had registered that morning's chest and wrist pulse rates and related endurance data, check how many people had signed up for his two afternoon step classes, grab a bite to eat in the ground-floor office behind the bar, head out to the bank and be back by three p.m. for more aerobic training.

After dressing, he remembered to make sure that all the rubber heart rate and wrist pulse monitor straps had been put back clean and dry in their place. Not every one of his cyclists was sufficiently committed to have bought his or her own. But, in fact, he had been pleasantly surprised that morning to greet a newcomer to his class, who had come fully equipped. And pleasantly surprised in more ways than this one, because the young woman in question was a natural blonde with grey blue eyes and one of the most gracefully athletic bodies he had seen in a long time. Serious women cyclists tended to develop unbecomingly muscular or bowed legs. Not that Isabelle Meunier struck him as one-dimensional in terms of her exercise and health interests: she had already lost no time on her first morning at the sports club to sign up for other courses, step and yoga, given by two of his colleagues.

Craig was manager of the *All The Right Moves Wellness and Fitness Centre* owned by a Dutchman who gave him pretty much of a free rein, within set budgetary limits, as to equipment purchases and hiring and firing of personal trainers. However, Craig had been given no say in the club's name. Not only did 'Wellness' strike him as an abomination, coined no doubt by some nerdish American who must have thought this the perfect antonym of illness, but Craig would have laid the stress on fitness first. All the same, having employed two full-time physiotherapists and a nail cosmetician and run a no expenses spared campaign advertising the centre's saunas and health bar, Piet van der Meulen had stamped the club with the seal of his authority. Hence, his new manager had no choice but to go with the flow, especially when Piet made it known that the weight training rooms, two squash courts and Craig's spin cycling were all very well for exercise freaks but hardly star attractions for saner health enthusiasts. And who was Craig to argue with the man holding the purse strings?

Nevertheless, Piet had not hesitated in his choice of the man to take over from someone who, after passing Luritania's civil service exam, had left to join the Ministry of Sports, where he had been charged with overseeing the Tour de France's upcoming *Grand Départ* from home soil. Craig had brought with him a membership motivational tool in the form of his home-grown software programme for detailed performance measuring. He had also gone up a notch or two in Piet's estimation after recommending Saturday and Sunday morning exercise classes for the very young in a room with plenty of soft rubber mats under the eyes of those parents who cared to stay to keep track of their infants' fun and games through the upstairs health bar's observation window.

Craig's most uphill battle with his boss had been to convince him of the good publicity to be had from offering spin cycling facilities to the residents of Luritania's home for the blind. Although this had been Vanessa Curtis's brainchild, Craig set about promoting it in earnest with his employer. Piet van der Meulen baulked at the idea of investing in an extra six *fietsen* (bicycles) used under supervision for only three days a week while installed on somebody else's premises outside the capital, Schönschlucht. Unwilling to take no for an answer, Vanessa, who spoke passable Luritanian, promptly booked an appointment with the Ministry of Health, and with Craig in tow succeeded in negotiating an appreciable subsidy with an unexpected bonus in the form of the unconditional backing of Luritania's female sports minister. In the light of this news, Piet dropped his original proposal to charge rent for the down time of half a dozen bicycles, the thought of which threatened his cash register mind with sleepless nights.

After checking the time once again on the wall clock opposite his desk in the main gym equipped with treadmills, rowing machines and exercise bikes, Craig decided that he could spare a few minutes to go through the morning's data input and print out the more interesting profiles. Then he trotted downstairs to the health bar, where he ate a tuna salad whole wheat roll and gulped down a freshly squeezed orange juice.

Picking up the small package that he had carried down from his changing room cubicle, Craig tapped his trouser pocket in search of the key to his red Jaguar XJS convertible and, after assuring the secretary on the front reception desk that he would be back in time for his first class of the afternoon, stepped out into the fresh air.

Slipping behind the wheel and placing the package by his side on the brown leather passenger seat, Craig paused to weigh up the pros and cons of storing this small item in his safety deposit box. The package contained an 1871 first edition of *Alice through the Looking Glass* complete with illustrations by Tenniel. It had been a gift from Tich on the occasion of Craig's 28th birthday three months ago. Appreciating its value, Craig had initially kept the book in his workplace filing cabinet, but Sunday's get-together with that 'Life's a game' mention had jogged his memory about Charles Dodgson and the need to find a more secure permanent niche for Tich's present.

Yes, he thought, as he turned on the ignition, the bank was the best solution. Motoring down the hill leading away from the club into the nearest village, Craig remembered Tich's praise of the second Alice tale, the one, he said, less well known than its predecessor but a fable with magic touches to it. And Craig had enjoyed rereading after all these years the story of Alice's adventures negotiating her creator's fantasy chess board.

When he reached the front of the local BLR Paribas branch, he found every parking place accounted for. But, as good luck would have it, just as he was about to swing the steering wheel around and head for the rear of the building, four rows ahead of him a BMW's reverse lights came on, and Craig pulled out to head off a less committed driver approaching from the other side whose chances of beating him to it were greatly reduced by the fact that the BMW would bar its way, allowing Craig to slip effortlessly into the vacant slot.

With the bank's entrance doors locked and the antechamber to the counter area unoccupied, Craig pressed the button activating a slow release mechanism allowing, at the most, two people at a time access to a cramped compartment with an exit door whose button stayed on red until the first door had come to a complete close. He waited for the warning light to turn to green, stabbed the button and watched the second door grind slowly open onto the inner sanctum, where he tapped on a touch sensitive screen's 'routine banking operations' flag and collected a numbered ticket placing him next in line in a queue already eight deep. However, with four of the six counters manned, Craig did not expect a long wait.

It was then that he recognised the young blonde spin cyclist from that morning's class sitting behind the bullet-proof glass of one of the counter windows. A further surprise, since he had never seen her in this branch before let alone known, when she had shaken hands with him, that BLR was her paymaster. He quickly decided to take two more tickets in the event that his first number was flashed up over another counter clerk or things got delayed at Mlle Meunier's counter by someone with a complicated transaction involving telephone calls to head office. And if this ploy failed to work, he would push in front of some unfortunate with the excuse that he had missed his number.

But mother fortune smiled on him: by the time he reached the front of the line his first number, 666, appeared above Isabelle Meunier's position.

After debating whether to address her in French or English, the language he had heard her use fluently to the Irish cyclist on the bike next to hers and with a fetching accent which, if anything, only increased his attraction to this young woman with not a single ring on her finger, Craig opted for English.

'What a happy coincidence. We meet twice in one morning. But I had no idea you worked here.'

'I'm on secondment from head office, covering for a girl on maternity leave.'

'How long for?'

'Could be up to six months, but you never know. You're a *pion*– I've forgotten how you say that in English – on their chessboard.'

Lewis Carroll's Alice, thought Craig. But more enticingly adult. 'A pawn? That's not a nice way to treat employees.'

She laughed. 'I was joking. What can I do for you, Craig?'

First name terms did not go unappreciated. He placed his ID and numbered deposit box key in the tray in the bottom of her window. 'I need to put something in safekeeping.'

'Hang on, then. You'd better go over to the end counter, while I get the ledger for you to sign.'

Craig followed her directions to the counter on the far right fitted with a door giving onto to the clerks' working area beyond which lay the bank's safety deposit room. Moments later, she appeared at and raised the counter window for him to sign the ledger and leave her to register the date and time of his use of the room. After which she opened the window to Craig's left, raised the fold-over counter above a half-door, ushered him inside and secured window and door back in place.

Craig followed Isabelle Meunier to another door, where she entered a series of figures into a keypad. The door opened onto a narrow corridor to the right of which stood the vault. While waiting for the vault's heavy-duty steel door to slide open on its ceiling and floor runners, his nose alive to the delicate fragrance of perfume sparingly applied, the headiness that had temporarily overcome him in the presence of his svelte five foot nine companion prompted him to have recourse to a quip.

'Certainly no pawn if they've already entrusted you with the keys to the kingdom.'

'Look at those doors. Would you call that fast track? That's what I'm supposed to be. Can I have your key, please? We won't get far without it.'

Craig covered his embarrassment with a smile. 'Here, of course.'

She preceded him into the vault lined on two sides by row upon row of numbered safety deposit boxes of different sizes. But Craig's attention was elsewhere, for he was amazed to see the roller shutter doors of the compartment opposite him wide open, displaying an abundance of bank notes of every denomination and row upon row of coins.

'Remind me of your number,' said Isabelle.

'Three hundred and eighty-four. Top right. Two rows down.' Craig's disbelieving eyes remained fixed on the horn of plenty.

Isabelle Meunier first inserted the bank's key into the left-hand lock on box 384, then Craig's key into the right-hand lock, turned both, opened the door and removed the bank's key. 'There we are,' she said. 'You know how to operate the outside door, I take it, after I lock you in? The button on the side wall.'

Craig had difficulty tearing his eyes away from the bank's treasury. 'Shouldn't that be closed?'

'You're not feeling tempted are you?'

'Hell, yes, I am,' he joked.

'Well, resist. See those cameras trained on you up there? You're on candid camera.'

'Isabelle, if you'll excuse my saying so, cameras or not, it's pretty irresponsible to leave clients in here with so much loot at their fingertips.'

'I couldn't agree more. But then it wasn't me who left it open. Another colleague is responsible for liquidity. Perhaps he got called away. Or had a bad day. Too much on his plate. Forgot all about it.'

'You're going to tell him, I hope.'

'As soon as I leave you. So be a good boy.'

'You should know that this goes against my better instincts.'

'I'm sure you'll do nothing stupid.'

It was hardly worth her leaving him alone for the little time it took him to store the first edition away into his deposit box. Craig had elected to pay over the top for the hire of a medium-sized box, which, he calculated, had enough room in it to accommodate a small fortune in 500 euro bank notes. He stared up at the two overhead cameras and winked.

'Not this time, guys. Too high a suicide rate in the prison down the road.'

However, after leaving the vault and standing aside for a security guard to open the end-counter door admitting him into the foyer, rather than making straight for the exit, Craig turned back towards the position no longer occupied by Isabelle Meunier. No doubt she had gone to iron out the fiasco in the vault.

As he was on the point of touching the button on the first of two doors leading to the street, some sixth sense made him turn around. Sure enough, Isabelle was returning to her seat. Furthermore, he had suddenly become the sole potential client left in the waiting area.

Craig seized the opportunity to rejoin Isabelle Meunier at her window.

'I hope you didn't leave you key inside,' she said. 'Because I can't let you back in there right now until a colleague has taken care of you know what.'

'No, Isabelle. The key's here in my pocket. And you'll be pleased to know I was as good as gold. Look, would you happen to be free for dinner tonight? There's a great menu on offer at the Château Vaugruge this week. I don't know if you know the place, but the open-air restaurant looks right down over the vineyards above the river. Quite something at this time of year.'

'Provided I can take you at your word. I'd rather not get caught sharing a meal with a wanted criminal.'

Craig could not have hoped for a more welcome answer. 'Perish the thought. Would eight o'clock suit you? You know the château?'

'Of course.'

'Fine. Let's meet in the parking lot below the steps leading up to the restaurant.'

'Very good. I look forward to an evening without Big Brother.'

Not an easy word for the French to pronounce that fraternal one. But for Craig, it was music to his ears.

※

After taking a Monday morning snack lunch behind her office desk, Vanessa caught the bus into town to visit Tich in his bookshop, *Bibliopole,* situated in a prime location behind the central post office, a national architectural heritage building.

Every time she visited Tich's shop, Vanessa was reminded of her Saturday coffee mornings with her close friend Gwyneth Hobart, who had died four years previously. Tich and Gwyneth had been married for just over ten years when she was diagnosed with pancreatic cancer. It took her life six months later.

Gwyneth (Tich's 'Gwyn') had been a professional photographer specialising in nature and wildlife. She worked for several top-flight magazines and exhibited in the Tate Modern before being invited to Luritania after winning an international competitive tender sponsored by the Ministry of Culture at the behest of Grand Prince Philippe Étienne. The sovereign wanted to put Luritania on the map at *National Geographic* level by way of fêting the country's National Parks centennial celebrations in tandem with inauguration of a zoo, 'setting the benchmark for ecologically responsible management', home to a number of endangered species, including two giant pandas gifted the country by the Chinese ambassador.

Gwyn was charged with producing a photo-book presenting the principality's nature preserves in the best possible light. Chosen to write the captions and complementary text, Justin invited Tich to the *vernissage* (private viewing) showcasing Gwyn's work, which was how the two first met. At the time, Tich was teaching English as a foreign language to the local Chinese community. When North Rhine-Westphalia and Rhineland-Palatinate's state authorities commissioned Gwyn on the strength of her Luritanian project to produce something similar for them, she decided to stay on in Schönschlucht. This led to the odd piece of photojournalism for Justin, another exhibition in Schönschlucht's showpiece museum, designed by China's renowned green architect Yang Changsong, and a contract with Luritania's *Naturbeschutzgesollschuft* (Nature Protection Society).

Because Gwyn and Tich shared the same love of literature, Tich, who was cheesed off with TEFL, decided to throw that job in and went along with Gwyn's proposal to compete with the mainstream book trade by offering people works at affordable prices. After Schönschlucht's mayor gave his blessing to the couple's civil marriage, Tich and Gwyneth managed to scrape together sufficient start-up capital to convert a disused bakery opposite the post office into the premises which Vanessa was about to enter.

On reaching the pavement outside the shop, Vanessa saw that its owner had been busy over the weekend arranging one of his themed monthly window displays: Our Environment – Our Future.

Tich had given pride of place to a variety of secondhand publications targeting man's mismanagement of the planet's natural resources and national economies: Nicolas Hulot's *Pour un pacte écologique*, Serge Latouche's *La planète des naufragés*, Stefan Rahmstorf's *Wie bedroht sind die Ozeane?*, Rachel Carson's *Silent Spring*, Jared Diamond's *Collapse: How Societies Choose to Fail or Succeed*, Al Gore's *Earth In The Balance* … These were, in turn, backed up by charts, graphs and posters illustrating the alarming rate of planetary deforestation, the indecent volume of toxic ocean waste, and a long list of species on the verge of extinction. According to one graph, the level of ongoing soil degradation brought about by a combination of intensive farming and erosion represented a time bomb set to exhaust the planet's topsoil within the next sixty years – with catastrophic consequences for the food supply chain.

'Nice end-of-days' work,' commented Vanessa, strolling through the open shop door, where she found Tich, a mug of coffee in one hand, the fingers of the other navigating his laptop's early afternoon news web site.

'Van, good to see you.' Tich set down his mug. 'Nice what?'

'The window.'

'Depressing, if you ask me. Looks like twenty years from now there'll be nothing left of the Great Barrier Reef, fifteen years later not a single glacier in the Alps.'

'Tell that to the multinationals. So, have you sold anything vaguely ecological?'

Vanessa cast a critical eye at the hyacinths presented to Tich the week before with a view to adding freshness to the bookshop's musty interior. 'Their water needs changing. And while you're at it, prune the stems – diagonally.'

Confronted by nothing other than cheerless news, Tich clicked across to Sport. 'Monday mornings rarely bring the punters out in droves. Had a young mother in. Bought *The Tale of Squirrel Nutkin*. A low-key, environmentally-friendly start to the week. She commented on your hyacinths. Said they looked droopy. Perhaps the water does need changing. But to what do I owe this honour? You in search of something specific? Or taking a breather from the daily grind?'

'A bit of both. Time-study engineers are not exactly everyone's favourite aunt, particularly when management's latest buzzword is rationalise. Everyone I interview sees me as Miss Downsize.'

'Offer you a coffee? The percolator's still warm out back.'

'No thanks, Tich. You really think corporate enterprise gives a fuck about the ordinary citizen's environmental gripes?'

The bookseller got up from his swivel chair, rubbed his lumbar region with clenched fists and cast a rueful glance at the window display.

'If you put it like that, no. But the important thing is not to let up. Ask *Fortune 100's* CEOs, do they really want their grandchildren to curse their memory?'

'From the mare's mouth, brave but futile, Tich.'

'O ye of little faith. That's fair trade coffee I'm drinking here.'

'And the chocolate on the biscuit?'

'Let's change the subject. How's your play coming on?'

'That's the other reason why I dropped by. I need two more copies of *Camino Real*.'

'Two of anything's asking a lot. Let's have a look.'

Vanessa followed her guide towards the back of the shop, where one section of nine rows of ceiling-high shelving given over to English literature was devoted to drama.

'Williams is going to be at the end,' said Tich.

He bent down to peer more closely at titles along the bottom row. '*Orpheus Descending*. Your namesake, Miss Redgrave, was great in the role of Lady under Peter Hall's screen direction.'

'Well, this Vanessa needs *Camino Real*.'

'If I have it, it should be here in front of *Cat on a Hot Tin Roof*, that is if nobody wandered off with that and stuffed it among the pet handbooks.'

Tich straightened up, rubbing his back again. 'Sorry, Vanessa, looks like we're out of luck.'

'Then I'll take you up on that coffee.'

'Of course. Just keep an eye on the shop front, while I pop out back. You get all sorts in here, including shoplifters.'

'Really?'

'Really. I get people carrying shopping bags to leave them with me at the till. Mind you, it's the ones wearing Clint Eastwood long coats with deep pockets that you need to watch out for. They can whisk half a shelf out from under your nose before you know it.'

Vanessa looked up at the ceiling. 'But you've installed CCTV.'

'Doesn't stop me from getting distracted with paying customers.'

'All the same, it's not as if your books are new. Some are tatty.'

'I'd prefer to say well used.'

'So why would anyone want to ... ?' A fluttering hand made further explanation superfluous.

'The temptation of getting something for nothing. What difference is one or two books less going to make to a shop on a par with Borges's Library of Babel? And, believe me, it isn't always the penniless who try put one over on you.'

Vanessa lowered her voice. 'In that case, I had better keep my eyes open. Someone's just come in dressed up to the nines.'

Tich turned to look at the slim young woman wearing a lace-detailed dress with black side paneling and peep toe ankle strap heels preceded by a white Pomeranian on a retractable lead. 'She's okay. No carrier bag. Mutt doesn't look as if it's got fleas. If she really needs Chekhov, you know your way around. Otherwise, give me a call.'

Moments later, Tich rejoined Vanessa at the counter, bearing a steaming cup of coffee and a plate of plain biscuits. 'Spot of milk, no sugar. That right?'

Vanessa interrupted her perusal of a paperback entitled *Sex, Anatomy and Punctuation* left on the plywood counter top. 'Thanks, Tich. Your second customer of the morning pecked around the cookery shelf, before walking out as empty-handed as she came in.'

'No harm in that. It would be a poor bookseller who stopped his customers from browsing. How are rehearsals going?'

'They're a long way off. We're into the early stages. Reading through the text, helping me to cast the play. How to divide the parts up among the male leads is proving a headache. The production stands or falls on getting that right.'

'Have you thought of asking Rashid whether he'd be interested? A good-looking young man with the necessary stage presence.'

Vanessa stretched down to pick up a stray sheet of paper blown in through the entrance. It was a post office advertisement for freshly minted coins, including one celebrating a, to her mind, overrated local cartoonist. 'You think he's into amateur theatricals?'

'Can't tell until you try.'

'Certainly wouldn't make a credible Don.'

'No.'

'Justin would be ideal in that role. But he keeps fobbing me off.'

Tich noted that Vanessa felt more comfortable steering the conversation away from Rashid.

'Where are you staging this?'

'In the courtyard of the Château de l'Aubaine. On one side we'll signpost *Terra Incognita*, on the other *Aeropuerto – Fugitivo*.'

'In the open air again like *The Taming of the Shrew* you put on in the gardens of the Villa Maximilian. Handy, having two magnificent chestnut trees as stand-ins for wings.'

'The setting this time is a dead-end Latin American seafront outpost on the edge of the desert. One side of the courtyard can be used as the terrace of the *Hotel Siete Mares* complete with tables and chairs. Enough to accommodate our audience. Ideal, because the characters will be able to circulate among the spectators. I'll get the château restaurant to serve margaritas and tacos. Having a fountain in the courtyard is the real bonus, though I still have to find out whether we can regulate it.'

'Makes a change from time-study engineering.'

'Almost anything's a healthy change from that. Now then, Tich, come clean. What kind of a weird book is this?' Vanessa held up the paperback. '*Sex, Anatomy and Punctuation.*'

'Unearthed after sorting through a box dumped on me *gratis* last week by a woman who said she'd been clearing out her husband's paperback collection.

'You get much *gratis* nowadays'

'More, I'm glad to say than ones I pay for.'

'I've always meant to ask. The rent. It must set you back a pretty penny?'

'I think you mean an ugly euro. In fact, no. Gwyn and I filed our application to buy these premises on a day when the mayor happened to be doing the rounds of the city offices. He remembered marrying us. Thought launching a quality secondhand bookshop in town was a great idea, especially since most people throw their used books away in recycling centres, where they either get pulped or snapped up by market stall sellers from across the border. He even went so far as to promise us two dozen boxes of books from his attic. Said that, if we undertook to donate a portion of our earnings to a good cause, he'd get his people to draw up a favourable lease. But, as I say, that's strictly between you, me and the doorpost. And we've come a long way from *Sex, Anatomy and Punctuation.*'

Tich took the paperback from her. 'Amazing the number of loss leaders that publishers turn out. It's only the last chapter that deals with punctuation. The author suggests using punctuation marks as euphemistic substitutes for fornication, body parts and cuss words. It's a pity I can't do a Victor Borge on this.' He started reading from the text in front of him: '"Jim and Wendy liked Spanish question marks, although Jim usually went in for exclamation marks before he worked Wendy up to a row of asterisks." That believe it or not is the expurgated version of *Jim and Wendy liked 69* (or soixante-neuf as people prefer to say, because it sounds sexier in French*), although Jim usually ejaculated before he stimulated Wendy to the point of multiple orgasms.*'

'Amazing rubbish.'

'Couldn't agree more. Periods, well, the less said about them the better. A comma is really a copula. Brackets denote intertwined limbs. And apparently dashes indicate bonking, because they have their roots in the Scandinavian for bashing. Hence, dash off represents a pathetically toned down version of fuck off. Oh dear, you'll never guess what this guy uses ellipses for?'

'Tell me.'

'Golden rain.'

'Gross. What about dicks and cunts?'

'Never one to mince your words, unlike this fellow. It appears a Hampton Wick, as I prefer to call it, is a long hyphen – a fanny, inverted commas. Hence, *he caressed her apostrophe* (no need to elaborate) *before inserting his long hyphen into her inverted commas.*'

'What if his dick qualifies as Lilliputian?'

'Obvious, no? A short hyphen.'

'And how does he make colons and semicolons sexy?'

'Colons are reserved for buggery, the semicolon for *coitus interruptus*. Oh, and a single exclamation mark signifies premature ejaculation.'

'He needs locking away.'

Tich dropped the book back on the counter. 'Yes, plain stupid, but, mark my words, if I leave it out here on the counter, it'll be sold long before Al Gore or Serge Latouche.'

'Not a patch on Rabelais. Remember his story about the monks toasting the health of their sleepover nuns.'

'I don't think I do, Van.'

'Glaze your arses to the pope.'

'That was Rabelais?'

She raised her coffee mug to his. 'Just possible I've got my Middle Age sources mixed up.'

Justin Hendry was grappling with the latest edition of Luritania's monthly city newsletter, *The Pulse*. Most articles were published in English and French, the two texts side by side, the language of authorship on the left, its translation on the right, a reflection of the fact that Luritania was a melting pot of nationalities with a working knowledge of one or the other of these *linguae francae*. In fact, foreigners accounted for close on half the principality's population. As for daily national, regional and world news, this was available to Luritanian speakers through their Catholic *Luritanische Bote* and a number of regional broadsheets. The *Bote's* journalists wrote predominantly in either German or French, rarely in Luritanisch.

A brief knock on door between his office and a neighbouring room tore Justin's attention away from the mock-up. He turned to face an excited Klaus Radetzky, *The Pulse's* sub-editor and cartoonist, resting his lank figure against the door jamb. The round-shouldered Radetzky, whose wife was continually telling him to correct his posture, seemed incapable of standing upright for longer than a minute or two.

'You've got to come and see this, Justin. Something I've chanced upon on the German net. About the protest march in Paris two weeks ago.'

Justin accompanied his colleague into the next room, an open-plan area divided into a number of cubicles, the nearest of which to his own office belonged to Klaus. The sub-editor directed his boss to a nearby seat. 'Take a look here.'

Radetzky pointed to his desktop monitor showing a broad semicircle of politicians and dignitaries, at least five rows deep, wearing black armbands and fronted by a line of ordinary citizens.

'See how the pavements on either side are deserted, while a cordon of police officers and riot troops contains the area behind, in front and on both sides of the big wigs? This group picture was taken in a quiet street within the French capital's business district. Now, look at this.'

The sub-editor used his touch pad to switch screens and enlarge one of a number of thumbnails.

'See the difference?'

Justin nodded. The new image showed a throng of peaceful demonstrators gathered behind the statesmen. 'Photo montage.'

'Exactly. Those bigwigs might have wanted to express their solidarity with the masses, but there was no way they were going to put their lives on the line by exposing themselves to rooftop sharpshooters.'

'The people in the front row in the first image were the family and relatives of those gunned down by the jihadists?'

'That's it. No doubt, Monsieur Pays-Bas and Frau Makrele shook hands with them, expressed their condolences, then stepped back.'

'But we saw this on the newscast. I don't recall getting the impression that the whole thing was set up.'

'Because you only ever saw the heads of state in the vanguard. The crowds accompanying them were filmed by cameramen ducking and weaving to one side and the other of the central mass.'

Justin could have queried the legitimacy of Klaus's images but, judging his sub-editor to be too keyed up to brook dissension, he gave a non-committal shrug. With Radetzky operating on automatic pilot, it was better to stand clear of the contrail. This was the self-willed man who, in the wake of the outpouring of public sympathy for the murdered Parisian cartoonists had the temerity to fashion two badges of his own, the first of which, *Je ne suis pas Charlie,* was meant to convey *I don't follow Charlie.* For, as much as Klaus Radetzky deplored the murder of that magazine's leading lights, he held them responsible for the slaughter of innocent people present in the building at the time of the attack. He also maintained that individuals who disseminated pictures of the prophet with a bomb in his turban or Christ with his cock hanging out and who didn't get the message were asking for trouble.

That badge he wore on the right side of his chest. On the left, he wore a badge proclaiming *Je suis Nigérien,* here taken to mean *I am Nigerian.* For, in Radetzky's opinion, Europe's headline-seeking politicians had turned their backs on the larger atrocities committed in northern Nigeria.

Justin edged closer as Klaus brought up the two images side by side. Now he was inclined to admit that the Germans had spotted something fishy.

'No wonder the French were running scared. Their intelligence messed up. Still, fancy the Germans showing this. Not the mackerel's state-run channel, I suppose?'

'Oh boy, no. How are things going with the galleys?'

'Still at the mock-up stage. Apart from my Q&A with the Transport Minister about the great tram project. That's ready.'

Justin was referring to a monumental capital investment scheme voted by the government with a view to decongesting road traffic leading into the city from the station and airport by introducing thirty sets of electric battery-powered trams serving park and ride stations at either end. The Poles had won the invitation to tender for the tram sets worth some 150 million euros, but the batteries powering their sets came from the Russian Federation. This was embarrassing, given that Poland and most other European States had imposed punitive trade sanctions against Russia in protest against its annexation of Crimea and support for the separatist movement in eastern Ukraine.

The Russian batteries were acknowledged to be the finest on the market. Furthermore, the price tag on batteries manufactured by their nearest European competitor was prohibitive. Transport Minister Günther Weizmann had rounded on his critics, claiming that the Russian batteries had formed part of the Polish contractor's inventory for the past four years, such that there was no question of authorising imports from a pariah state. Justin had not believed a word of this, but knew that it was more than his job was worth to take issue with verities from the mouth of a horse with such a distinguished pedigree, related as Weizmann was, albeit distantly, to Luritania's sovereign.

Klaus Radeztky removed three yellow Post-Its from the top of his desktop, gave them a cursory glance, replaced one and discarded the others. 'Which way did Weizmann lean?'

'What do you think? Denial.'

'Film reviews sitting pretty?'

'Not bad.'

'They are the only articles I haven't seen. Keeping them close to your chest, Justin?'

'Not at all. I gave priority to the trams.'

'What have you reviewed?'

'Christopher Nolan's *Interstellar* and Mike Leigh's *Mr Turner.*'

'And?'

'The first – pure soap opera. Michael Cain, ridiculous as a leading NASA scientist ponderously quoting Dylan Thomas. Matthew McConaughey spewing out bucketfuls of cheap sentimentality. The entire crew qualifying to be reduced to mush the moment its star ship penetrated the black hole.'

'Wow, you actually wrote that?'

'Not quite.'

'And the other film?'

'Timothy Spall, great as Turner. The whole artistic look of the film, marvellous.'

'So our lead story's the tram?'

'Yes, the sixty-four thousand dollar question being is this headed for another massive budget overshoot?'

Klaus nodded understanding, his mind elsewhere. 'I'm free to take over now, if you like. You have a flight to catch.'

Justin glanced at his watch. Wrapped up in his work, he had almost forgotten that he had to make that night's Luritanair flight to City of London airport to attend a funeral. Last week, he had receive a call from a south London nursing home informing him that his aunt, Clarissa, struck down by dementia three years ago, had died in her sleep. Justin, her sole surviving relative, had been hit by successive waves of shock, sadness and guilt.

The latter because he had been negligent in visiting Aunt Clarissa in her South Croydon nursing home. The last two visits had been six months apart. On each occasion, he felt that he might as well not have been there, for she failed to recognise him or to respond to pictures in his photograph album which he hoped might stir memories and bring a moment or two's awakening. Not that she turned him away when he reached out for her hand. But every now and then, she would start addressing an imaginary person standing beside her dressing table. Rather than Aunt Clarissa's dead mother or father, this seemed to be a stranger attracting mocking criticism for his behaviour. At least, Justin's aunt had conserved her sense of humour.

Incapable of mixing in with other residents, she had a room to herself, where, according to her carers, she could sit for hours on end troubled by irregularities in the patterned wallpaper or, if she chose to sit by the window, laughing at the birds swooping down to devour food put out for them on a table set up under a magnolia. She rarely ventured outside, fearing that 'those little rascals' would nip at her heels. But since Justin could not remember her ever mentioning being bothered by dogs, this made about as much sense as everything else she said.

Now that news of her death had reached him out of the blue, he felt mortified at being miserly with his visits. Aunt Clarissa had been a regular churchgoer and committee charity worker during her active years, which meant that she had not been without friends. But apparently only three had called by at the home to keep her company. One of these had taken in hand arrangements with the undertakers as well as organisation of the funeral service.

Since Justin's aunt had lived in a council house all her life until dementia had rendered her a danger to herself, she had left no property behind. As her only relative, Justin might have expected a brief mention in any will with, in view of his aunt's limited means, a modest bequest, but the poor lady had been robbed naked before entering the nursing home by a Jamaican social services worker responsible for seeing that her ward set neither herself nor her neighbours on fire. This unscrupulous character persuaded the seventy-year-old spinster to sign enough blank cheques to exhaust her account, then hightailed it to a certain Kingston far from the Thames and the long arm of the former coloniser's law.

As Justin understood it, the nursing home had donated his aunt's few belongings to a thrift shop, so that no tangible memento was to be handed down to him. All that remained on his side, as supposedly the chief mourner at Aunt Clarissa's funeral, was to pay due homage to her memory from the pulpit of the church where she had been christened and received communion and which she had faithfully attended for the best part of seven decades, a church whose good works in support of the local community she had unflaggingly supported. Hers had been a life fitting for a nun were it not for the fact that she had devoted herself to a perpetually ailing mother. Justin had been led to believe that when romance had entered his aunt's life, the mother had quashed it. All told, it was hard to decide whether a manipulative matriarch or faintheartedness lay at the roots of his aunt's maidenhood.

Justin looked at his watch. Klaus was right. He would soon need to order a taxi to take him and a carry-on suitcase to the airport.

'The interview with Weizmann is good to go. How about the cover?'

The sub-editor pulled two sheets from a stack of papers piled up on the floor next to his workstation, made space on a side table littered with proofs and spread out first one then the other poster-sized image. 'Your call.'

Justin pondered the choice between a cover page devoted solely to the Paris freedom of speech march and another the top half of which was devoted to Paris, the bottom to Nigeria, underpinned with the caption 'Slaughtered: France, 14. Nigeria: 2 000. Europe's leaders redefine the global village.'

'The second one. But not with that caption, Klaus. That's going too far.'

Justin's sub-editor smarted. 'But it's true.'

'Doesn't alter the fact that you're mixing apples and oranges.'

'What do you want me to do then?'

Justin ignored the petulance underlying the whine. 'Put *France: Europe's bloodied capital – Nigeria: Africa's forgotten war.*'

'A damn tragedy unfolding while the world stands by.'

Justin was in no mood to argue. 'Either what I suggested or Paris on its own.'

'You're the boss.'

'That's right. And I'm thinking about keeping both our breads buttered. Give me ten more minutes and I'll leave the final setting to you.'

'When can we expect to see you next?'

From Klaus's tone, Justin surmised that his sub-editor was still less than happy, but, knowing the man, expected him to get on with the job.

'Midday on Wednesday.'

'Sorry I can't wish you a pleasant break.' It was something of an attempt at reining back on wounded pride.

'That's how things are, isn't it? In the midst of life death.'

Klaus Radetzky glanced down at his rejected cover page and held his peace.

Undecided as to whether to offer to pick Isabelle up from home for their Monday evening dinner date, Craig had thought preferable not to rush things. He had no idea where she lived, whether she shared an apartment with someone else or even, which he doubted, had yet to fly the parental coop. All the more reason, he decided, to arrive at the château ahead of time so as not to keep his date waiting.

She, however, was the model of punctuality, pulling to a halt beside him in her bright new, peppermint green Renault Clio at eight p.m. on the dot.

Craig dismounted to greet her with a discreet French triple kiss on the cheeks.

Isabelle was wearing a smart, black short-sleeved jacket over an Indian cotton blouse on top of a black pleated skirt, which, without being eye-catchingly short, showed off her legs to advantage. Her finger nails were painted ebony decorated with a light yellow delicate fern motif. Apart from that, she had no need of make-up. Impossible, thought Craig, still enjoying the pleasure of a familiar fragrance, not to be won over by her natural good looks.

'A nice evening for sitting outside,' she said, pocketing the car keys in a small tote bag and turning to admire the château's lower gardens.

'Yes, I've booked a table for us on the other side, overlooking the vineyards. I hope that's all right.'

'Sounds good. Shall we go, then?'

They walked up the long flight of steps to the crushed gravel yard giving onto the bridge leading into the château. Isabelle paused to place both hands on the parapet and gaze down into the moat. 'I wonder if this place had oubliettes.'

'In the Dark Ages. I've forgotten how you say that in French.'

'Les temps sombres.'

'Well, on a lighter note, I like the way they've grassed over the footpath across this bridge.'

Isabelle pushed herself upright. 'Let's forget the forgotten, is that it?'

They were shown to a table at the front of the patio with a spellbinding view of the vineyards on either side stretching down towards the Vaugruge below. The air was still warm, the sun far from setting such that they needed the parasol to shade their head and eyes.

Isabelle ordered snails in garlic and parsley butter for her appetiser followed by an entrée of baked almond-dusted rainbow trout. Craig decided to order the same.

'Makes a pleasant change from my last boyfriend,' said Isabelle, once the waiter had moved out of earshot. 'He liked sharing different dishes.'

'Did that always work? Surf and turf?'

'Pardon?'

'I'm sorry. Fish and meat. Not sure my digestive system appreciates the wedding of opposites. Though, when it comes to that, I understand the healthiest way to start your meal is with the dessert. Fancy the idea of strawberry sundae first, then snails? I thought not.'

The waiter arrived with their mineral water complemented by bite-sized appetisers of tomatoes and chopped onions on toast. He opened the litre bottle of flat water and poured a measure into each glass.

Craig unfolded his bishop's hat napkin. 'Something,' he said, 'I've always meant to ask a true-blooded French person. Why *hors d'oeuvre*? Why unemployed?'

'You're serious?'

'Perfectly.'

Words were one thing, camouflaged mischief another. Isabelle eyed Craig quizzically.

'*Hors d'oeuvre* doesn't mean out of work. It means something aside from the main work. You knew that, didn't you?'

'Let's just say that I love hearing you pronounce *hors d'oeuvre*.'

'*Si vous préférez, nous pouvons parler français.*'

It was asking too much, Craig appreciated, not without disappointment, to expect her to be *tutoying* (addressing him familiarly as *tu*) this early on. 'No, no, no, Isabelle. Your English is head and shoulders above my French. What did you speak with your previous boyfriend?'

'French. He was Belgian.'

'Ah, the *n'est-ce pa*s race.'

When she burst out laughing, he wagged a point-scoring finger.

'There we are. I was right for once. The *frites* and mayonnaise brigade tack that on to the end of just about everything.'

'You include Marguerite Yourcenar in that?'

'I talk not of the written word, *n'est-ce pas?*'

It was at this point that the snails were served, a round dozen nesting in the hollows of each earthenware *gratin* dish. The waiter opened and dispensed a taster of *Pinot Gris* for approval before serving some to Isabelle.

'Dear me, so busy talking, we've forgotten about the appetisers. They've probably gone cold.'

'You'll hardly notice,' said Isabelle, 'if you eat them with the *escargots.*'

'Yes, well, it would be a pity to let them go begging.'

'May I ask you a personal question, Craig?'

'Go ahead.'

'You're not married?'

'Divorced. Married too young.'

'This was long ago?'

'*Les temps sombres.*'

'And since then?'

'A number of girlfriends, some slightly more permanent than others.'

'You've never felt like remarrying?'

'To be honest, no. Not sure I'm the marrying type. How are you enjoying the *escargots?*'

Isabelle Meunier took the hint.

When the trout arrived, they declined the offer to have it filleted.

Isabelle went about the task with surgical precision.

Craig offered the bread basket. 'Don't neglect the delicacies in the head, Isabelle.'

'Aphrodisiacs?'

'Not that I know of. Omega-3 in the fish. Roe, if you're lucky.'

'No roe in mine. Some liver like yours. Carcinogenic. Don't eat it.'

'Fair warning. How do you like the *Pinot?*'

'Nice.'

'Tell me something about your background, Isabelle. Before joining BLR.'

'Straight after the Université catholique de Louvain … ' She paused, eyeing him archly.

'I never said a word. After the Université de Louvain?'

'I went into publishing. Academic works. Research and conference papers, dissertations. Unfortunately, it was a small one-man business and the owner overreached himself. Misjudged the market. I'd been there for only eight months when he went bankrupt. But he was good to me. When it came to saying goodbye, he wrote a letter of recommendation to a banker cousin. Said he thought I was fast track material.'

'From words to figures. How are you finding the experience?'

'The pen is mightier than the abacus.'

'And did BLR take you on as fast track?'

'Yes. All it means is giving me more of a taste of front and back office than the average beginner. Then I come up against …' Isabelle wiggled the thumb holding her fish fork in search of the right words.

'BLR's glass ceiling?'

'Right.'

'You don't expect to be with BLR for the duration?'

'No, banking's all right as a stop-gap, but that's about it.'

'I see your people are building mammoth new premises on the fringe of town. And still they pay us a measly quarter of a per cent on our deposits. Wait much longer, and they'll copy the Japanese. Charge us negative interest for the privilege of looking after our hard-earned euros. I'm thinking of taking mine out and investing in a domestic, fireproof safe.'

'Not so loud. People might hear you.'

'All the better, if they happen to be bankers.'

'Don't let it spoil your meal.'

'No chance of that. The sauce hollandaise goes well with this fish. Think I overdid the lemon, though.'

She gave a quick, musical laugh. 'I saw the trouble you had with that.'

'Oh, the pip flicked onto the carpet?'

'Yes.'

'It's a crime, Isabelle.'

'The pip?'

'No, what I was saying before. It wasn't enough for fat cat bankers to bring the financial world to the brink of disaster with their bundled subprime mortgages. After getting bailed out by the taxpayer, they had the gall to go on raking in those indecent bonuses.'

'Yes, it's true. Some of BLR's top dogs must be living in clover.'

'And yet your bank employs people crass enough to leave a fortune in notes unguarded in one of its vaults. I could have …' Craig limited himself to hand gestures for the continuation.

Isabelle set her fork down to take a sip of wine. 'Naughty boy. But I lied to you.'

'You did what?'

'Those cameras are only turned on at night. I was told they kept them running for the first five years during normal banking hours, then decided it was a waste of money.'

'Really. They've never had cause to distrust their staff?'

'Apparently not.'

'Tell me, honestly. Did you not feel the slightest bit tempted today?'

'It would have been more than my job was worth.'

'That's not an answer.'

'I know. Of course, Craig, I was tempted.'

He took comfort from the fact that this was the first time she had spoken his name.

'I may not have been naughty this morning, but now that you tell me nobody was watching ...'

'Be careful. You're talking to a possible witness for the prosecution.'

If he had paused to question where his thoughts were leading him, Craig would not have known whether he was indulging in idle speculation or tempting fate. But he soldiered on.

'I suppose, had I known the all-seeing eyes were asleep, I might on the spur of the moment have shoved a number of high denomination notes into my deposit box. To teach your crowd a lesson, you understand?'

'Not quite as selfless as your *Robin des Bois*.'

'Well, once the shortfall was discovered the insurance would cough up, *n'est-ce pas?*'

'No, it wouldn't. Not after finding out that the cameras weren't working. And certainly not if it emerged that the notes were left out in the open.'

'Oh, tough t.... I mean, serve BLR right.'

'So, Craig, if you had helped yourself from the kitty in order to give us a lesson ...'

'Us, Isabelle? I don't equate you with that mob. Didn't you say ...?'

'All right. But if you were acting the aggrieved citizen getting his back on the banking fraternity, how would you then have spent your ill-gotten gains?'

'I would have donated them to a noble cause.'

'Such as?'

'The mortgage on my apartment.'

'You disappoint me.'

'Well, it never got that far for me to decide whether I wanted to emulate Robin Hood or Clyde Barrow. And surely, in the event of theft, BLR must circulate the serial numbers? The moment missing notes are offered over the counter of another bank ...'

Isabelle Meunier's gaze shifted to her plate. '*Vos carottes sont cuites?* (The game's up?)'

'Exactly.'

'Not necessarily. Are you forgetting how many banks turn a blind eye to money laundering?'

'Not worth getting my fingers burnt seeking one out.'

Isabelle's thoughts were following a different track.

'On the other hand, if today you had been an unscrupulous depositor with an accomplice on the inside, the two of you could have put one over on BLR.'

Craig set down his knife and fork, dabbed his lips with his napkin and began regarding his dinner companion from a fresh perspective. 'Well now, do enlighten me.'

Isabelle lowered her voice. 'The *coffre-fort* (safety deposit) box, immediately above yours is not rented out.'

'The large one?'

'Yes.'

'So?'

'I'll come to that in a moment. First things first. Had you been disreputable, after opening your box, you would have promptly transferred to it a modest four hundred thousand euros. That's eight hundred five hundred euro notes stored in eight packets of one hundred notes each. Next step, you would have locked the box, but told the clerk, there was something wrong with your key. The box would not open. The clerk would have informed you that it took up to a month to have a new key made. You could not wait that long. As it happened, you were thinking of renting a larger box. Was one available at the same convenient height? Really? Good. After taking out a contract on the box above, you would have used it to store away that innocuous-looking deposit brought in with you. Then you would have left the bank, having robbed it without spiriting one euro off the premises.'

'If my thoughts were naughty, yours, Isabelle, are in another league. Except that what would have been the point of all this?'

'Not to rush things. You wait for alarm bells. If the theft is detected before the week is out, you'll be called in for questioning, probably in the presence of the police. You explain that on the day of your visit there was a problem with your key requiring order of a replacement. This decided you to rent a larger box into which you could transfer the contents of your existing box later. Since the bank does not keep copies of owners' keys, you are asked to open your new box. No problem.

'By this time, the vault cameras will be working again during business hours. However, you have already given your accomplice, the clerk, both your keys. Each Wednesday morning at seven thirty, she is responsible for letting the *femme de ménage* (cleaning lady) into the vault. This leaves her free between eight and nine to switch the stolen bank notes from the smaller to the larger safety deposit box after packaging them in a sealed padded envelope. On Friday, you return to the same counter clerk, open your new box and leave BLR's Mensdorf branch with you know what.

'Better still, should the theft go undiscovered, with the cameras off there would be nothing stopping you before much longer from retrieving the eight packets from the smaller box after collecting the key from your accomplice.'

'Not that bright on my accomplice's part. If BLR wakes up to the fact that funds are missing, she stands to get hauled over the coals along with the rest of her colleagues.'

'Hauled over the coals?'

'Grilled. Not to the same extent as Jeanne d'Arc, but everybody authorised access to the vault's Midas compartment will feel the heat.'

'*Bien sûr*. She would …' Seeing the waiter ready to remove their plates, Isabelle held her tongue.

The interruption was not entirely unwelcome inasmuch as Craig was worried that he had caught the drift of Isabelle's suggestions. If his comely, fast track friend was seriously contemplating using him as a partner in crime, Craig did not relish playing the role of Jacques Mesrines.

Gathering up plates and the empty bottle of *Pinot*, the waiter enquired whether they would like more wine with their cheese. Craig ordered a small carafe of *Pinot* and a half litre bottle of mineral water. When the cheese board arrived, Isabelle limited herself to some *Brie de Meaux*, a slice of *Port Salut* and four white Muscat grapes. Craig chose *Roquefort*, *Crottin de Chavignol*, *Pont l'Évêque*, *Tomme de Savoie* and several purple table grapes. The waiter added baguette and butter to their bread basket.

'No copying this time,' said Craig. 'For once your boyfriend and I see eye to eye.'

'He's not my boyfriend anymore.'

Craig made a fair pretence of brushing this last remark off as something of little consequence.

Isabelle started on her *Port Salut*. 'All that spin cycling helps you work off the calories?'

'So far. That plus squash.'

'I've never played that. Volleyball. Hard on the fingers.'

'Compared to me, you're in great shape, Isabelle. I'm not getting any younger. Way back in the Dark Ages, I played field hockey for my county. The years have taken their toll. No longer the same speed or reflexes.'

'Well, only a handful make it to the Olympics. The rest of us content ourselves with recreational exercise.'

'Such as working out how to rob banks?' Curiosity combined with a sudden bout of elation brought on by more *Pinot Gris* made Craig curious to see if his suspicions were founded.

'I believe you were going to suggest we could escape Foucault's panopticon.'

Isabelle nodded, as if nothing could have been more natural than to resume the thread of the earlier conversation into which she was still wired.

'But surely not if a theft had been discovered? Then the cameras would roll twenty-four hours a day.'

'No, they are paused regularly each morning at eight o'clock, while the security guard reviews the previous night's images on his monitor before resetting the cameras to run from whenever. Why should BLR change that procedure? And the young Portuguese *femme de ménage* would be the last person to come under the loupe.'

'Well, now you put it like that, perhaps I, or *Monsieur Untel*, and his accomplice could pull off the perfect theft and give BLR a dose of its own North Korean sanction-busting medicine. On the other hand, has it not crossed your mind that we would be robbing other customers?'

'Not true. With the cameras working and showing nothing, and the bank falsely claiming the theft to be recent, the insurance would have to cough up.'

'But the bank would then be billed higher insurance premiums passed on to its customers in charges.'

'Spread thinly, Craig. Spread thinly.'

Isabelle cast an eye at the restaurant's generous cake trolley.

Unwilling to fault the flawed morality, Craig followed Isabelle's gaze. 'Ah, speaking of cupidity, do I detect *un faible pour le gâteau peut-être au chocolat* ?' (a weakness perhaps for chocolate cake ?)

'You're a mind reader?'

'Anything but.'

'How about you?'

'I think I could manage an ice cream.'

'Shouldn't you have eaten that before *les escargots*?'

'That would be as barbarous as spreading jam on my trout.'

The waiter presented both with the dessert menu. Craig lost little time in ordering a *poire belle Hélène*, while Isabelle indicated the cake trolley, inspected the calorie-rich contents, turned back to the menu and chose a *crème catalan*.

When their orders were trundled up, the waiter went unostentatiously about flambéeing the brandy spooned onto Isabelle's dish, leaving other diners to cast envious glances at what they took to be the flame of romance between a handsome young couple.

'I have to admit,' said Craig, 'that I envy your choice. No cabaret with this. Any idea which Helen my ice cream's named after? The one who inspired the quill of a bloody marvellous blind poet?'

'*Bien entendu*. Escoffier's way of commemorating Offenbach's Helen.'

'Indeed. Still, how would someone reputed to be a raving beauty like being remembered for her pear-shaped body? If she were African, perhaps. Might explain the hot chocolate.'

'Not if you remember the classical ideal of voluptuousness. Michelangelo's Eve was hardly anorexic.'

Craig was about to acknowledge this point when the shock of ice cream against his teeth brought home the reminder of their criminal peregrinations. Had Isabelle been a cat chasing its tail or had she taken pleasure from leading him on?

'Has it not occurred to you, Isabelle,' he said, grateful for the hot chocolate's palliative effects, 'that all our theorising about how to divest Harpagon of part of his loot is seriously flawed?'

'Of course,' she replied with a knowing smile before dipping her spoon into the caramelised surface of the custard crater. '*Ce n'est que tous les trente-six du mois qu'un confrère commettrait la même bévue en laissant ces portes-là ouvertes (Only once in a blue moon would a colleague make the same gaffe of leaving those doors open).'*

Craig poured another spiral of hot chocolate onto his pear. 'Furthermore, even if your idiot of a colleague were to commit the same blunder again, I'd probably stand a better chance of winning the lottery than of being in the same place on the same day.'

'Not if a little bird on the inside flapped its wings and let you know. Then you wouldn't need to play with keys and boxes. With the cameras off, you could stuff your pockets and briefcase and walk straight out.'

So that was it, thought Craig, Isabelle was prepared to pass from idea to deed. An enticing young woman with an alarmingly enticing proposition.

'That would be one very naughty little bird.' His spoon sculpted fruit or flesh. 'Any idea how much ready cash is kept in that vault's treasury compartment?'

'A good six million, of which four million in five hundred euro notes. That's eight thousand notes. You'd have a job carrying that much out.'

'Would there really be that many banknotes on offer?'

'Most probably.'

'Well, get thee behind me Satan.'

'Tell me, if you were caught, would you betray your canary?'

'Would I grass on it, to quote the jargon of a nation of gardeners?'

'*La perfide Albion.* (Perfidious Albion)'

'The answer is never. Cross my heart and hope to die.'

'Pardon?'

'Childish babble.'

It was not he who took the initiative to invite her back to his apartment. It was she who suggested her place; she who chose Leonard Cohen's *Suzanne* for them to slow dance to; she who undressed him; she who spurned the condom.

Two hours later, when their heated couplings had left them contentedly spent, Isabelle lay staring at the ceiling while slowly chanting Leonard's words about travelling blind.

'Craig,' she said at last, pushing herself upright on both elbows, 'be honest with me. Does every young woman who mounts a saddle in your gym end up with you mounting her?'

He burst out laughing. 'You've seen some of them, haven't you? What do you think?'

'I'm not to know how many attractive ones have been through your hands.'

'Rash, Isabelle, to mix business with pleasure. You can end up out on the street.'

'Are you saying I'm the first? The only one over all the years?'

'Two years.'

'In this club. Where were you before?'

'Another club. In Vancouver. Look, you've got me wrong. I don't go around sowing my wild oats like *la semeuse* on your coins.'

'That's not a smooth tongue talking?'

Craig propped himself up in turn and pulled the bedsheet over his head. 'Unkind woman. Incapable of recognising the voice of a maligned soul treading the bridge above his oubliette.'

She poked him in the ribs. 'I don't hear any chains.'

'That's because,' he said, letting fall the sheet, 'I may have shaken off my bodily chains but not those around my heart. I need a fair, blonde mortal to set me free.'

'And to help you swindle the swindlers.'

As if to be sure he had heard correctly, Craig banged his head against the back of the bed frame. He had. Suzanne was leading him down … to the river.

⁂

Rashid was analysing cash flow sheets spread out on the table next to his workstation when a knock came on his office door, followed by the head and shoulders of a white-haired, middle-aged stranger.

'Rashid Jabour?'

Rashid pressed the off key on his pocket calculator. 'Yes?'

The diminutive, round-shouldered visitor advanced into the room, holding a worn fedora in his left hand which he raised by way of introduction.

'Jack Mason. World Bank. My apologies if I've caught you at an awkward moment. Frank Welling suggested you might be able to help me.'

Welling was Rashid's departmental manager, which meant however much Rashid could have done without this interruption he had no alternative other than to stand up and extend the welcoming hand of interbank friendship.

'Do sit down, Jack. What can I do for you?'

Rashid eyed his visitor inquisitively as he placed his hat on a side table before settling into a metal frame chair designed with a view to privileging modernity over comfort. It only served to emphasise the World Bank man's stoop. Perched on the edge of his seat, Jack Mason put Rashid in mind of a feral cat.

Mason cast his eyes over Rashid's spartan, middle-management furnishings and the lack of any discernible personal touch other than a framed set of Arabic verses hanging alongside a map of the Middle East.

'The Koran?' he enquired with a nod towards the wall.

'Nothing so grand. A poem by my grandfather Najid Jabour. In praise of Lebanon's countryside.'

'Really.' Unimpressed or indifferent, Mason rubbed tired eyes. 'Haven't seen more than one skirt since I set foot in this building. MEDRIMCOMB not hot on gender equality? Or are you prejudging the Arab world – thinking they're happier doing business with men?'

'I wouldn't say that, Jack. We have quite a few women executives here. Two economists, one lawyer. Even one telecoms expert. Not bad going for a new organisation set to expand.'

'If it's anything like the World Bank, I imagine your managers keep the pick of the skirts for filling their PA requirements.'

Sensing that his preoccupation with flesh was beginning to pall on his host, Mason deftly changed subject.

'First year of operations. Well, I always say, get on board at the beginning, if you want to beat the others to the wheel house.'

'Well now, I'm curious, Jack. How can a beginner like me be of interest to someone of your experience?'

'Beirut.'

Sometimes a single word can convey a tome of information. But on this occasion, Rashid was none the wiser.

'I left Beirut for Paris when I was seven years old. I will probably have difficulty recognising the place when I go back there.'

Mason made the mistake of rubbing his knees only to grab hold of the chair's arm rests before saving himself from toppling over.

'But at least you know the lie of the land. A month ago, I attended a meeting in Washington with representatives of Egypt's Ministry of Public Works. We were told they planned to add colour to our next mission to Cairo with a sightseeing trip down the river to Luxor and Aswan. One of our young lions stuck up his hand and asked, "Which river would that be?" '

Rashid smiled. 'Not Ivy league. But there must have been a mistake. I suppose Welling thinks I know the city like the back of my hand.'

'He didn't exactly say that. Just told me you're due to fly out there on Wednesday.'

Rashid shook his head in confusion. 'Surely you've been misled, Jack? I'm still into my in-house probationary period. Not due for my business wings till the end of the year.'

'Well, Rashid, Frank Welling tells me you've already won your spurs. MEDRIMCOMB's management committee has given the go ahead to negotiating a package loan to the Bank of Beirut. Seems you're booked to fly out there with a couple of colleagues in less than forty-eight hours from now. No need to look exasperated. I'm willing to bet you'll be called into your boss's office the moment I walk out the door.'

Jack Mason's surprise announcement made sense of the cash flow analyses Rashid had been conducting when the man from the World Bank knocked on the door. The initial reaction of perplexed annoyance in the face of a stranger better acquainted than he with his work schedule rapidly dissipated, as the trainee grasped that he was to be spared months of deskbound boredom with a shot at winning his first stripes as a loan officer.

'That's great. Wednesday, you say ...' Rashid's fingers played a brief pitter-patter on a metal desk uncluttered of appurtenances save for a telephone, loose-leaf calendar, pen tray and blotter.' I didn't know that we were cofinancing with your people.'

'You're not. Yet. Next year, maybe.'

'So ...?' Rashid sandwiched the rubber from his pen tray between thumb and forefinger.

'Yes, unable, I regret, to give you the benefit of my experience with Bank of Beirut, because my and BoB's paths have yet to cross. No, I'm here for a different reason. Last month, I was flying back to Washington Dulles from Amman with a stopover planned at Rafic Hariri International. At the last moment, as always, they rescheduled the flight out of Beirut leaving me with precious little time to conduct some private business.'

Wondering what favour the World Bank man wanted from him, Rashid dropped the rubber back in its tray. 'Jack, I'm willing to help if I can. But I expect we'll have a pretty tight schedule of our own to keep to.'

'Don't worry. I'm not asking you to go far out of your way.'

Mason reached into his jacket pocket and extracted a card-backed envelope.

'I'd be grateful if you could deliver this for me, Rashid. Well, not for me so much as for all the good people who, at the initiative of the pastor at my wife's church in Annandale, have clubbed together to offer much needed support to Beirut's Christian community in the form of a handsome cheque.'

It was Rashid's second time to feel confused. 'You couldn't have dropped it in a letter box at the airport?'

'Something as important as this with message enclosed ought to be delivered by hand, which was my intention. The address was already written out in Roman characters. I hate to think what would have become of the cheque, if I'd left it to Lebanon's postal service.'

'Quicker to have wired the funds direct to a local bank.'

'Of course. One half of the donation is to be Swifted to the convent's Byblos Bank account. This cheque accounts for the other half drawn on a different bank.'

Mason handed the envelope across.

Rashid mused over the handwriting. 'Our Lady of the Sacred Heart Convent,' he said, translating from the French. 'I don't know this address. Where is it?'

'Out by the Martyrs' Cemetery.'

'But the Bank of Beirut's downtown, right?'

'Right. A taxi drive away.'

Rashid pondered Mason's words. The man's idea of a taxi drive away was probably an understatement. If that was the case, Rashid would find somebody on the spot to do the leg work for him for the appropriate baksheesh from his *per diem*.'

'You don't want it dropped off in the convent's letterbox?'

'No. Ask for the mother superior. If she's not there, ask for sister Ziara. One or the other is always on call.'

Holding the envelope vertically, Rashid tapped its lower end against his blotter. A nuisance, he thought. But no big deal. One way or the other, the cheque would get delivered. The decider: his manager expected nothing less of him.

'How can I say no to a fellow loan officer from the World Bank?'

'Economist, Rashid. The guy at the balance of trade end of the appraisal process.'

From both men's point of view the telephone could hardly have rung at a more convenient time. It was Rashid's team leader calling him into his office.

Taking the hint, Mason lifted himself out of an unforgiving chair and reclaimed his fedora by the crown. While waiting for Rashid to finish his call, he stood gazing out of the fifth floor window at the dual silver towers of Luritania's Central Bank, massive on the mid-distance skyline, all the time correcting the symmetry of the fedora's crown.

'Better let you get on with your work,' he said, as Rashid put down the receiver. 'Be sure not to lose that envelope, won't you? It means a lot to its recipients.'

After bidding his visitor farewell, Rashid walked up the stairs to the next floor, where he strolled down the corridor to the third door along bearing a nameplate labelled Marc Chevigny, *Directeur associé*.

By the time he left Chevigny's office half an hour later, Rashid had been given his assignment details plus flight, hotel tickets and a *per diem* cash allowance all arranged by one of Jack Mason's skirts, the charming and extremely competent Mademoiselle Nathalie Leblanc. Rashid's travelling companions would be Stephen Boyle – strictly speaking a Mashreq smaller businesses analyst, but until MEDRIMBCOMB's staff complement was beefed up this was better than nothing at all – and Horst Gottfried, one of the bank's environmental experts. Rashid concluded that Horst had definitely not drawn the short straw: since the team was charged with negotiating a microloans package, his input was likely to be minimal. But certain loan bible procedures were set in stone.

On the way back to his office, Rashid stopped by the coffee machine on his floor. After which, settling down into an office chair with, compared to Mason's doctor's waiting room model, all the bells and whistles attached (teal leather seat and arm coverings, head rest, height and angle adjustment, legs mounted on six castors), the young loan officer mulled over his good fortune. Not only had he been entrusted with a plum mission (the loan was sizeable) but he would be back in the office by late Friday night. This meant that, because MEDRIMCOMB personnel worked a 40-hour week from Monday morning to midday Friday, he would be given the Monday morning off. As the Beirut mission would not encroach upon his weekend, he would be able to attend next Sunday morning's Lenfindi Quintet get-together. He hoped the delectable Vanessa Curtis would be just as sure to attend.

Exiting London City airport, Justin boarded the DLR for Monument Tube station where he disembarked, walked the tunnels to the Circle line and jumped into the first train to arrive on the Centre line platform westbound for Oxford Circus, as he had booked into a hotel behind The Langham in Portland Place. With next to nothing to unpack, feeling anything but tired and with time on his hands, after running his eye down the evening paper's film list, he settled on Michael McDonagh's *Calvary,* which meant taking a bus down to Marble Arch. On leaving the theatre, he decided that Brendan Gleeson's anguished performance as an Irish priest confronted with the ineluctable against the background of untamed nature had put him in the right frame of mind for the morrow.

So much so that the idea of food made his stomach churn. He made do with the hotel room's fare of Garibaldi biscuits and camomile tea.

The next morning, his appetite recovered, Justin ordered poached egg on toast, baked haddock with scrambled eggs, toast and marmalade, and washed this down with strong black coffee. Before leaving for the funeral home, he stretched out on the bed in his room to trawl through news and weather updates: continued mixed messages from Russia concerning its position on Ukraine; another unarmed Afro-American shot by a white policeman, who needed seventeen bullets to get the job done; possibility of light showers in the Borough of Brent. Finally dragging himself to his feet, he pulled on the previous evening's light trench coat, stored his forgotten home apartment key in the room safe together with his passport and return flight booking tucked away there earlier, grabbed the bulky plastic room key and left for the underground.

Aunt Clarissa's mortal remains had been conveyed to a funeral home in Ladbroke Grove in preparation for the old lady's burial alongside her mother in Kensal Green cemetery. This meant that the journey was not going to be a long one: the Bakerloo line to Baker Street, followed by the Hammersmith line to Ladbroke Grove.

Ensconced in his seat in a fairly empty carriage, Justin began to reflect on life's transience and the cards dealt randomly by fate. The next moment, he was seized by the absurdity of the designation 'funeral home'. Did the undertaker live there? Did anyone, with their dying gasp, say: 'How I look forward to getting to my funeral home'? And had those who crowed 'home is where the heart is' ever read the story of Edgar Alan Poe's tell-tale heart? So, did funeral parlour sound any better? Perhaps. Though not cheek by jowl with a lip-smacking ice cream parlour. A parlour had to be a place where you sat and talked – in this case where you voiced gloomy thoughts or spoke affectionately of the departed. Don't talk ill of the dead was another piece of rubbish. Not that anything ill attached itself to memories of Aunt Clarissa.

And that euphemism, the undertaker. Justin shuddered: the damn draught, he supposed, from the carriage window opposite. Not that he could shake off his line of thought. What about funeral director? No, that sounded too upmarket. Incongruous even, since it implied a performance for someone beyond singing, shouting, clapping their hands, reading the lesson or telling the congregation what they thought of it. Mortician, then? Perhaps too bleak for some to stomach. Embalmer? That definitely sounded better for those not destined to be burnt to a crisp, were it not for the fact that undertakers were more schooled in dressing the dead than in removing their internal organs. On the other hand, Justin did not think that Aunt Clarissa would have taken kindly to the idea of having her brains reduced to pulp and flushed out of her nostrils.

This would be Justin's second funeral in the space of four years. Three years earlier he had lost both parents in a senseless motoring accident on the M6 outside Stoke-on-Trent, when an ageing ghost driver had ploughed into their car, bounced onto a second, killed herself, Justin's parents and turned a young mother in the third vehicle into a paraplegic.

Endeavouring to rid himself of these morbid thoughts, Justin sat back to survey his fellow travellers. But the more he became aware of his surroundings as his and the other carriages hurtled through another endless tunnel, the more he felt close to panic. What if it was his, their turn to fall victim to a deranged suicide bomber? Next stop Hades. Then the train emerged into the bright lights of the next station platform, and he came slowly to his senses. Better luck next time, Abdullah, he thought with no little relief.

After surfacing on the street outside Ladbroke Grove underground station beneath an unpromising grey sky, Justin reached for the A-Z street guide in his coat pocket to reconfirm which direction he should take. His goal lay down a road to the left of two traffic lights also to his left. With a strong breeze starting up, he regretted not having brought his telescopic umbrella with him. Noting that he was only just on time, he turned up the trench coat's collar and strode purposefully towards the nearest set of lights – all the while keeping an eye open for a florist's. As luck would have it, he chanced upon one on the corner at the crossroads. There were two customers in front of him and only one shop assistant. It called for patience, and he felt anything but patient. But by the time his turn came, he managed a taut smile in purchasing a small bouquet of friesias and a solitary violet tulip.

Both lights were against him and, although he was tempted, as the walking man had only just dematerialised, to make a quick dash across the second set, he decided against the wisdom of joining Aunt Clarissa quite so suddenly.

Jenkins & Sons Funeral Home proved to be a drab-fronted establishment. He thought it odd that no hearse was parked outside, until he saw the alleyway to a rear parking lot. Funeral homes were all the homelier with their Transylvanian death carts out of sight.

The manager greeting him at the front door made a good impression: a jovial individual with a warm grip, he contrasted with the stock figure of the dour, stove-pipe-hatted coffin merchant. Circumstances were depressing enough without the need for theatrical gloom and doom. It was not as if Aunt Clarissa had cut her wrists in the bath at the age of twenty-nine after composing visceral, mind-blowing poetry that would have made Ted Hughes hand back his laurels or as if the old dear, standing at the altar with an octogenarian bridegroom, had suffered the fate of Urma Thurman on her celluloid wedding day. Needless to say, it was heart-breaking to know that the poor woman had, like Iris Murdoch, left this world a shadow of her former self.

'All the world's a stage is it not, Mr Hendry?' said Mr Jenkins Sr. Justin wondered whether this was his routine philosophical opener when faced with the bereaved. On the other hand, a nephew was considerably less of a blood relative than a brother. In the event, he was relieved that Jenkins had not chosen the trite *one door closes, another opens*. Whereas Aunt Clarissa had been a fervent believer in the resurrection, Justin was convinced that the words spoken during the burial summed it up to perfection: ashes to ashes, dust to dust.

'I understand you've made the journey from abroad.'

'Luritania. A mere hour's flight into London last night. But perhaps I'm the last to arrive.'

'In fact you are, Mr Hendry. Let me take you through to the back room to view the casket and meet the other mourners.'

Another euphemism, thought Justin, while bound to admit that casket had the edge over the colder-sounding coffin. He wondered what had become of Aunt Clarissa's sandalwood jewelry box which he had seen on the dressing table in her care home. All gone to the thrift shop, Justin supposed, as he followed Jenkins Sr through to the rear of the funeral home bare, he was glad to see, of marble-topped tables decorated with sombre urns or miniature cypresses. Also mercifully absent were plangent background strains. His aunt, whom he had known to stamp her feet and hum along with Kylie Minogue's *Locomotion*, would have scorned the solemnity of being born aloft at the end of her days on the wings of Chopin's funeral march.

A small group awaited Justin. There were three women and two men, all seated bar one man standing with his back to the open casket and door through which Jenkins and Justin emerged.

But what captured Justin's attention as he drew closer was not the stranger, who, hearing the approaching footsteps, stood respectfully aside, but the open white-velvet-lined casket in which his aunt lay with her hands placed over a crucifix clasped to her chest. The embalmer, if such he could be called, had powdered the old lady's face, adding blush to her cheeks and a hint of rouge to her lips. Seeing Aunt Clarissa stretched out in this fashion, eyes closed, hair neatly brushed and wearing her favourite belted, blue cotton summer dress decorated with daisies, Justin wondered whether the impression gained of remarkable serenity was natural or the work of whoever had prepared her for this day. Moments later, his heart sank at the recollection of that numbing afternoon in the morgue where he had been summoned to identify the bodies of parents to whom he owed more than his existence.

The stranger facing Justin and his escort was a tall, florid-faced man whose ramrod straight back, squared shoulders, head held high and jutting chin lent him the air of a parade ground sergeant major in dressing down mood. This, he concluded, had to be the fellow who had undertaken (thoroughly correct use of the word in this case – Justin could not imagine such a character endowed with the finesse of an embalmer) the funeral arrangements.

However, when the stranger extended his hand and introduced himself gruffly, Justin decided that, rather than confrontational, he was ill at ease with the role thrust upon him.

'Stephen Cummings, lay preacher and friend of your aunt's. Saddened at your loss.'

If Cummings seemed embarrassed at having had to supplant Justin in assuming responsibility for his aunt's last offices, the nephew could not help feeling humbled in the presence of these people, who must have been in their own way very close to his aunt over the years.

'Your loss every bit as much as mine, Stephen. And thanks for taking care of everything.'

'Let me introduce you to Clarissa's other friends.'

Justin shook hands with Cummings's wife, Marjorie, another married woman called Bess, an elderly spinster named Phyllis and the only other man, who described himself as Aunt Clarissa's church sexton. Uncomfortable in an ill-fitting suit worn, Justin suspected, solely on occasions such as this, he nevertheless greeted Justin with the same unforced affability as Jenkins Sr.

Since the time was drawing close to when it would be necessary to close the casket, Jenkins Sr suggested that Justin might care to be left on his own with his aunt for a moment, while the others went through to the front until he called everybody out to the funeral cars at the back of the premises.

Justin kissed the old dear on her forehead and placed the friesias under her wrists.

'A shame you can't smell the scent. But those yellow, mauve and orange blooms are meant to brighten your soul's journey into the arms of Christ.'

Justin, Cummings and his wife Marjorie, sat in the passenger area of the hearse with to their rear Aunt Clarissa's now sealed casket bearing a number of wreaths, most of which, including one ordered from Luritania, had arrived at the funeral home courtesy of *Interflora*. The two other ladies and the sexton followed behind in a chauffeur-driven Lincoln funeral car. The two vehicles, moving at a snail's pace, were preceded by a tail-coated funeral home employee bearing a silver-headed stave with which he advertised their measured passage for a good fifty yards along the high street, before climbing into the hearse's driver-side passenger seat.

Only when Justin enquired as to why the choice had fallen on a funeral home so far from his aunt's church did he learn that renovation works were underway on the roof of Saint Cuthbert's. The vicar at a church conveniently close to Kensal Green had readily agreed to a brother vicar's using his church for the funeral service of one of his congregation.

On their arrival at Saint Mary's, the mourners found three women kneeling in the pews. Since they went unacknowledged by Cummings or the sexton, Justin gathered they must have been parishioners. Poor Aunt Clarissa, he thought, only six people to mourn your passing. Then it struck him that most of Aunt Clarissa's acquaintances would have beaten her to Saint Peter. This caused him to wonder how many would turn up for his funeral were he to die tomorrow. With no brothers or sisters, perhaps the same number: four of the Lenfindi Quintet, his secretary, Chantalle Boyer, and Klaus.

The vicar greeted each of the newcomers as they waited for the casket to be put in place in front of the pulpit from which he then paid warm tribute to Clarissa Heathcote's indefatigable support for his church's charities at home as well as in Africa, Asia and Latin America. Justin doubted whether much of his aunt's voluminous output of knitted woollen cardigans and pullovers would have gone to Kenya, Djakarta or Ecuador, although perhaps, as well as contributing to *Shelter*, it had served to clothe homeless earthquake victims in parts of North Africa.

The order of tributes must, Justin decided, have been drawn up by the vicar in collaboration with Stephen Cummings, because next into the pulpit was the lay preacher. He spoke without notes, praising Clarissa's successful door-to-door fund raising for *Shelter, The Samaritans* and *Great Ormond Street Children's Hospital*. He explained how she regularly helped out with floral arrangements at Saint Cuthbert's and contributed enthusiastically to decorating the Easter, Harvest Festival and Advent tableaux.

From a brief nod by Cummings in his direction as he prepared to step down, Justin understood that his turn had come to speak words that would never be heard by the very person for whom they were intended – unless, which he much doubted, notwithstanding the heartfelt words spoken softly over her coffin, Aunt Clarissa's belief in continued existence in some form and realm beyond the grasp of mortal comprehension was vindicated.

In view of his aunt's preference for the poetry of William Wordsworth, Justin rounded off his tribute by reading an abridged and amended version of a portion of the lake poet's *Tintern Abbey*. After reaching *'that best portion of a good woman's life'*, he continued:

'Her little, nameless, unremembered acts
Of kindness and of love … I trust,
To them I may have owed another gift
… that blessed mood
In which the burden of the mystery
Of all this unintelligible world,
Is lightened … that serene … mood,
In which the affections gently lead us on,
Until we are laid asleep
In body, and become a living soul:
While with an eye made quiet by the power
Of harmony, and the deep power of joy
We see into the life of things.'

No sooner had he regained his seat in the front row of the pews than he realised that his was the last of three eulogies to a gentle, unassuming being of seventy-three summers. There would be no obituary in *The Times*, no modified *Who's Who* entry for Aunt Clarissa. She was one of many whose memory of them would die with the last of their mourners.

By the time they walked out onto the front porch of Saint Mary's, the wind had picked up and dark cloud banks threatened rain. No sooner had the cortège reached the graveside than it started drizzling. All three women having had the foresight to bring umbrellas, Bess offered Justin the cover of hers. Long before the vicar had reached the closing words from *The Book of Common Prayer* and kissed the cross on his stole, Justin had drifted off into another world. At first, he thought that Bess's umbrella must have shifted away from him; then he understood the origin of the wet drops on his cheeks. He didn't know whether he was weeping for Aunt Clarissa, his parents, himself or all four. But the heavens seemed sufficiently lachrymose to compensate for the dry-eyed company around him.

There was no escaping the fact, thought Justin, that funerals reminded you of your own mortality. Worms or flames would not be denied feasting off his flesh. Nor need they wait until he was grey-haired. No matter how young and healthy he felt at present with his best years still in front of him, he was by no means guaranteed Aunt Clarissa's lifespan.

When the time came for the casket to be lowered into the grave, Justin bent down and let fall the violet tulip softly onto that part of the solid oak lid where he imagined her lips to be. While others scattered small handfuls of earth, he stepped back to find his shoulders encircled by a comforting arm.

'A great old lady,' said Bess. 'She made the best of her three score and ten years.'

'And now she's where she wanted to be. Reunited with her mother.'

'Seeing into the life of things.'

After shaking hands with the vicar, they made their way back across now muddy pathways and slippery grass to the waiting cars. Marjorie Cummings invited Justin to join the rest of the group for a modest reception of light food and drinks organised by her and the other ladies back home in Willesden. He had the impression that her offer was extended out of politeness rather than out of any genuine wish to get to know him better, and so felt no remorse in declining. Both he and they, he felt, understood they had little in common other than this now severed link with Clarissa Heathcote. It would be a relief not to have to endure the ritual of exchanging small talk over Mr Polly's *funereal baked meats*. On the other hand, after she left him to join up with her husband, this time in the sexton's car, Justin felt strangely lost seated alongside Bess and Phyllis in the back of the hearse where behind them part of the arrangement of one of the wreaths that had come loose as they were lifted out was sliding from side to side over a now empty platform. For a moment, he felt robbed, before realising that not he but his aunt had been robbed – by a nephew frugal with his affection.

Justin took the underground back to his hotel, where he washed, brushed up, collected his few belongings, checked out and walked in the direction of the previous night's outing. Vanessa had phoned him at work the day before to ask if he could hunt down a couple of copies of her forthcoming play in *Hatchards*. Remembering that one of his haunts, *The Stockpot*, was around the corner in Panton Street, he made up his mind to hop around there afterwards for bangers and mash, possibly followed by spotted dick, two of a nation of shopkeepers' culinary specialities yet to take the continent by storm. Aunt Clarissa, he felt sure, would never have begrudged him that.

When it came to seeking out the paperbacks of *Camino Real*, he found that *Hatchard's* only stocked this as part of a collection of Williams's plays, and Vanessa had made clear that if this was all that was available he should forget about it. However, Justin baulked at returning home empty-handed without trying elsewhere. He stepped out of *Hatchards* and continued on down the road to *Waterstone's,* where he came up trumps. After which, he saw that, with ample time to spare before catching his return flight, there would be no need to rush his meal. Perhaps, he thought, as he had had all he could take of the underground, he might make an exception for once and splash out on a taxi.

⁜

Tich's hobbies next to amassing literary collectibles were weightlifting and target practice, for which he owned licences for a .22 Martini International, a Remington pump-action rimfire rifle and a .38 Smith and Wesson revolver. But on his most recent visit to the firing range, after another club member had offered him to try out his 9mm Browning semi-automatic, Tich had been so pleased with the results that, seated at his desk by the shop entrance, he had begun surfing the web in search of local gun dealerships stocking this model.

There were a few customers browsing the shelves, one of whom would end up buying something since he had already had Tich put four hardbacks aside for him under the front counter, two of these devoted to the works of Chagall and Matisse, the other two to *Modern Conflict Archaeology* and *Sheng Fui Solutions for the New Millennium*. Because all were in near mint condition, none was cheap. Tich was heartened to see that there were still people prepared to pay good money for books at the higher end of the second-hand range such as expert or rare works. Since this fellow was still browsing, perhaps he was hoping to add to his purchases.

As if reading the shop owner's mind, the buyer in question chose this moment to sidle up alongside the front counter.

'I'm looking for a work on covert CIA operations written by a man called William Billings, purportedly a former employee of theirs, although it beats me how they could ever have allowed him to publish what he has.'

'What's the title?'

'*American Cloak and Dagger.* Not under Politics. Might it be somewhere else?'

Tich turned away from his monitor to take stock of the clean-shaven man in his late twenties or early thirties wearing a navy pinstripe suit together with what, in view of the man's soft transatlantic burr, could have been anything from an MIT to a Yale or Harvard University silk tie.

'That doesn't ring any bells with me.'

'Well, you can't be expected to know everything you have here. Could you not search through your data base?'

'Unfortunately, the firm I commissioned to set that up made a mess of things. They're still ironing out the bugs in their software.'

'Could Billings's title be stored under History?'

Tich tugged at a pained beard. 'I certainly wouldn't have put it there.'

'Do you think you could run an Internet search under Billings? In case I've got the title wrong. I imagine you know the right search engines.'

'Let's say I'm more familiar with metasearch engines than I am with chat rooms. My philosophy is simple. Twitter is for twits and Mugface – what else to call it? – is for mugs. I'd rather take the ice challenge every day for the next ten years than purvey my particulars online.'

'Somebody after my own heart. Try to see what comes up under William B.'

As the only William Billings of note thrown up by three different search engines was an American composer of psalms, Tich keyed in the title. 'Here it is, *American Cloak and Dagger*, published 1999. No mention of any D-notice. I suppose they have something like that in the States?'

'DA-notice. Any link to Amazon with reviews?'

'Yup. But no reviews. A single secondhand copy available online from …' Tich jiggled his cursor. 'One store in Ohio. No dustjacket, some underlining, worn pages, etc. Eighteen dollars plus ten for postage.'

'We can forget that.'

'Excuse my saying so, but this work hardly goes with your other purchases. A man, I take it with tastes as catholic as my own.'

'Those books are for friends.'

'And Billings?'

An urbane smile was a fraction late in dissimulating the downward turn of the eyes.

'Not so much a friend as an interested party.'

'Well, sorry I'm unable to help with that one. I'll make a note of it, though. That is, if you think you might be dropping by again. Or are you a bird of passage?'

'Hardly. I arrived here only last week for a stay of three years. At least, that's what I signed up for, but the diplomatic service likes shunting people from pillar to post at a moment's notice.'

Tich offered his hand in greeting. 'In that case, Humphrey Hobart at your service. Welcome to Luritania, Mr …?

'Palmer. Arnold Palmer.'

'Zounds, Arnold. How many people ask if you've been to one of those rejuvenation farms?'

'I tell them it was more a case of parental infatuation with golf.'

'Beats Bill Billings hands down. Diplomatic corps, you say. Up at the embassy on the rue Jacques Derrida, where they deconstruct the rest of the world?'

Palmer eyes shone a particularly intense blue. 'Not too wide of the mark, given that I'm the new cultural attaché.'

'Ah ha. So we, I, can hope to see more of you?'

'I should think so.'

'Let me present you, Arnold, with an ecologically-friendly hemp carrier bag for your purchases. On the house.'

'Why, thank you. No obligation to buy Diamond or Gore?'

'No, I doubt that either will lose any sleep over a rebuff from one of their own. Unless you're from Florida. I doubt whether Gore has got over that loss.' Tich finished tucking the four purchases into a pair of recycled paper bags, before slipping these into one of *Bibliopole's* hemp carrier bags. 'You'll be covering the local art and theatre scene?'

'Yes. I know, of course, that there's a strong American amateur theatrical group active here.'

'Right. Their latest Neil Simon production, *The Odd Couple*, sold out to packed houses.'

'Well, I'm also counting on enjoying some strong French, English and German theatre, professional as well as amateur.'

'In that case, look out for Vanessa Curtis's local amateur production of *Camino Real* slated for later this year. She's a powerful director, versatile and sure to grab your attention.'

The American picked up, read and pocketed one of the business cards stacked on the counter. 'I'll keep a note of that, Humphrey. Would that be as in Littleton or Bogart?'

'Neither, I fear. Humdrum Humphrey Hobart. Cash, debit or credit?'

'Cash. Here we go.' Palmer searched his wallet and came up with four notes to which he added the right number of coins.

'A refreshing change to see paper money. Most folk nowadays don't hesitate to pay plastic for as little as a Sunday newspaper. Maybe the odd South Sea Islander still pays with conch shells.'

'Civilisation's steamroller. Levels everything out.'

'Everything but not everyone. Therein lies the rub. Before you go, Arnold, I'd be interested to know … You look fit and trim. But it's not thanks to golf?'

'I try to work out in a gym, if I can find one.'

'Found anything suitable here yet? Because if not I can recommend *All The Right Moves* on the boulevard Auguste Lumière. It's got all the weights you need. Barbells, kettle and dumb bells, plenty of machines … I'm down there three evenings a week.'

'Boulevard Auguste Lumière. Named after one of the French brothers who beat Hollywood to the silver screen?'

'Yes, locals call it *le bal*.'

Palmer seized hold of his purchases. 'Humphrey, you're a mine of information.'

'Your best bet for keeping up with what's on in Luritania is *The Pulse*. Perhaps you've seen it already.'

'Indeed, I have. A smart piece of work.'

Palmer was about to turn on his heel when he slapped the counter with his free hand. 'Knew I'd forgotten something. If I'm not mistaken, you were looking up firearms on the net when I came in. You hunt?'

'Goodness, no. Would never have the heart to nail a hart. But no compunction about digging into venison, if it's served up to on a plate bloody and piping hot. How's that for double standards?'

'You belong to a gun club?'

'Rifle and small arms. Another of your non-golfing interests, Arnold?'

'You're forgetting my origins. All but born with a silver-handled Colt in my mouth.'

'In which case, you're right on target. Any time you'd like to accompany me down to the range, let me know. I'd be pleased to introduce you as a guest.'

'Thanks. I'll be sure to take you up on that, Humphrey.'

'Your speciality?'

'Used to be clays, trap and skeet out in the countryside where I grew up. Haven't shot clay in a long time. Nowadays, it's pistols over ten, fifteen and twenty-five yards, rifles over fifty yards indoors and a hundred yards outdoors.'

'Well, you've got my business card, Arnold. Give me a bell whenever you feel like checking out our club.'

'With pleasure. See you, Humphrey.'

Rarely had Isabelle seen her father in such good humour. Jean-Luc Meunier, the French embassy's *conseiller des affaires étrangères* (foreign affairs adviser) responsible for his country's external links with the Greater Luritanian Region had regaled his daughter with a wealth of spirited anecdotes while his wife, Charlotte, busied herself in the kitchen prior to serving up the evening meal.

Charlotte and Jean-Luc Meunier regularly invited their daughter around to their apartment for a mid-week chat over dinner. Tonight, Charlotte had prepared one of her signature dishes, *faisan cacciatore* in a cream sauce with fettuccini, chanterelle mushrooms, tomatoes, shallots and more than a *soupçon* of Armagnac. As her mother had been unable to share in much of the preprandial banter between father and daughter, Isabelle thought it only right, once Charlotte Meunier had settled down in her seat at the table, to enquire how her latest artistic projects were progressing. For her mother's creative talent expressed itself through diverse media ranging from water colours, copper engraving, acrylic painting and jewelry, to charcoal drawing, collage and, the latest experiment, papier-mâché. Upon learning how many different flowers and flower pots her mother had crafted during the past week, Isabelle insisted on being shown some before the evening was out.

'Your mother's forgot something in plain view,' said Jean-Luc, pointing to the Murano glass bowl in the centre of the table. 'Those eggs nesting there might look as if they are made of alabaster, but try weighing one in your hand.'

'Well,' said Charlotte Meunier, 'you two seemed to be having quite a bit of fun while I was slaving over my hot stove. Was there anything interesting, Jean-Luc, you were telling Isabelle, that I've missed out on?'

'Not really, my dear. In fact, I forgot to mention the best. A false alarm this morning at the German embassy. Apparently, the *Putzfrau* knocked over a lamp while she was dusting the ambassador's desk, and out fell what she thought was a bug. She ran straightaway to the security staff. They had a good laugh at the poor woman's expense. What she mistook for an electronic eavesdropping device turned out to be a piece of plastic from a transformer robot lodged in the base of the lamp. Mislaid there by one of the ambassador's children.'

Isabelle gave an amused shrug. 'Nevertheless, it is common practice, is it not, for you to bug one another?'

Her father flashed a glance at the reproduction of John Singer Sargent's *Oyster Catchers of Cancale* on the wall above the Meuniers' heirloom ormolu mantle-piece clock. Another acid pearl from his beloved Isabelle.

Determined to steer the conversation onto less potholed terrain, Charlotte Meunier first suggested her husband top up Isabelle's glass of *Crozes-Hermitage*, before adding: 'How does the only cyclist in the family feel about the fact that this year's Tour de France is to start in Luritania?'

'Helps put us on the map. Quite a few outsiders would be hard pushed to say where exactly Luritania is.'

But having conceded this much, Isabelle refused to be diverted from her private *cacciatore* course. 'Don't deny it, father. You all try to know each other's business.'

Jean-Luc used his napkin to dab the fine moustache beneath an aquiline nose. 'If it were so simple, Isabelle. However, I fear that, with the world becoming increasingly unsafe, it's only a matter of time before the microchip implants of science fiction become reality.'

After Isabelle had taken her leave of them, both parents concurred that their daughter had seemed more relaxed than during her previous visit even, in Jean-Luc's opinion, to the extent of playfulness. They knew that, despite not being ungrateful for the chance given her to make the transition from unemployed to employed at the drop of a kind word, she had kept her name on the capital's professional and executive register in the hope of finding something more stimulating than her current menial grind and the blurred prospect of rapid advancement along the financial conveyor belt. There was, she maintained, little joy to be had out of buttering the bread of a colossus bankrolling speculation at the expense of its depositors.

'A new boyfriend,' declared Charlotte on the strength of unerring instinct, bolstered by her daughter's announced intent finally to put down roots rather than continue to follow her parents to the back of beyond.

A new sense of purpose,' maintained Jean-Luc, although it bruised his ego to think that his daughter had inherited her strength of character from the distaff side.

One was closer to the mark than the other.

꧁꧂

Rashid was on his way out of MEDRIMCOMB's glass and steel HQ building to meet up with his colleagues in the downstairs foyer before they set off to catch their five-hour nonstop flight to Beirut, when he ran into his departmental manager, Frank Welling, in the corridor outside his office. The burly Yorkshireman had created a favourable impression on first encounter by touching upon non-work-related subjects, notably philately and numismatics (neither, as it happened, of interest to the new recruit) and the enthusiastic reception accorded Francis Huster during his recent stage adaptation of Albert Camus's *La Peste* in Luritania's *Théâtre moderne* (something easier for Rashid to identify with). A dedicated follower of world-class rugby football, Welling spoke French with exceptional, Camargue-accented fluency.

However, on this occasion, the manager's mood was anything but relaxed. 'Jabour. Off to Beirut, I take it?'

'That's right, sir. Everything I need, I hope, right there.' Rashid nodded towards the briefcase strapped to the top of his roll-on suitcase.

Welling accompanied him to the lift well. 'Some dreadful news, I'm afraid,' he said. 'I've just learnt that Frank Mason fell foul of the worst kind of mugger last night. The low life stabbed him several times. Two passers-by tried to come to his rescue after the rat took off, but Jack bled to death on the pavement.'

Rashid stopped in his tracks. 'Oh no, that's dreadful. Where did this happen?'

'Down by the Azaleengarten.' Frank Welling gave a weak, half apologetic smile. 'I remember from our World Bank days that Jack had a weakness for strip joints.'

Rashid shook his head in continued disbelief. 'Was he married?'

'Yes and no. More divorces than the average John.'

'And how did you hear about this?'

'Something of a fluke. News item on this morning's car radio. Report about a fatal mugging in town last night. Victim's only form of identification a Red Sox tie clip. That alerted me. As soon as I got to the office, I rang the police. Apparently, the bastard robbed Jack of everything. Wallet, passport – they learnt afterwards that he must have had it on him – and his watch. When the ambulance arrived to carry Jack to the hospital, they found a hat lying in the gutter. Later on, while adding it to the rest of his clothes in the hospital, one of the mortuary attendants chanced upon a card in the hatband. It had Jack's hotel details on it.'

The lift had arrived with Rashid free to ignore it, which seemed appropriate under the circumstances. 'Poor sod,' he said. 'What a way to go.'

Rashid's manager took the decision out of his loan officer's hands by being the first to step through the still open doors. 'Only five years off retirement. Life's a bugger, no doubt about it.'

Welling exited with a *Bon voyage* on the second floor. As the doors closed behind him, though it was not particularly hot, Rashid felt a single bead of sweat trickle down his back. Jack Mason's envelope lay in his left breast pocket, the only other belonging apart from the tie clip to escape the mugger's clutches.

⁂

After a satisfyingly stodgy meal in *The Stockpot*, Justin did not have to wait long before haling a minicab. Informing his fare that he was finishing his stint for the day, the swarthy driver cast a not dissatisfied glance in his rear view mirror at his Middle Eastern fare with the generic roll-on suitcase: the journey out to City airport guaranteed a paying customer back into town.

It was not until he had eased into his seat, and the vehicle had moved out into the traffic that Justin became aware of the neatly folded tabloid lying next to him. An unremarkable object had it not been for the yellow highlighting made by whoever's interest had been attracted to a particular news item. His professional interest aroused, Justin picked up the paper, then thought better and asked the driver whether he minded his taking the liberty.

The cabby threw a quick look into the rearview mirror. 'Not mine. Somebody must have left it there. What is it?'

'The Guardian.'

'Keep it, if you like. I'm a Telegraph man.'

Justin bent over the item:

Jim Mullins, a BBC freelance reporter back from Ukraine with eye-opening, behind-the-frontline footage, is bitter about his failure to open Downing Street's eyes to the death and destruction inflicted on the civilian population in the Donbass region in the east of the country. The government, he claims, has made its mind up about the rights and wrongs of 'a war fuelled by Russia whose rebels are sabotaging Ukraine's rapprochement with Europe'. Downing Street roundly repudiates Mullins's assertion that this war is largely misreported because of flawed monitoring of events on the ground around Donetsk and Luhansk by OSCE observers.

Justin checked through the rest of the tabloid without finding more highlighting.

When tossing the paper back onto the seat, his eyes fell for the first time to the floor and a smart leather briefcase, vivid crimson in colour, propped against his bench seat.

At first, he tended to dismiss this, unlike the newspaper, as none of his business. After all, the briefcase almost certainly belonged to the driver and had been thrown there by him. But the more Justin mulled it over, neither idea made sense: cabbies kept their private paraphernalia upfront, the tidier ones on the passenger seat (smaller items in the narrow central compartment), the not so tidy ones on the

47

far dashboard side and in the foot well below. But, however tidy or untidy they might be, none would leave any belongings, their own or somebody else's, where an unscrupulous passenger could lay his hands on them.

Then it occurred to Justin that a previous passenger, probably the one immediately before him must have forgotten this case. (Probably, The Guardian as well. Why go to the trouble of marking up something if you did not intend taking the newspaper away with you?) In other words, he should entrust the briefcase to the driver for handing over to his despatcher as lost luggage. Except that this cabby didn't appear to have a despatcher, because he wasn't wired into a waveband broadcasting traffic block and customer pick-up information to a fleet of cars. He was his own boss. Consequently, there was no knowing what would become of the case.

His curiosity piqued, Justin hoisted the briefcase onto his lap. It was made of sleek leather calfskin without straps to complicate fastening and unfastening. Just a flap secured with a lock and the finishing touch of polished brass reinforcements at the four bottom corners. But no shoulder strap, which might have explained how it had come to be left behind. He peered at the gold leaf under the lock: Giorgio Oliviero Benanti, Milan. Definitely left behind by a passenger.

On the point of leaning forward to draw attention to his find, Justin had second thoughts. Unworthy ones, he recognised, but pressing enough for restraint. The owner of this briefcase would never set eyes on it again. Of that he was sure. So why gift it to the cabby? He was bound to inspect the back of his vehicle before calling it a day. People probably left all manner of possessions on the rear seat which ended up in this fellow's home. No reason to add to the haul.

Justin hefted the briefcase to test its weight. Nothing exceptional. He shook it gently, taking care to keep the case near his waist rather than up in the air where the cabby might glimpse it in his mirror. Nothing shifted inside. He fingered the edge of the lock, at the same time glancing out at the blur of passing traffic and registering little. A few quirky head movements spelt indecision as to whether to risk looking worse in his own or, should he be caught in the act, the driver's eyes were he to pass to the next step. Justin moved a finger up onto the catch. The case was well and truly locked. He played at rotating the four-numbered combination lock set to prevent random opening. Pointless, he told himself, despite being unable to suppress regret that fortune had failed to smile upon him. Debating what to do next, he admitted that to hold on to his find was tantamount to robbery. But had he not himself been robbed? Of the nest egg accumulated over the years by Aunt Clarissa during her working life as a school bursar's secretary. Rancour brought a bitter taste to the back of his throat. Life had not been fair to his aunt at the end. Come to that, nor had it been fair to him.

Justin slipped the briefcase behind his back, a nervous but unnecessary precaution given that the driver had his eyes on the road and that the interior lighting was feeble. Opting for distraction, Justin began humming along in tune with the music on the cab's radio but soon tired of this as his ruminations wandered back to the question of moral and immoral behaviour. Why was a piddling temptation giving him so much trouble? Neither Aunt Clarissa nor Brendan Gleeson's priest would have hesitated to do the honourable thing. On second thoughts, Justin wasn't that sure about the father. Would he have lost sleep over a venial sin?

The fact was that nothing would be easier than to spirit away the briefcase and newspaper – the two had to be connected – together with his carry-on. Justin intended handing the cabby cash through the gap between the back and front seats, after which there would be no problem in whisking an additional briefcase out onto the street unseen and without giving rise to suspicion.

Which was precisely what Justin did upon arrival at City of London Airport, his task made all the easier by the sudden appearance of a woman out of the terminal's exit doors weighed down with luggage and loath to trek to the head of the queue. The vociferous reaction of two black cab drivers standing nearby was icing on Justin's cake.

However, it was only when Justin entered the terminal that it occurred to him that his new acquisition would have to be put through the X-ray machine. Moments later, waiting his turn in the baggage security check line, another awkward thought arose. What if they asked him whether the briefcase contained anything electronic? How could he tell? Supposing there was a cell or iPhone inside? Though certainly not a laptop. Of that he was sure. The briefcase would have weighed more than it did. And with the damned thing locked, how to answer that loaded question: 'Did you pack it yourself?' Possibly with a civil 'sir', added by way of turning the knife in the gaping wound of his embarrassment.

Justin decided to play it by ear. Let them see him remove the laptop from his own briefcase, after which he could try fooling them with some legerdemain in lifting both briefcases into the same tray with the new one at the bottom. As if nothing could have been more natural. Or remiss. Because if they picked up on this skullduggery, what then? No, nothing electronic there. Yes, he'd packed it himself but – would you believe it ? – he'd clean forgotten the new four-figure code set only yesterday.

Okay perhaps up to that point, but Justin's goose would be cooked if the bloke bent over the monitor on the lookout for plastic explosives saw something suspect in the case's innards and sent the red offending article back for detailed inspection. Then it would be better if they confiscated it. But they wouldn't. Not straightaway. They would have to determine what lay inside before deciding whether or not to bring charges against Justin for illegal conveyance of anything from lighter fluid, cocaine and counterfeit 500 euro notes to rhinoceros horn. So they would be obliged to force it open. At that stage, Justin's fate would be in the lap of the gods. The more he thought about it, the more he regretted not having left the briefcase where he'd found it in the back of the minicab. However, with no intention of handing the case over as lost property and no choice other than to continue on down the line, Justin resolved to brazen things out. Indeed, he felt counter-intuitively optimistic. Possibly because of Vanessa and her paperbacks. He was treading Williams's royal highway, guaranteed safe passage to his end station.

But was he? He suddenly recalled what Vanessa had pointed out about the double-edged *real* in *Camino Real*. Justin gritted his teeth.

It went without saying that the fumbled magician's switch could not go unnoticed. Which led to, 'Yes, I packed it myself … Nothing electronic. Kept the laptop in my old briefcase … Ah well, wish I could open it. Mental blackout, I'm afraid, about the combination. I'll have the devil's own job working that out when I get home.' Finding his patter greeted with condescension, Justin gave the tray a neat push onto the rollers leading to the mouth of the X-ray machine tunnel. Let that cyclopean device do its worst. As he walked past the tunnel toward the end of the roller conveyor, though he had intended to imitate an innocent passenger with nothing to hide, Justin could not help throwing a backwards glance at the official screening the briefcase's guts. In view of the time he was taking to make sense of what he saw on his monitor, he might as well have been conducting an MRI scan of Justin's head. But when a colleague standing behind the official bent forward to point at something on the screen, it was Justin's heart that felt the heat. Until the man ultimately responsible for passenger safety waved his colleague's objection aside.

To Justin's immense relief his several trays sailed through with flying colours. Milan's Benanti leather merchants had added a new fan to their roster.

⁂

At the end of her next spin cycling session at *All The Right Moves* led by Craig Roberts, Isabelle Meunier agreed with the recommendation that she should go over her bike's readout with him after showering and changing. Made openly in front of the rest of the class peeling off to the changing rooms or car park, none of whom would have found anything abnormal in their instructor's acquainting a newcomer with the results of his monitoring software programme, the recommendation was pre-arranged.

Remarkable, thought Craig, when she arrived at his side a mere fourteen minutes later, cheeks flushed, the picture of good health and indifferent to the stares of a middle-aged, overweight man exercising his pectorals with two expandable-retractable arm pulleys on wall-mounted blue steel cylinders.

Craig greeted Isabelle with a winning smile. 'Great performance.'

She smoothed a pleat in her cream-coloured skirt. 'I hope you mean what you ought to mean.'

'Of course. A compliment to your cycling skills. What else?'

'Well, are you going to offer me that print-out or sit there like a self-satisfied Buddha?'

'Miss Meunier, I am pleased to present you with the findings of Europe's premier health tracking programme. Read and consult at your leisure, but rest assured that you are in the pink of condition.'

Isabelle accepted the three proffered sheets of A4 paper, glanced at a set of figures on the front page giving pulse, heart and oxygen readings, turned to the back page packed with charts, Venn diagrams and a bell curve, folded the papers in half and tucked them away inside her shoulder bag.

'I should be,' she said. 'I've just taken a cold shower. I'm not sure about you, though.'

Before this point, the pair had lowered their voice to a level not patently below that audible to the man straining his chest and arms behind Isabelle. But Whitney Houston was now bolstering the privacy element with her full-throated *One moment in time* on the CD player one room over, where two of the club's personal trainers were at work.

Craig stopped nodding his head in time with the music, tapped the front of his laptop's keyboard and moved the icon across to a charm from which he selected sleep mode. 'I have another class straight after lunch hour. Feel like popping next door for a quick bite to eat?'

'Can we not settle for a snack downstairs?' All of which was shorthand for *Let's get going, there are things to discuss away from prying ears.*

After Isabelle had chosen a flaxseed salmon roll with carrot juice and Craig a tuna baguette, apple pie and orange juice, the couple repaired to a vacant back room reserved for personal trainers' time outs.

Isabelle insisted that it would be better to keep the door closed, until Craig explained that he could not afford the risk of someone with an axe to grind lodging a complaint of impropriety against him with the centre's owner.

'So,' he said, taking a plastic knife to scoop up some of the tuna's overflow, 'how are you feeling today? Everything all right?'

Isabelle gave a Gallic shrug.

'You're looking pensive. Something on your mind?'

'Yes. Gathering my thoughts.'

'Well, don't let the salmon go begging. It might help things along.'

Close to pushing the plate with her breadroll on it aside, she smiled, took the roll up in one hand, removed the top half, tided the salmon on the bottom half and started on a lettuce leaf.

'Have you thought about what we were discussing the other night?' The question seemed to be addressed as much to her slice of salmon as to her spin cycling instructor.

Its intended recipient narrowed his eyes. 'We discussed many things.'

'One in particular.' Her eyes were still down on her plate.

What followed, as Isabelle drew her gaze level with his, ran counter to what Craig was anticipating.

'I've been reading the latest report on the fall-out from the oil spill in the Gulf of Mexico. The authors renamed the platform Horizon Disaster. Do you know what they used to cap the wellhead? A toxic chemical agent. One that's seeping out, destroying millions of life forms. Imperilling the Gulf Stream. Bad news, Craig. You know why?'

'The Gulf Stream feeds into the Atlantic?' said Craig, attempting to digest this effusion of ecological earnestness on top of his tuna.

'Right. And if the temperatures start going haywire there because of BP's fuck-up, who's going to pick up the tab? You, me and everybody else on this side of the globe.'

Isabelle smiled at Craig's difficulty in reconciling espousal of the green cause with thoughts of taking BLR for a ride.

'Multinationals, Craig. Transnational corporations pathologically obsessed with profit. Bleeding the earth and consumer society dry.'

'You think the day will dawn when the little man says enough is enough? Forget it, Isabelle, the little man is walking blithely down the primrose path.'

Isabelle used her own exercise water to slake her thirst before starting on the orange juice. 'All the more reason for the likes of us not to kick our heels when opportunity stares us in the face.'

'Now it's my turn to say I hope you don't mean what I think you mean.'

'This can be done, you know. We can do it, you and I.'

At the sound of approaching footsteps, Craig threw an apprehensive glance at the open doorway. But whoever it was continued down the corridor to the nail parlour. 'I thought we'd exhausted fantasising about enriching ourselves at BLR's expenses.'

'Ourselves, Craig? Of course, not. We channel a fraction of one multinational's liquidity into deserving causes.'

'No we don't Isabelle, because, as you yourself said, we happened in on a unique banker's blunder. The rest is wishful thinking.'

'I told you less than the full story. You see, I know the code to the vault's cash compartment.'

For the briefest of moments, Craig wondered whether tuna could affect the brain. 'Come on, Isabelle. That can't be right. They must change it on a regular basis.'

'Eric Vandeweghe, our *directeur adjoint* (deputy manager), keeps the current code written on a card tucked in the back of a family portrait on his desk.'

'What?'

'*La preuve du pudding.* I tried the code out this morning and, lo and behold, my pudding was crammed with gold.'

Sudden loss of appetite caused Craig to push the apple pie aside. 'Isabelle, this is … You're risking big trouble.'

'The compartment's code consists of three letters followed by three numbers. The other day, when dropping work into Vandeweghe's in-tray, I noticed that the back of the family photograph frame on his desk was reinforced with a thin strip of cardboard lodged along one side. There were three letters inked in on it and three numbers in side-by-side columns. The letters were not that easy to make out because the card was upside down. The third letter could have been an R or a P. Then it struck me that it could well be a P. The P of AFP. I thought nothing of it at the time, but when I next dropped papers for signature into Vandeweghe's tray, I found the same piece of cardboard in place with no lettering on it. It had been turned around, grey side facing me.'

'What made you connect all this with the vault?' asked Craig whose response to the delicate hand gestures with which Isabelle embroidered her words in no small measure explained the hesitant shift away from his entrenched position.

'He has two ring binders full of AFP press releases. And I've discovered that he never changes the letters, only the numbers.'

'How did you manage to do that?'

'Went in one morning before he arrived while the cleaning lady was busy vacuuming and accidentally on purpose knocked over the frame, catching it before it fell. Only took a moment to remove the cardboard, taking care to remember which way round to put it back, and there they were, the letters AFP. The numbers alongside were different to those I saw before.'

'So even if this fellow were to drop his AFP in favour of something more original such as BLR, thinking no one was any the wiser – he would be kidding himself?'

Isabelle lent forward and clasped his hand in hers. 'We can do it, Craig. There are plenty of used high-value notes in there alongside the uncirculated ones.'

'With the cameras off. Perhaps. If you're sure the cameras aren't working. But...' (he hushed her with an index finger against her lips) '... so many things could go wrong. I could get caught red-handed. And ...'

'What? I'd walk free, while you went down. Is that what you're thinking?'

'No. Yes. No. I don't know, Isabelle. It's all too crazy for words.'

'Things won't go wrong. Not if you're slick and fast. After which we hide the money. Bury it in the woods. After all the fuss has died down and it's yesterday's news, we dig it up, drive across the border and bank it.'

'You seriously believe they'll open an account for two people arriving with a suitcase of banknotes, used or not, without questions?'

'That's the difficult part. We need a third party. A restaurant or shop owner willing to assure them that the money comes from his takings, that he's fed up with paying Luritania's high value added and business taxes.'

'So two become three, assuming, that is, that we find a willing partner in crime?'

'Have you any ideas?'

'No,' said Craig, flicking his eyes back towards the still open door. It was a lie. But whether the bookshop owner whom he had in mind would be as won over by the idea of consorting with bank robbers as he would be by Isabelle's concern for the environment was another matter. The sole burning question now was whether Craig Roberts was ready to commit himself to the point of no return.

'Anyway, few banks turn away respectable-looking, affluent customers. We could spread the loot over several accounts in separate banks.'

'You still haven't explained what you intend to do with the money after you've banked it.'

'I thought I'd made that clear. We write out cheques to Greenpeace, the World Wildlife Fund, Green Cross International, The Rainforest Trust, War on Want, *Médecins Sans Frontières*, Amnesty International ...'

'I should have guessed as much. Rebel with a cause or two. Have you stopped, Isabelle, to think how much will end up where it should compared to the amount gobbled up in administrative costs?'

'Enough to be better than nothing.'

'I'll come back to the main sticking point. What if I get caught?'

'Inside the vault?'

'Yes. With aluminium roller shutter blinds that should be locked fully open and the main vault door half open. What if somebody sees round it?'

'Half open? The gap is nowhere near as much as that. And you know it. Nobody will see a thing. Least of all the cash compartment.'

'I wish I shared your confidence.'

Isabelle gave Craig a smile as winning as it was complicit. 'There's something your fast track bank clerk forgot to tell you when she let you into the vault. I think you call it the clincher. On the right of the door is a button, which you should push when entering and leaving. On your way in, the button activates a red warning light above the entrance alerting staff to the fact that a client is inside. Push the button on your way out, as you're supposed to, and you cancel the light. In other words, nobody will trouble you.'

Craig looked up at the young woman who seemed to have an answer for everything. It did not help that he felt like cancelling his afternoon lesson and suggesting she call off work sick so that they could jump into bed at his place.

'Well, are you in or out?' Lack of persistence was not one of Isabelle's weaknesses.

Craig raised his hands against the table edge, splayed fingers calling for a moratorium.

'If I go ahead with this,' he said at length, 'I'll need to know how to lock down the compartment once I've finished.'

'Yes. That's easy. I'll show you.'

'But wait. I walk in with an empty holdall and walk out with a full one. Won't the weight factor look suspicious?'

'Nonsense. Nobody will give your holdall a second look. Apart from which, who among BLR's counter staff knows the size of your *coffre-fort* or whether you have heaps of Krugerrands stored in it?'

'True.'

'And it's not as if you're a weakling, Craig. A heavy holdall should be the least of your worries.'

Flustered by his readiness to grasp at straws, Craig uttered a nervous laugh. 'Perhaps.'

'So?'

One of Craig's personal trainer colleagues, a short, dark-skinned woman with an Afro hair style and ladybird ankle stickers, chose this moment to stroll into the room, flop down onto a couch beneath the window and start arranging the earbuds of her MP3 player. 'How are things, Craig? You on with step first thing this afternoon?'

'Fine, Caroline. Yes, why?'

'If your class isn't that big, think I could use part of the room?'

'No problem.'

'Great. Hope I'm not disturbing anything here. You two take no notice of me. I'm just going to crash out.'

'That's all right, Caroline. We're on our way. This young lady has to get back to work.'

Craig accompanied Isabelle to the car park, ostensibly to check his Jaguar's tyre pressures.

She paused, one hand on the top of her half-open car door, the other gently swinging her gym bag. 'Can we do this?'

'Can we? I would say yes. Should we, I would say no.' He raised a stilling hand. 'Will we? I would say perhaps. But first, I need to find our Harry Lime.'

'Who?'

'Our third man.'

Inaccurate but, Craig reflected, a moniker of which Tich might have approved.

On the way upstairs to his workstation and on the cusp of a decision, Craig questioned whether he was master of his own mind. Who was he trying to impress: the intrepid Isabelle Meunier or the unadventurous Craig Roberts? Swinging around the banisters at the top of the stairwell, he saw the familiar *All The Right Moves* poster facing him on the wall behind his desk. One of a series of extreme sports posters, it pictured a freefalling parachutist umbilically bound to his instructor. Craig was reminded of a remark made by Vanessa during the Sunday quartet's end-of-year meeting: *So much cosier to stay set in our ways than to reinvent ourselves.* Craig had concurred, nothing further from his mind at the time than stepping out into the great unknown. Despite that smile for the camera, not every landing was soft.

When Peregrine Musgrave texted J's private cell phone with news of the loss of the briefcase, the man from MI6 responded with a voice mail message, recommending an immediate get-together. The MP texted a second message to the effect that an immediate meeting was, for pressing private reasons, out of the question. The two agreed to rendezvous the following day.

Thus it was that the MP for Chelsea, Hammersmith and Fulham came to be treading the footpaths of London's Belgravia Square Gardens, a copy of the *New Statesman* under one arm and a fresh white carnation, bought only moments before, in his buttonhole. The tall, weather-beaten man awaiting him on a bench around the next curve was sitting with his head inclined in the opposite direction, absentmindedly twirling a bespoke, brass-topped, hazelwood walking stick from New Oxford Street's James Smith & Sons.

Some second sense alerted this taciturn individual to the approach of the rotund, beetle-browed individual with a thinning thatch of grey hair dyed black.

Musgrave, a seriously worried man, was in no mood to acknowledge the taste implicit in the Gieves & Hawkes light blue serge suit with matching Gucci leather shoes compared to his own off the peg John Lewis two-button seersucker

'Nice morning,' remarked J, staring into a bed of red tulips.

'For some, perhaps.' Musgrave placed the review next to him as a deterrent against foot-weary strollers.

J turned to face him. 'You look terrible.'

'I feel terrible.'

'Tell me.'

'A straightforward tale. Beginning, I get into a taxi, put the briefcase down. Middle, my cell rings. Dreadful news. End, I climb out of the taxi, leave the case behind.'

'Dreadful news?'

'From our son's school. While Stuart was ragging around with other kids in the playground, his head got banged against the wall. Badly. They had to call an ambulance. My wife and I spent the night at the hospital, taking it in turn by his side. Poor little beggar's still in a coma.'

'That is dreadful.' J delicately removed a caterpillar from the eye stitching on one lapel and set it down on the grass. 'I'm truly sorry. But young children can be amazingly resilient. Where is he?'

'Great Ormond Street.'

'The best. They work wonders.'

'Let's hope so.'

J turned his gaze back to the tulips. 'Have you given any thought to recovering the case?'

Musgrave loosened a tight collar. 'No. As you will appreciate, I've had better things to do.'

'We can't allow those documents to stay out in the public domain.'

'I don't see why not. They're hardly headline-grabbing material. No *for your eyes only* stamped on every page. No redacted sentences or paragraphs. Better still, they makes *Finnegans Wake* look as if it's plain sailing. '

'How can we be sure it hasn't fallen into the wrong hands?'

Conservative party and European Parliament member Peregrine Musgrave, whose constituents were beginning to comprise a worrying number of Brexit sympathisers, transferred his own gaze to the tulip bed.

'The next passenger the cabby picked up after me would have handed the briefcase over to him.'

'Did you see who his next fare was?'

'Did I …? What do you think?'

'Of course. Forgive me. All right, what about the taxi? Anything helpful you can remember about it?'

'It was a minicab.'

'You don't recall the company name?'

The MP's hesitation spelt a partial retreat from negativity. 'Wait a minute …'

Prolonged tongue biting culminated in a sigh of frustration. 'No good. Imagining things.'

'Perhaps the driver gave you his card. You put it in your wallet and forgot about it.'

Peregrine Musgrave scoffed at the suggestion, a cloud of doubt flitting across his face. Affecting weariness, he declined to reach into his jacket pocket.

'Any distinguishing features on the outside of the cab? Advertisements …?'

'All I can remember is white panelling on a grey background with the firm's name in black.'

'He gave you no receipt, the driver?'

'No. I paid cash.'

Both men ceased their exchange as a Labrador and a golden retriever on long leashes came sniffing around their ankles and under the bench. An elderly woman urged Rufus and Leo back into line.

'The cab's interior. Anything special? Think hard.'

Musgrave clenched his teeth. Think hard about the cab's upholstery? J had to be joking. But the next moment, a smidgen of recollection surfaced from otherwise lugubrious depths. 'Jordan,' he said. 'The driver was eager to chat. Told me he used to be a civilian airlines pilot flying Boeings in Jordan. After a while I tuned out, and he let me be.'

J's eyes lit up then shut down on this brief spark of hope. 'Sounded genuine? Perhaps he was out to entertain you. The better the entertainment the better the tip.'

'Must say, he sounded genuine. Pensioned off at 50. Retired with his wife to the UK. Joked that he must have been mad to decide to … Yes, wait now, something else … Start up on his own … transporting people at ground level. More dangerous than carrying them through the air'.

J nodded approvingly. 'I'll get our people to follow that up. Tell me, did he strike you as the kind of person … capable of robbing his own mother?'

'Difficult to say. Fact that a person sounds and looks honest needn't mean anything.'

'The combination was locked?'

'Of course. And with a briefcase as expensive as that I can't see my driver forcing it.'

'I'll try to get it tracked down. If your driver was not having you on, let's trust he's handed it in somewhere for tagging as lost property.'

'Well, good luck. Excuse me J, but I have to be getting back to the hospital. Be sure to let me know how things work out.'

The loss of the briefcase might have assumed the proportions of a nagging toothache for the man from MI6, but it had not blunted his sense of compassion. J shook Musgrave firmly by the hand. 'I trust your son will recover very soon.'

Musgrave left J sitting on his bench. A backwards glance a few steps later confirmed that he was still there rapt in thought. 'Counting the tulips', muttered the MP.

Walking past the gardens' Vitruvian Man sculpture, Peregrine Musgrave suddenly had the distinct feeling that J's efforts would go unrewarded. He was asking too much. Easier to square the circle.

After J, in turn, left the gardens, he cast a critical eye at the monument to Sir Robert Grosvenor with two faithful hounds at his side. My apologies, Sir Robert, he thought. Some things should never be for public consumption.

⁂

'Van, how nice to see you again,' declared Tich, shifting his feet down from the front counter. 'It's been a deadly dull morning. You've brought a ray of sunshine into this monk's cell.'

'I didn't think monks surfed the worldwide web for pornography.'

'There you do me a grave injustice. Apart from anything else, mental masturbation along those lines rots up your computer with everything from worms to Trojans. As a representative of your own fair sex might say, Not worth the candle.'

'Sorry to hear things are going slowly. One of those days?'

'I would like to think so, but then weekdays in general, apart from lunch hours and Fridays, are not electrifying. Can I offer you a drink?'

'Thanks, but I've had enough coffee to last me till tomorrow. I don't suppose you run to wheatgrass?'

'You suppose correctly, Van. Although I do stock grass of a different ilk. Strictly under the counter. Should you feel like getting through the rest of the day on a high.'

'Thanks, Tich, but I prefer to have my wits about me.'

'How's the play coming on?'

'In fits and starts. The fits outnumber the starts. I don't know whether it's a case of forty characters in search of a director or a captain in search of his submarine's escape hatch.'

'Forty! You have that big a pool of budding actors to draw on?'

Vanessa stopped turning over the pages of a paperback entitled *Meltdown: The End of an Era*.

'No, of course not. And I exaggerate. Tennessee Williams may have used a cast of forty or so for his first Broadway production, but Derbyshire Curtis has had to reduce that to twenty-five for her Luritanian premiere. A few will have to be quick change artists. Sometimes, I think I might have bitten off more than I can chew.'

'You have to admit *Camino Real* is not up there on most people's Tennessee Williams radar alongside *A Streetcar Named Desire* or *Cat on a Hot Tin Roof*. But then, of course, that's why you chose it.'

'I chose it, because of the way it breaks down the wall between audience and players. It's challenging at every level. Lighting, sound effects, wardrobe. I need volunteers to make up costumes for Don Quixote, Casanova, Lord Byron, the

58

Baron de Charlus, the twentieth century's Kilroy, a tinpot generalissmo shouting the scene changes … The list goes on, not forgetting the women. I take it you're not into sewing? Sorry, stupid question.'

'And the plot? I read the play so long ago, I've clean forgotten the plot.'

'Not so much a plot as vignettes.'

'Can't wait to see it. So to what do I owe the honour of your call? Before you say anything, let me warn you that I'm out of Aristotle's *Poetics,* Stanislavski's *My Life In Art* and Gielgud's *Stage Directions.*'

'If you ever had any of them in the first place. No thanks, Tich. I'm after something different. A gun.'

Tich guffawed, rocked back on his feet and threw a despairing glance at a ceiling flycatcher with no lack of corpses. 'What, for the play? Pop round the corner to the high street. Pretty good lookalikes, the plastic jobs they turn out nowadays.'

'I'm not looking for a water pistol. I need the real thing, damn it. A handgun. And you're the expert, right?'

Clasping the counter edge in both hands, Tich bowed his head apologetically, straightened up and eyed his svelte visitor with a look more critical than humble. 'Whatever for?'

'My morning jogs. Second attempted rape in the woods out on my side of town yesterday morning.'

'Change your route. No shortage of fitness circuits on the edge of town.'

'I'll be damned if I'm going to let some pervert dictate where I take my morning run.'

'Very well, buy a pepper spray.'

'No, Tich. I'm after the real thing. Not as in Stoppard. As in Smith & Wesson.'

He shook his head. 'The eternal tomboy.'

'Stop playing games Tich. I'm serious. Where can I buy a good handgun?'

'You can't buy a gun without a license.'

'You could buy one for me. Better still, let me borrow one of yours.'

'Out of the question. If the police stopped you, you'd be in deep shit, and I'd lose my license.'

'I see. You're not interested in helping me.'

Vanessa began to turn on her heels, but Tich reached across the counter and stayed her shoulder with his hand. 'Wait a minute, Van. Don't go ape on me. If you're dead set on this, I can help – but not overnight.'

'How do you mean?'

'First things first. Have you ever fired a handgun?'

'No, but …'

'Forget the buts. A beginner picks up a handgun and shazam, she knows how to use it straightaway?'

'I should say if she aims and pulls the trigger, yes.'

'After checking to see that it's loaded and the safety catch is off.'

'Niceties.'

'Wrong, Vanessa. Guns are dangerous things. They need to be treated with respect. And when a beginner aims and pulls the trigger, she's more likely to blast a toe off than to hit the target. What I'm saying is, if you're seriously interested in learning how to handle a firearm, you should accompany me down to the club, and I'll sign you in as a guest. If you're prepared to put in enough practice to have a reasonable chance of shooting this weirdo's balls off, we can think about enrolling you at the club and filing an application for a gun licence.'

'You'd do that for me?'

'Of course.'

"I really appreciate that, Tich. When can we start?"

'Wow, Miss Eager Beaver. In fact, it's one of my club evenings tonight. You free? No play readings?

'I'm free.'

'Great then. How about I pick you up around seven thirty?'

'That sounds fine. What should I wear?'

'Dress casual. Loose-fitting clothes. It's not going to be shotguns.'

'Sneakers okay?'

'Perfect. There's no dress code. Except, yes, you'll see veterans down there got up in all the macho gear – ammo belts and extras – but that's not for you just yet.'

'Glad to hear it.'

'So what have you decided to do about tomorrow morning?'

'What do you mean?'

'Change of route or rolling pin?'

'Oh, no. Pepper spray.'

'Pepper spray?'

'Yes, I've had one for some time now.'

'Are you having me on?'

'No. This shit doesn't need blinding. He needs castrating.'

When Peregrine Musgrave's cell phone started vibrating in his jacket pocket, he stood up to take the call in the hospital corridor outside his son's room.

'Hello, Peregrine, how is Stuart doing?'

Coming as it did from this caller, the question was unexpected. Musgrave could not remember having mentioned his son's name to J.

'Stable. His condition's stable.'

'That has to be good news, no?'

Musgrave shook his head as if both to clear it and to be rid of what, in his bleak mood, he uncharitably construed as empty civility.

In the absence of a response, J continued. 'We found the minicab driver.'

'Really? Oh, that's good.' Musgrave could scarcely have been less interested. His mind was elsewhere, his eyes on two trolleys being wheeled towards him, each bearing a frail, elderly male patient with all manner of tubes attached to him. Musgrave moved closer to the wall – a pointless gesture in view of the corridor's considerable width. Wrestling with the injustice of life's lottery – the pernicious hand dealt a nine-year-old boy and the curative hand dealt doddering septuagenarians, a burden for everyone, including themselves – he swung around, rested his head against the outside wall of his son's room and, muttering what one of the passing nurse's took to be gibberish, waited for his caller's next words.

'I need to see you again.'

'About the briefcase?' Musgrave turned around and propped his back against the wall. Flailing his free hand at the bubble of J's idea, the MP lowered his cell phone to listen for any change in the beep from the monitor in the room behind him.

'You still there, Peregrine? We need to meet.'

Musgrave gnawed at a knuckle. It was at J's insistence that they kept their phone calls short and to the point. But, as things stood at the moment, the father of a critically ill nine-year-old, was more open to talking things out remotely than to conferring face to face. On the other hand, was it even permitted for him to use his phone here? Might it not interfere with his son's monitoring equipment or the medical staff's pagers? The fact that Musgrave had not seen any notices to this effect didn't mean anything, given his current disturbed state of mind. Resigning himself to the inevitable, he pushed himself upright. 'When?' There was little point in asking where: they invariably met in one of three places referred to as B, LD or CH.

'Would mid-afternoon tomorrow suit you? Four p.m. in H?'

If there was no point in arguing the necessity for a meeting, Musgrave was not prepared to let J get away with thinking that his emergency outranked his own. 'Provided I'm not needed here.'

'Call me if you can't make it.'

The line fell dead before the words 'I will' left Peregrine Musgrave's lips.

After introducing Vanessa to the shooting club's secretary and registering her as a guest for the evening, Tich escorted his invitee out of the office down a corridor lined with photographs of competition winners and their trophies, then out of the building onto the small arms firing range.

'We'll try dry firing to start with,' he said, removing a brand new 9mm Browning from the shoulder holster in a carrying case containing more than one weapon. 'This here is a semi-automatic pistol with magazine. But another possible choice for you would be a revolver. Perhaps this snub-nosed Smith & Wesson 442.' He hefted the second weapon out of the case. 'Neither of these is loaded, of course. Chamber empty on the revolver. No magazine in the Browning. Safety first. Since you're right-handed, can I take it that's what we call the dominant hand? You're not ambidextrous?'

Vanessa punched him on the shoulder. 'Remember what you said this afternoon about shooting my toes off? Don't ask me to use my left hand. I'd hate to shoot my instructor.'

'Difficult to do dry firing.'

'I never asked Gwyneth what she thought about your fascination with firearms.'

'Gwyn? She would probably have told you it was pandering to the cowboy in me.'

'And was she right?'

'Let's put it like this, Van. You won't find my only copies of Owen Wister's *The Virginian* and William S. Hart's *Hoofbeats* on one of *Bibliopole's* ground-floor shelves.'

'Very well, Butch Cassidy, be sure to make a thorough job of teaching this Sundance Kid the tricks of the trade.'

'I'll do my best. Okay, after the dominant hand, what about the dominant eye?'

'That's a new one on me, Tich. Unless … Did I ever tell you that I grew up in the shadow of a super dominant father? No, I don't suppose your question is Freudian'

'Shall we concentrate on being serious for a change? Right or left-eye dominant?'

'How the fuck should I know? I think both eyes are pretty much the same.'

Accustomed to hearing Vanessa swear like a trooper, Tich had forgotten to suggest she moderate her language in front of his less outspoken shooting friends.

'Could we cut out the effing and blinding for a change tonight, Van?'

'Sorry. Carry on. I'll try to be a good girl.'

'Take your right hand and with both eyes open point at that target down there with the index finger.' Tich indicated the target immediately opposite Vanessa at the end of the 15-yard range where they were standing. Close your left eye. Now open it. Close your right eye. Open it. In which case did your finger shift off target when you closed your eye?'

'When I closed the left one.'

'Good. You're right-eye dominant, which is helpful because being cross-dominant, having a dominant right hand and a dominant left eye, would complicate things. Mind you it's more of a problem over long distances, and you're not interested in rifles. Right?'

'Not until there's enough snow on the ground for me to swap jogging for the biathlon. What next?'

'We get your grip sorted out. Here,' Tich took her hand, opened out the fingers and placed the Browning flat against her palm, the grip angled towards her wrist. 'Make a V with your hand as high as possible with your fingers wrapped around the front, thumb on top. Now bring your left hand up so that the second joint of your index finger is in contact with the bottom of the trigger guard. Then wrap those left hand fingers around the fingers of your right hand.'

Vanessa eyed her instructor quizzically. 'I really need both hands? Is this SWAT team country?'

'Believe me, for a beginner it's a damn sight easier than using just the one hand.'

'You sure about that?'

'In Olympic shooting, it's obligatory. We're not quite there yet, Van, are we?'

'No.'

'How does it feel? It shouldn't be uncomfortable.'

'This is okay.'

'Here let me help for a moment.' Tich adjusted the grip of her left hand so that the bone at its base nestled into the angle created by her right hand. 'How's that?'

'It's beginning to feel a bit awkward.'

'You'll get used to it. One more thing, since this is a semi-automatic, keep the thumb of your left hand off the top of your right hand. Otherwise, it'll get whacked when the slide kicks back. For the moment, relax. Hold the weapon down. Away from you, me and everyone else.'

'The weapon's not loaded.'

'Oh my, you'd be surprise how many people tell themselves that before finding their mistaken.'

'So now I aim and pull the trigger?'

'Hang on, let's not get ahead of ourselves. Next, get your stance right. Shuffle those feet more than shoulder-width apart. Good. Next, bend your knees slightly and lean forward from the waist. Whoa! Not that far. We're not the FBI training you for a shakedown. Ease back a little. Now relax. Take the gun back down.'

'Do I really need to bend my knees, Tich? It feels pretty damn ridiculous.'

'You do, Van, to help absorb the recoil when you fire. Now, bring your arms back up and try to form an isosceles triangle with them with your chest as the base. That's it. Elbows a trifle higher and slightly bent.'

'I'm never going to remember all of this.'

'Rubbish. It's child's play. Ready to take aim?'

'Longing to take aim.'

'Bring the gun onto your target. It's called zeroing. Some shooters prefer to bring the weapon down onto the bull's eye from twelve o'clock, some up onto it from six o'clock.'

'What's wrong with from nine or three o'clock?'

'Nothing. Whatever suits you. Okay, now level up the four corners created by the front and rear sights till you can imagine drawing a straight line across the top of them. Done that?'

'I think so.'

'Try to not to have more space on one side of your front sight than the other.'

'My grip's beginning to shake.'

'Perfectly normal. Relax. Bring the weapon back down. Then, when you're ready, try a dry fire. Shift your right foot back slightly, because that's where it needs to be to absorb the recoil when you fire for real.'

'I'm ready.'

'Use a firm grip, Van. Here, you're forgetting about that thumb.' He stepped in to correct the position of her left thumb. 'Can't have you injuring yourself first time out.'

'How's my aim?'

'Looks good.'

'One thing you don't need to tell me is not to pull the trigger. You have to squeeze this baby, isn't that correct?'

'I'm impressed.'

'Wait till I fire for real.'

'Everything in good time. Go ahead.'

Tich watched Vanessa conduct an unhurried, controlled dry fire.

'Not bad.'

'Let's load her, Tich. I can't wait to go for that round black bugger.'

'Okay. Patience. You're going to need those ear plugs and ear muffs we brought with us.'

'Really?'

'Better be safe than sorry.'

While Vanessa plugged and covered her ears, Tich tugged a loaded magazine out of the top of one of his shooting jacket pockets. 'Full clip. .22 rimfire. Minimum kick.' Placing it in her left hand, he raised his own muffs from around the back of his neck and secured them over his ears. 'Load her pointing down range.'

Vanessa slid the magazine into place, pressing it home with the heel of her palm. 'Let's go for it.'

'One last piece of advice. Best to get your breathing right. Take a deep breath, exhale but pause on the exhale to bring it all together.'

'Got you, captain.'

Tich watched his pupil settle into place and stood back with folded arms, his eyes switching between Vanessa's aim and the target.

He heard the sharp crack of the shot, saw the gun recoil and with no clear mark on the target's outer rings assumed she had missed completely. Then Vanessa took him by surprise by firing twice more. She lowered the Browning.

'Three's all I could manage without losing my concentration.'

Tich started rotating the target retrieval wheel. 'All right, place the gun pointing down range inside that shelf at your side.'

As soon as the wire conveyor brought the target within reach, he reached for and unclipped it, standing back in unfeigned admiration. 'Three bull's eyes. Two dead centre. One just below, breaking the ten ring. That is some shooting for a beginner.'

'Right-eye dominant, right-hand dominant. 'What do you expect?'

'Yes, well I was being pedantic about that dominant thing. It's no big deal over fifteen yards.'

'Can I go on?'

'Be my guest.'

Vanessa Curtis got through four more targets, firing thirty rounds and scoring well with her second and third targets, after which her shooting grew markedly less accurate.

'Enough for today,' she said. 'My eyes are tired, my arms aching. Perhaps we could try with the revolver next time, though I reckon I'm going to prefer this.'

Tich finished squaring up all five targets for Vanessa to carry home with her. 'A point to bear in mind with a revolver, he said, 'is that it's double action. When you pull the trigger, you first cock then release the hammer. Gives you time to think.'

'I prefer not to think.'

'Check the magazine and let me have that weapon back.'

She released the empty magazine and surrendered it and the Browning for packing away.

'My turn next,' he said, 'with the Smith and Wesson. You'll see what I mean about double action. But first pick up the cartridge cases and chuck them in that box over there.'

'Sure. Why the big grin?'

'You'd knock the socks off that poor sod in the woods.'

'That would be aiming a bit too low, wouldn't it?'

Peregrine was the first to arrive in Harrod's *Ladurée* tea room where he chose a secluded table and ordered a pot of jasmine tea, while 'waiting for a friend'. No sooner had the waitress left to attend to another table than he reflected that J might have been many things to him but friend was not one of them. There was something hardboiled about J which made the MP suspect that the toll exacted by tours of duty in war-torn parts of the globe had not been light. Not much had changed in that respect since he had been drafted in to assist the Secret Intelligence Service with its murkier business.

But in turning to regard *Ladurée's* other patrons bent over their afternoon cups of tea and cake stands and in noting the earnestness with which a middle-aged woman to his right was assailing the ears of a companion with no choice but to remain mute, he was reminded of the chasm separating him and his wife Margaret from the common run of mortals going about their everyday business unconscious of the kick in the teeth which life could deal them from one moment to the next. Margaret, his tower of strength, seemed to be bearing up better than he under the strain, though appearances, he understood, counted for nothing. On that first afternoon by Stuart's bedside, no sooner had she caught sight of the crucifix on the wall above his door than she had dipped into her cauldron of seething impotence and, with a venom equal to that of Lady Macbeth, ladled horror and rage onto the head of a trainee nurse with her shriek of 'Take down that witchcraft'.

Reacting with similar ill will to the woman whose trivial outpourings were beginning to irritate him beyond reason, Peregrine called on one of the Furies to hear his spell. But when his incantation failed to have the desired effect – instead of gumming the woman's mouth shut, it seemed to act as a spur to verbosity – the MP, deciding to seek distraction elsewhere, turned to his copy of The Times. Syria and IS, Ukraine and the separatists were still making headlines of sorts, although nothing compared to domestic political infighting. Since the latter was scarcely news to Peregrine Musgrave, he turned his attention to the snippets concerning those two major conflicts, the first on Turkey's border, the second on Russia's. More anti-ISS arms dropped from the skies by the no boots on the ground boys had fallen into the wrong hands. Par for the course, thought Musgrave. But the next two items made his skin creep: unverified claims that Kiev's latest abortive offensive was spearheaded by troops so drugged up to the eyeballs as to march fearlessly into death's embrace; and accusations that the Ukrainian high command, bemoaning a disgraceful desertion rate, was incinerating its cannon fodder to avoid compensating next of kin.

The MP folded his Times away and shook hands without stirring from his seat.

'How are things going at the hospital?' J, dressed in a less pricey suit than the one worn for their previous meeting, drew the chair opposite Musgrave from under the table and sat down taking care to avoid disturbing the other man's feet with his long legs.

'Still comatose. My wife's sleeping there permanently now.'

'His condition's stable?'

'Yes' said Musgrave, turning away as everything and everyone around him became blotted out by the image of his son's pallid face and feeble breathing under the oxygen mask. 'But the doctors say it's impossible to know whether Stuart's aware of our presence … You have to believe that being there for … with him … means something …'

'Unlike the old, the young, Peregrine, can prove incredibly strong in these situations. You should take heart from the fact that his condition remains stable.'

No longer inclined to dismiss J's interest in his son as an expression of polite concern and obliged to admit to his own prickly disposition, Musgrave suddenly found relief in opening up.

'It would be so much better if he responded to the pressure of Margaret's or my hand.' A pained father turned his head towards the ceiling, fending off the moisture dimming his eyes.

Both men were grateful for the waitress's arrival. J ordered cream scones, a selection of cakes and a pot of Lapsang souchong, Musgrave, toasted crumpet.

J waited for the girl to move away, surveyed his immediate surroundings with the air of someone lost in thought, then addressed the matter uppermost on his mind.

'So good that you remembered the Jordanian connection. The man has his own website: Come fly drive with me.'

Musgrave poured himself some tea and nibbled a complimentary Bourbon cream biscuit.

'But he wasn't able to help?' That much was obvious. Why else would they be meeting?

J seemed to have tuned out. As Musgrave watched him staring absentmindedly at the rambling-rose gilt artwork decorating the frame of a mirror on the far wall, the MP wondered whether, at times like these, his companion was back in some godforsaken outpost in Helmand province. J had chosen today to wear his tie clip with the blue on white enamel 29th commando regiment badge.

'No,' said J after a lengthy pause, following which he readjusted his focus onto the tiny vase of columbines on the table in front of him. 'Not for dint of trying.'

It was then that Peregrine Musgrave understood. 'What did you …?'

J shushed him with a wearily defensive hand. 'Denied having set eyes on it. Well, you would, wouldn't you? From a different culture to ours, Peregrine. Used to taking people for a ride, if you'll excuse the pun.'

Their orders arrived in a flurry of activity, one waitress depositing J's teapot and scones with all its trimmings, the other delivering Musgrave's crumpet and J's cake stand.

Musgrave spread melting butter over the warm crumpet. Should he have lost his appetite? On the other hand, what was the retired Jordanian airlines pilot to him, or he to the Jordanian?

'How did you leave him?' The question, out of false decency, before the first bite.

J had started spreading cream on his scone. 'Believe me, Peregrine, I abhor violence.'

J made a ritual of adding the strawberry jam after the cream, leaving Musgrave at a loss as to how someone could want to smother *Ladurée's* 'classic' clotted cream.

'But,' said J finally, sensitive to the need to break the hiatus, 'extreme circumstances call for extreme measures.'

'What our friends across the pond mean by appropriate tools to intercept and obstruct terrorism? Patriotism by any other name would smell less rank.'

J took a sip of his tea. 'Your Jordanian has survived treatment kinder than that meted out in Abu Ghraib.'

'All to no avail.' By now Musgrave had almost finished his crumpet and, though not hungry, was eying a slice off honey and lavender loaf cake on J's cake stand.

'Please,' said J, catching his companion's gaze. 'Do help yourself. All paid for by the Crown.'

'It's lost then, the briefcase?'

'Well, we're sure the driver never set eyes on it. It calls for exceptional fortitude to lie in the course of sacrificing fingernails.'

A mortified Peregrine Musgrave shifted nervously in his seat. Easier by elision to move on. 'A passenger helped himself to it?'

'So it would appear.' J licked strawberry jam from the side of an affirmative index finger.

'Hardly the end of the world, them against us.' Musgrave used the tea room's silver cutlery to halve the slice of loaf cake.

'All depends on whom we understand them to be.'

'Huh, could be anyone from a shoplifter to a knight of the realm.'

'Need one be the antithesis of the other?'

It was rare for J to crack a joke, however dry.

'Mr X manages to open the briefcase and finds your papers. What will he make of them? Nothing. Fit for firelighters. End of story.'

'That, Peregrine, presupposes prescience on your part. We cannot afford to leave it at that.'

'To my knowledge, taxi drivers don't keep passenger manifests.'

'True, but they do keep credit and debit card receipts. We found those for the day in question. There were none beyond two in the afternoon, and I understood you left that cab around three.'

'Yes, I received the call from Stuart's school at half past two and got the driver to drop me off twenty minutes later at the hospital.'

'In other words, our thief paid cash.'

'Taking you back to square one. Needle in a haystack.' Musgrave wondered where their circular conversation could possibly be leading. J had called this meeting for a reason. Uncharacteristically, he was taking his time to make that reason clear.

As if reading his listener's mind but preferring to delay enlightenment, J sat back, saucer and teacup in hand, savouring his Lapsang souchong. 'They say curiosity killed the cat but with the cat out of the bag, the creature's demise is, as far as we are concerned, academic.'

Musgrave gave the remark one of his take-it-or-leave-it sniffs. 'Rather out of the bag and up in smoke.'

'Not if it falls into the hands of vermin on a par with hackers.'

Peregrine Musgrave raised unsympathetic eyebrows. 'J, with nobody to point the finger at, your hands are tied.'

The taller man pulled his legs out from under the table and surveyed the cake stand at some length before removing a slice of Dundee in the manner of a player claiming a significant piece from his chessboard.

'Of course,' he said, 'we urged your driver to try to remember whether any of his passengers had behaved unusually … suspiciously … And, needless to say, bearing a red leather briefcase away with them. But it was asking too much.'

Musgrave decided that if he was in for the long haul, he might as well not let the tiramisu go begging.

But, as it turned out, J was nearing the centre of his labyrinthine meanderings.

'Our people went through the Jordanian's home from attic to cellar – not that he had a cellar. Garage rather.'

For once, Musgrave felt something other than indifferent self-interest take the upper hand. 'He was married, wasn't he?'

'Is married, Peregrine. Is. Don't make things sound worse than they are. The wife and two young daughters were locked in the bedroom – after it had been searched.'

'The Jordanian won't let you get away with this, J. He'll go straight to the police or press. If not both.'

'Set your mind at rest, Peregrine. He's not one of your constituents.'

'He won't take it sitting down.'

'I think he will. We had the good grace to indemnify him and his family.

Handsomely, I might add. It was the least we could do after acknowledging our error.'

'An error of State? The Jordanian swallowed that?'

'Whether he did or not is immaterial. What, however, may prove to be material is a pointer found after turning the minicab's passenger compartment upside down.'

'What pointer would that be?' asked the MP, glad to think that J was on the brink of getting to the point.

'A business card.'

'Which,' said a disillusioned Musgrave, 'could have been lying there for months tucked behind the back seat.'

'In fact, a crisp, freshly printed card found on the floor below the driver's drink-holder compartment, where a person leaning forward to tender cash could have dislodged it from his wallet.'

'So?'

'Your Jordanian high flyer did recall one significant drop-off. His last but one of the day at City of London Airport. The card we found was a European business card.'

Musgrave wriggled uncomfortably, as much from psychological blindsiding as from a chafing collar.

'Long shot, isn't it? Could mean sod all.'

J confounded his audience of one with a sleight of hand that all but produced the business card out of thin air. 'Schönschlucht. An address in Luritania. One of your stamping grounds.'

However worthy the piece of prestidigitation, the patter struck Musgrave as a letdown. 'But J, come on now.'

'Come on now?'

'Yes, I mean … for goodness sake … In the first place, you're taking something for granted, and in the second place how many people will that business card have been given to?'

J scrutinised the card more than was strictly necessary, its contents being known to him back to front after he had researched the business on the web.

'A publishing house. Its editor-in-chief with a very English-sounding name.'

Musgrave threw up his hands in a gesture dismissive of J's performance. 'And with a list of advertisers and subscribers as long as your arm.'

'But all known to him, no?'

The question went unanswered, because Peregrine Musgrave had felt his cell phone vibrate and was already taking the call.

'Margaret,' he said, 'that's wonderful. You're sure? No possibility that … No, no, that's so good. Just need to offload something, then I'll be along right away.' Musgrave delivered these words with a pointed glance across the table at a man still holding his ace of spades. 'How are you doing? Good. Me, I'm fine. Well, much better now. Ring me again if you need to and … take care.'

'Good news?' enquired J.

'Yes. They think that Stuart is slowly coming out of his coma. All the signs are promising. Restless leg syndrome, incoherent babbling, eyes opening and closing …'

'That has to be good news. You should be going, Peregrine. Leave me to settle up here.'

'Thanks. But before I go, what did you want to tell me that might change anything as regards those damn papers?'

'You're scheduled to fly across to Luritania next week for a European parliamentary committee meeting. I thought, Peregrine, you might call in on the editor-in-chief named on this card and tell him that somebody from his neck of the woods dropped in on you unannounced last week. You were busy and unable to spare this person the time of day, so you offered to look him up when you hopped over to Europe the following week. It's annoying, but somehow you mislaid his business card.

'However,' – and here J paused with the clear purpose of underscoring what followed – 'inside a copy of a magazine left behind by him in your office you found this business card and thought the editor-in-chief might be of assistance. Particularly since you weren't sure of the person's name. I suppose you could hazard one or two names for credibility's sake. I leave that to you. But be sure to ask him if he recalls handing his card out recently to anyone who might have flown to London.'

'And if it was a woman who picked up the briefcase?'

'It wasn't. The Jordanian remembered that much about his fare that afternoon.'

'Loads of business people travel backwards and forwards between London and Luritania.'

J grimaced. 'I'm sorry. I left out the obvious. Tell him your man was carrying a brand new red leather briefcase.'

'Frankly, J, I think we're on to a wild goose chase with this one.'

'It would be remiss not to try.'

Taking hold of the business card and his newspaper, Musgrave stood up. 'Very well, if things continue to look better in the hospital, I'll do your bidding and call in on …' he turned the card over in his hand, 'Mr Hendry, when I travel to Europe next week. If I can't make it, you'll have to send someone else.'

'Let's hope your son rapidly regains consciousness and that won't be necessary.'

'Thank you. Good day, J.'

'Good day, Peregrine.'

Craig had invited Isabelle to meet up with him in town to discuss at their leisure and in privacy 'a promising development'. He chose a salad bar popular with diet-conscious office workers and shop assistants. Bench seating along the walls of the *Ile aux Trésors* was interspersed with artificial palm trees and bird of paradise plants set in solid tubs arranged so as to offer patrons coves of calm and seclusion. He found Isabelle seated within an alcove towards the rear of the salad bar, where she was perusing a copy of the day's *Luritanische Bote,* while sipping mineral water.

Careful not to attract undue attention, they exchanged modest kisses.

'You're being watched over,' said Craig, motioning with his eyes towards the palm fronds above her right shoulder serving as perches for a pair of artificial parakeets.

'Unlike me they don't need feeding.'

Craig took up a seat on the cushioned bench alongside Isabelle.

'You should have ordered something, instead of waiting for me.'

'I feel like soup. Would you mind getting me a bowl?'

'Sure. What kind?'

'*Crème de poireaux au cerfeuil*. And a round of flax pita bread.'

When Craig rejoined her, he was carrying a tray with her order and his own, a dish of chilli con carne and a slice of cheese and asparagus pizza.

'You're not drinking anything?' she asked.

'No.' Craig set the dishes down on the table. 'I drank a good litre of water before I left the gym. How are things with you, Isabelle?'

'I'm surviving.'

'The healthiest policy,' he said, starting on the chilli. 'I couldn't help noticing what you were reading there. Belarus. Why the interest in what's happening on our eastern flank?'

'My father saw this coming.'

'Saw what coming?'

'The American octopus reaching out its tentacles into fresh territory.'

'Your dad said that?'

'Not in so many words. He's a diplomat, remember.'

'Could it be then that what you … what we are contemplating is partly a snub to authority?'

'That's preposterous.'

'Yes, I suppose it is. You're very much your own person.'

'And since when has my fitness instructor taken to reading *Jung for Dummies*?'

'Ouch, another one bites the dust.'

'Now that we've touched on the world news and whether I might be a suitable case for Jacques Lacan, I think it's your turn to explain what you meant over the phone by a promising development.'

'I've found our third man – our backer. Willing to participate, but on his terms.'

'Which are?'

'If he's going to be the one to open the account, then he has to be the principal accountholder, on the understanding that each of us would have power of attorney to make withdrawals.'

'He's trustworthy?'

'Yes, he's trustworthy. But that's not all. He favours placing the money with the China Reconstruction Bank in Haut Lieu les Lacs. In a renminbi account.'

To Craig's surprise, Isabelle took this suggestion in her stride. 'I like it. A man who sees the yuan as a future reserve currency. China's GDP has to all intents outstripped America's, especially bearing in mind how the U.S. Treasury keeps printing paper like it's Monopoly money. What line of business is our backer in?'

'He owns a bookshop. Second-hand books.'

Isabelle stopped stirring coolness into her soup. 'And he expects to walk into a Chinese bank in north-eastern France with a suitcase full of euro notes and make out these are the proceeds of second-hand book sales? What's the secret of his success, Craig, this friend of yours?'

Craig pulled a wry face. 'His shop's called *Bibliopole*. All that says to the Chinese or the French for that matter, because he'll probably be dealing with francophone bank staff, is that he sells books. And he will tell them, if necessary, that he has a long-running contract to supply Luritania's university and schools with textbooks.'

'Does he?'

'What do you think?'

'And how does he explain all these book purchases being paid for in cash? How many people pay cash nowadays, let alone for bulk orders?'

'He's got that worked out. He tells the Chinese bankers that, fed up with the derisory interest paid on his Luritanian deposit account compared to that on offer with them, he has cashed in his chips and decided to ditch the euro in favour of the currency of a new world order.'

Vanessa looked doubtful. 'He's the kind of person able to get away with that?'

'If ever a person could pull the wool over someone's eyes, it's my friend Tich.'

'What kind of a name is Tich?'

'It's slang for little. Tich is bear-sized. Have you read Steinbeck's *Of Mice and Men*? No. Well, one of the characters in that story is a giant of a man Steinbeck chose to name Lennie Small.'

'Like calling Gargantua *Tom Pouce* (Tom Thumb)?'

'Not really. Whatever you call him, Gargantua is still a brute. Humphrey Hobart – Tich's actual name – and Lennie Small are mild men. '

'And this Tich never so much as baulked at the idea of partnering us in crime? Tell me more about him.'

Craig set down his fork and relaxed against the bench's back rest. 'I've known Tich for three years. Two years before I arrived here, Tich's wife, Gwyneth, was diagnosed with cancer. Apparently, Tich pretty much worshipped the ground she walked on. So you can appreciate how devastated he was. They had just celebrated their ninth, I think, wedding anniversary. Gwyneth was given six months to live. She died within four. Tich has remained resolutely single ever since. Claims Gwyneth was irreplaceable.'

Craig took a deep breath before returning to his chilli. 'I'm sure you'll take to Tich. He's a big, warm-hearted man. And then there's Vanessa Curtis, a close friend of Gwyneth and still supportive of Tich. Gwyneth and Vanessa both read English at Clare College. But since Gwyneth was four years older than Vanessa, their paths never crossed in Cambridge. After leaving university, whereas Gwyneth went on to teach mentally challenged children, Vanessa branched out into time-study engineering. I must introduce you to Vanessa. She's a talented amateur theatrical director. Mind you, some find her tongue a tad rough. I happen to like her. She's one of a kind, capable of stepping in and, in her own inimitable way, lifting Tich's spirits. I guarantee the three of you will get on well together.'

Craig paused to sample his pizza. 'There's another reason why you and Tich should hit it off. His bookshop's window display this month is devoted to raising awareness of environmental degradation.

'But, to answer your question as to how or why he agreed to come in on this with us, I suspect that had something to do with Gwyneth. I'm told she liked kicking over the traces. Perhaps some of her non-conformist side has rubbed off on Tich. He said we should take BLR to the cleaners.'

'All right. When are you going to introduce me to your friends, Tich and Vanessa?'

'We meet up every Sunday morning at the airport together with Justin Hendry, editor of *The Pulse*. Four of us until last Sunday, when we welcomed a fifth recruit, Rashid Jabour, a young Lebanese working for MEDRIMCOMB. If you're free this Sunday, I'll take you along to meet the gang.'

'How can you be sure the rest of your friends won't view me as a gatecrasher?'

'I think they'll greet you with open arms.'

'Our plan is strictly between us and the friend you call Tich?'

'Of course. His lips are sealed.'

'Well, now that you've educated me about your friend and the rest of your Sunday band, can I take it that it's all systems go?'

'Perhaps better decide that after you meet Tich. In case you have second thoughts.'

'Why should I?'

'Frankly, I can't imagine why you should.'

'Then let's it get done tomorrow. Friday afternoon. Ideal. People are too concerned about clearing their desks to be focused on their duties.'

Craig agreed. There was no point in delaying. The longer they spun things out, the more likely he was to get cold feet. In fact, with the nuts and bolts of their scheme preying on his mind, he had revised his opinion about final execution.

'Only one thing, Isabelle. I've been thinking about the best way to go about this. I'm convinced your original plan A is the one we should stick to. Let me tell you why. If I go sailing in and out of your branch with a hold-all on the same day that those notes are filched from the vault's cash drawers and whoever checks on the contents of those drawers does so that evening or the next working day, then every visitor to the safety deposit room …' He held up his hands in anticipation of the obvious. '… and every bank employee present that day will be suspect. Yes, I can spirit the money away and bury it in the woods. They'll grill me, search my apartment, my locker and desk at the gym, perhaps turn *All The Right Moves* upside down and they won't find a thing, but why expose ourselves to all that unnecessary agro when taking things calmly ensures that no hint of suspicion attaches to me?'

Isabelle looked up from her soup. 'You'd still need to bring something along with you to camouflage what you stow away in your box.'

'Of course. Easy enough to conceal in my clothing. The only items exhibited in plain sight of the cameras in your reception area will be a couple of envelopes in which a client might be expected to keep bonds or share certificates in need of depositing.'

She picked up her paper, folded it into a baton and tapped him first on the right, then on the left shoulder. 'Congratulations, Sir Craig. Your noble contribution to our cause is not unappreciated.'

'I think,' replied Craig, returning to his chilli, 'that I should be kneeling for such an honour not sitting on the same level as majesty.'

'Pray first that I'm not *la reine Margot*. Her lover came to a sorry end. Beheaded.'

'With a newspaper?'

'All right, Sir Craig, your head is spared the block. In the interests of operation Chinatown.'

'Is that what we're calling it?'

'Why not?'

'Bad omen. The character played by Jack Nicholson had a flick knife stuck up his nose.'

'All right. Operation Mah Jongg,'

'That's better. But, as I said, no sense in rushing things. We take it in stages.'

'Then I suggest stage one, as you said, this Friday afternoon.'

Craig felt the heat of something other than chilli. But not for long. The fact that the two of them would no longer be acting alone told him to commit. If the readiness was all, Craig was ready.

'What time?'

'Around two o'clock. You don't want to be the last customer of the day before we close at four. People will remember you.'

'Trouble is I have a class from two to three.'

'Can't you get somebody else to take it?'

He thought for a moment, staring vacantly at one of the imitation parakeets with its head inclined towards an open tablet being scanned by a young woman with a fifties' bouffant hair style in the cove opposite.

'Probably.'

'Good. I'll ring you around one thirty. Bring your cell phone along. In the event of my having to warn you off, I can ring you inside the vault. With the red light on, you can be sure that back office staff will leave you alone in the safety deposit room. But we can't be so sure about Vandeweghe. He's an arrogant man and a law unto himself. If he makes a move out of his office, I'll see him from where I'm sitting. Since there's no way of telling whether he'll look in on you on his way to the loo, I'll give you a buzz.'

'*Merde.*'

'Let's hope that's all he'll be interested in. Anyway, once you've opened up the treasury compartment, closing it is child's play. I'll show you. Above all stay calm. Treat it like any other normal visit to your *coffre-fort*.'

On his way back to the fitness centre, Craig was forced to brake to an abrupt halt when a young man plugged into his MP3 player walked out blindly into the street from between two parked cars. Nerves frayed, Craig fumbled the gear lever and put his Jaguar into reverse, provoking a strident warning from the van behind. It was after he found drive and began moving that he heard a voice ringing in his ears – that of a budgerigar mimicking Isabelle's 'stay calm'.

⁂

Rashid and his two travelling companions decided to spend the ninety-five minutes stopover in Frankfurt Airport going their separate ways before meeting up at the departure gate half an hour before boarding time. There was no need to change terminals, since their flight was scheduled to leave from the same building into which they had disembarked. Glad of the opportunity to be free of his colleagues, especially after Stephen Boyle had persisted in tapping his brains about Beirut's recent unhappy history and differences between the country's Muslim, Christian and Druze communities, Rashid resolved to give the duty-free boutiques a miss, find a cafeteria where they sold coffee other than Starbucks and sort through his paperwork. Despite the streamlined efficiency of MEDRIMCOMB's working methods, the paperless office dreamt of by Boyle's environmental clan remained a distant prospect. And on business trips such as this bank practice required the exchange of numerous documents signed by the principals and witnessed by both sides' duly authorised deputies as well as by the intermediary bank's lawyer. In fact, this would be only the preliminary getting-to-know-you meeting. The loan contract, to be approved at a future meeting of MEDRIMCOMB's board of directors, would be signed at a later date between both parties in Luritania, when, Rashid was to make it known, it would be his bank's pleasure to welcome its Lebanese counterparts.

What the three European bankers were offering was a subsidised credit facility in answer to the Bank of Beirut's application for a package loan. The proceeds of this loan would underpin the borrowing bank's non-subsidised loans to job-creating smaller businesses in the manufacturing and service sectors as well as to subcontractors supplying the government's public infrastructure needs in the power and water purification sectors. Whereas Horst Gottfried and Stephen Boyle would be taken on a tour of prospective loan beneficiaries' plants, Rashid did not expect to set foot outside the Bank of Beirut's offices, where he had to get answers, the bulk on the spot, others only following his return to Luritania, to a raft of accounting and associated financial questions.

As it happened, the *Lessing Bar's* coffee was nothing to write home about, but the shelves lined with copies of *Laokoon, Minna von Barnhelm* and other of the writer's works made a refreshing change from the latest drumbeats from *Time* and *Fortune* magazines. Were it not for the fact that he had other things on his mind, Rashid would have dipped for inspiration into the pages of *Nathan der Weise*. But uppermost in his mind was the envelope tucked into his right breast pocket opposite the pocket containing his passport and flight tickets.

He set the envelope down on the table in front of him and pondered the writing. Easy enough to copy, but it would mean having to search for a replacement envelope among the stationery shelves or racks in one of the terminal's newsagents, and he could not be bothered. Did that not explain how one of the items gathered at the last moment from his pen tray on leaving the office had been a glue stick? A matter of subconscious anticipation.

Rashid withdrew a pencil from his briefcase, inserted the pointed end under one of the top corners of the envelope's flap, pushed the pencil deeper and, with one hand holding the envelope firmly in place, slowly rolled the pencil down towards the midpoint so breaking the flap free of the sealant, a procedure repeated from the opposite top corner. He ended up with a clean separation free of tears. Pinching the top and bottom of the envelope so as to hollow it out, he then tipped the contents, two folded sheets of stapled A4 paper, into his other hand. Rashid squinted into the concave chamber in search of something smaller lodged at the bottom or adhering to one side or the other. But there was no cheque.

He set down the envelope and opened out the two pages. They were a cargo manifest detailing, among other things: carrier (*TransMediterranean Shipping Company*), container vessel (*Le Marquis de Honfleur*), port of lading (Marseille), port of unloading (Beirut) and date of arrival (next week). The comprehensive list of the vessel's consignments included winterised canvas tents, tarpaulins, mattresses, sleeping bags, blankets, pillows, oil lamps, primus stoves, kitchen utensils, drinking water containers, infant formula, six hundred dried food packs, toiletries, medicines …

Rashid did not understand. Why had Jack Mason disguised the true nature of the envelope's contents from him? With every item bearing the stamp of either the UNCHR or International Red Cross, this shipment was clearly intended for the Shatila and Bekaa valley refugee camps. And what more natural than that the sisters of a nearby convent should play a part in distributing such essential humanitarian aid? The more Rashid tossed these thoughts around the less he could make sense of Mason's behaviour. Unless the American had been told only half the story.

Whatever the truth of the matter, this consignment removed one weight from Rashid's mind: the young banker could stop fantasising about the mugging having anything to do with the envelope entrusted to him by Mason.

Rather than using the glue stick to seal the manifest back in place, Rashid decided to wait until he had photocopied both pages in Beirut. Don't worry, Jack, he thought. Rashid the wise will deliver your letter.

❦

Arnold Palmer strolled past the embassy's furled stars and stripes hanging above side-by-side portraits of Barack Obama and Joe Biden, introduced his security card into the slot in the door to the corridor leading to his office, helped himself to a coffee from the pot left on a side table outside by Annabelle Fisher, the pert secretary shared between him and his colleague, the information officer, waved good morning to the consular officer and finally sat down in front of his desk on which Annabel had deposited the best part of the documentation requested by him yesterday.

In theory, he should have genned himself up on his new posting in advance of arriving in Luritania. But Palmer had reasoned that a country the size of a cornflake on the scale of world geography (he had won thirty dollars when not one colleague in the Port-au-Prince office managed to land a dart within inches of Luritania on the map pinned to a cork board in the strategy office) and with a population less than that of Toledo, half of which were foreigners, could hardly boast a mammoth history or cultural background. In other words, he would digest what little there was to digest after making landfall in the diminutive enclave. Not, of course, that it would do to come the Texan rancher over the Rhode Island hog farmer. Not unless he wanted to be sent packing on the next boat to the Aleutian Islands.

Suddenly caught with a hacking cough which left him clearing his throat of an unwelcome impediment, Palmer slapped the flat of his hand down onto the larger of two piles of documents and snatched up the topmost of Annabelle's papers entitled: *Luritania – Language and National Identity*. Not the best of starts to his morning, Palmer concluded, after finishing a rapid read of three pages devoted to a mongrel language which he had no intention of learning beyond a few polite phrases (*Benmirgen* – Good morning; *Wie maakt jo vandeg?* – How are you today?; *Danki, danki* – Thank you; *Tanki* – Please. Damn confusing.) The sole redeeming feature: place names were predominantly German, French or bastard versions of one or the other language. The national motto, *Sine ira et studio,* meant nothing to the cultural attaché until he read further. Coined from Tacitus, these watchwords were intended to convey the balanced impartiality of a tiny nation state sandwiched between its monolithic neighbours. Switzerland, he muttered, without the army knives, cheese and Alps.

Apart from one work of merit, an epic poem by Ludwig Giessheim about Lambricius, a mythical paladin whose heroic deeds were inspired by Amborix, a Gallic prince reputed to have made mincemeat of one of Caesar's legions, Luritania's writers had tended to favour German, French or Italian rather than their native tongue, presumably because this was the only way in which they could reach a wider audience, the vocabulary of the one Indo-European and two Romance languages being richer than that of their own. Translators had not been queueing up to immortalise their works in the tongues of Goethe, Voltaire or Dante. The sole epic, Oskar, *Der Retterhoun* (Oscar, the Rescue Dog) was based on an event recorded in the national press towards the close of the nineteenth century: when a Luritanian guard dog caught scent of a fire in one of his master's outhouses during the farmer's absence, this resourceful hound by the name of Oscar ran three kilometres to the nearest dwelling where someone was finally able, after a number of failed canine entreaties before uncomprehending bipeds, to grasp the significance of agitated barking and doggy motioning towards the evening skyline. Catching sight of a faint but unmistakable glow, Oscar's mind reader tied his horse up to his buggy and with Oscar at his side raced to the fire station down the road. Although by the time the fire brigade reached Oscar's place the fire had spread to a nearby barn, the firemen stopped it from reaching the farmhouse. When it emerged that the fire had been the result of arson at the hands of a disputatious neighbor, this individual was promptly clapped behind bars. Awarded the fire brigade's medal of bravery worn on a ribbon around his neck, Oscar was pictured alongside his proud master on the front page of the *Luritanische Bote.*

The country had sired its fair share of artists and sculptors, albeit none of international repute. The sole exception: an early nineteenth century photographer who had exhibited in New York, Toronto, London and Paris.

Reading on, Palmer learnt that in April 1944, in the aftermath of the outbreak of World War II, the current prince's grandmother had decamped to England from where she had joined forces with de Gaulle in issuing confidence-bolstering broadcasts aimed at denouncing fascism and assuring those under Nazi subjugation that liberation would not be long in coming – in the event four years later. On the other hand, Annabelle's sources indicated that a fair number of German sympathisers living in the south of the country had collaborated with the invading force, doubly complicating life for a brave but relatively small resistance movement.

Plenty of vineyards down by the Vaugruge River on the country's southern border, producing mainly dry white wine. Local cuisine a hodgepodge of everything from Austrian to Vietnamese, which Palmer took to mean that when the ambassador was entertaining prominent local figures to lunch or dinner, the culinary tune would be called by Bocuse.

Prominent among the recently elected government's 'new vectors for the future' were plans to: cut down on money laundering (here, Annabelle had added 'pull the other'); sever financial links between church and state; grant citizenship to long-established foreign residents (provided, Palmer concluded, that their knowledge of Luritanian extended beyond *Tanki)*; smile on gay marriages but draw the line at gay adoptions (earning this mention a pencilled *hooray!*); bolster an undermanned police force; and promote geothermal energy. Otherwise, it would continue where its predecessor had left off by investing heavily in public infrastructure, working on solutions to rush hour congestion (Annabelle's commentary: *see below – You must take the 'A' tram)*, and broadly endorsing the thrust of NATO and U.S. policy around the world.

As for the tram project, this should, by all accounts, have been embarked upon years ago and was unlikely to be completed by the time Palmer was shunted on to his next posting. But since the new cultural attaché had rented a flat in town twenty-five minutes' walk away from the embassy, other people's early morning and late evening rush hour headaches were irrelevant.

Tossing this last memorandum aside, Palmer picked up the next one and with a heavy sigh ran his eyes down a list of greater relevance to his duties: a Who's Who of local grandees. Luritania being a principality, foremost among these was Grand Prince Philippe Étienne, his consort Hippolyte (daughter of a wealthy industrialist from Brabant, a commoner with clout but no threat to the lineage, since the country's constitution provided for the prince's title too pass to the male heir apparent), their seven children and five grandchildren. Mention of the budgetary appropriations voted to keep the monarch, his consort and offspring in clover had Palmer whistling through his teeth. Next followed the usual enumeration of government ministers, politicians of every colour from green to black (far right on the rise?), national and European judges, ambassadors, a lone general (understandable insofar as the nation had no navy or air force), presidents of numerous European institutions, leading media representatives, the region's two finest burn treatment and eye-surgery experts, the Hungarian director of Luritania's philharmonic orchestra, the director of the capital's showpiece museum, the heads of the American and European schools, a chef credited with one Michelin star (Palmer thought it droll that France chose to champion its *haute cuisine* through a tyre manufacturer), two Tour de France cyclists, a 9th dan judoka and the country's only tennis Grand Slam semi-finalist. There were more names, but by now Palmer had had his fill. Time to turn to matters in need of more immediate attention itemised by Annabelle in a memorandum sitting on the lesser of the two piles of papers.

The previous attaché had already booked the next guest speaker for the annual Woodrow Wilson lecture but not his accommodation. As a renowned group of American gospel singers had suddenly added Luritania to their latest European tour programme, it fell to Palmer's lot to ensure that arrangements on this front went as smoothly as the group's *a cappella* music. There was also a Cassandra Wilson jazz concert in the offing and a visit by the Harlem Globetrotters to Luritania's multipurpose sports hall designed by cutting-edge Danish architects. Plenty to keep him busy, not to mention filling the quotas promoting international ties between Europe and his own country. That would mean singling out public affairs personalities for USA study and research grants.

Deciding that enough was enough, Palmer stood up, eased a crick in his neck and returned to the corridor for a second injection of caffeine, after which he dropped back in his chair, pushed the work papers to one side and picked up the latest copy of *The Pulse*. It was towards the end of the review among the *What's On* and *Future Events* columns that he chanced upon the article outlining Vanessa Curtis's planned production of *Camino Real*. This had to be the play alluded to by Humphrey Hobart, the owner of that second-hand bookshop in town. According to this article, Ms Curtis still had several roles left to fill and was seeking interested thespians. After treading the boards during his earlier postings, Palmer had the bit between his teeth and was keen to return to the amateur theatrical fold. All the more so since he was familiar with that play by Williams. Of the parts listed in *The Pulse* still up for grabs one in particular appealed to him: that of Gutman.

Gutman, an oxymoron of a name for a corrupt Latino despot who took pleasure in ordering people's lives. Yes, Palmer fancied that puppet master role. Of course, he'd have to give substance to the gut or paunch in Gutman, grease back his hair, put on an oily moustache, chew on a fat cigar – a handy prop for brandishing, when not used for spitting tobacco.

Palmer wrote down Vanessa Curtis's telephone number. After seeing her picture alongside the article in *The Pulse*, he concluded that this was a lady worth getting to know.

⁂

Craig was inside the BLR's customer entrance air lock at two o'clock on the dot with a smile on his face and two manila envelopes in his hand. As soon as he stepped into the reception area, he tapped the screen panel for the print-out of the next number for ordinary banking operations and took up his place third in line in the queue. His number – almost too good to be true – was 384, the number flashed up above Isabelle's counter, 381. The next second, a sharp ping jarred on Craig's ears as the counter clerk next to Isabelle pressed a button inviting forward the client holding ticket 382. One minute later, a clerk farther down the line invited the holder of number 383.

The minutes seemed to tick by as the client occupying Isabelle's attention continued her unfinished business. Although slightly on edge, Craig was glad to see Isabelle, completely unfazed by the delay; paying him no attention. Unless he had missed the briefest of eye contacts while looking down at the floor and shuffling his feet. His gaze shifted to the sign standing beside the yellow line painted on the floor at the head of the queue behind which customers were expected to keep their distance as if at customs checkpoints. Craig supposed that displaying the occasional notice in English was BLR's way of advertising its global reach. But some mischief maker had switched around the white lettering on a black Velcro background to read *Sweat In Line I Plea*. A similar wag had used an eraser and a biro to change the *Don't Forget to Remove Your Weights* instruction in his Vancouver weights room to *Don't Forget to Remove Your Tights*.

He looked back up at the numbers above each counter. Still no change. And it was his turn next. There were four counter clerks in all, but the fourth handled cash dispensing only. His screen showed 604, part of a different series. Craig fidgeted. The last thing he wanted was to draw attention to himself on camera by repeating his previous performance and jettisoning the present number for a new one. Perhaps the best solution was to act as if remembering that something had slipped his mind. He could step back and search through his wallet, take out his cell and make a call or walk across to one of the leaflet holders on a table against the wall behind him where stood documentation he risked forgetting if he didn't take it now. But the next moment, he was saved from indecision by a sharp ping and the flashing of number 384 above Isabelle's position. Her last client was stuffing papers into her handbag on the counter in front of the unmanned position to Isabelle's left.

'How may I help you today, sir?' Isabelle adopted the same tone as for her previous customer within earshot – neutral but businesslike.

Craig slid his driving licence ID and safety deposit box key into the slot below her window, dropping both into the retractable tray. 'I need to see my *coffre-*

80

fort, mademoiselle.' This last complimentary tweak to his request was not only unnecessary but even risky should a neighbouring counter clerk catch on to and recall the accompanying smile. But Craig, his composure regained, felt master of the situation. Under no circumstances, would he glance at the bank's overhead cameras.

Isabelle pulled the tray towards her, extracted the licence first followed by the key bearing a box number on the top of its loop end, verified his ID against her account data base, handed licence and key back to her customer, nodded and said; 'I'll fetch the ledger for you to sign, sir, if you wouldn't mind stepping down the counter.'

'Usual procedure,' he replied pocketing the licence but holding on to the key.

'Usual procedure,' she echoed matter-of-factly.

Craig had barely taken two steps when he felt a hand on his shoulder. '*Mijn Heer, zon diess von Uwe vergoss?*'

He turned around to face the customer with the handbag. She was pointing at the two envelopes left by him on the counter. '*Danki, danki hoekstens, die Dame,*' he said. (*Thank you very much, Madame.*) Then in French: '*J'ai dû me lever sans avoir la tête sur les épaules.* I must have got out of bed with my head screwed on the wrong way.'

'*Dot passiet mit chakein.* That happens to everyone.'

Weird pidgin language, he thought, snatching up the envelopes in his left hand and turning, no little flustered, in the direction of the far counter behind which Isabelle was awaiting him.

This time she raised the window for him to access and sign the ledger but not before duly placing a piece of paper over the day's entries preceding his arrival. Banking confidentiality gone mad, he concluded. There was next to nothing compromising to be learnt from the scribbled signature of the previous visitor to the safety deposit room. Craig took a biro out of its stand on the counter front and added his signature in the space in the far right column alongside his name, box number and the date.

Isabelle withdrew the ledger, closed it with the covering paper still inside, drew down the window, filed the register away on a shelf at the back of the room and returned to the counter with the bank key to the first of the two locks on Craig's safety deposit box, raised the flap and opened the door for her client to step inside.

Ever conscious of the need to avoid the cameras trained down on the bank's customers – he took it for granted that these had to be functioning – Craig followed behind, doubting whether the all-seeing eyes were up to capturing his appreciation of a shapely pair of legs or the soft down on the nape of Isabelle's neck. Nor, as he entered the mouth of the corridor leading to the vault, would they have caught sight of a second key wrapped in the handkerchief removed from his pocket with a view to blowing his nose.

When she reached the open vault door, Isabelle stood aside to allow him to precede her into the empty chamber, but only after he had pushed the button turning on the red 'occupied' light above the entrance. There were three bank officers in rooms down the corridor, but Isabelle had told him that these employees rarely entered the counter clerks' area from this side, because, however anomalous it might appear to anybody with a grain of commonsense, they preferred to follow the corridor looping around the back of the building to one of three doors. The first opened out into a smokers' yard, the second gave onto the indoor area immediately behind the lone cash-dispensing clerk and the third led to the toilets. The branch's manager and deputy manager had their offices on the upper floor.

'There's been a hitch,' said Isabelle, as she followed Craig into the chamber. 'I'll tell you about it later.'

Craig masked his disappointment. Everything, he thought, had gone smoothly up until now, apart perhaps from his oversight with the envelopes, but that could have been interpreted as the kind of mistake routinely made by people in a hurry to complete their various lunch hour errands.

'Remind me of your box number,' she said, the number engraved in her memory.

'Three hundred and eighty-four.'

She counted along the end of row three, inserted and turned her key in the lock on the left side of the box and motioned him to insert his own to the right.

A pained expression crossed Craig's face. For one drunken moment, the man set to play the part of Jacques Casanova in Vanessa's production of *Camino Real* half hoped the cameras might be working. 'It won't turn. I don't understand.' He made a show of tugging at the key to extract it then, doing a neat job of palming, held a second almost identical key up to the light. Almost identical because one of the teeth designed to turn the locking mechanism was slightly bent out of shape. 'Look at that, would you. How can that have happened?'

She took the key from him. 'Weak metal?'

'I don't think so. Rather something wrong with your lock. And that's a nuisance, because I not only want to deposit these documents. I need to take something out. Do you have a spare key?'

'I'll go and look. If there is one, I'll have to charge you for it. Fifty euros. If not, we'll need to order one. That would cost you sixty euros.'

The ensuing exchange was satisfying to both actors in that it proved, should anyone be listening in the corridor outside, that the clerk was keeping to the rule book in the face of a client venting frustration at the mercenary way in which BLR fleeced its clients for the slightest of services.

'Surely not.'

'I'm afraid so.'

'But why? Excuse me, mademoiselle. Why should I pay for a replacement when I haven't lost my key. Your safe has deformed it.' Without overdoing things, Craig had raised his voice sufficiently to convey justifiable objection.

It did not alter the fact that he was exaggerating the key's deformation. Both his and Isabelle's key consisted of a narrow tubular steel shaft finished at the top end with a metal eyelet and at the bottom with a pitted flange on each side designed to engage with specific notches in the safety-deposit box's lock. If Craig's key had become seriously bent during turning, it would have been impossible to withdraw it. Consequently, since the client was obliged to surrender his key to the clerk, simply inserting the good key in the lock with the complaint that it failed to turn would immediately arouse suspicion once an investigator found that there was not so much as a scratch on the key's flanges. Isabelle had to be provided with a defective key, the one now held up by Craig, his copy of the original, a copy minimally deformed in a vice in the high street's hardware store behind the shop assistant's back.

Isabelle turned away and removed the bank's key. 'Wait a minute, sir. Let me go and see.'

While she scurried off in search of the unfindable, Craig pulled out the single chair at the table in the middle of the chamber where clients, allowed in one at a time, sorted out the contents of their boxes. Except that there were no long, oblong black metal boxes to remove from behind the numbered lock panels. Everything had to be lifted out by hand from the small, medium or large-sized cavities let into the vault wall.

Waiting for her to return, sitting facing the wall opposite lined with row upon row of more safety-deposit boxes, Craig played with the envelopes in his hand without so much as a sideways glance at the sealed cash compartment to his right above which hung two supposedly unseeing cameras. After a while, a vein started throbbing in the side of his neck. He got up, stretched his arms and pulled out his wallet, opening and shutting it for no good reason other than that he felt in need of distraction. What had she meant by a hitch?

Isabelle was back before he had time to let unwholesome thoughts get the better of him. 'I'm sorry,' she said. 'I thought we had a spare key but apparently not. I'll go and order one for you.'

Craig frowned. 'I'm not sure that's such a good idea. You'd be better off calling in a locksmith. Otherwise, the same thing could happen again. This wasn't a case of weak metal. Look, do you have another box I could rent in the meantime? Something large. My own's becoming too small for what I need to store in it. In fact, I've been thinking of an upgrade. Perhaps you have something available.'

'Yes, there are a few boxes not yet taken, sir. What size were you thinking of?'

'Your largest model. There are things at home that would be better off in here.'

'The large ones are expensive.'

'How much more expensive than mine?'

'Eighty euros a month more than your present *coffre-fort*.'

'That is expensive. And the medium-sized box?'

'Thirty euros more.'

'Well, mademoiselle, could you please see what's available and fix me up with something right now?' Craig sensed that in her own quiet and highly controlled way she was enjoying this play acting as much as he.

'I'll go and see. It could take time. Perhaps you need to be somewhere else?'

'I do,' he said following her back out of the vault door and into the counter clerk's room. 'But I'd rather get this sorted out now, if possible.'

'Very well, but I'm afraid I can't let you stay here. If I find something suitable, we'll have to do the paperwork across the counter.'

Isabelle ushered him back into the clients' waiting area.

Craig was obliged to sign four different papers: the first, containing details of the new box (number and dimensions), authorised the bank to debit his account twice-yearly for the hire of the new box, on the understanding that this charge stood to be amended (euphemism for increased – banks never lowered their charges) the following January and each January thereafter; the second, reduced by half the hire charges on his existing box until such time as the bank's locksmith reopened it for Craig to transfer the contents to his new box. (Though of the opinion that BLR was skinning its clients, Craig was reluctant, even for appearance sake, to dispute the fifty per cent levy: the longer this whole song and dance took the more likely his nerves, under control up to now, were to start shredding.); the third, specified items which it was strictly forbidden to store in safe-keeping, including, which made him doubt the probity of fellow depositors, weapons, explosives, contraband and narcotics; the fourth made him responsible for replacement of the key, should he lose it, to the extent of sixty euros plus VAT (Isabelle had forgotten to mention the tax, which applied also to the hire charge), as well as for any damage to the vault. (Unable to remember having signed this document before, Craig wondered what could be meant by damage – until it occurred to him that there were people, not unlike himself, capable of trying to break into other people's property.)

'I have your key here,' she said. 'You're welcome to christen it with those envelopes.'

When they re-entered the vault, Isabelle indicated the new, larger box above Craig's existing one. Following the same routine as before, she inserted her key into the left-hand lock, turned it and waited for him to complete the opening with his own key. After which, Craig requested a repeat opening of the box with the allegedly jammed lock.

'Let's do this the proper way,' he said, transferring Lewis Carroll's work, a number of personal documents and shares together with three albums of a mint collection of commemorative Soviet space exploration stamps from the old to the new box together with both envelopes. 'We need this more or less empty.'

Under normal circumstances, she should already have turned her back on the client and walked out of the vault with the bank's keys, leaving him to finish his business.

These were not normal circumstances.

'The hitch,' said Craig, lowering his voice. 'What did you mean by a hitch?'

'He's changed the code.'

'Okay, so what? You've got it there?' He was looking at the folded slip of notepaper in her hand.

'He's dropped AFP and gone for something else.'

'What difference does that make?'

'The bastard's written down only two of the letters and two of the numbers.'

He took the paper from her and saw what she meant. Isabelle had copied down just four characters: DI 83.

'This means,' she said, 'that you have ten letters of the alphabet to choose from. A to J. And ten numbers. Zero to nine. '

'I have …?'

'Yes, the missing characters could be repeats. Look, I can't afford to stay here a moment longer. I have to get back to my station.'

'Hang on. The missing letter of the alphabet could be either side of that D and that I – just as the missing figure could be either side of your eight and three. On paper, that makes eight columns in all. And a hundred possible combinations for each column means eight hundred possible solutions. We're beaten before we've got going, Isabelle. We should call it a day.'

She looked him unflinchingly in the eyes. 'If you relish defeat, Craig. I leave you to decide. Believe me, if I could have, I would have texted you in advance. When I dropped off papers in you know who's office earlier this morning, there was no mistaking the code. But his lordship must have changed it later on. I only found out shortly before you arrived. If I hadn't, you would have been wasting your time.'

He nodded understanding. Now it was left to him either to abandon their gamble or to chance all on the ball's rolling into his groove in the roulette wheel within the presumably short time available to him.

'Any other customers you know of queueing up out there to get in here?'

'We average two a day. You're our second today. I checked through the ledger. For the past three months Friday has been the lightest day of the week.'

'That could change any moment. How long can I stay in here without arousing suspicion?'

'Some take up to half an hour. No idea what they get up to. Looking through their bling. Counting out their shekels.'

'Half an hour gives us a chance at it.'

'Then go for it, Craig. I must be off. Your cell phone on?'

He tapped his jacket pocket. 'Yes.'

'Then good luck.'

With that she turned on her heels and was gone.

Left to his own devices, far from feeling that his world was falling apart, Craig reflected that the challenge, though considerable, need not be that taxing provided he approached it methodically.

His first move was to re-open his original safety deposit box from which he removed two capacious folders with deep pockets and placed these to one side of the table. These folders had served to store Craig's birth certificate, passport, diplomas and shares now resting in the newly hired box. Next, he pulled free the tape securing several carefully folded sheets of kraft wrapping paper to the lining of his jacket, opened each out onto the table and stepped across to the cash compartment's combination lock situated bottom left out of sight to anybody passing by the vault door.

It was only when he bent over the panel that a disturbing thought struck home: what if the moment he entered a false code alarm bells started ringing inside the bank to bring the security guard running? But, no, surely the manufacturers had allowed for butter fingers on the part of their all too human bank customers? The moment he waved this worry aside, he was seized by a more crippling one. Suppose the system locked down after three abortive tries? That would be it. Game over. On the other hand, he could not see any reset button, which made him think that the code panel had no inbuilt protection against people such as himself. After all, what were the cameras for if not to deter miscreants from tampering with bank property?

Praying that his chances were fifty-fifty, making four hundred rather than eight hundred options, Craig entered his initial trial combination: ADI 830. No alarm bells. At least, none that he could hear. Crossing his fingers, he pressed ahead: BDI 830, CDI 830. No shutdown. No game over. With this boost to his confidence, he collected his thoughts and continued with the two outer column series. The trick, he decided, was to go about things unhurriedly. None of those banker's butter fingers. Five minutes later he had drawn a blank with the first two outside columns. Eight minutes later (he was slowing down) the inner columns starting DIA and 083 and ending DIJ 839 had also yielded nothing. Isabelle had told him there would be no mistaking the slight whirring of the opening mechanism once he hit the right combination.

Ten minutes later, he reached the end of the trail with the outer and inner series beginning ADI 083. His back aching, he straightened up to check the time on his watch. Twenty-three minutes' effort down the drain. So much for those fifty-fifty chances.

But when, at his very next attempt, DIA 830, the code panel lit up, blinking repeatedly, the message ACCEPTED appeared on the tiny touch pad, Isabelle's promised whirring sounded softly in his ears and the cash compartment's roller shutters (two on each side) retracted into their respective upper and lower grooves, Craig realised that he had hit the jackpot.

Used notes on the left she had said. And there they lay in all their abundant beauty.

His first thought that there was no time to discriminate between high, medium and low-denomination notes dissolved in the face of the quantity of purple, yellow and green currency. Thinking best to steer clear of the purple five hundred euro bills notoriously difficult to pass on, and given the quantity of two and one hundred euro notes at his disposal, he decided to privilege yellow over green.

Donning a pair of thin latex gloves, Craig set about stacking multiple bundles of the paper money, held together with paper bracelets specifying their quantity and face value, onto the sheets of kraft paper spread out on the room's table. Working as fast as he could, within eighteen minutes he had packed more than two hundred wads of notes into neat cubes secured with thick elastic bands, forty of these cubes stored away in the pockets of his two folders. He then placed the folders together with the bulk of the cubes wrapped in kraft paper into his old, lower-level safety-deposit box. Satisfied at finding this wide and deep enough to accommodate everything with room to spare, Craig closed and locked the door.

It was not until he turned to survey the gaps in the note racks behind him that he saw that he had let greed get the upper hand. But with no time left to undo what had been done he pressed the letter C on the touch pad, reactivated the roller shutters, extracted an opened packet of cleaning wipes from his pocket and removed all trace of fingerprints from and around the touch pad.

With the shutters all but closed, Craig took one leg of a wafer-thin tungsten steel compass out of his pocket, inserted this into the key hole and worked one of the notches in the lock's cylinder out of alignment. Introducing the original sound key into the lock, he was satisfied to find that it failed to engage or turn.

Having overstepped the half hour by a good ten minutes, Craig threw one last look around the room and under the table, pulled off the latex gloves, pocketed them, cancelled the red light above the vault door and, a model of self-collection, strolled out through the corridor into the counter area, where he saw Isabelle with her back to him dealing with another customer. A male counter clerk helped him to regain the reception area, where he paused to help himself to a couple of pamphlets before pushing the button on the bank's exit door, which flashed green before swinging open for him to enter the air lock and push the handle of the door opposite leading into fresh air and the bank's parking lot. Before leaving the street front, he took advantage of an unoccupied automatic cash dispenser to withdraw five hundred euros from his account, at the same time reflecting what a good boy he had been not to help himself to a few of the same notes from those bundles now sitting snugly in their brown paper wrapping in his dead deposit box.

As Craig climbed into his Jaguar, he thought of the irony of last night's play reading during which the impecunious Casanova suffered the indignity of having his portmanteau tossed out of the *Siete Mares* hotel.

As the Boeing banked steeply to make its line-up approach to the runway jutting out into a sparkling blue Mediterranean, Rashid looked down from his window seat onto the sprawling Lebanese capital. There was no mistaking the multiple cranes dotting the capital's skyline. All around them lay new buildings and infrastructure testimony to the fortitude of a people whose city seemed to be rising like a phoenix from the flames of the country's war-ravaged past.

The landing could hardly have been smoother. It was not long before Rashid caught sight of the yellow 'Follow Me' van leading the aircraft to its parking stand in front of Beirut-Rafic Hariri International Airport. The nearer they drew to the eastern arm of the giant magnet of the passenger terminal to which, it seemed, he and his fellow passengers were being drawn as if so many iron filings, Rashid recalled how during the 34-day war in the summer of 2006 the Israeli air force, claiming that weapons were being shipped into the airport to arm Hezbollah, had bombed several runways out of commission. Well, everything was back in working order on that front. Five minutes later, the aircraft's engines died down. and the cabin crew opened the forward doors to link up with the disembarkation jet way.

Since all three MEDRIMCOMB employees had carry-on luggage, they were spared having to cool their heels at the baggage carousel. And they went through passport control with minimum fuss: Reason for visit? Business. Length of stay? Three days. Thud of entry ink stamp. Next. (This terse processing in French for Boyle and Gottfried, Arabic for Rashid). The trio quickly exited the duty-free area sandwiched between passport and customs control. Rashid explained that taxis were the only form of ground transportation available in front of the terminal. If there were any airport shuttle buses, which he doubted, they were likely to be a hike away

The first thing that struck Horst Gottfried on stepping out into the open air was the heat. If he had expected a cooling breeze off the Mediterranean, he was disappointed. It was as if he had walked into a steel mill with every blast furnace working overtime. With no mitigating air currents, the atmosphere seemed thick with pollution. Too many taxis had their engines running. 'Enough CO_2 to send Al Gore into a flat spin,' he said.

Leading his companions away from the line of shared service taxis, Rashid headed for the next available yellow private taxi. No need to give the street address of the hotel chosen for them by Nathalie Leblanc. Resigned to the fact that it lay only a quarter of an hour away in the downtown business district, their driver grunted disaffectedly, left his fares to open the boot and pile in their carry-ons and took off before Boyle finished pulling his right foot in through the door.

During the short but eventful journey into town, Gottfried and Boyle felt as if they had entered a race track where the normal rules of the road no longer applied. A hornet's nest of vehicles threatened to converge on them only to sweep past or ahead, klaxons blaring their contribution to a dissonant concerto of eardrum-deadening hydraulic excavators, pile-driving hammers and cement mixers.

By the time their driver began wending his way in and out of less fluid traffic along downtown Beirut's boutique-lined streets, the trio found they were in a different world, that of chic Lebanese shoppers jostling with western tourists. It was only a matter of minutes before they pulled up in front of the massive modern glass, steel and brick structure of their hotel in Clemenceau Street. Rashid felt uneasy at the sight of this imposing edifice. Only a few minutes' drive away lay camps swarming with refugees enduring wretched living conditions. But his discomfort was short-lived. You had only to look around you, he told himself, to appreciate that the Lebanese people, who had had more than their fill of hardship, were not wearing sackcloth and ashes to atone for external conflicts that had displaced thousands into their refugee camps.

Finding the hotel's rates normal by European standards, Rashid was glad to learn that Mlle Leblanc had booked Boyle and Gottfried into one room and him into another. The thought of sharing did not appeal to Rashid, anymore, he imagined, than it did to Stephen and Horst. Perhaps Nathalie had consulted Frank Welling before favouring the mission's Arabic speaker.

The next morning, after a buffet breakfast in the hotel's top-floor dining room, whose panoramic windows encompassed the Mediterranean, city skyline and distant mountain range, the three MEDRIMCOMB agents set out on foot for the Bank of Beirut's offices in the rue Foch.

Horst Gottfried commented on the number of smartly restored French colonial buildings along the way, adding the observation that not a few streets, including the rue Foch and the rue Clemenceau, bore the imprint of France's post WWI mandate. Rashid remarked on Foch's clairvoyance. Following signature of the Treaty of Versailles, the Marshal of France had intimated that what others saw as peace Germany viewed as a twenty-year armistice.

The first sight that greeted them on turning into the rue Foch was the magnificent Mohammad Al-Amin mosque. Its sky-blue dome and four minarets towering above and beyond the far end of the street served as a vivid reminder, if any was needed, that the downtown area they were treading lay in the Muslim western half of Beirut. The architecture along this street combined colonial with modern, although the latter's high-rise residential and office buildings predominated. Rashid thought that the flowers planted in boxes the length of the middle of the street lent an additional touch of colour and elegance to surroundings that would have been the envy of many a town planner.

The welcoming party awaiting the group at the Bank of Beirut's handsome building on the corner of the rue Foch with the rue Uruguay insisted on offering morning tea or coffee before getting down to business. This was the Levant, where it would have been unthinkable to sidestep hospitality in the rush to crunch numbers.

But when it came to more serious matters, Rashid was mistaken in thinking that the workload assigned his environmental colleague in the Lebanese capital was less onerous than his own. Horst Gottfried could not be considered a hanger-on. Welling might have been generous with his new department's mission budget but not to the extent of sending one of his three mission staff out to Beirut simply to kick his heels. Whereas Rashid was tasked with throwing light on the Bank of Beirut's finances and investments, his smaller business and environmental audit colleagues were charged with getting out in the field to vet the bank's client portfolio. Since MEDRIMCOMB's management committee deemed Solidere, the principal body entrusted with urban rehabilitation and landscaping, a major client, this meant having to roll up shirtsleeves, don hard hats and, with the aid of the Beirut bank's interpreters, interview civil engineers, architects' assistants, quantity surveyors and site foremen.

To a certain extent, Rashid was happy with this division of labour, hoping that Horst and Stephen would feel too tired at the end of their first full day in Beirut to have much energy to explore the downtown shops, souks and bars. For this would leave him unencumbered to wander around as the spirit took him and perhaps even to fulfil his obligation to Jack Mason after photocopying that document and resealing the envelope. But, as it happened, Rashid's first day in the rue Foch headquarters went even better than hoped for due to excellent co-operation by staff equipped to answer a number of thorny questions e-mailed to them in advance as well as, in no small part, to the MEDRIMCOMB loan officer's buttoned-down approach, which privileged economy over hemming and hawing.

Consequently, after leaving his hosts with a number of points for clarification on the morrow and returning to his hotel room to change into less formal wear, by four o'clock Rashid was at leisure to explore downtown Beirut until later that evening. For the heads of the Bank of Beirut's Internal Audit and Risk Management Departments had invited him and his colleagues to dinner at nine o'clock in one of the capital's finest restaurants.

As soon as he had freshened up, Rashid turned his steps towards the square named after Samir Kassir, the French-Lebanese journalist and professor of history assassinated in the Christian half of Beirut shortly after the 2005 elections. Three and a half months earlier the fuse had already been lit to what was to become a string of political assassinations with the murder of former Prime Minister Rafic Hariri in a car bomb attack outside the Saint George hotel.

Following widespread condemnation of the murder of one of the most outspoken opponents of Syrian and Israeli intervention in Lebanon, the Kassir Foundation, set up by the journalist's wife and other admirers, erected a memorial to their fallen hero in the square which the town had renamed after him.

When he arrived in the square, Rashid, an admirer of Kassir and his writing, was heartened to see that flowers were still being laid at the foot of the bronze statue set in place to mark the anniversary of the journalist's assassination. However, this sculpture of Kassir seated with the writer's right leg resting over his left knee struck Rashid as gauche and too large. Had the choice been his, he would have commissioned a modest bust.

But after paying quiet homage to the man, his thoughts turned to Jack Mason and the shipment of aid intended to alleviate some of the misery of the Shatila refugees. Looking at his watch, he decided that he could make it out to the Lady of the Sacred Heart Convent and back and still have time on his hands before dinner. Furthermore, he was none too keen about venturing too far into the Christian half of Beirut in the dark.

As before at the airport, he stuck to the principle of avoiding a service taxi and hired the first private taxi that came his way. Contrary to expectations, the driver appeared to find nothing abnormal about ferrying the passenger he took to be a fellow Muslim to the doors of a nunnery. In fact, apart from running two red lights in a row, he proved to be a skilled negotiator of bottlenecks, albeit with a colourful repertoire of insults hurled through an open window. When the taxi finally drew up outside the convent gates, his fare's ears were still ringing from the latest tirade.

'Wait here for me, will you?' said Rashid, adding twenty dollars on top of the fare into a grubby hand by way of a retainer. 'I don't expect to be long.'

A shrug conveyed indifference one way or the other. Rashid debated extra insurance. Finding a taxi later on this far out would probably mean having to walk back to Martyrs' Square.

'There'll be more when I return.'

No sooner had he made the offer than Rashid had the distinct impression that the twenty-dollar deposit could be his downfall. Unless he was in and out of the convent within five minutes, his man would do a bunk.

The convent was surrounded by a low brick wall, the line of which was broken

90

at the front by a tall wrought iron gate. The grey stone building was five storeys high. And by the sound of clapping to music emanating from a few open windows on the ground floor, it was not Rashid's idea of a place of retreat from the world.

He made the mistake of trying to open the gate, before noticing the bell pull. Glancing at the overhead camera, he wondered whether an unknown male visitor might fare better at the tradesmen's entrance. A questioning look over his shoulder at the taxi told him that the driver was still there, his engine turned off and a copy of that day's *An-Nahar* spread over the steering wheel.

Unsure whether the bell had rung somewhere within the convent, Rashid gave the pull a second tug. The next moment, a voice sounded over the intercom above his left shoulder. Since the nun was asking him what he wanted in French, he switched to that language.

'I'm here for the mother superior with a message from ...' (He hesitated to give Jack Mason's name for fear that this would mean nothing to his respondent and that it might end up unintelligible in her mouth when she came to inform the mother superior.) '... from a charity in the United States.'

'The mother superior is not here at the moment.'

Impossible to tell whether this meant the mother superior was here but otherwise employed or genuinely absent.

'Then could I please speak to sister Ziara? I was told that she stood in for the mother during her absence.'

'One minute please.'

Rashid put on his best understanding smile and stood back from the gate. There was no garden on the other side of the wall, just a red brick drive with a semi-circular black slate pathway. Laid out like interlocking diamonds, the slate rectangles made the pathway look longer than it actually was. Several potted plants were set out under the convent's ground floor windows from which Rashid now thought he could hear the sound of children's laughter. He turned back towards the cab and shrugged. Three minutes must have elapsed, and he had yet to enter the convent. The driver threw him a disinterested glance and applied a wet thumb to turning the page in his newspaper.

At last the intercom crackled back into life. 'Hello, I'm sister Ziara. How may I help you?'

'I apologise about disturbing your afternoon, sister, but Mr Jack Mason from the World Bank has asked me to deliver an ...' (Rashid decided that the occasion warranted an adjective – the stronger the better.) '... important message.'

Rashid heard the gate lock click open. 'Do come in. And be sure to close the gate behind you. Neighbourhood children are not past throwing live mice through our windows.'

By the time Rashid reached the steps leading up to the front porch, the convent's door was open and a bright-eyed, fair-skinned woman (He wondered whether all nuns really did use scrubbing brushes instead of soap by way of penance.) of indeterminate age was standing on the threshold, a wooden rosary hanging from her belt.

'Sister Ziara,' he said, accepting her handshake. 'Pleased to meet you.'

'You weren't interrupting anything,' said the sister, turning to usher him into the convent, while she closed the door behind them. 'But I'm afraid the Reverend Mother Veronica Laura is out of the country at the moment, visiting another order in Alexandria. Like our own, it caters for abandoned and disabled children.'

Rashid understood the sounds of merriment in the background. Far from being contemplative orders cut off from the outside world, orders such as The Lady of The Sacred Heart pursued true missions of mercy.

'Can I offer you some tea? I'm afraid we have no coffee.' She gathered that her visitor's hesitation stemmed from not wishing to put her to any trouble. 'Water, perhaps?'

Now that he had had time to take stock of her more clearly, Rashid saw that this bareheaded sister with the close-cropped grey hair and blue-veined hands was probably older than he had thought. Presumably the sister chosen to replace the mother superior in her absence would never be a novice. 'No, thank you. I'm perfectly all right without a drink. Apart from which, I have no intention of keeping you from your work.' From the look on her face, Rashid wondered whether he had caused offence. Perhaps he had been rash. What if Sister Ziara thought he had come all the way from the United States on an errand of charity?

'You're not keeping me from my work, Mr ...?'

'Jabour. Rashid Jabour.'

'So, please do come through with me to somewhere you can sit down in comfort and, if I really can't offer you some liquid refreshment, take time to tell me your news for the Reverend Mother.'

The conviction that his taxi driver was already headed back towards West Beirut killed the seeds of an idea to make this encounter as short as possible. Apart from which, it would be discourteous to treat the sister as nothing other than a go-between by delving into his pocket, handing over the envelope with a succinct explanation and bidding her adieu. Rashid began to wonder whether he might learn something of interest about the man who kept his hotel key in the headband of his fedora.

He followed sister Ziara into a side wing of the convent which appeared, as far as he could judge from glances into open doorways along the corridor, to be given over to craftwork of one sort or another. She stopped halfway down and invited him into a low-ceilinged room, the four walls of which were painted in springtime colours. Once again, not his idea of the drab environment befitting an order of anchorites. The bottom half of one wall was fitted with a whiteboard, and there were a large number of alphabet tiles of varying sizes stacked nearby on a table fronted by a thick rubber mat.

'We have several dyslexic children in our care,' she explained, seeing his questioning stare directed at these items as well as at two rows of chairs designed for children of primary school age. 'They have speech therapy lessons here in the morning.'

Directing him to a chair more his size in front of a desk on which stood a telephone, an old-fashioned tape recorder and four sets of tapes, she took up her own seat behind the teacher's desk, her back to the window through which he could see a small herb garden. Another sister, supervising children engaged in weeding, bent down to dissuade one of her charges from uprooting coriander.

Sister Ziara straightened the white scapular over her light blue habit. ' Now. Monsieur Jabour, are you sure I can't offer you some light refreshment?'

Rashid took the hint. 'If you're intending having something yourself … thank you, yes. Mint tea would be fine.'

She picked up the telephone and pressed a button which, he imagined, connected her directly with the kitchen. The phone rang at the other end without response. 'I should try the refectory,' she said. A few moments later, she had placed her order.

Rashid thought that the sister must have been quite attractive in her youth. There was nothing matronly about her, nor did she appear diffident in the presence of a young man like himself. For the past few minutes, he had been pondering how best to break the news of Jack Mason's death. Now that he had accepted her invitation to sit down and explain in a relaxed manner the purpose of his visit, it would be inexcusable to skirt around how he had come to stand in for Mason.

If anything, the sister's next question made broaching the matter that much simpler. 'You work at the World Bank alongside Monsieur Mason?'

'No. We both work' (wrong tense, he thought) 'in the banking sector. But whereas he's based in Washington, I'm based in Europe. I'm afraid Sister Ziara, that I have some …' (Rashid debated the respective merits of 'bad' and 'sad') '… sad news about Jack Mason.' But this was Lebanon. Why sugar the pill? 'He was murdered only a few days ago when visiting my bank in north-western Europe. By a mugger.'

Sister Ziara put one hand to her lips, while the other grasped the silver crucifix hanging from her neck.

'Oh no, that's awful. Such a good man.'

Rashid nodded, not so much out of agreement with her character verdict as out of sympathy for the shock and distress occasioned by his news.

'A senseless act of brutality. I believe the police are still looking for his murderer.'

''That won't bring Monsieur Mason back to life.'

'True. But it might save someone else's. Sister Ziara, believe me, I would far rather not have been the bearer of these tidings.'

A knock on the door heralded the arrival of their tea, brought in on a tray by an altogether younger sister, who, rather than averting her eyes from the male visitor, gave him a friendly smile. 'The griddle cakes are freshly made,' she said, setting out two glasses nested in their silver holders, a long-spouted silver teapot, cutlery, plates, sugar and a dish of warm raisin-filled griddle cakes together with a set of butter pats each impressed with a different botanical design. Rashid suddenly felt hungry.

'Thank you, Sister Marie-Noël,' said the elder sister.

Rashid was amused to see the younger sister backing out of the room, the tray at her side, eyes still on him. No, it must have been my imagination, he told himself. But I could have sworn she was flirting with me.

Sister Ziara started pouring the tea into the nearest glass, alternately raising and lowering the spout to aerate the warm liquid. She served Rashid first, then herself. 'Those griddle cakes are Sister Marie-Noël's speciality. She'll be most upset, if you don't do her justice.'

'I won't argue about that,' replied Rashid, taking a cake from the proffered dish.

'Don't forget the butter.'

Rashid nodded. 'Tea first, I think.'

'Sugar?'

'No, thank you.'

'So, tell me, Monsieur Jabour, you are our new Monsieur Mason?'

'Very good tea,' he said, before setting his glass back down and using one of the butter knives to pick up an oak leaf butter pat. 'No, sister, I regret to disappoint you. I'm merely a messenger.'

'But you know … knew Monsieur Mason … well?'

Rashid noticed that she was confining herself to the tea. Sister Marie-Noël had brought an odd number of griddle cakes. Did that mean she thought he'd cope with all three?

'To be perfectly frank, no. Monsieur Mason was visiting my bank, MEDRIMCOMB, in Luritania last week. When he learnt from my manager that I was booked to fly out here on business, he called into my office to ask me to deliver a letter to your convent which he had intended delivering himself while passing through here. But things didn't work out, so … here I am.'

Rashid finished buttering his griddle cake, reached into his breast pocket and handed Sister Ziara Mason's message. The 'letter' part of his explanation was deliberate: best, if he had come in the role of postman, to disown all knowledge of whatever lay within that manila envelope.

But, of course, if the intended recipient was the mother superior, the sister would leave the envelope unopened. And she did.

'Thank you, Monsieur Jabour. The Reverend Mother always deals with such matters appropriately.'

This unexpected response left Rashid with but two options: to let matters lie, express feigned interest in the convent's good works while disposing modestly of a second of Sister Marie-Noël's three griddle cakes and then politely bow out; or to embark on a fishing expedition. Having come this far and unwilling to leave with nothing to show for it, Rashid decided to cast his line.

'Jack told me the envelope contained a sizeable cheque, representing charitable donations raised by one of his wife's church's back home. It's encouraging to know that not every American believes in feeding his country's war machine.'

For the first time, Rashid caught a glimmer of embarrassment in Sister Ziara's downturned eyes. She offered him more tea, which he accepted. For all that it had in common with Rashid's explanation, her next remark might as well have been directed at the satyr-like ghost standing behind her guest's shoulder.

'As I said before, Monsieur Mason was a good man. But prejudiced. On his last visit, he alarmed the Reverend Mother with his talk of punishing the transgressors.'

'Who would they be?'

'The ones who preferred to spare Barabbas. The Jews.'

Rashid was genuinely surprised. 'But that was all of two thousand years ago. And didn't Jesus say, "Forgive them, father, for they know not what they do"?'

The sister's fingers caressed her crucifix. 'Yes, and wasn't the Holocaust punishment enough? Not that I believe for one moment that God saw it that way. But Monsieur Mason was categorical. Time, he said, would tell. Such a pity that the Reverend Mother's last memory of the man should have been one of refusal to pardon fellow human beings.'

Rashid reflected that for the brief time during which Jack Mason had sat facing him in his office, he had sensed that the American was a man of contradictions.

'There must have been a reason for this somewhere in Mason's past?'

'If there was, he remained silent about it.'

Thinking it best not to dwell on the negative, Rashid abandoned further angling.

'Well, Sister, whatever the truth of the matter, I'm sure that your convent will put that donation to good use.'

'Yes, thank the Lord for his generosity, I'm sure we will. But you have no idea who will be replacing Monsieur Mason?'

'I'm sorry, no.'

When the time came for Rashid to pay farewell to Sister Ziara on the convent's front porch, it was obvious that he was in for a trek back to Martyrs' Square in search of transport. The walk, he decided, would do him good. He needed to clear his head. What, among other things, did the sister mean by 'The Reverend Mother always deals with such matters appropriately'?

When his cell phone sounded later that evening, and Isabelle's name appeared on his monitor, Craig answered straightaway.

'Did you have a good day?' she asked. 'Mine was as boring as usual.'

'I feel like stretching my legs,' said Craig, slipping into the same banal mode as his caller. 'Are you interested in joining me for a walk down by the river?'

'Nice idea. Want to pick me up? No point in taking two cars.'

'Is that the friend of the environment talking?'

'No. I like the idea of being driven for a change.'

'Have you eaten?'

'Yes. *Toast aux deux saumons*, green salad and a banana juice. You?'

'Spaghetti Bolognese and raspberry tart.'

'Which did you eat first?'

'I thought briefly of putting the tart on the plate with the spaghetti and trying both together. But I wasn't too bowled over by the idea.'

'Traditionalist.'

'What time should I pick you up?'

'Give me half an hour. I need to finish my ironing.'

It was still daylight when he pulled up outside her apartment building. Craig switched off the ignition and bided his time watching a woman busy watering the potted plants dotted around her penthouse balcony.

The next minute the front entrance door opened and Isabelle walked down the flight of steps leading to the building's red-tiled forecourt. She was wearing an Indian cotton dress that flattered her slim figure and showed off her legs to advantage. Craig was not to know that she had thrown on the first thing to come to hand from an altogether modest wardrobe.

'Full moon,' she said, as he got out to open the front passenger door for her. They exchanged triple cheek kisses.

Craig eased the car smoothly out into the road. 'Good or bad sign?'

'Pilots have been known to get jittery on full moon nights.'

'Crazy moon phases. I'd better keep my eyes on the road rather than on your knees.'

She pulled her hemline lower. 'You broke the code?'

'When I was close to calling it a day. The two missing characters were an A and a zero. In other words, if I'd started going across the columns one after the other punching in A and zero, I'd have broken the code in a minute. Instead of which, it took me …'

'Thirty-five minutes.'

'Well, not quite that. But far too long. Can we thank our lucky stars that nobody else was sitting out there in reception fuming at the time I was taking?'

'We can.'

'And as all this happened only a few hours ago on the eve of the weekend, *la merde n'a pas encore frappé le ventilateur* (the shit has yet to hit the fan)?'

Craig slowed down and pulled into the side to permit an ambulance, its siren blaring and blue lights flashing, to surge past him.

'Not before I packed up and left.' Isabelle watched the glare of the ambulance's tail lights diminish as the vehicle continued to gather speed along a road notorious for its accident black spots. 'So you succeeded?'

'The truth is,' he said, looking straight ahead, both arms holding the steering wheel with the stiffness of a man at sea hanging on to a life belt, 'I may have overdone things. Couldn't resist the colour of money.'

'What do you mean?'

Craig refused to meet her eyes. 'I jammed as many notes as I could into that box of mine. No idea how much. But a lot.'

'Well done.'

It was a response that took him by surprise. Craig turned to look at her. 'You think so? I had the sense to avoid the five hundreds.'

'Good. They'd be the first thing to raise another bank's suspicions.'

'Well, let's wait and see how much I've cleaned out. When it came to the crunch, I thought I might as well be hanged for a sheep as for a lamb.'

'They don't hang bank robbers nowadays, Craig.'

His face broke into a sickly grin. 'I filled the box to capacity. Too greedy. And I don't like myself for it.'

'A bit late for regrets. You planning on putting it all back?'

'Very funny, Isabelle.'

They sat for a while in silence, which turned out to be the right choice, because as they rounded the next bend in the road leading to a usually busy roundabout, Craig was obliged to come to a sudden halt. A police officer, armed with a blue traffic baton, was directing vehicles to a halt on the verge. Behind him two police cars formed a barrier across the road in front of which stood the ambulance. It looked as if a Peugeot had crossed the median, crashed into the rear end of a Renault travelling in the same direction and sent it headlong into a tree trunk at the side of the road. Isabelle looked from the Renault's shattered, bloodstained windscreen down to the earth and saw two misshapen bodies. Lifeless. She turned away. The Peugeot lay flat on its roof in the middle of the road. Paramedics were endeavouring to free a trapped female driver and her passenger. Seconds later, confirming Isabelle's suspicion that the ambulance men were going to get nowhere without metal cutters, the air was rent by another siren heralding the fire brigade's arrival from the opposite direction. Glancing into his rearview mirror, Craig waited until the last of the cars in front of him had completed its three point turn and then tacked on behind.

'Full moon,' he said, anxiously regarding a distraught Isabelle.

'Slow down,' she urged. 'We don't want to end up like them.'

'We can still make it down to the Château Vaugruge, if we take the second turning up ahead.'

'No, I'd rather not. Drive out to the Château du Vieux Moulin. Let's park there and walk down by the old mill race.'

It was not far to drive and, after parking and strolling down to the mill, they sat on a bench beside a cycle path running alongside the bank of the stream which curled out from behind the château. There were several apple trees behind them laden with dark red fruit some of which had fallen to the ground. Isabelle saw three boys further along the path tossing what looked like cores into the stream.

'So the code, Isabelle,' said Craig, placing a comforting arm around her shoulders, 'was DIA 830. Does that mean anything to you?'

She shook her head as if coming awake from a dream. 'Your guess is as good as mine. Perhaps the wife of our *directeur adjoint* is called Dianne.'

'As in Keaton? A laugh a minute?'

'If one moment he had her on a pedestal wearing a diadem, the next in bed wearing a diaphragm.'

'And 830?'

'I haven't the faintest.'

'Why did he have to spring this surprise on us just now?'

'I suppose he got tired with his routine.'

'But why make things more difficult by dropping two of the characters from his reminder?'

'More difficult for us, not for him.'

'That's what I meant. Did he twig somebody might catch on? Or worse. That they might suggest to the manager that he was as good as advertising the code?'

'We'll never know. Does it matter? You cracked it.'

'I suppose you're right.'

They both mused for a moment, Isabelle mesmerised by the efforts of a branch downstream to free itself from the cleft where it had become lodged between rocks, the water passing over and around it unhampered, Craig wondering whether a moon as white as the one above their heads, so many thousand miles away yet so close, really could curdle one's brains.

'So what happens next?' he said at last, hugging her that bit more tightly. 'When are the alarm bells likely to go off at BLR?'

'Monday morning. That's when Vandeweghe opens up the cash compartment to dole out notes for the week to each of the counter clerks. The largest share goes to that guy you saw sitting on his own at the top of the row, the one to whom shopkeepers and restaurant owners bring their takings in the form of prepacked coins and notes for running through his money counting and fake note detection machines.'

'Is Vandeweghe Dutch? Another Amsterdam capitalist?'

'No, Eric's Belgian – from the Flemish-speaking north. Why should he be a capitalist?'

'Bias on my part. *All The Right Moves* is owned by a Dutchman with his fingers in umpteen property pies.'

'Well, I heard that our Eric is having a large private villa built for himself down by the Vaugruge complete with swimming pool, sauna and wine cellar. Does that make him a capitalist?'

Craig laughed. 'What have we just become?'

Isabelle appeared either to ignore or miss the point. 'This means that first thing Monday morning, after he gets the shock of his life, he'll be thinking the finger of suspicion has to point at him. Okay, he's been gifted a 1% mortgage loan on his villa, capital and interest repayable over fifteen years, but even so, if his new place is going to be as palatial as he gives to believe, that represents a slice of Eric's salary big enough to hurt his disposable income.'

'But then, Isabelle, he'll say to himself, wait a minute, this is absurd. No one in their right mind is going to suspect a deputy manager of plunging his snout into the very trough for which he's responsible.'

'I agree. Absurd. But what will the police think? They'll be called in along with the insurers. Well, perhaps not with the insurers. The bank's got too much egg on its face.'

'They might deduce that your Eric is in league with an accomplice. Not an insider, of course.'

'Why not? An insider would be just perfect.'

'I was thinking more of a mirror image of our set-up. Let's suppose the law thinks he and a client have got together to spring a similar trick to ours – which I doubt very much. What will they do?'

'Order all recent visitors to the safety box room to trot along with their key. Because, although I pretended otherwise, we don't keep duplicates. And ordering copies takes time.'

'Suppose someone says they've lost a key? You believe them?'

'Makes no difference. The lock gets drilled out and a new one is put in.'

'Sensible. But the police would never bother looking in the unrented boxes.'

'They'd be stupid not to.'

'Why would any member of the bank's staff leave the loot within feet of where he'd stolen it?'

'You're asking me that question after what you've just done? And what's to say our hypothetical thief hasn't gone one better by smuggling half the notes out with him? Unlike you. So dazzled by the colour of our money that you left the pot of gold in place.'

'I'm willing to bet it never crosses the police's mind to open any of the boxes, rented or unrented.'

'You hope.'

Craig gave the matter some thought. 'All right then. Look, Isabelle, supposing Eric's imaginary partner books a box from abroad while out of the country on business. In the meantime, his key is mailed registered to his home address awaiting his return. The police would say, forget about it. Wouldn't you agree?'

'I suppose so.'

'They would chase other leads.'

She snuggled her head against his shoulder. 'Put that way, perhaps you're right.'

'Another thing that occurs to me,' he said, smoothing her hair and stopping short of calling her Marguerite, 'is that we should be careful about being seen too much together.'

Isabelle drew back her head. 'I hope you're not trying to tell me I should stop coming to the gym?'

'No, of course not. If anything, the fitness centre is the one place where it's the most natural to be seen together. But phone calls. We ought to continue to be careful on that front. The police might start searching through call records.'

'You think people incapable of putting two and two together are going to ask for wire taps on every BLR employee and every *coffre-fort* client who visited the vault over the past week? Be realistic, Craig. This is not the war on terror.'

'Okay, you could be right. Let's stop worrying our heads about what Monday morning will bring. I'm looking forward to introducing you to my friends the day after tomorrow.'

'What did you say Tich's real name is?'

'Humphrey?'

'What a very English name.'

'None of his friends calls him Humphrey, not unless they're looking for trouble. His full name is Humphrey Robert Hobart. Although he says he's never forgiven his parents for that middle name, some of his handkerchiefs are monogrammed HRH.'

Isabelle looked bemused.

'His Royal Highness.'

'Tich should think himself lucky. My middle name is Bernardine, after my maternal grandmother.'

'Ouch. I see what you mean. How did your parents manage to fall into that trap?'

'Somehow it never occurred to them. Did your parents give you a middle name?'

'Yes, Mortimer. Not the most joyous of choices, bearing in mind the prefix. Mortimer implies death at sea, although I can think of at least one Mortimer, an archaeologist, Sir Mortimer Wheeler, who died on dry land. So I plan to follow in his footsteps by escaping death by drowning.'

'I thought the English liked naming their cats Mortimer. Isn't it more likely that your parents thought you a cuddly baby?'

'I doubt it. Apparently, I was screaming all the time.'

'What a pain. Tell me, the rest of the band is certain to be there on Sunday?'

'I'm not sure about Rashid and Justin. Vanessa, yes. She's given me a role in her next play.'

'Really? What role might that be?'

'Casanova.'

'And it's taken you until now to tell me that?' Isabelle pulled away from him in impish disbelief. 'How appropriate.'

'Not quite. Casanova on his last legs. At the end of his days.'

'I like the sound of it. In giving you a foretaste of what lays in store for people after a life of debauchery, this role should teach you a lesson or two.'

'A bit late now. I've gone one better than Jacques Casanova by adding theft to my list of sins. As far as I am aware, he never robbed anyone.'

'Oh no? A good few girls of their virginity.'

'Didn't the term consenting adults exist in those days?'

'You think Casanova never touched a minor?'

'Well, there you have it, you see. The difference between lover boy and me. I've never been a Lolita man.'

'Thank goodness. Anyway, you're too young to be a sugar daddy. What's this play called?'

'*Camino Real*. You know it?'

'Can't say I do.'

'By Tennessee Williams.'

'I'd like to read it. Poetic?'

'I should say the most poetic of his works. But very much in tune with life's harsher realities.'

'As we should be, if we want to avoid putting a foot wrong.'

Vanessa's auditioning rules were inflexible: if a person turned up late, they were turned away. Those cavalier about punctuality in the early stages were likely to be as lax when it came to rehearsals. Productions, particularly ones as demanding as *Camino Real*, had to run like well-oiled machines. Any form of backsliding was given short shrift.

Saturday night's play reading, advertised in *The Pulse*, was being held in the back room of a restaurant with a bowling alley hired by Vanessa for games later that evening once she had got some way towards casting her play. The waiters, recognising Vanessa as a regular patron, made no fuss about limiting their service to drinks and light snacks.

Arnold Palmer was the last to arrive, albeit in the nick of time, the restaurant's front desk and bar staff having been instructed to tell latecomers they had missed the boat. The warning 'Camino Real Auditioning. Stay Away – We've Started' taped across a closed door was for those who failed to heed the first message.

Palmer got off on the wrong foot with Vanessa after introducing himself as the American embassy's new cultural attaché. This provoked a withering question as to what people like him were up to when Baghdad's cultural heritage was being spirited out of the country while his countrymen were digging for WMDs at the bottom of Saddam Hussein's garden. But Palmer, his interest in Vanessa Curtis and her play fuelled by *The Pulse's* article to the effect that the director set the bar for her productions high, took the criticism in his stride.

The principal male roles still to be decided were those of Don Quixote, Sancho Panza, Gutman, Kilroy and Lord Byron. Vanessa had the various postulants swap parts as she took them from one block or scene of Williams's play to another, the excerpts, decided in advance, marked by her with a highlighter. Not one for prolific notes, she contented herself with the odd comment on the back of a beer mat.

'Right,' she said, as the readings came to an end. 'I'll be honest with the menfolk. I don't think any of you is suited to play Byron or Kilroy, not, that is, the way I see these roles. Arnold, it's always nice to be able to welcome new talent. I'd be happy to cast you as the don.'

Palmer held up a stick of salami from the dish in front of him. 'Isn't it easier to pad someone out than to slim them down?'

'No need to worry your head about that. We can dress Quixote in enough gear to disguise his frame.'

'I was hoping for a …' (he waved the stick playfully) '… more substantial role.'

'Tell me, Arnold, in the play's opening and closing scene, who occupies centre stage?'

'Yes, of course, but …'

'Sancho, then.'

'Substantial in terms of corpulence but not in terms of dialogue. I'm good at remembering my lines.'

'So?'

'Gutman.'

'You fancy having the last word, is that it?'

'Let's say I'm happy to let the don have the first.'

'As far as Williams is concerned, he also has the last.'

'Well, speaking as the man who served as his country's cultural attaché to Bogota, permit me to suggest you won't find a better impersonator of a tinpot Colombian autocrat.'

'You're very persuasive, Arnold. In fact, I was testing you. I had you down for Gutman all along.'

If the innuendo was not lost on others, notably the envious, Palmer took Vanessa's remark as a compliment.

Out of respect for the Sunday Club's founder, Craig approached Tich before bringing Isabelle along as a guest to the group's next Lenfindi Quintet meeting. He guessed correctly that the group's doyen would welcome any young woman uniquely combining intelligence, environmental commitment and athleticism with beauty.

Craig therefore decided it appropriate for Isabelle and him to be the last to arrive at the airport on what proved to be a bright sunny weekend morning with the scent of hyacinths perfuming the air in the gardens along their walk up to the kiss-and-fly parking area fronting the terminal building. As the two drew near to the tables reserved by Tich in the café's breakfast area overlooking a runway bare of aircraft, Craig saw that Justin was back from his trip to London and Rashid from his mission to Beirut. The three men rose to greet Isabelle.

Isabelle felt somewhat daunted by the professorial look of the tall bear of a man at the centre of this trio until his face broke into a welcoming smile.

'My congratulations to Craig,' declared Tich, 'on his unequalled good taste.'

'Pleased to meet you, Isabelle,' said Justin, a rangy individual with deep blue eyes and a not unattractive five o'clock shadow.

'Craig's a lucky fellow,' added Rashid, the youngest of the three, his Levantine charm not lost on Isabelle.

Vanessa was the last to extend.her hand, which she did from across the table. 'I need a virgin with looks. And you, my dear, certainly fit the bill as regards looks.'

Embarrassed and alarmed in equal measure, Isabelle accepted the chair pulled out for her by Craig.

'No need to take it personally,' continued Vanessa. The virgin I need is no virgin. But miracles being what they are, the full moon restores her virginity as regular as clockwork, after which she is free to give herself to whoever takes her fancy.'

Isabelle's face relaxed into a smile. 'Including Quasimodo?'

'No, my love, afraid not. You'd have to make do with Kilroy. Although, with no writing on the wall, I've yet to find him.'

'Wouldn't Williams's Marguerite be more appropriate?' asked a suddenly coy Isabelle, referring to the courtesan rendered famous as *La Dame aux camélias* by Alexandre Dumas's illegitimate son.

'I always think it's a mistake to pair real lovers up onstage.'

Tich chuckled. 'That would rule out Claire Bloom and Sir Larry, Liz Taylor and Richard Burton, Emma Thompson and Kenneth Branagh ...'

'Those are pros. I'm talking about amateurs.'

Tich opened and closed bear trap interlaced fingers. 'Can't see the difference.'

Vanessa turned back to Isabelle. 'Has Craig tried to recruit you for our production?'

'Not directly. Though he lent me his copy of the play.'

'Would you be interested? I can guarantee you the men in the audience would be delighted to see you naked on a divan. Well, not birthday suit naked, which, let's face it, tends to be less alluring than scantily clad. And I'd rather avoid creating a shindig with the pope's man on the spot. So, you'd be wearing a veil, a see-through skirt over a vagina wig and a pair of emerald snakes twirled around what look to be glorious tits. Once Justin posts a photo of you in his rag, the tickets will sell like hot cakes.'

'Everything's fair in love, war and art is that it?'

'Definitely.'

'Well, I have acted before. But a long time ago.'

'What in, dear?'

'Molière's *L'École des femmes*. I played Agnès.'

'Agnès starts out in a nunnery, doesn't she, before tasting the fruit of corporeal love? Not ideal training for a gypsy's daughter. But I shouldn't be so choosy.'

'A Spanish gypsy. What about my accent?'

'French, Spanish – what's the difference? Romance tongues. Used properly, they cross all manner of barriers.'

As a waitress chose that moment to approach the group, holding a tray of used crockery and leftovers, Tich clapped his hands to signal the need for those with tea or coffee already on the table to decide what they wanted to eat and for Craig and Isabelle to choose whatever they felt like from the breakfast menu.

After the waitress had scurried away, Craig turned to Justin. 'How did things go for you in London?'

'Never easy, funerals. Part of life's not so rich pattern.'

'She was your aunt, right?'

'Yes. A devout Christian, kind-hearted, charitable. Never heard her speak ill of anyone.'

'Was it a burial or a cremation?'

'A burial. In the same plot as her mother. United in death and all that jazz.'

'Cremations are a lot cleaner,' said Vanessa. 'I want to go out in a violent burst of hellfire.'

Tich rubbed the bridge of his nose. 'I think they try to eliminate the violent burst part Vanessa, by sticking a rod up your arse. It sucks the methane out. Not that, thank the Lord, you'll know anything about being buggered.'

Justin finished pouring himself more coffee from the large pot in the middle of the table. 'Where would you like us to scatter your ashes? I take it not from the white cliffs of Dover. You wouldn't want a rerun of *The Big Lebowski*.'

'Haven't really thought about it. Somewhere poetic. Perhaps in the bluebell woods I jog through every week.'

'You'd be in good company, Vanessa,' said Rashid. 'Shelley was cremated. On the beach at Viareggio.'

Vanessa gave Rashid one of her man-eating looks. 'Don't tell me you've been reading *Camino Real* as well?'

Rashid returned her gaze unwaveringly. 'Sorry to disappoint you, Vanessa, but no.'

'Well, there happens to be a vivid account of Shelley's cremation in it with a touch of poetic licence. When we hear Lord Byron's account of what occurred in and around the funeral, we're not in bedtime story land.'

'Yes, I knew that Lord Byron was present at his friend's funeral.'

'I think you'd make a good Byron, Rashid. The part's still going begging, if you're interested.'

The young man blushed. 'Would I have to put pebbles in one of my shoes?'

Before she could reply, two waitresses arrived with the food orders. The first handed out a grilled ham and cheese sandwich to Justin and Rashid and another with a fried egg on top to Tich. The second set down a puff pastry slipper of roast chicken in a cream sauce for Vanessa, an almond croissant for Isabelle, and a salmon wrap for Craig. She returned a few moments later with a *crème* espresso for Isabelle and a *noisette* espresso for her companion.

'Pebbles?' said Justin, taking up where Rashid had left off. 'Like Brando stuffing his cheeks with cotton wool?'

'Calculi,' chimed in Tich. 'Highly appropriate for a man working with numbers.'

'No,' said Vanessa, 'I don't think we need to go that far. Apart from which, it's said that Byron was good at disguising his limp. In other words, forget Lee Strasberg.'

'Well, Craig,' said Tich, peppering his fried egg, 'are you and Isabelle planning on turning us into a sextet?'

'Please, not,' said Justin. 'Haven't we had enough sex for one morning?'

'Nothing wrong with sextet. Are you casting aspersions on Charles Mingus, Miles Davis, Benny Goodman …?'

'Not to mention,' added Vanessa,' sextuplets and sexagenarians, the first too ignorant when they pop out of the womb to understand what Justin's on about and the second, well most of them, more interested in a book than a cock or cunt at bedtime.'

'Do forgive Van,' said Tich, casting an unoffended glance at Isabelle. 'Not one to mince her words.'

Justin finished chewing on a mouthful of ham and cheese. Forget my objection. But does the Lenfindi Sextet have quite the same ring to it as the Lenfindi Quintet?'

Isabelle looked embarrassed. 'Please, everyone, I explained to Craig that the last thing I wanted was to gatecrash your club. If you're happy to have me along from time to time as a guest …'

'The problem,' interposed Vanessa, setting down a chicken-laden fork, 'is that Tich was toying with the idea of making our emblem the quincunx. The five-spot in dice. The spot in the middle being Tich, the rest of us revolving around him like planets around their sun. That wouldn't work with a six-spot.'

'Come on, Van,' protested Tich, 'I've been called many things in my time, but the sun around which … Oh, boy! Roll over Galileo.'

'If I may just make a suggestion,' said Rashid.

Justin set down his cutlery. 'Is that your best imitation of Woody Allen?'

Tich motioned Justin to pass him a coffee pot which seemed to have migrated permanently to his corner of the table. 'Go ahead, Rash.'

Rashid nodded. Like Vanessa, he took no exception to Tich's use of the diminutive.

'As someone weary of working with numbers all day, this humble newcomer proposes calling ourselves the Lenfindi Club.'

'Well, that has my vote,' said Tich emphatically. 'If the rest of you agree, it simplifies welcoming Isabelle into our midst as a fully-fledged member.'

The others agreed unanimously, Justin deciding against voicing the opinion that this brought them back to square one as regards voting deadlock.

'Now, the agenda for this morning. I take it, Isabelle, that Craig has explained the nonsense we're getting up to this month. You ready to go first, Van?'

'That's all right. I don't mind starting.'

Once the food plates had been cleared away, the coffee pot refilled and Isabelle provided with a bottle of mineral water, Vanessa delved into the sling bag over the back of her chair and pulled out two folded sheets of paper crammed with handwritten notes.

'There's too much here,' she said, 'to go through it all this morning, so I'll try to pick out the best of the bunch. 'First, something that really gets my goat. The prevalent cheapening of awe among American teenagers capable of describing everything from key lime pie to bubble gum as awesome.'

Tich cleared his throat. 'While we're at it, let's not forget shock and awe, coined by that smart ass predicting people's reaction to a judgment day rain of American cruise missiles.'

'Yes,' agreed Rashid, interrupting his ruminations on amateur dramatics and a certain freedom-fighter honoured by the Greeks with a cenotaph. 'Careful to put six thousand miles between him and the action.'

Justin tore his eyes away from watching a Boeing 747-8F defy gravity as its immense mass surged into the heavens, the sunlight glancing off a distinctive Luritancargo golden eagle tailfin logo. 'That went hand in hand with the axis of evil. But didn't that expression depend on which side of the East-West divide you were standing? I mean – Cheney and Rumsfeld, did the Iraqis picture them with haloes or pitchforks?'

'To return to the pursuit of literacy,' said Vanessa, reading through her notes, 'we have this beauty: *Thanks to intensive chemo- and radiotherapy bombardment of her brain lesions, Mrs Thingummybob died on the operating table'*. If Mrs Thingummybob's wraith had popped up after the event, I doubt it would have thanked the surgeons for a great job.

'Next, a couple of puzzles for foreign learners of English hoping for literacy in our tongue. Why should guilt-ridden mean overwhelmed by guilt rather than guiltless? Why should flea-ridden mean flea-infested and not flealess?

'Then a Queen's English no-brainer. Why do we regularly say *try and* understand instead of *try to understand*? Okay, *go and see what's happening* seems as acceptable as *go to see what's happening,* because we're talking about separate actions.

'But who, in their right mind, would say *I hope and win the lottery*? And what self-respecting farmer would say *I love and fuck goats*?'

'Yes,' said Justin. 'But to avoid giving the dog a nervous breakdown, he'd be advised to lock it indoors before staring on the goat.'

Tich wiped his lips with a serviette. 'Interesting, Van. From which TEFL textbook did you lift those shining examples?'

'I didn't note that down, Tich. But I was disappointed to hear my favourite female BBC World News presenter say with reference to al-Zawahiri that *his whereabouts is unknown*. Though I did like one television advertisement for Dubai, where the Arab singing this city's praises sounded as if he had a mouthful of halva, because *endless opportunities* come out as *and less opportunities*.

'What about you, Tich? I think that just about does it for me for today. I trust it makes up for last Sunday's next to nothing.'

Tich scratched his cheek. 'An honourable effort, Van. As for me, I've been digging into our rich linguistic heritage, as a result of which it may interest you good friends to know that the word *mob* is an abbreviation of the Latin *mobile vulgus* (vacillating crowd). Villain, a word of opprobrium nowadays, originally meant a farm labourer, but perhaps they only have themselves to blame. Look at the wanton use of pesticides leached into our water courses and those GMOs (God-awful Monstrous Oddities) the thought of which would have given Mary Shelley nightmares. Let it also be known, good people, that the word *ambition* derives from the Latin *ambitio*, which used to describe the walkabouts of Roman politicians canvassing for votes. It would tend to suggest that what we now know as ambition was not that highly regarded when the concept put down its roots. Finally, it appears that nice originally meant ignorant. So, in saying about somebody that he was "such a nice person", you were in effect calling him a nitwit.

'As to the damage visited upon our language by today's untutored, permit me to quote you these marvels of degenerate semi-literacy: *Nobody has what they did when we were kids in Brooklyn; Like one of her breasts, his cell phone was always within reach; a negative expostulation broke forth from the private eye's larynx*, and; *he could not help but notice that none were as aware as him of her gaping décollage*. Need I say that not one of these was found in gems of literature of the first water. While on the matter of water, I shall conclude by citing the workl of a local graffiti scribbler. The other day, while crouched on one of Schönschlucht's subterranean Vespasian facilities, I spied facing me the following inscription: *I only needed to spend a penny but it cost me a euro to open this fucking door*.'

'So now we know Isabelle,' said Craig, 'how Tich spends his working day. Reading Mickey Spillane.'

'Ah Craig, you do me an injustice. To sell those books of mine, I have to familiarise myself with the low as well as the highbrow. And what, may I ask, have you brought to today's feast apart from your divine companion?'

Craig took exaggerated interest in a callus on the side of one thumb. 'Sorry, folks,' he mumbled, 'I've been too busy mugging up my lines. Amongst other things.' With this last mention, he raised his eyes to engage with Tich, who refused to acknowledge the slightest understanding.

'All right, you're excused. As is Rashid, who has been busy flying between here and the other side of the Mediterranean on business.'

'In fact,' said Rashid, 'I did manage to work on a small puzzle on the flight back from Beirut. Something that I thought might be of interest.'

'Congratulations, Rash. Please go ahead.'

'It's to do with the carol about the twelve days of Christmas. What my true love brought to me.'

'Do tell us,' said Vanessa. 'I'm dying to hear what your true love brought to you this Christmas.'

'If you remember how that carol goes, each day the caroller brings his paramour more fresh gifts on top of the preceding ones, which in turn become repeat gifts. In other words, by the time he reaches the twelfth day of Christmas, he's given her twelve partridges in twelve pear trees. But, taken together with the cumulative amount of all the other gifts, this means that by day twelve he has showered three hundred and sixty-four gifts on the poor girl. She's the recipient of an entire menagerie, a chorus line of entertainers, at the very least forty-two goose eggs, the milk, I assume from forty cows, and four times as many gold rings as the fingers on her hands. It's enough to send any woman completely spare.'

Vanessa cocked her head to one side. 'Not three hundred and sixty-five gifts?'

'Yes, strange, Vanessa. But not according to my calculations. And that's treating each partridge in a pear tree as one gift. If not, you'd end up with three hundred and seventy-six gifts.'

Tich applauded. 'Well done, Rash. You've just gone to show that the spirit of commercialism was alive and kicking long before Harrods closed down for the day to allow royalty to buy up half of Knightsbridge or, should I say, Cairo. And what about you, Justin? I don't suppose you've been in any mood for fun and games?'

'No, though I have brought something to the table.'

'And what might that be?'

'An item and a confession. Of which I'm not proud.'

Justin lifted the red briefcase from the floor at his feet and set it on his lap.

'That's nice leather work,' remarked Craig. 'Must have set you back a pretty penny.'

'That's the crux of the matter. You see, I didn't pay anything for it. Because it's not mine. I nicked it.'

Vanessa put on a look of wide-eyed exaggeration. 'You did what?'

'Picked it up in a minicab, instead of handing it to the driver.'

'My sainted aunt.'

'Rather mine. Wagging a disappointed finger at her errant nephew.'

'Whatever made you do it, Justin? Nabbing another person's property?'

'Because … How should I know? An impulse. I realise now after the event that I was in the wrong. The proper thing for me to do is to return it. But my only chance of doing that is to find out who the owner is by opening the dratted thing. And it's locked. That's why I brought it along this morning. Perhaps one of you will be luckier than I was guessing the combination.'

'May I look at it for a moment?' asked Rashid.

'Go ahead.'

Rashid inspected the lock. 'Four figures. Not that difficult to work out. It means you have ten thousand possible combinations.'

Craig stared long and hard at Rashid. 'You call ten thousand chances of hitting the right combination not that difficult?'

Rashid responded with a polite smile. 'Not if it takes you three seconds to try each four-figure set. That's thirty thousand seconds in all. That's approximately eight hours and twenty minutes. Yes, I know, it seems a lot, but with a fifty-fifty chance of picking the right combination, the code can be cracked within four hours and ten minutes.'

'Feel free to have a go.'

'No, thanks. I don't fancy my chances. Perhaps someone else cares to give it a try.'

Rashid handed the briefcase to Vanessa, who passed it straight on. 'Idiotic,' she said. 'Justin should have known better in the first place.'

Craig experimented haphazardly with the numbered rotary dials before offering the briefcase to Isabelle, who followed Vanessa's example. Hence, by the time it reached Tich, its end station, the briefcase was as firmly sealed as ever.

Tich shook the case with no discernible shifting of its contents. 'How do we know there's no letter in here laced with anthrax?'

Justin puckered his lips. 'We don't, but something this expensive is hardly likely to be used for spoiling someone's day.'

'On the contrary. The ideal cover. You brought this back through the baggage check at London City Airport?'

'It was screened along with everything else.'

'Seems pretty lightweight. Can't be much inside here. What if it's brand new out of the shop?'

'Then why would it be locked?'

Tich inspected the leather merchant's lettering. 'Made in Milan. Interesting.'

Justin was beginning to look bored. 'What's interesting?'

Tich threw his head back and deliberated. Then twirled the lock's dials. Fingers as thick as his called for several readjustments, but when he finally lined up the four numbers of his choice in a neat row and pressed the catch, the lock opened.

'*Miercoles!*' exclaimed a no longer derisive Vanessa, who had been boning up on her Spanish.

'You can say that again,' said Craig, 'But don't.'

Justin and Isabelle joined Rashid's hand clapping.

'That's knocked the stuffing out of my four hours and ten minutes.'

'How on earth …?' mouthed Justin.

Tich gave a self-satisfied smile. 'I said to myself, supposing you had just bought this fancy piece of leatherwork, but couldn't for the life of you dream up a handy four-figure code, what would you do? Search for a mnemonic. Maybe something staring you in the face. Like the manufacturer's name.'

'Remind me,' said Rashid. 'In fact, I'm not even sure I noticed it.'

'Ah, Rash, my friend, that's a result of not being present in the here and now. Who was it that said: *To live is the rarest thing in the world. Most people exist, that is all?*'

Vanessa snorted. 'No need to rub it in, Tich. You got fucking lucky, admit it.'

'No, Van, my love, not with odds of forty thousand to one 1. I used nous.'

A now wide awake Justin, sat forward in his seat. 'All right, put your sleepwalkers out of their misery.'

'Giorgio Oliviero Benanti,' said Tich. 'Those initial letters ring any bells?'

Craig tried some of the coffee from the pot, but found that by now it was cold. 'G O B. Obviously, Tich, not as in shut your …'

'And where would that get us, Craig, even if your objection was unjustified? Government of Belarus? No. GBS would have been nice. George Bernard Shaw.'

'Stop,' said Vanessa, delivering a thwarted kick at Tich's ankles, 'messing with us.'

'That's fine,' blurted Justin, 'coming from an arch pisser.'

'As I was saying before I was rudely interrupted by the Royal Luritanian Theatre Company's Petrina Brook, GBS would have been nice. I might have chosen 1897. *The Devil's Disciple*. But then I asked myself, what about A.C. Milan? Might Silvio Berlusconi hold the answer? Not that I could see. So I turned to my schoolboy Italian. I had the same George that I would have liked for Shaw, then Oliver, then meaningless *Benanti*. I put my thinking cap on. What if the initial O of Oliver stood for *or*? From there, *Ben* being as near as damn it *Bene*, it was less than a millisecond to make the connection: George … Or … Well. What if Justin's briefcase owner's

Italian was as rudimentary as mine and he couldn't be bothered with Benanti's suffix? I was right. He plumped for 1984.'

Justin reached across the table to shake his friend by the hand. 'Tich, you're a bloody genius.'

'Sadly, unrecognised in my time. However, Justin, since I would rather not expose myself to an asp's bite, yours should be the privilege of exploring this case's contents. Here, take it.'

Justin turned back the flap containing the locking tooth and stretched the briefcase's expandable compartments open with a view to inspecting the interior. 'No snakes, Tich. No cell phone. No tablet. Just a folder.'

He pulled out a black cardboard folder with a buttoned-down flap.

'No anthrax here, I hope.'

'Open her up, boy,' said Craig. 'In for a penny, in for a pound.'

Justin unbuttoned the flap and withdrew several sheets of A4. 'Weird,' he said. 'No names, no dates, no addresses. The top sheets full of zeroes and ones. The others ... a dozen or so ... Well, see for yourselves. Nothing but a series of unintelligible letters.'

Rashid leant forward. 'May I have a look?'

'Help yourself.'

It took Rashid next to no time to come to a conclusion regarding the first two pages. 'Binary computer or text coding. What you have here, Justin, is reams of bit strings of encoded data. As for the other pages ... this looks like ciphertext. In other words, encrypted plaintext.'

'Why would anyone be carrying this and nothing else around with them?'

'I don't know. If you like, I can scan the binary code into my computer and get it translated. The other stuff is next to impossible to decrypt without the cipher. Apart from which, whoever prepared this might also have employed steganography.'

'Meaning?' said Isabelle.

'At its simplest level, invisible ink between the visible lines of a message. At a more advanced level, the microdot. When introduced into any normal text, a microdot is indistinguishable from your ordinary full stop. Nothing like these texts, where encryption shouts out at you from the page. And microdots have been superseded by more sophisticated methods of digital concealment. Perhaps that is what's at work here. The tiny hummingbird image at the top of the first page of the second document could be ideal cover for uncoded or, better still, coded stegotext. I can have a go at it. But, frankly, my chances of getting anywhere are minimal.'

'Let me photocopy it all then,' said Justin. 'And I'll drop the pages into you next week.' He paused for a moment, prodded by a recollection. 'Something else I forgot to mention.' He held up a newspaper and passed it across to Tich. 'I also found this on the minicab's back seat alongside the briefcase. As you will see, whoever it belonged to was interested enough to highlight mention of the war in eastern Ukraine. Perhaps the paper and the red leather job were owned by the same person. In which case ...'

Tich filled out the thought left hanging. 'The article might tell us something about the owner. Possibly a Russian or Ukrainian expat.'

'Your guess is as good as mine. Perhaps the documents are not entirely unconnected with the highlighting.'

'Fine,' said Rashid. 'But if I were you, I wouldn't go around advertising what you've found here. Someone has something to protect or hide. What's his agenda? If protection of privacy, what right have we to interfere in his affairs? Then again, if he's into something dubious ...' Rashid shuffled the pages back together, as the image of Jack Mason loomed larger than life in his mind's eye. 'Well, aren't we venturing into territory best left to the security services to tread?'

'Possibly,' said Tich. 'But with things getting, to quote Alice, "Curiouser and curiouser!", difficult not to take up the golden key handed us and try to open the garden door.'

⁂

Police officer Claude-Henri Weiland, taking notes on his laptop with the fluency of a touch typist, was recording the salient points of the interview conducted by his superior, Chief Inspector Georg Hoffarth, with BLR branch manager, Heinrich Katzenberger. The latter, a pasty-faced, corpulent man in his late forties had three reasons to be annoyed that a theft of this magnitude (the loss to BLR was put at four million two hundred and forty-eight thousand euros) should have occurred on his watch: first, because he had a mere two months to go before transfer to a more senior position overseeing BLR's Head Office SICAV (unit trust) activities; second, because only last week he had written to that same office recommending that Eric Vandeweghe's efficient stewardship of the branch's liquidity qualified the deputy manager, once he had seen in his own replacement, to fill the post of manager in BLR's large Schwarzfels-les-Étangs branch on the border with France; third, and by no means least, the *Luritanische Bote* had published that very morning a full-page article, lauding the unveiling of a magnificent oil painting of the Luritanian sovereign – together with wife, family and bloodhounds – by Frau Odile Katzenberger-Beerentopf, an article in which explicit mention was made of her husband's contribution to the country's economy, including the fact that he was about to move on to greater things after twelve year's faultless leadership at the helm of BLR's Mensdorf branch.

One of Schönschlucht's most senior police officers, who made no bones about forgoing the Chief in his title, Georg Hoffarth was a rawboned man with a pencil thin moustache, ears like mushrooms and a habit of throwing his chin out towards the end of each question. In the course of his enquiries, he, had already learnt that, rather than being on the blink, the cameras in the bank's safety deposit vault had been timed to switch off during working hours (as a result of which, he concluded, strictly off the record, BLR's insurers would be joking about this till Christmas, while BLR's shareholders would be shedding the odd theatrical tear at the minor dent to their dividends). He had also been told that the theft could have taken place anywhere between nine a.m. the previous Monday and four p.m. on Friday, when the branch closed its doors to customers for the weekend. To Katzenberger's chagrin, he did not conclude from this information that the robbery was necessarily conducted by outsiders. And this led the chief inspector to his next question.

'Can I take it that your *directeur adjoint* enjoys your absolute trust?'

'We have worked together for the past twelve years. He has fulfilled his duties to my complete satisfaction whether alongside me or covering for me in my absence.'

'Yes, but I'm talking about the man's integrity ... He enjoys your complete trust?'

As if asked to pronounce on the trustworthiness of Luritania's bishop emeritus, Katzenberger held up his hands in a gesture of defeat in the face of human nature. 'What can I tell you? François Villon wrote poetry. Himmler abhorred cruelty to animals.'

'I will, of course, need to question him after you, as well as the rest of your staff. Are any of them off work today?'

'You'd have to ask Eric that.' This time the hands were remonstrating. 'Don't worry. He'll get his secretary to give you a print-out of everyone present today and on each day of last week.'

'She'll need to include absentees.'

With Hoffarth pondering his next question, the fingers suspended above Weiland's laptop reminded Katzenberger of claws awaiting their prey. In fact, the recorder was more preoccupied with thoughts of lunch – *bouchée à la reine* and a glass of *Avranche blanc* – than with anything else.

'How often, Herr Katzenberger do you visit the safety deposit room for the purpose of checking liquidity?'

While recognising that this was a question no self-respecting investigator could fail to ask, the Mensdorf branch manager nonetheless took it personally. 'I hardly ever venture in there. Certainly never to check the contents. That's Vandeweghe's domain.'

'You know the code, of course?'

Simulating a bout of weariness, Katzenberger lowered his head, closed both eyes and used a fluttering hand to cover one half of his face. The mummery was obvious. 'I believe Vadeweghe keeps it locked in his office drawer. He changes it every week.'

'Without notifying you?'

Katzenberger's brows achieved the surprising feat of rising out of unison. 'The fewer people who know the code the better.'

'But you, his boss ...?' The inspector clasped his hands beneath a probing chin.

'If he falls ill, I have a spare set of keys to his office.'

'And where, may I ask, do you keep those keys?'

If nothing in Claude-Henri Weiland's expression hinted at anything other than neutrality, the officer's fingers seemed to attack their task with added fervor.

'Locked in that cabinet over there.' Katzenberger indicated the first of a set of grey metal wall cabinets behind Weiland.

'The keys to which?'

'On a chain in my pocket.' It was a lie. They were in his secretary's desk. But Katzenberger was prepared to sign the pledge, if Hoffarth asked him to stand up and empty out his pockets.

'I think we need to interview Monsieur Vandeweghe next. Alone. In his office.'

Katezenberger rubbed cleansing hands. For once, he was glad to be left on the sidelines. Let these two fish in Eric's pond, for all the good it would do them.

'Please, go ahead. I shall be here if you should need me further.'

'In fact, you can be of great assistance while I'm speaking to your deputy. We need to have a room set aside for interviewing each of your staff after we finish with Vandeweghe. Kindly have your secretary draw up the lists of presences and absences, including the age, length of service and duties of each employee.'

'Well, that's really Vandeweghe's …'

'No, Herr Katzenberger, I'd rather you do this for me. Agreed?'

The Mensdorf branch manager did not agree. But he was not the one calling the shots.

※

Eric Vandeweghe might have had plenty of time to prepare for the inevitable grilling from Luritania's law and order servants, but that didn't mean that he felt any the easier when the knock came on his office door announcing the two officers' arrival. Nevertheless, having told himself repeatedly that the only sin of which he was guilty was one of omission – for which he stood to pay dearly by losing out on that promotion to Schwarzfels-les-Étangs and his end-of-year bonus – he decided that if straight answers were all that was wanted to straight questions, let them fire away. He had nothing to fear.

After the customary introductions with superfluous apologies by Vandeweghe for the fact that his office was darker and more cramped than Katzenberger's, and once officer Weiland had settled into his seat, his laptop open and a new document already set up, rather than floating like a butterfly the hitherto inoffensive inspector stung like a bee with what his aide took to be a low punch untypical of the great heavyweight boxer whose framed picture hung on the wall in his boss's office.

'If some aberration prompted one of BLR's employees to commit this theft for reasons they had come to regret, would you not agree that it would be best for all concerned for that person to confess as much now and save us all a lot of trouble?'

Coming as it did out of the blue, this suggestion aroused Eric Vandeweghe's ire. 'If you're insinuating what I think you are, inspector, you're sorely mistaken. I'm sorry to disappoint you, but you're going to have to work to solve this crime. I assure you that I am just as interested as you, if not more so, in finding out how this theft was committed and by whom – insider or outsider.'

While Claude-Henri's fingers completed their staccato routine, Georg Hoffarth took stock of the man facing him, whose physique had more in common with a lumberjack than a paper pusher. He felt relieved that they were sparring solely with words. All the same, had Hoffarth been a gambling man, he would have bet his bottom dollar on Vandeweghe's innocence, despite the deputy manager's poker dealer's sleeve garters.

'Well, I'm glad to learn we're both on the same wavelength about one thing. So now perhaps, yes, we should concentrate on how this crime could have been committed. Who apart from yourself has access to the vault code?'

'Only Heinrich Katzenberger.'

'In what way.'

Vandeweghe tapped the bottom drawer on the right side of his desk. 'Katz's secretary has the only spare key to this drawer, where I keep the code.'

'That would be …' Hoffarth flicked through the pages of a notebook drawn from his breast pocket. 'Mlle Sophie Berenger?'

'Correct.' Vandeweghe adjusted to its full forty-five degree angle the cardboard flap holding upright the family photo from which he had earlier removed and pocketed a certain cardboard strip.

'How long has Mlle Berenger been Katzenbergen's secretary?' Vandeweghe could get as familiar as he liked, but the inspector was damned if he was going to refer to the branch manager as Katz.

'He inherited her from the previous manager. She knows the workings of this branch better than anyone.'

'Thoroughly trustworthy, then?'

Officer Weiland thought that if Hoffarth had been in a courtroom with Vandeweghe on the witness stand, the judge would have ruled him out of order for tendentiousness.

'Look, inspector, you're not going to get me to say a bad word about my colleagues. Let's leave it at that shall we?'

An unperturbed Hoffarth consulted his notes. 'How often do you change the code?'

'Fairly regularly.' This was no answer at all; rather than lie outright Vandeweghe preferred to fudge.

'How regularly?'

Vandeweghe glanced out of his second-floor window, hoping in vain to catch sight of a passing gaggle of wild geese. 'It varies. Sometimes I go a whole month without changing it. Sometimes I change it every week.'

'And when did you last change it?'

'As it happens, last Monday.' The deputy manager realised too late that this lie by no means facilitated the inspector's task.

'I understand it consists of three letters followed by three numbers. What combination did you choose last Monday?'

'DIA 830.'

'Any particular reason for choosing that combination?'

'For the DIA? My wife and I had been watching a television programme about Diaghilev, the Russian ballet impresario, the previous evening.'

'And 830?'

'The telephone area code for San Antonio, where my sister-in-law lives in Texas.'

'In other words, quite impossible for anyone other than perhaps your wife … Excuse me, Monsieur Vandeweghe, don't imagine for one moment that I am suggesting …'

'I should hope not.' Eric Vandeweghe forced a laugh.

'The only way to acquire the code would be to break into that drawer. But it has not been broken into, correct?'

'Correct.'

'Forensics will need to check the paper on which you noted that code. A long shot. But you never know.'

Vandeweghe was quick to improvise. 'A very long shot, inspector, because once I learnt of the robbery, I put it through the shredder.'

'You don't keep a record of the code anywhere else? On your computer, for example?'

'I'm afraid not.'

'Ah, that is a pity.' Hoffarth returned to his notes. 'While on the same subject, can you explain how there come to be no fingerprints on the key pad to the safety deposit room's cash compartment?'

The deputy manager scratched the nape of his neck. 'Our *Putzfrau* (cleaning lady) is the meticulous type. I can only think that she wipes it down each time.'

'The last occasion being?'

'Around half past seven this morning.'

'Ah.' The inspector uttered a long sigh. 'A case of imperfect perfection.'

'So it would seem, unless the criminal removed the evidence himself.'

'Himself?'

'Or herself. Why not themselves? Take your pick.'

Vandeweghe's darted sarcasm bounced off its target: the inspector was already pursuing a different line of thought.

'I understand you have contracted a substantial long-term BLR mortgage. Can you tell me whether you have any other significant debt exposure?'

In getting off to a bad start with the deputy manager with thinly veiled accusations of his guilt only to follow these up with fresh insinuations, rather than unnerving Vandeweghe Hoffarth had reinforced the man's self-righteousness in the face of what he held to be bigotry.

'I'm repaying a loan on my E-class Mercedes. Three hundred and fifty euros a month over the next eight years.'

Hoffarth transferred his attention to the window, where a butterfly was flapping its wings against a visible yet impenetrable exit.

'That's all? You're not paying subsistence to anyone? Part of your extended family?'

'Such as my sister-in-law in San Antonio? I don't think assistant district attorneys are in need of food stamps.'

'No, I expect not.'

Given the faraway look in Hoffarth's eyes, Vandeweghe was unable to decide whether the inspector was on the verge of repaying him in his own coin or making use of a filler.

'Do you own a deposit box in this branch?'

'Yes, of course. Katz and I both do. Part of BLR's perks for senior appointees. The boxes come free of charge.'

'What size is your box?'

'Large.'

'Do any other employees own boxes?'

'No. The rest are reserved exclusively for BLR clients.'

Georg Hoffarth added a flourish to the tail end of his note-taking, before looking up tellingly at the deputy manager. 'We will need to examine your box later today.'

Vandeweghe reflected briefly. 'Along with Katz's?'

'Along with Herr Katzenberger's.'

'I don't know what Katz keeps in his, but in mine you'll find a collection of rare paper money. Great Wall of China ten-yuan notes, Peter the Great five hundred rouble notes, McKinley ten-dollar notes …'

Anxious to stem the tide, Hoffarth broke in. 'McKinley, the president who embraced the gold standard. Assassinated, I seem to remember, by a man with an unpronounceable name. Worry not, Monsieur, we shall not disturb your prized collection. A pure formality.'

'Glad to hear it.'

The inspector returned to his notes, readjusting his position in a chair designed to make people less patient than he feel in need of an osteopath. He assumed that Katzenberger either remained standing or, which was more likely, invited his deputy into his spacious, well-appointed inner sanctum. This further pause gave Weiland the opportunity to stretch his fingers, ease taut neck muscles and admire a couple of Japanese pen and ink drawings hanging in glass-fronted frames on the wall behind Vandeweghe. He sensed that his boss was nearing the end of his questioning, a feeling born out the next moment as Hoffarth gave his notebook an emphatic double tap with his biro.

'What, Monsieur Vandeweghe, are your ideas about this theft? Now that you've had ample time to mull things over.'

The deputy manager's frown was such that his low hairline all but met his brows. 'I suspect, inspector, that your definition of ample is not the same as mine. I have spent the best part of this morning like the survivor of a plane crash. Scarcely knowing who I am or what to think of this blow to my … bank's reputation.'

The fraction of a second that it took Vandeweghe to paper over an unseemly gap was not quick enough to fool the inspector. Hoffarth refused to pander to his interviewee's self-importance.

'Yes, I fear that once the press get their teeth into this, they won't be happy until they've drawn blood.'

Vandeweghe nervously fingered the back of the family photograph, a source of greater sympathy than the inspector.

'At all events, only after I came to my senses did I ask how this could have happened. It had to mean that the robbery was the doing of a colleague or colleagues from this or another branch. Worse still, whoever was behind the theft knew it would sully my name.'

'How often do colleagues from other branches call in here?'

'Not that often.'

'Do any of them, to your knowledge, own safety deposit boxes here?'

'I'd have to check. But, I think not. Why should they?'

'They might live in the neighbourhood.' Georg Hoffarth paused. Troubled by the butterfly's agitation, he rose to his feet, crossed to the window and freed the creature. Returning to his seat in front of the banker, he recovered the notebook and pencil left on Vandeweghe's desk. 'Let's look at it another way. If, and this is a big if, … if they were planning to rob your bank, they could either rent a box or, better still, access your safety deposit room anonymously in collusion with a key-holding acquaintance?'

'They'd have to know that the cameras were turned off during the day.'

'Might not word slip out of that unfortunate decision on your bank's part?'

'It might.' The deputy manager's voice was edged with impatience, his features lacking embarrassment. 'But any such person would also need ID.'

'How often do your counter clerks check the photograph on the ID against the face in front of them?'

Vandeweghe nodded reluctant agreement. 'Perhaps not always that thoroughly.'

'And anyone with a bit of practice can forge a signature?'

Another nod of assent.

'So perhaps we should not be in such a hurry to rule out colleagues from other branches.'

Eric Vandeweghe decided that the time had come to play his only face-saving card. 'You asked my opinion, and my opinion is that you should look closer to home. Katz and Mlle Berenger had a long-running affair going between them, until Katz started bedding another younger employee. I must be one of the few people to know that Katz stopped paying the rent then on Mlle Berenger's apartment in town. Quite an upmarket apartment by all accounts.'

'A kept woman? Herr Katzenberher is married with two children.'

'And his wife has just finished her second oil painting of the *fürstliche Familie* to decorate the walls of its palace in the town centre.'

Georg Hoffarth mused for a moment, tapping the side of his nose with a premonitory biro.

'Might you be suggesting blackmail on the part of Mlle Berenger?'

Eric Vandeweghe's smile put the inspector in mind of a chorister denying his part in showing up the boy next to him for hitting a false note.

Hoffarth decided that this might not be a bad point on which to wind up the interview.

⁂

Katzenberger having instructed his staff to tell clients that the safety deposit room was off limits due to the ongoing police investigation, Hoffarth and his aide used the half hour before their lunch break to examine the manager and deputy manager's safety deposit boxes in both men's presence. It got them no further in the search for all or part of the missing funds. Furthermore, every one of the unrented boxes inspected earlier that morning were, as Claude-Henri put it in a whispered aside to his boss, emptier than a banker's heart.

Over salad and ham rolls brought from the local supermarket together with a quarter bottle of red wine for the inspector and mineral water for his sidekick, Hoffarth mulled over Katzenberger's news of success in tracking down those clients who had visited the safety deposit room the previous week. Suspecting, upon mention of the word theft – though BLR had kept its information economical – that the contents of their boxes had been rifled, all, bar two clients out of the country, had heeded the call to report with their key to the Mensdorf branch by no later than seven o'clock that evening. Before the pair resumed questioning the rest of the bank's employees, Weiland, who had not been happy about his boss's insistence that they stay put for lunch, took a break outdoors to clear his lungs of the musty atmosphere he had been breathing all morning. Ten minutes stretched into twenty after he bought himself a strawberry mousse and coffee in the café a stone's throw from the bank. Shoppers reassured by the sight of an armed law and order enforcement officer had yet to learn of the four million euros snatched from the bank in which many of them held an account.

⁂

By the time inspector Hoffarth got around to interviewing Isabelle Meunier, it was late in the day. Katzenberger had given the two police officers use of a room normally occupied by a bank assistant responsible for marketing bond and other security issues, this person having been absent for the past fortnight on special unpaid leave to care for an elderly handicapped parent. It was a small, sparsely furnished room without windows. The sole wall decorations were one poster putting Luritania on the Tour de France map and another, the worse for wear, advertising an exhibition in Schönschlucht's premier museum.

The first employee interviewed at the beginning of their afternoon session had been Sophie Berenger, an elegant, statuesque woman in her mid-forties. After undressing her in his mind's eye, Hoffarth baulked at the thought of such a stately woman consenting to play the role of Katzenberger's closet odalisque. Did she not have better taste? But sexual prejudices aside, the inspector's neutral line of interrogation bore scant fruit. Mlle Berenger was loyalty and honour personified.

Either that or she was putting on a superb act worthy of Sarah Bernhardt. Furthermore, Hoffarth felt sure that monitoring Sophie and Heinrich's bank accounts would lead him nowhere. Both suspects, if such they were, could run rings around the authorities in terms of financial camouflage: for either individual, setting up an offshore shell company linked to one or more accounts in a separate offshore tax haven had to be a piece of cake.

But, as it happened, although not one of the lesser employees questioned in the wake of Mlle Berenger's regal departure offered grounds for suspicion, during the ten-minute break which the two men took between one interview and the next in order to compare notes and clear the fog from their minds, Hoffarth insisted on keeping an open mind until completion of the last of his interviews.

Weiland was impressed by the attractive, intelligent-looking young woman with unclouded grey-blue eyes, who had just entered the room and taken up the seat indicated to her in front of the two officers seated behind a desk on which Weiland was viewing his open laptop, while the inspector added a final tick to the bottom of Katzenberger's list of branch employees. Isabelle Meunier's open expression contrasted with that of the previous interviewee, who had spent the entire time fidgeting, biting her nails and acting as if generally uncomfortable about having to answer to authority. Unknown to Hoffarth, the previous week this bundle of nerves had been hauled up before the local magistrate for lifting four packets of tampons from the city hypermarket. But her behaviour paled in comparison to that of the employee before her, a frizzy-haired counter clerk with low-cut blouse and concertina bracelets, who had rolled her eyes, thrown up clanking wrists and declared that any bank systematically ripping off its clients deserved a ten million euro (front-office rumours outstripping the rate of inflation) slap in the face.

'Mlle Meunier,' began a by now weary police inspector, 'are we perhaps talking to the daughter of the respected French diplomat, Jean-Luc Meunier?' It went without saying that Hoffarth, having studied Isabelle's résumé, knew that he had hit the nail on the head.

'That's correct.' Isabelle trusted that this deadpan Lowry character was not going to pry too deep into her family life. After falling in with the wrong crowd in her first-year student days, Marion Meunier, Isabelle's younger sister, had almost died of cardiac arrest through overdosing on crack. Following a period of nine months spent in a rehab clinic outside Fontainebleau, she had abandoned any further thought of study and taken off with a group her own age to explore Latin America. The last postcard received by Isabelle and her parents informed them that Marion was paying her way by washing dishes in a Santiago hotel.

'I see that you graduated from the Sorbonne *avec mention très honorable*. What, may I ask, is someone with your credentials doing behind the counter of a village bank branch?'

Slightly surprised that the inspector had not been provided with fuller details, Isabelle proceeded to explain how, following her previous employer's business going into receivership, she had gained appointment as a fast track trainee with BLR, a bank which gave better educated beginners experience of everything from doling out cash to clients to assuming line management responsibilities under the tuition of experienced supervisors. As she had only just signed up with BLR, to start with she had been put on counter duties.

'A taste of money,' said Hoffarth abstractedly to nobody in particular unless himself.

Isabelle smiled modestly, motionless fingers interlaced in her lap as she watched a not unfriendly Claude-Henri Weiland touch the concluding keys of his input.

Questioning the need to go through the same rigmarole with Mlle Meunier as he had with other counter clerks, two of whom had not even finished secondary school, Hoffarth returned to the present moment and his notes. Professional thoroughness dictated that he accord this young woman the same treatment as those who had gone before.

'Between nine a.m. last Monday and four p.m. last Friday, fifteen visits were paid by clients to the bank's *coffre-fort* room. Three of these were by the same person. In other words, thirteen different clients accessed that room over the past week. On conclusion of my investigations, I intend to make a number of recommendations to BLR, including the proposal that from now on whenever an employee asks a client to sign the *coffre-fort* ledger, as well as recording the date the employee should note down the exact time of day together with his or her initials.'

Hoffarth caught his breath. Isabelle was unsure whether the inspector expected her to compliment him on his recommendation or to improve upon it. In the event, she thought best to remain silent.

A slightly disappointed Georg Hoffarth pressed on. 'Mlle, are you able to remember how many times last week you showed a client into the safety deposit room?'

Isabelle managed to hide her amusement at seeing the young officer beside Hoffarth finish typing before his superior reached the end of his question. Perhaps inevitably routine dogged everyone.

Isabelle appeared to give the question, which came by no means as a surprise, serious thought. The fact was that she had shown several clients into the room now sealed off to her and everyone else with the Luritanian police force's yellow crime scene tape. But remembering how many and who, apart from one obvious case, and when was an altogether different matter.

'I would guess perhaps three times. Possibly four, because now I come to think of it one was a repeat.'

Hoffarth scanned his notes. The answer accorded with the figures he had jotted down from the other counter clerks' estimates.

'Do you remember what these people carried into the safety deposit room with them? By which I mean whether or not they brought along large bags or briefcases?'

'That's asking a lot.'

'Think hard.'

Isabelle concentrated. Actually, she could remember one old lady in particular fussing at the counter over the contents of her handbag, which resolutely refused to yield up her key until it occurred to her to open her purse. She had arrived at the counter dragging a small suitcase on wheels.

'There was an elderly lady with a suitcase.'

Mastering mounting impatience, Hoffarth followed the rule book. 'Did it look empty or full?'

'I remember her being out of breath tugging it. So, yes, it must have been fairly full. On the way in.'

The inspector adjusted the knot in his tie, at the same time smothering the desire to tighten a noose around the neck of every old lady who dragged half her shopping into the bank's vault simply to pull out some keepsake dusted down from her mantelpiece. 'Much lighter on her way out?'

'I couldn't possibly say. By then I was probably busy with another client.'

'Anything you recall about her or another client spending an abnormally long time closeted in the safety deposit room?'

'They're not really closeted there in the sense that the vault door is left permanently ajar. That's partly to ensure they remain visible to employees passing by along the corridor outside and partly, I suspect, to guard against exposing the more sensitive ones to claustrophobia. But no, in answer to your question, I can't recall anybody having spent too long in there.'

'What's your definition of too long?'

Despite having walked into a trap of her own making, Isabelle found herself smiling. "How long's a piece of string, inspector? I've never thought to time anyone. And, as I said, I'm usually too occupied with something else to notice who is leaving the building.'

'But clients don't turn up at the rate of one a minute, do they? How do you spend your time between clients?'

For Isabelle, the speed with which Weiland anticipated the last question verged on the comical.

Far from being amused, Hoffarth was wondering if the investigations by the extra help he had called in from head office had turned up anything with the ten summoned key-holding safety deposit clients. At least, they had taken off his hands the unproductive drudgery of going over the premises in search of clues. The mere thought reinforced his fatigue. It was his own fault: he should have spread these interrogations over two days, not tried to solve the insoluble at one fell swoop.

Isabelle's Meunier's voice brought the inspector back to the present.

'We get plenty of phone calls requesting information. People enquiring about the price of gold, whether they can cash in their semi-annual coupons at our branch, how to apply for Internet banking security tokens or open a child's savings account. And, of course, there are walk-ins requesting similar information on the spot or for for pick-up later in the day.'

'No time to twiddle your thumbs,' said Hoffarth, making a statement for once as he exchanged glances with an assistant whose fingers hovered aloft after tracing what could have been mistaken for an arpeggio.

In the absence of a response, the inspector continued with what might as well have been a catechismic ritual for all the joy it was bringing him. 'Thinking back again, Mlle Meunier, can you remember anything unusual in the behaviour of your three or four *coffre-fort* visitors? Anything, however slight it might seem to you. Nervous hand movements, downturned eyes, forced affability …?'

'I think I would have remembered something like that,' said Isabelle without hesitation. 'Even mentioned it to a colleague.'

'Speaking of colleagues, the same question. Have you noticed any of them behaving as if they have something to hide?'

'Not a few have domestic problems. Children to pick up from the crèche. Lunch hours overseeing plumbers' repair work.. These aren't the kind of people to have the time to hatch plans to rob their employer.'

Claude-Henri nodded in unison with his boss. With the end in sight, both men were ready to dispense sympathy where it was due.

And then Isabelle Meunier offered them her spoiler. 'On reflection there was one visitor to the *coffre-fort* room whom I remember more clearly than the others and not only because he was probably one of the last people to enter it.'

As if aroused from somnolence, Hoffarth sat up and looked his interviewee squarely in the face. It was needless for him to prompt continuation.

Isabelle requested a sip of water. The inspector removed the upturned plastic cup from the neck of the mineral water bottle in front of him and poured her a measure.

'I say this,' she continued,' not because he acted at all strangely but because his box refused to open. Even damaged his key. We've had to order a replacement.'

Hoffarth's face resembled a slowly deflating balloon. 'Yes,' he snapped with ill-concealed exasperation, 'that man was the last client to visit the room on Friday afternoon. Unfortunately, Mlle Meunier, as helpful as that information might seem to you, there's every possibility that the vault was robbed long before Friday. Even as early as last Monday.'

'*Mon Dieu!*'

'A wasted visit.'

'I'm sorry?'

'Your client with the faulty lock.'

'Not really. As he had been thinking of an upgrade and needed to deposit something, I signed him up for a new box.'

'I suppose you didn't see what he placed in it?'

'No, once we've helped open a box, we respect clients' privacy. But though I never actually saw what he placed in the new box, I do remember that when he walked up to the counter he was carrying two slim envelopes.'

'A quick in and out, then?' remarked Hoffarth, persuaded that the real waste of time had been his.

'I imagine so.'

'Well, I think that just about rounds up all I have to ask you. My apologies for keeping you behind till this late hour.'

'No problem, inspector. All in a good cause.'

Rising to her feet, Isabelle pushed her seat aside to give herself room to exit the room's cramped quarters: there was a coat stand and metal waste bin behind her which allowed the door to open only so far before encountering one or the other obstacle. Prior to the farewell handshakes, while Weiland stretched back in his chair, massaging stiff fingers, Hoffarth thumbed through his paper work. But when tired hands dislodged Isabelle's résumé from the top of the pile and the inspector reached out to catch it, his attention was caught by a forgotten note.

'If I could crave your indulgence for just a minute longer, Mlle, there was one question to which I'd be most interested in hearing your answer. Strictly one professional to another, so to speak.'

In two minds as to whether to remain standing or to sit down, Isabelle decided that it would be impolite not to reoccupy her seat.

'Of course. As it happens, you're not keeping me from anything important.'

Hoffarth held up Isabelle's résumé. 'I'm tempted to suggest that you have missed your vocation. A student of psychology and philosophy might be thought to be wasting her contribution to society by choosing a career in banking.'

Half inclined to treat this evaluation of her person as a non-question, Isabelle was on the point of responding, when the inspector held up an apologetic hand. 'Well, it's true. I think we've already covered how you came to be where you are. But, Mlle Meunier, my question from one professional to another is this. In your opinion, was this robbery the work of someone slightly more senior than a counter clerk?'

Isabelle blushed. 'I'm sorry, inspector, you'd do better asking those questions of a police profiler.'

'Nonsense. You must have your suspicions.'

'Well, your people turned our offices upside down and came up with nothing. Not that you really expected them to find anything. Unless ...'

'Unless?'

'Unless some ill-intentioned employee with a grudge against a colleague had deliberately hidden some of the money in that person's office.'

'Which would not appear to have been the case.'

'Right. So I'm telling you nothing that isn't obvious, if I suggest you're up against an inside job with or without outside help.'

'And such people would probably lie low and continue to go about business as usual?'

Since the inspector sounded in total accord with his own reasoning, Isabelle saw no need to chime in harmoniously.

'And what would you do, Mlle Meunier, if you were in their shoes?'

Her face broke into a bright smile. 'As you suggested – sit on the money until the heat wore off.'

'So we think as one. The people behind this cannot be unintelligent. Which complicates our chances of apprehending them.'

'Oh, I don't know about that, inspector. Sometimes the cleverest of people commit the most ridiculous mistakes.'

'Indeed, only time will tell. I wish you good evening, Mlle. And thank you for your co-operation.'

'The pleasure was all mine.'

A police officer waiting by the door outside the interview room, because he had thought better not to interrupt the inspector until he had finished his questioning, stood aside to let Isabelle past before knocking and entering.

'We've completed our examination of the contents of every safety deposit box visited last week, sir, bar the ones belonging to two owners away on holiday.'

'And?' Georg Hoffarth's monosyllable was freighted with disaffection.

Drawing himself up to his full height, the officer flicked open his notebook. 'For the most part, the usual run of what you'd expect to find: gems, gold bars, coins, stocks, shares and savings certificates, property deeds, wills, diplomas, one mink, one sable and two ermine stoles …'

The officer handed over his list, which the inspector scanned briefly, the name Roberts making as little impression upon him as the names of the other clients who had obeyed the call to turn up that day with their key.

'For the most part?'

'Yes, sir. One owner came unstuck trying to filch three packages. Eighty grams of crack, two hundred ecstasies and a dozen child abuse photographs.'

'He's been taken into custody, I hope?'

'Yes, sir. Not very ecstatic now.'

'Something to show for your efforts. We should be grateful for small mercies.'

The officer shifted awkwardly on his feet. 'I don't think any of us believed for one moment that we'd turn up four and a quarter million in used euro bank notes.'

'No, Jean-Paul, I suppose that was asking for the moon.'

After reading through Rashid Jabour's summary of MEDRIMCOMB's mission to the Bank of Beirut passed on to him by the young loan officer's superior, Frank Welling invited Rashid for a chat about his trip over a cup of coffee in the staff canteen. In shaking hands with his departmental manager awaiting him in the queue, Rashid reflected that one of the advantages of being in at the beginning of any new organisation destined to grow with time was the sense of camaraderie and pride felt by its pioneers in helping to launch their fledgling institution. Because, as experience went to show, with thirty shareholder member states hungry for results, within four or five years MEDRIMCOMB stood to become another monolith on a par with Europe's long-established development finance institutions.

Welling chose a medium-roast espresso and Rashid a capuccino, after which both men settled down at a window table overlooking the Carrera marble Neptune fountain in the bank's forecourt flanked by well-tended lawns and flower beds sloping down from the roadside.

Rashid had been warned that if the manager contented himself with one espresso, it was best to be the first to return to your desk; with two espressos under

Welling's belt, you could hope to accompany your departmental manager to the lift bay.

'Successful mission, I see,' said Welling. 'What sort of a welcome did the Bank of Beirut give you?'

'Warm. Thoroughly upfront and helpful. Their draft microloans portfolio well prepared. They'd like us to consider a full loan with interest subsidy for the Solidere museum project.'

'Something, I'm sure, our Board would be happy to approve.' Welling crunched on the almond crescent biscuit offered with his coffee and took his first sip. A busy secretary-general, escorting a party of visiting Moroccan bankers to a far table, waved greetings. 'How did you find Beirut after all these years? Won back the privilege to be called the Paris of the Middle East?'

'Well, the number of French boutiques around Hamra took my colleagues by surprise. As did the traffic pollution. But what struck me more than anything else was the level of reconstruction achieved in the downtown area.'

'Devastated by Israeli shelling in the summer of 2006 in that war against Hezbollah.'

'Right. All Solidere's good work again. And after the civil war it's made a fair job of urban renewal along the Green Line.'

'Did you get to see much of eastern Beirut? I imagine not compared to Boyle and Gottfried.'

In rising to his feet after noting the short queue in front of the coffee counter, Frank Welling spared Rashid concocting a plausible explanation on the spur of the moment for his foray into the Christian east side of Beirut.

By the time Welling returned to their table, it seemed as if, after engaging in small talk with another departmental manager at the head of the coffee line, he had forgotten all about east Beirut. Rashid wondered whether when taking time out with his peers or superiors his boss saved shoe leather by ordering a double espresso.

'Thought it only right to tell you about Jack Mason,' said Welling, after confining himself to a doubtful bite of his new biscuit, a hollow roll of the kind normally used to decorate an ice cream dessert. 'The embassy arranged to have his body flown back to the States. Seems he had a brother and sister over there, one out in Seattle on the west coast, the other in Delaware, which is where he was buried.'

'They never caught the mugger?'

'Did they hell?'

'So, no family?'

'Last wife untraceable. And Jack died intestate. Not sure how the law works out there, but eventually, if she doesn't turn up, I suppose Jack's estate will revert to his blood kin.' Welling stirred his espresso. Dark roast this time. 'Funny fellow, Jack,' he said absently, one eye on Neptune's double-ended trident. 'Rabidly anti-semitic. Not something that won him any favours on the Beltway. But never a good idea to argue the toss with Jack about the rights and wrongs of the Palestinians.'

While nodding understanding, Rashid could not help thinking that a man who went out of his way to lend succour to Lebanon's refugees, whether Palestinian or Syrian, could have been all that bad. And then Rashid recalled the words of Sister Ziara as well as the memory that had come to him upon landing on his native soil a few days earlier. The memory of missiles raining down on Beirut-Rafic Hariri International Airport only six years into the new century in a conflict that left more than a thousand Lebanese and just one hundred and sixty-five Israelis dead.

'Was Mason the peace-loving type? Perhaps he was protesting about the disproportionate use of violence.'

Finishing his second injection of morning caffeine, Frank Welling patted his stomach, glanced across in the direction of the secretary-general's Rabat party, then down at the fountain which had suddenly run dry. Not a good omen by feng shui standards, he thought. Necessary to get facilities management on the job as soon as he regained his office, a prime location from which Welling enjoyed a view not only of the fountain on the bank's forecourt but also of the landscaped gardens fronting the road.

'Peace-loving,' said Welling, giving Rashid the false impression that he had been according the suggestion serious thought, 'is not an adjective you could employ in Jack Mason's obituary without causing a few sniggers.'

Rashid wondered how his manager would have reconciled this judgment with the bill of lading delivered to Our Lady of the Sacred Heart convent. But even if Mason's mugger had been seeking that rather than hard cash, theft with or without assault and battery was still theft.

Isabelle could not have hoped for a better turn of events on the morning following her interview with Hoffarth. Late the previous night, an overhead lightning strike had caused a power surge serious enough to crash the BLR Mensdorf branch's hard drive, wiping out every recent time-stamped image captured by internal and external video surveillance cameras. Whereas the security officer had spared Heinrich Katzenberger added misfortune by backing up key financial data on the head office's multi-terabyte hard disk drive, he had neglected to copy password-protected files of the bank's video recordings across to a remote server. Technical constraints ruled out getting the cameras up and running again until Thursday.

It followed that, as soon as she had finished her midday spin cycling session at *All The Right Moves,* Isabelle asked the group's instructor for a word or two upstairs.

With a tug of war under way in her newfound partner's mind between testosterone and clear thinking – whether to welcome another *tête à tête* or to question Isabelle's failure to keep a low profile – Craig made the point a little too obviously, for the benefit of anyone listening, that although his time was at a premium, he could spare Mlle Meunier a few minutes after showering and changing.

When Isabelle pulled up a chair alongside his workstation, Craig was pleased to see the last late lunch hour exercisers laying down their weights and stepping off their tread machines. The only likely disturbance once they cleared the room would come from pensioners, shift workers or university jocks. Fortunately, most of these who showed up as regular as clockwork were not Tuesday people.

'There's no guarantee we'll be left this alone for long,' he said, careful to strike the right formal body language in the eyes of members leaving the changing rooms at the top of the stairs facing his desk. 'So I had better get my printer to issue today's performance read-out.'

Aware that she was crossing and uncrossing too much bare leg, Isabelle pulled down her skirt.

Craig was looking elsewhere. 'I'm afraid I'm too rushed to go over this with you in detail,' he said, reaching across for the print-out and setting it down between them. 'But not bad. Every indicator an improvement on last time.'

'And improvement is what's brought me here today.'

'I hope not of the *I could a tale unfold* variety.'

'Pardon?'

'Hamlet.'

'Shakespeare today is it? What's become of Tennessee Williams?'

'Casanova, you mean? I need a prop for that role. My cane. Williams's Casanova is no longer his old self. He doesn't approach fetching flesh with a bounce in his step. He hobbles towards it.'

'Poor you. Ageing before your time.'

Craig waved farewell to a couple of members on their way out of the building. 'Let's not abuse time, Isabelle. What news have you got for me?'

'News to act upon. In other words, forget Hamlet.'

'Casanova then? A fresh conquest every night?'

Although sardonic rather than suggestive, this remark was met with dismissiveness by someone in no mood for what she saw as frivolity. 'Hardly. Sherlock Holmes. Calm, decisive and methodical.'

'What's happened?'

Craig groaned inwardly at the sight of the fitness centre's eighty-two-year-old marathon runner, heading up the stairs into the men's changing room, from which, because already kitted out for exercise, he quickly reappeared clutching his towel and bottle of water. The next moment, the lanky Irishman was standing in front of Craig's workstation, swiping his microchip performance card across a sensor guaranteed to register data fed to it by any exercise machine into which he cared to insert the same card.

'How're things, Pat?' asked Craig. 'Haven't seen you for some time.'

'Pulled a hamstring five weeks ago. Just got over it.'

'Well, take it easy. That is if you insist on continuing to put our younger members to shame.'

Isabelle watched the elderly beanstalk sidle off in search of his preferred rowing machine which, she was relieved to see, turned out to be the one furthest away alongside the window overlooking the car park. Craig surprised her by whispering that Patrick, immensely shy of women, had intentionally chosen to put as much space as possible between him and the gym's new Siren.

'What's happened,' said Isabelle, taking up the thread where they had left off, 'is a window of golden opportunity. BLR's hard drive went down in last night's storm. Not a single video recording from last week saved. But that's not the only damage. Apparently, it will take security a good three days to get their cameras back in working order. This is the opportunity to finish off what we've started.'

Both she and Craig were thankful that a trainer in the next room's media centre had turned on a Shakira video clip for showing on the first floor's overhead screens. The singer's sea nymph rendition of 'Whenever, Wherever' drowned out their conversation in more ways than one: the self-effacing Patrick was plying his oars with renewed vigour.

'How much time have we got?'

'It would be pushing our luck to delay beyond tomorrow.'

'Are you telling me the police have finished looking under every carpet and cabinet at your branch?'

'Yes. They've taken down that spooky yellow crime scene tape.'

'When is the locksmith due to do his bit?'

'Forget about it, Craig. It's Vandeweghe's job not mine to book the locksmith. And our *directeur adjoint* has other priorities at the moment.'

'Damn, that means I have to find a way of moving the cylinder back in line.'

'What?'

'I thought it advisable. Of course, if I'd known this was going to happen …'

'Are you suggesting you don't know how to move it back?'

'Hell, no. But there's no guarantee that it will be easy.'

'Brilliant. Weren't things complicated enough without your adding to them?'

'Insurance, Isabelle. In case your bank smelled a rat when the locksmith said there was no way my key could have got damaged without damaging or displacing the lock at the same time.'

'Why didn't you let me in on this brainwave? I thought we were supposed to be a team.'

Craig flashed an angry look at his monitor which displayed Isabelle's near perfect performance.

'We are. But I was the one working down to the wire on this remember, not you.'

'Very well. I'll be praying you haven't let one bright idea undo all our good work.'

'I think it's time you got back to the office,' said Craig with ill-contained resentment, before it occurred to him that it might be better if he did fail to re-open the lock. That would give them more time to work out an action plan for the day the lock was repaired.

Isabelle rose to her feet. 'Treat my criticism constructively, Craig. And stay true to your role. More doors opened than closed, remember, to Casanova.'

When his secretary, Chantalle Boyer, phoned through to inform him that a visiting Westminster MP by the name of Peregrine Musgrave had dropped by, while on European Parliament committee business in Luritania, with a view to speaking to the editor-in-chief of *The Pulse*, Justin wondered whether there might be some mileage to be had out of this for his next edition. Although he had never met the MP, Justin knew him by reputation to be something of a paradox insofar as he was both an outspoken advocate of ever wider European economic as opposed to political integration and a staunch defender of the United Kingdom's position outside the Eurozone.

Declining Chantalle's offer of tea or coffee, Musgrave shook hands with the editor before taking up seat alongside him in a leather club armchair by the window overlooking Luritania's Place de la Concorde, where vendors were setting out their weekday vegetable and flower stalls.

'This is the first time it's been my pleasure to welcome a member of my home parliament to our offices.'

'Well, Mr Hendry, I'm here in Luritania because, as you probably know, I wear two hats, one with a tricolor cockade for Strasbourg, the other with a teal feather for the mother of parliaments. All of which is highly appropriate, given that our committee spent the whole of yesterday afternoon debating how to counter illegal bird trapping, including that of my namesake the peregrine falcon.'

'How can I be of help to you? An article promoting wildlife protection? That would be well received here. The government likes to parade its nature conservation credentials.'

'I was thinking more of the possibility of placing an advertisement. That is to say, unless you can save me the trouble.'

'Tell me more.'

Musgrave turned away from watching a stall owner carefully setting out rows of parsnips alongside bunches of radish and some strange white vegetable not, to his mind, unlike a landmine. But the MP saw no need to tread delicately.

'A gentleman dropped by my London constituency office last week unannounced at a time when I was particularly tied up. He wished to discuss European business of undoubted interest to me. I never like turning people away, but it really was an impossibly difficult day, and so I asked my secretary, similarly up to his eyes in constituency work, to tell this fellow that I would be glad to hear him out at a more convenient time. Taking this proposal in the spirit in which it was intended, he duly left me his business card.'

Politicians, thought Justin, born loquacious and honing circumlocution into a fine art over the years. 'I see,' he said, which, coming from a listener willing his man to get to the point, could scarcely have been further from the truth.

'Only afterwards did I discover that the card left me by this gentleman was that of the Innova Press Corporation's editor-in-chief. Yet it is obvious that the individual in question cannot have been you, otherwise you would have admitted as much the moment I walked through your door.'

'Yes. It appears he must have mistaken my card for his own.'

'Indeed, these things happen,' said Musgrave, producing the editor-in-chief's business card from his wallet and musing over it.

The false sense of security brought on by the MP's genial expression left Justin unprepared for the sting in the tail.

'But circumstances conspired to make me think that you could be of assistance. Especially since, a couple of days after visiting my office, this fellow telephoned to say that he had lost his briefcase somewhere on London transport. Not only was the case brand new, but it contained papers touching on matters of government that should on no account fall into the wrong hands.'

Not wishing to signal that he was treating his armchair like a life raft, Justin relaxed his grip on the compact leather arms.

'To return to your visitor's problem, did the man not identify himself or make things any clearer as to what he meant by matters of government?'

'At first, I thought he might have been cuckoo, but the urgency in his voice gave me second thoughts. I told him to come around to my office to explain things frankly, which he undertook to do that afternoon. He never turned up. That was the last I heard of him. So perhaps I was right all along. The man was deranged.'

'Sounds like it.' Only a politician, for whom it went against the grain to confess to any personal failing, would, thought Justin, go to such lengths to disown responsibility.

'On the other hand, I asked myself, what if he was genuine? Supposing the briefcase contained sensitive government contracts? But then, why had he not recontacted me? What had happened to him?'

'I can't see why ...'

'I apologise, Mr Hendry. I have not told you the full story. You see this fellow managed to track down the driver of his cab. Yes, he lost his briefcase in a minicab. The driver told him that, on the day in question, he dropped off his last but one fare at City of London airport. Well, what if that person had taken the briefcase to Europe with him?'

Musgrave drifted off for a moment, causing Justin to fear that the MP was deliberating whether to deliver a direct ethical reproach.

'Perhaps,' continued an increasingly unwelcome visitor, 'I should take my unknown visitor at his word. If that briefcase really did exist and contained sensitive material of direct concern to me and to one of our ministers, should I not make an effort to persuade whoever misappropriated the case of the wisdom of returning it?'

'My apologies.' In need of gathering his thoughts, Justin stood up, went over to his desk, pulled open a drawer and extracted a tube of tablets. 'Upset stomach. Last night's shellfish. '

'Too often the trouble with crustaceans,' said Musgrave with practised equanimity. 'Which restaurant was that in?

'Home. Supermarket microwave pack.'

'I've always maintained that microwaves should carry the same health warnings as cigarettes.'

'That would have half the restaurants between here and Strasbourg up in arms.'

'I fear you are right.'

Justin resumed his seat. 'Did your secretary not give you an idea of what this individual looked like?'

'Middle-aged. Average height. No distinguishing features that he could recall.'

'An accent, perhaps?' Sensing that the battle might not be lost, Justin found that he was almost enjoying playing Musgrave at his own cat and mouse game.

'I was told that the man sounded Italian. He kept interspersing his English with *ma* and *allora*.'

'That rings no bells with me. Perhaps he obtained my business card from reception. Anyway, best I post a classified for you in the next edition of *The Pulse* and have it copied across to our sister European publications. There would, of course, be no charge.'

'I'd appreciate that,' said the MP. 'Particularly since I happen to know that your online publications are viewed in France, Belgium, Germany, Italy … Europewide, so to say. Well, may I leave the wording to you? Something along the lines of sensitive classified material. Guesswork, needless to say on my part. But I can't afford to ignore the possibility that something bad might have happened to my visitor.'

'I understand.'

'Look, here's my card. Give the e-mail address, not my phone number. Crank e-mails you can delete at the touch of a key. Crank callers less easily.'

'Any description, in particular, of the briefcase?'

'Did I not mention that? How careless of me. Red calfskin leather.'

'How red?' asked Justin, voice untroubled, gaze neutral.

'Carmine, I was told.'

Sensing an unwelcome edge to Musgrave's voice, Justin tried to make light of of the pause.

'Not as in Carmina Burana?'

'If you view fortune as inimical.'

He's taking pleasure, thought Justin, in leading me on.

'At all events, not the most common of colours for a briefcase.'

'Agreed. It comes to us from cochineal. The dye, I mean. Cochineals are scale insects. The dye used to colour that leather carmine came from the female of the species.'

The editor understood the need for patience. Like all of his tribe, the MP preferred the indirect to the direct ambush. 'Really.'

'Her habitat is the prickly pear. More precisely, its pad or stem. Have you ever tried, Mr Hendry, to rid a prickly pear of its thorns?'

'I can't say I have.'

'A fruit to beware of. Its needle-sharp filaments can turn your hand into a pin cushion in a matter of seconds.'

Rankled by Musgrave's barb, Justin cast a less than tactful glance at his watch, a signal that the time had come to get down to business.

'Right, well, I'll have your small ad inserted in both our next printed and online issues. As you correctly suggested, your best chance of feedback will be from our website visitors.'

'Thank you. Most helpful. Don't forget to mention that the briefcase was made in Milan. A refreshing change from the People's Republic. Now, I think I've probably taken up enough of your time, Mr Hendry, and ...' Musgrave checked his watch against the clock on the wall. '... I really should be getting along. More things to debate up in the Jacques Delors building.'

Justin heaved himself out of his chair to escort Musgrave to the door to his secretary's office. 'Before you go, Peregrine ... I hope you don't mind my calling you by your Christian ...'

'Not at all, dear boy.'

'Our readers would welcome learning about anything of environmental importance under discussion up there.'

'Of course. I'll drop you a few paragraphs after I get back home.' The MP paused reflectively, his eyes lit by an enigmatic smile. 'Perhaps you could be sure to tack on a note cross-referencing the classified.'

'Of course.'

'I wonder, might I prevail on your secretary's goodwill to order me a taxi *tout de suite*? I'm running a trifle late.'

'No problem.'

'I trust you have no objection to my holding onto that business card of yours belonging to our Mr Mystery man? Fair exchange is no robbery.'

Hearing Justin and his visitor move towards the door to her office, Chantalle Boyer was already standing diplomatically nearby with a sheaf of papers in her hand. The MP bowed courteously, stepping aside to allow her entry.

'Chantalle,' said Justin, 'would you mind ordering a taxi for Mr Musgrave? He needs one as soon as possible to take him up to the *Heilige Kapelle* plateau.'

Returning to his office desk, the Innova Press Corporation's editor-in-chief threw Chantalle's papers onto the blotter, sat down heavily into his swivel chair and cast a vexed look out of the window at a now bustling marketplace before turning back to his desktop. He brought up his web browser and typed in a search request. As he already knew, the peregrine falcon was a bird of prey. But what he did nott know was that it was *the fastest member of the animal kingdom*, its high speed dive of over 200 mph leaving its victims scant chance of survival.

Five minutes later, Chantalle knocked and re-entered the room with a second stack of papers.

'More proofs, Justin, for *Les Nouvelles du Soir*. We need your *bon à tirer* (go-ahead to print) by five p.m.'

'Where's Radetzky?'

'Finishing his cartoon.'

'Why's it taking so long?'

'I don't know. But be warned. He says it's explosive.'

Justin hung his head in his hands. 'As if I haven't … ' He gave Chantalle one of his resigned smiles. 'Sorry, bad day. How did you get on with seeing Musgrave back to his committee meeting?'

'Funny fish.'

'You mean bird.'

'Pardon.'

'Never mind. Why funny?'

'After I suggested he relax until his taxi turned up, he insisted on chatting.'

'Think he fancied you?'

'Couldn't take his eyes off my top drawer.'

'You're talking about a man of the people.'

'The worst offenders.'

'Was that it then? Another lubricious politician?'

'No, for some reason he wanted to know whether you had visited London recently.'

'Shit. What did you tell him?'

Justin's secretary looked perplexed. 'That you were there only last week.'

Standing behind her BLR Mensdorf branch counter, the normally quick-witted Isabelle was slow to register the full extent of the surprise pulled on her by Craig.

There could be no mistaking the tall distinguished, red-headed man with the trim russet beard, who had just come forward and dropped his numbered ticket into the box on the counter top in front of her. The embodiment, she thought, of Peter Ustinov milking one of his authoritative improvisations.

'Mlle Meunier, I presume,' said Tich with the air of a Stanley who had tracked down his Livingstone. 'I come bearing gifts.'

He slid a folded piece of paper into the counter tray and, after satisfying himself that the clerks on either side of her were otherwise occupied, added: 'It is a true pleasure to be served by your good self.'

The compliment was wasted on Isabelle who, having taken out and opened up the sheet of paper, was trying to digest its contents:

Isabelle, my dearest, I hope you will find it in your heart to forgive me, but something in my bones has told me that it would not be a good idea for me to undertake our task today. No, I realise that the full moon has come and gone, so I cannot claim to be afflicted by madness or melancholy. However, I have found a worthy stand-in, for the bearer of this letter (whom you will, of course, call only Monsieur Hobart) has come fully equipped and willing to fulfil more than his role in our partnership. I leave him in your good hands.

   P.S. Be sure to shred this note promptly.

   J.C. (not, you understand, your Saviour)

She folded the note into quarters before tucking it under a sleeve. 'How may I help you, Monsieur Hobart?'

'I'd like to deposit something in my safety deposit box,' replied Tich, nodding down at the two sturdy hold-alls by his feet.

'Of course. You have identification?'

Tich obliged.

Isabelle opened up the blue resident's card, stared at the photograph of Craig Roberts stamped by the Luritanian Ministry of Foreign Affairs and acted out comparing this with the man facing her. 'I'll need your key as well.'

Tich obliged again.

Isabelle Meunier went through the motions of checking Craig's deposit box details on her monitor. 'Right' she said, handing back the resident's card, 'if you wouldn't mind stepping down to the other end of the counter ...'

'Of course, you need my signature.'

Isabelle wondered whether the real reason for Craig's crying off lay in last-minute fear of being unable to reopen the lock. Better have that ill luck fall to somebody else.

After Tich signed the ledger, she invited him into the vault.

'And this room, I believe,' he said, setting both holdalls down on the table, 'has been the scene of a daring robbery. By some barefaced villains, no doubt.'

'No doubt.' Despite the self-assuredness of the larger than life character played by Tich, the theatricality was testing Isabelle's nerves.

She inserted and turned the bank's key, then stood for a moment uncertain as to her next move. On the one hand, she should wait for him to insert and turn his, pull on it and open the door. On the other, she knew that that second good key held by him would not work.

Tich solved the problem for her. 'Thank you, Mlle. I'm sure I can manage from now on.'

And he did. Mere seconds after introducing Craig's compass arm, Tich found a toehold in a different notch and delicately rotated the cylinder into its proper position. After which the key turned effortlessly.

Ten minutes later – Humphrey Robert Hobart was not one to waste time – the BLR Mensdorf branch's client for only a day was ushered out into the reception area carrying two holdalls which, no longer giving the impression of being as light as a feather, contained four million two hundred and forty-eight million euros in stolen used banknotes.

When Isabelle, occupied with another client, saw Craig's friend exit the building, it was impossible to tell whether she was witnessing defeat or the dawn of a fruitful, three-way partnership.

The fact of the matter was that Craig had been economical with the truth. It had belatedly occurred to him that they would have to execute removal of the notes in two stages. And he had confided as much to Tich. 'Only someone as strong as an ox,' he said, 'would be capable of doing it in one.'

Humphrey Robert Hobart had carried two holdalls weighing in excess of twenty-one-and-a-quarter kilos each out of the BLR Mensdorf branch without breaking sweat.

By the time he had closed the car trunk and climbed behind the wheel, the bogus depositor had finished singing, 'As I walk along the Bois de Boulogne with an independent air, you can hear the girls declare', and reserved 'He must be a millionaire' for the attention of the face smiling back at him in the rearview mirror.

'Well, Gwyn,' said Humphrey, turning on the ignition, 'this, my love, is the closest we'll ever come to breaking the bank at Monte Carlo.'

⁂

For once, Peregrine Musgrave arrived earlier than his caller for their rendezvous in Belgrave Square Gardens. On this occasion, he had entered the gardens from the south-east entrance, which took him past the statue of Simon Bolivar and its inscription from a bygone era, which failed to raise a smile from the MP: *I am convinced that England alone is capable of protecting the world's rights, as she is great, glorious and wise.*

Finding their customary bench occupied by a woman pigeon feeder, whom, if he had the choice, he would have bundled off to Trafalgar Square to join the throng impersonating Saint Francis of Assisi without the inconvenience of his stigmata, Musgrave selected one farther along that was relatively free of bird droppings. The dedication read: *In fond memory of David Edward Balfour who spent many happy hours in these, his favourite London gardens.* Nothing as grand as Bolivar's monument. A simple piece of garden furniture dedicated to an ordinary citizen. Musgrave transferred his attention to the pigeon feeder's bench. Strangely enough, he had never seen that inscription because J covered it with his back. Still, Musgrave doubted that J's choice of seat was determined by anything as mundane as a memento to where somebody once enjoyed eating his cucumber sandwiches. The fact was that the bench faced onto some magnificent flower beds. J talked of retiring to the countryside to study philosophy and tend his roses. His paragon, Voltaire, had, as J liked to quote, said: *Life is bristling with thorns, and I know no other remedy than to cultivate one's garden.*

But cultivating roses was not an answer to the thorn piercing the heart of Peregrine and Margaret Musgrave's life. The MP glared at the woman with a pigeon perched on each outstretched arm, glared at the bed of tulips to his right, then cast a supplicating, dry-eyed glance at the heavens. No sign of J, he was glad to see. Musgrave could do without more condolences, however well-intentioned.

'Peregrine.'

The sound of his name spoken from close behind startled Musgrave out of his reverie. Turning around, he realised that J had walked up to him from across the lawn.

'My apologies if I alarmed you. What a sorry use that woman's putting our bench to. The feeding of pigeons and squirrels should be prohibited, don't you think?' J eased his six foot two inch frame into the seat. 'David Balfour. Whoever he was. Not a patch on Eugene de Havilland. At least, I'm assuming our man was related to the designer of the Mosquito.'

Musgrave curled his lips. 'Who wouldn't have appreciated bird crap.'

'Indeed not.' J subdued the volume of his blue silk foulard. 'How are things progressing with your son?'

'Definitely out of his coma, I'm glad to say. But the doctors fear meningitis. They're going to conduct a lumbar puncture to find out one way or the other.'

Sensing the extent of Musgrave's disquiet, J addressed the matter of direct concern to him. 'Under the circumstances, I should not have got you to run that errand for me on the continent. Not if it held up your return home.'

'It didn't.'

J flicked blades of grass still wet from that morning's dew from the side of a brogue polished to parade ground standards. 'Did you learn anything?'

Inclined to point out that Fortuna often proved to be blinder than Justitia in the bestowing of favours, Musgrave reluctantly converted bitterness into artfulness.

'When you were a child J, did you ever play that game pin the tail on the donkey?'

The look turned on Peregrine Musgrave was a cross between perplexity and concern for the MP's mental well-being.

But the Westminster man continued staring straight ahead. 'Your stab in the dark was right on target. *The Pulse's* editor snatched our case.'

J uncrossed his legs and dipped into a pocket for his cigarette case. 'Well now.'

There was a lenghty pause in the course of which, after making his selection, J ordered the remainder of his cigarettes into a serried rank. 'You caught him off guard?'

'I should say, judging by his reaction, that he knew what I was talking about. But ..'

'He refused to admit culpability?'

'Would you, if your interrogator was a member of the House of Commons?'

J took out a gold plated lighter and lit up. 'You let him off the hook?'

'What else could I do? He agreed to place an advertisement in the next editions of his various online and printed European reviews.'

J set the hand holding the cigarette downwind of his companion 'Face-saving, is that it, Peregrine? You're betting on Hendry's coming up with an anonymous finder of our lost property?'

'That's about the size of it.'

'And how do you see the briefcase being reunited with you?'

'I gave Hendry my e-mail address. My guess is that he'll contact me to announce that the case has been found. In fact, he's already e-mailed me to ask how best to proceed if it does turn up. Should he keep the case in his office for collection next time I'm over there? Or, if that's too long to wait, should he send it by registered post, and, if so, would I mind footing the bill? I liked that last bit'

'That's one possibility. Another is that there will be no response to your advertisement, because our documents have fallen into the wrong hands.'

'They're encrypted. What if, before I happened on the scene, Hendry succeeded in opening the briefcase, decided the papers were meaningless and binned them? He'd be too embarrassed to return the case empty.'

'If Hendry's our man as you think, Peregrine, he'd never burn or throw away such papers.'

Although Musgrave had had plenty of opportunity to think the matter through, preoccupations closer to home had led to his shelving the question of the fall-out from the briefcase's loss.

'The devil of it is, Peregrine, that even if your Mr Hendry – let's put it kindly – recovers the briefcase and returns it with the documents intact, how are we to know that he hasn't copied them?'

'We can't know. If he has made copies, perhaps he's sitting on them.'

'Why would he do that? Curiosity will demand that he decrypt them.'

'J, you know as well as I do, that the only document he could decrypt is the background paper. The code underlying the larger document, your exchanges with K, is unbreakable.'

'That's what they thought about the Rosetta stone.' J waved a lingering trail of smoke aside and shook his head. 'I'm afraid we're obliged to assume the worst. And that means strangling the cat before it's let out of the bag.'

Despite the seriousness of J's expression, Musgrave found it impossible not to smirk. 'Aren't we a little too late for that?'

'The problem is we can't be sure that K's listening post won't pick up on this.'

The bank of tulips which Musgrave had been regarding to his right opposite the de Havilland bench brought to mind the ceramic poppy stream of WWI blood in the Tower of London moat.

'You're willing to go down that road? Hendry looked harmless to me. If he coughs up, we should leave it at that.'

'He's an editor, a news hound. It wouldn't be so bad if his reviews were circulated only in a principality unknown to half the world, but that's not the case. Take this further. What if he tries selling his find to a major broadsheet?'

'He'll be brushed off with a polite *Thank you, we've seen it all before*.'

J got up to dispose of his cigarette stub in a nearby waste bin. 'Not,' he said upon returning to the bench, 'if he finds someone capable of deciphering the second text.'

'You know as well as I do that's next to impossible.'

'Do I?'

Peregrine Musgrave felt hollowed out. Hendry had impressed him as personable and outgoing. All right, the editor had succumbed to a moment's weakness in expropriating the MP's briefcase, but now that he had been given the opportunity to salve his conscience by returning the case and its belongings intact, surely he would rather than compound his crime?

J patted Musgrave on the knee. 'You've done your bit, Peregrine. Leave the follow-up to me. We don't want K catching scent of this.'

The MP cast a bleak look at J. 'Luritania is not some godforsaken hole in the back of beyond. You should talk to this fellow. Get him to see common sense.'

'The trouble, Peregrine, is that Hendry sees you as a man with access to ministers of Her Majesty's government. He knows the store you set by recovering those papers. Can we afford to consider him a friend, let alone an ally?'

'I understand,' said the MP with ill-concealed truculence. 'But no more heavy-handedness. And, if K does get wind of this, tell him to keep his pit bulls off.'

J turned from watching the pigeon feeder dispense the last of her bag of peanuts. 'We'll stay in touch. I hope your son's doctors are wrong about the meningitis.'

For several moments following J's departure, Musgrave sat immobile unable to tear mournful eyes away from the bed of tulips. When finally he hauled himself to his feet and retraced his steps out of the gardens, he threw *El Libertador* a glance both resigned and regretful. Thank God, he thought, you didn't live to see these days.

❧

'Ólaf,' said Tich, after introducing Arnold Palmer to Ólaf Thoroddsen, the *Cercle du Tir Hollenbach's* club secretary, 'this makes the second new club member I've brought along in the space of a week. I hope that qualifies me for a rebate on my next sub.'

'I tell you what, Tich, the next time you shoot a three ton over three hundred yards with that Lee-Enfield bolt action of ours, I'll stand you a box of Mark VII 303s.'

'How's that for a generous sonofabitch?' Tich turned to Arnold. 'I'd stand more chance of getting blood out of a stone.'

Ólaf grunted. 'I wouldn't bet on it. Arnold, you don't need to fill that form out now. Bring it along next time with your credit card. Tonight's on us.'

'Lucky Arnold,' said Tich. 'And lucky club, because my guest's brought his own sidearm.'

'How's that?'

Palmer opened his jacket to reveal a shoulder holster with weapon. 'Beauty of diplomatic bags.'

'You need ammo?'

'It's loaded and I've brought an extra magazine with me, but, yes, I could do with some more cartridges.'

'What's that? A Browning?'

'Yep.'

138

'Fine. Have to charge you for the cartridges, though.'

'Of course. I can pay cash here and now.'

'No need. Next time will do fine. If you do a bunk, Tich can pick up the tab.'

'If I'm the second of your latest recruits,' said Arnold on his way with Tich down to the pistol range, 'who got in the door before me?'

'Vanessa Curtis. Remember, I mentioned her name in connection with your dramatic interests?'

'Well, who would have thought …? She's given me a juicy role as a pistol-packing Latino in her latest production.'

'A plastic one, I hope, Arnold.'

'Naturally. Wouldn't do to scare the natives. What's Vanessa's speciality? Let me guess. Long-range rifle?'

'Wrong. Short-range pistol. Like us today.'

'Would you believe it? Wonders never cease. And what's a Swede doing in charge of a Luritanian shooting club?'

'Ólaf's not Swedish. He's Icelandic. And he's not the owner. That guy's Greek.'

'I keep forgetting. This place is like a miniature United Nations.'

'Right. With Luritania holding a seat on the Security Council. Say, speaking of security, is it normal for cultural attachés to carry weapons?'

'I wouldn't dream of going without one in Baghdad or Islamabad.'

'Well, no risk of a jihadist jumping out at you here and screaming *Allahu Akbar*.'

'*Charlie Hebdo* wouldn't agree.'

'How about suicide bombers? Your pistol wouldn't be much use up against one of those.'

'Unless I got one into his brain pan before he had the chance to take us both out.'

'Well, let's see how you do against friendlier fixed targets.'

Palmer went on to shoot three perfect cards over ten yards, scored almost as well over fifteen yards and recorded a decent score of eighty-eight at twenty yards. This compared to Tich's scores of three nineties, one ninety-five and a final ninety-seven at twenty yards.

Schönschlucht's second-hand book dealer wondered how the American would fare in competition against a learner of Vanessa's ability.

It was while Rashid was checking out the BBC world's news website on his iPhone that one item in particular jumped out at him. According to the breaking news headline, *Le Marquis de Honfleur* had just been boarded and ordered to change course by the Israeli navy. He clicked on the item to bring up the details:

The *Marquis de Honfleur*, a container vessel owned by the *TransMediterranean Shipping Company* was boarded in the early hours of yesterday evening off the coast of

Cyprus by members of the Israeli Navy, who had reason to believe that, contrary to its manifest, the Marquis de Honfleur was transporting not North American humanitarian aid but weapons. After these suspicions were confirmed, the Marquis de Honfleur was taken under naval and helicopter escort to the port of Limassol, where customs officials proceeded to unload the cargo. This was found to contain a considerable number of small arms, assault rifles, light and heavy machine guns, together with more serious firepower in the form of MANPADs (shoulder-launched surface-to-air missiles), TOWs (Tube-launched, Optically-tracked, Wire-guided Missiles), M20 Super-Bazooka antitank rocket launchers, anti-aircraft artillery and mortars.

At the time of boarding, the Marquis de Honfleur was bound for the port of Beirut. While Israel's Mossad and Ministry of Defence were prepared to concede that the shipment was destined to arm various Syrian cells opposed to the regime of Bashar al-Assad, it was not prepared to risk the chance of such weapons falling into the hands of Hezbollah. It therefore intended to lodge the strongest of protests with the U.S. Department of State.

When Rashid heaved a sigh, it was not for himself but for Sister Ziara and the Reverend Mother Veronica Laura.

Deciding that he had hung on for too long to that Beirut photocopy of Jack Mason's bill of lading, Rashid promptly destroyed it.

Although Vanessa and Justin had been lovers off and on for the best part of the past three years, theirs was a relationship where each respected the other's need for breathing space. For his part, Justin understood that, after working hours, her immersion in amateur theatrical productions as demanding, for instance, as Lorca's *The House of Bernarda* Alba left Vanessa too drained for anything other than sleep. For her part, Vanessa appreciated that Justin needed to be left free to buckle down to the occasional media study presentation commissioned by BAFTA, for which he had worked in England before arriving in Luritania. In fact, Justin, as well as editing *The Pulse* and providing significant input to several other Innova Press Corporation publications, was the capital's resident *Kinothek* lecturer, specialising in the cinema of Alfred Hitchcock, Michelangelo Antonioni, Federico Fellini, Luis Buñuel and the French *nouvelle vague*.

Vanessa's familiarity with Justin's weekly schedule had been enlarged as a result of according his secretary, Chantalle Boyer, the role of Marguerite Gautier in the upcoming production of *Camino Real*. Consequently, the two women had got their heads together to ensure that Chantalle kept unwanted callers at bay during one of the editor-in-chief's sacrosanct midmorning breaks, while Vanessa bearded the lion in his den.

When Justin, his feet up on his desk, a cup of camomile tea in one hand and a half-eaten Brie and tomato ciabatta in the other, heard the connecting door between his office and Chantalle's thrown open, he expected to see his secretary

140

bringing him the extra tea bag requested over the intercom. His feet crashed to the floor at the sight of Vanessa sweeping in with a tea bag looped around one raised finger, her face wreathed in smiles.

'¡Hola, amigo! ¿Qué tal? No hay que mirarte y tengo hambre.' (Hi, friend! How are things? I only have to look at you and I'm hungry.)

Justin did not know whether to blame his sudden indigestion on the ciabatta or on Vanessa's theatrical entrance.

'Here,' she said, tossing him the tea bag. 'It'll help calm the nerves.'

'My nerves were perfectly calm until … What's with this Hispanic charade? *Camino Real* gone to your head?'

Imitating a schoolmistress lavishing affection on one of her kindergarten favourites, Vanessa kissed Justin sweetly on the forehead, before dropping into the nearest chair. 'Thanks for the offer of a seat. *Camino Real*? Perhaps. That and the fact that I was so blown over by your showing of *Les Olvidados* the other night that I've been walking around in a dream ever since.'

Eyeing his ciabatta with suspicion, Justin took another bite, chewing long and deliberately. 'You're not the dreamy type, Vanessa.'

'Unlike Don Quixote. True. Well, to be frank, honest and above board, I have come to you as a supplicant, Justin, my dear Hispanophile. You see, I have come to the conclusion that irrespective of the number of people beating down my door in the rush to secure the part of the Man from La Mancha in a surreal production guaranteed to set the Luritanian theatre-going public afire, nobody, but nobody, is better suited to take on that role than your noble hidalgo self.'

'You mean nobody else is interested in taking on the part of a candidate for the loony bin who mistook windmill sails for gesticulating giants.'

'No, I mean they were all too overweight.'

'So no problem filling the role of Sancho Panza?'

'No, none. Look Justin, it's a small part. You walk on in Scene One trailing clouds of glory and walk off in scene Seventeen – well Sixteen, strictly speaking, but that's neither here nor there – leaving the audience the better for your imperishable, poetic vision.'

'Not anyone's idea of a meaty part.'

'I thought that would appeal to you. Not so much hours of hard graft as minutes of inspired brilliance.'

'You're mounting this in the open air in the Château de l'Aubaine?'

'Correct. Especially since it features a fountain, the source of a miracle brought about by no less a person than the don. Justin, I'm offering you an opportunity too good to miss. Take up your lance and shield and transform my production into the dramatic highlight of the year. Don't forget that Luritania is hosting the annual European anglophone amateur theatrical festival this May. Your performance could put us on the map. Picture your name posted up on billboards the length and breadth of the land.'

This last incentive was not without its appeal. *The Pulse's* design team had been selected to produce the poster advertising *Camino* Real, and even if the only billboards on which it would appear were those in the capital, Justin suddenly fancied the thought of seeing his name in the next best thing to lights.

'Put like that, I might just … You're not having me on? Only a few lines to memorise?'

'Right, but telling lines, Justin, telling.'

'Of course. Pronounced by a man qualified to play the lead in One Flew into the Cuckoo's Nest.'

'However,' said Vanessa, hard put to keep a straight face, 'there is one itty-bitty catch.'

'Ah, now. The moment of truth. As the priest says to his spellbound congregation, some unable to stop themselves from hoping for the worst: *Speak now or forever hold your peace.*'

'You've forgotten your extra tea bag. Just when you might need it.'

'Too late. The water's gone cold. Like my enthusiasm.'

'In fact, the longish interval of inactivity between entrance and exit is all about imitating a log, Justin. You see at the end of Scene One, which is really a prologue, the don lies down and falls asleep onstage … All right, in the château forecourt … until Block or Scene Sixteen when he wakes up. In other words, he's stuck there for a tad more than fifteen scenes.'

'Great. By which time, he or I will have gone batty with cramp. I think you've just lost your star attraction.'

'I see. Well, Justin, I suppose we could make things that bit easier for you by having you fall asleep out of sight behind the fountain. Then you profit from the first distraction to disappear before the audience is any the wiser. Leaving a pair of dummy legs sticking out for you to fold away after you sneak back for the grand finale.'

'That's more like it. Means I could bring my laptop along and put the waiting time to good use.'

'Actually, I've a much better idea. You act as prompter for those fifteen or so scenes. It will give spectators the impression that the play is being dreamt by you.'

'Not if your actors know their lines. Sorry, Vanessa, if I had an Equity card I'd wave it at you straightaway. This ciabatta will have to do. I'm pretty damn sure that asking an actor to double up as prompter goes against the rule book.'

'You're forgetting something. We're not professionals.'

'Worse still, then. You're exploiting naïve volunteers.'

'If that's your last word.'

'Sí, eso es mi última palabra.'

'In which case, forget the prompting and feel free to spend your down time with anything from a laptop to a lap dancer. Out of sight.'

'I should be so lucky. Do I take it from the beady look that your bag contains something more than a purse, lipstick and other feminine accessories?'

'How astute, Justin. Yes.' Vanessa dipped into her shoulder bag. 'Here. One copy of *Camino Real* in mint condition, you lucky man. People with longer parts have to make do with photocopies.'

'This wouldn't happen to be one of those I bought in Waterstone's? What a chump! I should have guessed as much. In for a penny, in for a thousand pesos.'

※

'How are things, Pascale?' asked Rashid the moment he heard his sister's voice over his iPhone.

'Rashid, so nice of you to remember Rebecca's birthday.'

'Yes, well, I'm trying to make up for the fact that I posted her card and gift too late for it to arrive on time.'

'I shouldn't let it worry you. Five-year olds are happy to open parcels whenever they arrive.'

'I didn't phone only to talk to Rebecca, Pascale. How are you? We haven't spoken for a long time.'

'A tiring day today. Almost lost a patient on the operating table. Severe anaemia responding badly to the blood transfusion. But we pulled her through.'

Rashid's sister worked as an anaesthetist in Paris's Salpêtrière-la-Neuve hospital. Monitoring patient's life functions, often for hours on end, required an uncommon degree of focus allied with unhesitating responsiveness to life-threatening developments. Incomparably more stressful than shuffling balance sheets. Few patients who came around in reanimation appreciated to what extent they owed their survival as much to the anaesthetist as to the surgeon.

'You still working those long shifts?'

'Yes, but with two days off in between. Gives me more time for Rebecca.'

'And Bernard?' If Rashid was enquiring about his brother-in-law, it was out of politeness rather than because of any real interest in the doings of an ophthalmologist whose short-sighted, right-wing political views clashed with his own.

'Pulled his back out carrying a chest of drawers he bought in a *brocante* (secondhand market) up three flights of stairs. How are things with you in that new bank of yours?'

'You won't believe it, but I was sent on mission to Beirut last week, sounding out new business.'

'You're not serious? Father is out there at the moment. Working for MSF (*Médecins Sans Frontières* – Doctors without Borders). Treating war-wounded Syrian refugees, among others.'

Leaning against his living-room wall, Rashid buried one side of his head in the heel of his hand. 'If only I had known.'

'Where were you?'

'Downtown.'

How much better, thought Rashid, to have found a way of meeting up with his father, whom he had last seen all of two years ago, than to have wasted his time on a poisoned errand.

'How long has he been out there?'

143

Rashid and Pascale's father, Philippe Farid Jabour, a senior trauma and orthopaedic surgeon, also worked in the Salpêtrière, albeit in a department other than Pascale's. Rashid knew that the hospital had given its blessing to one of their most experienced surgeon's secondment to humanitarian field surgery.

'About a fortnight. Mother got him to promise to ring her regularly. Listen, Rashid, don't torment yourself needlessly. Think how difficult it would have been.'

'Nonsense. Had I known, I'm sure I could have managed to seek him out.'

'Well, what's done is done. How was Beirut?'

'Hot. Sticky. Appalling traffic congestion. Some streets ridiculously chic, when you stop to think about what's going on all around.'

'I was too young when we left to remember much about the place. You as well, no?'

Apart from what he had taken to be olfactory memories stirred around the herb and spice stalls in the souks, Rashid had to agree.

'Did you get any time to yourself?'

The moment had come to admit that what had motivated the present telephone call was not so much the desire to wish a five-year-old happy birthday as the need to confide.

'A man from the World Bank asked me to make a charity call on a convent in East Beirut. Only afterwards did I learn that it was a strange form of charity.'

'What do you mean?'

Now that it came to it, Rashid, embarrassed to confess to being duped, decided against selfishly offloading his worries onto his sister.

'Rather like robbing Peter to pay Paul.'

'Tell me some other time,' said a Pascale no longer focused on Rashid, because her daughter was tugging at her skirt. 'Rebecca is standing here in her pyjamas after brushing her teeth. She's rubbing her eyes. Are you ready to speak to your niece before she falls asleep on me?'

A stowaway could not have abandoned his vessel more willingly than Rashid jumped at the idea of striking out into the safe harbour of childhood.

⁂

Justin's idea of knocking on his sub-editor's door was to give it a knuckle rap loud enough to wake the dead before launching himself into the room. There was a reason for this precipitate behaviour: the editor-in-chief had caught Klaus's predecessor enjoying himself doggy style with an Italian temp bent over her desk at a time, seven o'clock on a Monday morning, when neither expected to be caught in the act by a boss who had told everyone that he would be late in that day due to a blood donation appointment with the Red Cross.

It made no difference that the nearest Klaus Radetzky had come to philandering with a member of the opposite sex during the working week had been to offer Chantalle Boyer a heart-shaped chocolate truffle from the box he had been presented with on his birthday. Justin had programmed himself to expect the worst.

Consequently, when he burst into his sub-editor's office on the mid-week afternoon before the setters were due to be handed the pass for press for the next edition of *The Pulse*, Justin found Klaus, with his trousers firmly belted, standing over mock-ups of two cartoons, an index finger over pursed lips as he looked from one to the other without the slightest sign of surprise at what any normal person would have interpreted as a forced entrance.

'Chantalle told me,' said Justin, 'that your cartoon material, Klaus, could be contentious.'

'I should hope so,' replied the sub-editor who was using an animation pencil to retouch one of the drawings displayed on his Apple monitor.

'What's this week's choice?'

'On the left you have my answer to Obama's belated response to the Chapel Hill slaughter of those three Muslim students. Care to look at that first?'

Justin preferred to inspect the hard copy rather than the screen version. It showed a turkey, perched on the roof of a chapel, gazing down at three bloodstained college diplomas. The bubble above the bird's head read: *It says a lot about this country when I get to beat the bald eagle to it.*

'And on the right,' said Klaus, 'you have Ukraine's president playing to the gods.'

Justin looked down at the cartoon of Poroshenko holding six dark green passports in one hand and a piece of broken fuselage in the other. A matador's hat was perched on his head over which the bubble read: *Rumours that the Spanish air traffic controller monitoring flight MH 17 has gone missing are unfounded.*

The editor-in-chief cracked a smile. 'This one. We live and work in Europe. What Obama does or doesn't do about defending human rights in his back yard is irrelevant compared to how Malaysia Airlines flight MH17 came to be flying where it was.'

'So we go with it?'

'Aren't the passports and the scrap metal overkill?'

'It's all about staging a performance.'

'But you want to send this guy up. Could you change what he's holding in the next hour or so?'

Radetzky scratched a stubbled chin. 'Depends what you want.'

'A cape instead of the metal and a copy of Lorca's *Bodas de Sangre* instead of those passports.'

'That's a tall order.'

'Tall, but not beyond the skills of *The Pulse's* art director.'

※

'As you can see,' said Rashid, after handing out decrypted copies of Justin's binary-coded text at the Lenfindi Club's extraordinary midweek meeting after working hours up at the airport, 'this paper is headed *Plenum Ducentorum*, which I understand from what follows to mean Assembly of Two Hundred – by the sound of it, influential policy and decision-makers. And their agenda, spearheaded by a smaller *Consilium de Viginti* or Council of Twenty, the Assembly's power brokers, is, if we are to believe it, none too healthy. Read for yourselves.'

Tich, Justin, Vanessa, Craig and Isabelle settled down to digest Rashid's translation:

With the Earth's population expected to run to nine and a half billion by 2050, the strain which growth of this order is likely to put on sustainable resources will force the inhabitants of agriculturally impoverished areas to migrate into more fertile neighbouring regions.

We strongly recommend forestalling the impact of this growth on our economies by expanding our theatres of influence in and around land masses whose natural resources offer significant potential for future exploitation.

Territorial expansion allied with **acquisition and control of natural resources** *being our priority, it follows that we need to ease the strain on these resources by unburdening the relevant land areas of as much of their population as possible.*

Demographic goal: *reduction of global population by one seventh.*

Foremost among the means at our disposal: **cultivation of pathogenic viruses** *in the Third World capable of causing widespread fatalities in the absence of known antidotes.*

We are also progressively persuading Third World countries to close down outdated vaccination facilities and to give preference to our vaccines in the form of humanitarian aid targeting the young. A comprehensive inoculation programme is to be set in train in schools throughout the undeveloped nations. Those administering and monitoring use of our vaccines will be ignorant of the fact that they promote sterilisation or carry a dormant, disabling virus.

In addition, we should, wherever and whenever possible, not hesitate to maximise our ability to set one tribe or faction against another and to fuel interethnic warfare through covert arms sales.

For present purposes, the territory of the Russian Federation offers the most prized agricultural, energy and mineral resources available to us not through counterproductive force of arms but through continuing initiatives aimed at transforming the country's leadership in waiting into a colonial administration.

Hence, it is vital to continue undermining the Russian economy in the hope that sanctions combined with mismanagement by our fifth columnists will eventually sink the ship of state, resulting in calls for regional independence guaranteed to play into our hands through territorial dismemberment and the demise of the no longer elite oligarch class.

A further strategic advantage has been our success in **Ukraine**, *where we have been welcomed with open arms by a strong nationalist movement, descendants of those ultra-nationalists who fled the country for Canada when Hitler decided that they had become a hindrance to his cause. Our agents of influence (NGOs, numerous religious sects, etc., breeding grounds for fresh recruits) have spurred on this nationalism by persuading Ukrainian youth that its historical roots hark back to a race nobler than the Slavs.*

Any movement, be it populist or fascist, inciting russophobia plays admirably into our hands. Ukraine is an economic basket case and will remain so for years to come. Irrespective of what the Russian residents of eastern Ukraine might say to the contrary, no right-minded economist has ever suggested that people are more important than land. And once we, for our part, establish NATO bases close to the Russian Federation, arming these with missile defence systems ostensibly intended to counter threats from rogue states such as North Korea and Iran, we will be one step nearer our goal.

In tandem with Ukraine, our allies in **Lithuania** *have outspokenly promoted the idea that Russia is a threat not only to the Baltic States but to Europe as a whole. Let us acknowledge that Russia has neither the resources nor the inclination to saddle itself with economic cripples living off European hand-outs. But the more that we and our allies reinforce the spectre of the land-hungry Russian bear, the more we strengthen an ailing NATO and a mindset fearful of coming under Russia's yoke.*

In **Siberia**, *which we see one day as the real jewel in our crown, we are pleased to report that influential elements in Ekaterinburg are fanning the flames of a healthy secessionist movement.*

Developments look promising in **Belarus**, *where a number of our NGOs are patiently laying the ground for another Independence Square (best-case scenario) or velvet (worst-case scenario) revolution.*

Georgia *is, of course, already in our camp. But continued work is needed on drawing the Federation's breakaway Asian republics into the fold. In view of the level of impoverishment there, it is essential to step up support for ultra-right-wing nationalist movements, not least Daesh, by inculcating the young with the benefits to be had from switching camps at a time when the march of history should be telling them that the future lies in their hands.*

Our sole setback has been **Crimea.** *Its bloodless annexation snatched the gem of the northern hemisphere's Black Sea naval bases from our grasp. Matters were not helped after the event, when Gorbachev slated Khrushchev for gifting Crimea to Ukraine without consulting the Crimean people.*

The **information war**: *as world leaders in mind-influencing propaganda, we must continue to ramp up news streams discrediting any power that stands in our way. It is imperative to exploit the vast swathes of cyberspace under our control with a view to spreading any number of false rumours, however far-fetched, provided that these are guaranteed to fall on fertile soil. If this calls for rewriting history, we should not hesitate to distribute the new teachings as widely as possible, especially among the young and impressionable with little idea of or scant interest in history.*

Our clarion call: **Land, the commodity of the future**. *The more swiftly we lay claim to new territories the more surely we lay the foundations of prosperity for succeeding generations.*

Finally, the Assembly takes due note of the fact that the Council of Twenty's secretariat is to issue, under separate confidential cover, a full list of sponsors, their contributions and complementary tactics.

Rashid waited until everyone had finished reading their copy.

'I don't know about the rest of you, but I feel this document poses more questions than answers.'

Sitting slouched with both feet straight out in front of him, Justin threw his copy onto the table, pulled himself back upright and turned to Tich. 'I agree. How about you, Tich?'

'I suggest we take it in turns to say what we think about Rashid's text. Starting with you, Justin, the person who lifted it out of obscurity into the light of day.'

'Yes, well, I can't help thinking the fact that a member of the House of Commons is anxious to recover something that comes with all the trappings of a crackpot conspiracy theory should make us think twice. Craig, what do you think?'

'Tempting but perhaps a mistake to dismiss it out of hand. I suppose what I'm trying to say is that if this fellow Musgrave, who Justin has told us about, had not turned up, you could interpret this as a scam. The briefcase was left deliberately for somebody to discover in the hope that they would unlock the contents and take them straight to the BBC. The idea being to discredit America and its propaganda to the effect that Russia is a bigger threat to world peace than IS. Leaving coded documents in an expensive briefcase adds to the credibility. But then Musgrave waltzed along and spoiled that theory.'

'Isabelle?'

'Why use a minicab for a scam rather than go upmarket with a black cab? Anyhow, I would treat the document as genuine. But, to be honest, perhaps that's only because it reinforces my prejudices.'

'Vanessa?'

'Taken at face value, too ridiculous for words. Sterilisation and territorial rape. Both of which go well with the briefcase's lock code. But the policy makes sense. Why should eugenic manipulators and land grabbers copy Adolf, when they can achieve their ends by stealth? '

'Rashid?'

'I'd feel a lot happier if I knew what the second larger set of papers contained. But my IT skills don't extend to that level of decryption. How about you, Tich?'

'Puts me in mind of Maggie, who is reputed to have said that a land as rich as Siberia deserved a better fate than being a part of Russia. Be that as it may, I would tend to take the text at face value, were it not for the Frankenstein viruses and vaccines. I find those particularly hard to stomach in more ways than one. In other words, perhaps somebody is playing games here. Perhaps what we are looking at is only a draft, and the reason why Musgrave wants the briefcase back without any hullabaloo is that HM's government has plans for these documents. Then again, I could be totally wrong. Perhaps Musgrave is up to no good and fears for his reputation.

'Anyway, to sum up. The general feeling appears to be that there's something in this. A politician with a foot either side of the Channel hopes to avoid any of this leaking out. So, should we return him his briefcase *virgo intacto*, knowing that he will suspect his goods have been interfered with? Or should we get Justin to tell him that nobody came forward in answer to his advert?'

Justin finished making a note at the top of Rashid's photocopy. 'I have to return the briefcase. Musgrave caught me and my secretary off guard. He knows I took it.'

'So the next question.' said Tich, 'is how will the dishonorable member for Chelsea, Hammersmith and Fulham react to guessing his goods have been tampered with? There are various choices open to him. Leave well alone. The fellow caught in the next best thing to *flagrante delicto* has learnt his lesson. He was after the case. Whatever it contained was merely a bonus. But since all he found inside were documents meaningless to anyone but the owner, and he is returning them – no big deal…'

'Except,' interposed Justin, 'that the guilty party belongs to the news hungry class.'

'You took the words straight out of my mouth.'

Isabelle leant forward to add her contribution. 'A news hungry editor in a European backwater. And how much capital could he hope to make out of publicising this more widely? Apart from which, there's the matter of his publishing house and its shareholders. What if Luritania's political top dog happens to be a member of this Assembly of Two Hundred? He could well be.'

Justin objected. 'Nothing's stopping me from syndicating the article.'

'But would you be able to? Any journalist approached with this would turn his nose up at such a blatant conspiracy theory. After all, the Internet's full of them. Dreamt up by screwballs maintaining that aliens are already down here among us preparing their takeover, that the White House ordered 9/11…'

'But all the same,' said Vanessa, 'certain elements of the press like nothing better than a whistleblower. Justin would find takers. That's not the point, though, is it? The point is that whether he goes out looking for the modern-day equivalent of Zola's *L'Aurore* or incinerates his copy of these papers, it's all the same to the people he's robbed.'

'Hang on,' said Justin. 'Only a moment ago you more or less dismissed these plans as crackpot.'

'Yes, well, I'm no longer so sure. Some of them, at least, echo what certain neocons have to say about American exceptionalism. In short, you might need to think about joining me down at the shooting range.'

'Well,' said Craig, 'if Vanessa is right with her extreme times call for extreme measures, perhaps we should let Musgrave know the message is out. He and the people behind him would have to accept that they were stymied.'

'Fine,' said Rashid. 'How would you propose going about that? Getting Justin to publish a summary of what he found in a briefcase thought to belong to a conservative MP?'

'I suppose so.'

'But those papers were never meant to be seen by more than a select coterie.'

'Wait,' said Isabelle. 'If Rashid hasn't managed to decipher the second set of papers, what's to say that he or anyone else succeeded in translating the binary-coded paper into comprehensible text?'

'Yes,' said Rashid. 'That's even more of a case not to publicise. The longer things go with no word leaking out of this committee's real or fictitious plans, the safer Justin remains.'

Tich nodded. 'Yes, perhaps you're right. Return the briefcase and let sleeping dogs lie.'

Vanessa closed her copy of *Camino Real* in which she had been making marginal notes on timing the arrival of the streetcleaners with their undertaker's barrel. 'I still think Justin should join Tich and me down at the shooting range.'

Every Wednesday afternoon Vanessa endeavoured to leave work early in order to visit Clara Bogen, a forty-six-year-old inmate of Schönschlucht's blind home befriended in response to a mention by Justin about an article in *The Pulse* inviting readers to devote a portion of their free time to residents of *La Maison des Aveugles*. Vanessa had taken immediately to the warm-hearted, partially sighted Austrian, a sentiment reciprocated by someone appreciative of companionship.

Wednesday being swimming pool day, Vanessa found Clara waiting for her in the home's reception area, a duffel bag on the carpet at her feet.

'Clara,' said Vanessa, taking her hand before exchanging kisses, 'how are you? You've had your hair cut. It really suits you.'

'Thank you. Easier to control shorter.'

'And where's Bismarck?' Vanessa was referring to Clara's guide dog, a German shepherd.

'Resting. I walked him to the library and back this morning.'

Clara tended to talk as if she were the guide not the dog.

After both women had completed their laps without Vanessa needing to guard Clara against colliding with anyone in an adjacent lane, they stretched out side-by-side on loungers in the solarium, where the warmth of late afternoon sun seemed to be penetrating down through the glass shell roof.

When the two had rested sufficiently, they changed back into their everyday clothes and climbed upstairs to a self-service cafeteria to enjoy chocolate eclairs with fennel tea at a table overlooking the pool.

'You're wearing a different scent today, Vanessa.'

'Ah, you noticed. Yes, it's called *Vivace*. It's supposed to make you feel more awake.'

'In that connection, I hope you're arranging for someone to pick me up to come and see *Camino Real*.'

Accustomed to hearing Clara use that last verb without so much as a second thought, Vanessa made a mental note to ensure that her players polished their elocution and voice projection.

'Of course. The play's being performed in the courtyard of the Château de l'Aubaine. We don't do matinees, so you should bring a shawl to cover your neck and shoulders.'

'And who is playing Casanova?'

'Craig Roberts. He takes your spin cycling lessons.'

'A man of many parts. Very fit.'

'Yes, though I think Giacomo's way of staying fit was to jump from one bed to another.'

'How is that editor friend of yours?'

'Not without his problems.'

'Sorry to hear that.'

Clare's mention of Justin had brought a series of uncomfortable thoughts to the surface. Would she be able to stop herself from bedding Lord Byron? She still prickled at memories of those jealous boarding school bitches, who had it in for her after her lapses with the gardener's son and the cook. But now she, Justin and Rashid were in the same boat of an unenviably different nature.

Vanessa turned back to face her friend. 'Justin's too demanding. Works himself into the ground. Then ends up frazzled.'

'Sounds like a carbon copy of you.'

Vanessa drew a line across the table with a tremulous finger. A fault line, she thought.

'Clara, could I ask you a favour?'

'My goodness, please do. I'd be only too willing to do something for you for a change.'

'I'd like you to take care of a … private letter … a document for me. That is to say, if I should be called away for any length of time commuting between here and Brussels.' Now that she had come out with it, Vanessa could scarcely credit the feebleness of her logic.

'Oh dear, is that a real possibility? How I'd miss our weekly get-togethers.'

Vanessa berated herself for having caused unnecessary worry. 'Let's hope my boss changes his mind and sends someone else. In any case, next week is guaranteed.'

Since the last thing she wanted was to end the outing on a negative note, Vanessa reached out for Clara's hand.

'Chances are you can forget all about the letter.'

But circumstances beyond Vanessa's control would ensure otherwise.

After being taken on a guided tour of the fitness equipment, changing and shower rooms and sauna in *All The Right Moves*, Arnold Palmer filled out his membership application form at the front desk, paid for an initial three months subscription, trotted upstairs, changed and introduced himself to Craig Roberts, who issued him with his performance data chip card and accompanied him across to the nearest free tread climber.

'We call this a Nordic track elliptical. Useful if you're training for cross country skiing. Feel like setting it for a fifteen-minute workout, then moving on to something else?'

'Sounds good.'

Craig talked Arnold through the various functions while demonstrating the monitor's real-time performance levels. 'If there's nobody on hand to help with the bench press later on,' he said, turning back towards his workstation, 'give me a call.'

Not having exercised for the past fortnight, Palmer found the tread climber heavy going and had to scale down an ambitious resistance level. Following this warm-up, he moved into the next room and opted for two machines designed to build up pectorals, before stretching out on a mat to go through a series of abdominal and back strengthening exercises. By the time he walked across to the bench press, with nobody on hand to help him he decided to take Craig up on his invitation

'Mind acting as my spotter?'

Craig finished typing something into his desktop and put it into sleep mode. 'Sure. What are you trying out?'

'Triceps extension using an E-Z curl bar. I usually manage on my own, but it's been some time since I last lifted, so I'd rather be safe than sorry.'

On the eighth lift, Craig helped return the bar to its rack. Arnold gave a dissatisfied grunt. 'That's what comes of being out of condition.'

'I don't know about that, 'said Craig, tightening one of the collars holding the dumb bells in place. 'You've been lifting 25 kilos. Maybe you should have started with something a bit lighter.'

Arnold eased himself up and rolled his shoulders. 'Do you think Vanessa Curtis can pull off the *Camino Real* challenge?'

'Yes, she loves experimenting with novel ideas. Expects a lot of her players, though. I see you enjoy playing the manipulator.'

'As much as you enjoy playing the gay Lothario.'

'Careful with the gay, Arnold. You feel like doing any more lifts?'

'Frankly, no. My shoulder's complaining. Think I'll do some cycling, then call it a day.'

Craig followed Palmer into the next room, where the American climbed into the saddle of a model with dual action arms offering the advantage of an upper body work-out in addition to leg exercise. After Craig returned to his desk, he continued chatting to Tich's latest recruit to his fitness centre.

'No lack of culture this month, what with a jazz festival down the road, Nigel Kennedy and that Portugeuse fado group.'

'The first one's my baby, but I'll certainly be patronising the other two.'

'The Irish hosted an interesting lecturer last month. Gave us the lowdown on MIT's Noam Chomsky and his thoughts on massaging the truth.'

'Lowdown says it all,' retorted Palmer, flashing Craig a smile which told the fitness centre's manager the importance Americans in general attached to cosmetic bleaching.

※

Isabelle took a tea towel and began drying the wine glasses which her father had deposited in the rack on the kitchen draining board. Jean-Luc Meunier rolled up his shirtsleeves the better to apply elbow grease to refractory stains inside a set of Le Creuset cast iron pots.

It suited Isabelle's purpose that her mother had prepared a lavish meal supplemented with numerous vegetable side dishes inasmuch as Jean-Luc's unhurried thoroughness gave her the opportunity to chat to her father without fear of interruption or criticism.

'Papa, why is Europe all smiles about welcoming into its arms a country whose administration is riddled with corruption?'

'The Kiev cake empire? If you're expecting to see the Commission's president kissing his Ukrainian counterpart on the lips in the near future, Isabelle, I think you will be disappointed. And even if Ukraine were to defy the odds by becoming whiter than white, some pundits say that, in filing for membership of the European club, Ukraine is risking geopolitical hara-kiri. You see, technically speaking, once Ukrainians get to sip Bénédictine in the members lounge, Poland can bring the country before a quite different bar by demanding restitution of land and property lost as a result of WWII. Were Hungary and Romania tempted to do the same and all three succeeded, that would leave western Ukraine emasculated and eastern Ukraine lined up for a bear hug.'

'Well, how do you view the current situation in eastern Ukraine? The media keeps screaming about invasion. Russian tanks sighted one moment, gone the next. Presumably hiding behind some large bushes or trundled back into Russia.'

Jean-Luc paused to rub an itching nose with the back of a hand gripping a soft cleaning pad. 'Invasion? I doubt whether there are many regular army troops on the ground. Mind you, there's no lack of young and not so young Russian and Chechen volunteers fighting alongside Novorossiya. That's counterbalanced by the number of Poles and Romanians on the other side. As for tanks, what's Ukraine using? What it's always used. Russian tanks. And the Russian army? NATO knows full well that this is stationed behind the border.'

'So why the insistence that Russia wants to gobble up Ukraine and the Baltic States?'

'You can forget about the Baltic States. Despite the capital investment ploughed into them over the years, Putin's glad to be rid of them. But after plucking the Crimean plum from under Ukraine's and the West's nose, he miscalculated the blood cost of deserting ethnic Russians in eastern Ukraine. Russian patriots seeking federalisation for the Donetsk and Luhansk regions clamoured for him to order his troops into eastern Ukraine. He turned a deaf ear.'

'Because whereas Crimea was a walkover direct military intervention in Ukraine would have meant war?'

'Yes, the taking of Crimea without force of arms was an inspired move on the world's chessboard. Armed invasion of Ukraine would have won Putin even fewer friends on the international stage.'

'Apart from the Chinese, how many has he as it is? The Americans and their allies view him as warmonger.'

'Yes, my dear, ironic is it not? The Stars and Stripes is hoisted over around

153

eight hundred military bases worldwide, while the Russian tricolor waves over a mere fifteen foreign military bases, thirteen close to home. I believe the other two are a naval base in Syria and a logistical centre in Vietnam.'

'So who, in your opinion, papa, is the greatest threat to world peace?'

Jean-Luc upended his third *Le Creuset* dish on the draining-board beside an already full rack of plates and cutlery, dried his hands on the apron around his waist and threw Isabelle a smile part roguish part reprimanding.

'Dear daughter, never allow international politics to overshadow domestic priorities. You've missed a spot on one of those glasses.'

⁂

Each time that Tich drove into the village of Baalbek on the outskirts of Maastricht he asked himself what had possessed the communal authorities in this corner of the Netherlands' to name their village after a historic site in the Lebanon counted among the wonders of the ancient world. There was nothing to suggest the vestiges of a magnificent outpost of the Roman empire: no ruined columns or splendid mosaic floors. A windmill or two. Grain silos. Tich wondered whether a slip of the mayoral tongue had corrupted Daalbek to Baalbek. Daalbek might have made some sense inasmuch as the village lay close to the Jeker river, a tributary of the Meuse.

But such thoughts, including what Rashid would have made of this misnomer, soon took a back seat to Tich's more pressing concern: the need to start getting himself into a cheerful frame of mind before entering the sanatorium where his younger brother, Horatio Maddox Hobart, had been confined for the past four years. Tich drove up to the Netherlands midweek twice a month, either leaving his shop closed or getting his part-time assistant, Horst Völkling, to stand in for him. His brother received no other visitors, both men's parents having separated long ago, the mother to live with her sister in Auckland after the father had eloped with an artist to British Columbia – the last news Tich had heard of his father had been in a cryptic Christmas card postmarked Victoria: *Moira's latest exhibits created a sensation in Fairfield. We might be moving on.*

Humphrey Hobart reflected that it had been almost nine years to the day that he and his brother had been belting hell for leather along the Jabbeke highway between Ostende and Bruges with Humphrey at the wheel, when an eighteen-wheeler had pulled out in front of them. Forced to brake sharply, Humphrey had sent their Saab sedan careening into the safety barrier from which it had bounced back into the middle lane, struck the rear of a VW beetle, spun into the nearside lane, rolling over once on the road surface then twice onto the grass verge before finally sliding to a halt on the lip of a dry-bed ditch littered with glass and plastic bottles discarded by passing motorists. Whereas Humphrey, wearing a seat belt, had survived the accident with no more than a sprained right wrist, fractured kneecap and whiplash, partial failure of the passenger-side air bag had led to his brother's being projected into the windscreen. Once the ambulance rescue team arrived on the scene and freed the two men, it became apparent that the younger man, severely concussed, required urgent hospitalisation.

Comatose, Horatio was put on a ventilator for three weeks and remained in the hospital's trauma intensive care unit for a further five weeks before awakening. MRI scans revealed brain damage to Horatio's frontal and temporal lobes. The result: loss of sustained attention, memory and sense of identity. In short, Horatio no longer recognised his sibling. Solution: transfer to a secure psychiatric care facility equipped to cater for acute mental health disorders. Humphrey took immediate steps to seek out a suitable sanatorium in Luritania, where his brother could receive the best possible treatment for his condition. Faced with a long waiting list for admission to the only suitable local facility, he had no alternative other than to approach what his general practitioner judged to be the finest psychiatric care facility closest to hand: the Holistische Welzijn Sanatorium (HWS) in Baalbek on the Dutch-Luritanan border.

Since Humphrey's GP did not use superlatives lightly, Humphrey booked the earliest possible appointment with the sanatorium's director, closed up shop and made the journey to Baalbek by hire car, settlement of his claim on the insurers for the written-off Saab complicated by the fact that although one of the two witnesses to the accident, both of whom attested to seeing the heavy goods vehicle pull out without signalling, remembered the firm's logo on the rear panel, neither recalled details of the vehicle's licence plate.

The sanatorium's director, Frans van Landewijk, an outward-going man with luxuriant white hair and a neat matching Van Dyke, heard his visitor out sympathetically, explained that the HWS's excellent three to one staff:patient ratio came at a certain cost as did accommodation, the charges for which varied depending upon whether the patient was lodged in one of the general wards, which normally meant sharing with five other residents, or in a semi-private or fully private room. While none of the residents – Humphrey noted the director's systematic avoidance of the word 'inmates' – posed a danger to himself or those around him, a fair number, such as those suffering from Parkinson's, were under medication. HWS was unique in boasting an arts, crafts and music centre, where occupational therapists catered for stroke victims' aesthetic talents and motor skills. There was also a small on-site theatre in which films were shown twice a week and where the occasional play was mounted by a touring theatre company. The director stressed the importance of having his patients follow a strict regime, starting with early morning tai chi exercises and ending with yoga and lights out at 10 p.m. Of course, there were exceptions: not every patient was amenable to having his day ordered in this fashion.

Humphrey was shown around the extensive, well-groomed grounds. They passed one patient declaiming poetry at a bed of hyacinths. Others seated at tables on the verandah seemed to be engaged in board games, although on closer inspection several looked singularly unfocused. Two got to their feet to interfere in a game of croquet on the lawn below. It was clear from the vacant expression in many eyes that most, not just a few, were on medication.

The absence of female patients struck Humphrey as sad, although, he supposed, inevitable. What caused him the most concern was the thought that his brother, suffering from nothing more than concussion, would be thrown together with substance abusers, whose mental impairment was self-inflicted. While reassured by the fact that the sanatorium was not fenced off from the outside world and that there were no security guards patrolling the grounds' periphery with their dogs, Humphrey was reminded of Lovelace's lines: *Stone walls do not a prison make, nor iron bars a cage.*

What, he enquired, kept residents from fleeing the coop or losing their bearings and wandering into the village high street? .

'As you will have observed,' said van Landewijk,' each patient is allotted one of four identifying colours. They are, in effect, clothed head to foot in blue, black, yellow or green over white trainers. This permits us to see at a distance whom we are dealing with. White was ruled out from the start as a demeaning badge of institutionalisation. As for our freer colour scheme, I won't bore you with the clinical details. Suffice it to say that were anyone to wander out of the grounds into the village, they would be immediately recognisable to our local residents, who have undertaken to let us know straightaway. The local bus, taxi and railway services will never allow an HWS patient to leave the village.'

Humphrey decided not to ask what colour clothing his brother might be allotted, although he could not imagine Horatio, however impaired his sense of identity, taking kindly to being dressed up like a daffodil for months on end.

The director continued in a fashion devoid of grandstanding. 'In the fifteen years since HWS has been in existence not one patient has run away. I trust that is because they feel more secure here than they would in the outside world. Yes, there have been a few occasions when a patient has roamed into the village high street and attempted to buy a bar of chocolate in the hairdresser's or an ice cream soda in the post office. But the villagers are, for the most part, understanding people, who are quick to give us a call while entertaining or keeping an eye on our waifs.'

'I'm impressed by the noticeable lack of confinement. It makes a refreshing change from my preconceptions of how sanatoriums are normally run.'

'There are no high or medium-security units here, Mr Hobart. No potentially dangerous patients. No therapy through confinement. Your brother will be in safe hands.

'Of course, this is no holiday camp. Come ten o'clock in the evening, everything gets locked down until seven thirty the next morning. But it's true that we strive to create a family atmosphere. Nobody is called by anything other than their Christian name, and we try to involve each and every one in as many day-to-day activities as possible from gardening – we grow our own vegetables – to helping in the kitchen, and from laying the breakfast, lunch and dinner tables to changing the bed linen… Inclusiveness. It gives some, but not all, I'm afraid, a sense of identity.'

'Which, I regret to say, is precisely what my brother is endeavouring to recover.'

The director stood aside to allow a nurse escorting two patients back towards the main house to pass by. 'Some never do, you know, Mr Hobart. I hate to have to say it, but it's so. Not that we ever rule out the possibility of recovery however partial. But experience has taught me that in cases such as your brother's, where severe damage has been done to that part of the brain governing memory, full recovery of identity is rare. That is not to say that the individual cannot be made to feel more or less whole in himself, but probably in ways which would seem irrational to those like yourself who have grown up with him.'

Humphrey drew to a halt. 'That sounds defeatist,' he said, unable to look the other man in the eyes because his own were close to watering. 'As good as saying Horatio's condition is incurable.'

While casting an understanding glance at his visitor, the director continued in the same matter-of-fact vein as before. 'Not in the least. I'm simply warning you that Horatio is likely to be in this for the long term. There are no quick fixes.'

'Right, but there's one thing I must make clear. I don't want to see my brother stuffed up to the neck with opiates that turn him into little better than a vegetable.'

'I thoroughly understand, Mr Hobart. We don't rush headlong into treating disorders of Horatio's kind. Perhaps he might be a candidate for mild doses of L-DOPA to combat neurodegeneration. We'll have to see. But, no, we do our best to give our patients a sense of meaning amid their bewilderment and loss of orientation. Nobody here is maxed out on Prozac, if that's what you're thinking.'

Reluctant to label Frans van Landewijk as a smooth-tongued salesman, Humphrey could not help wondering how many of the director's patients were at that very moment lying forcibly immobilised in their beds behind locked doors. But when, after asking to be shown the kind of accommodation to which his brother would be confined, he was taken on a tour of the wards, Humphrey's mind was set at ease. The tranquil environment at HWS bore out his GP's and van Landewijk's reassurances. Humphrey spied not one patient kept under restraint.

So it was that Humphrey Hobart registered his brother for indefinite care (try as he might, he could not think of 'confinement' as anything other than a euphemism for incarceration) in Baalbek's *Holistische Welzijn Sanatorium*. Since Horatio's insurance cover together with Humphrey's limited resources fell short of the prohibitive cost of semi-private accommodation, the elder brother resigned himself to signing on the line for a bed in one of van Landewijk's general wards. It came as a pleasant surprise when van Landewijk informed Humphrey Hobart not only that a bed had just become vacant in the sanatorium's only four-bedded general ward, the monthly rate the same as for the larger wards, but that, if he agreed, Horatio would be sharing with a Welshman, an American and a Kiwi. Scope, as the director put it, for a bar joke.

Although visiting hours at the HWS were fairly flexible, Humphrey had come to learn that the mid-afternoon interlude between lunch and five o'clock tea was the best time to drop in on his brother. Weather permitting they would sit on the verandah before taking a stroll around the garden. When it was too wet or cold outside, they would get together in the lounge over a glass of lemonade and play the odd game or two of draughts or Connect Four, which Horatio took particular delight in winning while Humphrey pulled a convincingly long face at his repeated ineptitude.

Today being bright and sunny, Humphrey was looking forward to stretching his legs alongside his brother around the sanatorium's grounds. Drawing to a halt in one of the parking slots reserved for visitors, Humphrey stepped out of the Renault Espace finally paid for almost in full by his insurance company and walked up to the entrance to the limestone building. He had long ago deduced that the overhead cameras stationed around the grounds, entrance doors and the building's interior were there as much to monitor visitors' as patients' behaviour and movements.

On being informed that his brother was awaiting him outdoors either on the verandah or on the croquet lawn, Humphrey directed his steps back out through the front entrance and around the side of the building leading to the rear garden. Horatio, wearing a blue Indian cotton shirt and blue slim-fit chinos, was sitting with his back to Humphrey at a glass-topped metal frame table, watching one of his three ward mates, Probyn, build a house of cards. Horatio's two other ward mates, Maynard and Farley were nowhere in sight. Horatio abbreviated all three names to Probe, May and Far. In spite of the marked physical dissimilarities between this trio – Probyn, rotund, Maynard, cauliflower-eared, Farley affecting a Salvador Dali mustache – Horatio frequently mistook one for the other.

As if to prove this point, with Humphrey unseen drawing nearer, Horatio started applauding. 'Far,' he said, 'what a far, far better thing you're doing than you have ever done.' The next moment, he stretched out a hand and demolished Probyn's splendid pagoda.

'Ratio,' said Humphrey, now alongside a brother known to him as much by this familiar abbreviation as by his full Christian name. 'That was a considerable engineering feat by Probe. Could you do the same?'

Horatio gazed at his brother, then back at Probyn curled up in a ball of laughter.

'Where are my strawberries, Trevor?' said Probyn at last, after regaining sufficient breath to address Humphrey by yet another new name.

Humphrey failed to reply, his undivided attention reserved for his brother. 'How are things, bro?'

Horatio eyed the newcomer querulously. He remembered seeing this stranger before but was unable to decide whether he was another member of the sanatorium's medical staff called in from outside (because he was dressed quite differently to his usual carers), a gardener interrupting his weeding, or a postman delivering mail.

'My strawberries,' insisted Probyn. 'Why haven't you brought my strawberries?'

Humphrey had come to learn that Probyn had an unhealthy relationship with strawberries. After eating only a few of the first and only box of *gariguettes*, which Humphrey had brought as a present for sharing between his brother and Probyn, Probe had developed a bad case of hives. Yet this had by no means dampened a perverse craving for the little red fruit.

'Sorry, Probe. The market garden was plumb out of them today. Looks like they got snapped up by a bunch of restaurants.' Humphrey turned back to his brother. 'How are you today?'

'How am I today? How is he today? How is she today? How are they today? Rosita stone conjugal conjugating.'

Faced with Horatio's idiosyncratic responses, intermingling balderdash with lucidity, Humphrey wondered from where his brother had dug up that memory of *A Tale of Two Cities*. No Proustian taste or smell sensation could have prompted recollection of Sydney Carton's last thoughts. Surely, this augured well. Or did it? Humphrey did not know what to think.

Before that unforgettable driving accident, Horatio Hobart was poised on the cusp of a brilliant career. A graduate of Gonville and Caius College with a double first in mathematics and computer science, he had turned down the prospect of a research fellowship tied to completion of a Ph.D. thesis in preference to a handsome offer from the European Space Agency, which had recruited him to its European Space Astronomy Centre (ESAC) outside Madrid. Humphrey felt sure that Horatio's reference to Rosita could only have surfaced because of his brother's involvement in the Rosetta project, culminating in that maiden robotic space probe's landing on a comet. Despite the fact that Horatio had watched that historic achievement on the sanatorium's lounge television – Humphrey had telephoned the HWS to make certain that his brother did not miss the event – when Humphrey brought the matter up on his next visit, his brother went off at a tangent to talk about what he had eaten for lunch.

All of which made the elder brother feel doubly guilty as the man behind the wheel. Not only had he survived the accident with minor injuries but he had reduced to rubble his brilliant, fun-loving brother's future.

But that was not all. While working at the ESA's Spanish agency, Horatio fell in love with a young MIT alumnus, Jacqueline Pinebrook. During the first year of his confinement at the HWS, Jacqueline made the trip up from Madrid to visit him once a month. Van Landewijk arranged for the two to share a room during each weekend visit. However, after eight months of failure to communicate with Horatio on any meaningful level (whether intellectual, emotional or physical), Jacqueline reduced the frequency of her visits to one every two months. The breaking point came half a year later when she could no longer bear having her Skype calls to Horatio, routed through an HWS workstation, ruined by another patient in his ward. Disenchanted with his brother's girlfriend and her lack of staying power, Humphrey, unwilling to admit to prejudice, concluded that short-lived attachments could not be expected to stand the same test of time as the bond forged between brothers.

Not for the first time Humphrey felt his conscience pricking him for leaving Horatio with his elder brother as his sole outside visitor. Should he not have done more to persuade Jacqueline to last the distance, however indefinite that seemed? The fact was that instead of sympathising with her lot Humphrey had given the girl a complex about not being up to scratch.

Putting his arm around Horatio's shoulder, Humphrey was heartened to find the gesture not shaken off. 'Feel like a ramble around the gardens?'

Horatio stood up, paused briefly, collected a number of playing cards from Probyn's earthquake-stricken house, fanned them out in his hand and said. 'Bricks, Far, or I'll huff and I'll puff and I'll blow your house down. Bob and I are going for an Eric Ambler.'

Try as he might to resign himself to the wall erected between the two of them, Horatio's lack of recognition struck Humphrey as the cruellest of fortune's arrows. As he had always been Humph to his brother – the nickname Tich having originated with the shooting club's secretary, Ólaf Thoroddsen – Humphrey found it hard to stomach the regularity with which Horatio invented new names for him (last time, it had been Kev).

However, the fact that Horatio had suddenly seized on his middle Christian name gave Humphrey cause for optimism. Until he reasoned that, since Horatio had never called him Bob before, it was difficult to tell whether this was a flash in the pan or something suggestive of his brother's memory bank finally paying dividends.

The brothers stepped down onto the lawn and began walking across to the nearest pathway. Seeing the driver of a red electric golf cart, one of the sanatorium's many utility vehicles, about to pass by, Humphrey took hold of his brother's elbow. Unperturbed, the driver waved hello on his way to feed the pike in the lake on the ground's northernmost fringe.

'What have you been up to recently?' asked Humphrey, puzzled by the time it was taking one croquet player to decide whether or not to use his own ball to push another player's through the same hoop. Until he saw the red admiral that had settled on top of the hoop.

'Up to, down to, along to, through to …'Rhythmic repetition was one of Horatio's favoured modes of responding to questions.

By now they had reached the gravelled pathway wide enough to accommodate two golf carts. Horatio turned and started to walk backwards. 'Good training for Nole and the Fed,' he said.

It was a cheering reminder of van Landewijk's comment that Horatio Hobart's motor skills had not suffered the same setback as some of his neurocognitive functions. Not that Horatio had ever picked up a tennis racquet before the accident, but apparently he demonstrated considerable poise, balance and fluidity of movement during morning tai chi warm-ups. Humphrey supposed that one of the sanatorium's fitness trainers had pointed up the benefits to be had from walking backwards in terms of strengthening the quadriceps, gluteal and calf muscles.

'Do they serve you the fish in that lake at mealtimes?' said Humphrey, one eye on his brother's blind navigation skills the other on the cart taking what he assumed to be a further unauthorised short cut across another patch of lawn.

'Fish dish, lake bake. Puffer chests for tea, Bob.' Horatio was referring to the miniature fluffy Dutch pancakes called *poffertjes* made from wheat and buckwheat.

Part of the problem in maintaining a dialogue with Horatio was that he rarely asked a direct question. All the hard work lay with the interlocutor, who had to understand the need for patient perseverance.

'Think they'd let me stay to sample one? Careful, Horatio, move to the left. Otherwise you'll end up in that rhododendron bush.'

One of Horatio's heels hit the grass verge in front of a bed containing a large pink rhododendron in full bloom. Horatio stopped, turned around, laughed, clapped his hands and resumed walking forwards with his elder brother at his side. 'You should see my hammock,' he said. 'Red. For the Indian Ocean.'

Humphrey was encouraged to learn that Horatio had become the HWS's star macramé pupil. His brother had picked up this craft more quickly than most, mastering in record time knotting and hitching techniques that tested the staying power of the average beginner with no experience of weaving.

'I'd like that.' Humphrey counted off two positive interchanges on the fingers folded behind his back: *poffertjes* and this red hammock invitation.

'Remember,' (always a loaded feed, that one word) 'remember the marvellous macramé wall hanging Ma made with that fox hunting scene worked into it?'

But once again Horatio's voluntary recall failed him. It troubled Humphrey that the slate appeared to have been wiped clean for pre-accident family memories. Literary dribs and drabs were all very well but scarcely contributed towards giving Horatio a sense of continuity. His thoughts were as fragmented and shifting as the slivers of glass reflected in a kaleidoscope's mirrors. On the other hand, according to van Landewijk, Holbein the younger (it was the director's habit to name his patients after dead artists or writers) was an example of the exception proving the rule, for post-trauma Horatio continued to solve complex mathematical problems as spontaneously as ever.

One aspect of the HWS which fell short of Humphrey Hobart's expectations was its library. He had brought his brother a choice miscellany of secondhand novels, biographies, autobiographies, life science and historical studies from the overloaded shelves in his bookshop only to find these works appropriated by Maynard, who underlined entire paragraphs and scribbled offensive marginal glosses. Unable to elicit a straight answer from Horatio as to whether he had read any of the titles by his favourite authors before they were defaced by the manic May, Humphrey restricted himself to plying his brother with scientific and number puzzle magazines out of May's league.

As they followed the path serpentining around an immense sward dotted with the occasional rose bush, whose leaves, Humphrey noted, were remarkably free of blight, Horatio began singing with verve *Con te partirò*. It was a clear and comforting indication that his brother was not tiring of his company.

'Do they put on concerts in that theatre of yours, 'ratio? I ask, because…' (Humphrey reined himself in from saying 'one thing you haven't lost') 'that voice of yours is as strong as ever.'

'Concerts, dead certs, excerpts, perverts … We have them all.'

Exchanging glances, the brothers burst out laughing simultaneously.

'Would the gardeners let you hang your hammock between those two elm trees over there?' asked Humphrey, pointing to a stand of four elms planted well back from the path around the next bend.

'They bloody better had.'

Unable to believe his ears, Humphrey stopped in his tracks. Some neurons still firing as they should, he thought.

'With Sarah Brightwoman,' Those three words positively exploded from Horatio's lips.

'What?'

'In my hammock. Red sails in the sunny set.'

'Must be a big hammock.'

'Big?' Horatio was roaring again. 'As big as this.' He flung his arms out wide, narrowly missing the head of a pretty nurse escorting a lost-looking patient back towards the main building.

Much as he would have liked to think that a hidden switch had opened memory's floodgates, Humphrey was too circumspect to bank on these joyous outbursts being anything other than one-off.

'How long did it take you to make it?'

'Long? How long is a chain letter? How far to the moon? Let's roll a sixpence and see.'

After returning from their stroll – all the way out to the lake, where they saw the pike being fed, and back again – the brothers spent a pleasant half hour sitting on the verandah enjoying a pot of lemon tea and a dish of warm *poffertjes*.dusted with powdered sugar. Then Horatio led Humphrey to the art and craft centre to show him a magnificent red macramé hammock suspended from the ceiling.

'That's quite something,' said Humphrey. 'Ma would be proud of you.'

When the time came to part, Humphrey gave Horatio a long, moist-eyed hug. Pulling himself together, he looked his brother squarely in the eyes and said, 'I'm going to try to get you a room of your own at last. How would you like that? A room without Probe, May or Far.'

'A bridge too far?'

'Just the opposite, I hope.'

Driving out of Baalbek, Humphrey pointed the Renault Espace towards Maastricht, where he regularly did the rounds of the town's second-hand bookshops before heading on home. By the time he left Maasstricht, he had snapped up a number of bargains, including a 2006 edition of Robert Chandler's English translation of Vasily Grossman's *Life and Fate* and a first edition of J.M. Coetzee's *Waiting for the Barbarians*.

But if these bargains fuelled his enthusiasm as he batted down the E25 towards Luritania, they were small beer compared to the prospect, courtesy of the China Reconstruction Bank, of transferring Horatio out of his small general ward into more comfortable private accommodation free of the Probyns, Farleys and pencil-wielding Maynards of this world.

However, it was not long before euphoria gave way to gloom. If he had been unable to save Gwyn, what chance did he stand of saving his brother?

Rashid Jabour opened the topmost red folder of a package of inhouse mail deposited in his in-tray by the eighth floor messenger, Paul Schwarzneigen, a genial Luritanian, who helped his brother out at weekends on their jointly owned campsite in the north of the country near one of the country's more well-known châteaux. Paul had told Rashid that the Ministry of Tourism touted the château by claiming that Honoré de Balzac had penned *Les Illusions Perdues* while staying there. But the truth of the matter, Paul said, was that the author had written only a fraction of the novel in the château while trapped indoors with three foot of snow outside.

The folder contained his Bank of Beirut loan proposal for the attention of MEDRIMCOMB's Board of Directors submitted for prior approval to Rashid's boss, Marc Chevigny. The proposal incorporated three other contributions: one by Stephen Boyle, outlining the web of smaller businesses eligible for microloan finance; another by Horst Gottfried specifying the attention to be paid to compliance with European anti-pollution legislation and Lebanese waste recycling norms; the last by a prolix economist, whose three-page text on Lebanon's GNP, GDP and balance of trade profiles Rashid had pruned to three quarters of a page. Satisfied to see that his boss had written 'Approved' next to his tick alongside the comments box on the cover sheet, Rashid found the report file on his computer, filled out another covering form and sent both as e-mail attachments to MEDRIMCOMB's print room.

Next in order came more newspapers and magazines than he could cope with, but to which he subscribed in order to keep up to date with as wide a range as possible of media reporting: *International Herald Tribune*, Al-Hayat, *Frankfurter Allgemeine Zeitung, El País, Le Monde, Le Canard Enchaîné, Corriere della Sera, The Wall Street Journal, Time* and *The Economist*. Beneath this stack he unearthed a superfluous mission expenses form: Rashid's advance allowance had handsomely covered out-of-pocket expenses in Beirut. The only remaining work folder contained a list of loan applications filed by public works ministries in the Mashreq countries, rated by Frank Welling in accordance with their perceived furtherance of Europe's Mediterranean Framework Advancement Programme (MEDFAP) and flagged with the names of various loan officers under his command. Rashid noted that his next assignment, in conjunction with Horst Gottfried, was to vet a loan application from the Lebanese National Hydrocarbons Consortium for a feasibility study on development of Lebanon's offshore oil and gas resources.

Rashid picked up *Le Canard Enchaîné* and turned to the sports section, where his attention was caught by a report on the fracas that had broken out fifteen minutes before the end of the Europa League football match between Dynamo Kyiv and Guingamp. Apparently, supporters of the home team, mistaking the *tricolore* for the Russian flag, had set upon the small crowd of French fans. Commenting on the brawls after the match, a spokesman for the Ukrainian club had said that the French fans should have known better than to turn up with a flag whose colours matched those of the Russian flag. To which the reporter added the observation that it said a lot about the level of education of the Ukrainian supporters and their country's desire to align itself with West European values that they could not tell the difference between vertical and horizontal stripes or the order in which blue and white stood in relation to each other in the French and Russian flags. This had led a cartoonist to add his contribution in the form of a sequence of three drawings. The first pictured Frank Sinatra, the second, Elvis Presley, and the third, Stepan Bandera, while the caption below read (translated from the French): *This year would have been Frank's 100th, Elvis's 80th, and Stepan's 106th birthday.* Sinatra was shown holding his 'Telly' (Telefunken) microphone, Presley playing his Martin guitar, and Bandera brandishing a smoking submachine gun, the bubble words in his mouth: *I did it my way … In the ghetto.*

Rashid knew enough WWII history to recall the atrocities attributed to Bandera's fascist followers in butchering over one hundred thousand Poles, Jews, Hungarians and Russians in the name of ethnic cleansing, deeds that had won Bandera the status of hero in the eyes of Ukraine's right-wing extremists and of monster in those of the survivors of his militia's carnage.

The young loan officer was about to turn to the front page, when a knock sounded at his door, and Frank Welling walked in accompanied by two clean-shaven men wearing expensive blue woven wool and mohair suits, light blue, thin-striped poplin shirts and black oxfords. The sole difference in their dress lay in the duo's silk ties: while the younger-looking man wore a pale gold herringbone tie, the older man's choice was blood red. Rashid's first thought was that Welling had trundled in a couple of visiting MEDRIMCOMB directors. But he could not have been more wrong.

'Rashid,' said Frank, his customary affable self. 'Allow me to introduce you to Mr Stenning and Mr Chamberlain from the CIA.'

For one heart-stopping moment, Rashid thought that the two agents had been sent by the NSA after it had exfiltrated incriminating data from his home laptop, and that he stood to be accused of purloining a certain briefcase.

But the next instant the firm handshake he was given by the man he took to be the senior of the two, quashed that assumption.

'Warren Stenning. A pleasure to meet you, Mr Jabour.' The accent reminded Rashid of Jimmy Stewart, not that this man looked as if vertigo was a problem for him faced with the floor-to-ceiling windows on the eighth floor of MEDRIMCOMB's sixteen-storey stone, glass and titanium building. 'Mr Welling suggested you might be able to help us with our enquiries concerning Jack Mason.'

The shorter of the two men stepped forward. 'Hugh Chamberlain.'

'Pleased to meet you both, gentlemen,' said Rashid with a tense smile hinting that pleased was perhaps not the most apt of adjectives.

'Well,' declared Welling with the air of a man contemplating matters of managerial import. 'I think I'll leave you gentlemen to it. Should you need me again, I regret that you might have to wait until tomorrow. I have a committee meeting downstairs likely to stretch on into the late afternoon.'

Rashid invited his two guests to sit down. The man he later referred to as Earl Warren (after the Chief Justice presiding over the Warren Commission) was the first to break the silence as the door closed behind Frank Welling.

'We understand that Jack paid a special call on you a few days before his death.'

Feeling less vulnerable now that his worries had turned from first-person cybercrime to third-party weapons smuggling, Rashid was confident that he could put up a respectable defence. However, much depended on what Mason had told Welling before being introduced to his latest recruit. Rashid decided to play safe by leaving his visitors to raise the matter of the message.

'I wouldn't say there was anything particularly special about it. Mr Welling told him I was due to visit Beirut and, since it was one of Jack's old stamping grounds, he decided to chew the fat with me about Lebanon.'

'How did he appear to you?' The question was put by the younger, bull-necked man, who, finding little of interest to attract his attention in Rashid's spartan office, had been surveying the triple gold towers across the way housing enough European patent officers to make the CIA seem understaffed. A smoker's cough explained the scratchy voice.

Uncertain whether a Jungian or a run-of-the-mill interpretation was expected of him – given that, to judge by the other man's expression, what started out as a pointed question had dwindled into feigned indifference – Rashid fussed with his pencil sharpener.

'Like a World Bank employee glad of the chance to go over common ground with a colleague in a sister institution.'

'Not hunted?'

'Hunted? No. Uncomfortable. Yes.'

'How do you mean?'

'Those chairs.'

The two men laughed. 'No wonder,' said Stenning. 'You get world-class architects to design this building, then find some jackass to furnish it.'

Rashid decided it was time for him to take the initiative. 'Have you people got any closer to solving his murder?'

Chamberlain shot his cuffs. Gold cuff links and a gold wristwatch to go with the tie, thought Rashid.

Stenning unclasped his hands from around a knee. 'No, but we're pretty sure of the motive.'

In other words, Rashid concluded, you wouldn't be here if you viewed Jack's murder as no more than a random mugging.

'Jack Mason was involved in gun running, Mr Jabour.'

Rashid tried not to overdo the surprise. After all, the CIA didn't waste their time on petty theft.

'Oh.' That one well-rounded syllable seemed to suffice, like the hollow in the net that had just swallowed its butterfly.

'Legal gun running,' added Stenning, favouring one of the three golden towers with an admiring glance.

'Is there such a thing?'

'A U.S. senator helped finance the shipment of a large consignment of weapons to Lebanon for combatting those IS bastards after his daughter, a Syrian aid worker, was beheaded by jihadists. Container shipping being Mason's speciality, and the senator's wife and Mason's wife being members of the same church, Jack organised the freight forwarding.'

Stenning paused, as if to give Rashid time enough to digest this information.

'I see.'

'Unfortunately, the senator went about things covertly. We were never in on the deal, which didn't help when the Israelis boarded the container vessel off their coast, had the captain steer a course for Cyprus, got the custom's authorities there to inspect the cargo and decided that the weapons could fall into the wrong hands.'

'I recall reading about it in the press.'

'As you know, the Israelis are a law unto themselves. The vessel, the *Marquis de Honfleur*, was outside Israel's territorial waters off the Gaza strip. Which meant that, strictly speaking, there were only two reasons why the Israeli navy should have intervened. The first, and weaker of the two, nervousness. The suspicion that Hamas, weary of burrowing under the ground from the Egyptian side, had switched weapons infiltration from land to sea. But the *Marquis de Honfleur* was too far north to be bound for the coast of Israel. It was either headed for Turkey or Lebanon. Hence, the second and stronger of the two reasons. A tip-off that the vessel was delivering arms to Bashar al-Assad's men.'

Hezbollah, thought Rashid. But who was he to correct the CIA? Failing to understand the CIA man's motives in recounting these details, he decided to let Stenning continue full steam ahead. But at that moment, his cell phone rang. Rashid picked up the Nokia beside his blotter and looked at the caller ID: Vanessa. Apologising for the interruption, he waited for the call to be switched to voice mail.

'Of course,' said Stenning, unaffected by this temporary distraction,' the ship's captain contacted his office in Marseilles, and someone there got straight through to the senator, who nearly had a coronary for not thinking to keep us in the loop.'

'Because,' said Rashid, thinking that perhaps by now something more was expected of him than mute acquiescence, 'your people would have forewarned the Israelis not to intervene.'

'Correct,' said Chamberlain, perhaps for no other reason than that he had tired of playing second fiddle.

Rashid doubted whether the shift in the American's gaze from the window was due to his wondering whether Dominique Perrault, the architect of those anodized, gold-metal fronted towers, was related to Charles Perrault, author of Jack and the beanstalk.

'But,' said Stenning, ' the senator recovered enough to come running to us. We let Tel Aviv know where that shipment was headed. Of course, by then it was too late. They modified their excuse for boarding the *Marquis de Honfleur* outside territorial waters to one of fear that the consignment was intended not for Hamas but for Hezbollah.'

Yet, thought Rashid, that was not the end of the story, otherwise the CIA wouldn't be here confiding all this to a complete outsider – unless they had made their minds up that he was anything but a complete outsider. The next moment, his cell phone alerted him to the fact that he had received a text message. Rashid did not find it easy to read Vanessa's SMS (*That was one marvellous night last night, Lord Byron. Looks like I miscast you.*) with the detachment of a banker noting the ECB's latest set of key interest rates.

'And that, 'said Chamberlain, 'was the last peep you or anyone else heard from the press concerning the *Marquis de Honfleur.*'

'Because,' continued Stenning, 'after the vessel finally docked in Beirut and its cargo was offloaded, it looks as if the senator's weapons never reached the people for whom they were intended. At the worst, they were sold to IS by a middleman out to make a quick buck. At the marginally less worse, part were sold to IS, part to Hezbollah. Of course, if Jack Mason were standing here today, he'd deny double-crossing the senator. He'd say the arms were meant to help Hezbollah in its fight against IS. And once the Israelis seized hold of the cargo, who could tell where the arms would end up? But Jack isn't here. The worms are banqueting off him, while Hugh and I lose weight trying to fathom what he was up to.'

As if this lengthy summary had taken its toll, Warren Stenning paused to draw breath before assuming the air of a long-suffering prosecuting attorney. 'Now, Mr Jabour, are you still going to tell us you knew nothing about this shipment of Jack's?'

As much as Rashid took exception to Stenning's sudden change of tone from that of lecturer to prosecutor, he refused to flinch. 'The suggestion that I knew ...'

Wishing he could have assumed the cloak of a Don Juan in a hurry to leave for the shores of Greece, Rashid pocketed the cell phone and held both hands in a manner suggesting surrender to idiocy. 'Have you gentlemen bothered to think this through? Why would Mason choose an unknown quantity to help him achieve his ends? Until he walked through that door, I had never seen or heard of the man.'

'Perhaps, you could tell us what you were doing at Our Lady of the Sacred Heart Convent in East Beirut?' This sidewinder was all the more unexpected, coming as it did from Chamberlain, the man viewed by Rashid as supernumerary.

'Before I left for Beirut,' said Rashid, rising to the occasion, 'I learnt that my father had gone out to Lebanon to work as a field surgeon for war-scarred Syrians fleeing Islamic State. My family didn't know where he was stationed or even if he was still there. But I thought to contact the sisters at that convent because I was told they helped out as nurses in and around the Shatila refugee camp. Unfortunately, they knew nothing of my father or his whereabouts.'

167

And that, he told Vanessa later the same evening, while assuming the role of her Byron's Don Juan, not only seemed to satisfy the CIA but had them apologise for taking up so much of his time.

But both agreed that it would be premature to celebrate. Once on the CIA's books, you probably stayed there till the grave. After all, if they had trailed him to East Beirut, what was to stop them bugging his phone, computer and apartment? And if they chanced upon his decoding of Justin's document? Rashid need to erase all records of that work from his hard disk. Unless, of course, it was too late to close the stable door. In which case, what if the horse had already responded to a Silicon Valley Apple?

Vanessa recommended Rashid to recount his Lebanon experiences to the rest of the quintet at their next Sunday morning meeting. By which she meant 'the Security Council, including Isabelle.'

'It looks,' she said, 'as if you're out of the quick sands for the time being, but what's to say more of us won't get dragged under?'

Recognising that Isabelle's talents were wasted on front counter work, Heinrich Katzenberger transferred his fast track trainee to the back office to assist Eric Vandeweghe's trust fund management operations.

After losing no time in picking up the rules of the game, Isabelle was soon relieving the *directeur adjoint* of a significant amount of business which he had been unable to entrust to his previous assistant, a plodder of a secretary, obsessed with nail care, whom Vandeweghe had finally foisted off onto the bonds office on the grounds that she was the one in need of a change of scenery.

Within a few days, Isabelle was making diplomatic suggestions as to her boss's choice of investment decisions with respect to cash held in trust for the grandchildren of Luritania's Finance Minister.

With lunch hour only ten minutes away and most of the morning's major dossiers satisfactorily dealt with, Vandeweghe switched on his intercom and, adopting an unusually steely tone of voice, invited Isabelle in to discuss *encore une affaire* (another piece of business).

The moment she stepped through the door, he reflected that not only did she beat her predecessor hands down in terms of intelligence but she made the woman, obsessed with cosmetics, tight-fitting skirts and high-heeled shoes, look like the plainest of plain Janes.

'Yes, monsieur, what have you got for me?' Isabelle, who had hoped to be able to fit in a session of spin cycling followed by a snack lunch before returning to work, wondered whether the deputy manager intended keeping her behind for more trust work.

'Sit down, Mademoiselle Meunier. I wish to tell you how pleased I am with your performance. So much so that it occurs to me that you can be of particular help with a rather important matter.'

'Of course. I'd be delighted.'

'Of that I'm not so sure.' For all the attention he was paying to one corner of his polished mahogany desk, Vandeweghe might have been mistaken for a fisherman about to cast his line, But the next moment, as if snapping awake, the deputy manager rubbed his hands together, tucked both thumbs of interlaced hands under his chin and looked Isabelle straight in the eyes. 'You see, I have come to the conclusion that you know what became of our vanished four and a quarter million euros.'

As if confronted by someone talking in riddles, Isabelle stared back gamely. 'I'm sorry, I don't understand.'

'Ah, but I think you do. And all too well. You see, the *femme de ménage* remembers hearing you knock over my family photo frame. Need I say more?'

Isabelle kept her calm. 'Yes, I think so.'

'Well, obviously, you put it back together after it fell apart.'

'I don't remember it falling apart. I caught it. The *femme de ménage* must have heard me cry out.'

'She thought it dropped onto the carpet. Anyway, it always fell apart whenever I dislodged it. I kept having to replace the stiffener at the back.' Vandeweghe held up the frame to indicate the space no longer occupied by the finger of cardboard bearing his liquidity code.

'Yes, I remember that. Holding the photograph in place, was that it?'

'Perhaps you also remember that there was some writing on that little piece of cardboard?'

'Frankly, no,' said Isabelle, refusing to be cowed by Vandeweghe's manipulative persistence. 'And I take objection to your insinuations that I had anything to do with the loss of **your** treasury money.'

If she had wanted to sting Vandeweghe, she could not have done so more successfully than with this innuendo.

Vandeweghe repaid the jibe by wetting his lips in a manner that Isabelle found repulsive.

'You can object till the cows come home, Mademoiselle Meunier, but I'm sure I know what I'm talking about. You're too clever. Too clever by far. *Voilà votre chute.* (There's your downfall.)'

Isabelle smarted at Vandeweghe's deliberate use of the word *chute* with all that it implied in terms of original sin. He might as well have compared her directly to Jean-Baptiste Clamence in Albert Camus's novel. She got to her feet.

'Monsieur Vandeweghe, I cannot believe what I am hearing. That you should think I could be responsible for … It's unworthy of you. But if this is how you feel, I shall have to go to Herr Katzenberger and demand to be given other duties.'

'Sit down, *chère mademoiselle*, sit down. I'm sure we can come to an understanding.'

'An understanding!' After an evening spent, with Vanessa Curtis as voice coach, reading her part in *Camino Real*, Isabelle was equal to her role. 'How can that be possible, when all I hear is one unfounded accusation after another?'

'No need to get on your high horse. I can see how difficult this must be for you. But you would do well to bear in mind the *femme de ménage*. She knows on what side her bread is buttered. I don't want to have to call Hoffarth and Weiland in again, unless I really have to. To clear my good name. Because I believe that you, aided by one or more outsiders, robbed BLR of that money. I have no idea how you did so with only two thirds of the code to go on, but, as I said before, you are a clever woman.'

A stilling hand quelled further indignation. Vandeweghe took hold of the photograph frame, clutching it as if minded to wave a damning exhibit in front of judge and jury, before finally setting it gently back in place. 'But enough heated argument. Let us be pragmatic. After all, Mlle Meunier, I'm a reasonable man. Willing to let bygones be bygones, provided ...' Here the deputy manager paused to avert his eyes from those of his assistant. '... provided that you count me in ... for fifty per cent.'

Dumbfounded by Vandeweghe's proposal, Isabelle grasped the arms of her chair for support.

'Count you in? You persist in this madness?'

'Oh, yes, I do. And before I forget, there's the matter of a sweetener. I shall expect ,' said the deputy manager with renewed lip wetting, 'certain private favours in return for my promise to remain silent.'

'*C'est déguelasse, ce que vous venez de dire.* (What you just said is disgusting.)' For once, Isabelle was no longer acting. 'Excuse me, I can't take any more of this.'

'Well, before you rush off in a huff, think of your poor father ... what it would do to his reputation, were it to become known that his daughter was a common criminal. I give you till Friday to make up your mind, Mademoiselle Meunier. If I don't have your agreement to my terms by then, I shall have no choice but to invite our two police officer friends to set the records straight.'

Isabelle left the deputy manager's room in a daze. Bending over a bowl in the ladies' toilet, she felt her stomach heave repeatedly in a series of dry retches that caused her to slump exhausted to the floor, where she knelt, both hands locked around the bowl, fighting to control fear, loathing and recalcitrant stomach muscles.

Later that day, Isabelle and Craig met up with Tich behind *Bibliopole's* closed doors to discuss the latest developments at BLR's Mensdorf branch.

'Blackmail pure and simple,' said Tich, who had cleared aside his quarterly VAT returns to create space for three coffee mugs on the battered desk in his rear office. 'And if we were living out a *film noir*, reason enough, especially in view of this bastard's filthy mind, to lace his afternoon cuppa with rat poison. However, since none of us, I imagine, wishes to add murder to his or her cv on top of what our transatlantic cousins call grand larceny, we need to find a way to spike his guns.'

Craig turned away from admiring a standalone copy, in one of Tich's locked collectibles cabinet, of a 1930 *Argosy* magazine with its signature galleon cover image. 'Easier said than done.'

'And time isn't on our side,' added Isabelle.

The relaxed way in which Tich stroked the hairs on the back of his hand seemed to convey the contrary. 'First, let's be sure we're all agreed on two points. No admittance of guilt. No bargaining.'

'Agreed,' said Isabelle.

Craig voted silent support with a raised hand.

'But can we afford to call his bluff?'

'Definitely not.' Isabelle had thought this through with Craig before arriving at the bookshop. 'Vandeweghe would make it worth her while for the *femme de ménage* to lie through her teeth. He'd get her to say that she glimpsed me through the half-open door knocking over the photograph. That I removed and studied the card at the back. He'll have to confess to keeping the liquidity code jotted down there. But then, why shouldn't he, provided I take the flak?'

'Another thing I don't like about this slimy character,' mused Tich, 'is his greed. He doesn't know how many we are, though it would be normal to reckon on Isabelle plus one outsider. But instead of expecting a third of the pie, he's asking for half. That plus his other dirty demand means that on no account should we cut a deal with him.'

Craig pulled a face over a sip of Tich's chicory coffee. 'I thought we were already agreed on that. How do you see us spiking his guns? Perhaps I ought to offer him a discount on my spin cycling classes and push him to a heart attack?'

'No, Craig. We need to be more subtle. Play the man at his own game. Did you check out his home address, Isabelle?'

'Yes, across the border up north. He and his wife bought an old farm house and had it done up with cheap Bosnian labour. At least, that's what I was told by another BLR employee.'

'How far across the border?'

'Not far at all. Brevency.'

'Right. Well, what I propose is the following. Tomorrow morning, I hop across the border and withdraw one hundred thousand euros in cash from our China Reconstruction Bank account. Late tomorrow night, Craig makes the journey out to Brevency, parks well away from Vandeweghe's place and finds a convenient spot to bury that cash in a metal box. Isabelle uses one of the town library's laptops to compose a letter to the police, informing them that Vandeweghe has dug part of the proceeds of the robbery into his back yard or wherever. The police pounce, find the loot and take Vandeweghe in for questioning.'

'All very well and good,' said Isabelle. 'But his first reaction will be to point the finger at me.'

'And,' said Craig, 'what about fingerprints?'

Tich finished savouring his coffee. 'You and I had the sense to wear disposable gloves when handling those notes, so I'll use gloves again to collect and store the money. Isabelle should wear cotton gloves to handle the letter to the police.'

171

'But,' said Isabelle, 'Vandeweghe will still …'

'Yes,' said Tich, 'I heard you, Isabelle. Let him accuse you till he's blue in the face. He hasn't one shred of evidence against any of us. Do you remember how long you took looking at that piece of cardboard?'

'As a matter of fact, yes. Hardly any time at all.'

'Fine. And on the day of the theft, Vandeweghe had jotted down just four of the six numbers, making it even less likely that you could have known or guessed the full code.'

'Oughtn't I to go straightaway tomorrow to Katzenberger to complain about Vandeweghe and refuse to continue to work for him?'

'Yes. I suppose it would have been better to have done so today. But you can always claim that you were too upset. Did you have any dealings with Vandeweghe this afternoon?'

'No, we both stayed out of each other's way.'

'Are you all right with this, Craig?'

'I don't have much choice. A stranger your size lurking around at night would be sure to attract suspicion. I'll pay a visit to the hardware department of the nearest garden centre and buy a folding shovel.'

'Muddy your number plates and try to park off the beaten track.'

'A couple of things I don't like, Tich,' objected Isabelle. 'We're talking about giving away one fortieth of our takings. That's a lot.'

'I disagree. If it's a toss-up between chicken feed and *filet mignon*, I say we go for the fillet steak. What else?'

'Where will the police think Vandeweghe has stashed away the rest? My message won't help them work that out any more than to understand why he's limited himself to burying this amount in his back garden.'

'All right, add a note in your message to the effect that you were Vandeweghe's accomplice and that he made a joke of telling you he was salting some of the notes away in his garden to see if they came up roses.'

'And why would I say this if I was his accomplice?'

'Guilty conscience. You thought you ought to come clean.'

'Anonymously? Why not simply blackmail Vandeweghe?'

Tich threw up his hands. 'Hell, Isabelle, how should I or the police know? Perhaps you were frightened that Vandeweghe would bury more than the notes in his garden.'

'I suppose so. Well, what language should I write this message in? Not French, I take it?'

'I hadn't thought about it. But yes, not French. German all right for you?'

'Of course.'

'That would definitely be better. Perhaps they'll think Katzenberger is the accomplice.'

'Poor man. He's the last person I would want to impugn.'

Tich cast a look at his watch followed by a disapproving glance at his VAT returns. 'Is that it then, folks? We go ahead with this? By the look on your Romeo and Juliet mugs, I gather my proposal has carried the day. In that case, before we break up for the evening, I'd like to raise another money-related question.'

Since Craig had not told Isabelle about the tragic accident four years before on the motorway north of Bruges, Tich was obliged to explain his brother's situation in full. An extra one thousand euros a month would pay for a private room, where free of disturbance from other residents Horatio could, if it was not too much to ask, enjoy greater piece of mind. Tich also wanted to buy his brother a laptop in the hope that it might permit him to spread his wings.

Isabelle's initial reaction was to maintain that the purpose of their theft had been to parcel the funds out to deserving environmental and humanitarian charities. Surprised to find her resistant to what he thought to be a not unreasonable proposition, Tich pointed out that had it not been for his last-minute intervention the four million euros would not be sitting where it was now. After Craig, equally surprised at Isabelle's reluctance, fell in with his friend's proposal, Isabelle clammed up. Neither man, she concluded, appreciated what she had been through that day.

⁂

Learning, during evening rehearsals, that Arnold Palmer was due to visit the U.S. embassy in London's Grosvenor Square before the weekend, and that he was not averse to delivering a certain package to another London address while staying in the capital, Justin invited the cultural attaché round to his office the next morning to explain the nature of the package.

When Palmer arrived at the publishing house's building, he was surprised to see graffiti paint-sprayed across some of the windows: *Menteurs luritaniens. L'assassin, c'est Putin pas l'Ukraine.* (Luritanian liars. The murderer is Putin not Ukraine.) Imagining that Justin had his hands full, the American hesitated before finally ringing the doorbell.

'Yes?' barked a voice over the intercom, conveying an unambiguous message to intruders.

'Mr Palmer here to see Mr Hendry – if he's not too tied up.'

'Wait a minute.'

While the attaché stood biding his time, he wondered why the Ukrainian patriots had used red paint rather than their own bilious blue and yellow combination. Furthermore, although he had read that Luritania was a melting pot of nationalities as diverse as Icelanders, Montenegrans and Rwandans, he had no idea that Ukrainians had migrated here in any great numbers. Stepping back from the doorway, he noticed for the first time a banner stretched across the rooftop of the building sideways on to the Innova Press Corporation's main premises. It showed an image of Russia's president above the caption: *Je suis heureux que mon avion ne volait pas à plus basse altitude l'autre jour, sinon mon propre peuple m'aurait abattu.* (I'm glad my plane was flying no lower the other day, otherwise my own people would have blown me out of the air.)

173

Wise, thought Arnold, to contact the fire brigade before more busybodies recorded the publishing house's embarrassment.

After the door lock clicked open, Palmer found a troubled editor-in-chief awaiting him at the top of the staircase.

'So easy to upset people nowadays,' said Palmer, shaking Justin by the hand.

The Pulse's editor pulled a wry face. 'Freedom of expression. The nutters' inalienable right. Come on in.' Justin shuffled the cultural attaché into his office past a harried Chantalle Boyer fending off telephone calls from rival pressmen overjoyed at the prospect of running stories about the competition's misfortune.

'Well,' said Arnold, after the editor had closed the door behind them, 'what have your people done to upset the latest band of barbarians clamouring at Europe's gates?'

'Published a cartoon.'

'I didn't know that Kiev was bursting with Muslims.'

'It's not. Any more than this is a repeat of *Charlie Hebdo*. Ukrainians up in arms because we took a tilt at their president.'

'The chocolate billionaire?'

'And owner of a funeral parlour empire doing particularly sound business at the moment.'

Palmer dropped into one of Justin's leather armchairs, flinging a casual arm across the back rest. 'Your cartoonist walks too fine a line between parody and insult?'

'Nothing new for cartoonists. Anyway, our owner has ordered me to make sure that all future cartoons lay off international figures. He said the *Luritanische Bote* and the country's leading French rag are spoiling for a fight over who should pillory us on tomorrow's front page.'

'With or without your cartoon?'

'The *Luritanische Bote* is majority catholic-owned, so they'll steer clear of inviting trouble. But the other paper could well reproduce it.'

'All in all, good publicity.'

'That's one way of looking at it.'

'You know how fickle the public is the moment one day's bad news gets overtaken by the next day's calamity.'

Justin concluded that Palmer was well suited to the role of Gutman. 'Let's not hope for any calamities.'

'Despite the fact that the media likes to turn brush fires into wildfires.'

'Hang on, Arnold. We're not all scaremongers or phone hackers.'

'Of course not, Justin. I wasn't directing my comments at *The Pulse* …'

Palmer broke off to allow Justin to respond to the strident ringing of his phone. Chantalle's voice sounded over the intercom.

'The television van and camera crew have arrived. They want to interview you.'

'I bet they do. Tell them, they'll have to wait. I'm busy.'

As if scattering mites immune to the cleaning lady's feather duster, Palmer flapped his hand along the stiff leather back rest. 'Justin, Justin, I'm sorry. Here I am taking up too much of your time, when you have more pressing matters to deal with. The package. Give it to me, tell me where it's to be delivered, and I'll be off.'

Justin walked across to a side cupboard and drew out the red leather briefcase. 'As you can see, I was using the term package loosely. I have every reason to believe that this briefcase belongs to Peregrine Musgrave, a Westminster MP. Have you heard of him?'

'Can't say I have. What happened? Was he out here visiting and left it behind?'

For a moment, Justin felt inclined to go back on his original intention of confessing all and to fabricate a tissue of lies, but the morning's events had sapped his willpower.

'No, yours truly, totally out of character and not knowing what he was doing after attending a funeral in London, lifted this from a minicab on the way to City of London airport.'

Palmer scratched a puzzled forehead. 'You did what?'

'Yes, I know. Unbelievable. I should have handed it to the driver, but something told me it didn't belong to him.'

'You looked inside?'

'No, I couldn't. It was and still is locked.'

'And you brought it all the way over here through customs without knowing what it contained?'

'Yes, even more incomprehensible, when you think it could have contained drugs.'

Palmer stood up to inspect the briefcase. 'Made in Milan,' he said, reading the manufacturer's name in gold lettering. 'Classy. So how come you found it belonged to this Musgrave?'

'He was over here on parliamentary committee business. Showed me my business card, which must have dropped out in the back of the minicab when I opened up my wallet to pay the fare.' Justin did not need to be telepathic to read the question forming behind Palmer's eyes. 'You're wondering why I didn't hand it over there and then.'

Reacting to the ear-piercing screech of brakes, the editor looked down out of his office window into the forecourt where a television broadcasting van had just drawn up.

'I was ashamed to admit candidly to what I had done.' He continued speaking towards the knot of passers-by congregated on the far pavement. 'And Musgrave was charitable enough to give me the benefit of the doubt not only by suggesting that the business card belonged to the briefcase's owner, but by having me place a classified in *The Pulse* for the present holder of the briefcase to come forward and return it.'

'I see. And where does this fellow, Musgrave, hang out in London?'

'I'd be grateful if you could drop the briefcase in to the reception at the House of Commons together with a letter I've taped to the back explaining the whole dratted affair.'

'Well, no problem, Justin. I'll see that this gets delivered.'

'Just a minute, Arnold. Before you go, something I'd be interested to know – unless cultural attachés are obliged to stay clear of politics.'

'Try me, but never quote me.'

'What's your take on this Ukrainian conflict?'

Palmer clutched the briefcase to his chest. 'I think you've backed the wrong horse. Another lame nag for Europe's stables. But a Kentucky derby contender for us because it gallops us right up to Putin's front door.'

'I was thinking more of the conflict itself. Where it will end.'

'At the moment, Kiev is having to boost its army's numbers with convicts and derelicts functioning on alcohol and drugs. Drop-outs who don't give a damn about discipline. Our people have tried teaching them how to use multiple rocket launchers. In one ear and out the other. They blow themselves up forgetting to clean the tubes after firing. And since they rarely follow orders, they've been known to shell their own positions. In financing these jerks, we're only throwing good money after bad.'

'What about the other side? Putin's boys.'

'Mostly Ukrainian miners and tractor drivers. But there's a fair number of volunteers fighting alongside them from Russia, Chechnya and elsewhere. Just as everyone from Chechens and Poles to fucking jihadists is fleshing out Ukraine's excuse for an army.'

'No invasion?'

'Of course not. If the Russians really wanted to up the ante, they'd be in Kiev in the space of a fortnight.'

'But NATO says ...'

'What you'd expect it to say. To justify its existence.'

'Well, thanks for your straight-from-the-shoulder analysis.'

'Not for publication.'

'I wouldn't dream of it.'

'Good luck with those television goofballs.'

Justin nodded, and the pair shook hands. As Palmer left the office, *The Pulse's* editor-in-chief decided that after being given a roasting by the owner, it was time for him to give others one.

Craig reported back to Tich in a tea room behind Schönschlucht's central post office. The first-floor customer seating area overlooked the capital's Place de la Libération, where a visiting brass band was playing Sousa on a rotunda decked out with boxes of geraniums. The two men had secured a table to themselves near the window. The patterns on the drawn back curtains showed slim women in saris drinking tea on a palace terrace, while in the gardens below elephants carried the maharajah and his retinue back from the hunt in opulent howdahs.

'Green tea,' said Craig, whose suggestion it had been to meet here. 'Makes a change from coffee.'

'If I was living in Amritsar I might agree. But this is Luritania. A stone's throw from the Arctic.'

'Oh, yes? The winters are pretty rude in Nepal and Tibet, but how often do you see the natives grinding coffee beans?'

'Coffee keeps me awake.'

'Caffeine's a killer, Tich. You're safer with that oolong. Did your Chinese TEFL students never tell you that?'

'No. At my farewell dim sum party we drank beer. You're saying this is supposed to be good for me?'

'Spot on. Polyphenols.'

'Polly who?'

'Antioxidants. They fight free radicals.'

'Sounds political. But nothing, I suppose, to do with fascists?'

'Nope. Free radicals eat away at your DNA.'

'Nasty.'

'Care for a piece of my marble cake?'

'I'd rather have a piece of your news. You're looking and sounding too smug. Things went well last night, hunting out this creep's house and garden?'

'I heeded Vanessa's advice: improvise.'

'Tell me.'

'Drove the Jaguar to a wooded spot across the border. Took my mountain bike out of the boot and cycled over to reconnoitre his converted farm house. After which, I went back to the car and drove a mite closer. Sure you wouldn't like some?'

'I'm trying to lose weight. And I'd hate to have those free radicals muck around with my genes.'

'This cake's harmless.'

'I'm willing to bet it's packed with artificial sweeteners. Go on, Craig. You drove closer. Then what?'

'Put on my night running gear and rucksack. All the right moves. Emil Zatopek. Won three gold medals at the Helsinki Olympics after endurance training with a backpack.'

'Am I meant to be impressed? I'm impressed.'

'The street lighting wasn't that great. I was dressed in black. Didn't meet a single person out walking his dog. Three cars passed me by. I doubt the drivers gave me a look.'

'What are you pausing for? I'm hooked. Carry on.'

'The marble cake was looking neglected. Okay, our man's burglar deterrent is a *beware of the dog* sign. Which had me worried me, until I decided that, with no kennel or chain outside, the mutt had to be sleeping indoors.'

Seeing a bored-looking, middle-aged woman at the table behind straining to catch every word, Tich telegraphed one of his most disarming smiles. She applied knife and fork to a croissant and her confusion.

'Are we going to get to the interesting bit before midnight? Where did you dig the hole?'

'Who said I dug any holes?'

'What's that supposed to mean?'

'It was a large garden with a dry well out back. With a corrugated metal cover. I opened it up, tossed the packs in and replaced the cover.'

'Dry? You sure?'

'No bucket. No pump handle. No smell or sign of water that I could see with my flashlight. Tossed a couple of stones down. Clunk, clunk.'

'The goods packed in watertight plastic?'

'Of course.'

'Congratulations.'

'Coming from you, that's the next best compliment to the order of the garter.'

'I think Isabelle would look a darn sight better wearing one of those than you would.'

'You're beginning to sound like you know who.'

'You told Isabelle?'

'Yes, she put that piece of information in her letter posted this morning. Addressed to the police inspector who interviewed her.'

'Careful about fingerprints?'

'Very.'

'So now we wait for the balloon to go up for our Belgian friend – he of the wolfish appetite and impure mind.'

'That's it.' Craig was staring out of the window at the military conductor, who had just rapped the music stand with his baton. A row of red-faced percussionists lowered their instruments and turned towards the band leader.

'But,' said Tich, 'in spite of being the one to sire this idea, I have to admit it's a gamble. There's no knowing which way Mr Frites with everything will jump.'

'He's got nothing on us other than a hunch.'

'And the police? What if they reckon our fellow's been set up and start jumping Isabelle through more hoops?'

'Like I told you, Tich. Isabelle's a first-rate actress.'

'It's one thing playing a cross between a virgin and a nympho and another acting the innocent abroad.'

Craig nodded. The band struck up with *The Gladiator*.

Peregrine Musgrave strolled past the statue of the man who had once said that the United States was fated to plague America with woes in the name of freedom. Musgrave wondered whether, had he been alive today, *El Libertador* would have substituted 'the world' for 'America'. He surely would have cast bitter tears at the sight of the sorry state of his native Venezuela.

The Westminster MP, in no mood to appreciate the scent of hyacinths, arrived grim-faced in front of J, proprietorially planted on his de Havilland bench, sat down beside him and deposited the Milan briefcase between the two of them.

'Patience has its own rewards,' he said, either preferring not to look J in the eyes or disinclined to give occupants of neighbouring benches the benefit of the doubt.

It followed that there was nothing more natural than for J to treat the briefcase as if it were invisible.

'How are things with your son?'

'Not good. Poor kid underwent one EEG and two CT and MRI scans. Then, as I told you, they tapped his spine to draw off fluid and found confirmation of bacterial infection.'

'Meningitis?'

Musgrave had the impression that the sour look on J's face had less to do with life's injustices than with the sight of a teenager sailing towards them through the gardens on a shabby skateboard.

'They're treating him with intravenous antibiotics.'

'And he's holding up well?'

Musgrave decided that he had let acrimony colour his judgment. 'As well as can be expected. We're ...' Hesitating to reveal that he, a lapsed Catholic, got down on his knees each night away from his wife to pray for his son's recovery, Musgrave was grasping for the right words.

J squared his shoulders. 'Not easy for you. Either of you.'

'Well, that's life, isn't it? Full of nasty surprises. Unlike the briefcase. Must say I was surprised to see it returned.'

'The editor admitted to the error of his ways and trotted it back to you?'

'It was waiting for me at the House of Commons with a note of apology.'

'I see.'

If there was one thing the MP had come to learn about J, it was that the phrase 'I see' never boded well.

'Has it been opened?'

'How should I know? It's still locked.'

J placed the case on his lap and twirled the combination until the lock clicked open. Folding back the flap, he extracted the two documents and accorded them the briefest of inspections.

'Everything appears to be in order,' he said, replacing the papers and relocking the case. 'You can go ahead, Peregrine, and deliver them to your minister.'

From the even tone of J's voice, Musgrave suspected this was not the end of the affair.

'You don't sound all that happy at being reunited with our briefcase.'

'Because I know that it's been opened.' J beckoned to a young gipsy selling nosegays of carnations, gardenias and cornflowers. A hawker might have been as *persona non grata* as a skateboarder, but the old Harrovian could not resist the attraction of a blue cornflower for his forlorn buttonhole.

'How can you tell?' said Musgrave, declining the girl's offer.

J waited until the gipsy finished pocketing her money and moved away.

'Peregrine, ever since Assange and Snowden made the headlines, sexual and corruption scandals have taken a back seat to mega-leaks. The press is constantly nosing around, eager to sniff out proof that there are no greater falsehoods than freedom and democracy. What better potential source of classified information to this effect than a locked briefcase belonging to a member of the House of Commons?'

'But Hendry didn't know to whom the briefcase belonged until I appeared on the scene. And even then he could not be one hundred per certain that the case was mine.'

'Only a naïve fool would believe that, Peregrine, and you are neither naïve nor a fool. Put yourself in Hendry's shoes after you tipped him the wink. Would you sit on the briefcase?'

Since Musgrave appeared to have no cogent argument to the contrary, J drove his point home.

'Of course, you wouldn't. And once you opened it – a matter of patient child's play – and chanced upon encrypted documents – hallelujah!'

The MP was about to intervene but J pre-empted him. 'No, no, I'm not blaming you. Who asked you to run this errand, if not I?'

'So why the worry?'

'Because Hendry has been anything but honest with you. He was intrigued, even frightened, by what he found.'

'How can you know what he found?'

'He will have recognised the binary code for what it is and had it translated. Bingo. Grist to a journalist's mill.'

'Innova Press Corporation?'

'Or something with more clout.'

'I thought we agreed he would get nowhere peddling that to anyone.'

'True. Another far-fetched conspiracy theory. Like the one maintaining that Bill Gates favoured seeing the world's population halved by the middle of this century, and that nature could be lent a helping hand by cultivating GMO rice and wheat crops guaranteeing female sterility across Africa, the world's second most populous continent.'

Musgrave wished that the school holidays had not brought out so many cheerful children.

'Or that JFK was assassinated because he wanted to strip the Federal Reserve Bank of its exclusive right to issue U.S. currency and transfer this responsibility to the U.S. Treasury Department …You get my gist, Peregrine?'

'Of course. As Churchill said: *A lie gets halfway around the world before the truth has the chance to get its pants on.*'

'Except that, Peregrine, our problem is that these meddlers in our affairs out in Luritania will suspect that what they are sitting on is not preposterous theory but harsh reality. Because it's been found in the personal belongings of a member of HRH's House of Commons.'

'But if you're right and the easier of the two texts has already been decoded, nothing, as far as we know, has leaked out.'

'Our trusting Peregrine. Hendry has won you over.'

'Nonsense. Intuition. I'm sure we can sleep calmly, J.'

'If we weren't dealing with an editor, I might agree. But I think you've been taken in, Peregrine. Hendry is holding fire while waiting to crack the second code.'

'Wait a minute, J. You told me that document contained a code flagged immediately by your data interception people the moment somebody went online with it.'

'That's correct.'

'Well, has it been flagged?'

'Of course not. I would have told you, if it had been. But prevention, Peregrine, is eminently preferable to cure.'

'The second document is doubly encrypted, is it not?'

'Yes. But why kid ourselves that no minds are sharper than those of our encrypters? If hackers succeed in penetrating government and corporate data banks, why should they throw in the towel at the sight of what they see as a different challenge?'

'What are you suggesting?' A question to which Musgrave already knew the answer.

'As I said last time, steps must be taken to ensure that Hendry sees reason and leaves well alone. Don't worry, my affair not yours.'

The MP envisioned J behind the controls of one of de Havilland's Mosquitoes, poised to fire the aircraft's four Browning machine guns as he came in at the enemy from out of the sun. A fanciful idea dismissed the next moment, when he acknowledged that, should the genie ever be let out of the bottle, the individual most likely to prove Hendry's nemesis was not the man working out of Vauxhall Cross but the man working out of Langley, Virginia. It was a fate he would not have wished on anyone, let alone a personable, inoffensive young journalist.

J broke across the MP's uncomfortable train of thought. 'All that remains for you, Peregrine, is to deliver the contents of our little red friend here to their intended recipient.'

Musgrave reclaimed possession of the briefcase. 'Just like that,' he said, lost in a world of his own.

'Everything all right, Peregrine?' A genuinely concerned question prompted by J's failure to divine that Musgrave's thoughts were of a man who, after serving in Monrtgomery's Desert Rats, had in later life become one of the MP's favourite comedians. The briefcase's lock had been set to coincide with the year of Tommy Cooper's death.

'No,' replied a world-weary Musgrave, his sunken stature leaving him dwarfed by the man with the bearing of a Grenadier Guard.

⁂

Isabelle Meunier had been one of the last to hear the news; she had been working in one of the back offices when Inspector Georg Hoffarth together with two armed members of Luritania's police force marched into BLR's Mensdorf branch and demanded to see the deputy manager. Five minutes after confronting Eric Vandeweghe, Hoffarth, accompanied by one of his men, led the handcuffed Belgian out past the other officer standing guard in the reception area and bundled him unceremoniously into one of two waiting Ford Crown Victorias. An astonished Heinrich Katzenberger confirmed that the deputy manager had been taken away for questioning.

Crowded around the television in Isabelle's apartment later that day, Craig, Tich and BLR's fast-track trainee watched reconstruction of the dawn raid on the grounds of the converted Vandeweghe farmhouse in the course of which one million six hundred euros in banknotes had been recovered from the bottom of a disused well. In next to no time, the banker had been charged with the Mensdorf branch theft.

While Craig and Tich were high-fiving each other, Isabelle was endeavouring to come to terms with this bolt from the blue. In view of the amount involved, it was clear that Vandeweghe had been milking funds not only from Mensdorf but also from his preceding branch, since there too he had been responsible for liquidity. And this could not have been achieved without cooking the books. It made completely empty his threat of denouncing her.

'Craig,' she said, 'did you make a wish when you threw those packages down there?'

'That nobody would see or hear me.'

'Your lucky night. No full moon and somebody up there smiling down on you.'

'On us,' said Tich. 'Our lucky night and a weight off our minds. Let Eric scream his innocence all the way to the clink. One thing we can be sure of – when Inspector Hoffarth and company go looking for the rest of the Mensdorf heist, they won't come knocking on our doors.'

On the fourth day of intravenous injections, Stuart Musgrave slipped into deep unconsciousness. It was late at night when maternal intuition pulled Margaret Musgrave awake from her slumbers to the feeble rasping sound issuing from her son's throat. Half an hour later, Stuart breathed his last in her consoling arms. Refusing to admit that she had lost her only child, Margaret Musgrave clung on to the nine-year-old's lifeless body, sobbing the lines of *All Through The Night* over the youngster's tear-stained face.

When the night duty nurse arrived to check on Stuart's condition, it was no easy task to prise the grieving mother away from her son. A doctor, young enough, thought Margaret, to be an intern, was called upon to confirm death. Horrified and enraged at the callous way in which he treated her son as another of the hospital's early-morning-hour corpses, she chased him out of the room with a mouthful of splenetic invective. The doctor narrowly avoided bumping into an anguished male rushing along the corridor outside. Peregrine had been shaken awake by another night nurse.

Bereft of speech, Musgrave stumbled to a halt beside his son's bed before taking Stuart in his arms and emitting a loud wail.

Later that night, after Peregrine had made the necessary heart-rending phone calls to grandparents and relatives from his cell phone in the family kitchen where Stuart's last sketch of *Spaceship Infinity* was pinned to the refrigerator door, Margaret turned the full force of her desperation and fury on the sole person whom she could hold responsible for this cruel blow. 'It was your fault, all your fault. If you had been more of a father to him, taught him how to deal with bullies, this would never have happened.'

'But there was nothing deliberate about what happened in the playground. They were playing tag with a medicine ball under the eyes of the gym instructor, and Stuart got accidentally barged into the wall.'

'Accidentally? You believe that guff we were given? The school was protecting itself against a charge of negligence. The father of the boy who pushed Stuart into the wall helped raise fifty thousand pounds for their new cricket pavilion.'

'You think starting criminal proceedings against an eleven-year-old or his father is going to bring Stuart back?'

Margaret Musgrave jumped up from her seat and, tears streaming from her eyes, pummelled her husband on the chest, until, a spent force, she collapsed sobbing into his arms.

'All you've ever truly cared about has been that bloody career of yours. Stuart and I were second-class citizens compared to those freaks strutting around Whitehall and Strasbourg.'

'You know that's not true, Margaret.'

'Do I? Why, you were even sparing of your time with Stuart while he was in that infernal hospital.'

Peregrine felt a hot rush of anger, shame and remorse suffuse his face. 'That infernal hospital did all it could to save him. It's those freaks who are a complete waste of time. Look, Margaret, we need to tell ourselves and Stuart that he hasn't really left us. He's everywhere around us. In need of our love and prayers. Yes, whatever you might think to the contrary, I believe he needs our prayers. Creatures his age don't vanish overnight. They hang on, because we, Mischief' (Peregrine was referring to their son's Jack Russell) 'and all his toys and books and other belongings won't let go of him until he understands that letting go isn't the end for him but a new beginning.'

Margaret Musgrave drew away, staggering slowly back towards her seat. 'I'm sorry, Perry, I shouldn't have said what I did.'

'I can forgive just about everything apart from the playground accusation. That hurt.'

'It was mean, and I'm sorry.'

Musgrave walked across to where his wife lay slumped on the floor beside an armchair. Kneeling down, he took hold of her by the shoulders and pleaded.

'Stuart's still with us, Margaret. You've got to believe that. The angels aren't ready for him.'

'Angels, what bloody good are they? If one of God's angels was there for Isaac, why couldn't he have been there for Stuart?'

Bowed down by the meaninglessness of his life, Peregrine Musgrave sunk, in turn, onto the carpet.

⁂

The Lenfindi Club's Sunday morning breakfast club started out on a subdued note after Rashid recounted the private side to his trip to Lebanon and the call made on him by two visitors from the CIA.

Justin delved into his pocket and produced a typewritten note. 'I'm sorry, folks, but on top of what Rashid's just told us, I have bad news from the man to whom I delivered that damned briefcase. His message is short and to the point: *Mr Hendry, I feel I should tell you that whoever touched that briefcase while it was out of my possession needs to look out for his back. There are people of ill will whom it is dangerous to cross. Burn this and the envelope.*

'It's unsigned but the envelope's postmarked Fulham.'

Vanessa finished scrawling a side note into her master copy of *Camino Real*. 'That means we're sitting on somebody else's goldmine. Publish and be damned, Justin.'

'What's there to publish?'

'Rashid's deciphering of the first document, which you came by through an unnamed official source in the UK.'

'That could end up implicating the very man who wants me to forget about this for my own good.'

'For whose good? Are you completely bonkers?'

'I agree with Vanessa,' said Isabelle. 'That first document is all about the one per cent of the world's wealthiest and their unsavoury scheming.'

Craig was the first to dissent. 'At the expense of Justin's security?'

Vanessa waved her referee's copy of *Camino Real*. 'Can't we stand together on this? *Un pour tous, tous pour un?*'

'With muskets, I suppose? Mind you, I thought Dumas's heroes preferred swords to muskets.' Justin's attempt to make light of the affair concealed deep-seated unease.

'Brownings,' said Vanessa, 'not muskets. You're forgetting that Tich and I know how to use pistols.'

Tich waded in with one of his prefatory, silencing grunts. 'Hang on there, Van. You've only just got your licence and you want to play bodyguard?.'

With the conversation too alarmist for his liking, Justin overrode Vanessa's response. 'I could go around disguised as the don in *Camino Real*. That should throw anyone barging into the editor-in-chief's office with a Luger and finding himself facing a Spanish scarecrow.'

'I think you should take that note seriously,' said Rashid not without reflecting on his own recent brush with the authorities. 'The bugger about today's global village is that we're all subject to scrutiny. I disagree with Vanessa and Isabel. Leave well alone. If nothing gets published, why should these people of ill will bother to raise a finger against you?'

'Because,' said Tich, 'they'll be forever wondering whether he's biding his time. In which case, they'll try to nip any unwanted move on his part in the bud. Not that anybody's threatened Justin directly. That would be clumsy, and I imagine the nasty-minded guys our Serjeant Musgrave has in mind go about things differently. Justin's best bet is to give to believe that their text has gone viral. Trying to close the lid after that would be like trying to nail jelly to the wall.'

'Do I have a say in this?' said Justin, the marked change of tone signalling a more level-headed approach to his predicament. 'After all, I'm the one with my head on the block. Publish and be damned, is that it?'

If Isabelle looked chastened, Vanessa, Craig and Tich, more used to reading their friend's mind, remained unmoved.

Vanessa waited several beats before responding. 'Better than don't publish and be damned.'

'It's hardly material for *The Pulse*, Vanessa. And even if we were to give it space and shunt it around our European websites, it would never have the same impact as in a mass circulation tabloid.'

'So sell it to *The Guardian, Le Nouvel Observateur* or *Der Spiegel.*'

'I thought we'd been through this. They'd laugh me out of court.'

'Not if you tell them, you've had death threats.'

'Oh, great, Vanessa. That's quite a step up from paint-sprayed graffiti. My reading of Musgrave's idea of ill will wasn't as up close and personal as a knife in the ribs.'

'Sorry, Justin. But you have to admit, it's not a bad selling point.'

'Vanessa,' said Rashid, 'don't forget that none of those three publications will be satisfied with the starter alone. They'll want the main course.'

'Encrypted?'

'They'll bust a gut to get it decrypted.'

'Not,' said Isabelle, 'if they're hand in glove with the Council of Twenty. Then this would rebound on Justin.'

'I thought you were for publishing.'

'I've changed my mind.'

'Look everyone,' said Justin. 'I've brought along photocopies of both papers. You're welcome to help yourselves. But they're not for playing with. Strictly for placing in safekeeping. Just in case, Vanessa is right and Don Quixote comes up against more than his delusional brain can cope with.'

Tich was the first to take up the offer, followed by Vanessa and the rest.

'Well,' said Tich, after more beard stroking, 'are we going to vote on this?'

Justin crossed his arms and sat back in his chair with eyes closed. 'What's the motion?'

'Publish and be damned. Those for?'

Vanessa raised a solitary hand. Tich looked at the others, then joined her.

'Those against?'

Craig, Isabelle and Rashid each raised a hand.

Justin continued sitting motionless both eyes firmly shut.

'You have to cast your vote, Justin.'

The Pulse's editor-in-chief opened his eyes. 'For.'

'In which case we're deadlocked.'

'No, we're bloody not. This is my call, Tich.'

'Is it?' objected Craig. 'What if you drag us all down with you in the process?'

'Why should I do that? You're squeaky clean, the lot of you.'

The glances exchanged between Isabelle and Craig did not go unmissed by Justin.

'No,' Isabelle demurred, 'wait, good people. You're a quintet, remember. I'm not entitled to vote. You have to disregard my vote, Tich. And that means Justin publishes.'

Tich wrinkled his forehead. 'I thought we'd agreed to follow Van's "One for all and all for one" credo.'

'You, we, still can,' said Isabelle. 'But as a group of six, we'll always risk deadlock.'

'Much as I dislike the result,' announced Craig. 'I say we go with Isabelle's suggestion.'

'Right,' said Tich, 'that wraps up the main business on this morning's agenda. What have we got left to take the bitter taste of Musgrave's Gatling gun warning out of our mouths? In view of last week's prior engagements, Justin and Rashid were spared contributing. In my round robin, I suggested limiting ourselves to word oddities. Who feels like starting? Van? Craig? Isabelle?'

'I don't mind going first,' said Vanessa, 'though what with *Camino Real* and the office treadmill, I've had precious little time to devote to lexical peculiarities. But I finally plumped for the nomenclature of nosh.

'First off, Jerusalem artichoke. Not found growing near the Dome of the Rock, because it's native to North America. And it's a sunflower, which is why it's thought that Italian settlers called it *girasole* after the plant's habit of turning towards the sun. Later on, it looks as if other tongue-tied settlers chewed *girasole* into Jerusalem. Of course, you and I are more familiar with the artichoke's edible tubers than with its flowers.

'Next up, ambrosia, the food of the gods conferring immortality. Even gluten-free, over-indulgence in today's high sugar content rice pudding by the same name guarantees diabetes, if not an early grave, for the sweet of tooth.

'Then, credenza. A piece of furniture, you'll say. Right, but one used in medieval times as a sideboard on which food and drinks were placed for sampling by a dogsbody, the first to drop dead if anyone had poisoned something intended for his lord and master. *Credenza,* meaning confidence, probably tripped off Lucrezia Borgia's tongue whenever she was handing around the drinks or canapés.

186

'I'll conclude with pork from Latin *porcus* (pig), downgrading to *porcello* (little pig). That's one snort away from *porcellana* (porcelain) named after the cowrie shell. Why? Because the ancients, in common with Botticelli, thought the opening on the side of that shell resembled a woman's you know what. So next time you menfolk are eating or drinking off porcelain try not to behave like a *porcello*.'

'Perhaps I should go next,' said Craig, 'since I am able to match Vanessa's quartet. If it hadn't been for Isabelle egging me on, I might have arrived today empty-handed and fattened our kitty by ten euros. So, what have I got?

'Apothecary. A source of headache and other cures, you might think, were it not for the fact that the Latin *apothecarius* referred to any kind of shopkeeper. Perhaps Woolworth-type drug store owners are truer to the word's origins than are pharmacists.

'Next, caprice from Italian *capriccio*. That word originally conveyed "shiver of fear" comprising, as it did, *capo* (head) and *riccio* (hedgehog). Presumably, anyone whose hair stood on end after reading Dante's *Inferno* merited calling "hedgehog head".

'Staying with Latin and Italian, I give you *sclavus*. Used by one Roman finishing off his letter to or taking leave of another, this would have meant "Your servant". Watch the centuries fly by and, lo and behold, *sclavus* was transmogrified into *ciao*. So next time you wish someone *ciao*, be sure they don't take that as an invitation to tread all over you.

'Finally, let me end on the cheerful note of "hearse". This has its roots in French, where the word referred first to a farmer's harrow, then to a similar-shaped wooden candle-holder placed on top of a coffin, after which it was applied to the carriage transporting the coffin. The connection with "rehearse"? Well, that's French again, in the sense of "repeat". Thus, each time Vanessa puts people through their paces in rehearsals, she is smoothing things out in much the same way as a farmer repeatedly evening out the earth with his harrow.'

'Really?' said Vanessa. 'I hope you're not going around, Craig, saying I treat my actors like clods.'

'No,' said Isabelle, drawing a slip of paper from her sling bag, 'he tells people you're like our Marianne sowing the seeds of inspiration. My turn now. I trust you'll excuse me, if, as a first-timer, I offer less than Craig and Vanessa. After all, English is not my mother tongue.'

'No need to apologise,' said Tich. 'I didn't expect you to bring anything to the table.'

'Well, then ...' Isabelle held up her short shopping list. 'My humble contribution. First, as evidence of my fascination with some of your quaint English alliterative expressions: dilly-dally, harum-scarum, helter-skelter, higgledy-piggledy, hocus-pocus, honky-tonk, hotchpotch, hugger-mugger, hunky-dory, hurdy-gurdy, hurly-burly, hush-hush, hustle and bustle, jiggery-pokery, mumbo-jumbo, namby-pamby, roly-poly, shilly-shally, tootsie-wootsie and topsy-turvy.

'In responser to which, *Guillaume le conquérant* left his mark with *bric-à-brac, cul-de-sac, fleur-de-lis, laissez-faire, papier-mâché, pêle-mêle, pince-nez, pot-pourri, sang-froid, savoir-faire* and *tête-à-tête*.'

'Touché, Isabelle,' said Tich. 'A neat way of paying us back in the coin of the realm rather than in sous or those damned euros. And allow me to congratulate you on masterful aspiration of the letter which takes such a back seat in your alphabet. I shall follow close on your heels with a few abstruse dribs and drabs. Starting with poppycock. That, my friends, it appears, is our anglicised euphemism for what the Dutch call soft crap.

'Next, skulduggery. This comes to us via uninhibited Scotland, where sculduddery meant adultery or fornication. We English seems to have transplanted it from the bedroom to the Cabinet Office.

'Next balderdash. That has its origins in the unwholesome mixing of beer, wine, milk and, for all I know, lemon barley water. Though what you and I currently understand as balderdash begs the question how well Baldacci's books sell in Russia, where *balda* means fool.

'I've also dredged up a number of expletives familiar to me from my childhood reading material. It never occurred to me at the time that these were toned down religious oaths. My favourite was zounds, a contraction of by God's or Christ's wounds. A close second came gadzooks, God's or Christ's hooks.

'Strewth, I subsequently came to learn, means God's, and, presumably, Christ's truth. Though I never noticed my dad cross himself after hearing a football commentator declare: *Strewth, that was a clear foul on the defender*. Apart from anything else, I'd be delighted if some kind soul could enlighten me as to what they understand by God's truth.

'Gor or cor blimey, as you may or may not realise, is a corruption of the more risky profanity, May God blind me. Mind you, anybody declaring *Gorblimey if I tell a lie, but isn't that Monica Bellucci a knockout*? ought to get off lightly.

'As for crikey, I'd hate to count the times I must have seen that in *The Beano*, *Dandy* or *Hotspu*r, while blissfully unaware that it was a watered down version of that most indefensible of oaths, Christ kill me. Strange, I would have expected it to mean Christ strike me.

'Cripes was another familiar exclamation which I never suspected of being anything other than a tepid expletive, although I can't be sure that it crossed the lips of Dan Dare or Desperate Dan. In fact, cripes is an alliterative euphemism for Christ's stripes, the ones inflicted by order of Pontius Pilate.

'Finally, golly and gosh. Those harmless utterances of surprise are euphemisms for the Almighty used by those fearful of taking the Lord's name in vain. I doubt whether the lesser Lord Snooty was aware of that or whether any of my examples have meant anything to Isabelle, more familiar with *Boule & Bill* and *Titeuf* than with Dennis the Menace or the Bash Street Kids.

'On the other hand, this posy of genteel oaths attests to nothing so much as the potent influence of religion among us Anglo-Saxons on language not imbibed with our mother's milk. Time then for our chain-reaction super collider. Perhaps Rash wouldn't mind starting us off today. Name your preference, Rash. Theatre, cinema, literature or art?'

'Let's try cinema this time.'

'Of course. In that case, should anyone find themselves at a loss for a title or director, they can cite an actor for the link.'

Rashid: *Groundhog Day*. Bill Murray.

Vanessa: *Long Day's Journey Into Night*. Sidney Lumet.

Craig: *Dog Day Afternoon*. Al Pacino.

Isabelle: *Reservoir Dogs*. Tarantino.

Justin: *Straw Dogs*. Peckinpah.

Tich: *The Wild Bunch*. Twins.

Rashid: *The Wild One*. Brando.

Vanessa: *The Godfather*. Coppola.

Craig: *Bram Stoker's Dracula*. Twins.

Isabelle: *Tinker Tailor Soldier Spy*. Gary Oldman.

Justin: *Bridge of Spies*. Spielberg.

Tich: *Catch Me If You Can*. Twins.

Rashid: *Shutter Island*. DiCaprio.

Vanessa: *The Aviator*. Scorsese. Twins.

Craig: *Taxi Driver*. Triplets.

Isabelle: *Mean Streets*. Quadruplets?

Tich: Yes. Great, Isabelle.

Justin: *The Good Shepherd*. De Niro.

Tich: *Hereafter*. Matt Damon.

Rashid: Handed me on a plate: *Groundhog Day*.

'Hold on,' objected Craig. 'On a plate?'

'Yes. Punxsutawney Phil prophesies the future.'

Tich stroked kinks out of beard and head. 'That's stretching things, Rashid. But I'm prepared to give it to you for bottle.'

'Bottle?

'Tich means you should be ashamed of yourself,' said Vanessa. 'Following *Hereafter* with *Groundhog Day* is about as legit as tacking *Jaws* onto *Reservoir Dogs*.'

'Please not,' said Justin. 'Reminds me of the character played by Robert Shaw.'

'A man for all seasons?'

'No, a man named Quint. Ended up as shark food.'

⁂

After the loss of her first child through miscarriage, Margaret Musgrave had lived through many a long dark hour until the day finally dawned when she was able to rejoice in the arrival of Stuart Alexander. Not that his had been an easy delivery inasmuch as breech birth risks had necessitated a cesarean section. But if losing her first infant had been unbearable, the death of her only child whom she had cherished and nurtured through nine all too brief summers left Margaret a shadow of her former self. As for her devastated husband, Peregrine Musgrave was forever reproaching himself for past failings: his warnings that excessive doting on Stuart risked doing the boy no good; his time spent at weekends pouring over papers rather than kicking a ball around with his son in the park; and last, but not least, seeking to gain favour with a certain cabinet minister by tacitly peddling the thinking behind J's MI6 missives.

Recognising the pointlessness of continuing to heap blame on her husband, Margaret Musgrave turned the full force of her diatribe away from the school authorities (where was the master who should have intervened in the schoolyard to forestall dangerous bullying?) onto the Almighty. Peregrine's suggestion that Christ would welcome Stuart into paradise met with a stinging retort:

'Where was Christ when the Aberfan colliery spoil tip collapsed and left one hundred and sixteen children dead? Twice now He's robbed me of my flesh and blood. What have I done to deserve this? Better that He had made me barren than let me reproduce only to suffer this agony.'

However, despite all her railing against the deity, Margaret finally agreed that, like her stillborn, Penelope, Stuart should be given a 'wishy-washy' Church of England funeral. 'The Humanists are out,' she said. 'No woodland burial for my son stuffed upright in the ground in a wickerwork sentry box like an ecologically space-saving domino. Given half a chance, the hospital would have treated Penelope like clinical waste – but I didn't let them. We gave her a church burial, and so Stuart must be buried next to his sister.'

It cost Peregrine no little effort to dissuade his wife from reading her own abbreviated version of WH Auden's *Funeral Blues* from the pulpit. 'Think of the effect it will have on the grandparents and others.'

'Why should I concern myself about upsetting my parents-in-law? They barely approved of me.'

'Your own parents then. More particularly, Stuart's closest friend and school chum.'

That last argument seemed to carry more weight than any other, though Peregrine could not be certain that she would keep her promise. He feared she would pronounce the words:

Stop all the clocks★, cut off the telephone
Silence the pianos …
Let aeroplanes circle moaning overhead
Scribbling on the sky Stuart Alexander Musgrave is dead.

He was my North, my South, my East and West,
My working week and my Sunday rest.
My noon, my midnight, my talk, my song.

The stars are not wanted now, put out every one;
Pack up the moon and dismantle the sun
Pour away the ocean and sweep up the wood
For nothing now can come to any good.

★ By W.H. Auden, 1938

Instead, during the memorial service, Margaret spoke of how nothing made her son happier than to be able to sleep out in the garden under canvas on summer weekends with his beloved Jack Russell puppy, Mischief, or to take him on cycle rides in his front-mounted biker bag. For his part, Peregrine explained the pleasure Stuart derived from his collection of Summer and Winter Olympics stamps and from two pond-worthy bolsa-wood galleons built by his own hands. The grandparents paid tribute to Stuart's fun-loving nature, while his form master praised his pupil's enthusiasm for mathematics and cricket.

When the time came for both parents to offer their closing words, Peregrine was unaware that Margaret had Auden's verses in her left and Mary Frye's funeral poem in her right pocket, but it was only after looking down on the wretched face of Brian Heathcote, Stuart's best friend – one of the reasons why she had rejected the suggestion of an open casket – that she reached into her right pocket to read:

> *Do not stand at my grave and weep*★.
> *I am not there; I do not sleep.*
> *I am a thousand winds that blow.*
> *I am the diamond glints on snow.*
> *I am the sunlight on ripened grain.*
> *I am the gentle autumn rain.*

Stepping up beside his wife for the continuation, Peregrine placed his arm gently around her waist:

> *Do not stand at my grave and weep.*
> *I am not there; I do not sleep*
> *When you awaken in the morning hush,*
> *I am the swift, uplifting rush*
> *Of quiet birds in circling flight.*
> *I am the soft star-shine at night.*

Husband and wife concluded in unison:

> *Do not stand at my grave and cry.*
> *I am not there; I did not die.*

A dry-eyed Margaret bestowed a weak smile on the bowed head of Brian Heathcote. After which she stood immobile, eyes riveted to the casket, until Peregrine helped her down to the front row of pews.

The hardest moment for everyone came at the graveside, where the headstone

---

★By Mary Elizabeth Frye, 1932

lay ready with the inscription proposed by Peregrine and, to his surprise, consented to by Margaret:

Except ye ... become as little children, ye shall not enter into the kingdom of heaven. Mathew 18:3.

A grandparent aided Peregrine in catching the distraught mother as she came close to fainting at the end of the minister's committal, which she interpreted as an incantation, the priest as a soulful orison:

Father, the death of Stuart Alexander has created a void in our lives. Separated from him, we feel broken and perplexed. Give us confidence that he is safe, that his life is complete with You, and that we shall all one day be brought together with Stuart before the glory of Your presence in heaven.

We have entrusted Stuart Alexander to God's mercy, and now we commit his body to the ground alongside our angel Penelope; earth to earth, ashes to ashes, dust to dust; in sure and certain hope of the resurrection to eternal life through our Lord Jesus Christ.

'And death,' muttered a woebegone father under his breath, 'shall have no dominion.'

Two days after the funeral, Peregrine Musgrave took up the envelope sent him by the Great Ormond Street Children's Hospital containing a handwritten letter of condolence from the consulting surgeon expressing regret at his inability to save Stuart. Within minutes, he had tippexed out his name and address, covered this with a stick-on label bearing an address in Luritania, inserted a brief typewritten note and a thin paper pouch of the kind used by banks to communicate clients' PINs, sealed the envelope and added postage celebrating Bradley Wiggins and Team GB's London 2012 gold medals.

⁂

'Well, 'ratio, how do you like your new room?'

Humphrey Hobart was pleasantly surprised to see what difference an extra one thousand euros a month made. As opposed to the scuffed grey linoleum on the floor of his previous shared ward, his brother now had wall-to-wall, floral-patterned carpeting. He also had his own bathroom, where the same cordless electric razor brought in by Humphrey after the accident sat in lieu of Horatio's preferred wet shaving kit on top of the wash basin alongside his toothbrush and other toilet articles.

The watercolour of Lake Windermere that had hung above his brother's bed in the ward now hung where Horatio could see it upon awakening each morning against eggshell blue wallpaper decorated with songbirds and butterflies. It was a third-floor room with a view of the gardens, neighbouring woodland and a valley from where Humphrey heard the sound of a carillon as clearly as if it had been pealing from a belfry at the edge of the sanatorium's grounds. The sash window's upper panel was fixed, while the lower one could be raised only so much.

'Sheep shearing,' responded Horatio in reference to his recent haircut, which made him look five years younger.

'Not as bad as that. Think yourself lucky you're not in the army.'

'Army barmy.'

'Couldn't agree more. Nothing crazier. How do you like your new room?'

'Are we going for an Eric Ambler?'

'Whenever you feel like it. How's the room?'

'Did you bring strawberries for Probe, Bob?'

The man taken for Bob shook his head. Had he heard correctly? Horatio had asked him a direct question.

'Has he been up here?'

'Probe, May, Far. Gone home. When can I go home, Bob?'

Humphrey gave a start. His first thought was that his ears must have deceived him. But no, he knew that was not so. Could it be that the brother used to being treated, at best, as a welcome companion, at worst, as a total stranger had suddenly been recognised as a connection, however indefinite, with Horatio's past? Humphrey told himself not to jump to conclusions. It remained to be seen whether this turn of events was a game changer or a flash in the pan.

'Horatio, didn't you see Probe and the others at lunch time? I'm sure they're still here.'

'No, gone home. Gone away.'

Humphrey, who until now had forgotten that a nurse had seen him into the third-floor corridor with an electronic card, began to query the wisdom of his re-accommodation gesture. Had it left his brother friendless?

'When was this?'

'Vermurr lent them his bikes.'

Horatio was referring to the HWS's director whom he invariably associated with a Flemish or Dutch painter – in this instance, Vermeer.

The cycling mention making no sense to Humphrey, he suggested they go for their customary walk around the grounds.

Humphrey was pleasantly surprised to see the freshly mown rear croquet lawn home to an open-air yoga class.

'Ever thought of trying some yoga, 'ratio?'

'Toga gives me headaches.'

'Looks very relaxing,' said Humphrey, unable to see Probyn or his brother's other two former companions among the group on the lawn. 'I don't see anyone standing on his head.'

'You need to be born by the Gangcheese.'

On this occasion, Humphrey decided to follow the path leading to the sanatorium's rose garden, where there was a choice of benches, some of which were always shaded from the sun. It took them twenty minutes to reach the spot, by which time he knew Horatio would welcome resting his legs. They sat down opposite a dogrose alive with bees.

Following what Humphrey took to be his brother's earlier promising kinship allusion, he wondered whether fate might not have offered him a golden opportunity to reopen remembrance's door.

'Just look at those industrious bees, Horatio. Doing better than ma's hummingbird recipe.'

His brother's attention appeared to be elsewhere: after removing a trainer, Horatio was trying to free worrisome grit from under his sock.

'Ratio, she said,' continued Humphrey, 'remember the ratio. One portion of water to four of sugar.'

Horatio's face lit up with a smile. 'Nectar, Bob. Nectar.'

It felt to Humphrey as if his heart had jumped in his chest. In the space of less than an hour his brother had made two connections with his past, this latest traceable to their boyhood. While her sons were gathered around the kitchen table watching Julia Hobart roll dough, she had taught the sweet-toothed Horatio the recipe for artificial nectar relayed to her by friends freshly returned from Trinidad and Tobago.

'Hummingbird nectar.'

'Busy buzzers.'

Now that Horatio had removed his sock, Humphrey feared that his grappling iron was doomed to lose its fleeting hold on the edge of a chasm growing wider by the second.

'Bees buzz. Hummingbirds hum.'

'Flip-flop flappers,' said Horatio, his sock and shoe back in place. 'My feet don't like this Eric Ambler.'

On the return walk to Horatio's room, Humphrey decided to concentrate on how to make the most of his brother's new laptop connected to the sanatorium's wifi network.

After the nurse had let them back into Horatio's corridor and room, Humphrey shepherded his brother across to the workstation which Horatio had played a helping hand in assembling and on top of which sat the open Apple with a flatbed scanner to one side and a laser printer to the other, a pack of copy paper stored on one of the shelves below. Humphrey was praying that having these devices and facilities to himself would help Horatio regain his enthusiasm for surfing the web's scientific and sports sites.

'Shall we try to set up your favourites? Make everything just a click away?'

To Humphrey, it seemed that Horatio's mock castanet clicking combined playfulness with enthusiasm.

Want me to find the Coal Cats?' Humphrey was referring to the English premier league's Sunderland A.F.C., which had captured Horatio's support long ago following a protracted affair while at Cambridge with an economics undergraduate.

'Cats not allowed.'

'Not real cats. Black cat footballers.'

'Cats playing football. Nice game. Let's try.'

'No, 'ratio, Sunderland.' Humphrey spaced out pronunciation of the three syllables in the hope that this might cause his brother to make the connection.

'Wonderland? Not interesting. Prefer Natchee.'

It took a while for the penny to drop before Humphrey recalled Horatio's passion for numbers. 'Fibonacci?'

'Yes, Fibber Natchee.'

'Now we're into counting something other than goals, let's see what I can find.'

Ten minutes later Humphrey had set up a full folder of mathematicians ranging from Archimedes, Euclid and Newton to Laplace, Gödel and Yitang Zhang via Srinivasa Ramanujan. Heartened to see his brother enthusing over these names and accompanying biographies, he sat back to watch Horatio focus on an article about the Indian astronomer and mathematician, Aryabhata. Humphrey remembered one occasion in particular when Horatio had been at his most lucid, albeit briefly, after dipping into a copy of the *New Scientist* not defaced by May. Despite witnessing the inevitable curtailment of articulateness, Humphrey sensed that the same cloud had not fallen over an inner landscape.

'Pi man' exclaimed Horatio. 'Sunlight man!'

While ignorant of his brother's meaning, Humphrey felt encouraged. Might working rather than playing with numbers rekindle lost habits and memories? Then again, although the past could not be undone, how different things might have been had Horatio been able to enjoy Skype sessions with Jacqueline free of interference from his ward mates. Except that who should have leant on Frans van Landewijk to see that Jacqueline's calls were received in private? Humphrey preferred to but could not forget that.

Concluding that it would be a mistake to drag his brother away from the monitor, Humphrey patted Horatio on the shoulder, promised to take him for another walk on the next visit and bowed out. But not before tucking into the bottom drawer of his brother's bedside table a copy of Peregrine Musgrave's coveted papers.

Worried about Horatio's loss of contact with other inmates, Humphrey searched out and accosted a middle-aged nurse whom, he imagined, still worked on his brother's old ward. She informed him that Horatio had been cycling that morning in the sanatorium's gym alongside Probyn.

'Probyn,' she suggested, 'told your brother that Maynard, Farley and he had entered for the Tour de France.'

'Isn't eating strawberries at Wimbledon more Probyn's style?

'I thought he was allergic to strawberries.'

'Don't I know it.'

'How is your brother faring upstairs in a room on his own?'

'A new chapter, nurse. I'm hoping it will give him a sense of stability.'

'He does have moments when he's particularly alert, you know. Too many patients here are in a perpetual mental fog. We can't say that of your brother.'

'Thank you nurse. First Horatio now you have lifted my spirits this afternoon.'

After turning on his heels, Humphrey wondered whether he should have asked the nurse if his brother had made new friends on the third floor. He checked himself, deciding that Frans van Landewijk was better placed to know this. But the manager was nowhere to be seen as Horatio exited the building.

Because both *La Maison des Aveugles* and the local library stocked a limited supply of books in Braille, and both carried not that many audio books of interest to Clara Bogen, Vanessa spent part of her visits to the blind home reading to her friend.

'You know, Vanessa,' said Clara, 'I heard Bismarck stir several times in his basket while you were reading *Timbuktu* last month. I'm sure he was pricking up his ears. Did you notice?'

'In fact, I did. Yes, he seemed to be paying attention.'

'I liked the way you made Auster's story come alive. Bismarck must have felt the same.'

'Until Bismarck, I'd never known what it was like to have a four-footed friend in the audience.'

'Speaking of audiences, why not read me some of *Camino Real*?'

'Oh dear, that would probably try your patience and my skills. Tennessee Williams has written a bundle of stage directions into the script, and I'd have to keep changing voices. I'm a director, first and foremost, remember.'

'False modesty. You're an actor director.'

'Giving my all to directing at present. Not that I aspire to rank alongside Deborah Warner or Kenneth Branagh.'

'What's that supposed to mean?'

'Warner's modern-dress take on *Julius Caesar* at the Barbican had Caesar assassinated in a board room. And Branagh's production of *Macbeth* in a deconsecrated church in Manchester was so visceral spectators close to the action lived the blood, sweat and mud of the battle scenes.'

'What next? *Othello* set on the International Space Station?'

'Don't they float around up there? That might work for Oberon and Titania in *A Midsummer Night's Dream* but not for much else.'

'Well, what surprises have you in store for your audience?'

'I have to admit they'll be close to the action. I believe I told you that I've hired the Château de l'Aubaine's courtyard. So it will be an open-air production. But no blood and gore. A voluptuous semi-naked virgin, though, for the men to get the hots over.'

'Including Casanova?'

'A good point. But no. Casanova no longer has the same spring in his step as he did in his youth.'

'Well, I've nothing but praise for Craig Robert's attentiveness. The other day I came over dizzy during his cycling class. It must have been one of my low blood sugar mornings. I could have had a bad fall, but he came to my rescue. The next day, he called round to see how I was doing and presented me with a box of chocolates.'

'Not the best of choices, if you happened to be diabetic.'

'I thought it was a nice gesture. Anyway, Vanessa, won't you read some of the finer parts of your play to me?'

'Not today. Today I've brought along a collection of short stories by Somerset Maugham. I thought you might like *The Three Fat Women of Antibes.*'

'Well, I've yet to be disappointed by anything you've selected for me, Vanessa. But I take it this one will leave Bismarck sound asleep?'

'Yes, otherwise he'll be the first German shepherd I've known to be interested in bridge or chocolate eclairs.'

'Have you also brought along that envelope you talked about last time?'

'No, Clara. Perhaps I'll remember it for my next visit together with *Camino Real.*'

'Why did Tennessee Williams have to confuse things by giving his play a Spanish title?'

'Not confusing to west coast Americans familiar with the Californian mission trail. It ran six hundred miles from San Diego to Sonoma.'

'Williams saw Don Quixote and Lord Byron as missionaries?'

'Let's say defenders of lost causes.'

'Williams was very alive to human frailty, wasn't he?'

'I think he saw us as flawed products of a divine potter who fell asleep over his wheel. A sentiment shared by Maugham. Imagine entering this world with a club foot, losing both parents by the age of ten, being brought up by an unloving uncle and finding you were gay in an era when homosexuality was a criminal offence.'

'Does any of that show through in *The Three Fat Women?*'

'No, but I guarantee that by the time I get to the end, we'll have either worked up a good appetite for tea or decided to go on a starvation diet.'

'If the first, you'll have been as bad as Casanova in encouraging diabetes. Still, I forgive you both. All right, Vanessa, you and Maugham do your best to make me hungry. Why was he called Somerset?'

'No idea. That was his middle name. His first name was William. I don't think *The Razor's Edge* would have sold brilliantly under the name of Bill Maugham.'

Later that evening at the shooting range, Vanessa confessed to Tich that she had treated it as a bad omen when, after opening Maugham's collected complete short stories, she had chanced upon *The Appointment in Samarra* – written in the same year as *The Three Fat Women of Antibes.*

Chantalle Boyer latched on to her first error in the proofs of the next edition of *The Pulse,* which she was reading through with a temp whose sour expression was due to Chantalle's refusal to conduct this work with somebody cut off from the rest of the world by ear buds attuned to Taylor Swift.

'An homage. Yuck, strike off that n.'

'What's wrong with it?'

'Well, Deirdrie, we don't say an omage, do we? Unless we're Alfred Doolittle.'

'Who?'

'Any more than we'd say Ennery Iggins.'

'I wish you'd speak English.'

'We're trying to write it, dear. An homage is a solecism.'

'Solar what?'

Chantalle resisted suggesting that if Deirdrie spent less time clicking her fingers to *Blank Space*, she might fill the gap between her ears with something a tad more profitable.

'Perhaps not as bad as a pleonasm, which we ran into a moment ago in that piece where Klaus must have had his head in the clouds when he wrote 'the new tram sets will make a large, gaping hole in the Ministry of Transport's budget.'

Deirdrie's mouth mirrored a crater.

'I'll give you that that pleonasm is not as common a word as sarcasm, Deirdrie – unless you work in this business.'

The other woman's face relaxed into a smile. 'Nothing to do with orgasm?'

'Not unless you have an orgasmic climax. Which neither of us is likely to experience while reading about trams, tax havens and territorial disputes. Shall we continue?'

But at that moment, the phone rang. Noting that it was an incoming call, Chantalle reached out for the receiver. 'Innova Press.'

'Good morning. Perhaps you can help me. I've been trying to run down Mr Hendry's home telephone number.'

As this was not a voice that she recognised, Chantalle opted for discretion. 'Well, Mr … I'm sorry, I didn't get your name.'

'Fairweather. Magnus Fairweather.'

Chantalle knew of no advertiser or subscriber with a name as barometrically memorable as that.

'I'm afraid, Mr Fairweather, that I'm not at liberty to disclose Mr Hendry's home phone number. He's here today. I can switch you through to him. Oh, no, sorry, I can't. He's in conference. Let me give you his direct dial extension, and you can try again in half an hour.'

'I didn't want to bother him with private matters at the office. Perhaps you could tell me where he lives. I checked through the town listings, but he's not there. Unless, of course, he's ex-directory.'

Hugh Chamberlain aka Magnus Fairweather sensed from the look on Warren Stenning's face that he was pressing his luck.

'My boss doesn't appreciate my divulging personal information to strangers, Mr Fairweather. I'm sure you can understand that.'

'But I'm no stranger. Justin and I were at varsity together.'

'All the same, I'd rather you phoned back later.'

'Very well. What's the extension?'

After Chantalle Boyer had finished with the unknown caller and replaced the receiver, her first thought was to make a Post-it note of the call for attaching to Justin's telephone, but the urgent proofreading in front of her and the feeling that the American-sounding Magnus was not putting business their way made her drop the idea. It was a decision she came to regret.

⁂

'What do we do?' said a less than happy Hugh Chamberlain. 'She won't help. Respecting his privacy. Why isn't he on the net?'

'He is, Hugh. It's just that he doesn't advertise his inner leg measurement or the name of his corner shop.'

'So we drive round to his office, sit outside until he leaves and follow him home?'

'No, too much trouble. We talk to the guy responsible for that Ukraine cartoon.'

'Why should he speak to us? He doesn't know us from Adam.'

'Leave that to me, Hugh. I'll get him to meet up with us for a drink after work tonight.'

'I thought you told me he was married. What if has to go straight home?'

'I said, leave it to me.'

By six thirty that evening, the three men were gathered together around a table in the *Café Grundschoss* in a village on the outskirts of town on the road leading to the Vaugruge. Klaus Radetzky's house lay in the next village but one.

Introducing himself as Guy Banks and his colleague as Terry Irving, Warren Stenning started the ball rolling by congratulating the sub-editor on the courage of his convictions.

'We liked your cartoon, Klaus. Fact is, because we both work for the OSCE, we see a fair bit of what is going on behind the scenes in Ukraine. And it's not all as one-sided as people make out.' Read what you will into that, thought the fake Guy Banks.

Klaus Radetzky took a sip of Riesling. 'Everyone here is convinced that Poroshenko's people are the victims of Russian aggression.'

Warren Stenning was not to be led on. He and Hugh had their own agenda. 'Have you found out who daubed paint all over your windows and walls?'

'The police aren't going to round up Luritania's Ukrainian residents for questioning over misuse of a pot of paint, are they?'

'There are that many to round up?'

'More than you'd think.'

'We hope whoever did this hasn't taken his indignation about that cartoon out on you personally.'

'What do you mean?'

'Organising protests outside your home. Harassing your wife and family.'

'Thank goodness, no.'

'And your editor. Have they set their hounds on him? Daubed his house with slogans?'

'Hendry doesn't live in a house. He rents a fifth-floor flat. They'd be pushed to spray paint that high up without a ladder.'

'Especially in town.'

'Who told you Hendry lives in town? He has a place in Oberfriesing on the south-west side of the city.'

Stenning scratched his nose. 'Funny, I was sure he lived in town. Who told us that, Terry?'

'To be honest, can't remember. But, yes, I thought he was a city man.'

'So what can I do for you gentlemen? It's not every day that the OSCE knocks on my door.'

Warren Stenning decided that it was time to hand the baton to his partner. 'I'll let Terry tell you, Klaus.'

Hugh Chamberlain ran a finger around the rim of his glass of *Waldaner Preisgau*.

'We like your style, Klaus. Professional. So we have a proposal for you. Another cartoon, but without the risk element. Ukraine's president wants to put us out of a job by bringing in UN peacekeepers. One of our guys back in Kiev suggested making fun of Poroshenko by drawing him in a blue helmet, brandishing a popgun. The caption: Pop goes the weasel. The man's initials are P.O.P. If you agreed to draw this for us and ran off fifty copies to take back out east, we'd be willing to pay you a hundred bucks.'

'Colour photocopies,' added Stenning, pouring out the last of his quarter carafe of *Pinot Gris*. 'We need to make our point in blue.'

Klaus Radetzky eyed both men wryly over the rim of his green-stemmed wine glass. 'To use one of your sporting expressions, Terry, that figure shows you're way off base. Two hundred dollars would be nearer the plate.'

Hugh Chamberlain played pat-a-cake with his fingers while ruminating. 'You fellers get paid that well? I guess you deserve it. Okay, if Guy here gives the nod, we have a deal.'

Deciding that his partner's shrewd reaction made up for the earlier telephone gaffe with Hendry's secretary, Warren Stenning extended a deal-making hand.

Klaus finished his drink, glanced at his watch and hoped that nothing more was needed of him. 'When do you need this by?'

The man calling himself Terry Irving handed over two light blue bills.

'Thanks. You still call these greenbacks?'

'Yeah. Look more closely.'

'Independence Hall.'

'Where the declaration was signed. City of brotherly love.'

'The building's green?'

'Not last time I saw it.'

'With money the root of all evil and green the colour of envy, maybe Jefferson should have chosen a different colour.'

Stenning rolled his tongue around some *Pinot Gris*. 'Greenbacks came after his time, Klaus, during the civil war.'

The sub-editor pocketed the two crisp banknotes in a wallet that had seen better days. 'You haven't answered my question. By when do you need those copies?'

Hugh Chamberlain smiled across at his colleague. 'We're out here on leave visiting friends. Can you get them to us by Saturday? We fly back to Kiev via Munich on Sunday.'

'No problem,' said Klaus, knowing that he could fit the work on the cartoon into his overtime hours.

'Here's our telephone number,' said Warren, offering the sub-editor a card with the name Guy Banks, OSCE Project Coordinator, Special Monitoring Mission (SMM) and a nine-digit cell number.

'You guys carry arms out there?'

Warren Stenning threw his questioner an unbelieving glance. 'Hell, no, Klaus. Guns are for the gung-ho guys. We're the heigh-ho guys. All work and no play. Apart from times like this.'

Justin was in the middle of a late Chinese take-away dinner when the front entrance phone sounded. The only people he thought likely to be calling in on him at this time of night were Vanessa or Tich. When he pressed the speaker button, a bowl of stir fry in one hand, a fork in the other, he heard a young, agitated female voice addressing him in broken French.

'Hello, I'm sorry to trouble you at this hour, but my car has broken down outside your building, and I have no phone to call the Automobile Club. I've been standing here pressing all the buttons. You're the only person to have answered.'

Swallowing a mouthful of noodles, Justin wished he had lashed out the extra euros for a video phone. He was loath to let a complete stranger see the messy state of his living room. Rather than inviting the woman upstairs, the simplest solution would be for him to ask for her Automobile Club membership number so that he could ring for assistance on her behalf.

'Not a flat tyre?' he said.

'No, some engine fault. A few minutes ago a warning sign started flashing on my dash. A skidding symbol. Every time I take my foot off the accelerator, the car shoots forward.'

'Have you just come off the motorway with your vehicle in cruise control?'

'Off the motorway? Yes. But I never use cruise control.'

'Perhaps you touched it accidentally using the windscreen wiper stick.'

'It's not been raining.'

Justin was well aware of that. But at this time of year drivers used their windscreen liquid to wash off viscous insect remains.

'Well, maybe you moved the switch using the indicator.' Justin realised that hunger and irritation had combined to create a distorted image of his unexpected caller. She was probably the antithesis of the plain, dumpy person he imagined her

201

to be in his present uncharitable frame of mind. But somehow he could not bring himself to be chivalrous.

'Why not go and check, then call me back?'

'All right, if you insist.'

The note of petulance only served to reinforce bloody-mindedness. Yes, Justin said to himself, I do insist, you silly bitch.

Since his living room looked out over the street, he went across to the window, parted the curtains and peered down. The only vehicle he could see by the kerbside was a green Volkswagen Golf parked under a street lamp with its side lights on. But there was no sign of the woman or, come to that, of any pedestrian taking the late-night air to whom she could have explained her problem. Justin waited and kept watching. Still no movement from the front entrance of the Résidence Éméraude.

The now familiar voice sounded again over the door phone. 'Hello, are you there?'

'Yes,' said Justin, taking an unhurried mouthful of stir fried sweet pepper.

'What I think you mean by cruise control … the button on the steering wheel stick … it's in the off position. So it must be something else. You see, you didn't let me finish. I wanted to tell you that the brakes are fading. That's dangerous. I daren't keep driving if the brakes are going to fail on me.'

Now who's insisting, thought Justin, as his stomach gave a twinge that had nothing to do with peppers, coming as it did after switching his gaze to the hand-addressed envelope from the Great Ormond Street Hospital lying beside his glass of Saint-Émilion Merlot and waiting for him with the rest of the day's post.

Justin steadied himself against the wall. Careful, he thought. Don't let your editor's imagination get the upper hand. But, all the same, play safe.

'I tell you what, mademoiselle.' Perhaps not the best approach, he thought the next second, if she was a mother of three, though this struck him as unlikely. 'Your car is not the only thing that has broken down. Our lift is out of action. So to save you climbing up six flights of stairs, I suggest you give me your Automobile Club membership details and I'll ring the breakdown service from up here.'

It was an idea greeted with prolonged silence. But then Justin fancied that either she was muttering to somebody else or his mind was playing tricks on him. In the absence of a reply, he crossed over to the window again. This time he saw a shapely young woman walk rapidly away from the entrance and out onto the pavement, where she regained her vehicle, started the engine and drove slowly away down the street. If he had waited a minute longer, he would have seen two men in business suits emerge from the same front entrance and walk in the opposite direction to a red Audi parked out of reach of the nearest street lamp. As the Audi moved away from the kerb, its driver pointed the vehicle towards the tail lights of the distant Golf.

Klaus Radetzky had just finished reading Hans Christian Andersen's tale of The Tinder Box to his six-year-old daughter Rosalie, when the front doorbell rang. Knowing that his wife was busy sorting away freshly ironed bed linen, he kissed his daughter on the forehead, wished her sweet dreams, tucked the bed clothes around her, plugged in her friendly night light, retraced his steps softly to the half-open door, stepped into the upstairs hallway and, crying out, 'I'll take it, Gisela,' trotted down to the front door. Probably, he thought, people collecting money for the Red Cross or the local brass band.

After checking through a side window, Klaus opened the door to an attractive young woman, who was clearly not out to collect money. Such people always went around in pairs at night ready to thrust a clipboard at residents, daring them to part company with neighbouring donors.

'I'm sorry to bother you,' she said. 'But something dreadful has happened. I was driving down the road when a deer rushed out of the woods and crashed into the side of my car. The poor creature is lying on its side out there in the road. I think it must have broken its neck. Could you possibly help move it onto the verge? I've got a tow rope. Then I suppose I should ring the Automobile Club.'

As opposed to his daytime excitable self, the relaxed father reacted to the situation with aplomb. 'Rather the fire brigade. Let me get a pair of strong gloves. Have you put out the red warning triangle?'

'No, I forgot. I was too upset.'

'Best to do it as quickly as possible. Don't worry, I'll only be a moment.'

True to his word, Klaus was soon back at the front door, wearing a pair of sturdy gardening gloves and shouting a message up to his wife. 'Won't be a minute, Gisela. There's been an accident. Someone needs help.'

No sooner had he reached the green Golf GTI than the CIA agents posing as Guy Banks and Terry Irving converged on him as if from out of nowhere. It happened so rapidly that all Klaus could remember upon coming to later bound hand and foot to a chair in what he took to be the office of a warehouse or garage repair shop was the fact that, rather than standing by the roadside, the young woman had been sitting behind the wheel, that somebody had seized him in a bear hug from behind and that another person had clamped a damp pungent-smelling cloth over his nose and mouth.

The two unsmiling, self-styled Ukraine ceasefire monitors sat facing him at opposite ends of the base of an equilateral triangle of which he formed the apex and centre of their attention. It took Klaus a while to realise that his arms and legs were immobilised.

'What kind of a bad joke is this?' he said, attempting to shake off the muzziness that threatened to drag him back down into a netherworld.

'No joke, Klaus,' replied Stenning.

'You're no more OSCE officials than I'm Father Christmas.' Klaus could hear himself slurring his words.

'We wish you were, Klaus. We wish you were. You see we need a present or two from you. Give us those and this will be over with before it's started.'

'I don't understand a word you're talking about. Untie me, for Christ's sake. What the hell is going on here?'

'You warned Hendry off us?'

'I did what? You're making no sense.'

Like a juggler catching a club flipped up in the air from his companion a few paces away, Hugh Chamberlain took over from Warren Stenning. 'What have you and Hendry got planned for the next edition of *The Pulse*?'

'Shit, are you both out of your tiny minds? Nothing about Ukraine. More's the pity.'

'And if I was to mention the word two hundred to you?'

The fact that Klaus Radetzky felt like a prisoner under interrogation did not mean that he was unprepared to give as good as he got now that his mind was clearing. 'That's two words.'

'Which tell you what?'

Klaus scowled at the man called Irving. His mouth was dry, both his arms were numb, the flow of blood constricted by the cord securing them to his chest, and he needed to urinate. 'You want your two hundred dollars back? God knows why. I should have charged you jerks five hundred.'

Chamberlain nodded sagely before producing something from his jacket pocket that, to Klaus, looked like a futuristic toy pistol.

'Know what this is, Klaus?'

Sudden understanding struck home. Radetzky was unable to hold back from wetting himself. 'I need to pee. Set me free, damn you.'

'I need to pee. Set me free. Congratulations, Klaus. You're a poet as well as a cartoonist.'

The sub-editor tugged unproductively at his bonds. 'I need the toilet. You want me to shit my pants?'

'Well, let's put it like this, it took us a helluva long time to tie you up that neatly, Klaus. I really don't fancy going through that boy scouts' badge stuff again.'

'Who are you guys?'

'Just answer our questions and you can crap cow pats in the room out back.'

'What questions?'

'Like the one we already put to you.'

'About *The Pulse* or about two hundred?'

'Maybe they go together like a horse and carriage.'

Stenning's imitation of Frank Sinatra went unappreciated by Klaus Radetzky, who abandoned struggling against his restraints only to feel a warm rush of urine filling the fabric over his crotch.

'Jeez, Klaus,' tut-tutted Chamberlain. 'That's gross.'

Radetzky's motor controls failing him completely, the prisoner continued urinating until the last of the liquid running down one trouser leg had pooled onto the rough grey carpet at his feet.

'I'll have to hold my nose when I introduce you to my pain compliance tool –

as the law and order profession call it. Nice, eh? Unless you comply, it causes you pain. Feel like complying, Klaus?'

Despairing of his situation, the man who could have done with Andersen's monstrous tinderbox dogs to extricate him from this surreal situation resorted to shouting for help. When the second of his interrogators called Banks got up to silence him, Klaus used his weight and the thrust of his heels to tip his chair over backwards and bring himself crashing to the floor. It took both men to pull their prisoner upright.

The back of his skull had hit the floor with such force that Radetzky felt surprisingly clear-headed enough to fight back with his tongue.

'You're both crazy. Fuck your two hundred. Keep them.'

The next moment Chamberlain took his colleague off guard by crossing a line which both had agreed was off limits.

He pressed the taser to Radetzky's chest and pulled the trigger. As the full force of the electrical shock hit home, the sub-editor emitted a shrill scream, his body bucking violently against its bonds.

'Comply, you fucking cartoon freak,' demanded Chamberlain, reactivating the weapon thrust against his victim's body. 'Comply.'

Aware that their man had nothing to hide, a seriously worried Warren Stenning grabbed his companion by the arm. 'Leave off, you imbecile.'

But Chamberlain refused to relent. An exasperated Stenning dealt his partner a crippling chop to the kidneys.

By which time it was too late. Klaus Radetzky had suffered cardiac arrest. They had a corpse on their hands.

'You crazy half-wit,' stormed Stenning. 'Couldn't you see? He knew nothing.'

'Perhaps. But he knew about us. How could we let him go?'

'With money. Plenty of it. And an apology. Our bad mistake. Whatever. Not easy after you did a Guantanamo on him.'

'God, he stinks. He really has crapped himself.'

'What do you expect? You fucking killed him. Systems shutdown. In common with your dumb brain.'

Hugh Chamberlain stared down at the hand holding the taser in a fruitless bid to transfer blame onto its manufacturers. 'What do we do now?'

'Make it look like an accident. No, that won't work. Suicide.'

'How?' The blank expression on Chamberlain's face was a barometer of mental confusion.

'Chuck him over one of the city bridges.'

If the clouds seemed to lift from the back of Chamberlain's mind, it was only temporarily. 'Which?'

'Well, what do you think, Hugh? The one plumb in the middle of town?'

Out of his depth but reluctant to admit as much, a sickly Hugh Camberlain tucked the taser back into his pocket. 'Okay, Mr smart ass. I've got the message. My foul-up. How was I to know the guy had a weak ticker?'

Not for the first time Stenning reflected that having this oaf foisted on him was the cross he had to bear for a honey trap two years before in Tel Aviv. Unable to rein back on his frustration, he resorted to spelling matters out. 'You're missing the point, Hugh. This isn't shock and awe territory. There's no such thing as the Assembly of Two Hundred. It's the product of warped minds, remember? Meaning we're expected to go about things differently than we would if we were dealing with WMD merchants or lunatic jihadists.'

With more than a glimmering of understanding of the enormity of his actions, Hugh Chamberlain bowed his head. 'I suppose we'd better clear up here.'

'No, Hugh. Leave that to me. We need to lug him into the back of the Audi. There's a tarpaulin downstairs on a rack at the back of the garage. Fetch it and we'll wrap him in that. Then we'll drive out to the supermarket behind the Exhibition Centre and hope to find a dumped trolley.'

'We'll never get it inside the trunk.'

'Yes we will, on its side. Fold down the back seats. We'll drive down to the Blue Bridge, park on the slip road and wheel our tarped bundle over to the bridge.'

'Now who's crazy?' said Chamberlain, fortified by the thought of being able to turn the tables on his not so bright master. 'They've installed plexiglass safety barriers the length of the bridge. There's no way we can toss him over without giving ourselves a hernia. And we try to do this in front of cyclists, joggers, traffic travelling in and out of town? Somebody's bound to get out his cell and alert the police. They'll catch us before we get back to the Audi.'

'I wasn't planning on doing it right now, Hugh. More like three o'clock in the morning, when traffic's at a minimum. And we don't need to trolley our friend all the way to the middle of the bridge, do we? As for the plexiglass, I'll stand in the trolley, haul him up and push him over while you hold on to things so that we avoid doing a Harold Lloyd.'

'What about cameras? Aren't they everywhere nowadays? They'll capture us taking onboard the trolley, loading it and then shoving our bundle over.'

'This is Luritania, Hugh. Sleepytown. The odd lens snapping red light runners. No cameras where I'm expecting to pick up a trolley. And as for the bridge, none there after they installed that plexiglass.'

'What's the owner of this place going to think when he discovers someone has snuck in here and pissed on his carpet?'

'I'll try soap and water on it. If he still notices anything, he'll likely as not think it was some animal. I doubt he'll see straightaway that the tarp is gone. Not when his high value equipment is left untouched.'

'A good job we parked the Audi inside.'

'Hugh, I try to think of everything, but I'm only human. That's where I wish I could look to you. Picking up on things I might forget. Which reminds me. What do you think we should search our man for?'

'The two hundred dollars?'

'That and what else?'

'His ID?'

'I don't think so, Hugh. Perhaps our business card?'

'Oh, sure. Yes, I forgot.'

'Your job then to go through his pockets. With gloves on.'

'Do I have to? He stinks to high heaven.'

'Whose fault is that?'

Despite a thorough search of Klaus Radetzky's wallet and few other belongings in various pockets, Hugh Chamberlain came up empty-handed.

'Not good,' said Stenning, forced to admit that his Blue Bridge plans now looked as if they had more holes in them than a double colander. 'But I don't see how we can leave him here without bringing the police down on us.'

In the early hours of the next morning, Warren Stenning stopped the Audi short of the intersection with the semi-motorway taking traffic over the Blue Bridge towards town and the Frisian Islands on the one side and from town towards Andorra and Vaduz on the other. After parking the car out of view on a hard gravel bed behind a temporary worksite hoarding and opening the trunk, he got his partner to help remove an empty supermarket trolley and a large bundle, which Chamberlain was obliged to untie in order to bend Radetzky's knees up to his chest, a task made none the easier by rigor mortis, before rewrapping and resecuring the corpse so that it could be made to fit inside the trolley.

As they neared the Blue Bridge, so named because it had been built under the stewardship of Luritania's Christian Democrat Party back in the early 1950s, Stenning realised not only that his idea of lifting the body out of the trolley was flawed – he would never be able to do this on his own while standing in the shopping cart, itself a difficult feat in cramped conditions alongside the corpse – but that, as his partner had said, the amount of effort required to haul a body weighing seventy kilos over the curved plexiglass barrier was more than anyone could manage. He therefore instructed Chamberlain to push the trolley back towards where they had left the Audi, while he went ahead to reconnoitre the land giving onto the gorge on the bridge's airport side. Following the path running along a low stone wall which curved around the edge of the gorge, Stenning was soon out of sight of the road with his right side fully covered by a wooded area. Advancing further, he came across a semi-circular observation platform equipped with a telescope and a chest-high granite slab showing compass points and distances to Paris, London, New York, Beijing and Sydney. Ideal, he thought.

After rejoining Chamberlain who, he was glad to see, had had the sense to seek cover under the trees fronting the gorge's wooded slopes, Stenning explained that their task promised to be easier than anticipated. However, in wheeling the trolley out from the edge of the wood, Chamberlain tripped, all but twisting an ankle, and let the cart slip from his grasp on an incline. The load factor obeying the law of gravity, the trolley began rolling towards the roadside. Obliged to hare in pursuit, Stenning caught up with the cart sideways on and thrust out a braking foot in front of the rear wheels. Deflected from its course, the trolley struck a mound of earth, wobbled, keeled over and spilled the lifeless Radetzky, bundled in his tarpaulin, to the ground.

'Hugh,' shouted Stenning, alarmed that so far not one vehicle had passed by on the roadway. It could not continue like that for much longer. At this time of night, security firms were called out to investigate burglar alarms, the police to cover break-ins, brawls or drunk-driving road accidents, ambulances to ferry geriatrics to the mortuary. 'Get over here double quick and help me put our man back in his wheelchair.'

But they were in luck. Although it cost them no little time and exertion to raise the body back into the shopping cart while keeping this stationary, not a single siren assailed their ears with its banshee wail, no Polish HGVs thundered past them nor were they disturbed by any transcontinental coaches with attentive front-seat guides and drivers.

By the time they reached the observation point the night sky's thin cloud cover had disappeared, revealing the northern star and a number of constellations. Stenning pointed one out to his colleague. 'See those seven stars up there? The Big Dipper. Well, Klaus is in for a different kind of ride. So let's get this over with.'

Hoisting Radetzky out of the cart proved more cumbersome than lifting him in. But Stenning had wedged two large stones against the trolley's front and rear wheels, which meant one problem less.

'We need to straighten him out,' said Stenning, as they laid their bundle on the ground. 'Easier for us to chuck him over.'

Hugh Chamberlain laboured with the unconventional knots tied by him around the tarpaulin. But, finally, the body was uncovered and its limbs unfolded, giving Chamberlain a stark reminder, if one was needed, of the price of his hot-headedness.

With Stenning holding Radetzky's corpse by the arms and Chamberlain holding the feet, both men stood poised – catching their breath and, despite the cool night air, sweating – on the edge of the observation platform.

'Okay,' said Stenning. 'Ready?'

'Yup.'

'Keep a tight hold of him. We swing him three times. Stronger each time. The third swing super strong. Because we want this baby to dive through the air like an eagle swooping down on a field mouse.'

Chamberlain concealed his impatience: first, stars, now an eagle. Perhaps Stenning belonged up there on a different planet. 'I'm with you,' he said. 'On the third swing we let go.'

But on the second swing, Chamberlain called a halt. 'Shit, Warren, can we move further back? This damn wall is too low. I don't want to copy the cartoonist.'

The taller and stronger of the two, Stenning laughed, relaxed his grip, shuffled his feet and took a couple of steps away from the wall. 'This far then.'

Chamberlain sidled back in line with Stenning, his chest heaving asthmatically, sweat pouring down his face. 'I'm out of breath. Give me a second.' Though he would have given anything to be rid of his burden there and then, Chamberlain feared that he did not have the energy for the final heave.

Stenning controlled his impatience. 'Take your time. Let's do it properly.'

The next moment, the sound of rustling in the undergrowth behind them caused both men to spin around. Standing a mere five yards away on the fringe of the woods was an adult deer, ears erect under fully grown antlers, eyeing them fixedly.

It was hard to tell who was the more rooted to the spot, man or beast, but as the deer continued to hold its ground, Hugh Chamberlain panicked and let go of the corpse's legs. It was enough to make the deer turn and bolt back into the woods.

'They're vegetarian, Hugh,' said Stenning. 'More frightened of us, unless there are any young around to protect. But I guess not. So pick those legs up before he or she brings back reinforcements.'

'You think …?'

'That was meant to be a joke, Hugh. Let's be done with it.'

Although the third swing had more heft behind it than the first and second, Chamberlain's end lacked the muscle power to ensure that the corpse was cast far out into the void. Hastening to the rim, Stenning gazed down into the gorge below.

'Can't see a thing. No idea where he's landed or if he hit anything on the way down. I checked to be sure there were no trees growing out of the side, so I hope he made it all the way to the bottom.

A panting Chamberlain joined him at the edge and rested both palms against the granite orientation slab. 'What's down there?'

'Try breathing through your nose, Hugh. You look like a damn fish out of water.'

'What's down there?'

'I heard you the first time. Houses, gardens, streets, allotments, the Leiseflösschen, a rivulet foreigners call The Dribble. It's too far over for him to have landed in that. My guess is either he's on somebody's roof or he's spoiled their prize zucchini.'

Chamberlain heaved himself upright and dabbed his forehead with a handkerchief. 'Can we go now? This place gives me the creeps.'

'But the best of it, Hugh, is that we're invisible. And only somebody as familiar with the city as our cartoonist would know about this scenic observation point which the authorities didn't have the resources or the inclination to make safer than it is.'

'What do we do about the trolley?'

'We can't leave it here.'

Chamberlain rubbed tired eyes. 'I suppose not. Push it out of sight into the woods?'

'No, Hugh. We wipe it clean and take it back where we found it. You can wheel it to the Audi, while I take some dead wood and wipe out the tracks we've made.'

'And the tarp?'

'Maybe we can leave that here. I'll toss it behind a stand of trees.'

'Watch out for the deer.'

'If there was one thing that failed to make an impression on Warren Stenning, it was a clumsy attempt by the likes of Hugh Chamberlain to give him a taste of his own medicine.

'Good advice. I'll try not to let them think I'm a rutting buck.'

Memo from K to J

With the opposition's media presence on the western front thinner than Salome's seventh veil, our propaganda machine is enjoying a field day. Sheer nonsense to suggest that Urodina is dishonouring the truce agreed with the Nevskian leadership, the Invigilator, the Dutchman and Amchuk (the man who makes Dick Nonix look like John the Baptist). The more so when our lackeys monitoring the conflict attribute nine out of ten ceasefire violations to the rebels. By now, there can be no mistaking the bad and the ugly in this drama. That, my friend, allied with systematically outlawing use of the label 'separatists' in referring to the ragtag and bobtail rebels, is the beauty of propaganda.

Response from J

I view the dearth of counter-propaganda differently. Aware that the Nevskian leadership would rather wash its hands of Urodina's Stalino and Voroshilovgrad rebel movement, oligarchs on both sides have colluded to sap rebel morale by systematically assassinating the breakaway movement's top brass.

Response from K

The fact of the matter is that Nevskians and Urodinians, irrespective of colour, stripes or ethnic origin, are of secondary importance compared to their territory. Let them stew in their own juice provided they do our bidding.

The news of Klaus Radetzky's death cast a pall of gloom over the Lenfindi Club's Sunday breakfast meeting.

Tich thrust aside one of the regional French newspapers taken from the pile on a seat at a nearby table.

'The fellow who wrote this needs his head examined for suggesting Ukrainian extremists were waiting in the wings to torch Klaus's home unless he paid for that cartoon with his life.'

'Right,' said Rashid. 'Heaven help us if people are beginning to put Poroshenko on the same footing as the prophet Muhammad.'

'But if this clearly was a case of murder,' said Isabelle, 'then perhaps Ukrainians are behind Klaus's death. Look, Klaus wasn't suddenly overcome by a dizzy spell.

In more senses than one. Firstly, in walking out on his young wife and daughter in the middle of the evening to travel – goodness knows how – all the way out to the Blue Bridge – a good four miles from home. Secondly, in losing his balance while gazing up at the pole star on that observation point. So why aren't the police getting off their backsides and treating this as homicide?'

'They are, believe me,' said Justin. 'Tich's newspaper is taking a tasteless sideswipe against the *Bote's* policy of turning a blind eye to the fact that people used to jump off the Blue bridge like lemmings. What can you expect from a journal in a god-fearing Roman Catholic country where suicide is as taboo as the priesthood's pederasty? Suicides get dressed up as death by natural causes.'

'You're saying,' said Vanessa, 'that after somebody leaps three hundred feet into the Leiseflösschen, the only way for him to qualify for an obit is for his nearest and dearest to tell the press he must have been pissed out of his mind?'

Tich pursed his lips. 'Only you could have put it so delicately, Van.'

'Well,' said Craig, 'that is about the size of it.'

'My fault,' said Justin. 'I got carried away just as I was about to explain that the police are treating Klaus's death seriously. Signs of postmortem lividity suggest Klaus was dead before he ended up in the gorge. After talking to his wife, the police are sure Klaus was abducted that night, perhaps tortured, then dumped into the valley in the early hours of the morning.'

'By angry Ukrainians?'

'Ridiculous, I know. But, apparently, that's the theory they're pursuing.'

Isabelle looked up from scraping the sugar icing from the top of her raisin-studded pastry 'My father says the situation in Ukraine is grossly misreported. There are no regular Russian army troops in eastern Ukraine. Volunteers, yes. Just as you'd expect if your sympathies lay with fellow Russians combatting fascism. It's a battle of Ukrainians against Ukrainians not Ukrainians against Russians. But it suits America and NATO to shout from the rooftops that Russia is the aggressor. If you ask the average Russian inhabitant of Donbass what he thinks of Putin, he'll tell you that Putin has betrayed the people of Donbass. On the one hand, the Russian leader crows on about his victorious annexation of Crimea in a bloodless coup, and, on the other, he turns his back on the daily slaughter of his compatriots across the border in Ukraine. Why? Because the Kremlin's oligarchs are hand in glove with Kiev's oligarchs and don't want to upset the west. And the OSCE plays a duplicitous game of fake neutrality. At one stage, its monitors were headed by a Canadian whose Ukrainian antecedents made the men under him as unbiased as a hanging judge.'

'Your father,' said Vanessa, 'pours state secrets into your ears as if they were common knowledge?'

'On the contrary. There's nothing secret about them. It's a question of targeting the right web news sites with the right search engines.'

Justin interrupted his scanning of the *Luritanische Bote's* many obituary pages. Klaus used to refer to these as the *Hammer Horror* supplement. In other words, the *Bote* was the last paper that Gisela Radetzky would choose for announcing her husband's funeral arrangements.

'The OSCE connection you just mentioned, Isabelle, is interesting. One of the first calls I made after learning about Klaus's death was a visit to his wife, Gisela. She told me that when she looked through her husband's desk drawers for a credit card he had borrowed from her the day before, she came across two one hundred dollar bills and a business card in the name of an OSCE mission officer called Guy Banks. Gisela had no idea what the bills or the card were doing there.'

'You're assuming they're related?' said Tich.

'I'm assuming nothing other than that it sounds fishy. Why did Klaus mention neither to his wife? Because he had only just come by them?'

'Or,' suggested Vanessa, 'because they'd been there some time and he was keeping them secret.'

'It's possible. But why?'

Rashid held up his iPhone to show the results of a Dogpile search on the OSCE's monitoring mission in Ukraine. 'According to this, most of the time the OSCE's monitors are incapable of telling who's firing at whom, partly because the separatists make life difficult for them and partly because the Ukrainian army tells them there are too many of its landmines around for it to be safe for them to venture out. In other words, lame ducks more likely to sympathise with a prospective NATO member than with its opponents.'

Tich shifted his considerable weight in a chair fashioned for lighter individuals. 'Did Klaus mention having been contacted by the OSCE since publication of that cartoon?'

'Did he heck? And he would have. Of that I'm sure.'

'So we and the police are assuming that somebody from the OSCE paid your sub-editor two hundred dollars before luring him away from his home in order to chuck him over the Blue Bridge. Why the two hundred bucks?'

'A bait?' suggested Craig.

'I haven't told you the full story,' said Justin. 'At least, not how I have come to view things since a certain note arrived in my mail box.'

Unzipping a slim document case, he removed a business envelope from one of the case's many pockets and leant it against the coffee pot in the middle of the table. 'Last week Tich was educating us about the word gosh. What I have here is a gem of a different water. The GOSH that stands for Great Ormond Street Hospital. Those of you who keep abreast of the news back home may have read about the death from meningitis of Stuart Musgrave, the only child of Margaret Musgrave, an intellectual property and business lawyer, and Peregrine Worsthorne Musgrave, Member of Parliament for Chelsea, Hammersmith and Fulham. Stuart was being treated in London's premier children's hospital. The envelope is postmarked Fulham.' Justin paused to take breath and coffee.

'Why,' asked Tich, 'would Musgrave be writing to you so soon after the death of his son?'

'The letter, if you can call it that, because it's only a brief typewritten note, is unsigned. The accompanying and more important enclosure purportedly contains the decryption key to the second of our documents found in that red leather Milan

212

briefcase. It would appear that Musgrave who, preferring to remain anonymous, advised me to destroy his first note and its envelope, experienced a change of heart and loyalties following the loss of his nine-year-old son. I'm faced with an open invitation to publish and be damned.'

'Assuming,' said Rashid, 'that you know how to use the decryption cipher to uncover the meaning of that second document. As I recall that was an ADFGVX cypher text. One awful headache to decrypt. Have you looked at the key?'

'No, it's in here.' Justin handed over the small rectangular slip resembling a PIN communicator. 'Go ahead. You're welcome.'

Rashid tore along the perforated edges, unfolded the slip and looked at the six letters of the alphabet printed dead centre in capital letters. 'This certainly seems to be the key. I could have a go at decoding, but I can't guarantee anything. We'd be better off looking for an expert code hacker. Whoever compiled the text used a transposition cypher. To crack that you need to carry out frequency analyses. This is no piece of cake, I assure you.'

'Wait a minute,' said Craig. 'Do we really want to go ahead with this, Justin? I mean, sticking our necks out even further?'

Justin spoke with feeling. 'Well, I should bloody well say I do. The bastards who killed Klaus weren't Ukrainians. They've probably got next to nothing to do with that mess. They're into something bigger. And we need to expose them.'

Vanessa was unconvinced. 'How can you be so sure that Klaus's death is connected to the red briefcase?'

'Call it a feeling in the bones, if you will. And I've told you only half the story. On the night that Klaus was abducted – it can only have been that – a woman rang his front doorbell to tell him there had been an accident in the road outside. He went to lend a helping hand, and that was the last that Gisela and his daughter, Rosalie, saw of him. Less than an hour before this, a woman called up to my apartment from the downstairs front entrance to say that her car had broken down and that she needed assistance. I was eating at the time – it must have been around a quarter to eight – and so the only helping hand I felt like offering was to ring the Automobile Club's breakdown service, because she was without her cell phone. I guessed she wanted me to come down to investigate what was wrong. Instead, I suggested she go back to the car to check a few things out. She agreed reluctantly, so I decided to take a peep at her from my window. But there was no sign of movement out front. I waited. Still nothing. After a couple of minutes, she called back up to say she'd acted on my recommendation. That was enough for me to give her short shrift. Only then did I see her move away, climb into a green VW and drive off.'

Tich nodded. 'These people were after you, but when they couldn't get what they wanted they went for second best, thinking that you would have confided in Klaus.'

'And,' added Rashid, 'the fact that they murdered him says they could not afford to be identified had they set him free. They're still out there somewhere.'

'Yes, and there's more to this. The morning following Klaus's death, my secretary, Chantelle, told me that a stranger with an American accent had phoned her at the office the day before enquiring about my home telephone number and address. Made out he was an old university chum, but didn't leave any name. I never had any American friends at Durham.'

Justin cast hurt glances around the rest of the group. 'You can guess how I feel now, can't you? I should never have given into the temptation of stealing that briefcase. Klaus has paid the price for my stupidity. And what if his insurance company doesn't pay out on suicides? The moment the investigators get a whiff of that newspaper report, Gisela Radetzky might as well say goodbye to compensation.'

'Surely,' said Isabelle, 'not if the coroner gave the police to believe that your colleague was already dead before he was found at the bottom of the gorge?'

'Let's hope, you're right. Two police officers, an inspector and his assistant, came around to the office to question me about Klaus's mental health following the graffiti protests about the Ukraine cartoon. Asked if I thought the balance of his mind might be disturbed. I told them it was hard to imagine anyone less likely to suffer a nervous breakdown over something like that than our sub-editor. Yes, at first he was upset that he'd turned the spotlight on our publishing house for all the wrong reasons. Luritania's conservative press moghuls were having a field day at our expense. But that was short-lived, because, before we knew what had hit us, we were bombarded with sympathetic tweets, phone calls and emails. And Gisela confirmed that there were no financial worries or family problems that could have caused her husband to take his own life.'

Justin covered his face in his hands. 'The poor woman. Married for eight years with a devoted husband and loving daughter. Suddenly, for no apparent reason, Klaus is snatched away from them both and murdered. Christ, how guilty I felt facing her. She had decided that the Ukrainians were behind this.'

After a lengthy pause, Justin looked up and threw a helpless glace at Vanessa. 'She works in a travel agency selling package holidays to well-heeled Luritanians who can't do without their winter injection of Tenerife or Antalya sunshine. It can't pay that well, her job. And Klaus was too young to have built up much by way of a pension, so she'll probably get peanuts, if anything at all, from the state, and a miserable excuse for a pay-out from his private pension fund managers. Mind you, one thing to be thankful for, our owner has come forward with a generous up-front compensatory payment in recognition of Klaus's contribution to the success of his publications.'

Isabelle looked interested. 'Might I ask the names of your inspector and his sidekick?'

'Of course. A grizzled guy, thin and sharp as a pencil, called Georg Hoffarth and his young assistant, sergeant Claude-Henri Weiland. Why do you ask?

'A feeling, which you've just borne out. Those happen to be the same two officers who visited my BLR branch to question us about the bank theft. It seems they also cover major league homicide.'

'What did you think of them?'

Isabelle exchanged glances with Craig and Tich. In two minds as to whether to arrogate the right to divulge a secret which was not hers alone to reveal, she opted for discretion. 'Efficient but, with Luritania's police force thin on the ground, lacking the back-up to pull out all the stops. It makes me doubt whether they'll get far investigating Klaus's death.'

'Gisela told them about the Ukraine monitoring mission card and the two hundred dollars. Hoffarth suggested that Klaus might have been bribed. She refused to accept that possibility. They're following up the OSCE lead.'

'And,' said Craig, 'you intend to go ahead and publish something that accuses a nebulous supranational committee of murdering Klaus Radetzky, because it thought he knew too much about their covert plans for dismembering the Russian Federation, gobbling up Siberia and sterilising half the population of sub-Saharan Africa? That's hardly going to have the world's media beating a path to your door. Shouldn't we wait until Rashid has decrypted the meaty stuff?'

'I agree,' said Tich. 'Although I was all for publishing last time, I think that Klaus's death has put a different complexion on things. We need stronger ammunition than we've got at the moment. What we have is too wild and woolly.' He held up a restraining hand. 'No, no, wait. I understand you want to atone for this tragedy. Publishing in haste is never a good idea. And it's not going to bring Klaus back, is it? You said he was impetuous, but I believe that if he could shout across at you from the grave …'

'He's not been buried yet. The funeral's on Tuesday. I'll be there together with Chantalle, our setters, the owner …'

'Fine, but if Klaus were here now, I bet he'd tell you to hold fire until you have something that can rock these buggers' boat.'

Justin was staring into empty space with glazed eyes. 'I suppose you're right. I'm in a hurry to correct a wrong that's past correction. I don't suppose the land-swallowing story would shake many rafters. But the sterilisation scandal surely would.'

Having undergone a change of mind, Isabelle looked across at Tich and Craig. 'About Gisela Radetzky, what do you think?'

All three had agreed that sooner or later they would have to make a clean breast of things in front of Justin, Vanessa and Rashid. Craig was the first to respond.

'I think, yes.'

'Tich?'

'If ever there was a deserving cause, this has to be it.'

Thus a subdued Isabelle Meunier, taking due care to lower her voice so that only three pairs of secular ears heard her confession, explained how she had robbed BLR Paribas of more than four million euros in used banknotes with the assistance of her two partners in crime, Craig Roberts and Humphrey Hobart. While the other half of the Sunday morning group greeted her announcement with a mixture of wide-eyed disbelief and open-mouthed amazement, she went on to describe her environmental and other motives, Tich's journey across the border to open an account with the China Reconstruction Bank and, finally, how a certain avaricious deputy manager had been hoisted with his own petard.

'Therefore,' she concluded, 'if Tich and Craig agree, I propose that we draw on these funds to make an appropriate donation to Gisela Radetzky.'

'And how,' asked a now only slightly less than dumbfounded Vanessa Curtis, 'would you manage that without arousing the suspicions of her bank?'

'No problem,' volunteered Rashid. 'I could set up a legitimate offshore account fed by a generous fundraising event in support of a fatherless child and her mother widowed after the murder of her husband.'

'Well,' said Justin, taken aback by discovering how little he knew about the workings of Tich and Craig's minds, 'You do realise, I suppose, that you've made us accomplices after the fact?'

'Technically, you're right, of course,' said Tich. 'But since none of you banks with BLR, lays claim to a share in our illicit proceeds or has understood, let alone remembered, a word of what Isabelle just said, I think that argument is purely academic.'

Isabelle summoned a weak smile. 'And I thought you agreed, Justin, that we had already burnt our boats in siding with you over the briefcase.'

Feeling that he had had his fill of bad news for one morning, Justin got to his feet. 'Wait a minute,' he said. 'I won't be long.'

True to his word, he was back in next to no time, holding two small bottles of cognac which he proceeded to unscrew.

'I don't know about the rest of you,' he said, pouring short measures into each of his friend's coffee cups, before adding the last of the brandy to his own, 'Vanessa and Rashid, in particular – but I need this like the hair of the dog that bit me.'

Vanessa raised her glass. 'Tich, Craig, don't believe for one minute that I approve of what I thought I heard Isabelle say a moment ago. But the three of you appear to have dragged the rest of us into Dumas territory. Decision time. What do you say, Justin and Rashid? Do we tell these malefactors to get lost or is it *One for all and all for one?*'

Seconds later, Justin, Rashid and Vanessa were not only accomplices after the fact but confederates sworn to exposing the people behind Radetzky's murder.

Any stirrings of guilt outweighed by satisfaction at the success of her fishing expedition, an emboldened, Isabelle Meunier, the last to chink cups, declared loudly enough for those at neighbouring tables to hear: *Un pour tous, tous pour un.*

As far as Peregrine Musgrave was concerned, J could not have chosen a worse time to call for a meeting. The Westminster MP had mistakenly thought that immersing himself in his constituents' concerns might assuage his grief but as most of these concerns were petty, Musgrave soon lost patience with his petitioners and their gripes. It helped that his male factotum was expert at addressing written or e-mailed complaints so as to give the impression that these issues were under serious consideration by a man who refused to cite his dual portfolio as an excuse for laxity. But even when he managed to escape from the drudgery of constituency work, it took little to upset Peregrine. What particularly angered him was the lack of expressions of sympathy for his loss. The stony-faced Chairman of the Members Estimate Audit Committee, for example, bumped into in White's had shown no sign of understanding with his sullen harping on about undocumented expenses. Loath to concede that some might feel embarrassed in his presence, their own inexperience of death rendering them inept in the face of another man's loss, Musgrave took immediate objection to this mandarin's insensitivity.

And now J had resurfaced like a festering wound in need of lancing. What the MI6 man could have wanted at this stage defeated Musgrave. He had called for a meeting in Harrods. But with a difference this time, the venue CH rather than LD, meaning luncheon at the Caviar House Oyster Bar. When Peregrine turned up at twelve thirty, he found J seated near the wall at one end of the counter, where both men stood to be shielded from passers-by and busy-bodies. The MP eased himself onto the vacant stool in front of the reserved sign, found a purchase for his feet on the rail below and accepted the waiter's offer of champagne.

The older man raised his own glass by way of modest salutation. 'Nothing to toast, I regret to say.'

'No,' agreed Musgrave, allowing the ice cold Taittinger to freshen his palate. In the past, he had tended to exaggerate J's glacial side, all too often forgetting the veteran's mental scars. Yet this same battle-hardened Secret Service agent had touched Peregrine with his thoughtfulness in sending a wreath of bright blossoms (sunflowers, daffodils, yellow roses and tulips) to the funeral home. It had been necessary to improvise when Margaret had asked who had added the simple signature J under his or her condolences.

But today, J, for his part, seated cheek by jowl with the Westminster MP, was struck by the drastic change in Musgrave's appearance: haggard and hollowed out with stress lines around eyes and mouth, the bereaved father resembled a cadaver ready to be measured for its coffin. Deciding that the spoken word, however banal the utterance, meant more to Musgrave under these circumstances than silence, he placed his champagne flute on the counter and accepted the menu handed across by the waiter to the unseeing Peregrine.

'Something deeply wrong about the young losing out in life's lottery before they've hardly got started.'

'A senseless accident,' said Musgrave, staring vacantly at the peacock wall mural behind J's shoulder. Margaret and he had finally accepted the headmaster's assurances – all the more so when borne out by Stuart's school friend – that horseplay rather than malice aforethought explained the shove that had sent their son crashing into the playground wall. The boy responsible for this tomfoolery had accompanied his father to the Musgrave's house to offer a contrite apology.

J knew something about accidents. Such as when the crew of a Canadian helicopter gunship high on amphetamines had mistaken for the enemy a patrol led by him to flush Taliban insurgents out of Marjah, mowed down eight of his best men and put three others, including himself, in hospital. That shabby euphemism 'friendly fire' had put an end to his days on the front line.

A ruddy-faced waiter, who put Musgrave in mind of the lead member of a barbershop quartet, beamed down at his two customers from across the counter. 'What can I get you gentlemen to eat? Today's *fines de Claire* are particularly *fine*.'

'Complete with pearl?'

Musgrave was hard put to remember when he had last heard J crack a joke. It made him wonder what was up.

Sensing his companion's bemusement, J wagged a reproachful finger at the waiter. 'My friend doesn't know this, but last time I was served *fines de Claire* by Jules, a customer further down the counter came across a pearl. It was amusing to see the number of hands that went up to order more of the same, but less amusing when Jules returned from the kitchen to report that, sad to say, they had run out of these beauties. Shame on you, Jules. How many did you find?'

The waiter imitated disbelief by throwing innocent hands out wide. 'My dear sir, that was a red letter day for but one person.'

'Very well, give me half a dozen. What are you having Peregrine? I can recommend the soup.'

The MP finished scanning the menu card for the third time without having taken in more than a handful of words. His focus shifted to a man lower down the counter, with a napkin tucked into his collar to prevent soiling shirt and tie, sedulously buttering a slice of bread before dipping a large peeled prawn into a dish of sauce. 'I think I'll take the jumbo Madagascan tiger prawns.'

The matter of ordering their food dispensed with, the two men began discussing the latest international news. J pointed to an article on the inside front page of his newspaper reporting on the situation in Ukraine.

'Have you seen anything more pathetic than this, Peregrine? Ukraine's leader, plastered out of his mind while doing the rounds of the war wounded in a Kiev hospital makes a gift of a football to a soldier who has lost both legs. It is with such leaders in need of Dutch courage that we forge alliances. They don't have to be educated enough to know the difference between Janus and Perseus or civilised enough to appreciate that routinely torturing their opponents wins them few friends. All that is required of them is to do our will. And they do so, because we line their pockets. Who, I ask, is the more reprehensible: the vassal or his overlord?'

As this was the first time Musgrave had heard J slate the very policy he was instrumental in implementing, the MP put the momentary testiness down to *ennui* rather than to a profound change of heart.

But the next moment, when J welcomed the arrival of his oysters and his companion's tiger prawns with an enthusiastic smack of his lips, Peregrine decided that the Vauxhall Cross recruit had been modelling himself on Janus.

'Are you sure, Peregrine, I can't tempt you with one of these magnificent *fines*?'

'Thanks, I've never been a great lover of them.' Musgrave had stopped short of saying that he thought oysters in general overrated. To start with, you didn't eat so much as swallow the things. Then there was the myth about their being an aphrodisiac. Perhaps thought to symbolise the riches awaiting devourment from that most intimate of caverns. No doubt the taste of brine went to some people's head like the salty tang of sweat.

Seeing no need for the bib solution, Peregrine let the napkin reside where it was meant to: on his lap. He started in on the jumbo prawns. Sooner or later, he told himself, J would get to the point of this meeting. Carroll's Walrus would take possession of him.

J squeezed lemon onto three oysters and began delicately buttering the thin scallops of toasted brown bread, a smile playing around his lips.

'That would have made a good cartoon,' he said.

'Not sure I follow you,' replied Peregrine, despairing of the mindreading expected of him. J's unpredictability made the man a living conundrum.

'The hospital football.'

'For those who like black humour.'

'I fancy it would have appealed to *The Pulse's* cartoonist, had he lived to draw it.'

Musgrave swallowed prawn and incomprehension. 'What?'

'Suicide. The response to that Ukrainian cartoon of his tipped him over the edge, literally.'

The MP set down his fork and dabbed his lips. 'That doesn't make any sense. Cartoonists are used to brickbats. And from what I understand, the fellow was thick skinned.'

'So there must have been other factors at work than spitting at the spittoon.' J turned to face his companion. 'You don't understand what I'm talking about?'

'No.'

'My apologies. Why should you?' J finished munching on a slice of toast. 'The Ukrainian president's real name is Valtsman. He and half his henchmen are Jews who changed their names to hide their origins. The president's choice of surname was most unfortunate. It has made the man the butt of Russian spittle bucket jokes.'

'How did you learn about this suicide?'

'We have people on the spot. But it was on the Net. A passing mention, mind you.'

'Hard to believe.'

'Not as bad as other news from the same quarter.' J's eyes were fixed on the aquarium by the wall across from the counter. 'Such a lengthy lead time between laying bait and reeling in the catch.'

More riddles, but this time Peregrine Musgrave sensed all was far from well. He followed J's gaze. Didn't sharks behave similarly? Circling their prey before homing in.

'Somebody out there in Luritania has been trying to decode our second paper with the decryption cypher.'

One of Musgrave's shoes lost its toehold on the smooth metal footrest. An observer might have been excused for mistaking the pallor in the already wan face for that of a wraith.

219

J switched his eyes from the fish tank to his companion, whose lips looked singularly bloodless. The MI6 man wondered how an MP as thin-lipped as Musgrave managed to win people over from the hustings.

'Worry not, Peregrine. He'll get nowhere. Someone slipped up in passing you the wrong cypher.'

No, thought, Musgrave, it was deliberate. They were testing my loyalty to their worthless cause.

'How did you find out?' By which the MP was referring, as he was sure J understood, not to the source of the leak but to remote processing of the cypher.

'Lady luck played in our favour. The laptop used to work on the code was purchased in Washington State, Seattle, only a year ago. The retailer followed Patriot Act instructions. Only certain models were sold to people of Middle Eastern extraction, models capable of flashing warning lights to us the moment something as sensitive as this was uploaded. The purchaser was Lebanese. He's currently working for the MEDRIMCOMB in Luritania. A computer-savvy friend, I take it, of Mr Hendry's.'

Musgrave opened and closed a fist as weak as his mind on its grasp of things. But the shark was not baring its teeth. J pushed aside a fourth empty shell, motioned the waiter for more Taittinger in both glasses and sat back from the counter to rid his lungs of the strong perfume wafted his way by a tarty-looking woman with a cobra tattooed below her neckline.

'I can understand how you acted as you did. Life has been, how shall I put it, excessively unkind to you and Margaret.' Musgrave could not recall the last time when J had referred to Margaret by name. 'For want of a better scapegoat, you lashed out at us. Disaffection. I forgive and sympathise with you. Believe me, I do.' J paused. Aware that he could not soften the blow, he inclined his head backwards and regarded the nearest orb light suspended from the ceiling by a pyramid of golden wires. 'My superiors told me they can't afford a weak link in the chain. I told them to look elsewhere. Not my style, Peregrine.'

After finding solace in the Château de la Marquetterie's white Chardonnay champagne, the veteran used to advising others to look out for their own backs refused to admit to feeling as if he were under observation.

'But if the cypher was the wrong one?' Musgrave felt as if his fist was closing on straws.

'That overdone justification for all manner of ills. A matter of principle.'

Feebleness being a quality he despised in others, it went against the grain for the MP to have to admit to this failing with what amounted to an entreaty. 'What should I do, J?'

'Well, now that I've given you advance notice, you could, of course, go public and do the Lebanese's work for him. But I fear that would rebound on Margaret. Would you want that? No, of course not. You could both pack up and set sail for the horizon. Other couples less scrupulous might fake the husband's disappearance overboard and hope to collect the life insurance. I really don't know what to say to you.'

Musgrave switched from thoughts of self-preservation to the well-being of the man he had come to think of as puppet master.

'How can you be sure you weren't followed here? That we're not both being watched right now?'

'I left a message for my secretary telling her I was taking a stroll through the gardens. And we never meet in Harrods on a Tuesday.'

'They'll not forgive you for refusing to …' Musgrave waved an empty fork in the air by way of his own cypher for the fate of a man on death row. 'Why should you have to foot the bill for an oversight brought about by *force majeure*?'

'My dear Peregrine, don't trouble yourself about me. I can take care of myself. Some red lines they cannot afford to cross. I know, better still, understand too much for them to chance their arm against me. '

Looking back on it afterwards, Peregrine Musgrave couldn't work out whether it was the champagne or the mentality of a condemned prisoner facing his last meal that persuaded him to do justice to his full portion of Madagascar's prime tiger prawns.

⁂

As opposed to the day of his aunt's interment, on the morning Justin left the office to attend his sub-editor's funeral service the sun was shining brightly. Not that, once the last of the eulogies was over and the strains of Eric Clapton's *Tears In Heaven* had faded away, the mourners needed to gather in the open air around the graveside, because Klaus Radetzky had made it known that he wished to be cremated. According to his wife, Klaus felt that this gesture would be his modest contribution towards lightening the toll taken on the planet by the ecologically irresponsible and their multitudinous landfills. Justin had not thought fit to ask Gisela where she intended scattering her husband's ashes.

Also pursuant to Klaus's preference, there were no priestly sermons, prayers or blessings, simply warm tributes by family members, friends and colleagues in memory of a man who on his last birthday had celebrated reaching half the biblical life span of three score years and ten, which, as Vanessa later put it, meant one year less than Lord Byron at the time of his death.

While the cremation was taking place in the wake of the memorial service, the congregation intermingled in the courtyard outside the chapel. Justin found that Gisela held up remarkably well in no small part, he suspected, because she felt the need to be a tower of strength for a puzzled daughter convinced that her mother and all the other adults were laboring under a misunderstanding. She knew that the father who had read her to sleep with that premonitory fairy tale had climbed down into a hollow tree from which he would sooner or later reappear clutching a bag of gold coins.

Acknowledging that she could not hope to insulate her daughter from the hurtful remarks which children her age were capable of meting out to their less fortunate peers, Gisela had nevertheless prevailed on her employer and Rosalie's headmistress to agree to the six-year-old's keeping her mother company in the travel agency for a fortnight, during which time Gisela intended to work out how best, without shattering Rosalie's world, to correct the little girl's impression that her daddy was going to return. Gisela knew that she would need counselling before taking on this challenge.

Under the circumstances, it was understood by all concerned that nobody was going to betray what was happening out of sight, while they stood gathered in front of the chapel.

When Gisela brought Rosalie up to meet Justin, she introduced him as daddy's boss.

Intuiting that enough had been said about the young girl's father in the past tense, Justin resolved to steer clear of what he called the obituary mood. 'A great cartoonist, your Daddy. Does he draw many cartoons for you?'

'No, but he's got a whole collection of Peanuts we look at every now and then.'

'I believe you have a dog. Is he called Snoopy?'

'No, Groucho.'

'Oh, I like that. Has Daddy told you why he called him Groucho?'

'Because his growl is worse than his bite.'

Gisela looked around to be sure that nobody was hovering nearby anxious to take their leave to the land of the living. 'Justin, do you think you could pop round to our place tomorrow evening? I'm due to meet those police officers in the morning. Inspector Hoffarth told me over the phone last night that there have been some interesting developments.'

'Of course, Gisela. When would you like me to drop by?'

'Come for dinner. At seven.'

'No, I couldn't presume …'

'Don't be silly, Justin. Look, you're the only male friend I feel I can count on at present. I'll probably get weepy. I know I will. But I need company. Don't disappoint me.'

'Will Justice read me a fairy tale, Mummy?'

'Justin, Rosalie. Justin. Well, I don't know.'

'Love to,' said Justin, whose wish for children had been one of the bones of contention between him and Vanessa.

'That's settled then,' said Gisela. 'Tomorrow night. Dinner and Hans Christian Andersen.'

❧

Memo from K to J

The robber barons who plundered the Nevskian League of its wealth in the 1990s consider themselves business titans, the nation's elite. They are parasitic moral midgets, no more elite (chosen) than are drug lords. And their ratpack scions run rings around the law. However, it suits our purpose that the populace is too busy aping Western ways to appreciate that its insatiable captains of industry are mindlessly bleeding the country dry.

Response from J

Ah K, but even if the populace were to wake up, where could it hope to find its standard bearers when the puppet opposition parties are government-funded? And the moment a new independent party of businessmen appears on the scene with solutions to turning the economy around, the establishment's propaganda machine decries them as extremists or blackshirts, i.e. little better, in its book, than terrorists fit for imprisoning.

Peregrine Musgrave returned home early at a time when his wife was still at work, because she too despite her physician's advice had refused to forswear the opium of work. Without the drudgery of the daily grind, both wife and husband knew that tidal waves of misery, guilt and worthlessness would keep flinging them against the rocks of their own Cape Despair. This was not to say that their psyche allowed them to fend of bouts of unmitigated sorrow, impotence and self-flagellation exacerbated by sleep-deprived nights.

In fact, Peregrine had spent last night's early morning hours at the kitchen table labouring over the note which he had now read for the last time before placing it on the living-room dresser, where his wife invariably left her handbag after returning home.

The end product was uncharacteristically brief for a man of words.

Dear Margaret,
I cannot expect you to forgive me. What I am about to do is unconscionable. But you deserve better than this deluded wretch. Were I to continue to breathe the same air as you, I would only make your life more miserable than it is already. You see, while playing my humble part in safeguarding the security of this country of ours, I foolishly let sensitive papers fall into the wrong hands. Now that I have lost the trust of the very people whose endeavours I respected, I should be and am fearful of the consequences. But now that the time has come to pay the piper, I am ready. It means that no harm will come to you. That I guarantee.

Dearest wife, lover and partner through years good, indifferent and bad, I beg you to start afresh after I am gone. Find yourself a good man. Remarry. Have children. Give meaning to your life.
    Your wayward falcon,
    Perry

What had first struck the MP as a straightforward task proved unnecessarily complicated. To start with, the nozzle at one end of the hosepipe he intended using refused to budge, and he was obliged to take a fretsaw to cut it off. Then, after making a second cut, his flawed rule of thumb approach to judging how much hose he needed left him two feet short of the proper measurement. This meant he had to start all over again, laying the severed length alongside the rest of the hose unwound from its wheel beside the folding garage door.

But even then, by the time he reached the driver-side door with the hose in his hand, he found that he had been so flustered as to insert the wrong piece in the Rover's exhaust pipe. A lesson, he thought, in how to bungle your suicide.

Matters got worse: when he walked to the back of the car, he saw that end of the hose on the floor. 'No method in my madness,' he muttered, before searching out an oily rag and stuffing it around the hose so as to lodge this firmly in the tail pipe, guaranteeing no escape of exhaust gases other than through the hose. Next, in scrambling into the front seat, he hurriedly slammed the door, forgetting that in doing so he had cut off the desired supply of carbon monoxide.

After coming to his senses, opening the door and checking that he had not made the hose useless by squashing it in the frame, Peregrine Musgrave collapsed back into the warm leather seat, his heart racing, his mind sending him a succession of mixed messages prompted by fear, irresolution, culpability, anxiety and hopelessness. Music. Perhaps some soothing melody was called for to calm shredded nerves and send him on his way. Musgrave uttered a feeble laugh. How to find the most fitting valedictory musical accompaniment? He stretched across and flicked through the selection of CDs in the passenger-side glove compartment. After rejecting Vivaldi's *Four Seasons* and Dvorak's *New World Symphony* (Peregrine refused to snuff it to the tune of dog food), he plumped for the Beatles and *Let It Be*. His own mother, like McCartney's, had been called Mary.

He slotted in the CD and pressed the play button only to learn that he had inserted the disk the wrong way up. After pushing the eject button and re-inserting the disk correctly, he began singing along with McCartney.

Cack-handed. What ageing does to one, he thought. Not to mention the once youthful singer, who now could have been mistaken for a dowager. Dame Paul. Well, that was one advantage to quitting along life's highway before you became bent, raddled and preoccupied with liver spots.

Musgrave took the dread decision and turned on the ignition. The hose, looped around the steering wheel, took time to emit fumes into the front seat area. But when they did arrive, Peregrine coughed, spluttered and finally turned off the ignition. Get a hold of yourself, he thought, after an interval spent wondering whether J's veiled threats of assassins waiting to push him under the wheels of a Routemaster were designed to scare him into forcing his hand. He counted up to three and turned the ignition back on.

Memories of his mother caused him to smile at life's circularity; he had entered the world through his mother's birth canal, and now he was about to embark on a one-way ferry trip down the Lethe into Hades. But the man who had definitely not been born with a silver spoon in his mouth had not even an obol, the equivalent of a measly halfpenny, to put in his mouth to pay that ghastly oarsman. Still, if he dipped his hand into the waters of Lethe, his would be the bliss of eternal forgetfulness – although one German philosopher had called this the concealment of being. On a par with Sartrean being and nothingness. Bliss or cowardice?

Feeling his head sagging, Peregrine righted himself, loosened his collar and adjusted the rearview mirror. The face staring back at him looked waxen, the eyes lost. He turned away. It was growing warmer in the car, and his head was becoming increasingly muzzy. He took a deep breath, which only made things worse, because the drowsiness swept up on him like an all-enveloping cloud of fatigue.

Had the church not modified its stance on suicide? No longer a mortal sin if committed in conditions of diminished responsibility. Pathetic, thought Musgrave, a papal let-out clause should be the last of your concerns compared to the judgment of your own flesh and blood.

Because that was it. Peregrine would soon be rejoining his son. The next instant, the bereaved father was gripped by a spasm of shame at the thought of the inevitable filial reproach. 'Why did you leave Mum all alone in the world?' At the same time, somebody was uttering words of wisdom. But whose? Those of mother Mary? Would his mother have not beseeched Peregrine to stop now? Those of Marcus Aurelius? Had the stoic philosopher not maintained that whoever favoured vice over virtue was justified in taking his own life? Somebody else was telling Peregrine, let it be. The hand holding the hose fell limply into the lap of the man who was turning down substantially more than appointment to the Chiltern Hundreds.

Should he slap his cheeks? Or was someone else trying to slap him awake? Had Margaret come home early and found him slumped over the steering wheel? No, nobody was trying to waken him. They were calling him into the arms of sleep. Perhaps what he had imagined hearing was the Zen koan's sound of one hand clapping. How did you describe that or the colour of rain, let alone the taste of success, the smell of defeat or the touch of moonlight on water? Moonlight, tugging him back to the shore and wakefulness, when all he wanted was to sleep. But slapping? His mother had slapped him only once on the cheek as a child. When she thought he had pronounced that four letter word. The seven-year-old Peregrine had read the expression blue funk in some penny dreadful. Hadn't understood what it meant, but liked the sound of it. And now, as if to make amends for her mistake, his dear mother was smoothing his hair, singing him a lullaby. Let it be, let it be.

Gisela Radetzky was a firm believer in the benefits of eating a goodly number of vegetables each day. The dinner she prepared for Justin was a prime example of dedication to this principle: diced courgettes, onions, carrots and peppers sat alongside parsnips, celery, fennel and tomatoes as the perfect complement to a mouthwatering number of boletus fresh from the frying pan where they had been basted in the lightest of cream sauces.

'Those mushrooms are full of vitamins, protein, dietary fibres and minerals,' she said, handing Justin a basket of warm pitta bread. 'Klaus and I picked them a couple of weekends ago. Shit, this is no good. Pour me some of that wine. Klaus is everywhere. But nowhere.'

Aware of the thin dividing line between trite and genuine words of comfort,

Justin reached out for and held her hand. 'Don't hold back the tears, Gisela. Nothing more natural than you should feel like this.'

'It's not good for Rosalie to see her mother transformed into a weeping willow.'

'Well, she's not here at the moment. She's in her room waiting for us to finish so that I can read her that fairy tale.'

Gisela gave a croaky laugh. 'Did I just say willow? I meant widow.'

'Ah, Hans Christian Andersen at work there.'

Gisela dried her eyes on her apron, raised a frail smile extinguished almost as soon as it had formed and touched wine glasses with her guest. 'Some of Andersen's tales are harrowing.'

'Perhaps not if you're a child. Children, can be a lot tougher and wiser than we care to think. Where did you gather these boletus?'

'In the woods behind our house. The humid weather had brought them on. Klaus said I had a nose for boletus, but it's the eyes not the nose that track them down. The trick is to be patient. Klaus tends … tended to be in a hurry. These little creatures rarely advertise themselves. Nature teaches them the prudence of invisibility.'

'I can't believe that truffles taste any better.'

'You need a nose to sniff those out, I believe.'

'A pig's nose.'

Gisela set down her fork and took a sip of *Rosentraublinger*. 'Talking about sniffing things out, Justin, I told you that inspector Hoffarth came around to see me.' She stopped playing with the stem of her wine glass. 'He had news. Serious news, Justin.'

Justin nearly said 'Good news?', before realising the inanity of greeting any news as good under present circumstances. 'The police have a lead?'

'More than that.'

It was his turn to put down his fork. 'What did this Hoffarth fellow say?'

'First of all, that the OSCE had no Guy Banks on their records. Nobody by that name was currently working for them out in Ukraine or anywhere else for that matter.'

'But Klaus had obviously met up with this guy. Why otherwise would he have held on to a business card he believed to be genuine?'

'He was conned. And the two hundred dollars almost certainly came from the man calling himself Banks. Hoffarth said that your secretary described the unknown quantity who phoned up to ask about your home address as having an American accent. The same man for sure as tricked Klaus into believing in him.'

'What else did Hoffarth say?'

'Plenty. The police checked out the main car rental agencies at the airport and around Schönschlucht. There were eight recent bookings by Americans. Of these, three vehicles had been returned and were still sitting in the agencies' parking lots. Hoffarth instructed each of the firms to hold on to those cars.'

'Had they already been cleaned inside and out?'

'Apart from checking to see that everything was in order and that the renters had left nothing behind, not one hire farm had vacuumed or wiped down its vehicle.'

'And?'

'Two of the three rental vehicles seemed interesting. The other one had been hired by a family of four. Hoffarth and a forensics expert travelled out to each agency. The first car they inspected had been hired by an American business woman …'

'But the woman who rang my bell that same night, Gisela, had a European accent.'

'You didn't let me finish, Justin. The police seem to think that your woman was or is no more than incidental.'

'Sorry. Please go on.'

'Although they found nothing of interest in that first car, they conducted fingerprint tests and made a note of the driver's particulars. Then they moved on to the second agency. The model was an upmarket Audi, which partly explained why it was still sitting there unhired.' Gisela hesitated. 'Can I serve you more mushrooms, Justin? There's quite a bit left in the pan.'

'Later perhaps, when you've finished yours. You've hardly taken a bite.'

'I've lost my appetite.' Gisela's usual fresh complexion, which allowed her to be sparing with make-up, looked drawn and wasted. The strands of blonde hair twisted nervously between her fingers were blighted by split ends.

'You need to eat, Gisela, to keep up your strength. Rosalie doesn't want to see her mother falling ill or fading away.'

'I eat all I need, Justin. The fact that you're enjoying what I've prepared is enough for me. Do you think you could finish my wine? If not, I'll pour it back into the bottle. I don't want to turn into an alcoholic.'

'No risk of that after less than half a glass. All right, I'll help you out. Now, what did the Audi tell them?'

'They took samples of the dirt and gravel in the front floor wells, and these matched the site of the observation point overlooking the town valley.'

'My God.'

'It gets better. The rental firm has a camera mounted in its front office. Probably because it hires out top-of-the-range models. The police took the memory stick away and ran through all the images for the two days on which the Audi was hired and returned. The same man turned up on both occasions, the first time together with another man, the second alone. And, by the way, according to his driving licence, the fellow renting the car was a Gerald Bancroft from Oregon. We have no way of knowing whether his companion went by the name of Banks or not.' Gisela paused, used her fork listlessly to poke food around her plate and finally abandoned the idea of eating.

Deciding that this information called for a level head, Justin poured himself more Icelandic mineral water. 'They've checked with the airport to see if either of these guys has lit out?'

'Yes. Nobody called Bancroft or Banks has flown out of Luritania over the past week. And nobody with either of those names has booked into or out of a hotel anywhere in the principality.'

'On the basis of that fake business card, I'd say that's scarcely surprising. But then they go and get themselves on camera. How do you work that out?'

'They think Luritania's behind the times.'

'Well, I take my hat off to inspector Hoffarth. You haven't mentioned fingerprints. I believe the police call them latents. Did his forensics expert find any?'

'Several. They're running checks on them with Interpol. Apparently, these things take time. In the meanwhile, Hoffarth's men have alerted local television broadcasters. They've undertaken to show pictures of both men on their prime time and late night news channels.'

'Sounds good. Except that with today's porous borders, the two could be miles away by now.'

'Yes, but all regional airports and every cross-channel ferry operator plus Eurotunnel have been told to be on the look-out for them. Hoffarth says they've burnt their bridges.'

'Not if they're as adept at disguising their appearance as they are at counterfeiting documents.'

'I suppose a lot depends on whether Bancroft and Banks realise they're fugitives from justice. If they watch the television or buy a newspaper, yes, they're likely to do as you suggested. Perhaps not otherwise. Anyway, Hoffarth expects the French, Belgian, Dutch and German media to advertise both individuals as dangerous men on the run. And, in case they still happen to be around, he's issued instructions for their photographs to be pasted up around town.'

'I should watch the late night news.'

'No need to, Justin. I have a spare copy of these individuals' photographs here.' Gisela stood up and walked across to a sideboard from where she lifted two sheets of paper off a pile of magazines.

'Have you seen either of them before?'

'Can't say I have. Not the best of photos – especially for the character in the background. But thanks for showing me. May I keep these? Make my own copies?'

'Of course. Anything you can think of that might help track these criminals down. I need to find out why they took my husband from me. What can he have done to deserve …?' Gisela Radetzky's eyes focused blankly on the mawkish *lladró* porcelain wedding gift from her in-laws, which the *femme de ménage* should have dropped and broken on the floor long ago, after lifting it week in, week out from its place on the mantelpiece for dusting down. What could you say about a father and mother who were 'regrettably unable' to cut short their maiden trip around the world to attend their son's funeral?

'There's one thing I forgot to tell you. We can't be absolutely certain but, according to the coroner's report, Klaus could have suffered a heart attack before he was thrown from the observation point. In other words, it's possible that these people might have tortured him. We need to find them.'

228

'I agree,' said Justin after a protracted silence brought about by inability to come to terms with his sense of guilt. 'We need to catch and bring these brutes to justice.'

'Above all I need to know why they did what they did.'

No, thought Justin. I know why they murdered your husband. I am responsible for his death. And if you ever learn that, I'll never be able to face you again.

'Are you sure I can't tempt you with more mushrooms?'

'They're delicious, Gisela, but I'm not sure I could manage any more. Do you think Rosalie's still awake? If so, I ought to pop in and read her that fairy tale.'

'I'll go and see. She was excited before you arrived, looking forward to her bedtime story. Knowing Rosalie, I doubt whether that will have tired her out.'

Gisela returned a minute later. 'No, Justin. Off you go. A promise is a promise.'

Rosalie wanted Justin to read her the story of *The Ice Maiden*. Her father, she complained, had kept finding excuses to put off telling her that tale. But after Justin had scanned the short story, he decided that it was the worst possible choice for Klaus's daughter. After proposing several titles, upon Rosalie's insistence he read her the story of *The Nightingale*.

'We have a wood behind our house,' said the little girl, after Justin had put back the book on its shelf beside Rosalie's collection of Winnie the Pooh. 'Do you think you could open the window, Justice, so we can hear whether a nightingale is singing in the trees?'

Justin did as bid, but the only sound to be heard outside was the cawing of crows.

'I expect the nightingale will come later, while you're asleep, Rosalie. It's probably too early for him now.'

'And will he bring Daddy with him?'

Justin steadied himself against the window ledge. 'That would be marvellous, wouldn't it?'

'We don't need to be Chinese?'

'No, Rosalie.'

'But I have a clockwork clown. If the real nightingale hears him, will he think I'm Japanese and fly away?'

'I'm sure not. Does your clown sing?'

'No, he plays a tune.'

'Always the same one?'

'Yes.'

'Well, the nightingale won't have anything to worry about.'

'I suppose not. Could you tuck me in now like Daddy does?'

Gazing down at the pink-cheeked little girl snuggling under her bedclothes, and persuaded that his solicitousness towards Gisela amounted to more than threadbare self-justification, Justin was besieged by doubt in the face of a hopeless situation.

When he returned to the living room, hearing Gisela busying herself with cutlery in the kitchen, he stepped inside to take up a dish cloth.

'What did you read her?'

'*The Nightingale.*'

'Ah yes, I know that one. Did she stay awake until the end?'

'She did. Hung on my every word. So I tried to put on a good performance.'

'How was your Chinese accent?'

'More up to Little Red Riding Hood than to Little Red Book standards.'

Gisela hung her head over the sink, casting a bleak smile into the sudsy water.

'She likes you, Justin. Don't desert us, will you?'

As embarrassed as he was anguished, when Gisela Radetzky turned to face him, Justin took her in his arms and let her lay her head on his shoulder.

'Whatever makes you think I'd do that?'

'I don't know what to believe in any more. Everything's become so damn rotten.'

'Not with Rosalie beside you, surely? A little lighthouse brightening your darkest hours.'

'I know. I have to be brave for her sake.'

'And you will be.'

'If only I had been the one to open the door to that woman. I'm sure I'd have seen through her. Then Klaus would still be here. Oh, this is no good.' Gisela lowered her head and, with her back to the sink, gripped the edge of the draining board with both hands for fear she was losing anchorage on more than the physical. 'Why did this have to happen to us?'

Aware that predominant among his own storm-tossed emotions was a burning desire to make love to this grief-stricken woman, Justin found himself striving to banish the thought of wishing to supplant Klaus in Gisela's affections with such indecent haste. The memory of the words spoken by Hamlet, *The funeral baked meats did coldly furnish forth the marriage tables*, rang accusingly in his ears.

Gisela raised her eyes to his. 'I want to see these evil men brought to justice.'

Justice, he thought. That's how Rosalie thinks of me, the personification of injustice.

'So do I, so do I. The world's all the poorer for the loss of a gifted cartoonist and sub-editor, not to mention a fine husband and father. And somebody has to pay for this.'

Memo from J to K

Have you heard the latest uproar on Urodina's military front? Intent on reigniting the conflict in the east on the grounds that the rebels kept breaking the ceasefire, Veki HQ ordered the lieutenant colonel of one of Urodina's right-wing battalions to storm and take immediately a rebel-held village on high ground.

But without being given adequate time to prepare his ground attack, the battalion commander quickly found his men outfought and outgunned.

Having already committed the gaffe of anouncing that the heights had been retaken, Veki, desperate to cover up for the fact that the attack had been repulsed, denounced the incident as a further flagrant sabotage of the ceasefire by Nevskian insurgents.

Resenting the high command's insistence that the right sector played no part in spearheading offensives, the lieutenant colonel made it known loud and clear that Veki's regular servicemen were the first to down weapons, abandon tanks and take to their heels the moment things heated up, leaving his men to lead the battle and sacrifice lives which others were unwilling to put on the line.

He attacked Vespuccia, in particular, for turning the screws on Veki to disown right-sector involvement in the ongoing combat.

Response from K

Yes, our people caught wind of this and quickly stopped news of it from leaking out. It's true that the Veki army is a shambles with most of its enlisted men untrained and unprepared to risk their lives. But, no, we can't afford to let the outside world know the extent of our and Veki's reliance on the right sector.

Memo from J to K

It is essential that your people stifle reports of the number of incidents of Urodinian fascists torturing battlefield wounded. One of our left-wing periodicals carried news yesterday of the contrast between the way in which the rebels treat and feed Urodinian combat casualties in their field hospitals and the way in which their opponents break the limbs or ribs of injured rebels they come across on the battlefront.

Response from K

I beg to differ. I suspect that the source of that information is one of your side's go-it-alone war reporters, who ought to be banned from returning to Urodina.

Response from J

Sorry to correct you, K. But the source was a Vespuccian from a large corner of that country of yours where people still fantasise about independence. He posted a damning video on the Web. One of our journalist's latched on to it, after which there was enough hullaboloo from the opposition during Wednesday's PMQ to make our Mr Titanic turn bright salmon pink and punish his hand on the despatch box.

❧

To ring the changes between swimming and serialised or short story readings, Vanessa took Clara Bogen to the Hampstead Playhouse to sit through a performance of Alan Bennett's *The History Boys*, a play which she had read to Clara the previous year. After discovering that it was being produced locally, Vanessa bought two tickets for the Saturday matinee performance nearest to her friend's birthday. Under normal circumstances, scenes in which action took precedence over dialogue – such as when the Headmaster walks into his General Studies teacher's lesson to introduce the new history supply teacher only to be confronted by one of two boys with his pants down as both test their French, acting out a meeting between a prostitute and her client – would have been lost on a sight-impaired audience member ignorant of the text. But even if Clara was unable to appreciate body language and facial gestures, fortified by a strong memory, she chuckled along with others around her.

'Thank you so much,' said Clara, grasping Vanessa warmly by the hand, as they prepared to leave the auditorium after the curtain had been rung down on the players' last bow. 'That was a perfect present.'

As agreed beforehand, the two women caught the first bus back to the *Maison des Aveugles* with a view to taking Bismarck for a walk around the nearest park. On the way down to the playhouse they had been able to sit on the lower deck, but on the return journey this was fully occupied, and they sat on the upper deck's front seats.

'What did you think of the acting, Miss Actor Director?' asked Clara.

'Not bad. Good sense of timing.'

'Did you see the original cast? Nicholas Hytner's production?'

'At the Lyttleton? Yes. It deservedly got rave reviews.'

'Were you taught history the Lintott way?'

'Afraid so. Not encouraged to think outside the box.'

'Would you have preferred Irwin or Hector's approach?'

'Although my sympathies lie with Hector's somewhat dodgy Renaissance man teachings, I could see myself being taken in at that age by Irwin's sleight of hand approach to dazzling the examiners. '

'Yet Irwin's ends up as a government spin doctor confined to a wheelchair.'

'Yes, presumably expert at defending the politically indefensible. In line with the time-honoured tradition of historical denial and falsification.'

'Time-honoured?'

'Starting with those pharaohs who disliked their predecessors enough to erase all mention of them throughout the land. Followed by the compilers of that unbiased history of the Jews we know as the Old Testament. Skip a couple of millennia, and there's no end to historical distortion through denial.

'Claims that the British empire's opium wars with China were motivated by greed and that colonial imperialism plundered India's economy: gross misinterpretation of the facts; Turkey's part in the Armenian genocide: pure fabrication of events; statistics showing the unholy number of comfort woman forced into sexual slavery by the Japanese military during World War II: gross misinterpretation of the facts; Russian pre-Bolshevik history: pure fabrication, according to those charged by Stalin with doctoring the country's history; Saddam Hussein, enemy of Al-Qaeda: gross misinterpretation of the facts by the pacifist class; accusations that Turkey's army thinks nothing of torching scores of Kurdish families in their cellars; pure fabrication of events by those in the west who should know better, given the country's membership of NATO.

'In other words, it's a rare country capable of unbiased propaganda about its record or alliances.'

'Yes,' said Clare, 'human nature never changes. Today's politicos continue to build careers out of peddling half-truths and rewriting events.'

'Now who sounds as if she's in Irwin's camp?'

'They say seeing is believing. The fact that I can't see doesn't mean I don't know how to read between the lines. By the way, Vanessa, when are you going to give me that confidential document?'

'I brought it along with me today together with a small gift for you.'

'Another gift? Vanessa, you've done enough already with the ticket to today's play.'

'Thought you might like an Ernie bond, especially since it starts with the number eleven. Remember what you told me about the Spanish blind association, ONCE?'

'The lottery ticket sellers? Yes, but I'm not Spanish, Vanessa.'

'Ah, how do you know you don't have Spanish blood in your veins – all the way down from Catherine of Aragon's daughter?'

'What a compliment! She had almost three hundred Protestants burnt at the stake. Shame on you for fabricating my history.'

When Justin read the news of Peregrine Musgrave's death accompanied by an obituary tending towards the fulsome (*architect of entente between a disillusioned British electorate and its European cousins*), he picked up the telephone to be sure that Tich would be manning the front counter of his shop during that day's lunch break.

It was a pleasant summer's day, making for a refreshing walk to Tich's second-hand bookshop from the Innova Press Corporation's offices at the railway end of town across the temporary catwalk erected to do duty for the pedestrian equivalent of the existing bridge under redesign for the city's major tram project. The catwalk traversed the gorge between Schönschlucht's lower and upper halves. According to the myth perpetuated by the nation's poet laureate, Edmond Lentz, in his romantic verse-tale *Die Riesengebrueder*, in ancient times two giant brothers, vying for possession of the land on which today's capital stood split it between them by carving the Leiseflösschen ravine out of the landscape with mighty sweeps of their legendary *Diamantklingen* broadswords. In contrast to Freiheitstrasse, on the railway side of the catwalk, notable for its many boulevard cafes, the pavements on Kronstrasse, the central boulevard threading through the city's northern side, were lined with banks and finance houses, each new building as much a testament to the originality of its design – soaring grandeur combined with creative experimentation – as to the power of money.

But whereas modernity screamed down on Justin from on high on the uptown side of the catwalk, once his steps took him into the old town's Gothic quarter, the feel of cobblestones under his feet and the sight of the half-timbered stores behind the central post office made for more congenial surroundings compared to Kronstrasse's chill, corporate soullessness.

As always on a weekday when Tich was present, *Bibliopole's* front door was held open with a wooden quoin bearing the greeting SALVETE. On this occasion, Tich was noting down details of e-bay's offer of a signed first edition of Laurence Sterne's *The Life and Opinions of Tristram Shandy, Gentleman,* while pondering how to win Isabelle and Craig's consent to a withdrawal from their joint China Reconstruction bank account in the form of a temporary loan repayable with interest from the shop's takings.

'Afternoon, Tich. How's business?'

The shopkeeper looked up from the tantalising image on his monitor of nine calfskin volumes with gold-tooled Moroccan labels.

'Ah, good day, Justin. A mixed bag. One customer wanted me to knock twenty per cent off my first edition of *The History of Pendennis,* enriched by one of Thackeray's illustrations, on the grounds that a number of the pages were creased. He took the hint when I suggested that a flat iron used on those pages would get him further than if it were used on his wallet. That scoundrel was followed by four children herded in by an enterprising young mother, whose offspring walked out with copies of *Treasure Island, Swiss Family Robinson, Robinson Crusoe* and *The Coral Island* – none of which, their mother lamented, while I rejoiced, could be had from Schönschlucht's central library.'

'I didn't know you stocked children's books.'

'Tut, tut, Justin. Adults have been known to enjoy rereading those titles. I for one.'

Justin had his ears open for the sound of shuffling feet, whispering, books being taken down from or replaced on shelves, pages turned, hardbacks snapped shut. From where he stood, there was no other way of knowing how many customers, if any, were ensconced behind the compact ranks of Tich's towering bookcases. But then, he had failed to notice the overhead CCTV nestled near the ceiling behind him.

'Perhaps all quiet for the moment on the western front?'

'It is. Can I offer you a drink?'

'No thanks. You've seen the news about Musgrave?'

'Not until you told me, and I looked on the web. Yes, poor sod gassed himself in his garage.'

'Couldn't cope with the loss of his son, so his wife said.'

'Yes, tough when a nine-year-old dies on you.'

'You believe that was the sole reason? Coming as it did right after he sent me that warning in the GOSH envelope?'

Tich stroked his beard. 'Now who's been reading too much Mario Puzo? Safer, Justin, to stick with *Wind In The Willows.*'

'Come on now, Tich, a banker's found hanging under Blackfriars Bridge and an MP dead from carbon monoxide poisoning in his garage. Might the two not have something in common?'

Sensing that it was a mistake to treat his friend's alarmist version of events as another of Sterne's cock and bull stories, Humphrey Hobart checked himself from further flippancy. 'You're saying ghosts from Musgrave's past caught up with him and it was too much to handle on top of seeing his son buried at such a tender age?'

'No, I'm saying that Puzo vendetta merchants from the present were getting to Musgrave. And that we need to ratchet this up a notch. Ask how does this affect us? Because there's no denying we're party to sensitive information. The type of information that gets people killed. Innocent people like Klaus Radetzky. Now we've dragged Rashid into the arena with us, and not one of us can hope to emulate Russell Crowe once the lions and charioteers are set loose. Should we ask for police protection? I'm thinking of the women, Vanessa and Isabelle. Supposing our opponents make all the right connections?'

'Van can look after herself. So, I hope, can I. But there's no doubt the rest of you are vulnerable. Still, what are you going to say to the police, if you go to them? You've chanced upon embarrassing classified material which, you're pretty sure, got Klaus killed. That same information is known to five other people, all of whose lives are at risk. They'll make all the right sounds, type out a statement for you to sign and tell you they'll refer the matter to their superiors.'

'And if I or Rashid should turn out to be next on some shady organisation's shopping list?'

Tich shifted awkwardly in his seat, turning self-consciously away from the calfskin collectors' pieces.

'They might wake up then.'

'Thanks, Tich. It's great to know I won't be a prior beneficiary of their civic solicitude.'

'The shady people who did away with your sub-editor are either long gone out of town or holed up somewhere until the heat is off.'

'That's as maybe. But they're not fucking windmills, are they?'

The warning wave of Tich's hand fell short of alerting Justin to the fact that a customer had moved from inspecting the window display to enter the shop. The not unamused male customer sauntered past both men at the counter, eliciting a welcoming smile from Tich. 'Any questions, feel free to ask,' he boomed.

Before continuing in a lower tone of voice, Justin waited for the newcomer to disappear into the thick of Tich's book labyrinth. 'I need you to teach me like you did Vanessa how to use one of your automatics.'

'Well, Justin, You're welcome to join the gun club. You do realise, though, that it's against the law to carry firearms around with you? This is Luritania not Texas.'

'You're joking, of course?'

'Of course.' Tich opened one of the drawers below his counter and, with one eye on the overhead CCTV screen, pulled out a fully loaded Browning. 'Tough luck, if I or Van, my latest recruit, see them coming first. And that, by the way, Justin, is a lesson you should remember. If we get you reasonably proficient in the use of one of these little darlings, shoot first. None of the James Bond crap. Questions can wait till afterwards. That is, if there's anyone left to answer them.'

'Shouldn't we bring Rashid in on this?'

'Invite him along, by all means. You free tonight?'

'Yes.'

'Eight p.m. down at the shooting range. Here's the address. On the outskirts of Teufelswald.' Tich handed over the club card. 'You know the area?'

'Not that well, but I'll tap the address into my Tom-Tom.'

'Okay. While you're at it don't forget beating the jungle drums to Rash.'

'Vanessa never told me what prompted her to join your club.'

'She wanted a stronger deterrent than pepper spray to scare the shit out of weirdoes on her morning jog through the woods.'

'How good a shot is she?'

'Damn good.'

'I should have guessed. Vanessa does nothing by halves.'

'How are rehearsals going?'

'Fine, seeing as I'm supposed to spend most of the play asleep.'

'Your dream world. Vanessa said you're the play's alpha and omega. Playing to the gods.'

'No, Tich. To the groundlings. Van's staging this as an open-air production.'

'I took it to be her way of saying that if the play's a sandwich, you're the bread either side of the meat.'

'So long as it's not turkey.'

The unknown customer chose that moment to step up to the counter with a copy of a book held close to his chest.

'The cover's scuffed,' he said. 'Think you could knock the price down?'

'Well, pal,' said Tich. 'You're the first customer I've met who buys a secondhand book for its cover. Give it here.'

Justin stood aside to allow the prospective buyer to hand the book over. It was a copy of Michael Connelly's *Blood Work*.

⁂

Memo from K to J

In a recent Internet video clip, a group of beer-swilling men and women in a bar in one of our south-western states was asked to vote yes or no to the question 'Should an atomic bomb be dropped on the Nevskian League'? It took a moment for the hotdog chewers to digest more than their food before the overwhelming majority punched the air with an emphatic 'yes'.

As to what your average Erubuan views as 'that kerfuffle in Urodina' on the League's western border, we get the impressiom that he is so remote from and indifferent to the conflict that the number of civilian dead and injured, the many children left blind or without arms and legs, the families made homeless, all this is meaningless to him. Likewise your average western Urodinian sleeping soundly in his bed. Why this indifference? Largely because of the excellent results achieved through superbly skewed media coverage of events on the ground.

Response from J

Indeed, K, and when the Invigilator lambastes the Nevskian League for sending nine thousand foot soldiers to aid the rebels, her press felicitously fails to suggest that this figure has been pulled out of thin air or that the Veki junta is pitting itself mostly against local volunteers without helmets, bulletproof vests, boots or decent rations.

───※───

When Arnold Palmer drove up to the unpaved track leading to the farmhouse on the outskirts of Deerglingen, it occurred to him that as safe houses went it would have been hard to improve on this isolated set of buildings down by the Silberstrom, a tributary of the Vaugruge. According to the embassy's information manual, following the original owner's death and the eldest son's decision to turn down sheep herding, dipping, shearing and slaughtering in favour of playing lead guitar with a local rock band, the then ambassador had accepted an offer by the state to subsidise purchase of the smallholding, sell off the livestock and install a bachelor tenant farmer ready to turn the arable land over to leguminous cereals and forage crops, it being understood that the his farmhouse and outbuildings could be made available for operations in the interests of national and European security. The sealing of lips was assured by the guarantee of dire consequences in the event of infringement of state secrecy laws.

Arnold turned his jeep past the fence with its dusty mailbox labelled A. Mouton into the rutted driveway. Not for the first time did he ask himself how the embassy had managed to find an owner whose name better suited his predecessor. If anyone had seen his approach, it would have been through binoculars, and Palmer found it hard to believe that the arrival of a weather-beaten, four-wheel drive could be a source of curiosity for neighbours sitting two kilometres down the road.

He manoeuvred the vehicle off the dirt track around two massive blocks of concrete intended to deter casual passers-by from making the journey up the drive to see whether the owner dealt in horse manure for their vegetable patch or free-range eggs for their refrigerators. The outbuilding to which he next directed the jeep was a white painted bungalow with gable roof and a set of steps leading up to the front porch. Not that anybody was enjoying a sundowner on the porch, the occupants having been strictly instructed to remain out of sight.

Pulling to a halt to one side of the steps, Arnold waited for the dust to settle before alighting. When he climbed down to the ground, he heard the bird-scattering propane cannons resonating loudly across the early evening air from the vineyards to his right down by the Silberstrom. The front door was opened to him by a less than happy-looking Warren Stenning with four days of stubble on an unshaven face.

'Am I glad to see you,' he said. 'Keep me cooped up much longer with Huey and I'll be ready for the funny farm.'

Arnold eased his way past Stenning into the front living area, where he cast an eye around the room. The air was heavy with smoke, one patch of the white stucco ceiling above a corner armchair discoloured a murky grey. The coffee table's ash trays overflowed with cigarette stubs. A beer-stained playing card lay beside an otherwise neatly stacked pack in the centre of the table. *National Geographics* were heaped on a side table. The television was showing an NFL match transmitted from the States by satellite to a parabolic dish on the main farmhouse. The New England Patriots trailed the Pittsburgh Steelers by 14 to 21. Following closely behind Arnold, Warren Stenning walked across to the set and turned the sound down.

Palmer flopped down into the armchair opposite the fume-begrimed corner ceiling. 'What have you guys been playing?'

'Texas Hold'em.'

'What for?'

'As in why or what with?' Stenning sounded petulant. Palmer liked to beat about the bush. Given the present fraught situation, the CIA agent had little patience for small talk.

'As in for dollars or euros.'

'Neither. Match sticks.'

'Who's winning?'

'I've enough to burn the place down. If we had a power outage in the middle of the night, Hugh would be tripping over the furniture.'

'Where is the man of the moment?'

'Sleeping off a hangover. How much longer are we going to have to sweat it out here?'

Arnold picked up the spare card, added it to the deck, shuffled the pack and cut it in half to uncover the topmost face card: the joker.

'Since when has anyone played poker with the joker?'

Warren Stenning pulled a face. 'Hugh's idea. His way of improving on his chances. A fifth ace.'

'And you humour him?'

Stenning refused to be drawn. 'Where's the change of clothes you were supposed to be bringing us?'

'You think you need them? They've stopped showing your pictures on the box.'

Hearing footfalls down the corridor, Arnold turned his gaze towards the living room door.

A bleary-eyed Hugh Chamberlain stopped on the threshold, both hands resting for support on the lintel. 'Look what the dog's brought in. Our never-had-it-so-good mission rescuer.'

'You keep getting your wires crossed, Hugh,' retorted Arnold for whom the dislike was mutual. 'I'm in the salvaging not the rescue business. Who got us into this mess, if it wasn't you?'

Chamberlain dropped his arms and ambled into the room. 'When are we leaving?'

'Soon.'

'Together or separately?'

'Separately. You guys still use Brownings?'

Stenning tapped his left shoulder. 'As always.'

Palmer hoisted himself to his feet, turned with his back to the two men, went across to the curtained window and looked down the empty driveway.

'Nice to know,' he said, before spinning around and shooting Hugh Chamberlain through the heart. His victim could not have toppled down backwards more suddenly had he been felled by a metal bolt from a slaughterhouse stunner.

The next second, Arnold's Browning was centred on the chest of a man, convinced that his visitor had taken leave of his senses, fearful for his life. 'Take it easy, Warren. You're not on the retired list. When I said separately, I meant separately. You walk out of here. Hugh leaves on his back.'

'Jesus, Arnold,' said Stenning, who had known better than to make a move towards his shoulder holster. 'Are you out of your mind?'

Had he suspected that Palmer was on drugs or otherwise unbalanced, Stenning would have thought twice before voicing this sentiment, but the man who had just killed his partner had clearly committed a premeditated act.

'I think not, Warren.'

'You think this neighbourhood's so dozy nobody will alert the police?' Stenning was hugging his ears in protest against the deafening sound caused by Palmer's automatic, which might as well have not been silenced for all the difference the suppressor made within such an enclosed space.

Palmer lowered the automatic. 'Considering how far we are from the nearest building, the sound of that single shot will come across like part of another vineyard cannon burst.'

Warren Stenning was still in a state of disbelief: 'You retired Hugh on whose instructions?'

'Calm down. Guys like him give your organisation a bad name. Clowns in action.'

'Why should anyone associate Hugh with Langley?'

Arnold Palmer mused for a moment, one eye on Stenning, the other searching for the spent cartridge. 'No reason. Look, he blundered. We can't afford a repeat.'

A suspicious Warren Stenning regarded Palmer uncertainly.

'Trust me, Warren,' said the cultural attaché, returning the Browning to its holster. 'You're not for the meat wagon. You're being sent home. Mind you, don't count on Langley strewing posies at your feet. '

The fact that Palmer had reholstered his firearm was less than reassuring for the CIA agent. His ears were still ringing, his armpits were staining the sleeves of a shirt that had stuck to his back and his mouth felt as dry as sawdust. What could have brought Palmer to murder a fellow member of the company in cold blood? Staving off a wave of nausea, Stenning found the strength to stand his ground. 'I don't like this one bit. You could have sent us both home. Instead of this. Way over the top. I would have recommended demoting Hugh to a desk job. Tell me, Arnold, since when have you been carrying that weapon?'

'Pastime of mine, Warren, competitive shooting. From the day I captained my college shooting team to victory against Carnegie Mellon, until the present day. And, as you well know, customs never poke their noses into diplomatic bags.'

Judging from Arnold Palmer's more relaxed expression that his life was no longer in danger, Stenning began to get enough of a grip on his nerves to risk two unforgiving questions. 'On whose authority have you taken Hugh out, Arnold? Is this going to get pinned on me?'

Arnold Palmer slumped down onto a sofa designed for couch potatoes: the depth of the seat such that his legs stuck out in front of him like two thick sticks of celery. 'Authority?' Extending one arm along the top of the backrest, he tapped the fabric with the flat of his hand. 'No need to trouble yourself on that score, Warren. The ambassador's in on this. Yes, I know, not one of our country's finest. Closet boozer. Touchy temper. Went practically apoplectic over Hugh's botch-up. Who was I to argue with Nussbaum? Why stymy my career?'

'You could have protested to HQ.'

'Really? You think HQ would give any credence to complaints from a greenhorn compared to the words of an ambassador with twenty-eight years' service behind him? And, by the way, Warren, I persuaded the ambassador to do his best to clear your name with Langley over this. It goes without saying they're not happy about the way things have turned out.'

'Great. And what about the police here?'

'No big deal. What matters is how the people back home view this.'

'I still think you could have argued the case with Nussbaum. Talked sense into the man rather than …'

Catching Palmer's eyes narrowing, Stenning decided to leave well alone.

'Rather than what, Warren?'

'In your shoes, I'd have tried to talk him into getting us both home and giving Hugh enough black marks to put a permanent damper on his career.'

'You're wrong in thinking I didn't try, Warren,' said Palmer, the lie tripping smoothly off his tongue. 'But the old man maintained that getting you both home safe and sound would have been tricky and could have ended badly for you. This way, you fly out of Europe safe and sound. The customs and police authorities are looking for two people fitting your descriptions not a loner.'

'Come off it, Arnold. They're not that dumb. It would make more sense for Hugh and I to split up.'

'Perhaps. But they won't be looking for a blind man, will they?'

'A what?'

'You heard me. I've got a nice white folding walking stick for you, Warrren, and a pair of cloudy white extra large contact lenses opaque only on the outside. You'll have twenty/twenty vision with those babies. And no need to act like a stumblebumb. After all, not every blind person out there is stone-blind.'

'Shit, Arnold, is this your crazy idea?'

'Stop worrying, Warren. Your change of clothes is in the car. By the time you don them and your lenses and take up your cane, nobody will associate you with either of the men wanted in connection with the murder of a Luritanian cartoonist. Put on a pair of dark glasses, if it makes you feel any easier.'

'And how do I get home?'

'I drive you across the border to a railway station from where you catch a train to Brussels *Gare du Nord* and a connecting train from there to Brussels National Airport. After which you fly to Oslo before returning to Washington D.C.'

'Why not directly to Washington?'

'Two reasons. First, nobody will be expecting either of Luritania's most wanted criminals to be flying to Norway. Second, we have some business for you in Oslo. Data to collect at the *Radisson Blu Gardermoen* airport hotel. Everything's taken care of, Warren. All the tickets and intel here in my pocket. We should get going soon. Can't have you missing your train.'

Warren Stenning bent down and picked up the cartridge case which had spun near his feet. 'Haven't we got something more important to attend to before that? You don't intend leaving Hugh here, do you?'

'Of course not. I'll back the jeep up to the kitchen door. There's a sleeping bag in the trunk together with your things. We can zip Hugh up in that and take him with us.'

'Take him with us where?'

'To a disused, off-road quarry between here and the border. We'll weigh down Hugh's sleeping bag with stones and dump him there in a pit full of groundwater and rain. He'll never be found in a month of Sundays.'

'And the bloodstained carpet?'

'We have people to clean up after us, Warren. Safe houses have to be kept safe. You wait here while I bring the sleeping bag in.'

Stenning bent down to inspect the corpse and was reminded of Radetzky. 'Smells like he shit himself.'

'Nasty, I know. Try to make the best of a bad job.'

'And what about loose ends?'

'Fill me in, Warren.'

'I'm talking about turning our backs on Hugh's fuck-up. Someone needs to settle Hendry's hash.'

'Well now, leave that to me, Warren. Leave that to me.'

⁓❊⁓

But equally well in a world where the dividing line between fact and fiction is so thin as to make little or no difference, Arnold could have driven into town and taken the short walk from the Azaleengarten parking lot to the boarded up *Kinothek* premises used temporarily by the CIA as a safe town house until such time as the building was pulled down to make room for yet another bank.

A long-established institution enjoying considerable popularity among Luritania's film buffs for the emphasis it placed on vintage art house movies as opposed to mainstream blockbuster productions, the *Kinothek* not only devoted entire weeks to a specific director's works but invited guest speakers from France, Germany, Italy, Spain and Great Britain to share and discuss with viewers their analyses of films from the monochrome era. But when the chief projectionist, a fifty-nine-year-old who had been with the *Kinothek* from the start, came down with lung cancer, the cause of which was traced to the use of asbestos in the building's water pipes and flues, Luritania's Ministry for Sustainable Development and Infrastructure ordered the premises' closure, while the Ministry of Culture supported the *Kinothek's* relocation.

Since the building was slated for demolition in the fairly distant future, the American Ambassador had struck a deal with Luritania's Prime Minister in accordance with which his people could use the flat at the top of the building formerly occupied by the deceased projectionist as temporary safe house accommodation for limited-stay personnel.

As Arnold approached the front of the *Kinothek*, he saw from the posters on the hoarding outside that the last film to be shown there had been Michel Hazavanicius's 2011 black and white silent film, *The Artist*. What comes around, goes around, he thought, letting himself into the side entrance with no giveaway glance over the shoulder and without waiting for the nearest passers-by to clear his path. Warren Stenning and Hugh Chamberlain might have been smuggled into the premises late at night, but there was no need for Arnold Palmer to act other than as if he had every right to be here.

The first thing to strike the cultural attaché whenever he set foot in the old cinema was the lack of air. On this occasion, the atmosphere felt mustier than usual. After making his way through the rear side corridor into the main entrance hall, he turned the lights on and took the carpeted steps leading up to the foyer and ticket office two at a time. The familiar *Nosferatu* poster greeted him at the top of the broad staircase, which would have done credit to a Busby Berkeley movie. Today, Arnold sensed an unhealthy kinship with the blood-lusting count played by an actor with that most appropriate of names, Max Schreck.

The corridors on both side of the ticket office led to an area taken up with exhibits of cinematography memorabilia, including a 1930's dual format projector for 9.5 and 16 mm silent movies, a life-size cardboard cut-out of Alfred Hitchcock and a series of posters ranging from Bergman's *Wild Strawberries* through John Huston's *The Maltese Falcon* and Orson Welles's *Touch of Evil* to Alain Resnais' *Last Year at Marienbad*. This area fronted the red-curtained first-floor auditorium, which was of no interest to Palmer, who directed his footsteps towards the stairs up to the next level, where spectators had been able to stretch back and enjoy their film from the comfort of plush red velvet armchairs in the balcony overlooking the lower auditorium. Deciding to pause for a moment, he pushed aside the entrance curtain, chose a seat in the back row, deposited onto the next seat the large reinforced supermarket carrier bag which he had brought with him, and gazed down at the blank screen below. The walls at that level were also decorated with posters: one of Chaplin in dungarees perched on top of and adjusting one of the nut and bolts on a giant cogwheel in *Modern Times*, another of Harold Lloyd hanging from the minute hand of a clock at the top of a skyscraper in *Safety Last!,* a third of Randolph Scott and Joel McCrea in *Guns In The Afternoon*, a fourth of Tony Curtis, Jack Lemmon and Marilyn Monroe in *Some Like It Hot*, for although the *Kinothek* had won its spurs showing black and white films, the owners came to recognise that many of the best early colour motion picture films would attract additional *Kinothek* patrons. In boosting box office takings, that decision had helped to replace sit-up-and-beg seating with the current comfortable armchairs kinder on viewers' backs.

Palmer's information sheet had told him that the *Kinothek* was due phoenix-like to rise from the ashes of the present building in new, smarter premises uptown. He assumed that the downstairs memorabilia would be whisked safely away before the demolition gangs moved in with their wrecking balls, bulldozers and excavators.

It was not surprising for him that his two wards sitting one level further up in an apartment that used to be let to the *Kinothek's* founding member projectionist for a peppercorn rent had failed to register his presence. No doubt because of the sound of the familiar music filtering down from above: the concerto de Aranjuez. In harmony, Palmer thought, with *Guns in the Afternoon*. This comparison prompted Arnold to deliberate over his plan of action. For what he had intended was serious. With little if any experience of field work most of the stuffed shirts in Langley pushing paper from one desk to another lived by the rule book. And those framing the rules frowned on any form of resourcefulness departing from the norm. Given what Arnold had in mind, this meant that he had to dress things up in such a way that nothing rebounded on him. Others in his position might have hesitated to go ahead without sounding out their ambassador, but Arnold knew that the present incumbent would never have approved of so drastic a remedy as his. It suited this *film noir* environment in which the person playing *Camino Real's* Gutman could have been said to slip into the personality of his namesake in *The Maltese Falcon*.

Well, the ambassador need never know the truth of the matter. Let him swallow the icing around the bitter pill which Arnold had prepared for him and Luritania's boy scout police force. The sole sticking point was that Warren Stenning deserved better. Why should he pay the price of his partner's ineptitude? Because he was Chamberlain's minder and should not have lost the plot? It suited Palmer's frame of mind to think so, though not without discomfort as to his readiness to take on the role of judge and executioner. Reluctant to admit to a sadistic streak to his nature, the man who fancied himself as a diplomat cut out for higher office eased the crick in his neck, took hold of the carrier bag and headed for the door giving onto the last set of stairs leading up to the projectionist's private apartment.

Palmer paused in front of the *Kinothek's* topmost door, reflecting that it suited his purpose that someone had just turned the volume up on the music. He did not bother to knock. His colleagues were expecting him.

The cultural attaché was familiar with the apartment's uninspiring décor: the living-cum-dining room minimally furnished with three wickerwork chairs, a battered table on one end of which stood a gramophone – the source of the music which had first reached him downstairs – with a stack of long-playing records to one side, a full-length easel mirror in need of resilvering, an upright piano with a scratched folded down lid and a glass-fronted Welsh dresser advertising a set of Wedgwood bone china. Palmer conjectured that if Stenning and Chamberlain had chosen to drink out of Styrofoam coffee cups and to eat off yellow plastic plates – those in evidence on the table across from the gramophone – this had not been out of respect for the deceased projectionist's belongings but rather because they found his chinaware too effete to handle. Although everything – porcelain excepted – created the impression of a shabby bachelor garret.

But one item that had escaped Arnold's attention until now was the telescope trained on the night sky visible through the room's sole source of natural light, a large dormer set in the building's nineteenth century mansard roof. That fine piece, which was in fact a 10" computerised Casegrain-Maksutov must, he reckoned, have cost a pretty penny – but perhaps the projectionist had not been one to invest his savings in more earthly possessions.

Neither Stenning nor Chamberlain, seated at the table, rose to greet him. Chamberlain declined to interrupt perfecting his one-hand card shuffle. Stenning acknowledged the newcomer with a nod, before putting his laptop into sleep mode.

Arnold placed the carrier bag on the nearest unoccupied wicker chair. 'First time I've seen that telescope. You guys been star gazing?'

'Yeah,' said Chamberlain, surprising Palmer with the speed of his next series of riffle shuffles. (What a pity, thought Arnold, that Hugh's mental adroitness was no match for the CIA agent's manual adroitness.) 'We've been looking for a galaxy light years away from this hole.'

'Maybe you should be aiming for something closer to home, like the international space station. Although I doubt whether our bosses would be willing to shell out on something that would mean paying Putin's boys.'

Stenning stood up, went into the kitchen behind the open door beside the mirror and returned with an extra disposable cup and a pot of coffee. 'What have you brought us, Arnold? Good news or bad?'

'You guys had the sense to come unarmed?'

'What do you think? Langley expects humint staff to get by with pea shooters.'

Palmer reached inside the carrier bag. 'That's good news.'

Hugh Chamberlain might have been fast with his pack of cards, but Arnold Palmer was lightning quick with his silenced Luger, shooting both men squarely through the heart.

'Good news for me. Bad news, I'm sorry to say for you, Warren,' he said, having chosen to eliminate Stenning first, partly because he could not afford to have second thoughts about taking out the senior, more respected of the two agents, partly because Chamberlain presented the closer target.

But now that he was standing there gazing down at two corpses, his stomach churned over. Warren Stenning's wide open eyes seemed to be boring into him accusingly. Furthermore, unless this too might have been his imagination, one of Stenning's arms was not entirely lifeless: the fingers appeared to be fluttering spasmodically.

It was not the first time that Palmer had killed. There had been the Czech runner in Prague suspected of being a double agent after passing on tainted intel. The fellow had tried to squeeze more money out of him, until Arnold had blown a fuse. A heated argument at dead of night on the Legion Bridge. The Czech ended up in the Vitavia with a bullet in the back of his head.

This was different. Stenning deserved better.

Relieved to see that Stenning's fingers had stopped twitching, Palmer bent down and closed both men's eyes. There was something repulsive about the fact that Chamberlain's jaw had sagged open. Or was the repulsiveness to be found elsewhere? Palmer went through to the kitchen and helped himself to a handful of water from the tap. Why did his head suddenly feel as if it was splitting? He had done the right thing, hadn't he? Prevented Chamberlain from getting the company into deeper shit. But why Warren? He knew why. Self-sufficient, level-headed and competent, Warren Stenning reminded Arnold of his college's star linebacker. People looked up to him. Arnold Palmer might have been an ace shooter on the pistol and rifle range, but compared to Jeff Swanson and his phenomenal success in fending off touchdowns, Palmer was a sideshow. And Swanson, like Stenning, was modest. Palmer couldn't abide that blend of accomplishment and unpretentiousness that won Swanson so much admiration.

Shaking these thoughts from his pounding head, Arnold closed the tap, wiped it and the sink surround down and returned to the front room, where he removed the suppressor from the Luger, wiped the weapon down, placed the silencer back in the carrier bag, took out and pulled on a pair of latex gloves and, finally, lifted out a second Luger which he had fired earlier with the same silencer in the woods behind his apartment. After making sure that each weapon bore not his but the right fingerprints, he dropped them individually beside their respective owners. Deciding to leave the first two spent cartridges where they had fallen – let the Luritanian forensic experts, for all the good it would do them, take the entry angles of each bullet to indicate the presence of a third party – he grabbed hold of the carrier bag, turned on his heels and left the room to the continuing strains of John Williams's guitar.

In two hours' time, one of the embassy's service staff would raise the alarm after calling in with that evening's takeaway meals. If the ambassador recommended that Palmer handle this mess, his first step would be to summon the police. He was damned if he was going to return to the *Kinothek*. Nobody, he felt sure, had taken any real note of his arrival or departure. The buildings opposite were office blocks closed on a Saturday. And there were no video cameras in this or the next street.

Despite these assurances, a shiver ran down his spine. Were he by some twist of fate to be incriminated for these murders, he would plead functional immunity. Not that that would do him any good with HQ. Langley would wash its hands of him.

No, once again, he was letting his imagination run wild. This was a cut and dried case of two felons losing their cool. As for how they had come by the weapons, not only had Arnold never seen a Luger on show or in use in Hobart's shooting club but he could cite more than enough witnesses ready to assert that the sole weapon he took to shooting practice was a 9mm Browning.

⁂

Memo from K to J

> *Never underestimate the importance of the language of propaganda. That ragamuffin band fighting in the name of Urodina's breakaway eastern republics is not nine tenths miners, tractor drivers and bricklayers and one tenth Nevskian League volunteers but nine tenths the latter and one tenth the former. When reporting the number of fatalities in this conflict continually emphasise casualties on the side of the Urodinian army and downplay the role of independent fascist units operating outside central government control.*
>
> *We have, at all costs, to avoid accusations of having boots on the ground in Urodina. Vespuccians are there solely to train and advise in co-operation with our Erebuan partners defending Urodina and Erebu's eastern flank against the warmonger.*
>
> *All the more reason to reinforce our alliance's raison d'être by ramping up fear and loathing of the Nevskian League throughout the Erebuan Union, notably among those three sprats on the League's north-western fringe.*

Response from J

> *Yes, you Vespuccians have taken the art of manipulating public opinion to a new level. Who else transmutes fiction into fact so tellingly?*

Response from K

> *Well, as Goebbels said, propaganda should be popular, not intellectually pleasing. And never forget one of linguistic programming's golden rules: in giving the ring of truth to seven pieces of mendacity in a row, never fail to ensure that the eighth piece tells the unvarnished truth.*

Rashid had not expected to be given a return mission to Beirut so soon after his first business trip, but it appeared that the nascent bank needed more fare to offer its Board of Directors for their upcoming meeting. And the project put forward for financing by Lebanon's Ministry of Culture, the Beirut Palace of Archaeological and Cultural Heritage, represented a major, eye-catching public relations investment that had taken priority over the feasibility study on development of the country's offshore oil and gas resources. This new project was of particular interest to Rashid insofar as it promised to make his grandfather's poetry known to a wider Arabic-speaking and francophone public.

In the wake of pressure exerted by UNESCO and other influential players, including the cultural ministry's antiquities department, *Solidere,* the company charged with redeveloping central Beirut's city centre had been reproached for failing to guarantee that its building programme respected the capital's five-thousand-year-old archaeological heritage. In particular, greater care and attention, it was told, needed to be paid to excavations under the souks along the Rue Weygand, aligned with the ancient Roman east-west *decumanus* road, where Roman and Byzantine mosaic floors had been uncovered. Now, tasked with helping to establish the planned Palace, *Solidere* hoped to add lustre to its somewhat tarnished image by laying the foundations for a flagship museum and cultural complex in the middle of an artificial lake on the city's outskirts. The design contract had been awarded to a German architectural firm. Accessible on two sides by a mosaic causeway, not only would the low-lying glass and steel structure be mirrored in the surrounding water but its wavelike roof would reflect Beirut's Mediterranean credentials. The lead contractor for the building work was the renowned French firm, Bouygues.

While teaming up again with MEDRIMCOMB's environmental specialist, Horst Gottfried, on this occasion Rashid was also accompanied by Jean-Yves Lefebre, a young civil engineer who had won his spurs working on Bechtel's *Jubail* project in Saudi Arabia.

The fact of the matter was that Rashid's part in this mission was less of consequence than that of his colleagues, for the trio's departmental director already had a clear picture of *Solidere's* finances thanks to the study drafted by the World Bank, joint project sponsor with MEDRIMCOMB. However, the IBRD harboured doubts about the project's impact on the environment: despite recognising that businesses and residents adjacent to the proposed vast building site would have no choice other than to relocate for the duration of the construction work because of intolerable noise and dust pollution levels, the city planning office had yet to come up with reasonable alternative accommodation, while, for their part, the relevant Lebanese ministries had conducted only cursory public enquiries. Horst's environmental impact assessment and Jean-Yves's civil engineering analysis would therefore be determining factors in the report put together by loan officer Rashid Jabour for submission to the hierarchy back home. Although this was not to say that Rashid was absolved from a thoroughgoing analysis of *Solidere's* finances by way of corroborating, enlarging upon or adding to the World Bank's findings, it did mean that the heaviest burden would be shouldered by his colleagues. As it happened, Rashid had reservations about the way *Solidere* was managing its operations, but Frank Welling urged him to play these down and to paint the same favourable, broad brush picture of the company's finances and policy as that presented by the prime lender.

Although in no position to argue with his manager and obliged to follow Welling's guidelines, Rashid decided to cover his back by adding his own pleadings in a separate paper. Should this ambitious project go down the tubes nobody could accuse him of negligence. Consequently, he would confine his contribution to the loan proposal to the bare essentials, fleshed out with Jean-Yves and Horst's input plus the summary review of Lebanon's economic situation, a carbon copy of the analysis appended to his earlier Bank of Beirut project report.

Faced with a reasonably light workload and free of outside commitments (no mother superiors to visit), Rashid had hoped to track down his father but, after contacting his sister, Pascale, and learning that Jabour senior had been drafted to a field hospital well south of Beirut on the border with Syria, was forced to accept defeat.

Under the circumstances, with his first full day and a half of business at *Solidere's* head office under his belt, Rashid felt at liberty to saunter down to the old quarter at midday to look up the address given him by Pascale and to see whether the house in which they had spent their infancy was still standing. The law of coincidence being anything but frugal for those awake to the moment, Jabour crossed paths with a jaunty young woman carrying a clear, water-filled plastic bag containing a goldfish, which he imagined to be a present intended for a child. For in no time at all his thoughts had returned to the fish pond in the courtyard of his parents' house here in Beirut and remembrance of toppling into it one Sunday morning when bending over the edge to investigate what had become of the cupful of tadpoles poured in by him the day before. More frightened than angry, because convinced that someone had crept up from behind and nudged him into the pond, after struggling out of the water, a badly soaked boy, who had just celebrated his seventh birthday, looked vainly around for signs of the culprit. To this day, the adult man recalled shaking plant matter from his hair and shoulders before glancing back into the water to see the goldfish scurrying around in fear for their lives.

Memories of that soaking reminded Rashid of one of the distinguishing features of the courtyard's sturdy double iron-studded oak doors: a solid brass knocker in the form of the head of an old greybeard with ivy growing out of his hair, who, despite his wild mien, was, according to Rashid's mother, a benign guardian spirit. After the goldfish pond incident, her son begged to disagree: that character with the green tangled hair meant nothing but trouble.

After walking to the eastern corner of the *Solidere* downtown reconstruction project, Rashid headed towards the rue Gouraud in the Gemmayzeh neighbourhood. Once there, he discovered more gentrification, notably in the form of café bars and restaurants which had taken over from a series of hole-in-the-wall butchers, bakers and other small retail outlets serving the local community. It was as Rashid was passing one of these café bars that a pale grey Renault Touran pulled up alongside him. The front seat passenger, a swarthy man dressed in a smart business suit and tie, rolled down his window and flashed a gold filling smile.

'*Monsieur Jabour, Shafeek Aoun nous a dit que vous aviez l'intention d'explorer le quartier Achrafieh. Permettez-nous de vous offrir un tour. Plus confortable avec de la climatisation.* Mr Jabour, Shafeek Aoun told us you intended to explore the Achrafieh district. Allow us to give you a ride. More comfortable with air conditioning.'

Rashid recognised neither of the men in the Renault. His first impression of the less nattily dressed stranger behind the wheel was of a bull-necked, shaven-headed bouncer. The man's face was rendered flat and expressionless by wraparound sunglasses making it impossible to see the eyes.

These thoughts melted into the background as the man in the passenger seat opened the car door, stepped onto the pavement and held out his hand. He was taller than Rashid and had a hare lip from which the young loan officer found it difficult to tear away his eyes. 'Hakim Berbera. Mansoor,' (the tall stranger, indicated his companion who made no attempt to look Rashid's way) 'and I are due to meet your colleague Monsieur Lefebre tomorrow. Knowing that we were relatively free this afternoon, Shafeek suggested that we might act as your guides. Unfortunately, by the time he had this idea, you had already left the building.'

Unable to remember telling *Solidere's* Shafeek Aoun that he was headed for the Achrafieh district, Rashid was tempted to say that he would rather pursue his peregrinations in the open air, but realised that this would not go down at all well with fellow countrymen who expected hospitality to be met with due courtesy.

'Well, that's most kind of you, Monsieur Berbera. But no need to address me in French. The fact that I've spent most of my life outside Lebanon doesn't mean I've lost use of my mother tongue.'

Berbera revealed more of his gold fillings 'Jayyid jiddan (Very good). Why speak in the language of the colonisers, when we are blessed with our nobler Levantine Arabic?'

Rashid, who was feeling thirsty, ventured a suggestion. 'How about my offering you both a drink first?'

Berbera threw a quick, disapproving look at the interior of the café bar behind Rashid.

'A good idea. But not here. I can suggest a better place farther up the road.'

Berbera opened the Renault's rear door, and Rashid climbed into the back. The tall businessman walked around the other side to join his guest in the seat behind the driver, who finally acknowledged Rashid's presence by turning, extending a hairy hand and confining his greeting to: 'Mansoor Saad.'

Berbera removed a cigarette case from his breast pocket, opened and offered it first to Rashid, who declined, then helped himself. Rashid saw that his guide's taste in cigarettes ran to upmarket Sobranie Black Russians rather than to the local Cedars brand.

'I see no need for formality, Rashid. Let us continue on first name terms. After all, we are not on a business outing. I shall not bore you with details of how many tonnes of concrete our workmen intend pouring on this project.'

MEDRIMCOMB's loan officer could not decide whether the gurgling sound from the front seat denoted efforts to clear a windpipe irritant or to smother a laugh.

Rashid decided that Berbera's idea of farther up the road was elastic. Saad drove about seventy yards along the rue Gouraud before taking a sharp turn into a narrow side street where gentrification had yet to reach. The Renault stopped alongside a café-restaurant with the name *Maxim's* emblazoned on the red awning above its façade. Only afterwards did the Byronic Rashid reflect on the irony of the fact that the renowned restaurant to which the Beirut eating house seemed to be paying homage stood in Paris's rue Royale.

To the annoyance of a delivery man carting crates of wine into the restaurant's side door, Saad reverse parked the Touran tight up against his van's lowered tail lift. Dark glasses firmly set in place, Saad dismounted together with Rashid and Berbera, his face all but set in stone in view of the lack of emotion displayed in the teeth of the man's protests.

On stepping inside the entrance, Rashid found tables and benches at the front of the establishment given over to customers reading the day's news over multiple espressos or pots of cinnamon anise tea, with tables farther back set for three-course meals.

A broad-shouldered man with bad tooth decay who, judging by the way in which a nearby waiter moved dutifully to one side, Rashid took to be the manager, came up to Berbera and shook him warmly by the hand. 'The rear room is all yours,' he said in guttural Arabic.

Reading the puzzled expression behind Rashid's eyes, Hakim Berbera raised his voice above nearby table chatter. 'Quieter back there. Jawad has let us have the place to ourselves. I've bought a map along with me. We can spread it out and decide which sights take your interest. What can I offer you to drink?'

If warning bells were sounding in the back of Rashid's mind, they had chosen too late to make themselves heard. 'Mint tea would be fine,' came the answer from a man whose mouth felt dry from other than thirst.

But the next moment, faced with Berbera's disarming smile, Rashid concluded that he was fantasising.

Hakim Berbera led the way to the back of the cafe, where the door giving onto the main restaurant area opened into an oblong room down both sides and along the far end of which ran long wooden tables with enough chairs, Rashid guessed, to accommodate large parties. There were two pictures on the walls: one of a crewed catamaran cresting the waves, the other of a polo game. Rashid recalled being told by his mother that the most challenging subjects for oil painters were water and horses in motion. Looking at these poorly executed examples, he had to agree.

But no sooner had Saad closed the door behind them than Rashid was trying to quell a feeling of claustrophobia faced with the room's airlessness and lack of daylight. It put him in mind of an experience several years before trapped in a crowded lift between the thirty-first and thirtieth floors of an Atlantic City hotel: the lights had failed, plunging the occupants in darkness and calling for an uncommon effort on Rashid's part not to panic at the thought that the stranded capsule's oxygen supply might be limited. But, the lights were not long in flickering back on, after which the lift gave a reanimated shudder and resumed its descent.

There was no point in Rashid telling himself that this windowless room was a hundred times larger than that lift or that his two companions were unperturbed by their surroundings; claustrophobia was not responsive to reason.

This unsettling line of thought was interrupted by Berbera and an invitation to take a seat halfway down the side table to their left. It meant that Rashid found himself sat facing the polo match. A player in a green jersey defending his team's goal mouth was about to clash sticks with one of two red jersey opponents. Berbera pulled out the chair opposite Rashid, drew the city map from his pocket and unfolded it between them on the table. The next moment the door opened, and a waiter brought in a pot of mint tea for two and an espresso. Saad waited for him to leave before taking up the espresso and settling down in a chair which he placed with its back to the door.

Rashid watched as Berbera poured the mint tea, a ceremony punctuated with the accompanying 'Insha'Allah' incantation, although the young banker sensed there was more to this than mere ritual. After Berbera finished filling his glass, Rashid raised his own in its silver holder by way of salutation and reciprocated with 'Insha'Allah'.

Berbera took two sips, set his glass back down on the table beside the tray with a teapot that, thought Rashid, would have been the envy of many a European silversmith, and, after fishing a red highlighter from his jacket, coloured over an entry on the map, turned this around so that it was facing Rashid and said pointedly: 'What can you tell us about this?'

When Rashid leant forward, he saw that Berbera had highlighted The Lady of the Sacred Heart Convent in east Beirut. If a first taste of the tea had soothed his nerves, the sight of the blood-stained convent leaping off the map at him in tandem with the steely look in his questioner's eyes set Rashid back to square one. He began to think that his claustrophobia had been brought on by that earlier sense of foreboding as much as by anything else.

His first solution, dismissed no sooner than it was formulated, because Saad's impressive bulk effectively blocked his sole exit, was to stand up, protest at being hoodwinked for some inexplicable or mistaken reason by bogus *Solidere* employees and stride out of the room. The second, more practical but by no means attractive solution was to tough it out. All very well, but he had yet to learn whom he was dealing with: undercover officialdom or people a law unto themselves? Not much to choose between the two, on reflection, be it in Lebanon or in any showcase western democracy.

Best to play along with Hakim and wait for him to lay his cards on the table. 'First and foremost,' replied Rashid, 'it's home to sisters of mercy catering for the destitute in the Shatila refugee camps. But apparently it's also a dead letter box for international messengers.'

'And since when, Rashid, have you been assuming the role of courier alongside that of investment banker?' The fact that Hakim was stirring honey into his mint tea did not make his expression any the sweeter.

Rashid gave a dispirited sigh. 'What's this all about, Hakim? If you mean what I think you mean, let me tell you that I've been through all this before.'

'How interesting. With whom?' Hakim flashed an impatient look at Saad, who looked as if he might be falling asleep. Rashid caught the glance and deduced that a heavy lunch had put paid to the espresso's kick-starting Mansoor's afternoon.

'Representatives of a country, I fancy,' said Rashid, 'whose people are in the grips of Islamophobia.'

'But whose government specialises in global interference?'

The rhetorical question took Rashid by surprise, denting what little composure he had managed to muster until then.

'You choose strange bedfellows, Hakim.'

It was an infelicitous remark, but one that appeared to leave Berbera unmoved. There was a brief, reflective pitter-patter of fingers against the table edge, before Berbera retrieved the highlighter and threw into red relief the Bashoura and Martyrs cemeteries.

If this left Rashid as much in the dark as that time in Atlantic City, on this occasion he felt no need to fear the worst.

Hakim tapped the highlighter against a gold filling. 'We understand that two CIA agents gone missing in Luritania are presumed dead.'

A suddenly worried man, Rashid tried to get a hold of himself. He opened and closed his mouth without articulating anything intelligible.

Hakim glanced at a note jotted down at the bottom of the map beside the legends box: *Hobbies include acting. Amateurish.*

The adjective, almost tacked on as an afterthought, came across slightingly.

His power of speech regained, Rashid leant forward across the table. Swamped as he was by dread of what Hakim and his sidekick might be capable, he told himself not to back down. 'Dead?'

'Perhaps because they didn't buy your story.' Hakim highlighted a third area, Beirut's Jewish cemetery. 'And because you killed Jack Mason.'

A burst of indignant laughter only underlined the fact that Rashid was unnerved. 'That's arrant nonsense, Hakim. A twenty-eight-year-old investment banker starting out on his career. Why on earth ...?'

'The purpose of the note you delivered to the convent,' said Berbera, cutting Rashid short, 'was to inform its recipients of an arms shipment for Hezbollah in the battle against Israel and Islamic State.'

Rashid held exculpatory hands out wide. 'I was told it was a shipment of humanitarian aid for Syrian refugees.'

The crash of Saad's chair legs against the parquet floor as the Lebanese shifted his bulk forward made Rashid doubt whether Mansoor really had fallen asleep. Had he noticed how the man's stubby fingers danced across his iPhone's touch screen and pad, he would have known better.

Without bothering to turn in Rashid's direction, his eyes fixed on cascading screen tiles, Mansoor Saad broke his silence in a way that made Rashid change his mind about writing Saad the silent Lebanese off as a heavy-cum-factotum. 'Tell him, Hakim. We're losing time.'

Berbera poured himself more tea, leaving the handle turned in the direction of a man who, no longer his guest, but somebody striving to mount his defence unaided, was beginning to appreciate what it felt like to be the accused in the dock awaiting sentence.

'We're Hezbollah,' said Hakim at last, leaving time, if, by the look on Rashid's face, any was needed for the message to sink in. 'We've been cheated out of what's rightfully ours. Those arms ended up with Daesh for use against us and Bashar al-Assad and his regime.'

Saad heaved himself off his chair, loosened his belt a notch and walked across to join the other two at the table.

'The consignment was due to be delivered at this point along the coast,' he said, seizing Hakim's highlighter and marking the location on the map. 'But a group of Daesh militants delivered it to this point here' (another red scar) 'closer to the border with Syria.'

Rashid was ready with his objection. 'Wait a minute. The Israelis commandeered *Le Marquis de Honfleur*, had it dock in Cyprus, had the cargo offloaded and confiscated it.'

Mansoor came the nearest he would to smiling. 'You heard only part of the story. What Israel wanted the world to believe. Because the truth was too embarrassing. In the early hours of the day following impoundment of the cargo, thanks to a well-paid harbor master Daesh stole every crate from under Israel's nose.'

'In other words,' said Hakim, eying Rashid over the rim of his glass, 'weapons intended for us were snatched by our enemies. This pains us, Rashid. What can you tell us about it?'

Sensing that the very person he expected to be the more hardheaded of the two was less interested in apportioning blame than in sketching out the facts, Rashid ventured to try to clear his name by directing his reply at Saad. 'All I can tell you is what I told those two CIA men back in Luritania. I was a simple messenger delivering post from A to B at the request of C. The first I learnt of the death of C was upon my return to Luritania. And now, I learn for the first time from you that both agents might be dead. Don't you understand? You're talking to somebody on the sidelines with no idea what this is all about.'

Saad flicked his fingers at Berbera. 'Hakim, we're getting nowhere. What's done is done. I don't think either of us seriously thinks that Jabour had anything to do with our waylaid shipment. I suggest you move on.'

Finding consolation in warmth, Hakim cradled the glass in his hands.

'Rashid, Rashid, you would have us believe you are innocent of misdoing. So how to explain your latest adventure, which is quite out of character for the respectable, low profile banker you make yourself out to be?'

The sense of reprieve given the MEDRIMCOMB loan officer by Saad's intervention dissolved into perplexity. 'My latest adventure? What's that supposed to mean?'

Berbera replaced his glass on the tray, extracted a folded sheet of paper from his jacket pocket, opened it up on top of the map and used the highlighter to draw more blood by underscoring the printed heading: **Symmetric-key cryptography**.

Rashid blanched at the sight of the copy of the same article downloaded by him from the Internet only days before.

The whites of Hakim's knuckles stood out against the tightly clasped highlighter. 'Decrypting classified documents. Stolen classified documents.'

Rashid squirmed in his seat. 'I like puzzles.' It was a feeble response and one that immediately had Rashid feeling like an embarrassed juvenile dragged up in front of the magistrate with no better excuse than inquisitiveness for shoplifting a book about pseudo-random number generators

Rashid took a gulp of by now cold tea, before turning to the pot for an injection of warmer liquid. How had these Hezbollah agents come by that article? Who could have hacked into his computer? All too aware that flippancy was the wrong road to travel down, he decided to tread carefully.

'People should know better than to leave sensitive documents lying around in public places.'

'In public places.'

Rashid did not for one moment believe that Hakim's lengthy musing meant that he was debating whether his informant might be referring to a railway station waiting room or a subway toilet.

The tall Lebanese used a toothpick to ease a mint leaf from the spout of the silver teapot with the precision of a surgeon removing a stitch. 'Where precisely did you come by those classified documents?'

As opposed to living through the ordeal of telling the truth the whole truth and nothing but the truth, give or take the odd omission, Rashid was faced with the dilemma of either betraying his friends' trust or cutting a more credible figure as a liar than he had as a truth teller. He was reminded of Vanessa's words on that first night after they had made love. In taking on the role of Lord Byron, she had said, he should remember Stanislavsky's advice to his players: create believable. The next morning, over brunch, she had lent him her copy of Harold Clurman's *Lies Like Truth*.

And suddenly it came to him, almost light-headedly, that he felt more relaxed about lying than he had about telling the truth. He was even looking forward to crossing swords with Hakim and Mansoor.

Rashid started out, as he intended to follow on, with an unabashed piece of nonsense. A gamble. But he doubted whether whoever had paid these two Hezbollah recruits to do their discovery for them had vouchsafed the full story.

'Together with a copy of a Royal Opera House programme.'

Hakim's eyes clouded over with a mixture of suspicion and incomprehension.

'The Royal Opera House in London's Covent Garden. The programme for an evening performance of *La Traviata*. Left on the back seat of a taxi side by side with a briefcase.'

'So tell us why you didn't leave well alone or draw your find to the driver's attention.'

Rashid had a ready answer for that. 'The driver was a shifty type. Jordanian. I didn't trust him to do the right thing.'

'Which was?'

'To take it back to his employer's office and enter it as lost property.'

'But it was all right for you to …' Hakim pondered his choice of words. '… purloin it?'

'I like puzzles, particularly mathematical puzzles. The briefcase had a numbers lock. Child's play to open. I decided to take it home and …'

'Home being Luritania?'

'Yes.'

'So once you got home, opened the briefcase and saw what was inside, why didn't you try to trace the owner?'

'Ah, yes, well, you see, Hakim, the owner failed to leave his or her name and postal or e-mail address inside, not to mention his or her telephone number.'

'Your curiosity piqued, you wondered whether you might be able to decrypt the contents?'

'Indeed, Hakim, indeed. Perhaps I should be ashamed to admit to as much, but it's true.'

'And,' said Mansoor Saad, revealing a pair of not unfriendly, nutmeg brown eyes, as he at last removed his sunglasses to start polishing them with a soft cloth taken from his shirt pocket, 'you went ahead and gave it a try.'

Rashid all but chortled. 'Gave it a try, Mansoor. Gave it a try. But, I'm sorry to say, got nowhere.'

'And had you got anywhere, what would you have done next?'

'Good question. I must admit I hadn't got around to thinking that one out. I suppose it would have depended on what I came up with.'

In the middle of extracting a second mint leaf, Hakim paused to give an artful smile. 'And all this decrypting, attempted, should I say, decrypting, you did on your own without sharing the news with anyone?'

Watching Berbera spread the second leaf carefully out beside the first near the lip of the tray, Rashid wondered whether his questioner was emulating Cassandra.

'That's right. I didn't.'

'Didn't what?'

'Share it. What you call the news.'

Mansoor Saad removed his jacket to reveal upper arms the size of hams. It occurred to Rashid that if his interrogators voted for violence, he would leave this infernal café-restaurant and its rear hell hole nowhere near as in one piece as when he crossed the threshold. On the other hand, as opposed to his foxier associate, Saad was still acting the personification of forbearance.

'As I said before, we're prepared to believe you had nothing to do with the fact that those weapons destined for us fell into Daesh hands. A joint American-Israeli fuck-up. Something the Americans are more famous for than our neighbours, wouldn't you agree?'

Rashid might have agreed with Saad, had he not known better than to side with the enemy.

'Whether you would or wouldn't makes no difference, but those same bastards capable of using a cruise missile to swat a fly have paid us handsomely to extract the truth from you about the other matter. Their pissant idea of a consolation prize.'

The way in which Saad lingered over the word extract made Rashid revise his opinion: the show of patience of the man he had mistaken for no more than a chauffeur was wearing thin.

'Do you persist in telling us that you said not one word about your decryption efforts to anybody else?'

Catching the drift of Saad's question from the first four syllables, Rashid put on a convincing low-key smile. 'Who likes admitting to failure? If I had got anywhere, yes, it might have been a different story.'

Irrespective of which of Rashid's interrogators took precedence over the other, Berbera was unwilling to hold his tongue any longer. 'We only have your word that you got nowhere. According to our information, there were two documents. Compared to the second, decoding the first should have been plain sailing. Are you saying that defeated you as well?'

If Rashid hated to think how Likud would react to learning that its allies in Washington thought nothing of doing deals with Hezbollah, it was only momentarily, because Berbera might as well have landed him a right uppercut. Having foolishly persuaded himself that Hakim and Mansoor's paymasters were shitting their pants about the second, hard-nut-to-crack document, not only had he completely downgraded the importance of the first document about which there could be no denying that decrypting it was a piece of cake, but by no stretch of the imagination could he expect either properly briefed questioner to believe that he had come up short with that one.

Rashid had no alternative other than to play the truth card, knowing that this could prove his downfall. 'Ah, yes, I clean forgot about the short document. Nothing that sensitive in it, I would have thought.'

'Bull,' said Berbera, clicking his cigarette case mechanically open and shut. 'It was sensitive enough to encrypt.'

'And,' continued a thoughtful Mansoor taking up the slack in the midst of ruminating on the seaworthiness of a catamaran listing perilously to one side, 'in addition to conveniently forgetting about your success with the first document, you have difficulty perhaps in remembering whether you might have mentioned its contents to a friend or two. Or three. Or four.'

Faced with a now anything but benign Saad and feeling as if he had dug his own grave, Rashid temporised in the wishful hope that the Americans had limited Mansoor and Hakim's understanding of that first document to the bare bones. Careful, he thought, whom you drag into this. No names, no pack drill.

'I might have mentioned something to a couple of friends over coffee. But wait, before you say anything, that document contained nothing that an inquisitive blogger couldn't find searching the Internet. Plenty of conspiracy chestnuts out there which people like to latch on to. Particularly if they bear out the belief that we're all pawns in a game played by the Rothschilds and the Rockefellers.'

Mansoor splayed out both hands, as if inspecting his meaty palms for signs of Rashid's future. 'These friends, what did they have to say about your memos?'

This was the first time that Saad or Berbara had spoken of memos. Could this have been a slip of the tongue, revealing elementary knowledge of the second document? Or was it a trap sprung to catch him flat-footed should he show a moment's hesitation in rebutting the idea? Rashid thought best to avoid ambush. With denial. 'They reckoned that the briefcase with its mysterious documents had been deliberately planted so as to lure some naïve idiot to take their find to the press.'

'And,' said Berbera, his highlighter poised over the Al Amine mosque as if, Rashid reflected, in search of illumination, for it would surely have been desecration to colour red either of the twin domes of that masterpiece of Lebanese architecture, 'who did they think would be so prodigal as to give away a tooled leather briefcase?'

Once again, Rashid felt himself foundering against the next outcrop of intel, the cumulative effect of which threatened to sink him for good.

'A mischief maker who gets the same kind of kick out of deception as a hacker gets out of disruption.'

'Yet,' pursued Hakim, the highlighter now resting harmlessly on the top of his cigarette case, 'you never mentioned the second document?'

That, concluded Rashid, contained the memos which had the Americans worried enough to shower largesse on Hezbollah. But at the same time, all Vanessa's lessons about acting out believable truths and all those polygraph-cheating tricks he remembered about how to ride out the rough patches of an interrogation were valueless now that he had steered his own suicidal course to a merciless reef.

Scowling at the polo player who seemed too hemmed in to be able to save the situation for his side, Rashid flapped a feeble hand illustrative of submission. 'It's possible that I might have.'

'And your friends discouraged you from continuing with your decryption?' Mansoor had the fixed look in his eyes of someone counting the seconds until he sprang his trap.

'Absolutely.'

'How did you react to that recommendation?' Eyes hitherto concentrated on the off balance catamaran drilled into Rashid's eyes.

With the strength born of the desperation of a drowning man, Rashid willed himself to withstand the heat behind Mansoor's twin gimlets. 'Told them they were probably correct, but went ahead anyway. Getting nowhere again.'

'But reported back to them?

'No, why should I? There was nothing to report.'

'Good. So now you can inform them you have succeeded.'

For Rashid it was no longer a question of a trap but of brain failure. 'I can what?'

'You're not deaf, are you? Show him, Hakim.'

Berbera delved into his breast pocket and produced an envelope, which he laid on the table.

'You destroy that indecipherable second document and take on deciphering another in its place for which the Americans have helpfully provided the key. All here in this envelope.'

Whatever he might have thought of Mansoor before, Rashid reverted to his original assessment of the man: someone capable of breaking a few fingers. Best, therefore, to accept the offer, but without jumping at it. After all, there had to be more to it than this.

Hakim's smile was overlaid with gold. 'You wish to object?'

'Well, I don't see …'

'You don't see your friends reacting any differently to the contents of this new document than they did to the first?'

'Right. But I suppose a lot depends on the nature of those contents.'

'Another conspiracy theory. With little of substance in common with the first.'

'So why should I or my friends believe in it any more than in the first?'

'Our employers doubt whether you or they will.'

'Then aren't they, we, you, all of us wasting our time?'

'Not if the results get published,' said Saad, pulling Hakim's map towards him and perusing it as if the present conversation was of only partial interest to him, which it patently was not.

Rashid looked as baffled as he felt. 'What?'

'Yes, you, Rashid Jabour, will make sure that the decrypted text is given to the media outlets listed in Hakim's envelope.'

It seemed evident to Rashid that whatever the new text contained either in no way reflected badly on its drafters or was as politically loaded as the first document. But if so, why did the Americans need him or his friends to release this red herring into the media ocean? It could only be because they were making his cooperation conditional upon burning the original. But how could they bank on that?

The man who had been reading Rashid's mind rather than the map looked up with the answer.

'If this text fails to make the headlines within a week of your return to Europe, we will deliver your father up to the jihadists.'

Rashid felt as if the ground was opening up under him. 'You bastards. What's my father got to do with this?'

'You're insulting the wrong people, Rashid. Your father has nothing to do with this. But when we tell the jihadists of the new caliphate that your father refuses to treat any of their war wounded taken to his field hospital, they will post a video on the Internet decrying the policy adopted by *Médecins Sans Frontières* of discriminating between those it treats.'

'But that's not true.'

'Perhaps not in your father's case, but who will know the difference once they see him pleading for his life? Think carefully, Rashid. The action you take – destroying the original of that second document and seeing that its replacement gets maximum publicity – will save you and your mother the ordeal of watching Daesh parade images of the beheading of an eminent French surgeon.'

'Yes,' added Berbera, picking the highlighter up and balancing it between his forefingers, 'and should the original document ever resurface, whether decrypted or not, know that the Americans will track you and your father down and put paid to you both.'

Rashid viewed both men with stony, half-dead eyes. What point was there in taking out his anger and resentment against them? The tables had been turned. Fate had propelled one messenger into the unwholesome company of two others.

Mansoor reached over his associate to push the envelope across to Rashid. 'Valuable item. Be sure not to lose it.'

An already sickened Rashid Jabour felt no better for recalling that Jack Mason had offered the same parting advice.

※

Memo from K to J

Our State Department spokesperson has excelled herself by announcing that President Falseman ordered the dropping of Little Boy and Fat Man on Niponia to deter the Nevskians from invading that country. The fact that Falseman targeted residential areas, killing two hundred and fifty thousand civilians, while visiting atrocious after-effects on survivors and their offspring, won Vespuccia few friends. To my mind, citing geopolitical justification for that ignoble act at a time when Niponia is commemorating its seventieth anniversary can only create more ill-feeling.

Response from J

And man's inhumanity to man gets no better with the passing years. Fascist elements in Urodina have started murdering priests and celebrants in Orthodox churches answering to the Nevskian patriarchate. In seeking to eradicate all Slavonic religious influence, while vaunting the superiority of Catholicism, their stated aim is to bring Urodina closer to Erebu. I am amazed that not one Erubean head of state or government has protested. Evidently, acts such as these, which would normally be considered indefensible, are acceptable insofar as they serve further to weaken and isolate the ethnic Nevskian population.

※

Because of exceptionally warm weather, Tich, the first of the Lenfindi Club to arrive at the airport, texted the rest of the group to meet him for breakfast out in the open air terrace on the second-floor observation deck overlooking the aprons and runways. Vanessa and Rashid, the first to turn up, found Tich leaning on the railing at the front of the deck, watching the gravity-defying ascent into the heavens of a Turkish Airlines Boeing 737. Vanessa shielded her eyes from the sunlight glancing off the aircraft's white-on-red wild goose tailfin logo.

'Dreaming of mosques and minarets, Tich?' she said, adjusting an errant tortoiseshell barrette.

Easing himself away from the balustrade, Tich turned to greet Vanessa with a kiss on each cheek, Rashid with a handshake.

'I try to limit my dreaming to shut-eye time, Van. If you were inferring that my head was in the clouds on a par with that Boeing, I beg to correct you. Who, in his right mind, would want to set foot on a land which makes nonsense of prayer mats and muezzins by persecuting its religious minorities? No, I suggest we wake up and smell the coffee. See those tables over there?' Tich indicated two round, wood-slatted outdoor tables to the left of the terrace's entrance doors. 'Reserved for us.'

They sat down under a green awning flapping gently in the morning breeze. It was not long before the rest of the party arrived: Craig and Isabelle followed by a sunburnt Justin.

'Someone with as many moles as yours,' said Vanessa, 'ought not to overdo sunbathing.' It was a remark met with embarrassment by Justin, confusion by Rashid and amusement by the others.

'I went out into the park yesterday to learn my lines, Vanessa. Clobbered by the next best thing to La Mancha's heat and aridity, this method actor got so much into character that he fell asleep. That merits praise not opprobrium.'

'Oh dear, Justin, we have make-up for the tan. And if you are going to fall asleep, keep it for rehearsals. I don't want to hear titters from the audience brought on by your snoring.' This further revelation left Justin smarting and Rashid wishing he were somewhere else.

A young, fresh-faced waiter appeared as if from out of nowhere to take their orders. Unclipping an android smartphone from the top of his green and black-striped apron, he buzzed their requests through to the kitchen.

'The times they are a-changing,' said Tich. 'Mark my words, the lead pencil will soon be as old hat as the quill pen.'

'With Hitachi renting duty-free space here,' said Craig, 'it wouldn't surprise me if they start using robots to serve us.'

'Not all bad,' said Vanessa. 'Despite dire warnings about artificial intelligence, I don't think Cambridge's foremost theoretical physicist has got the jitters about the next generation of robotic vacuum cleaners.'

'Really?' said Tich. 'Those flying saucer ones? Killers on staircases.'

'I don't live in a duplex, Tich.'

'How about robot bookshelf dusters?'

'I believe the Japanese have yet to get around to robots in black fishnet tights tall enough for their feather dusters to reach *The Snows of Kilimanjaro*.'

'That's what I don't like about advanced technology. Short on *joie de vivre*.'

Neither rolling mechanically on wheels nor spirited out of an oil lamp, the waiter resurfaced to set out the group's food and drinks orders.

'Talking of which,' boomed Tich over the roar of an incoming Lufthansa Boeing 747-8's turbofan engines, 'what have you all been able to come up with about the suggestions e-mailed you for today's get-together?'

'I found a ridiculous piece of local environmental journalism,' said Justin, unaware of the white powdered sugar moustache created by his almond croissant, which Vanessa refrained from commenting on as very much in character. 'I suppose most of you, apart from Rashid, will have seen it. Tich's killer vacuum cleaners are nothing compared to Luritania's killer trees. *Killer trees to be axed,* says our leading French-language rag. After totting up the number of deaths caused by people driving head-on into roadside trees, Luritania's Minister for the Environment has recommended felling dangerous timber along our forest road network. Naturally enough, this prompted a barrage of letters to the press. One tongue-in-cheek writer enquired whether Luritania's trees were uprooting themselves with a view to stalking everything on four wheels driven by stone-cold sober Luritanians.'

'No, I didn't see that,' said Tich. 'Another fine example, though, of one governmental step forward meaning two steps back. Is that all, Justin?'

'Sorry to say that between managing my seven to six o'clock grind and mugging up on Williams's Don Quixote, I had precious little time to devote to your linguistic suggestions.'

'Oh, well,' said Tich, who had his own good reasons for not reproaching others for backsliding, 'does anyone else care to continue?'

Isabelle raised a hand. 'Another tree story pretty much replicating the behavior of Justin's *Lord of the Rings* trees. Apparently, a British family in the north of France has received handsome compensation from the local authorities after their retired 62-year-old mother was flattened by a tree. And not just any old tree. The tree that fell on the poor old dear had originally been planted as a tribute to Napoleon's only son.'

Rashid interrupted munching of a tuna and sesame seed roll. 'Nature's revenge for Waterloo.'

Isabelle looked up from the vortex caused by stirring sugar into her cappuccino. 'Hardly. Napoleon's son, Francois Bonaparte, died of tuberculosis at the age of twenty-one after a short and misspent life. I don't think he carried quite the same historical clout as his dad.'

'No more tree stories?' asked Tich, looking around the gathering.

When nobody came forward with an offer and Rashid's roll triggered memories of Ali Baba and the Forty Thieves, the young man cast as Lord Byron spoke up. 'Yes, in a way, Tich. About a monkey puzzle tree which I succeeded in climbing. But better left till later.'

'Why not now?'

Rashid flashed a glance at Vanessa. 'Well, we might not see eye to eye about fun and games.'

'Sounds portentous, Rash. All right, till later. Craig, your turn.'

'Sorry Tich. Mother Hubbard's. Blame it on *Camino Real*. But I did help Isabelle out with her contributions.'

'Sounds,' said Tich, 'as if the stakes you lot are playing for in *Camino Real* rival those in *Casino Royale*.'

'Come off it,' said Vanessa, 'he doesn't have nearly the number of lines to learn as some of the characters he plays opposite.'

'You mean Kilroy, Marguerite and Gutman?' Craig pulled a face. 'That's as maybe. But how would you like it, if I missed one of my cues?'

'Wait a minute, I'm the villain of the piece, Vanessa,' said Isabelle, extracting a note pad from her sling bag, 'not Mr Casanova here. He came to my linguistic rescue.'

'That's it, Vanessa. So cut me some slack.'

Vanessa raised her eyebrows. 'Oh dear, another temperamental actor. Don't expect me to take a powder.'

'Can we cool it, please?' said Tich. 'This isn't school, where you have to hand your homework in on time. Let's hear about Isabelle and Craig's joint contribution.'

'Right,' said Isabelle. 'I started out by asking Craig why, if you can be nonplussed, can't you be nonminussed? If level-headed, why not uneven-headed? If stick-in-the-muds are square, why are innovators not circular? Why do we call construction site derricks cranes rather than giraffes? Are they free-flying? Mind you, I have to confess that the French language follows the same twisted logic here.

'Then again, how to explain to an extraterrestrial that we sentence people to life imprisonment for genocide and regicide, but rehabilitate them after attempted suicide and allow them to walk free after committing pesticide and herbicide?'

'And,' said Vanessa, 'how did Mr Casanova respond to all this?'

'By telling me that every language had its fair share of illogicalities.'

'*Le mei congratulazioni, Giacomo!*'

'That's what I like to hear,' said Tich. 'Keeping an even keel. Sail on, Isabelle.'

'Well, next we compared the name differences between a few similar English and French parlour games. Whereas Craig used to play snakes and ladders as a child, I was into goose – *le jeu de l'oie*. What he knows as ludo, I know as *petits chevaux*. As for your pencil and paper game noughts and crosses, we French call that *morpion*. And just as one man's meat is another man's poison, we call your tiddlywinks *le jeu de puces*. The fact that *puces* and *morpions* also mean lice might explain why the British unjustly accuse the French of lack of hygiene.'

'What bothers me,' said Justin, 'is the thought that once Brussels gets its teeth into these differences, they'll want to harmonise. Depending upon whether they plump for *jeu de l'oie* or *jeu des serpents et des échelles*, one of us will have to redesign our board game. And if they get proscriptive about noughts and crosses and prescriptive with *morpion*, we British will have to eat humble pie as a result of scratching our privates in public. Apologies, I interrupted.'

'That's all right, Justin. I was nearly through. Yes, so finally, a French girl's tribute to Monty Python. Whereas you English use *rhubarb, rhubarb* for crowd mutterings, we descendants of Astérix prefer *murmures* or *brouhaha*. Since brouhaha is closer to your hubbub, *murmures* strikes me as ideal, because it could be confused with *blackberries, blackberries*. And, in case you are thinking of asking … no, we have nothing that I know of as colourful as the *raspberry* used in your expression to *blow a raspberry*.'

'No,' said Tich. 'You would need a French berry prefixed by your wind-breaking *pet*. But perhaps Craig didn't tell you that a raspberry is English shorthand for a fart? All part of the beauty of our rhyming slang. Too many raspberry tarts, too many farts.'

'I'm too much of a gentleman,' said Craig. 'Runs in the family. The last thing my parents thought of in naming our sooty-coloured cat Smutty was that less pure minds would view the creature differently. Anyway, enough of me. What does the maestro have to offer to counter or complement our *pot-pourri*?'

'By our, do you mean Isabelle's fragrant contributions or your rotten pot?'

'I don't smoke pot.'

'Glad to hear it. But I have always been one for ladies first. And we seem to have forgotten, Van.'

Vanessa set down her coffee cup. 'I suppose I ought to apologise about rubbishing other people's *Camino Real* excuses. Because the fact is that I've had to devote a fair bit of my spare time to breaking in the International American School student I chose for the part of Kilroy over a more experienced candidate. That one walked away from the auditions in a huff, shouting, "The kid's hoping to pass his baccalauréat, and she goes and gives him a fat bunch of lines to learn."'

'So, what have I come up with? Material more suited to Isabelle inasmuch as it touches on the seeming illogicalities of English pronunciation.'

Vanessa unfolded a piece of paper tucked between the pages of her copy of the play. 'Right, why should the bough of a tree be pronounced in the same way as the bow an actor makes to the audience? Why is cough not pronounced in the same way as rough and tough? Not to mention thorough. So heaven help the wretched foreigner obliged to ask for directions to Loughborough. Similarly, how should Franz and Heidi, twisting their tongues around furlough and dough, be expected to remember that that last syllable sounds like "oh"?

'But since we English like to complicate matters, we have plough and sough (as in the piggy noise the wind might make in Justin's trees) pronounced in line with "how". And, of course, let's not forget to add trough to this rich mix together with a bird called a chough.

'Anyway, last but not least, however stupid it might seem, why should English learners not pronounce manslaughter man's laughter? Over to you, Tich.'

Clearing his throat, Tich avoided the eyes of those around him. 'Well, I regret to confess that I was so immersed in my *Rosetta Stone* Mandarin beginners' course that I fell behind in my lead responsibilities.'

'That's news to me,' said Vanessa. 'Why the sudden interest in Chinese? Oh, yes. I'd forgotten. Your new cosy relationship with the triads, whom you were teaching the difference between *gilt* and *guilt* before needing their help with your laundry.'

Tich paused to loosen the shirt button above his midriff nearest to parting company with its cotton thread. 'No need to cast aspersions, Van. Chinese, as you well know, is the language of the future. Spoken by the people of the future. Their economy, the economy of the future. Forget the dollar. The yuan, the world reserve currency of the future, is backed by gold.'

Rashid lowered his coffee cup. 'Right, the dollar like the euro is intrinsically valueless.'

'However,' – Tich reached into his shirt pocket – 'I did manage to spare the time between grappling with basic hanzi and the four tones, to jot a few things down for your delectation today on the back of a paper place mat from the *Moulin à café.*'

He brushed his shirt front clean of croissant flakes before starting to read from a grubby folded sheet of paper, the back of which showed the coffee shop's logo: two millers taking a coffee break outside their mill.

'A nice tautology from an article I was looking through by a respected writer: *a chance coincidence*. Let's say, I have yet to encounter a deliberate coincidence.' Tich faltered, screwing up his eyes. 'Shit, it's a sign of the pitiless march of time when you can't decode your own writing.'

'Decoding's more my line,' said Rashid. 'In fact, Tich, if we've finished with the fun and games, I can tell you about that monkey puzzle. You see, I've managed to crack the code for Justin's second document.'

'I thought you said it would be a bugger to break even with Musgrave's cypher?'

'That's right, but in view of our agreement not to let Klaus Radetzky's murderers off the hook, I burnt the midnight oil.'

'And that means *le nostre congratulazioni, signore Turing?*'

'No, Tich, don't let's make out that I can hold a candle to Alan Turing. And, in the present case, I'd appreciate remaining anonymous.'

'You've brought the translation with you?' asked Justin, his journalistic antennae focused on Rashid.

Rashid dipped into the briefcase by the side of his chair. 'As before, I made copies for everyone. But there's something you ought to know. What I'm giving you here is an abridged version of the original. I doubt whether any of you is interested in the findings of a report on last year's Afghan poppy harvest. For reasons best known to them, the compilers of this more contentious material chose to tuck their text in among the paragraphs of the poppy report. Frankly, printing that out separately was not only too much of a hassle but a waste of paper.'

On giving the same sham explanation to Vanessa the previous evening, Rashid had limited himself to retailing the gist of the print-out in order to put her on the same footing as the rest of the Lenfindi Club and to avoid giving the impression that the two of them were colluding.

The first to put the text down, while waiting for the rest to finish, was Tich, who scribbled a note on his folded paper place mat, then, again vexed by lack of precision, sat counterproductively fiddling with its legibility.

The last to put her copy down, Isabelle gave a dissatisfied frown before returning to her cappuccino.

'Your opinions?' asked Rashid.

Leaning back in his chair, Craig stretched linked hands above his head. 'Another variation on the conspiracy merchants' propaganda.'

'Isabelle?'

'Disappointment, since it supports those in the same camp as the first document's policy makers.'

'Justin?'

'Credible, but hardly groundbreaking news.'

'So why did someone go to the bother of camouflaging it?'

'You have a point. No idea.'

'Vanessa?'

'Whether true or false, I don't believe that Justin should put his head on the chopping block by publishing it.'

This was not what Rashid expected to hear. As at no stage had he confessed to Vanessa that he had been blackmailed, they had spent the night arguing about how to treat the decrypted document. In the end, before they both fell asleep in the early hours of the morning, an exhausted but restive Vanessa had relented, siding with his suggestion that they should talk Justin into turning the material into an exposé. Now she was avoiding Rashid's eyes.

'Tich?'

'It's a *non sequitur.*'

'I'm sorry?'

'I expected the red leather briefcase's second document to contain a list of the Council of Twenty's action plans together with sponsors and the number of dollars to be put on the table. This is no such thing.'

'Easy enough to explain,' said Rashid, who had foreseen this objection. 'Three possibilities. One: whoever stashed these documents in his briefcase forgot to pick up or print out what we can now call the third one. Two: each of these documents was intended for different consumers. Three: both were going to be delivered to one and the same person already in possession of your missing text.'

Tich was watching a couple taking a selfie at the front of the observation desk, where they appeared to be trying to get more into the frame than just the tail fin shamrock of the Aer Lingus Boeing behind them taxiing out to the runway. Of the uncharitable opinion that selfie sticks had taken narcissism to new depths, he turned away.

'I'll grant you that. But if you want my honest opinion, I can't help thinking we should leave well alone. Because Musgrave's code has brought us back to where we started.'

'I thought you and Justin were all for publication. Why the change of heart?'

'Perhaps the fact that we've been given to understand that certain people are prepared to stop at nothing to prevent this from leaking out.'

'But,' said Craig, 'you would have to be a few sandwiches short of a picnic not to read this as yet another fanciful conspiracy. Them, Russia and China, against us.'

'And who's driven them against us?' said Isabelle.

Tich raised a moderating hand. 'Let's stay off politics. Frankly, I don't know what to make of it. Fanciful or as real as tomorrow.'

With a broad bank of cloud about to cross the sun, Justin removed and folded his dark glasses. 'If, as Craig suggests, it's fanciful, why should there be any threat hanging over it?'

'Aren't we all rather missing the point?' said Vanessa. 'I mean forgetting the first document. Compared to this text that, if genuine, is the more incendiary.'

So that was it, hoped Rashid: Vanessa playing careful not to side with him without first giving to believe she wanted to consider the counter-arguments.

'But, nevertheless,' said Isabelle, 'we shouldn't forget the fallout for Justin in leaking the less incendiary document. What do you think, Rashid? We haven't heard from you.'

'It's hard to believe that Justin will risk polonium poisoning, if he releases the present text for public consumption. Whereas the earlier text is certainly tendentious. Justin?'

'That squares with how I see things, except that this latest text is hardly going to set the world on fire.'

'The way I see it,' added Vanessa, 'to release this text would be to play into the hands of the Council of Twenty and its rapacious Assembly. It justifies their outrageous schemes by throwing into stark relief threats so awful that it would be a sin to conceal them from the public.'

Rashid was forced to conclude that one prerogative a woman could never be denied was the right to change her mind.

'You believe,' said Isabelle, 'that the text is a tissue of lies?'

'Maybe. Maybe not. But publicising it is bound to win the authors no lack of support for their crusade against the perceived villains beyond the Urals and the Tibetan plateau.'

Tich held up stilling hands. 'All right, good people, what are we heading towards here? Pandering perhaps to the drafters of today's text by publishing it and dropping the first text, because publishing both would mean sticking our necks out? And by our necks, I mean Justin's, unless Rash is game enough to do the job for us over the Internet, wangling it so that nothing can be traced back to him.'

A diffident Rashid hesitated long enough before replying to enable Vanessa to preempt him. 'I don't think, Tich, that my Lord Byron needs to get so thoroughly into character as to measure himself against the poet's defence of freedom.'

Vanessa's dissuasion having given him time to formulate his reply, Rashid took up the baton.

'It's virtually impossible to post a blog on a site that can't be traced back to you.'

'Yet,' said Tich, who was having difficulty in deciding where Rashid stood on this issue, 'you're prepared to let Justin chance his arm?'

With the sun still behind the clouds the light breeze had become distinctly chiller. A shivering Isabelle reached for the long-sleeved cashmere cardigan over the back of her chair. Craig lent a helping hand. The two exchanged puzzled glances, Craig failing to realise that Justin's security meant more to Isabelle than her crusade against a coven of wealthy manipulators, Isabelle that Craig felt sure no harm could come of publishing, since the Lenfindi Club had fallen for a hoax.

But Rashid took Tich's criticism in his stride. 'No, not at all. In for a penny, in for a pound. As we said before, we're all in this together. I'm perfectly willing to put this latest text on the Net, because I share Craig's belief that it's innocuous. All I'm saying is that, even if plucked out of the rarefied digital atmosphere of the Cloud, any half competent hacker can trace the text back to me in Luritania.'

Tich scratched his beard. "So what should we do, people? Take another vote on whether to publish and be damned?'

'That's fine by me,' said Justin.

With dissenting votes cast by Tich, Vanessa and Isabelle – the latter reluctantly disqualifying herself – the motion in favour of publishing the second text was carried.

Seeing the last remnants of cloud clearing the face of the sun, Justin put his glasses back on.

'If we want to see this in *The Pulse*, I'll have to put it up for approval by the owner, though I doubt he'll find anything to object to. However, if we want to reach a wider audience, it'll be the same problem as before. Convincing the media we're not foisting another bummer on them.'

'Well,' said Rashid, 'as it happens, I've taken the liberty to jot down a list of media outlets. Those best to approach, those best to avoid. I'll e-mail you the details for you to see what you think. At all events, Justin, nobody's better placed to succeed with this than you.'

Justin brushed the compliment aside together with an ugly bluebottle hovering above his trousers. 'If that were true, Rashid, I'd be working in London or Paris.'

'Who knows?' said Craig. 'This could be the making of you.'

'Or the breaking,' said Isabelle, unable to share her boyfriend's confidence.

When the Club broke up, Vanessa dragged Rashid to one side behind the duty free boutiques. 'What's this about a list of media outlets, Rashid? Why are you dead set on seeing your text spread abroad? What are you hiding from me? From us?'

'Hiding? Nothing,' said Rashid with artfully simulated resentment covering the fact that he had no intention of coming clean. It's partly because I'm convinced publishing would never rebound on Justin ...'

'And what about you, Rashid? When Lord Byron set off for Greece, did he think he was invincible?'

'This is where we fail to see eye to eye, Vanessa. The fact is ...' Questioning the wisdom of giving voice to his thought, Rashid hesitated too briefly to correct its articulation. '...not one of us needs fear comeback from publishing.'

'Why should that be? You've had a visitation while out in Beirut?'

Momentarily thrown by the reminder of the unpalatable message delivered in *Maxim's*, Rashid hung his head in his hands. 'That's fatuous. Look, as Isabelle said, the incendiary text is the first one.'

'Okay, I'm prepared to give you that. You said partly?'

'Yes, partly because I think Justin has nothing to worry about and partly because I feel it's not entirely rubbish. You don't agree?'

'You're missing the point. Almost two decades after coining the expression "fools rush in where angels fear to tread", Alexander Pope went on blithely to write *The Dunciad.*'

'I never read it.'

'But Pope's enemies did, and he lived to regret it.'

It was news that Arnold Palmer could have done without. A new kid on the block, he had failed to do his homework. Except that underwater diving hardly came under his cultural brief. How could he have known that a local diving club used the abandoned water-filled quarry for Sunday morning practice purposes?

The *sapeurs-pompiers* (fire brigade) were called out along with ambulance men and the police after an eighteen-year-old's dive to the quarry floor revealed the fully clothed body of a corpse weighted down with bricks. Once it was ascertained, after delivery to Schönschlucht's *Krankenhaus Paracelsus*, that the lifeless man's left buttock bore the tattoo of a naked female astride a Harley-Davidson with Knoxville emblazoned on one of its twin exhausts, Tennesse on the other, the police wondered whether they might have come across a suspect wanted in connection with the murder of Klaus Radetzky. Although the face was in no fit state to stand comparison with the car rental agency's video recording, the height and build appeared to match the physique of one of the two fugitives from justice.

Thus it was that Dexter Nussbaum, the USA's ambassador to Luritania, received a telephone call from a certain Inspector Hoffarth informing him that it seemed that one of his nationals had been lifted deader than a dodo out of a 60m sandstone quarry used for dive training and was now lying in Schönschlucht's central hospital morgue with a bullet hole through his left sternum. Perhaps one of his assistants would like to call by the hospital to help identify the body and accompany the inspector downtown for further questioning? As the consular and commercial officers were away for the weekend on business in The Hague, and the public affairs officer was pleading a streaming head cold, the ambassador, to his great regret (Palmer gave the man full marks for hypocrisy), was obliged to rely on Arnold's goodwill to see that his country folk (Dexter Nussbaum tended to affect a cracker-barrel pose with his staff) were given a clean bill of health by the media hounds – particularly since the press was probably slavering (Nussbaum's idea of a joke) at the prospect of a juicy story of NSA or FBI extra-territorial meddling.

A worried Palmer, short on ideas, sat rigidly holding his cell phone to his ear after the ambassador had rung off. By the time he came to his senses, he was persuaded that there would be no sweat in dealing with Schönschlucht's Inspector Hoffarth and that the press would buy whatever he told them. Two more mistakes which he was to rue that weekend.

During the drive from his apartment to what he and other likeminded people took to be an architectural monstrosity – Schönschlucht's new central hospital opened the previous year by a perspiring Health Minister whose token three shovelfuls of earth towards planting a cherry tree in the hospital's forecourt left this stalwart gasping for breath – a hitherto confident Arnold Palmer, his mind preoccupied with anticipation of what lay in store for him at the morgue, found himself only periodically awake to his surroundings and wondering for how long he had been on autopilot, a danger to himself and to others.

The mammoth hospital building, with its brand new, state-of-the-art burns treatment centre, soon hove into view above humbler neighbouring premises on account of towering five storeys higher than its nearest steel and concrete rival. Palmer remembered reading that the *Krankenhaus Paracelsus's* inauguration had taken place amid a blaze of publicity – the ruling Christian Democrat party trumpeting the relocated premises as another jewel in the country's non-stop modernisation plan, which in the space of fifteen years had transformed one side of the capital's outskirts into a sprawling megalopolis, the opposition Social Progressives slamming the massive cost overrun and the way in which transnational corporations had been granted carte blanche to move in and seize real estate left vacant after four of the city's long-established, smaller hospitals had been pulled down, their staff and equipment relocated to the gigantic new facility. A popular francophone daily had dubbed the new building *le mastodonte incroyable* (the Incredible Hulk), partly because of its size and partly because of the architect's choice of exterior copper cladding set to take on a greenish patina through exposure to the elements.

It was Palmer's first visit to the hospital. Since he had no idea where the morgue was situated, after pulling into a space on level one of the tiered underground car park, he made straight for the ground-floor reception desk from where he was directed to the rear of the building. The lead corridor floor was painted with directional arrows: red for heart surgery; green for neurology; blue for the burns care centre; black for the X-ray department. For a moment. Palmer saw himself as a modern-day Theseus aided by a provident Ariadne. Except that it was mettle and not its homophone which he needed to outwit whatever Minotaur awaited him at journey's end.

Despite the instructive floor markings, Palmer took several wrong turnings before deducing that the brown-arrowed orthopaedics corridor branched off halfway along into a white-arrowed corridor indicating the way to the morgue. By the time he reached this point, he was roundly criticising the hospital's designers for not copying airport terminal practice: had he known from the outset how many minutes it would take him to get to the morgue, he would have put on a bit of speed. On second thoughts, there was no harm in keeping the inspector waiting; it did not pay to show too much willing.

The white arrow lines led Palmer alongside an open door bearing the word Chapel above the lintel. He paused to look down the aisle, where two women knelt before an altar draped with a blue cloth and surmounted by a wooden cross beneath which stood a finely sculpted Mary gazing at her crucified son, while at the same time cradling him as a baby in her arms. No point in going through the motions of praying for Chamberlain's soul, thought Arnold, any more than for your own – by these people's standards, damned eternally.

Finally, twenty yards further on down the corridor around the next corner, he saw a pair of double white laminate doors with the evenly spaced letters M O R G U E painted in black across them. The briefest of reminders of Alexander Poe gave way to mirth, as Palmer stepped up to the door on the right and encountered a small, black foam sign reading: S. Chang, Morgue Director – Office 581, Fourth Floor. Pushing open this door, he entered a wide, tiled lobby with a vacant, glass-fronted reception desk to his right on which stood a foot-long, blue plastic 'Secretariat' name plate. A nearby poster cautioned: 'Authorised persons only beyond this point'.

Palmer looked at his watch: a quarter of an hour late. Might the inspector have lost patience and taken his leave? Arnold had passed a number of people in civilian clothing in his long, winding walk any one of whom could have been a disgruntled police officer. But the sound of the door's slow-release closing mechanism having alerted staff in the office behind the desk to Palmer's arrival, the next second an inner door opened, and a balding, bespectacled man Arnold guessed to be in his early fifties poked his head around the jamb, looked the newcomer up and down and barked, 'Where's your pass?'

Palmer, who had neglected to slip on the ribboned pass handed him at reception, fumbled in his pocket before producing the rectangular card holding a photocopy of his ID photograph. 'Palmer,' he said. 'Arnold Palmer. U.S. Embassy. Here to see an Inspector Hoffarth.'

Arnold heard a chair scraping the floor in the next room. The fellow he took to be a morgue official opened the door and stood aside to admit a thin, keen-eyed individual in his mid-forties. Both men then emerged via a side door into the lobby. 'Ah, good afternoon, Mr Palmer,' said the inspector, shaking Arnold's hand. 'Georg Hoffarth. Pleased to meet you. You managed to find us.'

'Thanks to the 21st century's answer to Daedalus.'

Hoffarth nodded understanding. 'And this gentleman is Jeroen Vanderheyden, the morgue's manager, although it is someone else who will be showing us through to the cold chamber.'

The white-coated manager extended a hand Arnold thought as cold as those of his temporary wards. 'The badges are important. I was ready to redirect you to ophthalmology. Let me page the chief medical examiner.' Vanderheyden pulled a two-way pager from his shirt pocket and tapped out a brief message. 'The coroner ordered a full autopsy,' he said, putting the pager back in its place. 'Unavoidable in a case of murder.'

This was nothing new to Palmer, who, though he could have done without

Chamberlain's body being found this quickly, felt sure he had nothing to fear from a post-mortem.

Vanderheyden returned behind the counter to search out a pair of elasticated, blue plastic, anti-bacterial footwear slip-ons.

It was while Palmer was donning the second of these that a tall young woman with raven black hair tied back in a neat bun emerged through a set of aluminium doors on the far side of the lobby.

'Good. Here she is,' announced the manager. 'Permit me to introduce you to Mademoiselle Patricia Roussel, our chief pathologist and star graduate of the venerable University of Montpellier's Faculty of Medicine.'

Confronted by the slim forensic medical examiner, Arnold Palmer had to make an effort not to betray signs of sexism, for, as much as he had readied himself for this moment, he had not expected to find the heart and lungs of the man murdered by him to have been removed by a woman.

Her handshake was firm and business-like. Her brown eyes assessed him coolly before switching to Vanderheyden.

'He's sewn up and tagged. Have you told these two gentleman to be prepared for the drop in temperature when we go through to the cold chamber?'

As if mindful of more pressing matters, Jeroen Vanderheyden threw a glance at the wall clock before steering Hoffarth gently by the shoulder in the direction from which Mademoiselle Roussel had just come. 'Minus thirty degrees. The inspector knows. No need to spend long in there. Bring them back out as soon as you can. Then let Mr Palmer and the inspector ask whatever they need to.'

So that's it, thought Arnold. 'Mr Palmer and the inspector.' They're playing me for a fool. This Hoffarth fellow has already been there, seen and heard it all.

No sooner had the cultural attaché set foot in the cold chamber than he started shivering. Roussel strode purposefully towards one of a set of five hermetically sealed doors, which she proceeded to open and from which she rolled out a heavy gauge, stainless steel tray. Whereas it seemed to Palmer that his and Hoffarth's face had to be turning blue – both men had sought warmth for their hands in their trouser pockets – their guide gave the appearance of being as at home here as in the lobby outside. She had, he concluded, to be wearing the next best thing to a merino wool sweater under that flimsy knee-length uniform.

So this was it, the moment of truth. The bulk filling out that body bag in Miss Roussel's tray was whatever was left of Hugh Chamberlain after too many hours spent submerged in a brackish quarry pit.

The no fuss pathologist unzipped the bag down to neck level. 'As I've removed all his vital organs,' she said matter-of-factly, 'it's best to spare you the sight of the body. Can't have you puking over our nice clean floor.'

Hoffarth, who so far had, in fact, only seen the post-mortem photographs of the corpse, took one look at the bloated face and turned away. 'Recognise him?' he asked, his breath all but freezing on the air in front of his lips.

Arnold Palmer gazed down at the livid features of the man whose life he had cold-bloodedly taken two days before. Under the circumstances, 'it' was more appropriate than 'him'. Immersion in quarry water had so disfigured Hugh's face as to make him virtually unrecognisable, such that even Arnold would have had difficulty in contesting his eventual answer.

'No, poor bastard,' he said at length, all the while aware that the inspector's eyes were fixed on him. 'What a way to die.'

Fortunately, for Palmer, neither Hoffarth nor the pathologist was sensitive to the remorse underlying his look of overt horror and repugnance. Unable to back off or tear his eyes away from the ruined features, Palmer felt the bile rising in his gorge.

'Can I zip him back up?' said Mlle Roussel, who, having seen all this before, was keen to be done with the identification.

Seeing Palmer turn aside, a handkerchief clamped to his mouth. Hoffarth nodded. She closed the bag, rolled the tray back into its chamber and locked the door, a slot in which contained a card with the words *'Mâle mort: carrière Feltgen'* (Dead male: Feltgen quarry).

Both men were relieved to regain the lobby, where they found Vanderheyden on the phone behind the front desk. He beckoned all three through to the side door from where Mlle Roussel led the way into an office looking out onto a perfectly tended lawn with flower beds brightened by grandiflora and petunias. Palmer wondered whether anything that colourful would get planted above Chamberlain's unmarked grave.

A minute later, they were rejoined by a phlegmatic Vanderheyden, who had not failed to note Palmer's sickly complexion. 'Help yourself to a drink,' he suggested, indicating the water dispenser on a side table.

Georg Hoffarth peeled off his plastic overshoes. 'Well, thank you, Monsieur. I think we've seen all we need to. No questions on my side, Mademoiselle, that, I feel sure, won't be answered in your report to the coroner. How about you, Monsieur Palmer?'

'No questions.'

'Good.' The inspector turned to Vanderheyden. 'So we'll leave you both to get on with your work. Mademoiselle, if you could kindly e-mail me a copy of that report?'

Patricia Roussel accepted the inspector's business card. 'It'll be in your in-box later tonight. Nothing complicated as far as cause of death is concerned. Some deaths by drowning pose more questions than answers, but not when the cadaver's heart has been pierced by a bullet before submersion.'

This piece of information being nothing new to Palmer, he was grateful not to have to fake surprise. With one eye on the serpent-entwined staff motif on the cup he had filled from the water dispenser, the other on the thrust of the pathologist's breasts under her white coat, Arnold nearly let his *Camino Real* persona get the better of him. But the cultural attaché had more sense than to express the thought: 'One job less for the street cleaners.' Instead, feeling in no fit state to rush out behind the inspector, Palmer took a welcome seat by the window, where he quaffed the last of his water. 'Not the sort of thing our ambassador appreciates having happen on his watch.'

272

'That's just what I wanted to talk to you about, Monsieur,' said Hoffarth. 'But not here, of course. We should leave these good people in peace. If you're feeling okay now, I think we should make a move.'

Palmer not ungrudgingly heaved himself back onto his feet to exchange polite parting handshakes with the comely Mlle Roussel and the morgue's bluff manager. If he found the latter forthright and his slick chief medical examiner not one to waste her words, the inspector struck Arnold as diplomacy personified. But no sooner did he feel relieved by the fact that Hoffarth had avoided mention of any questioning 'down at the station' than Arnold realised his psyche was overcooking things. There was not a shred of evidence to connect America's cultural attaché to Luritania with the unidentifiable body fished out of that quarry. In short, it was hard to imagine anyone less of a murder suspect. Palmer's earlier confidence surged to the fore. This was not *Crime Watch Daily*. Nobody was about to remind Arnold of his Miranda rights.

※

It was a short drive from the hospital to the central police station within a stone's throw of Schönschlucht's mainline railway station. Compared to the building they had just left, Luritania's no frills police headquarters struck Palmer as drably utilitarian. But perhaps this accorded with his version of the chocolate box caveat: don't let a snazzy outside fool you into taking it for granted there's no crap on the inside. What if the worker bees, for whom this dreary hive was home, brought back their weight in gold each day? Palmer remembered reading that there were only two prisons in Schönschlucht: the larger of the two located on the outskirts, the smaller unit down in the valley where Radetzky had met his end. Both establishments had shameful suicide records.

As the construction budget for this box-like building, thrown together as if by someone who had run out of the right Lego pieces, omitted underground parking, Arnold followed the inspector's hand signal and stationed his car in one of the vacant surface slots marked 'visitors'. By the time Palmer had turned off the ignition, Hoffarth had already parked in the numbered space reserved for him and was standing talking into his cell phone. Arnold began to wonder whether the man's physical fitness might be paired with mental acuity. Not that he had any cause for concern on that score.

They walked through the front entrance to a reception desk, where Hoffarth signed in his visitor before leading him past the lift area and up three flights of stairs – another sign of a healthy life style applauded by Palmer – to a corridor lined on one side by a large open-plan office, on the other by a number of closed doors, the third of which along bore a smart brushed copper name and title plate identifying this as Hoffarth's private office. Arnold was puzzled as to why a 'chief inspector' would hide the more authoritative half of his title under a bushel.

Georg Hoffarth ushered Palmer into the office in front of him. Everything about the room spoke of a tidy, uncluttered mind, though the number of orderly ring-binder files stored on shelves inside master-lock, glass-panelled oak cabinets indicated that the Ministry of the Environment's promotion of the paperless bureau cut no ice with the upper echelons of the country's police force. To Arnold's mind, the sole anomaly was the framed photograph of Muhammad Ali on the wall behind Hoffarth's desk. Perhaps, on reflection, not that incongruous: the boxer was punishing a punch ball in preparation for his next opponent.

At the same time, Arnold was slightly taken off balance to find a uniformed police officer, who looked on the young side to be wearing three blue shoulder chevrons, at work on his laptop to one side of the desk fronted by Hoffarth's wooden wedge name plate. Waking up to the newcomers' presence, the officer removed his headset and stood up to acknowledge his superior.

'Monsieur Palmer, permit me to introduce you to Claude-Henri Weiland, my assistant. Weiland is a *stagiaire* (trainee) learning the ropes, so to speak. I hope you will not take it amiss, if he sits in on our meeting. Being able to rely on his touch-typing skills spares me the pain of playing back audio recordings.'

With no alternative other than to go along with this *fait accompli*, Arrnold Palmer accepted the young officer's handshake with a firm grasp and one of his more cordial Gutman smiles. 'Not at all. Your office. You're call.'

Hoffarth motioned Palmer to take any of the three seats arranged in front of his desk. Arnold settled into the middle one. 'How can I help you, chief inspector?'

Georg Hoffarth waved a dismissive hand. 'Please, chief inspector is too much of a mouthful. Although this is the first time that I've had a member of the diplomatic corps sitting in front of me, I don't think we need to go overboard with the protocol.'

'Fine by me,' replied Palmer, falling into the more suave side of his *Camino Real* persona. 'So, as I said before, how can I help you?'

Hoffarth interlaced his hands above a stomach as flat as a pancake and sat tapping his thumbs together in a private Morse code indecipherable to third parties. Palmer waited calmly, favouring silence: the inspector's roadshow; best not to steal his thunder.

'Would you mind thinking again,' said Hoffarth at last, 'about not recognising the face in the morgue. We're pretty sure the man is or was American.'

'There are hundreds of Americans living and working in Luritania. Only a few register with the embassy. We can't be expected to know them all. Apart from which, I've only just joined the staff in the rue Eisenhower, so I've yet to rub shoulders with many of our local contingent.'

'But you keep abreast of the news when your fellow countrymen make the headlines.'

'You're referring to the Radetzky murder case?'

'What else?'

'Yes, I saw, we all at the embassy saw the grainy pictures of the two men wanted in connection with Radetzky's death. But I honestly couldn't say that the man lying in the morgue looks like either of the two you're hoping to catch up with.'

'Well, it's true that we released minimum information to the local press about our suspects. Blurred photos of a couple of men in business suits. One standing behind the other. The fellow signing for the hire car speaking with a nasal American twang.'

Palmer nodded understanding. Broadcasting the fact that the police had the lowdown on men a tad more wanted for questioning than the cultural attaché would only hinder their prospects of apprehending them by forcing the duo to go to ground.

'But it went without saying that the one who took out the car hire agreement in the agency where the video camera recorded those overhead shots presented a driving licence.'

Palmer suppressed a smile half in anticipation of what was coming, half out of admiration for the CIA's methods.

'The man you saw less than an hour ago stretched out on that cold chamber tray was called Walter Bernard Walburton Jr. At least, that's what his driving licence said. The only problem is that Walburton Jr is currently serving a twelve-year sentence for multiple identity thefts in an Illinois correctional facility.'

This time it was impossible to smother a smile.

'You find that amusing?'

Arnold used a cough to bring himself back into a more serious frame of mind. 'You have to admit it shows a certain amount of chutzpah.'

There was the slightest hesitation in the rapid scampering of Weiland's fingers. Nothing, Arnold speculated, that a subsequent spellcheck couldn't put right.

Georg Hoffarth finished flicking back through his tear-off desktop calendar. From the way in which the folded over pages were fairly evenly distributed between both halves it appeared that the inspector tore nothing off. Perhaps, thought Palmer, belatedly regretting his facetiousness, Hoffarth had an unequalled memory for dates.

The inspector's next words served as a warning, if any were needed, for the cultural attaché to remember where he was and with whom he was dealing.

'Unlike you, Monsieur Palmer, I have two murders to account for.'

'I'm sorry. Of course.'

'I believe that you Americans are used to high crime figures. We, I am glad to say, are not. Our stock-in-trade runs from drunk driving and burglary to drug peddling and prostitution.' Hoffarth's index finger settled on a recent date. Time to switch tack. 'Monsieur Palmer, what motive do you think an American could have for killing a Luritanian cartoonist?'

Arnold collected his thoughts. 'Might it be that these guys were Canadians posing as Americans? Quite a few Ukrainian fascists emigrated to Canada after WWII. To escape retribution.'

'Just as your own country welcomed in Nazi war criminals?'

'Well, I'm not sure where you got that idea from.'

The inspector consigned the pages under his left hand back where they belonged: into the past.

'Hard to believe descendants of Ukrainian emigrés happened to be passing through Luritania, bought a copy of *The Pulse* and felt incensed enough to plan and carry out the murder of a cartoonist ridiculing Ukraine's president. As a cultural attaché, would you not agree that poking fun at world leaders is a natural enough safety valve for your man in the street at the mercy of those lampooned?'

'Put like that, yes, I would have to agree. But as you just said, I'm a mere cultural attaché. There's nothing in my background to equip me to understand what motivates the criminally minded. You'd be better off interviewing one of our intelligence officers.' The last suggestion, delivered without the trace of a smile, was the source of no little satisfaction to someone tutored in intelligence gathering.

'But your ambassador sent me you. I was hoping you might be able to breathe fresh life into our "pedestrian approach" to these linked affairs.'

Although smarting under the backhanded swipe at a U.S. journalist's recent criticism of Luritania's police force for failing to apprehend the wanted leader of a Latin American drug cartel visiting his Schönschlucht bankers, Arnold had the sense to stay tight-lipped.

'Isn't this talk of Canadians leading us nowhere except down the garden path, Monsieur Palmer?'

'Come again?'

'Did Monsieur Nussbaum not tell you that the drowned – correction, murdered – man had Tennessee inscribed on one of his buttocks?'

'Ah, yes, that's something I forgot.'

'Hard to imagine forgetting something that memorable.'

'Not after you've been shaken up by a visit to the morgue rounded off with the sight of a face that looked as if it had been pecked at by fish.'

The inspector followed up Palmer's parry with the equivalent of one of his gloved hero's body blows. 'Would it help if I told you that we retrieved the drowned man's passport along with his body?'

Palmer refused to flinch. 'Not in the name of Walter Walburton Jr?'

'Right. In the name of Archibald Leach.'

'Doesn't ring any bells with me.'

It was Georg Hoffarth's turn to smile. 'I realise that most cultural attachés would never associate Hollywood with culture. But for an American like yourself …'

Palmer's eyes settled on Weiland's motionless fingers poised above the keyboard like a partnership of vultures sensing carrion.

'I'm afraid you've got the better of me.'

The inspector opened the top right-hand drawer of his desk and pulled out a transparent plastic ziplock wallet containing a passport with a familiar blue cover all the worse for wear for lengthy immersion in filthy quarry water.

It could, thought Palmer, have been a navy blue Canadian passport were it not for the eight letters PASSPORT still visible at the top. 'An American sportsman named Archie Leach. Is that the guessing game?'

'No, originally a British stilt walker, Archibald Alexander Leach. Became something of a household name in America. Cary Grant.'

Of course, thought Palmer, chiding himself for his mental block. 'And Cary Grant,' he said, 'died in …'

'Nineteen eighty-six.'

'Another case of identity theft. So, clearly, our man fished out of the quarry had something to hide.'

'His companion also.'

'Have you searched the quarry for a second body? Wait, I can see your objection. Surely it was the companion, Mr X let's say, who shot his friend before dumping him in the quarry water? Otherwise, you would be looking for different killers. But perhaps this was just that. A case of revenge for the cartoonist's murder.'

'By who? Radetzky's wife? A fellow journalist? A Russian expat loyal to Ukraine's separatist cause? From the look in Georg Hoffarth's eyes, Palmer sensed that the inspector was daring him to agree with any such absurd suggestion.

'It sounds unlikely, I know. But in the words of Sir Arthur Conan Doyle: "When you have eliminated the impossible, whatever remains, however improbable, must be the truth".'

'So you tend to think that Mr X shot Mr Leach before throwing him into the pit?'

'Yes, though I'm beginning to doubt my own logic. Why would he shoot his partner?'

'Any number of reasons. They had a falling out. He thought he had a better chance of escaping our dragnet alone.'

'Speaking of dragnets, did you dredge the pit for weapons?'

'Our own divers searched the bottom and found nothing.' Hoffarth paused and glanced across at his assistant. 'I could do with an espresso. How about you, Claude-Henri? And Mr Palmer?'

Inclined to think that he had thrown enough sand in the inspector's eyes, Arnold Palmer welcomed the idea of an injection of caffeine. 'Thank you.'

'Let's take a pause then, while Claude-Henri does the honours.'

Standing up to stretch his limbs, the inspector walked over to the window from where he could see the blue bridge spanning the city gorge from the rim of which Klaus Radetzky had been hurled to his death the week before.

'A bright fellow, Weiland,' said Hoffarth, continuing to drink in the view. 'I hope to see him back with me as my permanent assistant one of these days after he's done the rounds of our different departments.'

Since the inspector seemed to be giving voice to musings only indirectly intended for anyone else, and Palmer knew the folly of obsequiousness, instead of seconding this judgment the cultural attaché held his tongue.

His preference remaining with the view below, the inspector threw Arnold a quick glance. 'Tell me, what are your first impressions of our principality, Monsieur Palmer? Favourable, I hope.'

'Very. You're not cursed by industrialisation. On the contrary, you're blessed with stretches of woodland and forests the envy of town-dwellers used to pollution from smokestacks and vehicle exhausts.'

'I can assure you we have more than our fair share of vehicle exhausts, mostly visited upon us from across our borders.'

'Still, for the most part, Luritania remains unspoilt. A very green and pleasant land.'

Palmer, who had joined the inspector by the window, felicitously refrained from mentioning one biting judgment by the embassy's commercial attaché to the effect that Luritania was a principality the size of a pocket handkerchief passed from the hands of one European owner to the other over the centuries such that everyone had blown his nose into it but none had thought to launder it for a good many years now because they were too busy laundering money.

'I've already taken my mountain bike out a couple of times to ride along your *pistes cyclables* (cycle tracks). You can't breathe air as fresh as that back in my hometown.'

'Where would that be?'

'If you wanted to butter someone up, thought Arnold, why not lay it on thick. 'LA.'

'Yet it's called the City of the Angels.'

'Named that before the Ford Motor Company saw the light of day. It probably verged on the angelic for people living in the age of the horse and cart.'

The next moment, Weiland reappeared bearing a tray from which he set out an espresso each for his boss and Palmer and an opened bottle of still mineral water for himself. The two men by the window resumed their seats.

Not bad for an office espresso machine, concluded Palmer, for whom the first taste of coffee felt almost as good as a shot of something sniffed out by the inspector's drug hounds.

After taking his own first sip of the reviving beverage, rather than picking up from where he had left off, Georg Hoffarth reversed tracks. 'Identity theft, one of the banes of our technological society. Nowhere near as prevalent in Alfred Hitchcock's day.'

Arnold Palmer could not decide whether it was because of the coffee, but somehow he felt increasingly well disposed towards the foxy inspector Hoffarth, a man after his own heart.

'Ah now, there you have me again.'

Georg Hoffarth allowed his nose to dwell over the espresso's rich aroma. Certain people liked to down their *petit noir serré* in one gulp. To the inspector's mind, that showed disrespect for everyone from planter to packer. There was too much rich goodness in the drink to be thrown back like a shot glass of vodka.

'Cary Grant was a favourite of Hitchcock's. He cast him in several leading roles, including one which revolved around a pet theme of the director's. Mistaken identity.'

Hoffarth eyed Palmer quizzically. Although Arnold had a fair idea of where the inspector was heading with this line of discovery, he stood by his original intention of waiting for the mountain to come to a different Muhammad, which it did in the next breath.

278

'Klaus Radetzky paid the price for somebody else's sins.'

When there was no point in resisting, better, decided Palmer, to go with the flow. 'Not a matter of the wrong name? Rather someone else in Radetzky's entourage?'

'That would seem to make sense. Such as the editor.'

'I didn't know he had a reputation for rubbing people up the wrong way.'

'He doesn't. But, of course, there are cranks out there ready to take offence at the slightest thing. You only have to scroll through some of the drivel posted on Facebook to realise what potential there is for lunacy.'

'As I understand it, the graffiti plastered over the publishing house's façade targeted the cartoon. Hendry was presumably responsible for okaying the cartoon. Ergo, it was his head your two suspects were really after. But they got the wrong man.'

The inspector took his second sip of sustenance. 'Possibly. I had Claude-Henri scan every magazine put out by Hendry's people over the past three months, including, of course, *The Pulse*. He came up with nothing remotely likely to cause offence. Correct Claude-Henri?'

Weiland made use of the direct question to massage cramped fingers and to slake his thirst. 'Correct, except, as you pointed out, chef, you can never rule out the nutter factor. Like that character who waved a fake hand grenade at the prime minister in protest against the death of his dog, which had keeled over after licking a manhole tainted with rat poison.'

Palmer chuckled. He could see how these two were good for each other. Although it looked as if the inspector had reached an impasse at the end of one of his assistant's sewers.

'What can one do in such circumstances?' From the way in which Georg Hoffarth averted pensive eyes from the ceiling to the coffee cup and saucer in his interviewee's hand, Arnold knew that this question was anything but rhetorical.

'Question the editor. Grill him as to possible motives. Had he received any threatening messages? Was he aware of having upset any particular official, group or organisation?'

'Good, but no in answer to all those questions.'

'So we're back to square one.'

'Not quite. Not if Leach's companion, or killer, is still in hiding or on the run, and we find him.'

'You might strike lucky. Perhaps he'll give himself up.'

'Is the moon made of cheese?'

'You're right. Highly unlikely.'

'Highly unlikely perhaps because he knows too much. And can't afford to let what he knows fall into other hands.'

'That,' said Arnold, inwardly enjoying the realisation that he and the inspector were, unknown to the latter, on the same wavelength, 'could put his own life in danger. Indeed, perhaps your earlier implausible assumptions were not as flawed as all that. Leach has been taken out by people anxious to silence both men.'

'Particularly bearing in mind the way in which Y – simpler to call him that than Leach – was disposed of. We know he cannot have been lured to the lip of that quarry pit to be shot there, because Mademoiselle Roussel put the time of death as several hours prior to drowning. And no reasonable person would draw his victim out to the quarry to sit around for three or four hours after murdering him before tipping the body in the water. More to the point, how could one person lug the corpse all the way from the roadside to the pit unaided?'

Not a trap, of course, that throwaway question, acknowledged Arnold, but even so it would not do to betray any familiarity with the murder scene. 'Easy. The murderer could have driven up to the edge of the quarry.'

'Impossible. The quarry's surrounded by a three metre high stone wall, the gates padlocked after working hours. And only the diving club has a spare set of keys for their weekend training. No, two men at least disposed of that body. Perhaps a third one kept watch while they clambered up and over the gate.'

'Wouldn't you have found traces of that on the ground? Drag marks left on the other side when the killers pulled the body up to the edge of the pit?'

'Not after the diving club had driven their vehicles through the gates.'

Arnold hung an apologetic head. 'Of course, stupid of me. But what about traces of blood?'

'I forgot to say that our diver found a blood-stained carpet at the bottom of the pit. It must have come loose after the body was thrown in the water.'

Really, thought, Palmer, not that this changed anything.

'And how did your two murderers lift their corpse over the gate?'

'With a rope tied around the carpet. One hauled, the other pushed.'

Spot on, inspector, reasoned Arnold, remembering how he and Warren had got rid of the rope later in a skip laden with roadbuilding waste further up the road. But then how could the keen-eyed Patricia Roussel have missed the marks made by the rope around Chamberlain's waist – particularly with a carpet as threadbare as the one that he had found in one of the farm's outhouses and which Warren had agreed was more suitable than the sleeping bag solution?'

Arnold felt his cell phone vibrating in his breast pocket. 'Would you excuse me for a moment?'

The fact that there was no caller ID told him it had to be the ambassador. Probably chafing at the bit. Fretting that this affair would be seen as a blot on his copybook. The old goat should have been put out to grass long ago. A good job Weiland's fingers were at rest. The young officer might have been talented, but his many attributes did not run to mindreading.

His first guess almost certainly correct, Arnold decided to ignore the call. Pocketing the now silent phone, he picked up his coffee cup and finished a tepid espresso. 'Well, what are we left with, inspector, after all this surmising? Precious little hard evidence one way or the other. Almost makes me feel ashamed of moaning about the lot of being my embassy's lowest of the lows, a token cultural attaché.'

Georg Hoffarth straightened the knot in his tie, a signal to Weiland that the interview was about to come to an end. Claude-Henri stretched out his arms and poured himself more water.

'What are we left with? Too many unanswered questions.'

'That's life, inspector.'

His thumbs curled around the edge of his desk, Hoffarth pushed himself back out of his seat. 'Thank you for giving us your time. Monsieur Palmer. I hope you won't mind if I get back to you later should we come up with anything else relevant to the American connection.'

'Be my guest,' replied Arnold, persuaded that he would hear nothing further from either the astute inspector or his protégé.

Hoffarth removed a thin white card from a pen and pencil holder next to his telephone. 'Take this, do. It'll open up the car park barrier for you.'

The inspector waited to catch the last of his interviewee's footfalls in the corridor outside before turning to his assistant. 'You got everything down? No problem?'

'No problem.'

'What did you think of our American friend?'

'Started out acting a cut above us. Got better later on.'

'What they call a smooth operator.'

'Chef, when he mentioned that name Archie, I couldn't help wondering whether Palmer's colleagues call him Arnie.'

'Why's that?'

'Oh, I don't know – like wise-cracking Arnold Schwarzenegger.'

'Didn't he play the part of the Terminator?'

From the faraway expression on Hoffarth's face, Claude-Henri could not decide whether his superior was joking or serious. 'That's right, chef. Dead right.'

'Run a background check on him.'

'Will we get far with that? Palmer's *corps dipomatique*, remember. '

Georg Hoffarth tore the previous year's 31ˢᵗ December leaf from his calendar, scribbled down two names and a telephone number and passed it across to his assistant. 'Try Roggenskop's boys over in the Ministry of Foreign Affairs. Tell them I need to know all they can dig up about Monsieur MiniGolf.'

Memo from K to J

In announcing that anyone who disagrees with him is likely to be a terrorist, the sultan sitting in the six hundred million thaler Ak Saray presidential palace seems to have followed in the footsteps of President Shrub, who declared, 'Either you are with us, or you are with the terrorists'.

What does it tell us about the times we live in that both gentlemen have been caricatured as 'nuttier than a fruitcake'?

Some say, K, that the times make the man. If so, our times are sorely lacking in great men.

I share the sentiment 'East is East, and West is West, and never the twain shall meet.'

But further to the point raised by you, I beg to point out a parallel development at the helm of the League. The Wayfarer is said to be considering setting up his own national guard – after the fashion of the janissaries of old charged with protecting their sultan. If this is true, might it be that the uncrowned head senses his long-suffering subjects have had a bellyful of gruel and hanker after a change of menu?

That evening, down on the shooting range with Tich and Vanessa, where they were joined for the first time by Justin, Arnold was unable to hide his vexation at producing a mediocre score on his set of four fifteen-yard targets. After seeing Vanessa achieve a near perfect score four times in a row of three tens and a bull's-eye, his mood blackened to the point where he no longer recognised himself as the same person who fancied he had run circles around the Schönschlucht police force's answer to Columbo.

But over a glass of beer later in the bistrot, where the group were accustomed to take their nightcap before each went his or her separate way, Arnold rid himself of some of his vexation by relating how his Sunday had got off to a bad start with an arm-twisting call from the ambassador forcing him to stand in for an absent colleague at the Paracelsus hospital morgue. The police wondered if he could identify the corpse of a middle-aged American found at the bottom of a quarry pit by a local diving club. Following that unforgettable experience in the Paracelsus's sub-zero corpse cooler, the investigating police officer had dragged him down to headquarters for a grilling. As if he, of all people, a newcomer to Schönschlucht could have been expected to throw light on how a John Doe he had never seen before had ended up sleeping with the fishes after being shot through the heart.

'On the basis of tonight's score,' said Tich wryly, 'nobody in his right mind would think you capable of shooting a sitting duck at five yards.'

'Thank you, Humphrey. It's nice to know where not to turn to in my hour of need.'

'Wait a minute,' said Justin. 'I'm interested in knowing what the police thought about your dead fellow countryman. Did they make any connection between him and my murdered sub-editor?'

Arnold gave a non-committal shrug. Hendry's unexpected appearance at the range had been another factor to dent his equanimity. Nevertheless, if only to underline his unhappy lot as the victim of officialdom, the cultural attaché proceeded to fill his companions in on an expurgated version of his interview with Chief Inspector Hoffarth.

But the call made by U.S. Ambassador Dexter Nussbaum to his cultural attaché that Sunday morning and subsequent events could equally well have taken a quite different turn.

In other words, there is every possibility that the actual telephone conversation and what ensued between the *dramatis personae* went as follows:

Ambassador: Arnold, you can forget about this being a day of rest. We're in deep shit.

Palmer: What's happened, sir?

Ambassador: What's happened is that those two CIA agents you talked me into taking under our wing are lying in Schönschlucht's central hospital morgue.

Palmer (after appropriate shocked pause): How can that be?

Ambassador: They shot each other. Was that your doing?

Palmer (temporarily speechless): How do you mean. sir?

Ambassador: I understand you've joined a gun club.

Palmer: Yes, but, ambassador, surely you don't think I could have been stupid enough to supply Stenning or Chamberlain with a firearm?

Ambassador: One firearm each. No, to be truthful, I find that hard to believe, but how else could they have come by those weapons?

Palmer: They must have arrived with them.

Ambassador: That would require an almighty suspension of disbelief.

Palmer (staggered to learn that the ambassador was as familiar with Samuel Taylor Coleridge as he was with Charles Monroe Schulz): Well, sir, I don't know how else to explain it. Are you sure about this?

Ambassador (in a voice like thunder): Do I sound as if I'm talking about an embassy tea party?

Palmer: I'm sorry, sir. It's just that … Why would they …? I mean, we were working towards saving their skins.

Ambassador (sound of sucking on a cough drop): Saunders walked in on the scene this morning when delivering their breakfast order. After finding last night's pizza boxes unopened in the downstairs foyer, he trotted upstairs, and there they were stretched out on the floor, both with a bullet through the heart.

Palmer: It makes no sense.

Ambassador: That's as may be. But they're dead, Arnold, and you are now going to have to explain to the police why these two were holed up in one of our safe houses. Now meaning straightaway. You've got half an hour to get your butt down to the morgue, where a certain Chief Inspector Hoffarth is expecting you. With questions. So you had damn better make a good job of clearing our name.

Palmer: Yes, sir.

Ambassador: Then report back to me immediately. Use this number. If I'm not on the golf course, I'll be in the club house. Makes no difference. Just call.

Palmer: Right you are, sir.

Ambassador: And one last thing, Arnold. If the embassy comes out of this badly, your career is as good as down the toilet.

By the time a hurried Arnold Palmer reached the morgue after several missed turns trekking through the warren of corridors umbilically interconnecting the *Krankenhaus Paracelsus's* ground-floor departments, he began to doubt whether he was sufficiently composed to jump through a few more hoops without putting a foot wrong. It did not help that the morgue's manager, a Fleming by the name of Vanderheyden, acted as if his presence was an encumbrance – Palmer wondered whether the man was as gruff with next of kin – and made no bones about being glad to offload him as soon as possible onto Chief Inspector Georg Hoffarth, a thin, sharp-featured man of indeterminate age (anywhere, Arnold surmised, between thirty-five and forty-five) who insisted on being called inspector. After the manager paged his pathologist, Palmer found the person in charge of the hospital's forensic autopsies to be an extremely grounded young woman whose fine features brought to mind the Greek diva, Maria Callas. Not one for small talk, Mademoiselle Patricia Roussel lost no time in bustling Palmer and the inspector in their hygienically encased footwear through to the cold room. Hospitals, and morgues in particular, Palmer decided were no place for dilettantes.

Confirming the dead men's identities was a matter of seconds. Yes, Arnold told the inspector, relieved at finding Warren Stenning's eyes permanently closed, both were known to him, although he was appalled to see them in body bags. In view of the chill factor inside the cold room, neither Palmer nor the inspector objected to the fact that Mademoiselle Roussel was as prompt in ushering them back to the manager's office as she had been in hastening them in. There being nothing left to discuss with Vanderheyden or his pathologist after she had corroborated the undisputed cause of death, the two visitors left the hospital on the understanding that Palmer would follow the inspector to police headquarters with a view to completing the requisite paperwork.

Upon arrival in Georg Hoffarth's office, Palmer was introduced to the inspector's male assistant, a young sergeant responsible for making a written record of the proceedings. Offered a choice of tea, coffee or a soft drink, Arnold, aware of the need to remain alert, requested an espresso.

After they had dispensed with the formalities of name, age, nationality, address, occupation (production of his diplomatic passport spared Palmer further red tape), the inspector, who had also opted for an espresso, explained that once the interview proper was finished, his amanuensis would run off a printed copy for Palmer to read through and sign by way of endorsing its accuracy. If Palmer had second thoughts, felt he had been misquoted or wished to add anything, Claude-Henri Weiland, the young recorder, would make the necessary changes. Arnold was given to understand that his statement could be used subsequently as evidence in court. While alive to the fact that this last rider was intended to make anyone think twice before perjuring himself, Arnold felt confident that, should it come to the crunch, Luritania's Ministry of Home or Foreign Affairs would get nowhere in trying to obtain a waiver of his diplomatic immunity.

He was pleased that the interview was to be conducted in English. Not that he found French a struggle, because he had already seen postings in Vietnam and Haiti. But the inspector, educated, like many of his countrymen, in three foreign languages, was perfectly at home with English. The same obviously applied to his assistant. It was not the first time that Arnold had had dealings with the police in his official capacity abroad, and he had the impression that the dour inspector Hoffarth would be no more of a pushover than his counterparts in Hanoi or Port-au-Prince. If anything, the inspector struck him as someone to be warier of than the cheroot-chewing lieutenant in Clercine set on causing maximum political embarrassment over reckless driving by the ambassador's chauffeur accused of mowing down a fourteen-year-old street vendor orphaned by the 7.0 magnitude earthquake in 2010. It would not do to adopt the supercilious, quasi-Gutman air of a diplomat who, though deeply concerned about the loss of life, considered the affair something best swept under the carpet in the interests of bilateral relations.

The inspector removed his jacket, arranged it tidily over a side table partly occupied by an empty gilt bird cage with half-open door – viewed by Palmer as an ideal prop for Vanessa Curtis's open-air *Camino Real* production – loosened his collar and tie, returned to his desk, clapped both hands crisply like a ringmaster announcing the next act, pointed a starting-gun finger at Weiland and threw out his first question.

'What was the United States embassy doing harbouring two murder suspects?'

Although not unprepared for this bull's eye, Palmer had not expected to have to bring his wiles to bear in navigating the equivalent of the Cape of Good Hope this early in the proceedings. Looking from one man to the other – not that Weiland, bent over his laptop, seemed to be paying him the slightest attention - Arnold exhaled a deep breath, gritted his teeth and launched into partially charted waters.

'We wanted to avoid things getting blown out of proportion.'

Georg Hoffarth bestowed one of his less sympathetic stares on Palmer before sitting down and pulling two photographs out of a top drawer. 'By things, I take it you mean these,' he said, pushing both photographs across the desk to face the diplomat. The first, taken from the photo archives of the *Luritanische Bote*, showed a picture, too gruesome for publication, of the mangled remains of *The Pulse's* cartoonist above the caption 'Valley murder victim, Klaus Radetzky'. The second was the clearest picture Palmer had seen as yet of the two CIA agents in the car rental office: a head and shoulders shot of Chamberlain with Stenning hovering in the background.

After wincing at the sight of the first picture and trying to concentrate on the fuzzier image of Stenning rather than on the only slightly clearer close-up of the man he had had no compunction about killing, Palmer wrapped both hands around the back of his neck and fixed the vacant bird cage with a baleful stare.

'They came to us for help. Desperate. Unjustly accused of something that had nothing to do with them.'

'So why, if you believed them, did you choose to shelter them in a temporary safe house and not on embassy premises?'

'That was the ambassador's decision. He was sure of their innocence. You see, inspector …' Palmer shifted his gaze as if viewing Hoffarth and his desk through a zoetrope which brought the inspector into the cage. '… the two men lying in your city morgue are CIA agents. Whatever the rest of the world might care to think about the CIA, we, in the United States diplomatic corps stand by them in times of trouble.'

'Perhaps your definition of times of trouble contrasts with mine.'

'Every so often they get into deep water not of their making. We bail them out.'

As if testing not only the furniture's but his own resilience, Hoffarth pushed both hands against the lip of his desk, tipped the front legs of his chair off the floor, held them suspended there for a few seconds and then eased them back down. 'Bail them out …' The inspector pondered these words for what struck Palmer as an inordinate length of time, before finally collecting his thoughts. 'Do the innocent need bailing out?' Addressed as it was not to Pamer but to the minute-writer, the question verged on the sardonic.

'If falsely accused,' said Arnold without resentment.

'And how did your ambassador hope to establish their innocence?'

'That was to be my responsibility. As you are no doubt aware, the National Security Agency's outreach programme extends to diplomatic missions. Humble cultural attachés are sometimes called upon to fulfill more demanding functions.'

'For how long were these men in your care?'

'Just over a week.'

'You spent more than seven days endeavouring to justify their alibis?'

'No, after two days of intensive questioning and follow-up research on our part …'

'Our part?'

'We have helpers.'

'Go on.'

'After that, it was evident that they were concealing something which had nothing to do with the cartoonist.'

'That's as may be, but it doesn't change the fact that we have evidence linking their rental vehicle directly to the crime scene. I make no apology for saying that your ambassador's decision to place himself above the law in our country only serves to confirm his nation's lack of respect for international law in general.'

'Believe me, inspector, it was never his intention to deceive you.'

'Yet you and he have manifestly gone behind our backs. Well, let's forget for now the distrust and ill-feeling which this episode has caused on our side, and concentrate on the hard facts. We have proof that your CIA agents …'

'Excuse me, inspector. They're not – were not – our CIA agents. We're not responsible for them.'

'As you will. But we have proof that somebody drove the vehicle hired by those two Americans close to the observation point beyond the Blue Bridge on the night of Radetzky's death, because when they returned it to the rental office the next day, dirt and gravel in the foot well plus tyre track matching combined to build a damning case against them.'

'That proves nothing. How many tourists drive out there each day?'

'A brave, if not desperate, try, Monsieur Palmer, considering that your sole defense of these two men is that they were involved in something unconnected with the cartoonist but too sensitive to divulge. That in itself is enough to make a cat laugh.'

'Well, inspector, before you rush to judgment on these men, spare a thought for the fact that they aren't – weren't – convicted felons on the run.'

'And you and your ambassador should bear in mind that flouting the laws of guest countries wins you no friends in the short term. However, I can see that there is nothing to be had from going around in circles here.'

The inspector rose to his feet, turned his back on Palmer and crossed to the window, leaving an impassive secretary and a patient cultural attaché to commune with themselves. Hoffarth's attention shifted to the horizon where a cluster of motionless, cross-border wind farms were reduced at this remove to matchstick proportions. Drawing his gaze nearer in was the massive outline of the *Krankenhaus Paracelsus*, a behemoth in the belly of which lay two frozen corpses. Swivelling on his heels, he walked back to his desk and stood clutching the chair back. After turning this marginally one way then the other, while debating his line of attack, he let go of the chair, folded both arms over his chest and addressed his next question to a point just above Palmer's head.

'Their names. We need their names. For the record.'

It was a curveball unappreciated by Arnold Palmer, who kicked himself for not having thought of this in advance. 'Blake and Jacobson.'

The inspector cracked a cynical smile.

Arnold uncrossed his legs to ease numbness at more than one level. If only to buy time, he played ignorance. 'False IDs?'

'Fake passports. One in the name of John Rutherford Stanton, who perished at the age of three when his suicidal mother flung herself, with baby John in her arms, off Pennsylvania's Wissahickon Memorial Bridge. That was all of twelve years ago. The other in the name of Peter Kola Oniche.'

'Cola as in Coca-Cola?'

'No, with a K. Peter Kola Oniche, a native American Ojibwe, smothered to death in 1989 in a Montana health clinic.'

By no stretch of the imagination could Palmer guess which of Stenning and Chamberlain had consented to this colourful identity theft. 'Standard procedure,' he volunteered, 'for undercover purposes.'

'And what would you say, if I told you that the CIA denies outright that the two men shot dead in your care are or ever were on its payroll?'

'Inspector, come on now. Surely you understand that the CIA would have to deny all knowledge of those names. Mind you, now you've alerted them, I reckon they'll send out their bloodhounds.'

'No doubt. To sniff around the scent left by you people.' Hoffarth gave the top of his chair back a pat with both hands by way of cueing the next question.

'And what would you say if I told you that the men you identified were killed by a third person or persons?'

Palmer felt as if the inspector's eyes were all but hammering rivets into him.

'What? I thought it was a cut and dried case of one man falling out with the other.'

'Rather a cut and dried case of an amateurish attempt to dress the two deaths up to look that way.'

'But,' and here Arnold remonstrated with defensive hands, 'the only people who knew of our Blake and Jacobson's whereabouts ... the only people with access to the *Kinothek* where they were holed up were embassy staff.'

'Precisely. And I can't see why embassy staff, who had gone to such lengths to hide and protect their CIA wards, should suddenly turn on them and, so to speak, slit their throats.'

Simulating temporary loss of words, Arnold transferred his look of indignation to Weiland's immobile hands.

'You're right,' he said after several beats and with no little emphasis. 'That's absurd.'

'Might I ask, Monsieur Palmer, where you were on Saturday afternoon and evening?'

Arnold's face broke into a smile. Now that the inspector had showed his hand, any worry the man enjoying ambassadorial protection might have nursed about having the carpet pulled out from under him melted away.

'From midday onwards till around six p.m., catching up on the backlog at my desk at the embassy.'

'On your own?'

'No, at least two other people can vouch for me. Apart from which all our comings and goings are recorded by reception.' Arnold kept a straight face. The inspector was out of his league in matters of interdepartmental diplomatic solidarity. Palmer knew that and so did the inspector.

'So you weren't down on the shooting range?'

Arnold's shifted in his seat. The man had done his homework. 'In fact, I spent part of the evening there. In company.'

'Of course.'

Time, thought Palmer, to take advantage of the opening gifted him. 'Between what hours, might I ask, did the pathologist put the two deaths?'

There was a trace of submission in the way in which Hoffarth inclined his head. 'Between midday and five p.m.'

'Inspector, you're a bright man. What earthly reason would I have to queer my pitch with the Department of State? More to the point, what earthly motive could I have for murdering two members of the CIA? I'm sorry but you're beginning to annoy me.'

Resuming his seat, Georg Hoffarth eyed the empty birdcage with its open door. 'You're right, of course. It makes no sense. Come to that, none of this whole affair makes any sense.'

Palmer could have done with an apology; realising none was forthcoming he stretched out arms and legs and gave a less than polite yawn.

'Anything else, inspector? I'm sorry I couldn't help you, but if something should crop up, you know where to find me. Can I set the ambassador's mind at rest? I take it you won't be interviewing Mr Nussbaum? He's a busy man.'

Georg Hoffarth flashed Palmer his first look of irritation. 'I think that'll be all for now. My assistant will print out a copy of the *in extenso* for your signature. After that, provided no changes are needed, we can call it a day. I would ask you to accompany Claude-Henri into the next room. The printer's there, and I have phone calls to make.'

Interviewer and interviewee shook hands. Arnold Palmer put on his best man-to-man face. 'No hard feelings.'

The inspector echoed the same words – dully without emotion.

After Palmer disappeared through the door into the next room, Hoffarth placed both hands flat on the table, spreading his fingers wide as one meditating over veins and tendons displaying an enviable intricacy of design and order absent elsewhere. Several moments passed before he summoned the resolve to lift the receiver; they were moments spent contemplating his powerlessness compared to that of a famed African American athlete.

It was one of those lethargic starts to the working week: Justin, who had spent the best part of the previous evening turning Rashid's decrypted material into an article for publication in *The Pulse's* next digital edition, was willing himself to stay awake with the help of a second cup of strong black coffee, while Chantalle Boyer yawned undecidedly over imperfect nail gloss in the midst of clearing the decks of Friday evening's leftover filing. When the telephone rang on Chantalle's desk as she was searching through her handbag by a window box of geraniums in need of watering, the strident note shredded both silence and nerves.

'If it's someone wanting to post a free ad in *The Pulse*,' said a bleary-eyed Justin, 'tell them it'll have to wait till the next issue. If it's for a feature classified, we still have space.'

'It's for you,' announced Chantalle, after taking the call. 'The police. Inspector Hoffarth.'

'Feedback about Klaus?'

'He didn't say.'

'Put him through.'

Justin picked up the phone. 'Morning, inspector. What can we do for you?'

'I'd like you to post a news item for us in this week's online and printed versions of *The Pulse*. You have room, I trust?'

Although, thought Justin, it was probably this man's style neither to beg nor to demand, the inspector's tone left no doubt as to the implications of failing to accommodate Luritania's police force.

'We'll make room. How long and about what?'

'Short. I can e-mail it to you now. About what, you'll see for yourself. It's gone out to all the dailies. You're the last in a long line. Sorry, Mr Hendry, I'm a busy man. I'll send it across straightaway.'

'Very good.'

The line went dead. Justin replaced the receiver and called up his mailbox. Having checked through it earlier, with nothing better to do than await the inspector's message, and somewhat prickly about the "last in a long line" mention, he clicked on his spam folder. Two messages. Not a candidate for cialis and unimpressed to learn that he stood to benefit from a wealthy Nigerian's estate once he gave the sender his bank account details, he clicked on delete and was one step away from emptying his digital dustbin, when a ping announced incoming mail.

Justin opened the inspector's message:

Following the unexplained murder of two foreigners whose bodies were found over the weekend in Schönschlucht's boarded-up Kinothek opposite the Azaleengarten, the police are asking anyone who might have seen one or more persons entering or leaving the Kinothek or behaving suspiciously in the immediate area between noon and six p.m. last Saturday to contact the number given below as soon as possible.'

'Police giving us a hard time? asked Chantalle, seeing the fixed look in her boss's eyes.

'No,' said a puzzled editor-in-chief. 'The inspector wants us to publicise two murders.'

'Not journalists this time, I hope.'

'Next to no details. Inspector Hoffarth plays his cards close to his chest.'

'What a way to start the week. He'll have Luritanians looking over their shoulder.'

'Not only Luritanians.'

⁂

After reading the same announcement in the *Luritanische Bote*, Ambassador Dexter Nussbaum called Arnold Palmer into his office.

There was no invitation to sit down. The glowering ambassador stabbed a podgy finger at the offending article. 'You seen this?'

Indeed Arnold had.

'Congratulations, Arnold, because you've well and truly fucked us.'

'In what way, sir?' The suitably humble subaltern thought it foolish to understand this reprimand in its literal sense.

'One safe house down the toilet.'

Embassy staff were accustomed to this fondness for categorising anything that attracted the ambassador's wrath as worthy of the lavatory.

'Sir, the *Kinothek* was a temporary facility only – due to be demolished to make way for another bank.'

'God knows when. Not this year. Probably not even next year.'

As with the inspector, Arnold Palmer fancied that he knew when best to hold his tongue. He wondered what Radetzky, the cartoonist, would have made out of the ambassador's beetroot-red fulminating.

'I thought this was going to be hushed up, not splashed all over the media. Before you know it, every news hound across the four borders with a nose for dirt will be poking around to see what he can dig up.'

The ambassador knew, as did Palmer, that he was ranting for the sake of it. An earlier call to the Minister for the Interior had guaranteed that there would be no mention of the embassy's connection with the disused *Kinothek* nor of the murdered men's possible affiliation to the CIA.

'Sir, I'm sure the authorities will keep our name out of the mud.'

'Dream on, Arnold. Dream on. This very morning, that treacherous bastard who defected to Moscow leaked news about the NSA's bugging the former Luritanian prime minister's phone. If the present incumbent gets the idea that Washington is listening in to his every word – as he probably will – this *Kinothek* disaster will give him something to throw back in our face.'

Palmer did not think the ambassador naïve enough to believe that further scandal about American eavesdropping on the head of government of what Arnold had heard referred to in Washington as a pygmy European state could lead to anything more grave than histrionic posturing – after which bilateral relations would return to normal.

'What would you like me to do about it, sir?' In situations such as these, Arnold realised that what Nussbaum expected of underlings was grovelling not resourcefulness.

'Do about it?' For a moment or two, Ambassador Nussbaum took the question seriously before slamming an angry fist into the punch ball of his open left hand. 'Do? There's nothing you can do to undo what's done.' (The amount of splutter accompanying this declamation as a result of the ambassador's falling foul of his own tongue twister was met with an abnormally straight face on Arnold's part.) 'Just get your no good ass out of my office and find us a new permanently safe house.'

⁂

With Isabelle's mother away visiting her sister in Nantes, Isabelle thought to invite her father to meet Craig over dinner in one of Jean-Luc's favourite restaurants inside the château whose courtyard Vanessa had booked for five evening performances of her play.

Jean-Luc Meunier, for whom sartorial pride was one of etiquette's natural adjuncts, arrived at the young couple's table dressed in an impeccably cut white Canali blazer and chinos, his cracked-print Christophe Lemaire shirt topped by a Brioni gold paisley silk foulard. At first disposed to approve of her father's good taste rounded off as it was with a neat pair of Bruno Magli beige suede loafers, his daughter revised her opinion when factoring in the jarring dash of red in his claret-coloured, silk-twill pocket square. Coupled with the casual summer shirt advertising a compulsion to look younger than his age, this signalled overkill. It seeming unlikely that he had gone out of his way to impress Craig, Isabelle was pained to think that her flighty father might be anticipating another of his assignations later that evening in his wife's absence. Isabelle failed to understand her mother's pitiful *quid pro quo* for tolerating this raffish behaviour whenever she was away from home: the day that Jean-Luc Meunier kicked over the traces while the two of them were living under the same roof, she would pack up and leave him.

After first gratefully accepting her father's gift of a fragrant orange and pink rose, for which the waiter rapidly found a fluted glass vase, then introducing the two men to one another, Isabelle commented on the slim document case placed unobtrusively on a side chair.

'Not work from the office, I hope?'

'That?' said Jean-Luc. 'Reading material. You know how I never have enough time during the day to catch up on essential reading.'

No stranger to paternal complaints about the stultifying life of an underemployed *rond de cuir* (desk-bound office worker) counting the minutes before lunch, Isabelle responded to her father's play-acting by rolling her eyes.

This being his first encounter with a seasoned diplomat outranking a mere attaché, Craig thought better of asking Isabelle's father to define essential. Not that he was likely to confess to its including French men's magazines. On the other hand, from the few confidences Isabelle had let slip about her father's strictly off-the-record worldview, Jean-Luc could well have been a closet reader of *Le Diplo*. It pleased Isabelle and amused Craig to think so.

'What are you two drinking? Do you intend to stay with *Sorhafen Blau* all evening? Forgive my saying so, but you're both looking rather pale. You, in particular, Isabelle'

Tempted to chastise her father for feeling it necessary to speak English in front of Craig, whose French she adjudged passable enough. Isabelle decided it would be ungracious to object. After four years spent in Washington, Jean-Luc Meunier was perfectly used to conversing in English. It had become his second language, which he spoke with the slightest, to her mind charming, trace of an American accent.

'We've been on a diet, father. Are you forgetting that Craig is a fitness trainer? He's sticking with mineral water.'

'And you?'

'*En Luritanie, Raoul roule et ne boit pas.* (Isabelle was citing a popular designated driver commercial, recommending whoever drove when out with friends or family to stay sober.)

'And there was I imagining we might be celebrating something tonight,' said Jean-Luc, a twinkle in his eye. 'Or are engagements out of fashion for the young of today?'

'Father, neither of us believes in rushing things.' Isabelle knew that this was less than true: whereas Craig was keen for them to tie the civil marriage knot as soon as possible, Isabelle preferred to wait and see how their relationship matured over time.

'Which means you're cohabiting. Dreadful expression. Worse still, please don't say you're planning on entering into a *pacte de concubinage*. Craig's not already married, is he?'

'No, I'm divorced, Monsieur Meunier. You don't have to worry about polygamy.'

'Well, that's a relief. You should know that I'm behind the times in thinking that marriage is the moral cement of the family.'

Had she been on her own with her father Isabelle might have let her composure desert her to the point of accusing him of hypocrisy, but in the presence of Craig and faced with the almost saintly reverence with which these words were delivered, she decided to let things pass.

Jean-Luc corrected a kinked trouser crease. 'Forgive me Isabelle, Craig. I shall not press you any further in this highly personal matter. The night is young. Let us enjoy each other's company over a superlative meal, which I insist on offering you both to fête your ...' Reaching for the rose, the jovial diplomat breathed in the satisfying scent, replaced it in the vase and, fingering his wedding ring in search of the elusive compliment, finally settled for: '... togetherness.'

True to his word, Jean-Luc Godard insisted on treating the couple to a sumptuous meal. However, as they had just completed a three days' fast on lemon juice water, they asked the waiter to carry back to the kitchen what was too much for them to manage and, so as not to disappoint Jean-Luc, to put this sizeable amount in takeaway aluminum foil containers.

A devotee of Havana cigars, the diplomat decided to accompany his after-dessert *Kümmel* and dark roast *crema e gusto espresso* with a *Partagas*. Aware that neither Isabelle nor Craig approved of smoking, but determined not to allow this to spoil his pleasure, he took care to avoid polluting the air around them.

Isabelle, her *crème brûlée* unfinished, paused to take a sip of Yunnan green tea, before broaching a subject of mutual interest to her and Craig.

'Father, Craig wants to hold a fundraising event in his fitness centre in support of MSF. It's to be a thirty-hour cyclothon with relay teams of four taking a rest and refreshments every so often and spending the night in sleeping bags on the centre's floor mats. The owner, a Dutch businessman open to ideas for polishing up his gym's image, has agreed to lay on snacks and drinks. We'll be advertising ahead of time in local sporting equipment and sportswear shops as well as, of course, in the press, including *The Pulse*.'

'Yes,' said Craig. 'But perhaps more important is the fact that I've managed to interest the Town Hall, the Sports Minister, a number of hedge funds, banks and auditing companies to sponsor us. Of course, we expect friends and family members to come forward as sponsors for individual cyclists.'

Left unmentioned by Craig and Isabelle was the agreement reached with the owner of *Bibliopole* that a certain bank across the border in France would match every euro raised from sponsors with three of its own. *Bibliopole's* owner had seized this opportunity to suggest that his not insignificant part in the BLR Mensdorf branch heist merited recognition more solid than gratitude. Where else would the couple have found a human forklift capable of spiriting so much dosh off the premises from a storage point less than two metres from where it had been originally lifted? And whose inspired idea had it been to invest this booty offshore, so to speak, in a financial establishment owned by the world's largest economy? The commission duly approved by his two listeners, albeit on the back of Isabelle's objections that it flew in the face of jointly approved altruistic principles, had gone towards winning e-bay's *Tristram Shandy* auction, Tich having decided that it was undignified to tie this transaction to a loan.

Jean-Luc scratched an itch and a question from his forehead. 'Cyclothon. Admirable idea. Well, I suppose you wouldn't object to a non-physical contribution from me? I would never have the staying power to drive two pedals around for ...' He did a quick mental calculation. '... fifty-four thousand seconds a day for two days.'

'Not even the youngest participants are expected to cycle that long continuously, father. At the most, four hours at a stretch.'

'I'm relieved to hear that. Having your cyclists drop dead on you would hardly be a good advertisement for MSF. What, may I ask, Craig, made you decide on them for your charity drive?'

'A blog,' said Craig, 'about the latest trade pact which the Americans are urging us to sign up to. As well as flooding our markets with a lot of their junk products, it would give the pharmaceutical majors a stranglehold on prices, particularly those of medical supplies most needed by MSF.'

'That's how I understand it also. A bad deal for Europe. But then our governments are expert at leaning over backwards to please Washington.' Jean-Luc extracted two green euro notes from his wallet. Would this help?'

'Very generous, sir. Which team would you care to support? The *Tour de France*, the *Giro d'Italia,* the *Vuelta* or the Milk Race?'

'It would unpatriotic of me not to back the *Tour de France*. And isn't the Milk Race *dépassée*? Scarcely a day goes by without doctors advising us not to guzzle cows' milk.'

'You're right, but we're hoping to net Lurilait as a star sponsor.'

The diplomat pocketed his wallet before returning with unfeigned satisfaction to the *Partagas*. 'This is not just exercise for fat-burners and masochists? It's a competition?'

'Yes, those sponsors whose team records the highest number of kilometers have pledged to double their original *mise* or stake.'

'Ah, then I should pray that there will be no Bernard Hinaults on my team.'

'We've managed to recruit the American cultural attaché to head the *Giro d'Italia*. His team has agreed to stoke up on pasta the day before the event under *Barilla's* sponsorship.'

'And who have you got to sponsor the *Tour de France* and the *Vuelta*?'

'A bakery for the first. I'm still waiting for a reply from the *Instituto Cervantes* for the second.'

'None of whose riders will be expected to bear lances. Which reminds me of your American diplomat. A recent recruit, as I understand it. Can the embassy really afford to give him two days of their time?'

'Only one. We're holding the event over a Friday and Saturday.'

'I see. Well, his countrymen are in the news again. Has either of you read the latest editorial in *The Pulse*? No? I have a copy here.'

Jean-Luc Meunier unzipped his document case, pulled out Justin Hendry's magazine and held it up in plain view of Craig and Isabelle.

'Distinctive choice of cover compared to last week's picture of the prime minister cutting the ribbon inaugurating the country's new zoo.'

The waiter obligingly choosing this moment to clear the table of empty plates, Jean-Luc handed over the magazine for Craig to lay out on the table beside him and Isabelle. Both were unprepared for Justin's stark cover image depicting an apocalyptic mushroom cloud under the heading: *Is the Cold War Heating Up?*

On the other hand, the moment Craig turned to the front-page editorial, he and Isabelle recognised Rashid's decrypted text.

'I leave you to decide whether it qualifies as recommended reading or *Fahrenheit 451* material.'

After spooning up the last of her *crème brûlée*, Isabelle moved her chair closer to Craig's. Conscious that they should treat the editorial as something they were seeing for the first time, Isabelle hoped that Craig would have the presence of mind to moderate his reaction.

Her first impression, to judge by the opening sentence, was that Justin had taken editorial liberties with the original.

In an era where conspiracy theories have become as commonplace as tales of corruption among the highest echelons of the world's paramount sporting authority, chill news has reached our ears sounded by tocsins foretelling dark times ahead on the world political stage.

The message, reproduced below, is as stark as it is clear.

Last week, the Russian Federation let it be known at the highest level that should the USA's continuing addiction to illegitimate interventions around the globe presage the use of force of arms to rewrite borders at the expense of either the Russian or Chinese people and their respective territories, any hostilities mounted towards this end would be met by reprisals against the belligerent's home territory.

Maintaining that it has laid massive explosive charges in Pacific Ocean undersea trenches, which charges it is capable of activating, the Russian Federation claimed that it has the capacity to visit devastating floods on the west coast of North America and its hinterland with crippling effect on the region's infrastructure and economies.

Last month, the captain of China's Jin-class Cao Wei nuclear submarine successfully conducted a launch test off the coast of Los Angeles, demonstrating the ease with which a dummy ballistic missile could reach the Chinese mainland from this distance: a tacit warning to the North American government of the risks it runs in seeking to extend its zone of influence in South-East Asia and the South China Sea. Washington should understand that any violation of the red lines around China's disputed territorial waters will be met with a vigorous response.

In the light of these two, possibly joint, threats to American and world security, the U.S. military's commander-in chief is considering deployment of a significant number of land, sea and air nuclear strike forces to strategic, undisclosed sites around the globe.

Citizens of the free world are also cautioned to note with concern recent proselytising campaigns mounted by Russia and China towards winning non-aligned countries to their side with the intention of shattering the mould of the current world order.

The White House has informed the Congressional leadership of the president's wish for an immediate debate behind closed doors with a view to countering these confrontational policies.

Dear Readers,

The fact that April 1ˢᵗ is long behind us should not deter you from taking issue with the validity of the above warnings. However, in view of the unimpeachable source of this material, which, for reasons of confidentiality, your editor is unable to reveal, The Pulse's management is reluctant to contest its authenticity.

Justin Hendry
Editor-in-chief

'What do you think?' asked an inscrutable Jean-Luc, when Craig and Isabelle looked up from their reading. 'Scare-mongering of the worst sort or more than a grain of truth?'

From the glint in her father's eyes it was impossible for Isabelle to know whether, and to what extent, he was in earnest or leading them on.

She gave an indifferent shrug. 'I agree that this is weird stuff for a *Pulse* editorial. A pity Justin had no Klaus Radetzky to give the cover a less doom-laden spin.'

'And you, Craig?'

'Must say I'm inclined to believe a good piece of it. Perhaps because it coincides with my world view of each side forever provoking the other.'

Isabelle disguised her astonishment at this apparently off-the-cuff judgment, clearly meant to pander to her father, by simulating an eye irritation. 'How about you, father?' she said, tugging gently at a lower eyelid, her head tilted upwards as if disturbed by a wayward eyelash.

Taking hold of the review, the diplomat cast a lingering, stony gaze at the cheerless product of the Manhattan Project before stuffing the publication unceremoniously back into his briefcase.

'You'd be better off asking Craig's cycling cultural attaché. See whether he dismisses it with a snigger or wonders who Hendry's source might be.'

'I wanted your opinion, father. You're as bad as those prevaricators the straw polls call Don't Knows.'

'All right, eighty per cent blarney.' Jean-Luc gave his cigar a Churchillian puff. The red embers dancing briefly at the end of the *Partagas* might almost have borne out the tenuousness of his verdict. 'Remind me of the name of that cultural attaché.'

'I don't think I mentioned it,' said Isabelle, her vision genuinely blurred, her father having forgotten where he was exhaling. 'Don't your people circulate you with the resumés of all embassy newcomers?'

Jean-Luc regarded his daughter as if both thrown and gratified by the realisation that she had got the better of him. 'Indeed we do, indeed we do. All the same, refresh my flagging memory.'

'Palmer. Arnold Palmer.'

The diplomat might have been communing with his muse for all the time it took him to respond. 'You never heard this from me, of course,' he said at length, tapping bloodless fireflies into his ash tray. 'But cultural attachés from the other side of the pond rarely wear only one hat.'

'Well, Arnold Palmer's interest in culture is more than passing. He queued up to audition for a leading role in Vanessa Curtis's latest production.'

'Natural enough. It gives the fellow an intro into a wider circle. Helps him put out feelers.'

'With amateur theatrical actors? What joy could he hope to get out of that?'

'Joy?' Although good, Jean-Luc's grasp of English was not good enough to grasp this colloquialism.

'What inside information about affairs of state could he expect to tap into from ordinary folk like us?'

'If his people have bugs for affairs of state, they also have nature's antennae for corporate and everyday indiscretions.'

'Such as who's sleeping with whom?'

The diplomat's response came without the bat of an eyelid. 'For example. All grist to the mill. Especially if one embassy's military attaché is sleeping with another embassy's female cultural attaché.'

'The Americans have a military attaché here in Luritana?'

'Of course.'

Craig flicked a persistent fly from some sugary dessert residue marring the otherwise spotless patterned tablecloth. 'Whatever for? Think of the cost.'

'Primarily, liaising with the local NATO contingent. As for being a drain on the budget, in terms of value for money – aren't we all?'

'Why is it,' asked Isabelle unwilling to concede that she should pay lip service to her father because he was footing the bill, 'that those Europeans making the most rumpus about sovereignty never thought twice about relinquishing it to NATO? Oh dear, slip of the tongue there. I meant to say to America.'

Familiar with his daughter's Gaullist sympathies, Jean-Luc Meunier waved a patriarchal finger and signalled the waiter for a second *crema e gusto*. He waited until the man had left, before downing the rest of his *Kümmel*. After which the grey-haired diplomat sat pensively, the empty liqueur glass in his hand, his expression no longer jovial but clouded.

'Arnold Palmer is a liability,' he remarked with studied sobriety: 'Tread carefully with him.'

Despite finding such advice puzzling, Isabelle, knowing her father well enough to appreciate that this was his last word on the matter, stayed the makings of a rejoinder from Craig by nudging his foot.

However, she was pleasantly taken aback, when, after settling up with the waiter, leaving a generous tip and consulting his watch, their Lucullian host explained that he had become the lucky owner of a free ticket, offered him by an indisposed embassy colleague, to that evening's late-night, one-man show starring a versatile British comedian, whose manager had scheduled a single performance in the Luritanian capital as part of his artiste's European tour. The cherry on Jean-Luc's cake was that the visiting comic's show would be in French.

Left to their own devices, the young couple decided to order another bottle of mineral water to help down a small dish of chocolate truffles untouched by Jean-Luc out of consideration for his blood glucose level.

'Do you think,' said Craig, 'unable to resist the lure of a dark truffle which, as it turned out, had a champagne centre, 'that we upset your father by pecking at our food?'

'No, he never lets other people's fads affect his own appetite. You saw how much he enjoyed the braised lambs' tongues and his *Châteauneuf-du-Pape*.'

'Still, it made me feel ungrateful after he gave me those four hundred euros.'

'Silly. No need to feel that way. I though he was in his element tonight.'

'What was that nonsense about Palmer? Why the kick?'

'There are certain things you can't press him on. I sensed he regretted saying as much as he did. But if we were in Washington at the same time as Palmer or my father has heard something about the man through diplomatic channels, it's quite possible that he knows more than he's letting on.'

'What cause have we got to concern ourselves about Palmer? How can he know anything of our Sunday discussions?'

Isabelle eyed her second cocoa-powder-dusted Grand Marnier truffle. 'This is ruining all the good work started with that diet.'

'The flesh is weak.'

Out of the corner of her eye, Isabelle caught the waiter polishing first one then another toecap on the back of his trouser leg. She refocused on the dish of truffles.

'Forget Palmer. What do you think about Justin's cover? Isn't it over the top?'

'What do you mean?'

'Feeding the American war propaganda machine. If it's them or us, let's get ready to nuke them first.'

'That's crazy, Isabelle. No sane person would choose to go down that road.'

'Find me the sanity in today's international affairs.'

'Very good. But the spectre of mutual assured destruction? Enough to rule out being crazy enough to go for a pre-emptive nuclear strike.'

'That's as may be. But I'm beginning to think that Justin should follow this latest article up with the first deciphered text. Let the public see both sides of the coin.'

'That's inviting trouble. Aren't you forgetting Klaus Radetzky?'

'There's nothing to prove that Klaus's death had anything to do with the contents of that lost property briefcase.'

'What about the conservative MP, the one who committed suicide?'

'Musgrave? He was devastated by the death of his son.'

'So devastated that, before gassing himself, he went to the trouble to post a danger zone warning to Justin?'

Isabelle looked up from studying the label on the mineral water bottle advertising the therapeutic properties of the spring from which it was drawn in the grounds of Luritania's Trappist monastery.

'All right, I see your point. But why did we all agree to publicise Rashid's latest?'

'We didn't all agree, as you well know.'

'Well, you agreed on the assumption that it was trumped up by scaremongers. Just, as I suspect, some of us looked down our noses at the first text's chronicle of evil-minded plutocrats planning world resource domination. But that was our reading of things. What if the suicidal Westminster MP is to be believed? Then there's nothing to choose between the first and Rashid's latest decryption in terms of making troubled waters rougher than they already are. Therefore, we might as well publish the first.'

'But I thought you, Tich and Vanessa rated that the more incendiary of the two.'

'I did, it's true. But the more I think about it, the more I feel that once Justin publishes that first text there'll be no need for him to fear retaliation. After all, with nothing more to report, the damage will have been done.'

'Not if he acknowledges how he came by both texts and their connection with a member of the House of Commons. Perhaps I'm willing to go along with you for part of the way with this, but what I don't understand is why you're suddenly doing an about turn that makes Justin a sitting duck. Why should he agree to that? What right have we to ask him to stick his neck out, while we stand to one side?'

Craig's criticism together with the suspicion that Luritania's commercially-minded Trappists aspired to cash in on the Lourdes phenomenon made Isabelle question her logic.

'You mean, if we're going to do this, we should put our money where our mouth is?'

'Yes.'

'How?'

'Blogs. E-mails to a cross-section of European broadsheet editors.'

'Rashid has already covered that. Said he'd feed his ideas to Justin. So, no. Bad idea.'

'All right. How about approaching the BBC World News team. Suggesting interviews.'

'Be realistic, Craig. Who are we to them? Unknown quantities. The lunatic fringe.'

'Then YouTube. A podcast.'

'Come off it, Craig. You're that keen on looking ridiculous?'

'Well, what would Miss Clever Pants suggest?'

'Prioritise.'

'Meaning?'

'For a start, get the authorities on our side.'

'Which authorities do you have in mind? Interpol, MI6, the NSA?'

Isabelle turned away from the as yet unconfirmed holy water. 'Confession time. Following our last Lenfindi Club meeting I went straight to the police on Monday morning. Hoffarth. That inspector who interrogated me over the bank robbery.'

'You did what?'

'Gave him the bare outlines. How Justin's life could be at risk.'

'You did this off the top of your head?'

Isabelle gazed stolidly at the unholy thimbleful of spring water left in her glass. 'That's one way of putting it.'

Craig pushed the remaining truffles out of his and Isabelle's reach. 'Without appreciating the irony. An unrepentant criminal seeking help from the police?'

'I think,' said Isabelle, staring fixedly at a nineteenth century lithograph of the château on the wall behind Craig, 'that a person's life is more important than mere paper money.'

'I can't argue with you on that one. So how did this Inspector Hoffarth react? Did he humour you?'

'No,' snapped back Isabelle, switching her eyes to bring the full force of her glare to bear on Craig. 'He promised to keep a close watch on Justin, his apartment and workplace.'

'All well and good, Isabelle. But you went this alone. At the very least, you should have sought Justin's approval. Better still, left him to take the initiative. What's the betting that Hoffarth will rope him in for questioning? You need to forewarn Justin.'

'I suppose I should.' It was an admission forced out, while one of Isabelle's hands clutched at the tablecloth overhang, the index finger of the other ploughing a furrow across the surface.

'Make your peace with him. Say you didn't feel you could put off going to the police for another week.' Belatedly ruing his self-righteousness, Craig came to an abrupt halt on the heels of a different realisation. 'Hang on. Hoffarth must have asked you how you came by whatever you told him. What exactly did you tell him?'

There was an element of sovereign dismissal to the way in which Isabelle shook her head before deigning to reply. 'That Justin had been warned to be careful about what he published. I didn't say from where the warnings came. It left Justin free to claim he'd received threatening e-mails, which he'd brushed off and deleted.'

'Hoffarth's bound to dig deeper.'

Feeling vindicated and suddenly less at daggers drawn with Craig than with a middle-aged man ogling her from a nearby table, Isabelle reached out to lay claim to forbidden fruit. 'So Justin will throw sand in his eyes.'

'It doesn't alter the fact that you've put him in an awkward position.'

'He's not a kid. Journalists are used to seeing traps of this kind a mile off.'

'And who's laid this one for him?'

Isabelle flailed an arm out in exasperation. 'For heaven's sake, I was trying to help.'

Sensing that he had gone too far, Craig went to place a reassuring hand on her shoulder only to have it dislodged. 'I'm sorry,' he said, backing off. 'You meant well.'

Isabelle sat wrapped in a cocoon of silence. The waiting proved too much for Craig.

'Did Hoffarth ask how Justin came to confide in you?'

'I told him it was during a break while rehearsing our parts in Vanessa's play.'

'So?'

'So what?'

'Think it through. You're a police inspector. Someone comes to you with a story. You can't make your mind up whether to take it at face value. Perhaps others might help clarify matters. Like the rest of the cast.'

'Oh yes? Hoffarth would be here until the same time next month interviewing us all.'

'Rubbish. He only needs to tackle the principals. Justin would hardly have confided in one of the streetcleaners.'

'I don't agree,' said Isabelle, picking with diminished conviction at a loose thread in the tablecloth.

'Don't agree with what? Think of it. You've unwittingly dragged the rest of the Lenfindi Club into Hoffarth's catch net. That means we need to alert the others double quick.'

'Not the rest of the club. Only two others. Vanessa and Rashid.'

'In terms of who's directly affected, yes. But although Tich isn't involved in the play, we can hardly leave him out, for goodness sake. That means calling a full club meeting as soon as possible. During the lunch hour tomorrow at *All The Right Moves*. In the staff room. There's only one trainer with a course first thing in the afternoon, and I'll tell him politely to leave us undisturbed.'

'Shit, Craig, how am I going to face your friends? They never wanted me in their club in the first place.'

'Not true.'

'Yes, I'm sure of it.'

Craig hesitated for a moment before venturing a split-second solution. 'I'll make out it was my idea to go the police.'

A minimally placated Isabelle smoothed out the furrowed tablecloth. 'Now Casanova wants to play Sydney Carton.'

A reluctant one, thought Craig, having only half meant what he said, but with no alternative now other than to live up to his word.

'Reporting back, sir, on the little I've been able to glean about Palmer.'

Claude-Henri Weiland stood in front of his boss's desk, watching the inspector chance his luck with a national lottery scratch card bought earlier that morning by the trainee as part of a weekly set of six for the staff on Hoffarth's floor.

'And?'

'It seems that trouble of one sort or another has followed Palmer around the globe. Trouble reflecting on his employers, mind you. Nothing compromising laid at his door. The guy appears to have been something of a facilitator.'

'Facilitating his employers' interests.'

'Right.'

'But no dirt attaching to him?'

'Nothing obvious. But there is one point of interest. All Palmer's postings have been short-lived. The man barely has time to soak up the local colour before he's moved on. Does that tell us something?'

'I think it does. Monsieur MiniGolf is bad news.'

'Any luck with the card, sir?'

'Only if you call getting your stake back lucky. And you?'

'Four euros.'

'Careful, Claude-Henri. Don't let success go to your head.'

The trainee was on the point of taking leave of his boss, when the sight of the birdcage jogged his memory.

'Do you mind my asking a personal question, *monsieur*?'

'The first of my staff to do so in a long time, Claude-Henri, you're making me feel almost human. Go ahead.'

'It's the bird cage. I've been with you for a month now, and only twice have I seen the door latched. Was there a reason for that?'

'Something to do with catching our man? I'm afraid not, Claude-Henri. No, it's much simpler than you think. On most mornings when I arrive for work, the first thing I do is to open the cage door left closed overnight. It's a way of telling myself to unclutter my mind. Therefore, on those days that you saw the door latched, my mind was more cluttered than usual.'

'And what, if I may ask, *monsieur*, is the trick in uncluttering your mind?'

'Trick, Claude-Henri? I wish I knew, since I tend to have as much success on that front as with your miserable choice of scratch cards. Curiosity satisfied?'

The trainee made a subdued exit.

⁂

Upon learning from Chantalle Boyer's temp that Justin Hendry had left for Spain – on business, she thought best to say -, Craig was in two minds as to whether to call a meeting at all in the absence of the person directly in Hoffarth's line of fire. Swayed partly by contrition, partly by Craig's self-sacrifice and partly by the realisation that the longer they delayed things the more difficult it would be to justify her silence, Isabelle persuaded him otherwise.

The meeting could hardly have got off to a worse start. Only Vanessa expressed understanding of Craig's decision to cut the Lenfindi Club out of the loop by taking his concerns about Justin's safety directly to the police. Tich accused the fitness expert of going off at half cock, and reproached Isabelle for not talking her boyfriend out of it. She in turn insisted, not without bad conscience, that she had tried her best to dissuade him. For his part, Rashid was uncommonly ratty about Craig's action, saying that the fact that close friends called him Rash should not be taken to mean that he was headstrong. But after some heated exchanges, tempers calmed and all five agreed to keep to the same story if approached by the police: in the wake of the graffiti episode, Justin Hendry had spoken only in the vaguest of terms about threats from anonymous third parties.

Given Tich's uncompromising opposition to Isabelle's suggestion that the rest of the club should press *The Pulse's* editor to publish the first decoded document on the heels of the second, it was agreed to shelve further discussion of the subject until Justin's return.

⁂

Memo from J to K

Have you noticed how, despite being on all but a war footing with the Nevskians, Urodina continues to enjoy subsidsed coal, gas and electricity purchases from the League? Why does the latter refuse to hit the neighbouring economy where it hurts by charging market rates? And why, in addition to sourcing power at knockdown prices, is it bailing out the loss-making subsidiaries of its banks on Urodinian territory? Because not one oligarch on either side of the divide is willing to relinquish his profit-taking.

303

Agreed. Well-heeled Nevskians are more likely to flaunt wallets made of the skin of rebel war dead than to shell out in support of an independence movement threatening their illicit business interests.

And with oil and gas production in the private sector's stranglehold, these billionaires are throttling the life out of the League through price hikes driven by no other purpose than self-enrichment. In favouring the higher revenue gas export market, they leave four fifths of their country deprived of one of its prime natural resources. Unfortunately for us, the prospects of a grass roots revolt against leaders cut off from reality look dim. Accustomed to swallowing propaganda from the Wayfarer and the Bear to the effect that economic recovery is around the corner, Nevskians remain misguidedly long-suffering, hoping against hope for better days to come.

Mind you, should public discontent boil over, every one of the League's profiteers, not a few of whose bodyguards are supplied by private Vespuccian security contractors, has his private jet on standby at the country's major airports ready to whisk him away to the safety of one of his extraterritorial properties.

Following the last-minute cancellation of a symposium in Barcelona on *The Dangers of Honest Reporting from War Zones* which he and his lead cameraman had been invited to attend, Justin decided that, instead of getting Chantalle Boyer to go to the hassle of arguing a refund from the airline, he would ask Gisela Radetzky whether she and her daughter would like to join him for a three-day trip to Barcelona. When Gisela agreed, he told Chantalle to buy a third ticket for Rosalie on the same flight, and assured mother and child that they would occupy the two side-by-side seats reserved for him and his colleague.

However, waiting near the airport's self-service check-in machines with only thirty minutes to go before boarding and no call or text message from Gisela on his cell phone, Justin began to wonder whether she might have had a change of heart. Until he saw them both hurrying though the terminal's automatic doors, Gisela, dressed in a flowery summer dress (Klaus, she told him, had said never to wear widow's weeds on his behalf), pulling a lightweight hold-all, and Rosalie, wearing a denim jacket over a tropical print shift dress, carrying a soft toy under one arm, while tugging a metal *Jungle Book* suitcase with the other.

'Dreadful morning,' said Gisela. 'Duckling here took one spoonful of cereal and threw up over her clothes. Milk had turned. Still, she's better now, aren't you, Rosalie? We're not too late, are we?'

'Only hand luggage? No, no need to worry. I've got our online reservations printed out. Straight to the counter for our tickets, through security and plenty of time to draw breath before we board.'

Less than two and a half hours later, their flight touched down at Barcelona-El Prat airport.

Whereas Justin had made several trips to the Catalan capital before, this was Gisela's first visit to Barcelona. The wiser from experience, Justin had booked the three of them into a hotel in a calm area off *Las Ramblas*, the main pedestrian thoroughfare.

After learning that Gisela was a fan of Gaudí's mosaic art and the paintings of Miró, the widow's host had worked out a custom-made sightseeing programme using the hop-on, hop-off, open-topped tourist buses departing from the Plaça de Catalunya at the northern end of *Las Ramblas*. At the same time, while of the opinion that most of the street performers along *Las Ramblas* as well as the art work for sale there were the height of kitsch, Justin appreciated that it would be a pity to deprive Rosalie of the chance to miss out on some of the more imaginative live statues. Finally, an outing to Tibidabo way above the city rounded off with a ride on the *Red Aeroplane* was an absolute must for the six-year-old. This had necessitated reassuring mother rather than daughter, the inheritor of paternal feistiness, that the 1928 model of the first plane to fly between Barcelona and Madrid was fixed to one end of the arm of a crane around which it revolved sedately, leaving passengers to relax inside their panelled wood and leather cabin from where, clear skies permitting, they could enjoy unequalled views of Barcelona and the Mediterranean below.

***

On their first evening in Spain, Justin escorted his two companions to a family-run restaurant off the tourist track. They were lucky to find a table: most were occupied by locals tucking into red mullet, monkfish or squid, and not one was without its bottle of house wine. Gisela remarked on the menu chalked up on a blackboard above the counter

'Is that in Catalan?'

'Yes. They don't get that many tourists in here, so no plastic-coated menus with glossy pictures of fried eggs, sausages and beans.'

'Do you speak Catalan, Justin?'

'No. At first, I mistook it for a dialect of Spanish. It's not. It's closer to Occitan, the *langue d'Oc* spoken over the border in France.'

'On the flight across I read that it's the official language of Andorra.'

'Right and of Valencia, where, unsurprisingly, it's called Valencian.'

'Don't you know any words, Uncle Justin?' asked Rosalie.

'A few. *Paella,* for one.'

'But that's Spanish,' protested Gisela.

'Yes and no. For a Catalan, a paella is a frying pan not one of the dishes you eat out of it. The Spanish for frying pan is *sarten*.'

'What's a bird in Cattylan?' asked Rosalie, fascinated that afternoon by the feathery creatures peeping out from their cages along *Las Ramblas*.

'*Ocell*. Pretty close to Italian *uccello*, but very unlike Spanish, *pajaro*, which, I believe, comes from the Latin for sparrow.'

'But you know so much, uncle.'

'If only that were true, Rosalie. Apart from seeming to remember that a cat is a *gat* and a dog a *gos*, that's about the extent of my Catalan.'

'So,' said Gisela, 'how are you going to manage with that menu?'

'It looks as if it's scarcely changed since the last time I was here. And when it comes to food, my memory is phenomenal.'

'What do you recommend?'

'Personally, I'm a fan of *chocos*, fried cuttlefish in lemon juice. There's sea bass, if you prefer that.'

'I fancy something vegetarian for our first night in Barcelona. I don't think Rosalie should eat anything too heavy either.'

'In that case, how about aubergine with green beans and tomatoes?'

'Sounds good.'

'Ma, can I have some of those potatoes?' Rosalie had turned towards a dish of deep-fried *patatas bravas* on the next table.

'I don't see why not. Wouldn't mind some myself.'

'Well,' said Justin, 'I'll tell the waiter to serve Rosalie's portion plain. It usually comes with peppery tomato or garlic and olive oil sauce.'

'How will you manage that. if you don't speak Catalan?'

'We're not in Ukraine, Gisela. Catalans haven't declared Castilian Spanish beyond the pale.'

'So the latest incarnation of Don Quixote will make himself understood?'

'He did last time.' Justin paused, hesitating to mar an unclouded evening with what, he suspected, was the product of an overactive imagination. 'Have you noticed those two guys over there, who arrived just after us? Am I seeing things or do they keep staring our way?'

Gisela Radetzky waited a couple of beats before turning to look in the direction indicated by Justin. 'Scruffily dressed, aren't they? Perhaps they're admiring our taste in clothes. Or is it simply that we're the only tourists here?'

'You mean I don't look even remotely like the don?'

'You need to be thinner and older. A straggly grey beard would go better on you than that clean shaven chin. And you don't look like someone who's lost his marbles mugging up on the Knights of the Round Table.'

The service was unhurried so that by the time the food arrived Rosalie was close to falling asleep after a tiring journey and her enthusiastic capering along *Las Ramblas*, where she had her picture taken with the sad-eyed street performer imitating Edward Scissorhands.

Seeing that her daughter's attention was elsewhere, Gisela risked an oblique reference to the little girl's father. 'You mentioned Ukraine earlier, Justin. You know, I'm sure that had nothing to do with … Look, Ukraine trumpets its vendettas. You understand? It can't have been Ukrainians.'

'I agree.'

'Those dollar bills I found tell a different story. What could Klaus and you have done to put the Americans' noses out?'

Justin knew that it had to come to this sooner or later. Dodging the issue was no solution. He owed it to Gisela to make a clean breast of things.

'Your husband did nothing, Gisela. I fear he paid the penalty for my sins.'

'What?' Gisela Radetzky's look of alarm was all the greater inasmuch as it coincided with the need to catch Rosalie before she fell asleep off her chair.

'Mistaken identity.'

Justin proceeded to fill his widowed companion in on the background to and fallout from Peregrine Musgrave's documents. To his surprise, she heard him out with dry-eyed stoicism, never interrupting, never betraying the slightest emotion. It was as if intuitively she had been waiting for him to reveal something of the kind. And when he had finished his confession, instead of throwing her head back in despair, she regarded him straight in the eyes before saying: 'You were right. I was wrong. That couple definitely are interested in us. Pickpockets?'

Justin flashed a glance at the two men sitting at a table in one of the far corners over a bottle of wine and what looked, to judge by the inky black colour, to be a dish of *calamares en su tinta.*. Both wore grubby T-shirts and frayed, pebble-washed jeans. Caught in the act of watching the three foreigners, the balder of the two was a fraction of a second late in averting his gaze.

'If so, bad at disguising their intentions.'

As it happened, the walk back to the hotel proved uneventful. Despite repeated glances over their shoulders (by this time, Justin was carrying a somnolent Rosalie in his arms), there was nothing to indicate that three weary tourists were being followed by two down-and-outs or, for that matter, by anybody else.

When Gisela took Rosalie into her own arms outside her bedroom door, despite struggling to reconcile herself to the fact that she had been deceived by someone indirectly responsible for her husband's death, it was without recrimination or bitterness that she took her leave of a man condemned to failure in making amends for the irreparable.

Although the strains of the previous evening had left their mark on both adults, Gisela was the first over the next morning's buffet breakfast to resolve to make the middle of their three days in Barcelona a carefree one for all concerned, her daughter in particular. She needed no persuading by a Justin noticeably less outward-going than usual to agree to his proposal that the highlight of their morning should be a visit to Antoni Gaudí's acclaimed work in progress, the *Sagrada Família,* and the highlight of their afternoon an excursion to the Tibidabo amusement park on the heights overlooking the city.

'I'm afraid,' said Justin, as the three of them took in the warm early morning sun atop their sightseeing bus on the way to Spain's most visited edifice, 'that we'll find the church teeming with busloads of tourists like us. Once we get there, we have three choices: staying with the tour guide I signed up with when I booked our tickets online, peeling off from him or her, or going it alone with or without an audio tour. Having taken one myself, I can recommend the audio tour, although if you'd rather not fiddle around with plug-ins while climbing the spiral staircases inside some of the towers, I'm perfectly willing to act as your guide for the modest price of an ice cream in Tibidabo. Anyway, trying to fit in all the towers would not only be too much and too boring for Rosalie but, frankly, more than, I fancy, either you or I could take with so many people swarming around.'

Gisela patted the sling bag in her lap. 'I've brought along a guide book. So let's go it alone with you as our occasional cicerone.'

Rosalie pulled a face. 'What's a zitszeroni?'

'A guide who gets paid with ice cream.'

'Does he have a spotty face?'

'Well, ours doesn't.'

As they approached the church, Rosalie pulled another face and stuck out her tongue. 'That looks weird. All those spires stuck on any old how. Why's it called a church?'

Gisela extracted her guide book from the sling bag and sought the relevant page. 'Actually, when the last pope consecrated it, he called it a minor basilica.'

'What's a basilica?'

'Good question, duckling. Wish I knew.'

'Wait till you get inside,' said Justin. 'Minor's a bit of an understatement.'

'Orwell thought the building an eyesore,' said Gisela, seizing on one of the more disparaging comments made about Gaudí's project over the years.

'Yes, well, perhaps if he was able to set foot in it nowadays he might revise his opinion,' said Justin, who could have done without the red leather reminder.

'You know how I hate museums, Ma. Can I wait outside?'

'On your own?'

'No, with Uncle Justin. He's seen it all before.'

'Not all. And how am I going to cope without a zitszeroni?'

'It's all right, Rosalie,' said Justin, 'I'll give you a piggyback, if you start feeling tired.'

Gisela frowned. 'Rubbish, the exercise will do her good. Anyway, Rosalie, Uncle Justin knows I'm more interested in the mosaics than the sculpture, so we can focus on those and leave the crypt, museum and the rest for another visit.'

For the first time that morning, Justin's face broke into a grin. 'I suppose your guidebook tells you about the magnificent view from the top of the towers.'

'Yes. What's funny about that?'

'Nothing, just that, if you want to take snapshots of mosaics through the openings on the way up the spiral staircases, there are four hundred steps to mount.'

'I thought there was a lift.'

'Which you pay for. All in a good cause. The entry fee and extras like that help fund the never-ending work on Gaudí's project in the making.'

'Easier on the heart and lungs than carrying Rosalie all the way to the top.'

'Last time I was here, I took the lift up one side and the stairs down the other. And I was glad not to run into any diehard mountaineers on their way up. Those steps are narrow. The faint of heart are advised not to peer down over the inside edge without holding on to something.'

'Gaudí's idea of Hades?'

'Let's say the idea of installing a lift never featured in the great man's plans. I prefer to think Gaudí saw the climb up one of his towers as an expiatory pilgrimage.'

'Well, this pilgrim's idea of progress is one of Mr Otis's contraptions. Shouldn't we get going before the place is packed out?'

Although by booking in advance Justin had avoided the drudgery of queuing, neither he nor his companions could enter the building without first announcing themselves on time to their guide with proof of identity. Joined five minutes later by the last of the ticketholders for their tour, they entered the *Sagrada Familia* through a portal reserved for guided groups. After their escort had given her introductory talk, Justin politely explained that, because of time constraints, he and his party preferred to proceed separately, while reserving the right to blend back in with the group should their paths cross.

They had entered via the Nativity façade. When Gisela gazed up at the roof completed five years earlier she was struck by the contrast between her initial impression of the building: whereas from the outside it resembled a haphazard succession of baroque excrescences, from the inside it was blessed with an aura of the sublime. If Gaudí's original intention had been to respect the lines of nature, those following in his footsteps would seem to have remained true to the master builder's ideal. Gisela Radetzky stood mesmerised by the artistry which had made possible this forest of intriguingly angled pillars supporting a roof canopy transfused with colour from sunlight soaking through the stained glass windows. Rarely had she felt so moved.

'My head's reeling,' she said, as with one hand she found anchorage on Justin's shoulder and with the other she gently swung Rosalie's arm. The next moment, joy gave way to grief at the thought of how life had brutishly robbed her of the man who should have been sharing this sense of wonder. Yet instead of repelling Justin she clung on to him all the more firmly.

'Last time I was here,' said Justin, 'there was so much scaffolding with men working on the roof that this was no better than a building site. Now there's a real feeling of completion.'

They moved deeper into the interior, Gisela marvelling at the blaze of kaleidoscopic iridescence filtering down through the trunks and overarching branches of the forest of Gaudí's load-bearing pillars. The guidebook had told her that, in striving to remain true to nature in its variety, the Catalan architect had opted for four different kinds of stone.

As they were walking along the apse and approaching the High Altar, a table of polished Iranian porphyry, Gisela felt a tug at her arm. 'Why is Jesus on a parasail?'

'Ah, yes,' said Justin. 'I find that a trifle odd, Rosalie. But I don't think it's supposed to be a parasail. After all, I believe Jesus could walk on water.'

'It looks,' added Gisela, staring at the golden canopy from which a bronze effigy of Christ with knees raised was suspended above the altar, 'like an outsize Victorian lampshade. I suppose the artist is trying to show us how Jesus brings light into people's lives.'

'A pity,' said Justin, 'that the pope could not have brought some of his own to the consecration service. All right, Spanish is not his native tongue, but there was about as much enthusiasm in his voice as if he'd been reading from the Barcelona telephone directory. It was a miracle King Juan Carlos and Queen Sofia didn't fall asleep.'

'Well, I don't suppose the royals were sitting on uncushioned metal chairs,' said Gisela, indicating the rows of seats set out for visitors preferring meditation to shutter-release buttons. 'That would have kept them awake. In fact, I wouldn't mind resting for a moment.'

'Of course, why not. Tell you what, I'll trot across to the nearest tower, climb up the steps and take a few snaps of some Murano glass mosaics for you.'

'Take Rosalie with you.'

'No, it's too dangerous for kids her age. They're not allowed on the stairs.'

'And why would you use them, if there's a lift?'

'The exercise will do me good.'

Rosalie already unhappy about the number of children her age seen with the very handheld devices forbidden by her parents (after all, this was holiday not school time) began to act petulantly. 'Why can't I go, Ma?'

'You heard what Uncle Justin said.'

Justin pointed towards the roof. 'It's a very long way up, Rosalie. You need to keep your strength for the funfair this afternoon.'

'Will I get to fly on the Red Aeroplane?'

'Yes. And you'll be higher up than I'm going, looking down onto the top of these towers.'

Rosalie addressed her response to her soft toy tiger cub. 'Should we believe him, Tigger?'

'Yes,' said her mother. 'Now come and sit down with me over there. We'll stay put, Justin. That way, you'll know where to find us.'

He saw them both to their seats, counted how many rows they were from the front and kissed Rosalie goodbye. 'I'll try not to be too long.'

Gisela gave him a winning smile. 'Take your time. Better still, take good pictures.'

⁂

Justin chose to mount the stairs leading to the top of one of the four towers on the basilica's Nativity façade side. No sooner had he set foot on the first few steps than he was reminded of Craig's exploit: last year, Schönschlucht's fitness fanatic had made the sports headlines in the *Luritanische Bote* by helping to raise a goodly sum for motor-neuron disease research after completing the annual Empire State Building run-up in twelve minutes. If Justin remembered correctly, Craig had climbed half a mile vertically around twenty-eight flights totalling one thousand six hundred steps. Even if a mere quarter of that number now faced Justin, there were any number of solid reasons not to emulate Craig: conditions in Barcelona in mid-summer were hardly the same as those in New York in February; Craig had been kitted out in running gear; the steps up the Empire State Building were wide compared to those in the *Sagrada Família*, where they rose in an uninterrupted spiral; and while Craig had been able to use railing as leverage for most of the climb, apart from when overtaking other competitors, the ascent handrail here was on the left side, and Justin was right-handed.

Taking his time, he made it to the top in six minutes, stopping along the upper section alongside narrow, often low, wall openings for shots of mosaic work. Although the bridge at the top connecting two of the Nativity towers provided the ideal viewing platform for photographs of the city below, Justin knew that Gisela was more interested in the towers' finials than high-tech architecture such as the, in his opinion, ugly Agbar Tower.

With his attention focussed on capturing the mosaics spelling out *Sanctus, Sanctus, Sanctus, Hosannah in Excelsis,* Justin failed to notice the baldheaded man in the same worn T-shirt and frayed jeans from the night before. The fact that he was not plugged into any audio equipment, had no camera in his hand or slung around his neck and was hovering on the edge of a group bombarded by statistics thrown at them by their skirted Catalan guide would normally have been enough to attract attention, but Justin was more preoccupied about leaving Gisela and Rosalie too long on their own.

He was approximately halfway down the same stairs that he had climbed minutes earlier when he heard a voice from above cry '*Señor Endry*'.

Few people fail to react to hearing their name spoken, and Justin was no exception, despite the fact that this foreign speaker left the H unvoiced. While not instant, his recognition, upon turning to face the man behind him, was only briefly delayed. Justin stared behind the stranger, but could see no sign of his companion – or of anyone else for that matter.

'Yes,' said Justin in no need of a sixth sense to tell him that all was not well.

The baldheaded man with a bad line in greasy designer stubble gave a satisfied nod and edged down to within three steps of Justin. Heavy breathing from below alerted Justin to the approach of a third party. But Justin's hopes that this would be a tourist like himself were crushed as he glimpsed the head and shoulders of the bald individual's stocky associate. What happened next occurred so swiftly and unrealistically that, thinking back on it afterwards, Justin was at pains to grasp how he remained composed enough to cope with his attacker. For last night's stranger standing above Justin suddenly took it into his head to clasp both hands around the railing attached to the outside wall behind him and to launch both feet out at Justin's chest in an uncoordinated lunge. Had his bald assailant been an expert in taekwondo, Justin would have been propelled backwards down the staircase – probably helped on his way by the other half of the partnership. But either Justin's aggressor fancied that he was Spain's answer to Bruce Lee or he had rehearsed this acrobatic gambit solely in his head, because only one foot came near to doing any damage and that gave Justin, with Gisela's camera slung around his neck, the perfect opportunity to grab hold of the heel of the man's sneaker with both hands and to twist it violently. The failed kick boxer screamed in pain. Instead of relinquishing his hold, Justin followed up his disabling response with a yank that wrenched the man not only free of his handrail onto the unforgiving concrete steps but on past him down these into his associate, who, in trying to save him, lost his own balance and fell badly, knocking his head not once but twice against the side wall and ended up sprawled over the inside edge of the spiral staircase gazing unseeingly down into its eye. Deciding that there was little he could do for either man, the first as much *hors de combat* as the second, Justin stepped gingerly over their inert bodies and hastened to regain ground-floor level. Once there, he collared the nearest guide and advised her to call for an ambulance.

Before rejoining Gisela and Rosalie, Justin opted to recover his composure for a few minutes on a seat several rows behind them.

'You look hot,' said Gisela, when he reappeared at her side. 'I told you. You should have taken the lift.'

'Must have been part of the macho side of me wanting to prove something. Still, I think I got you a couple of good snaps.'

'Better than my guide book?'

'Far better.'

'Did you notice how the angels over the façade had no wings?'

'Can't say I did.'

'Apparently, Gaudí thought wings an aerodynamic non-starter for seventy-kilo bipeds.'

'Icarus proved him right on that one.'

'Icarus was no angel.'

Right, too human by far. What's wrong, Rosalie? Do I detect a bored six-year-old?'

Rosalie grimaced. 'Tigger says he's seen all he wants to of this technicolour forest.'

'He's only just arrived.' It took effort on Justin's part to say this, given that he would have preferred to leave the building without further ado. But this was Gisela's first visit to the *Sagrada Família*, and he was reluctant to rob her of a fuller experience.

Consequently, they spent a further two hours in and around the basilica, part of this time being spent with their guide, who had heard that the staircase to the top of one of the towers had been cordoned off to the public because of an accident.

'Lucky you,' commented Gisela.

'Yes,' said Justin. 'Lucky me.'

After leaving the basilica, they returned to the hotel for a wash, brush up and siesta. Justin cut short his rest time to visit the marketplace off *Las Ramblas* to buy provisions for their picnic up at Tibidabo. Later that afternoon, they took the blue tram and funicular to the hilltop Skywalk, where Justin bought tickets for the Ferris wheel and the *Red Aeroplane*, after which they ate their picnic on one of the tables set out on the observation platform overlooking the city. In the course of wooing Rosalie first with candy floss then with a toffee apple, Justin was suddenly beset by the sickening thought that one observation point could remind her mother of another. However, Gisela gave no indication of having fallen victim to a painful association of ideas.

As it happened, Rosalie and her mother found the *Red Aeroplane* tame, and Justin had to agree. In spite of the fact that the Ferris Wheel revolved at the same snail's pace, all three preferred the view from their yellow open-air gondola.

⁂

The morning of their last day in Barcelona was spent visiting more Gaudí attractions as well as the Joan Miró museum on Montjuïc, where both Gisela and Rosalie were much taken with some of the sculpture and artwork. After they had checked out of their hotel with time to spare before catching the bus from the Plaça de Catalunya to the airport, Justin suggested exploring *El Corte Inglés* department store a stone's throw from the airport bus stop. They had just crossed the road to the pavement outside the store's front entrance when the driver of a speeding white Seat Ibiza appeared to lose control of his vehicle in taking the turn too sharply onto the street alongside them. The first to whip around and appreciate the danger they were in, Justin scooped a frightened Rosalie up into his arms before rapidly pulling Gisela towards the store front. Apparently unable to correct his trajectory or brake in time, the driver spun his wheel desperately only to smash the rear of his Seat into the ground-floor window next to the one where Justin and his wards were huddled. Since he was not wearing a seat belt and the airbag failed to activate, the force of the impact projected the driver headlong into the windscreen, after which the Seat, an automatic, rolled forward at an angle off the pavement and onto a collision course with a passing bus. Despite swerving, the bus driver was unable to avoid damage to his vehicle's nearside bodywork.

'Did you see what I saw?' said a still shivering Gisela. 'The driver. The bald man you said kept glancing our way last night.'

'Yes,' said Justin, trying to calm Rosalie's sobbing. 'It means no standing around to fill out police reports. I need to get you and Rosalie on that flight, then home safe and sound.'

'I don't understand, Justin. What could you have you done to lead to …?'

'I wish I knew, Gisela. Forgive me. The last thing I wanted was to involve you and Rosalie in anything like this.'

'It's terrible. I don't want to see you harmed.'

Justin put a calming hand over her mouth. 'Let's not alarm the little one. And don't worry about me. I can fend for myself.'

It was not until Justin was tightening his seat belt in preparation for the take-off from Barcelona airport that the stupidity of those last words of his outside *El Corte Inglés* struck home. The two men in the *Sagrada Família* had been amateurs. Next time, the people coming at him from out of nowhere were likely to be professionals.

He gazed down the aisle at mother and daughter seated three rows in front and to his left. How fond he had grown of that high-spirited, freckle-faced little girl. But one day soon Rosalie would learn that her father was never coming home, and what then? Impossible to face her. As for the mother, what were his real feelings towards Gisela? No, there lay more stupidity. Had he not visited enough woe on her already?

By the time the aircraft had reached cruising altitude, Justin had decided that severing relations completely at this point would be nothing short of brutal. He had to continue to behave supportively towards mother and child, while slowly distancing himself from closer ties. Justin Hendry had no right to drag two complete innocents into the minefield planted by him the moment he lifted that damnable red briefcase.

Memo from J to K

> *The way in which the Nevskian oligarchs are fulfilling our ambitions verges on the spectacular, until you bear in mind that where their money is there is their motherland. Nevskian plutocrats with banks in Urodina are now making bargain basement loans to Veki for purchasing arms used to shell ethnic Nevskians in the eastern enclaves. Mammon truly knows no bounds. I'll wager you that the leader we love to denounce as Erebu's bogeyman is encouraging not clamping down on these money-grubbers.*

Response from K

> *How right you are. The statistics speak for themselves: our mini-Praetorian guard within the Nevskian administration effectively put to the sword no fewer than sixty thousand smaller businesses last year by doubling their tax bill. Of course, while feathering their own nests, our colonial administrators did not neglect to ensure that we benefited from this corporate slaughter. Dependence on imported goods, joblessness, poverty and the suicide rate look set to hurt an already fragile economy*

Response from J

> *Fine, K, but however useful they might be to us in their back yard, the League's oligarchs will not be permitted to flout the laws of our land by profiting from having a foot in both camps. We require documentary proof of the origin of all white money*

deposited on these shores, failing which such funds and associated property purchases will be subject to state seizure. However thankful we might be to see wholesale plundering of the League's economic wealth undermining the national economy, we cannot permit corporate felons to have the best of both worlds.

⁂

'There's a gentleman asking after you at the visitor's entrance. Says he's a member of the British *corps diplomatique* and that you know each other.'

Jean-Luc Meunier spoke back into his office intercom. 'Describe.'

'Tall, distinguished. To judge by his bearing, I'd say ex-military. Slight limp on his right side.'

'Name?'

'Jericho. Said you were expecting him.'

'I was. Admit him. And be sure to tell your security staff in the lobby there's no need for him to turn his pockets out. We won't be risking our lives if they turn their metal detector toy off for a minute.'

'But security protocol, monsieur?'

'Bugger protocol. My visitor's from MI6.'

'If you say so, monsieur. But I'll need to register the fact.'

'Make a whole novel out of it, Louis, if you like, but let the man in.'

After turning off the intercom, for the second time that morning Jean-Luc studied the photograph of Jericho and him taken outside Nangarhar University in Jalalabad, where he had been delivering a series of lectures on political science while Jericho had been liaising with two American professors ostensibly on sabbaticals from MIT and Caltech. He righted the cardboard picture frame's stand, angling the photograph towards the door.

The man known to his MI6 employers and the UK's General Register Office as Rex Alexander Jericho had sent him an encrypted e-mail to the effect that he was visiting Luritania on company business and hoped that they might be able to meet up. Wondering what company business could have brought Jericho to Schönschlucht, Jean-Luc, who was enjoying a markedly uneventful working day, threw the sole file requiring action in the medium-term back into the drawer of his metal cabinet marked classified, turned the key on a faulty lock cooperative only if turned repeatedly (on this occasion, France's *conseiller des affaires étrangères* gave up after the fourth attempt) and stood up ready to welcome his visitor. Let the consul think he was impressing visitors by bending over his desk in a poor imitation of Rodin's *Le Penseur* (The Thinker). That was not Jean-Luc's style. If there was no *pain sur la planche* (if you were not worked off your feet), why pretend otherwise? Nor did it dent the diplomat's pride to have to share a secretary with the consul. Even a bureaucracy as entrenched in its ways as France's *corps diplomatique* grudgingly accepted that times had changed.

Thus, when Lucie Picquet showed the man who was a stranger to her into Jean-Luc's office, Meunier felt no need to mention the fact that his previous secretary, whom Rex had dubbed *la sirène grecque* – on account of her captivating voice and statuesque neck – had been moved sideways.

The long-legged Lucie with the figure of a catwalk model – who thought her qualifications (a degree in Political Science and Philosophy from Paris-Sorbonne university) wasted on papering over consular blunders from ambassadorial eyes – stood in the doorway between her office and Meunier's, wondering what these two men could have in common: the one calling himself Jericho, a rugged, weather-beaten, middle-aged male, whose features betrayed signs of world-weariness, and the pale-faced, slightly built civil servant with a touch too much complacency for her liking, the embassy's switchboard operator having made it known that the *conseiller* complacently advertised his extra-marital dalliances over the office phone.

Not one given to time-wasting, Lucie Picquet limited herself to announcing, 'Your visitor, monsieur.'

Preliminary greetings between acquaintances who had not seen each other in a long time dispensed with, Jean-Luc motioned the man accustomed to being called *Géai* (jay), rather than Jhee (French pronunciation of the letter j) or the more fraternal Rex, to sit beside him on a splendid sofa upholstered in red Toundra leather. Jean-Luc Meunier had been so taken with this expensive item of Roche Bobois furniture as to have funded it partly out of his own pocket, since it was well beyond the means of his fixtures and fittings allowance.

'Can I offer you something to drink, *Géai?* Tea or coffee?'

'That's good of you, Jean-Luc, but no, thank you. I've come fresh from a breakfast of scrambled eggs, bacon, toast and marmalade and an inexhaustible coffee pot. Oh, and I forgot the *girolles.* Perfect, I might add.'

'I doubt they were gathered locally, unless the hotel buys its mushrooms fresh from the market. Where are you staying?'

'*L'Ambassadeu*r. Where else?'

'Well, they definitely wouldn't be using mushrooms gathered outside *la belle France.*'

'Not a bad hotel. Gym and rooftop pool. I managed to fit in a few laps before breakfast.'

Jean-Luc nodded understandingly. Morning exercise had always been part of Rex's routine. Not a custom which the *conseiller* felt inclined to emulate, despite the paunch which he was developing and of which, paradoxically, he felt more self-conscious in the company of the flabby-breasted men with whom he shared a sauna evening than under the sheets with his paramour, Michelle, PA to one of those ineffectual, overpaid *députés européens* (members of the European Parliament).

'Hence the appetite. What brings you to this godforsaken pinhead in the greater European patchwork?'

'God-forsaken? I thought the papists were strong on the ground in Luritania.'

'Strong on ritual. Weak on performance. The government made noises about holding a referendum on whether or not to separate church and state, then lost the stomach for it.'

'How much longer before they you move on, Jean-Luc?'

'Two years, which is two too many.'

'In a principality this size, I suppose you've got to know just about everyone who's worth knowing.'

'Well, let's say, compared to Washington this is a watering hole where the hyenas outnumber the big cats.'

'So the name Hendry must be familiar to you?'

'The Innova Press Corporation's *rédacteur en chef* (editor-in-chief)? Yes. A small fish in a small pond.' While sensing the drift of his visitor's conversation, the *conseiller* found it hard to believe that the recent nuclear apocalypse article warranted a visit from MI6.

'I've run into the fellow a couple of times at cocktail parties. Inoffensive type. Intelligent. *The Pulse*, his monthly review, is generally informative about local events, personalities, politics. His latest editorial, on the other hand, was a departure from the norm. Insinuations about Machiavellian geopolitics. Perhaps he thought he was beginning to sound too parochial.' Jean-Luc paused, eying Jericho like a blackjack dealer waiting for a decision: another card, or enough is enough?

But Rex's opening remark told Jean-Luc that he had mistaken poker for blackjack.

'I saw it. Not entirely claptrap, but our feedback told us that most of the tweets it invited were of the *Stick to what you know* variety, only a handful suggesting *A wake-up call for ostriches*.'

'Hard to strike an alarmist note with Luritanians. Though some lose sleep over demographics.'

Jean-Luc read the questioning look in his visitor's eyes. 'The possibility of becoming outnumbered by foreigners.'

Not one for whispered confidences, Rex pressed his back more firmly into the sofa's lumber support and tilted his head towards the ceiling in the manner of a lecturer contemplating how best to share his theorem with others. 'Jean-Luc, what I am about to tell you must remain strictly between us and these four walls. Provided that ...'

The other man gave one of the sofa's leather cushions a sharp slap. 'The only bug found in my office will be an acarian.'

'Good. Well then, the crux of the matter is that classified notes inadvertently left in a London minicab have ended up here in Luritania.'

'Really?'

'An oversight on the part of a go-between ferrying material from our people to the Foreign Office.'

'No longer a go-between?'

'No longer of this world. You read about Peregrine Musgrave?'

'The *député* who committed suicide?'

'Distraught ever since the death of his only child, a nine-year-old brought down by meningitis.'

'But if not by him, you know by whom the papers were transported here?'

'Possibly Hendry, possibly an acquaintance. The name Jabour mean anything to you, Jean-Luc?'

'I'm afraid not. Should it? You see, I am failing you miserably. Not that Jabour has much of a Luritanian, let alone a European, ring to it.'

'Right, he's Lebanese. A junior loan officer with MEDRIMCOMB.'

'And how did he come by your classified material? No, stupid question. He was on business in London, when he chanced upon it in that London taxi. Wasn't it at least under lock and key?'

'Nothing complicated enough to fool a quick-witted schoolboy.'

'And what stroke of luck made you think the theft of your documents might be traced to Hendry or this Lebanese banker?'

'Happily for us, Jabour is the owner of a laptop with software programmed to ring bells the moment anyone starts playing with certain decryption algorithms.'

'I see. Not one crime but two. First, Monsieur Jabour, Hendry or a third party steals your documents. Second, discovering that they are encrypted, instead of reporting his find to the authorities, Jabour tries his hand at cracking your code.'

'We can't be sure he succeeded. In fact, he had two encrypted documents to play with, only the longer of which presented a serious decryption challenge. Musgrave suspected Hendry of the theft but was unable to prove anything. The editor had just got back from London. Supposing, Musgrave asked himself, classified papers had dropped into Hendry's lap. Anyone else might have destroyed or, at best, returned them by registered post to the Home Office. But a journalist faced with the makings of a scoop?'

'You think Hendry passed the papers on to this Jabour character, because he thought Jabour could break the codes?'

'That's how it would appear. Jabour was nowhere near London.'

Hearing the phone ringing in Lucie Picquet's office, the *conseiller* craned his neck in the hope that he was not about to be roped in for something.

'In other words, Jean-Luc, I've come on a shopping errand, hoping you might be able to tell me what links Hendry to Jabour.'

From the way in which the *conseiller* was clasping his knuckles, Rex might have been excused for thinking the Frenchman was praying for inspiration. 'My dear *Géai*,' said Jean-Luc at length, 'I'm afraid I have no idea.'

Jean-Luc cast a glance at the photograph, which had yet to catch his guest's attention. Confusing the sudden lancing pain down the side of his head with a pang of guilt (he had Rex Jericho to thank for valuable intel about a mole in France's embassy in Islamabad), the diplomat wrestled with a half-formed thought pertinent to Rex's enquiries. Perhaps it was the air of the theatrical in the photograph of the two men that finally broke the mental logjam: there was Rex in his desert camouflage outfit looking the part of a military adviser fresh from the front and next to him Jean-Luc Meunier, the sanguine diplomat responsible at the time for liaising with NATO's French contingent.

'Just a minute. My daughter is taking part in an amateur theatrical production to be put on a few weeks from now. She mentioned that Hendry featured among the cast. There was an advertisement in his bilingual review inviting people to audition. Is it possible that Jabour might also be one of the players?'

'I don't know. There must be any number of ways in which the two could have met up. Cocktail party, game of squash, church fair, businessmen's luncheon. Still, any and every avenue is worth trying. Do you think you could sound your daughter out?'

'Of course.'

'What's the play?'

'*Camino Real*. Tennessee Williams. If you ask me, a bit of a gamble on the director's part. Tragicomic pantomime.'

'And what role is Hendry playing?'

'Don Quixote.'

'Fitting for a journalist. Forever tilting at windmills.'

'Except that in your case, if I understand correctly, the don is definitely crossing swords with the wrong people. Let me call my daughter now. Are you sure I can't offer you a drink?'

'No, thanks.'

Jean-Luc pulled out his cell phone. Isabelle was quick to answer and, unsuspecting of her father's motives, informative. When she expressed curiosity as to his interest in the young Lebanese, Jean-Luc fobbed her off with a promise to explain later: his secretary had just handed him a fax from Paris.

'Perhaps we are on to something,' said the diplomat, turning to Rex, 'and perhaps we're not. Rashid Jabour, to give him his full name, **is** acting in the same play as Hendry. However, it would seem unlikely that the two of them are on the best of terms. Rashid is sleeping with the director, who used to be Hendry's love interest.'

'All right. I was wrong. Maybe the director. Who is he?'

'A she. Mademoiselle Vanessa Curtis.'

'Well, maybe Miss Curtis was capable of going behind Jabour's back to Hendry with whatever her new lover succeeded in finding out. After all, what could be more foolish when starting on a career with MEDRIMCOMB than to risk being shot down in flames by divulging classified secrets?'

'You have a point.'

'I'd suggest it started out as a fun thing. A challenge. But then if Jabour did decode the papers, he'd be bound to think twice before burning his fingers. On the other hand, if Miss Curtis passed the results on to Hendry behind her new lover's back, perhaps she would placate Jabour by assuring him that he would fall under the radar.'

'But that's not so, is it, *Géai*? You said you'd got his number.'

While one side of Rex Jericho was entertained by the diplomat's use of colloquial English, another side was preoccupied with information control.

'Correct. Unknown to him. What concerns me is that now I seem to be up against an unhealthy *ménage à trois*: Jabour, Hendry and Curtis. My chances of containing things are looking slimmer by the hour.'

In need of clarity of vision of one kind or another, Rex rubbed bleary eyes. 'Your daughter, Isabelle,' he ventured at length. 'Rude of me not to have asked after her. How is she doing?'

'Not as well as she'd like. Started out in publishing, but the firm went bust. Got herself a job in a bank for the time being, while prospecting the ground for better things. '

Despite the fact that Jericho's gaze had finally settled on the photograph given pride of place on Jean-Luc's desk, the diplomat's words awoke the unsettling thought that there might be one more character to add to MI6's conundrum.

'Not the same employment market nowadays for young people with good qualifications as there was in our day.'

'I don't think she'll follow her mother and me around anymore, once my time is up here. She's had her fill of Asia and the Americas.'

Nothing venture, nothing gain, decided the man from MI6. 'If any loose tongue was to mention official secrets lost in a London minicab, how likely is it that Isabelle's first thought would be to report that to you?'

Jean-Luc uttered a clipped, mocking laugh. 'As likely as my waking up tomorrow morning to find the moon made of *gruyère*.' He raised a staying hand. 'Don't take that to mean she knows anything about this affair. I'm sure she doesn't. We were talking about Hendry's latest *Pulse* editorial the other night, and I'm sure that had she known anything she'd have given the game away.'

Not about to confess to knowing the identity of the instigator of that editorial, Rex rubbed the circulation back into a stiff right leg. The unspoken message behind Meunier's words counselled him against using Jean-Luc's daughter as somebody else's eyes and ears.

'We're getting nowhere fast,' continued Jean-Luc, aware that he had been told only half the story, if that. 'Plenty of suspicion and finger pointing, but nothing to show that your worst fears have been realised. Anyway, aren't your people's encryption techniques impregnable?'

'So we like to think.'

'In which case, why worry? The chances are that the gremlin you picked up on vanished up its own backside.'

'I'm not worried,' came the less than honest reply. 'But those higher up the tree are. They're already hearing buzz saws.'

'And so they send you out here on a fool's errand?'

'I think not. My remit is to serve notice to anyone suspected of illegal possession of sensitive information relating to national security that they are in breach of the Official Secrets Act. More than that. To make it crystal clear that should they fail to cooperate, we will bring the full force of the law down on them.'

'That should do the trick. Especially if you threaten to pursue them to the ends of the earth, though nowadays that seems to mean no farther than Moscow or the nearest Ecuadorean embassy.'

'I wouldn't have troubled you with this, Jean-Luc, if our people were still here, but, as you know, they upped sticks and skedaddled to *La Ville-Lumière* (Paris).'

'Can't say I blame them. It'll be a wonder if our side doesn't strike camp soon.'

With few items ticked off on his shopping list of questions, Jericho decided to call it a day. Rising to his feet, Rex Jericho held out an appreciative hand. 'Well, I ought to be going, Jean-Luc. You must be busy.'

'Doing nothing. Could explain why I'm in line for one of this year's order of merits. Please feel free, *Géai*, to stay as long as you like. The only work I have booked for this week is a consultancy meeting paving the way for greater bilateral co-operation on the Syrian refugee crisis. Enough to drive a *conseiller* to write his uncontentious memoirs.'

'Well, thank you, Jean-Luc, but I have a few more calls to make this morning. Still, I hope we can both find the time to fit in a lunch or dinner date before I leave on Saturday?'

'I'd like nothing better.'

'Drop me a call at *L'Ambassadeur*.'

'Right.' For the diplomat, it was too late in the day to be as chary as his MI6 friend about handing out his cell phone number.

Two thoughts that had been troubling Jean-Luc Meunier during that morning's conversation returned to vie with each other in his mind. But now that he was about to show his visitor to the door, the first, whether to warn Isabelle, was overtaken by the second to such a degree that the diplomat articulated it *sotto voce*.

'Those classified secrets, *Géai*. Nothing, I trust, to do with the Council of Twenty?'

With no perceptible sign of hesitancy, the man from MI6 turned to face France's former espionage mission head in Islamabad. 'No, Jean-Luc, you can set your mind at rest on that score. Nothing to do with the Council.'

It was a lie camouflaged with a smile reassuring to the man charged with writing and circulating the minutes of all Council of Twenty meetings held in northwestern Europe.

⁂

Memo from K to J

This year's Afghan poppy harvest funded by our agents is set to produce a bumper crop thanks to the development of a new strain of highly productive seeds. It will help flood the Nevskian market with opium and increase significantly the number of drug addicts among the young, one out of every six of whom is on the poverty line. Indeed, the greater inroads we make into debilitating the Nevskian population by promoting drug and alcohol abuse, the more we stand to undermine the moral fibre of an already uneasy society. No less that one hundred thousand Nevskians a year die as a result of drug addiction.

On the other hand, I am unhappy about the Octagon's decision to set up biological research laboratories in Urodina for developing epidemic viruses.

321

Response from J

While we share your concern about the laboratories, my people are also understandably troubled by the fact that your representatives have taken over operation of the strategic port of Assedo. This will give heroin and cannabis traffickers improved access to Erubuan markets.

❧

Once the embassy's front entrance doors had closed behind him, Rex Jericho took out the hotel's pocket guide to Schönschlucht, opened up the centerfold map and studied the crosses made by him that morning over breakfast. The French embassy was conveniently situated on the edge of town, and Schönschlucht was compact in layout, making most of the points of interest to him within easy walking distance. With a population of a hundred and ten thousand, excluding outlying built-up areas some more far-flung than others, Luritania's capital, thought the man from MI6, only just qualified as a city. Two boulevards uptown conveyed the bulk of traffic to their partner boulevards downtown across a pair of bridges spanning the city gorge. One of these bridges had already been widened to accommodate the planned tram service, while the other was closed to traffic because widening works were still under way.

It took a mere fifteen minutes for Rex to stretch his legs as far as the nearest gorge overlook from where he gazed down to the landscaped valley floor. A battery-powered, toy-town set of carriages led by an imitation locomotive was conveying tourists along the roadway on the far bank of the sleepy, willow-fringed Leiseflösschen. And yet, thought J, the theft of a set of classified documents in London had sparked off a chain of events culminating in the murder of an innocent man, who had finished his life, in a blood-soaked mess of fractured limbs, at the bottom of this same peaceful gorge. The next moment, the sound of a real train chugging over a third bridge across the valley to his left awoke Jericho from his ruminations.

Deciding it was time to collect his thoughts with more coffee, he directed his steps to the town centre, where he found an uncrowded café looking onto the main post office. The suggestive way in which the waitress advertised her tongue stud in conjunction with the menu made Jericho wonder whether he had chosen wisely. But when he turned down the menu card's offer of soups, salads and whole-wheat *baguettes* in favour of a double espresso, the girl backed away from his deadpan expression as if on the receiving end of a lesson in how not to win tips.

Rex shrugged off his jacket and, before hanging it over the back of his chair, removed a biro and the town map from the breast pocket. It had not surprised him that Jean-Luc had failed to bring up the affair of the cartoonist or the body in the quarry. The diplomat knew when to leave well alone and take his lead from others. Rex guessed that the *conseiller* would have been unable to throw light on either death. From which he concluded that he was back to square one as regards why and by whose hand Chamberlain had been removed from the scene. This was disturbing, because if the executioner was not Stenning, who had apparently vanished into thin air, then it looked as if K had engineered Chamberlain and perhaps Stenning's demise from afar through local agents.

Rex picked up his biro and map for the waitress to wipe down the table, before delivering his espresso together with a couple of sachets of sugar, a small square of dark chocolate and the bill from a tray deposited on the neighbouring table. Half expecting but glad not to see the initial gesture of cleanliness accompanied by an antibacterial spray, Rex settled up immediately with, to the girl's gratified surprise, a not ungenerous tip.

The first taste was always the best, he thought, particularly when you craved a quick revitalising shot of caffeine. Rex savoured the flavour, staring out of the café window at both the post office façade, which might have been mistaken for Portland stone, and the cast iron clock beside it mimicking London's Little Ben, then turned to refocus on his open map. Hendry's publishing house and printing press were on the other side of town, the MEDRIMCOMB building six minutes away by bus on this side. But two other crosses were of greater interest: the first, on a road conveniently close to where he was sitting; the second, against a street in a village on the outskirts of town. On the one hand, everything spoke in favour of the direct approach: beard the lion in his den. On the other, although it would mean descending to housebreaking, something might well be gained by combing through Hendry's apartment while the editor was at work. And why? For the very reasons Jericho had been unwilling to divulge to Jean-Luc Meunier. The most damaging material in those stolen papers were Rex's exchanges with K. MI6, more properly known as SIS (Secret Intelligence Service) could not afford to have them made public: to do so would be to jeopardise its penetration of the CIA in the person of K. For it had taken years of painstaking collaboration rewarded by fat payments into an account in Anguilla to convince K and the CIA of their good luck. In Rex, the Americans had surely won over a valuable double agent at the heart of Great Britain's intelligence agency.

The fact that K's people refused to subscribe to the European press's view of Great Britain's lapdog leadership made recruitment of the apostate Jericho all the sweeter. On the other hand, to Rex and his masters' confusion, K had proved to be a bundle of contradictions: in one breath, the epitome of colonial arrogance, espousing interference in other nations' affairs for their own and the greater good; in the next, his country's harshest critic, bemoaning the fact that it was considered better to exploit rather than to co-operate, preferable to recruit allies than to win friends and inacceptable to play second fiddle.

In other words, K was just as likely to come out with the mantra '*Those who are not for us are against us',* as he was to declare that the sole reason why neutrality was anathema to the White House was because 1600 Pennsylvania Avenue was run by control freaks.

Needless to say, MI6 knew the games which the CIA liked to play and vice versa, which, no doubt, from time to time left both sides wondering whether they might have backed the wrong horse.

However, now Rex was faced with a different headache: damage control. In short, Jabour had lived up to part of the deal agreed to in Beirut, but had he honoured his commitment to destroy the unencrypted papers? To do otherwise would be to put his father's life on the line. However, even if it stood to reason that he must have shredded the documents and deleted the scanned versions from his hard drive, where was the guarantee that he had not shared either document with Hendry or others? Well, there again, Jabour would surely have pulled out all the stops to stifle any leakage. In short, was Rex not fretting needlessly? It was a question that refused to go away for no simpler reason than Murphy's law.

If, by some freak of nature, the wrong people got hold of and deciphered the memos exchanged with the man in Virginia, not only would the CIA and MI6's respective operatives be as good as exposed but a game plan costing months of dedicated hard work stood to be sabotaged.

But, paradoxically, for the moment Rex Jericho was less concerned about his own future than that of the person or persons who had misguidedly become entangled in the filaments of a web from which escape would be nigh impossible after the same alarm bells had sounded in the NSA's SIGINT in Maryland as they had in Cyber Security in Cheltenham, when Jabour's laptop sent out its red alert. Following the much improved shake-up in inter-agency communication channels, GCHQ's SIGINT notification of the alert to HUMINT in Langley and the latter's notification of the same to Cheltenham had crossed each other in nanoseconds. Hence J had no alternative other than to apprise K of what was at risk. As soon as K learnt that his and Rex's encrypted Internet exchanges formed part and parcel of Jabour's texts, he had taken into his own hands the solution to ensuring the young man's silence. That solution had, J felt sure, been crowned with success. But things were never that simple, and K could be a loose cannon. Furthermore, in terms of numbers on the ground, his geographical reach surpassed Rex's. Consequently, if nothing had been learnt from the Chamberlain-Stenning fiasco, and the chances were that nothing had, J needed to intervene before more lives were put needlessly at risk.

Clara Bogen was feeling menopausal and at a loose end. After a troubled night's sleep, the morning yoga class had relaxed mind and body to the point where she had dozed off only to awake embarrassed by her snoring. It helped that the instructor and other class members made light of the incident. This was not the first time that somebody had fallen asleep. But the sound of rain hammering down on the roof, the wail of vehicle sirens and the prospect of a day without a visit from the mobile library service (the van's gear box had given up the ghost) or the promised talk on the life and works of Rimsky-Korsakov (cancelled, everyone had been informed, due to the guest speaker's 'indisposition', which, Clara thought, was a nice catch-all for everything from sleeping off a hangover to oversleeping with a girlfriend) reinforced the message that this was one of those days.

Left to her own resources and casting around for ideas as to how to pass the time, Clara decided to clear out the bottom of her room's wardrobe cluttered with boxes in which she stored old shoes, gloves, scarves and souvenirs. It was in the course of sorting through one of the last of these boxes that she came across the envelope containing the document entrusted to her by Vanessa Curtis, an envelope recognised by touch because of its bulk and because Clara had stamped it with a wax horse shoe seal.

Dusting down her skirt, Clara took the envelope back to her desk by the window. She had given the envelope scant thought since the day Vanessa had asked her to take care of it. But now that she began turning the matter over in her mind, she was at a loss to understand why Vanessa should have chosen to entrust her with private papers. Perhaps her friend preferred not to pay a lawyer custodial fees. Perhaps there were no safety deposit boxes where she banked. But why would she deposit a confidential document with a blind person (the more politically correct adjectives for her condition were anathema to Clara)? Then she remembered that Vanessa's mother had died four years ago and that daughter and father were at loggerheads. As Vanessa had refused to be drawn on this, Clara had not pressed for an explanation. There was a sister, a petrochemicals engineer, but stationed in Bahrein, she thought.

What could the envelope contain? A last will and testament? No, most unlikely. Vanessa was four months away from her thirtieth birthday. Not the age when people worried themselves about wills and estate tax. Apart from which the envelope weighed too much. Money? Perhaps. In the form of bonds or stocks and shares. Perhaps not. Might it be the draft of a play written by Vanessa, something she preferred to put to one side until *Camino Real* was under her belt? Something groundbreaking: Royal Court material? The more Clara thought about it, the more intrigued she became, until finally she was unable to resist taking up her ivory-handled paper knife and slitting open the envelope. After which, she drew out and unfolded a goodly number of sheets of A4 paper. Her next decision, formulated while staring, first, for inspiration at Bismarck asleep in his basket and, next, at the neighbour's marmalade cat prowling around the base of an untenanted bird house in the garden below her window, was to walk downstairs to the secretary's office. She and Maureen Prescott, PA to the blind home's manageress, got on well together. Clara felt sure that Maureen could be relied upon to keep a confidence.

The vivacious, strawberry blonde PA was busy word-processing at her workstation when Clara tapped on the door and walked into her office.

'Hello, Clara,' said Maureen, waiting until she had reached the end of her sentence before turning to face the older woman. 'Not good news about the library or the Rumskee Corkscrew lecturer.'

'No,' replied Clara. 'And perhaps you got that last name right. He uncorked one bottle too many last night.'

'No, dental abscess. Or so he said. What's that you've got there? Something you need me to read?'

'No. Something private, Maureen. I'd be most grateful if you could convert it to Braille. The person who gave it to me ...' Clara hesitated before compounding the bad start to her day with a brazen lie. ' ... insisted it was for my eyes only.'

'Wow, 007 and *La Maison des Aveugles*,' said the PA, removing her reading glasses and throwing Clara a quizzical look. 'You'd rather I didn't take a peek at it, is that it?'

'If it's not asking too much.'

'Well, give here. I'll have to name it when I save it. Sounds mysterious. Any ideas? Bogen's *Skyfall*?'

'No,' said Clara with a laugh, and then off the top of her head, '*The Spanish Tragedy*'.

'Really? Any connection with your friend's *Camino Real*?'

'I don't think so. Elizabethan drama. Not exactly Tennessee Williams's cup of tea.'

'Elizabethan drama? Now, you really have got me on tenterhooks. Should I ...' Maureen Prescott stopped short, knowing better than to suggest performing the conversion blindfold.

Clara began to regret treating the matter with kid gloves. 'It's just that I promised someone ....' At a loss for words and at cross purposes with herself, she came to a grinding halt.

'That's all right, Clara. Just joking.'

I'm sorry. But please delete the screen files after scanning, converting and printing it out.'

'Take a seat, then. I can do it for you know.'

'Are you sure, Maureen? It's almost twelve pages long.'

'Oh, that is a bit much. Never mind. I'm just about finished with this text. Hang on a second.'

As it happened, the matter of scanning, saving and converting the text to Braille took next to no time, such was the PA's familiarity with her software. The Brother laser printer coughed the pages out in quick succession.

Maureen handed Clara back the originals together with their Braille conversion. 'Are you absolutely sure you want me to delete both screen files?'

'Yes.'

'No problem.' Maureen clucked a philosophical tongue, her fingers dancing a private pattern across the keyboard, after which she rolled her swivel chair away from the workstation. 'Would you like a *petit four, Clara*? The box on the filing cabinet was left there this morning by Eve Bayliss's daughter. A thank you for getting Eve to hospital quickly when she fell and broke her hip.'

'Never say no to a *petit four*.'

'Don't you mean never say never? Sean Connery.'

'That was never say never again, wasn't it?'

The strawberry blonde rubbed her forehead. 'Think you're right. Anyway,

Clara, you'd be helping my waistline. I've scoffed four of the little dears already.'

'Franglais hypnotism.'

'Ah, you and Vanessa and your word games. Though what you've got there doesn't sound like a game.'

'I suppose not.' Because of the muddled state of her mind, in attributing thoughts to Maureen that had never entered the PA's head, Clara mistakenly sensed that her friend was angling for a connection between the Braille conversion and Vanessa Curtis. This made Clara all the more anxious to beat a retreat. But reluctant to do so only moments after exploiting Maureen's goodwill, Clara shifted the conversation in a different direction.

'That marmalade cat's been after the birds again.'

'Didn't catch one, I hope?'

'No, but not for want of trying.'

'Perhaps we should try to get Bismarck to scare him away.'

'Heavens, no, Maureen. Bismarck's too docile. The gardener's fox terrier is what's needed.'

'I don't think so. You weren't here the day it terrified another moggy and chased it up a tree. We had to call out the fire brigade to bring the petrified creature back down.'

'Oh dear, how do you treat a feline for post-traumatic stress?'

'I'm not sure you can. We never saw hide nor hair of that particular moggy again.'

'Well, I've kept you long enough, Maureen. Thanks for fitting me in. I can tell you're busy.'

'No. Only two more letters, and then I'll be ready for a coffee. Feel like popping back in a quarter of an hour for a chat?'

'Love to.'

When Clara returned some twenty minutes later, Maureen was finishing grinding Kona beans in readiness for their coffee break. Seeing Clara clutching what she took to be more paperwork for scanning, the PA pulled out a chair for her visitor next to her own.

'Hello Clara. What have you brought me there? Something else to process?'

'I wish I knew. Either something's gone wrong or we need Daniel Craig's people.'

Maureen shook a tousled head, before inspecting her purse mirror for traces of what felt like a mosquito bite. She blamed the fish pond. Her office window opened onto it.

'Daniel's welcome here any day,' she said, before transferring her attention from the pink swelling to the percolator, which was filtering its last drops. 'Dash of milk with two sugars?'

'Please.' Clara placed the originals together with their Braille versions side by side on the secretary's scanner lid. 'There must have been a mistake, Maureen. Your software has turned my Spanish tragedy into double Dutch.'

'How can that be?'

'Believe me. Nothing but line after line of jumbled letters.'

'Perhaps the print quality of the original was poor and the software couldn't read it. Do you mind if I take a look at the original?'

Clara gave a resigned shrug. 'I think you ought to.'

After consulting Clara's initial text, Maureen Prescott turned puzzled eyes on the woman she had come to count as a friend. 'But Clara, your text is just that. Line after line of jumbled letters.'

'Are you sure?'

'Positive. I don't know if you've noticed, but only the top and bottom sets of characters on each page seem to be the same. And in bold font. Mind telling me how you came by this gobbledygook?'

Clara accepted the mug of coffee held out to her followed by the offer of more *petits fours*. 'Sorry, Maureen, I can't do that. And I can't believe it's gobbledygook. The person who gave it to me …' Clara hesitated to commit herself further. 'No, it must mean something.'

'Perhaps it's computer programming language. Except isn't that written in binary code? Did the person who left you these pages give you no idea of the contents?'

If Clara found comfort in the warm drink, it was comfort without understanding. 'Frankly, no. You're saying this is all written in non-binary code?'

'Looks very much like it.'

'But how could I be expected to …?' Clara stopped in mid-sentence, allowing Maureen to complete her thought for her.

'Elizabethan drama. Spanish tragedy.' Maureen rolled the two concepts around tongue and eyes. 'Is it possible that whoever gave you this document knew you would make use of it only if something happened to them?'

'That's ridiculous. No, I'm sure I was expected to hold on to it only temporarily. You see, Vanessa …' (in spite of her best intentions, the name slipped out) '… this person thought they might be seconded to Brussels for several months, and so I suppose they didn't like the idea of leaving an important document in their place down here for that length of time. No…' Clara seized up in the face of her lack of logic in denying the fears voiced by Maureen. For why else had Vanessa asked her to hold on to these pages even if only temporarily, unless … unless …?'

'No,' continued Clara, backtracking. 'We're both guessing. Wildly. By far the best solution would be to put these pages back in the envelope where they belong and forget about them.'

'A trifle late for us to bolt the stable door.'

Had it not been for Maureen's 'us', Clara Bogen might have left it at that. Instead, she went through the motions of stalling.

'I don't like this one bit.'

'I'd suggest by far the best solution to ridding yourself of worry would be to ask whoever gave you this stuff what it's all about.'

'How can I? That would mean confessing to having opened an envelope I had no right to open.'

Maureen extracted a cell phone from her handbag. 'Very good. How about this idea? My latest boyfriend is used to trapping hackers. Why not give this to him to see if he can make anything of it?'

Rocked from one extreme to the other by the swings of her emotional pendulum, Clara Bogen shook her head vigorously. 'No, thank you, Maureen. I'd rather not. I think we ought to leave well alone.'

'You sure about that? I could give him a call now. Nice guy. Works in the American embassy. He'd jump at the opportunity to help with something like this.'

Clara wrinkled her brow. 'Let me sleep on it, Maureen. But for the moment, no. I'd rather not betray the trust placed in me any more than I have already.'

'I perfectly understand.'

And that was the end of that particular discussion. Though not the end of the affair as far as an inquisitive PA was concerned. For Maureen Prescott had simulated deleting the digital version of Clara's scanned originals. Before the end of her working day, she copied them to a flash drive for handing to her boyfriend, Greg Brinkman – on the understanding that whatever he discovered had to remain strictly between the two of them. The guarantee of that understanding was reiterated later that night when the virile diplomat slipped red lace panties off raised buttocks and reached for a pot of strawberry yoghurt an arm's length away on the bedside table.

⚜

An iPhone call to Hendry's office revealing that the editor-in-chief was away on business in Barcelona, Rex Jericho began seriously debating the pros and cons of whether to pay the journalist's apartment a visit. Having googled the green belt on the city outskirts for a closer look at Hendry's address, he decided that it was a toss-up between whether he should act legitimately (through the local intelligence agency) or go it alone. The tail side of the flipped two euro coin landed face up: go it alone. Rex regarded the laurel wreath decorating the head of the coin's stern-faced, aquiline-nosed aristocrat and wondered how someone accustomed to standing proud in his chariot would take to being slotted into a supermarket shopping trolley.

Preferring to use transport of his own, Rex Jericho walked back to *L'Ambassadeur*, where he took the hotel lift down to the underground garage, climbed into his Peugeot hire car and drove up two ramps to the surface. The sunlight was bright. After lowering both visors, he pulled into the side of the road and punched his target's coordinates into the dashboard's navigation device. Before much longer, a confident female voice was leading him on his journey to the village of Oberfriesing.

Twelve minutes later, with the red arrow on the GPS monitor blinking on a red bulletin board pin a third of the way along Oberfriesing's rue Baron von Stieglitz, the man from MI6 was greeted by the comforting though superfluous announcement, 'You have reached your destination'. Gratified to see that most Luritanians appeared either to covet their privacy or to fear the effect of the midday

329

sun on their curtains and wallpaper (the shutters were closed in every window on both sides of the road), he pulled to a halt thirty yards past Hendry's apartment block. A quick inspection showed three other cars parked along the kerbside within range of his Peugeot, only one of which was occupied. The young man behind the wheel was playing with one of those handheld devices that Jericho's boss called the lamebrain's lysergic lumber.

When he arrived in front of the apartment building's ground-floor pushbutton panels, Rex decided to sound Hendry's flat number if only for appearance sake, after which he pressed a button for another floor and was rewarded by a woman's voice speaking what he guessed to be Luritanian. Opting for French, he gave the name of the local electricity supplier, explaining that he had come to repair a faulty fuse box in the basement.

The entrance door clicked open. Rex crossed the mock parquet floor, climbed up a flight of steps to the lift area, punched the door button beside one of the two waiting cabins, stepped inside, hit Hendry's floor number and thanked providence that the lift was not fitted with an overhead camera. Similarly grateful that not a soul was in sight when he emerged on the fifth floor, Rex set about efficiently opening the quadruple-bolted, but by no means burglar-proof, reinforced steel door to an apartment which he hoped was not alarmed.

The door opened smoothly. Silence within. Rex slipped quickly across the threshold, shutting the door behind him. There was a musky smell in the air that he was unable to place. Perhaps the apartment needed airing. To judge by the disarray in the entrance hall – running shoes with stale socks thrown to one side next to a baseball bat (which, Rex thought wryly, might have been handy for beating the brains out of trespassers), a solitary down-at-heel slipper mangled as if by a dog, and a coat and hat rack festooned with clothes in need of hangers – it looked as if Hendry got by without a cleaning lady.

The nearer he got to the half-open door to his right opposite the open kitchen door to his left, the stronger became the scent of musk. The sight meeting his gaze when he walked into the living room took him by surprise. Clearly, someone had got there before him. Someone who thought nothing of taking a knife to the sofa whose stuffing was strewn over the floor. The fact that Hendry's laptop had been left open on the desk against the far wall under a poster of Philip Seymour Hoffman in an off-Broadway production of *Long Day's Journey into Night*, suggested that this had yielded nothing. Hence, the savage attack on the furniture.

Rex decided there was nothing to be lost from giving the laptop a try. However, when booted up on battery power, it proved to be password protected. He made a vain stab at things with *The Pulse* and, for the hell of it, *Snowdenia*, before closing the computer down. Then he turned towards a birch veneer, roll-front cabinet left unlocked. That, he concluded, meant one of two things: negligence or a waste of his time

But before he could test either of these theories, something leapt out at him from under the sofa in a snarling blur of fangs and fur and sank its teeth into his left calf. The sheer speed of the creature was as alarming as the searing pain exacerbated by its refusal to let go. Had the animal gone for his right leg, Rex would have tried to kick it free with his left. But after the army surgeon had removed more shrapnel than Rex cared to remember from his right thigh, there was no way in which he could use that leg as a battering ram. With the creature still clinging firmly to his calf and hot blood running down his trouser leg, Rex resorted to the nearest blunt instrument to hand. A blow to the animal's rib cage with Hendry's laptop had the desired effect. The creature, which Rex took to be a weasel, released its grip and darted as quickly as it had appeared back out of sight under the sofa.

Rex leant a steadying hand against the roll-front cabinet, tugged loose his tie and yanked up the torn trouser leg. A nasty-looking wound, he thought, berating himself for not having recognised the scent for what it was. Hobbling out of the living room, he made for Hendry's rear bathroom, where he searched through the wall cupboard for antiseptic and dressing.

Had it not been for the brown-stained label, Rex would not have known that the second bottle he picked up contained iodine. Taking hold of a dampened face flannel, he eased himself down onto the linen-basket lid, rolled his trouser up to the knee, wiped as much blood as he could from his leg, folded the flannel, kept it firmly in place against the wound by pressing his leg against the rectangular ceramic wash basin, picked up the bottle of iodine and began prising loose the cap.

The next moment, his heart sank as he heard a key turn in the front door lock. Rex Jericho, the decorated veteran of three wars and one of MI6's homegrown agents had been caught, transplanted out of his element, like a common thief with his hand in the till.

The door closed. Footsteps. A woman's voice: 'Good God, Pliny, how on earth …?' Followed by a sharp intake of breath. Whoever it was had probably seen drops of blood.

Better a woman than a man, reasoned Rex, relieved to think that the third voice in a row to greet his ears that midday was female and that she was English-speaking. But how not to frighten her out of her wits? To start with by staying put, not that he was in a fit state to move anywhere quickly, let alone decorously. What were the chances, if he sat tight, of her turning tail and fleeing? The trail of blood leading out of the living room would cause most women to panic or send them running, wouldn't it? But running where? To bang on a neighbour's door or to call the police from the street below?

This woman neither screamed nor bolted. She stood her ground. For a good two minutes.

'I'm in the bathroom,' he said at last, his voice raised in resignation. 'You have nothing to fear from me, which is more than can be said of that damned weasel.'

But there was no rejoinder, just as there was no sign of retreat. Only silence. Until, suddenly – a scampering sound. The woman's voice, calm and affectionate. 'Pliny, my love. What a stupid bitch. Justin will never forgive me.' Then footsteps in Rex's direction. A dark-haired young woman appeared in the doorway, nestling the pacified creature in her arms. She looked the type, thought Rex, whom K would have called whip-smart.

331

'And who, in fuck's name, might you be?' she said in a voice devoid of alarm, her blue eyes flickering with undisguised scorn and no little amusement.

'He's domesticated?'

'Of course. Why else would he be here? '

'I thought he might have crawled in through a hole under the kitchen sink.'

'No, Pliny, who's a ferret, by the way, not a weasel, should have been in his cage, but obviously this dolt bungled securing his door. Result? One no longer serviceable sofa-cum-pull-out bed. You haven't answered my question. I have every right to be here. And you?'

'Perhaps you'd let me finish looking after my leg first. That beast took a bite out of it after erupting on me as if spewed from Vesuvius.'

'When was your last rabies shot?'

'Thanks for your concern. Too long ago to remember.'

'Well, you're going to need several. Pliny might be domesticated but only since his owner, Justin, caught him chasing a cat in the garden out back.'

'Great. I escape the worst of an IED in Helmand province only to be dealt a sucker punch by a creature farmers use to hunt rabbits.'

Vanessa watched the stranger dab his wound with iodine. Satisfied that he was harmless enough to cause her no trouble, she put the ferret back in its cage and returned to help secure the dressing.

'Any other woman would feel threatened by me,' said Rex, feeling equally foolish and embarrassed by her matter of fact first aid.

'I'm not any other woman. And you look pathetically respectable. Too old to be a friend of Justin's. Family perhaps?'

Rex rolled down his trouser leg, pulled himself to his feet and stared absentmindedly at the mess he had created on the tiled bathroom floor. 'No. The family I belong to is no ordinary family. Do the letters SIS mean anything to you, Miss …?'

'Curtis. Vanessa Curtis. MI5 and MI6 stewing in each other's juices?'

'Oh dear, no holds barred, is that it? No, Miss Curtis, there's nothing incestuous about the new set-up, I assure you.'

'Illegitimate rather, seeing that your *modus operandi* includes breaking and entering. How else would you have got in, since your family has nothing in common with Justin's?'

Rex cast an exasperated glance at his first sight of Hendry's last entry on the calendar pinned to the wall above the toilet: *Remind Vanessa that Pliny needs exercise.*

'I only learnt at the last moment that Hendry was in Barcelona. As I couldn't afford to wait, I improvised.'

'Without knowing whether he had an alarm?'

'Not that clever, I agree. But I was lucky.'

'Until Pliny made a better job of things than an alarm. Well, here in Luritania, breaking and entering is as much a crime as it is in Queen Liz land.'

'Only a misdemeanor, I believe, if nothing is stolen. There's a world of difference between burgling and investigating.'

'Tell that to the beak. Although, I suppose, you won't need to. You people enjoy a free hand running rings around the justice system.'

Unable to shake off his vexation at being caught red-handed, discomfited by his amateurism and with his leg still stinging, Rex sank back down onto the linen basket.

'All right, you've made your point. If I'm the sorry face of MI6, we might as well pack our bags and leave town.'

It was the first time he had seen her smile.

'A bunch of grown-up schoolboys playing cloak and dagger in the next best thing to your underwear. Look, I think we ought to go through to the front room, find a couple of chairs Pliny hasn't made a meal out of and talk things over. But first I must clean out his cage, feed and water him. Which is what brought me here in the first place. Then you can tell me what brought you here.'

While Vanessa catered for the ferret, Rex carried two high-backed chairs across from the dining to the living area and sat down in front of a roll-top cabinet mute to his curiosity. By the time she returned, he was wondering whether O'Neill's play respected Aristotle's unities of time, place and action and questioning the poster's place in a living room.

'Did you put that poster up?' he asked, as she returned, pet care completed, from the kitchen.

Vanessa settled down into the chair next to his. 'You seem to know more about me than I know about you. In fact, I know nothing about you.'

'Everything in good time. You saw Hoffman in that role?'

'Yes.'

'Lucky you.'

'Lucky me.'

'I understand you're putting on a play at the moment.'

'Putting a play together, yes. Who told you that?'

'The same sources who told me all I needed to know about Justin Hendry. I wish they'd told me you were his ferret sitter. It might have spared me those rabies vaccinations.'

'I don't sit for Justin's ferret. I've been dropping by during my lunch break for the few days Justin's in Spain to feed Pliny and take him for a runabout in the park across the way.'

'On a long lead?'

'A very long lead. He chases just about damn everything else on four legs, unless I reel him in. I've told you my name. You've still to tell me yours.'

'J.'

'As in Douglas Jay, Privy Counsellor?'

'As in the tenth letter of the alphabet. Or, if you prefer, after the bird. Not that I'm one for jabbering.'

'If I prefer? Meaning it might just as well be J as in jay walking, since you're trespassing. But perhaps you're having me on. Whatever would possess someone from MI5 to tell me his real name?'

'MI6.'

'Of course. You're out of home waters.'

Rex turned to face her. 'But not out of my depth. Unlike Justin Hendry and Rashid Jabour.'

If Vanessa had felt paradoxically in control of this farcical situation until now, thanks partly to the Browning nesting inside an otherwise innocuous sling bag and partly to docile acceptance of her nursing ministrations, her self-assurance suffered a knock under the SIS man's unwavering glance.

'I don't understand.' It was the feebly prevaricating best she could manage.

'If you're saying that out of a misplaced sense of duty to protect, I would suggest you think again.'

Vanessa threw a look at the sling bag out of arm's reach by the window ledge near the bathroom door, where she had left it, when gathering up Pliny, on top of the large earthenware pot containing Justin's Philodendron. She stared back at Rex only for instinct to tell her that her imagination was in overdrive

His point made, Rex changed tack. 'You and Justin Hendry are good friends?'

Vanessa assumed that, if MI6 had done its homework, J would have had more sense than to suggest 'close friends'.

'I think we'd have to be for me to volunteer ferret walking.'

'That creature doesn't know the meaning of the word walk. He confides in you?'

Pliny? No. He doesn't seem to have inherited his namesake's flair for oratory.'

Rex nodded knowingly. A woman after his own heart, though hand in glove, if no longer sleeping with, the editor. 'A journalist such as Hendry should know better than to make public information jeopardising national security.'

'Is that a statement or a question?'

'A reflection.'

'If you're going to throw the Official Secrets Act at Justin, don't expect him to quake in his boots. The Tower of London is a tourist attraction nowadays not a staging post for the executioner to whet his axe.'

'You're wrong to make light of this, Miss Curtis. The fact of the matter is that should he go any further, he risks prosecution and a prison sentence of up to fourteen years.'

'Murderers do less time than that,' said Vanessa, mystified by the disconnect between J's warning and the material published by Justin, which seemed to be of as much consequence as a flea to an elephant. But then perhaps her idea of sensitive information was pitifully outdated. No, she was wrong. 'Should he go any further' meant that J was more worried about the sterilisation project

'An idiosyncracy of our justice system, is that it? Ah, but does your common or garden murderer pose a security threat? I think not.'

Rex punctuated this remark with a cross between a laugh and a croak, recalling how quick Langley had been off the mark with its substitution of bogus decrypted material, though K had declined to reveal precisely how this had been achieved. Of course, the ball had been in J's court then, since Langley had intervened on the understanding that Vauxhall Cross would live up to its responsibilities by nipping any further initiative on Hendry's part in the bud – all the more so since the leak had occurred on J's watch, the culprits practically on home ground.

But both sides knew that what was at stake had more to do with Jericho and K's survival than with the common good. Were Rex Jericho's cover to be blown, MI6 would have to kiss goodbye to a cosy relationship built up with Langley's man through long hard graft. And not only would K's people rue losing a valuable catch, but K might conceivably be viewed as a turncoat.

While these thoughts raced through Rex's mind, Vanessa remained silent, refusing to feed her interlocutor the line which sooner or later, she knew he was bound to extract from her.

'I'm afraid I clobbered Pliny with Hendry's laptop. No telling who or what came out of that experience the worst. Pliny, me or the Vaio.'

'I doubt the blow unlocked Justin's password.'

'As it happens, you caught me just before I was about to inspect that cabinet.'

'The top drawer probably contains a photocopy of *Camino Real* with Justin's part highlighted. The next my birthday present to him, a copy of Hašek's *The Good Soldier Schweik*. The one under that photographs of his parents' safari around the Serengeti National Park. Should I continue?'

'Not unless one of those drawers is home to state secrets.'

'We're chasing our tails here. Has Justin published anything remotely endangering your precious national security?'

Pondering this question, Rex Jericho wondered what was the more ridiculous: to suggest that his breast pocket was bulging with confidentiality declarations under the Official Secrets Act (a threat calculated to make less stern souls than Miss Curtis reach for their fountain pen) or to propose retiring to the kitchen for coffee (caffeine seen as a welcome distraction from the nagging pain in his leg).

'Well then, has he committed an indictable offence?'

'Let's say he's been skating on very thin ice. It would be inadvisable for him to venture out with a heavier back pack.'

This remark caused Vanessa further confusion over the difference between the two documents found in the Italian leather briefcase. Why should the less incendiary of these texts have been made so much more difficult to decrypt than the other? Rashid had convinced her that the explanation lay in the fact that the two were unconnected, each intended for a different consumer. And that a third more inflammatory document had either come to be left out of the briefcase or was already with its intended recipient. But then why was MI6 uptight about a text so easy to decypher?

Seeing no point in concealing her frustration any further, Vanessa fed J his line. 'You're talking about a fucking text that it would be an insult to feed to a Christmas sale robot in Hamley's. I wouldn't be surprised to learn that Justin rolled it up into a ball and gave it to Pliny to play with.'

'Ah, does this perhaps mean you have trodden the same not so royal road as your Don Quixote?' Rex did not know which he felt the more following this confession: relief or desperation Yes, he had made all the right connections, but how many more wrong ones had Hendry made?

Vanessa raised an eyebrow. 'MI6 finds the time to poke its nose into the European amateur theatrical scene?'

'When amateurs try to put one over on professionals. I hope your entire cast is not using our text as a bookmark.'

'If you think my solidarity with Justin extends to handing out classified documents like freebies, then you're a greater fool than I took you for when I found you sitting by the toilet nursing that gash in your leg.'

'Solidarity. An honourable Polish concept. But misplaced in the present case. Tell me, how many others, apart from Hendry, you and Jabour know about this document?'

Vanessa saw no point in dissembling. 'A handful.'

'And what's your definition of a handful?'

'I'd be a greater fool to tell you.'

'Of course.'

'So where do we go from here? Am I under arrest? Liable to prosecution? I suppose not. MI6 don't carry handcuffs. They leave that kind of thing to idiosyncratic justice enforcers.'

Rex Jericho rubbed frustration and weariness from his temples. Ever since setting foot in this dratted apartment everything seemed to have gone haywire. But now that his worst suspicions were confirmed, it was as if a weight had been removed from his mind. Except that he still needed to unglue this woman and her friends' eyes fully to the Pandora's box which they had opened.

Getting to his feet with some effort, Rex rescued Justin's Vaio from the floor, eased the lid open and, after ascertaining that the monitor was undamaged, replaced the laptop where he had found it. 'Nothing loose there. Japanese AI survives concussion.'

'You hope.'

Rex Jericho started pacing the room, one eye on the poster, the other on Vanessa's sling bag, appreciating the significance of the one without registering the importance of the other.

'I hate to sound dramatic, Miss Curtis but, not to put too fine a point on it, survival is what you and everyone else privy to those documents should be worrying about.'

'Dramatic? No, you sound Darwinian.'

'Jabour was given unequivocal instructions to destroy his documents. How can I, how can we be sure that he did? Or that, if copies were left floating around, all have been destroyed?'

'You can't.'

'Precisely. In other words, you have every reason to fear that others will leave no stone unturned to ensure that those documents' contents never see the light of day. Compared to them MI6 deserves canonisation.'

336

'I thought you had to be dead to qualify for sainthood. A mite early to be carving *hic iacet* on MI6's tombstone.'

'All well and good, but compared to your other foes we are philanthropy itself.'

'What does that make you? Andrew Carnegie? Should we take refuge from these unnamed foes in one of your libraries behind the shelf marked Security?'

'Miss Curtis, this is no laughing matter. Even if you and Hendry assure me that the originals and all copies of these papers have been destroyed or, if not, will be as soon as you give the word, I regret that I cannot guarantee that that will be the end of the affair – not with the ramifications to national security as complex as they are. I cannot impress upon you too firmly the warning that others will show less understanding.'

'Why not say what you mean – the CIA? I didn't think they troubled themselves with whistleblowers showing up the seamy side of democratic evangelisation. Nothing new in that, is there?'

Rex paused to draw breath. Time to lay it on thicker. 'After *Le Nouvel Observateur*, *The Economist* and *Der Spiegel* – not to mention a few other journals – gave space to that mushroom cloud editorial, it would be a grave mistake for Hendry to go viral with more material. He needs to understand that that way lies disaster. For him and his hangers-on.'

'Frightening.'

Rex Jericho spread his arms out wide in a gesture of piqued resignation.

'You can't say that I haven't told you.'

'Oh yes, Mr Jay, Magpie or whoever, I've got the message. Official Secrets Act and CIA bugaboos.'

'I intend to spell matters out to Mr Hendry as soon as he returns from Barcelona. Ask him to contact me at *L'Ambassadeur*, where I'm staying under the name of Maurice Chandler.'

'Well, if that's that,' said Vanessa, taking Rex's business card including his hotel room's telephone number, 'Perhaps you'll have the decency to leave here together with me.'

'Aren't you forgetting the ferret?'

'No. I think he's had enough exercise as it is.'

Claude-Henri Weiland looked up from his iPad to congratulate himself on his calculation of how long it would take Vanessa Curtis and the weather-beaten stranger to reach street level. After a brief chat at the kerbside and a handshake, the two went their separate ways.

Weiland punched the redial button on his cell phone. Hoffarth picked up on the call within seconds.

'Yes, Claude-Henri?'

'Want me to tail the stranger?'

'They left together?'

'Yes. No attempt to pretend otherwise.'

'Follow him.'

'He could follow her, of course.'

'No matter. Stay with him.'

'I'd better get going. He's off. I'll keep you updated.'

Georg Hoffarth replaced the office receiver in its cradle. The webcam installed in Hendry's living room had paid dividends, prompting Claude-Henri to suggest monitoring Vanessa Curtis's apartment. The inspector said he would think the matter over, but that his trainee could forget any idea he might have about concealing a webcam in that young woman's bathroom. Whether or not Mlle Curtis had acted the part of Florence Nightingale in Hendry's bathroom was irrelevant compared to what had been captured onscreen in the living room.

What nettled Hoffarth more than anything else was another of the force's false economies: his superior's refusal to run to the extra investment of a microphone. The inspector would have sacrificed his thirteenth month bonus to know what those two had been talking about.

Memo from K to J

> *As the months go by and nothing improves in Urodina, I am not alone in thinking that my people misjudged the February 2014 putsch. Now that the Nevskians see the hornet's nest we've stirred up across the border, our chances of achieving a similar coup d'état on their home ground look decidedly slim.*

Response from J

> *Yes, K, instead of staking everything on a thoroughbred, you backed a spavined nag with swastikas decorating its saddle blanket.*
>
> *I would suggest that there is scant difference between today's Wayfarer and his retinue of oligarchs and the tsars of old and their boyars. Certainly, today's oligarchs think nothing of appropriating the country's forests and lakes and selling them off to outside private interests. And safe in the knowledge that nothing rankles more with the west than imprisoning people because of their sexual rather than their intellectual orientation, they have no qualms about repressing dissent among the intelligentsia.*
>
> *In short, your guess is as good as mine as to whether domestic patience will finally snap as we approach the centenary of that first revolution.*

It was not until Rex Jericho regained his room back at *L'Ambassadeur* that he discovered the loss of his regimental tie clip. Not a good omen, he concluded, deciding that it must have come loose in the fight with that ferret. Well, he could hardly return there. And it was not as if the clip was irreplaceable. All the same, it irked him to think that he had failed to notice the disappearance of something he slipped on almost as regularly each morning as his watch.

Resigned to the fact that it had been an abortive day in more senses than one, Rex Jericho sat down in front of his makeshift workstation at the hotel's room's writing desk and, wondering what other surprises the day had in store for him, downloaded the latest encrypted message from K onto his iPad.

As both men used symmetric encryption, Rex was able to use the same key, but with the algorithm in reverse, to decipher the text which, in view of the time difference between EDT and CET, had arrived in his e-mail box at ten minutes past three in the afternoon. The contents were not unexpected.

J, I'm still teed off about learning from our intercept nerds rather than from the horse's mouth that our cyberspace correspondence fell into the wrong hands. Now that we've strangled one baby at birth, I'd like to know how much longer before you choke its twin?

Rex Jericho emitted a splenetic moan. MI6 had known from the word go that this affair could not be done and dusted without interference from Langley. Its only misjudgment had been as to timing.

Rex's reply was part recapitulation, part plea.

You didn't hear from me earlier, because I didn't want to alarm you unnecessarily. It's unfortunate that one of our runners inadvertently left classified material in a London minicab and that these documents were picked up by a journalist.

But, and this is something I omitted to point out before, I regret to say that once warning lights started flashing over there, Langley seems to have taken it into its head to despatch two emissaries to Luritania. Instead of pouring oil on troubled waters, that partnership added fuel to the fire by murdering an innocent bystander. Your guess is as good as mine as to what drove them to this. None too impressive, however you look at it.

I'm sitting in Schönschlucht, awaiting the return from Spain of Mr Justin Hendry, our principal antagonist. After speaking to a close acquaintance of his, I feel sure that I can not only convince Hendry of the error of his ways but sweep this whole sorry business under the carpet.

In short, the sole damage done so far can be considered trifling inasmuch as the majority of British, French and German readers of Hendry's latest editorial (your or Langley's tour de force?) will dismiss it as another cockamamie conspiracy theory – which is presumably what you wanted.

Langley's reaction cannot, I hope, have been motivated by fear of disclosure of our e-mail exchanges? They are so solidly encrypted as to defy unravelling by anyone other than an autistic savant.

I urge you to leave this to us. Give me two days more, and your worries will be laid to rest.

Dissatisfied with what he saw as a desperate fling of the dice, Rex Jericho pressed 'send' before deciding to add body to his coffee with whisky from the minibar. And waited for a reply that was not long in coming; before he had time to collect his thoughts, an ominous ping announced incoming mail.

J, I'm neither blind nor deaf to what's going on over there. We know that Hendry is not acting alone. Without so much as a squeak from my blue-feathered friend, what option did you leave us with? Don't count on my standing by, waiting for you to pull off one of your Vauxhall Cross coups.

The reply squared with Rex's guess as to the reaction from K's end: at best, Langley would give him forty-eight hours' free rein; at worst, it would let him know he had run out of slack. Either way made little difference. K's people rewrote the rules as they went along.

Rex Jericho had dug himself into a hole. A very deep hole. At least, that was how he saw it. Anyone else might have laid the blame for the fix Rex was in at Peregrine Musgrave's door. But Rex was not someone to bear grudges, especially against a man called to a hospital emergency ward where his son lay in a critical condition. A man driven to commit suicide. By what or by whom? Did he have that on his conscience? And what about the fate of Hendry, Curtis and the rest of their band? Would he come to have that on his conscience as well? With K stamping impatiently in the wings, Rex Jericho, fancying he heard the sound of trumpets, took a swig of laced coffee.

Greg Brinkman scratched dandruff and perplexity from his head. After fifteen minutes spent running decryption algorithms for Maureen Prescott's text, he had nothing to show for his efforts. Not that he could claim to know what he was doing other than wasting his and the embassy's time. Confident from the outset that he could crack this nutshell with a digital hammer, rather than admit that it had got the better of him, he concluded that some unkind person had to be playing a practical joke on the scrambled document's blind recipient.

On the verge of tossing the text into the waste bin alongside half a dozen fruitless print-outs, Greg told himself that, however worthless he deemed the document, a certain delectable strawberry blonde might not take kindly to his consigning her property to the shredder.

But Arnold Palmer chose this moment to barge into Greg's office cubicle, grab hold of a spare chair and sit down beside him.

'We're living in an eco-friendly age, Greg. How many saplings are you going to plant to make up for that wastage?'

However strongly Greg Brinkmann might have felt about his mentor's habit of jumping up behind him, he lacked the gall to object when caught shortchanging his employer.

'What have you got going here, Greg?' Palmer seized a handful of paper from the bin. 'Instead of poring over that manual I gave you yesterday, you're playing games? Or has someone in China hacked into your hard drive and left a nasty Trojan behind?'

'No, sir. A girl friend asked if I could help solve a puzzle.'

'She's hoping to win a bunch of money … some competition, is that it?'

'No, she was given a document to convert to Braille. But when she saw what it was, she realised she'd wasted her time. The text makes no sense. Here, see for yourself.' Greg handed Palmer the original.

'Now, you really are losing me, Greg. Braille, you say?'

'She's PA to the manageress of a blind home.'

'And somebody gave her this …' Palmer was studying the text with a mixture of incredulity and amusement. '… gibberish. Why, for goodness sake?'

The intern wondered how a mentor whom he had been led to believe had razor sharp judgment could be so slow on the uptake.

'If they were blind, they wouldn't have known that the text was nonsensical.'

'Yes, but why give it to your friend in the first place?'

'Perhaps she'd received it in the day's post,' suggested Greg, deciding against making Palmer look a complete fool.

'Doesn't somebody like your girlfriend open post for her residents before making her mind up whether to give it to them or not?'

'I don't really know. Perhaps.'

'Not perhaps, Greg. She does. So this blind person was in possession of something she had brought into the home with her or had smuggled in. Something important enough for her to need to read it.'

'Smuggled is a bit strong, isn't it? Why would anyone slip a blind person this kind of rubbish?'

'Because it would be safe with them. Safe from prying eyes. And, young man, have you noticed that each page begins and ends with the same set of letters …?'

'I can't say I did.'

'…implying that somehow or other this document does make sense. I'll shove it across to NSA's decryption team. See what they make of it.'

'Well, I don't see them getting far without the key.'

'You're not a code-breaking computer geek, Greg. Leave it to the experts.'

※

After Georg Hoffarth learnt that Vanessa Curtis had returned to work and the stranger to his upmarket hotel in town, the inspector decided to pay a quick visit to the young woman in her office.

When reception phoned her to announce the surprise visitor, Vanessa was in the middle of putting the finishing touches to a recommendation that her organisation benefit from the economy of scale of outsourcing processing of employees' health insurance claims and reassigning in-house processing staff to more productive operations. By the time Hoffarth knocked on her door, she was penciling in the last of three drooping-mouthed smilies beside those sections of the staff regulations itemising compensation in the event of temporary or permanent invalidity and the capital sum payable upon death to next of kin.

She rose to her feet to greet the keen-eyed police officer with a clownish blue and white visitor's badge pinned to his lapel. The man's reedy physique was belied by a straight back and a firm handshake.

'Inspector Georg Hoffarth.'

'What can have brought you all the way here, inspector? I warrant something a stage removed from a backlog of parking fines.'

Unsuspecting of the implicit connection between her visitor and her encounter earlier that day with J, Vanessa failed at the same time to understand what had spurred her lightheadedness.

Hoffarth accepted the offer of a chair. 'I'm here to tell you that, in the light of what befell Mr Radetzky... I trust you know what I'm talking about? Well, we have been keeping an eye on Mr Hendry's apartment during his absence.'

While there was no longer any need to put two and two together, Vanessa had yet to grasp what 'an eye' added up to. 'That's heartening to know.'

'You were there today. Also, before you, there was another man, Bernard Faulkner, poking around among Mr Hendry's possessions.'

'You installed cameras in Justin's flat?'

'One camera. It showed you having quite a long, earnest conversation with Mr Faulkner after that pine marten chewed up his leg.'

'It was a ferret. Bernard Faulkner, you say?' (A person of Jay's stature might have been many things to her but never a Bernie.) 'That's not the name he gave me.'

'Well, it's the name he's registered under at his hotel, *L'Ambassadeur*, in town. Who is he and what was he doing there?'

Vanessa saw no point in fudging the issue. If anything, as she saw it Hoffarth's arrival at this juncture might help stabilise the vessel on which J had set her adrift together with her friends.

'He works for MI6. Or so he said. I have no reason to disbelieve him. He warned me that Justin, Mr Hendry, risks bringing the weight of the Official Secrets Act down upon his head. Worse than that, he intimated that Justin and anybody else with knowledge of certain missing documents could be targets for reprisal by unprincipled individuals.'

The inspector scribbled a hurried note into a slim, hard-backed diary.

'And how did he gain entry to the apartment?'

Vanessa had no hesitation in deciding that Jay deserved to reap what he had sown.

'Well, Justin hadn't exactly made him a present of a spare key.'

'I see. And you understand what documents he was referring to?'

'Not really,' said Vanessa, relieved to learn that Hoffarth's eye had not been paired with an ear.

342

'Did Mr Faulkner mention Klaus Radetzky?'

'No. Why?'

'Because it's doubtful that Radetzky's death had anything to do with one of his cartoons.'

'Don't leave it at that, inspector. What do you mean?'

'We don't believe his death was an accident. And there was no question of suicide. One or more persons must have thrown him into the gorge.'

Vanessa recalled the mention she had just read in the staff regulations about the capital sum payable on death being forfeited in the event of suicide. Thank goodness, she thought, that Klaus's wife would not go begging. As for her own next of kin, it was sickening to think that she could end up enriching her domineering bastard of a father.

Then it occurred to her that the inspector could be a blessing in disguise.

'Inspector, do me a favour. Do all of us who are friends of Justin Hendry a favour. Pay a visit to Bernard Faulkner before he disappears back into his MI6 genie's lamp. Perhaps he'll be more forthcoming with you than he was with me. After all, you people work on the same side of the fence.'

'Not quite. But, yes, I intend to do just that. Is there nothing else of value you can tell me?'

'If I think of anything, I'll let you know.'

'Here's my card.'

Once Georg Hoffarth had taken his leave, Vanessa returned to her work. To little or no avail, her gaze riveted on the marginal *track changes* notes on her laptop's monitor beside the small print qualifying permanent invalidity. It triggered a macabre memory about something told her in confidence over a glass of wine at the time when the building in which she was now sitting was still under construction. In studying the topographical survey drawings, the architect's on-the-spot representative had seen that the Kreuzplateau site chosen for Vanessa's HQ had originally been called the Galgenplateau. In other words, contrary to what he had been led to believe by the Ministry for Urban Planning (that *Kreuz* denoted either the site of an early religious settlement or the plateau's subsequent importance as a major junction between mail coach arteries), these archival drawings showed the plateau to have, in reality, been named after the gallows (*Galgen*) erected there.

It was, as he put it, 'hardly propitious'. Vanessa had to agree.

Well, Messrs Hoffarth, Chandler or Faulkner, she thought, is it going to be a case of *The Long Goodbye, The Big Sleep, Light In August* or *As I Lay Dying?*'

<hr />

Arnold Palmer was mugging up his Gutman lines about signs in the sky, when an urgent call came through from the ambassador for him to get his ass over to the video conference room for a chat with Langley.

On joining the ambassador a few moments later in the room familiarly known as the bunker, Palmer found his chief in conversation with a middle-aged man he recalled from his days at CIA headquarters. The ambassador turned to signal Arnold to take a seat nearby. But not next to the great man. That would have implied a place in the pecking order unjustified by Palmer's status.

Arnold struggled to remember the name of the fit-looking, hatchet-faced individual with the swept back mane of black hair, who reminded him of Jack Palance.

'This gentleman,' said the ambassador, striking his most proprietorial tone, 'is Mr Lester Kayser, Principal Covert European Operations Manager. He has just told me that one of my officers sent a document decrypt request to Langley yesterday without my knowledge. Why was I not informed of this before?'

Arnold Palmer hid his confusion behind a mask of subservience. 'Sir, I'm sorry. I didn't want to bother you with something that probably amounted to nothing. Greg had a brainteaser, a game neither of us thought worth the candle. But I favoured pushing it through to the cyber decryption boys to see if they could make something of it.'

'Well, you got one thing right, Palmer,' said the man on the screen glaring down at Arnold from four thousand miles away. 'It was seriously encrypted. Now perhaps you can tell me in as few words as possible, before I have your guts for garters, how you came by that document.'

'I got it from one of our interns, Greg Brinkman.'

'And how, pray, did he come by it? Keep it short and sweet, Palmer.'

Arnold Palmer reflected that he had rolled with worst punches than Kayser's during his time at Fort Benning in the days before the CIA handpicked him for their HUMINT recruitment programme. 'From a secretary working in a local home for the blind.'

'I hope you're not guying me, Palmer.'

'Sir, Mr Kayser, I swear that was what Brinkman told me.'

'Well, Palmer, you or Mr Brinkman better find out double quick what that secretary was doing with this document. Understood?'

'Understood, sir.'

'And report right back to me in less time than it takes you to remember which hand you wipe your butt with.'

꧁꧂

After establishing that Bernard Faulkner had booked a hot seaweed wrap for six o'clock that evening with the hotel's massage parlour, Georg Hoffarth betook himself to *L'Ambassadeur* for late five o'clock tea and scones. The latter not to his taste – the pastry insisted on sticking to the roof of his mouth – he confined himself to a modest slice of Black Forest gâteau and a pot of camomile tea while reading the sports pages of a regional newspaper, his interest attracted by that summer's Tour de France running for eighty kilometres through southern Luritania. A box item at the bottom of one page advertised a charity cyclothon organised by a local fitness centre, *All The Right Moves*, to raise money for *Médecins Sans Frontières* Hoffarth gave a grunt of nuanced approval: too many people, to his mind, held up Luritania as the epitome of the acquisitive society without recognising the good work done by the sovereign and his wife, the *Croix Rouge* and sister charities supporting humanitarian projects around the globe.

With the time approaching a quarter to seven, he carried his newspaper across to the palm-fringed Hawaian lounge, where, according to a voluble receptionist, Faulkner invariably took his post-massage sundowner.

Georg Hoffarth scrutinised the extensive choice of drinks listed on the cocktail menu and decided on a negroni. When the barman, a flamboyant character, came to take his order, the inspector settled up straightaway with plastic money.

True to habit, five minutes later, the man from MI6 stepped into the lounge, occupied a table by the window giving onto the hotel's arboretum, its centerpiece a circular fountain with concentric jets playing set piece patterns. There was no need for Rex Jericho to consult the cocktail menu. Before long, the same barista who had served Hoffarth sashayed up to the window table with Jericho's customary cocktail.

Leaving his drink untouched, Jericho turned to his iPhone. Georg Hoffarth took this opportunity to get up from his seat and move discreetly across to the window table, drink in hand.

'Mind if I join you?'

Jericho looked up querulously. How had this complete stranger known to address him in English?

'By all means.'

The two shook hands.

'Don't suppose you know anything about dog bites? How to treat them?'

The inspector took up the seat opposite Jericho. 'Why? A call from home, perhaps? I hope it's nothing too serious. A child?'

Jericho put down his iPhone. 'You're looking at the child. I was taking a walk in the woods this morning, when some sickly mongrel started sniffing at my heels. When I lost patience and tried to shoo it away, the damn creature turned on me and bit me in the leg.'

'What bad luck. You're inoculated against rabies?'

'Too long ago to be of any use now. I've just been exfoliated, wrapped in seaweed and detoxified. Said to work wonders but, I regret to say, no cure for rabies.'

'Might that explain the stiff drink? It looks suitably ecological for these surroundings. What is it?'

'A fallen angel. Gin, lime and crème de menthe. Perhaps I should have ordered a penicillin. The Scotch might deaden the nerve endings. On the other hand, I doubt whether doctors prescribe acacia honey water for treating rabies. What's yours?'

'A negroni. More gin with Campari and vermouth.'

'As red as the blood that mutt drew from my calf.'

Hoffarth raised his glass hospitably, waiting for Jericho to return the gesture before taking his first sip.

'Something of a misnomer, sundowner, don't you think?' said Rex. 'Here we are with a good two hours to go before nightfall and a roof over our heads blotting out the sun.'

'No more of a misnomer than calling a ferret a dog.'

Rex stopped stirring his cocktail and cast a quick look around the lounge's other tables. Only two occupied, both by elderly couples of no significance.

'What's all this about?'

'People who break into other people's apartments in broad daylight are looking for trouble, Mr Faulkner. Especially when the apartment in question is monitored with a webcam.'

Feeling on more solid ground now that he knew this was a one-on-one situation, Rex Jericho studied the unsmiling man in the neatly cut business suit opposite him with a mixture of puzzlement and admiration. The slight accent told him that he was probably dealing with a Luritanian – almost certainly, in the light of this latest revelation, a member of the local police force.

'You have the advantage of me. Monsieur …? We haven't been introduced, yet you already know my name and how I came under attack this morning in one of your city's apartments.'

'My name is Georg Hoffarth. Chief Inspector Hoffarth.' (Outwardly urbane, the police officer was in no mood to pull punches.) 'And I take a dim view of outsiders who choose to break into other people's property on my home ground. All the same, I am not here to charge or arrest an apparent member of Her Majesty's Secret Service on official overseas business, however dubious that business might seem. Please, don't let me spoil your evening or your drink. Mr Hendry's ferret has done enough damage for one day.'

'How many citizens' homes in Schönschlucht are equipped with webcams and microphones connected to the police department?'

Hoffarth though best not to disabuse the man calling himself Bernard Faulkner. 'Not many. But our city has witnessed three violent deaths in the past fortnight, and I suspect that they are linked to the same intelligence you were trying to uncover in Hendry's apartment.'

'I can't fault your logic, inspector.'

'I would therefore appreciate your sharing whatever knowledge you have of these crimes with my department. Upholding the Official Secrets Act with due vigour is all well and good, but once murder intrudes its ugly face you no longer enjoy *carte blanche*, Mr Faulkner.'

Jericho stared at the barista, wondering whether it was this showman who had put the inspector on to him. But after the fellow had finished turning two bottles on his shelf so that their labels faced outwards, it was his hair that had his attention in the polished-edge mirror tiles above the bar not the two men at the window table.

'Inspector, believe me when I say that we do not consider ourselves to be above the law. On the contrary, our services and yours have a … long history of cooperation.' Chequered, thought Rex, would have been more accurate, but that was hardly the message to convey to this inspector. 'I am obliged to await Mr Hendry's return from his business trip, before making the severity of his situation clear to him. He will be required to return all illegally obtained classified material, failure on his and anybody else's part to destroy all digital records resulting in immediate prosecution. I would hope that this clinches matters. None of us wants to see further unpleasantness of the kind experienced with Mr Radetzky.' Jericho rounded off this peroration by smacking his lips over the cocktail cherry.

But if Rex Jericho thought the inspector would be sufficiently impressed to take him at his word or to deem breaking and entering part of the day's work for MI6, he was mistaken.

Before taking another sip of his negroni, Georg Hoffarth revolved the glass so as to avoid the wedge of orange. 'I would like nothing better than to believe that you will manage all this, Mr Faulkner, but how am I to know that you are who you make yourself out to be? Perhaps you have taken a leaf out of the training manual of the service you claim to represent, one that specialises in smoke and mirrors.'

Rex gazed into the depths of his fallen angel. Had their roles been reversed, he would have been equally skeptical. 'Who else do you imagine I'm working for, inspector? The lameduck Ukrainian parliament propped up by a USA which can never have enough feet in other people's doors?'

'I doubt they'd go to all this trouble over a cartoon.'

'Who then?'

'What proof can you give me that you work for MI6?'

Rex reached into his breast pocket, pulled out his wallet and handed the inspector a card. 'Ring or fax that gentleman, Clarence Swithinburn. My head of ops. No, inspector, those numbers are real enough. Check for yourself and you'll see. They'll put you in touch with SIS headquarters at Vauxhall Cross.'

'Will Mr Swithinburn know whom I'm talking about? You register here under the name of Faulkner, but give Mademoiselle Curtis a different name.'

'People in our trade have this thing about anonymity, inspector. Difficult to shake off.'

'Need I tell you that the two individuals murdered after Radetzky had a similar hang-up about anonymity.'

'Come now, inspector. Were they carrying passports as good as autographed by her Britannic Majesty's Secretary of State? I think not.'

'No, rather a question of the pot calling the kettle black.' Hoffarth turned to look at the grey-haired man and woman sitting at the table to his left. Bent over their tablets, they had not exchanged a word for the entire time since his arrival. Was that what came of knowing each other inside out to the point of indifference? How little he knew about the man opposite him. 'Everything gave to believe that those two men with fake IDs were responsible for Radetzky's death.'

'Yes, so I understand.'

'But do you understand why?'

'Why they killed the cartoonist? I have no idea. Was there Ukrainian blood in the family? Did one have a Canadian passport?'

'We believe they were Americans. Could it be that they were interfering on your pitch? After all, Radetzky worked for the man you're itching to throw the book at.'

It was Rex's turn to look at the old married couple, but to think how much less complicated life had to be for people in their vegetative years.

'You're saying they were out to steal our classified secrets? One set of government agents dying to get its hands on another's sensitive information? Aren't you forgetting the special relationship?'

Hoffarth grimaced. With Bernard Faulkner all but revelling in making things up as he went along, there was little point in pursuing the matter.

'So you will be staying on at *L'Ambassadeur*? I believe you are booked in for one more night. Monsieur Hendry's flight is scheduled to touch down the day after tomorrow.'

'Yes, well, I shall have to extend my stay.'

Georg Hoffarth took out his own card and proceeded to scribble a note on the back of it.

'Here,' he said at length. 'My contact details. I've written down the name of the hospital on the edge of town with the shortest emergency room waiting times. I suggest you drive out there tonight and get that leg seen to.'

'I was wondering. Is it really necessary? After all, the ferret was a pet. Domesticated.'

'Mr Faulkner, as in your average family, the worst bites tend to come from within not from outside.'

'The voice of experience. Are you not finishing your drink?'

Hoffarth viewed the rest of his negroni with a jaundiced eye. It was not just the traffic light colour that signalled stop. The vermouth, he suspected, was begging to differ with the combined might of whipped cream, cherries and chocolate sponge cake.

Memo from J to K

> *It looks as if funding and arming of Islamic State factions on the Nevskian League's southern borders will soon pay dividends once these cells make their presence felt within the hinterland. But on the hearts and minds side, you need to get IS to disseminate plentiful propaganda in support of what it believes to be its own rather than your agenda. Why? Because should you fail to prod Urodina into embroiling western Erebu in a war with the League over appropriation of the Tauric peninsula, your best alternative will be to increase destabilising territorial incursions.*

A question of great minds. But don't imagine we're neglecting the heartland. We have a number of recipes for eroding the Nevskian economy ranging from twisting the Central Bank's arm over continued purchases of our paper to obliging the Nevskian Defence Ministry to engage in heightened spending in answer to the stationing of our people's helicopters, tanks and heavy artillery on the League's doorstep.

As for the Tauric peninsula, our political pundits are keeping that card close to their chest.

Arnold Palmer lost no time in cornering Brinkman in his cubicle.

'Greg, I need to know more about that document you were given by your girlfriend. Where did she get it from?'

The intern, who had dutifully unplugged himself from Vivaldi, dog-eared a page in the thick ring-binder manual he was ploughing through with less than enthusiasm.

'I thought I told you. From one of her inmates. Somebody called Valery or Virginia. I can't remember for sure.'

'Are you screwing her again tonight?'

'No, I'm not,' said Greg Brinkman, resentful of his mentor's crude, intrusive familiarity.

An unruffled Palmer continued along the same reckless path. 'Well, for Chrissake, why not?'

'It's her Luritanian class night followed by aerobics.'

'Learning that monkey language? Hasn't she got better things to do?'

Tempted to take issue with this blatant piece of xenophobia issuing from the mouth of the embassy's cultural attaché, Brinkman finally decided to let things ride. 'What's up, Arnold? Why the hurry?'

'Why the hurry?' Palmer used the little space available to him in the cubicle to stalk his thoughts. 'The hurry is because that text I sent across to our people has hit a raw nerve. We need to find out lickety-split what the hell that document is doing in a blind people's home down the road from us.'

'Right away?'

'You heard me. Get on the phone to your broad and ask her the name of the woman who asked her to convert that text to Braille. What sort of a person is she?'

'How would I know?'

'Your broad, you halfwit. Is she featherbrained?'

The dual insult implicit in the judgment that Greg's choice of girlfriends and the blind home's choice of PAs ran to emptyheaded bimbos was the tipping point for the intern. 'No, she damn well isn't. What's got into you, Arnold? You're like a cat on hot bricks.'

'What's got into me, Greg, is that my future's on the line. I need to get to the bottom of this. Now, not tomorrow.'

'Okay, give me a moment. I'll see if she's there. You want to listen in on the other phone?' Brinkman indicated a handset in the neighbouring. unmanned cubicle. 'If so, press the hash key.'

'As if I didn't know it. Fine. Go ahead.'

To both men's relief, Greg Brinkman got through to Maureen Prescott without undue delay.

'Maureen, Greg here. How are you?'

'Monday-morningish. And you?'

'Are you on your own there?'

'Yeah. Betsy, the manageress is showing a new resident and her family the ropes. Why?'

Greg threw a glance at Palmer, who motioned him to get on with it.

'It's about that document you gave me.'

'Really. Have you got anywhere with it?'

The intern rubbed an unlined forehead and flashed another look at his mentor, who mouthed a 'No'.

'I'm afraid not. Who did you say gave it to you?'

'I don't believe I did.'

'Yes, Val or Virginia.'

'Why do you need to know? Look, Greg, I'm not at liberty to divulge personal information about residents.'

Brinkman floundered. Only moments before Palmer bounded in on him he had been scoffing at the manual's entry to the effect that that the best intelligence gathering reflected on the gatherer's intelligence.

Alive to the intern's quandary, Palmer placed a hand over his mouthpiece. 'Tell her,' he said as softly as he could manage, 'that a cryptanalyst colleague is willing to help in his spare time, but he needs to know more about the background.'

Greg promptly relayed the essence of this to Maureen.

'You mean he'd like to stop by and talk to my resident about it?'

Hooking the handset under one armpit, Arnold Palmer registered his approval with two emphatic, shoulder-high thumbs.

Upset that Maureen's idea had not occurred to him first, Greg was on the point of conveying Palmer's agreement, when he saw his mentor stabbing at his watch.

'He has a free moment now, if that would suit your resident.'

'Wait a minute, Greg. I need to go out into the hallway to check on the activities board. This might not be the best of times, if she has a tai chi class.'

'I apologise about the feather brains,' said Arnold, who had tuned back in to the two-way conversation. But before he could continue, his cell phone rang. Snatching the device from his pocket, he took a quick look at the caller's number and switched to vibrate. 'Tai chi can't last all fucking morning, can it?'

Fortunately for Palmer, who had raised his voice, Maureen returned to the phone at the tail end of the cultural attaché's exasperation.

'Someone else there with you, Greg?'

'Yeah, the person I was talking about.'

'Well, tell him he's in luck. She has nothing on until eleven thirty. If he comes within the next half hour, he'll find her reading.'

'Great.'

'He'll have to check in with reception like everyone else. What's his name?'

'Palmer. Arnold Palmer.'

Throwing both hands up to his face in disbelief, Palmer came close to throttling his intern.

'Well, tell Mr Palmer to ask for me when he checks in. In the meantime, so as not to spring a surprise on her, I'll let my resident know she's got a visitor.'

'My resident,' said Palmer mocking Maureen's voice, the moment the PA had rung off. 'Not one to give much away, is she, your wily little bird? But as for you, Master Greg, take the featherbrained dunce's cap and go stand in the corner. Why, by all that's holy, did you tell her my name?'

'Why not, for goodness sake? What happens if you bump into her somewhere? You're the one who keeps telling me Schönschlucht's so boxy the moment you swing a cat in it you hit someone you know.'

'This Arnold Palmer happens to be a cultural attaché not a fucking cryptanalyst.'

For once, Greg Brinkman felt sufficiently undaunted to hit back. 'Reinvent yourself, Arnold. Chapter Five, Section Two of the *American Intelligence Officers' Handbook*.'

⁂

Arnold Palmer had not expected to find the iinterior of Schönschlucht's *Maison des Aveugles* decorated in a variety of tasteful pastel colours. Unable to believe that this could brighten the day-to-day existence of the home's residents, Palmer concluded that the aim was to raise staff spirits. If he was correct on the second count, he was wide of the mark on the first: many of the partially sighted inmates confessed to feeling at ease with the warm colour schemes. Furthermore, the home numbered two married couples among its residents, the husband of each of which was partially sighted.

Shortly after Palmer signed in as James Rawlings Jr, Maureen Prescott came out to greet him from her side office behind the reception desk. Arnold reflected that not only did the home's designers deserve congratulating on their choice of decorators but Greg Brinkman had found himself a real gem in this woman, who addressed him with the same fetchingly Scottish-accented English he had heard over the embassy's phone.

'I'm afraid, Miss Prescott, that Arnold Palmer had to cry off at the last moment because of some fuss up at the airport.'

'Really? Will we be reading about in tomorrow's *Bote*?'

'An unruly American bundled off his flight to Amsterdam after harassing the stewardesses because of sitting too long on the taxiway without a drink.'

Given Miss Prescott's free and easy approach to diplomacy, Arnold made a note to follow up putting Greg in the picture about the fictional toper with a forceful reminder of what the rulebook had to say about interns keeping their mouth shut.

'Would that be the responsibility of an intelligence officer?'

'Whatever gave you that idea?'

'Oh, I don't know.' Maureen gave her mosquito bite a vexed rub. 'I understood that Mr Palmer was a decoding expert.'

'Our work isn't as cut and dried as that, Miss Prescott. Each of us is called upon from time to time to cope with all manner of problems involving our citizens.'

'All the same, embarrassing that this pest happened to be American.'

'Well, Irish-Americans tend to be in a class of their own.'

'Yes, I suppose that's it. Irish-American, Polish-American. The passport says one thing, your gene pool another.'

With the visitor's register open on the counter in front of her, Maureen cast a look at the latest entry. Aware of, but untroubled by, the fact that she had started off on the wrong foot, she decided not to question the preposterous Junior suffix. 'Mr James Rawlings?'

'That's it. Legal attaché.'

'Shouldn't you rather be at the airport?'

'No, Palmer is standing in for the consular attaché on sick leave. Don't worry, I'm fully briefed on the problem, and … Who is it I'll be meeting with?'

'Miss Bogen. Miss Clara Bogen.'

'Well Miss Bogen has nothing to fear from me. I'd just like to ask her a few simple questions. If she knows the answers, all the better. If not, *tant pis,* as they say.'

'But just a minute, Mr Rawlings,' said Maureen, her face turning red. 'I understood that the person sent by your embassy was to help Miss Bogen understand what her document was all about. Now you tell me you've come to interrogate her.'

'Interrogate? I intend doing nothing of the sort. If anything, I hope to set Miss Bogen's mind at rest. It's clear that she is innocent of any wrongdoing.'

'I should hope so,' said Maureen with a brief, controlled glare. 'That's the first I've heard of any mention of wrongdoing.'

Tripped over by his own clumsiness, Palmer fudged. 'I'm sure there's no such problem. However, Miss Bogen might think that if officialdom is interested in her document, it's because somebody feels she has something to hide.'

'I see.'

Maureen Prescott might as well have prefaced her rejoinder with 'I once was blind but now' for all the discomfort it caused Arnold Palmer, who felt the back of his neck prickling.

'Well, Mr Rawlings, let me take you straight up to Miss Bogen's room. It's hectic here this morning. We had a fire in the kitchen last night, and the safety inspectors have descended on us. On top of which the manager needs me to get out the agenda for next month's board of trustees meeting.'

'Of course, I perfectly understand. It was good of you to fit me in at such short notice. Is there anything special I should know about Miss Bogen?'

'I don't think so. Oh, yes, her German shepherd, Bismarck, is naturally wary of strangers. Don't go patting him on the head, unless he licks your hand.'

'I meant more how should I …?' At a loss for words, Palmer faltered. '… I've never had to deal with the blind.'

Maureen Prescott stopped in mid-stride. 'They're human not extra-terrestrials, Mr Rawlings,' she said, swivelling to face him, while annoyed at having struck a patronising note brought on by dislike of the man rather than of his preconceptions. 'Behave as you would with any normal adult.'

Palmer's cheeks flushed. He was not used to being made to feel small by a woman with a tongue to match her figure. 'Of course, of course.' But repetition only jangled his nerves.

Sensing that she had touched a sore spot, Maureen relented. 'I'm sorry. What's important is not to talk down to the visually impaired. Treat them as equals.'

Squaring her shoulders, Maureen Prescott led the way up the stairs to the first floor. As they walked down the wide, freshly hoovered corridor with rooms on either side, Arnold caught the sound of someone practicing on the violin. Maureen stopped at the fourth door on their left on the side of the building overlooking the garden. After knocking, she preceded Palmer into the room.

Arnold wondered if this helped reassure the German shepherd dog lying on a mat in one corner: the animal seemed to react to him with placid indifference.

The man who had reinvented himself in line with his intern's recommendation was impressed by the room's size and arrangement. Spaciousness made it possible to accommodate a quilted single bed, a workstation complete, to his mind incongruously, with laptop, a dressing-table, writing desk (equally anomalous), two easy chairs and one brown leather armchair in which sat the woman likely to prove either his salvation or damnation in the eyes of Lester Kayser.

Maureen Prescott did the introductions, though without explaining that the man called Rawlings was a legal attaché not a codebreaker. That, she thought, was better left to him.

Clara Bogen interrupted her reading of a Braille novel to stand up and welcome her visitor, Bismarck's large brown eyes following her every move. Arnold Palmer shook her warmly by the hand. He felt unusually nervous at meeting what he imagined to be this blind brunette's dead-eyed gaze. In the event, Clara Bogen kept her eyelids lowered for the most part throughout the encounter.

'Well,' said Maureen,' I have to get back to a hot stove. Can I order you both something to drink – lemonade, tea, coffee? Clara? Mr Rawlings?'

'Jasmine tea, please, Maureen,' said Clara, motioning her guest to take a chair while she resumed her seat.

'Lemonade would be fine for me,' added Arnold, gathering from Miss Bogen's tone of voice that all was not well between her and the secretary.

'Right,' said Maureen, turning to go. 'I'll have them sent up to you.'

Left to himself with Miss Bogen, a no longer young woman but one who retained something of the classical beauty personified by those film stars whose names he could not recall from Hollywood's silent movie days, Palmer began to feel surer of his surroundings. It helped that Bismarck prioritised scratching his ear

'I appreciate your giving up your time to me, Miss Bogen.' Despite being eager to get things over with, Arnold had more sense than to dive in head first.

'Yes, a precious commodity time, spent before we realise it. But you're not squandering my time, Mr Rawlings, though I must tell you that I am cross with Maureen for letting my private text fall into someone else's hands.'

Well, thought Arnold, no need to test the waters. Miss Bogen was nothing if not direct. 'I suspect she acted with the best of intentions.'

'Without consulting me first. Anyway, what's done is done. I understand you're a cryptanalyst with the American embassy. Does that mean to say you've succeeded in making sense out of nonsense?'

If there was any question that Arnold Palmer had come prepared for, it was this, though he preferred to delay disabusing the woman about his professional skills. 'No, I'm sorry to say we haven't. But your text does contain a number of characteristics indicating that it is more sophisticated than a run-of-the-mill substitution code. Might I ask you how you came by it?'

'It's been in my possession for years. I'd completely forgotten about it until I started turning out some cardboard boxes the other day full of old papers and photographs.'

'I see.' Confronted by Miss Bogen's first outright lie, Palmer wondered how many were to follow. 'But where, as far as you can recall, did it come from in the first place?'

No sooner were these words out than, and this did not escape Arnold's notice, the German shepherd dog pricked up his ears and began viewing his mistress's visitor with less than friendly eyes.

'I honestly can't remember.'

'Have you many written possessions not in Braille?'

'Very few.' Her distrust of Rawlings did not incline Clara, partially sighted from birth, to frankness. 'I began losing my sight at the age of eight.'

'What would you say, if I were to tell you that your text was probably composed within the last three years?'

'How could you know that if you haven't made sense of it?'

'Certain patterns, Miss Bogen. Certain patterns associated with modern cryptography.'

Clara's expression tautened. 'Are you are accusing me of lying?'

Palmer was disheartened to see the canine rising slowly to his feet and pawing the floor. A low growl, so low as to be barely audible, issued from the depths of the dog's throat.

The bogus legal attaché with a mission threatening to go up in smoke, adopted his most soothing tone. 'The idea never crossed my mind. Mistaken perhaps. We all forget things. Look, is it possible that you might have confused this text with something else? Could a relative or close friend have sent or given it to you since you entered this home?'

'Why would a relative or close friend send me a document I couldn't read?'

'Yes, there you have me.' Palmer paused, weighing his next words. 'Could they have given it to you temporarily? Used you as a safety deposit box, so to speak.'

'No, definitely not,' retorted Clara Bogen whose intuition told her that her visitor was not a man to be trusted. 'I would certainly remember something as obvious as that. Now, I think, Mr Rawlings, if you will excuse me, that I would rather you left me in peace. Frankly, I object to your insinuations.'

'I'm not insinuating anything, Miss Bogen. I came here wanting to help you get to the bottom of this mystery. Perhaps if you care to think harder about this, eventually something will trigger a memory.'

By now, the dog was definitely staring Arnold Palmer out. It took a knock at the door and the appearance of an aproned Filipino woman holding a tray with Clara and Arnold's drink orders to calm the creature down.

'That's good of you, Marisol, but Mr Rawlings is about to leave. He's welcome to take his drink with him. You can leave my tea here.'

There was little that Palmer could do in such a situation other than to accept that he had met his match. 'I apologise once again for taking up your time,' he said, withdrawing with a reverential bow, which, he reflected, was probably wasted on a blind person. He was wrong. Clara Bogen's sense of motion-associated hearing was particularly acute.

Much to his alarm, Palmer found Bismarck trotting close on his heels, until Clara called him back from halfway along the corridor.

On his way back to the front desk, his thoughts racing, Arnold Palmer decided to chance his luck with a closer look at the home's visitors' register. Fortunate to find the receptionist nowhere in sight, he rapidly checked through recent entries. Next to the columns recording each visitor's name, date and respective arrival and departure times stood a column showing the resident visited. There was no need for Palmer to write down the names of Clara Bogen's visitors over the past three weeks. Clearly the more frequent visitor, for reasons that escaped him, was Vanessa Curtis. But the other visitor, perhaps of more interest than the *Camino Real* director, because of his having paid Miss Bogen just one visit, was Craig Roberts. On the other hand, thought Palmer as, after signing out, he walked down the colonnaded veranda of *La Maison des Aveugles* into the bright July sunshine, it would be unwise to jump to conclusions. Even if Vanessa Curtis was no longer sharing beds with the troublesome man from La Mancha, who better placed than she to be Miss Bogen's text donor – though why? To his mind, that made Craig the wild card, and wild cards could be as troublesome as they were unpredictable.

Moments later, his mind clouded over with the realisation that if Maureen Prescott mentioned the name Arnold Palmer to Clara Bogen and word of this got back to Vanessa, as it surely would, the game would be up. Greg Brinkman had done him a gross disservice.

※

Memo from J to K

It serves our ends to malign the Wayfarer as much within as outside his League. The naïve might consider this policy self-defeating. On the contrary, as long as the Nevskians' top dog is fulfilling our objectives we should give to believe that he is everybody's sworn enemy. Particularly after he has played into our hands by: leaving his country's health service in tatters; closing scientific research laboratories; driving smaller businesses to the wall; permitting his cronies to make money out of anything from prohibitive transport infrastructure taxes to exports of timber better processed domestically. The list goes on – to our great satisfaction. In short, let us continue to vilify an unwitting ally.

Response from K

You may have cause for rejoicing on that front, but on another I see only cause for tears. Millions of Vespuccian dollars evaporated the other day when panicking Urodinian fighters turned tail and abandoned three of our mobile, state-of-the-art, anti-artillery tracking systems, which, despite our best training efforts, they were incapable of mastering. It pains me to think what a gift these pieces were. Each had a range of forty miles designed to lock onto and identify the calibre of thirty enemy artillery pieces simultaneously within eight seconds. In short, J, whatever possessed us to waste sophisticated technology on hicks?

Response from J

And, I'm afraid, there's more bad news, K. Only minutes after four international monitoring operatives vacated an army barracks, a secondary school and a hospital where they had planted target designators in rebel-held eastern Urodina, Veki arillery started bombarding all three positions. The advertisement could not have been clearer to the insurgents, who detained the four concerned before releasing them on the understanding that they were never to show their faces again in monitoring missions inside the conflict zone. Fortunately, this episode was accorded limited coverage by the media, the best part of which is paid to know when to keep its press, television and digital mouths shut.

※

Whether he liked it or not, Palmer was obliged to invite the ambassador to join him in the bunker for the follow-up video conference with Lester Kayser. Arnold had been warned that staff who failed to play up to the great man invariably rued their hubris. Dexter Nussbaum liked to think he had a finger in every pie. But if massaging his ego was part of the game, it had to be done subtly. On no account,

356

Arnold had been told, let the ambassador sense that he was being taken for a ride.

However, on this occasion, there was no need for discreet brown-nosing. After digesting the negative feedback from his underling's trip to the blind home, Nussbaum was, to Arnold's chagrin, relishing the proposed video conference with the 'you-rather-than-me' satisfaction of a guinea pig sensing a fellow creature's imminent vivisection.

When Lester Kayser's image came up over the video link with Virginia, it seemed to Palmer as if the hard-nosed executive had not budged an inch since their last talk, looking, as he did, as if chiselled out of stone. Such that when the two-dimensional image moved its lips, the cultural attaché had to pinch himself awake.

'Well, what's the news, Palmer?'

'The text reached the blind home's secretary through an inmate, a woman called Clara Bogen. I questioned Miss Bogen but got nowhere with her. She was covering up for someone. Of that I'm sure. I checked up on her recent visitors. Only two. One is a friend of a journalist guy. He created a stir last week with some souped up end-of-days scare in a local rag popular with English speakers. The other certainly knows the first and the editor, because all three of them are involved in an amateur theatrical production.'

'Would that production happen to include a Mr Rashid Jabour?'

'Yes, it would,' said Arnold, baffled as to how Kayser could have known or guessed this.

'Well, let me fill you in on a bit of background. We had a man-to-man with Jabour out in Beirut, as a result of which he undertook to see that not a shred of that text you mailed me ever saw the light of day. Either Mr Jabour is not a man of his word or the text was leaked before he could sit on it. That leaves us with a bitch of a headache. So let me lay it on the line for you, Palmer. Jabour you can leave to me. But Hendry, that fucking mouthpiece of the free press, who I'm damn sure passed our text on to Jabour, and the two other people you referred to have just become your business. *Capisce?*'

'Yes, sir.'

'Who are they? Names.'

Momentarily unnerved by Kayser's concept of 'business', Palmer lost his customary volubility. 'Craig Roberts and ...'

'And? I'm waiting.'

'A Miss Vanessa Curtis.'

'Friend of yours?'

'No.'

'Well, you damn took your time making up your mind about that one, sonny Jim.'

'You want me to question all three, sir?'

'Question them, young man? Yes, by all means. And after you've finished that pissing in the wind, find a way to spike their guns. By which I mean don't even think of trying to copy those imbeciles, Chamberlain and Stenning.'

Arnold Palmer's face fell.

'What's the matter, Palmer? Cat got your tongue? I guarantee you that trio is not acting alone. However many heads there are to this Hydra you've bred in your back yard, you'd better damn lop them off one by one.'

Ambassador Nussbaum, whose Christian name implied a skilfulness in effect foreign to him and who suddenly wondered whether he not Palmer might become the corpse in Rembrandt's *The Anatomy Lesson of Dr Nicolaes Tulp*, reached out a steadying hand on the table in front of him.

'That kind of talk won't wash over here, Lester. This isn't bongo bongo land.'

'Calm down, Dexter, I was speaking figuratively. My people invested a good year of their time and a bunch of dollars in priming Palmer for situations like this. He knows how to handle things, don't you, Palmer? Nothing ham-fisted. The keyword here is demoralise.'

Now that Kayser was putting Nussbaum in his place and lauding the intel officer, Palmer felt a surge of relief. For although Kayser had resuscitated two ghosts, he had done so with no hint of suspicion on his part as to Arnold's involvement in their removal from the scene. Consequently, employing velvet-gloved tradecraft to sealing Hendry and Roberts's lips should be child's play. Not that, taken on the hoof, Arnold was sure how to deal with Vanessa Curtis or Roberts's sexy girlfriend, Isabelle Meunier, particularly since he had yet to touch base with the girl's father. Perhaps if he impressed Kayser with his handling of the first two, he could sue for a helping hand. After all, he wasn't fucking Superman.

On the other hand, he had pulled the wool over Kayser's eyes with Chamberlain and Stenning, which went to show that granite face was not as hot as he cared to make out. And as for the ambassador, gut-scared about seeing his career besmirched inches from the finishing line, didn't he understand that Arnold had more sense than to foul his nest when to do so would be to foul his own?

'Leave it to me, sir,' he said, looking directly at the figure on the screen, a man who, he felt, knew how to reward work well done. But the next moment, this thought was jostled aside by a gnawing uncertainty. What if he had underestimated the ambassador? Could he trust Nussbaum to believe his version of events concerning the deaths of Stenning and Chamberlain? And should the prospect of scoring points rekindle doubts, what if the ambassador smelled a rat and dropped it straight in Kayser's lap? Who would the CIA man tend to believe? It came as a chilling realisation to someone only moments before brimming with confidence: Dexter Nussbaum would not think twice about stabbing his aide, Langley's flavour of the month or not, in the back.

⁂

'Curtis.'

'Vanessa?'

'Yes, is that you Clare?' Vanessa had never received a call from Clare in the

358

office before. In fact, she was not aware of having given her friend her work number. Then she remembered that her iPhone was on charge in her vehicle in the basement car park.

'I'm sorry to trouble you at work. It wasn't easy tracking you down. I rang the wrong premises. Your people have so many buildings. Anyway, the switchboard finally gave me your extension.'

'No problem, Clare.' Vanessa could tell from her friend's voice that all was not well. 'Is something wrong? I hope you haven't had a fall.'

'No, nothing like that. But, and I hate to have to tell you this, I've made a bad mistake. That confidential document you gave me…'

'Yes?'

'I should never have opened the envelope.'

'You opened it?' Vanessa could hardly have been more surprised. This was completely out of character with the lonely woman she had befriended and whom she thought she knew so well. But what right did Vanessa Curtis have to criticise, she who did not even begin to understand what it meant to live in Clara's world? How would she survive, if left to depend solely on her tactile and auditory senses? She recalled Clara's once telling her without the slightest pathos, 'The congenitally blind are like chrysalises that can never become the butterflies they long to be.'

'Yes.'

Despite Clara's all but palpable timorousness, Vanessa's was unable to prevent the fount of sympathy from running dry.

'Buy why?'

'No justifiable reason. I'd had a bad morning with everything seeming to go wrong. Oh, I don't know, Vanessa. Can't you forgive me?'

You insensitive bitch, thought Vanessa, alive to having turned the knife in the wound. 'Of course I can. And I do. Is that all you're worried about, Clara? It's not as if the envelope contained anything of…' As if adrift on a sinking vessel, Vanessa faltered between 'importance' and 'value' before donning the worst possible life jacket, one with a leaking air chamber: '… interesting.'

'But that's just it,' said her friend. 'Somebody else thought it very interesting.'

'What do you mean?'

'It's a long story, Vanessa. I don't know whether I ought to tell you over the phone. Could you possibly pop round tonight?'

'I'm afraid I've got rehearsals this evening, Clare. Can't it wait?' A stupid question, thought Vanessa, if Clara's shaky voice was anything to go by. And then a connection was made somewhere in the back of her brain that refused to allow Vanessa to let matters rest. 'Clare, who was this somebody else? Can you tell me that over the phone?'

'I asked Maureen to convert your document into Braille, and it came out as … well, just a string of meaningless letters.'

'I'm sure it did.'

'You know then?'

'Know what?'

'That it's coded and of interest to the Americans?'

'You've lost me, Clare. Wherever did you get that idea from?'

'Maureen took it into her head to show a copy to her current boyfriend, an intern at the American embassy. And then an attaché turned up at the home to ask me where I got the document from. An objectionable man called James Rawlings. Bismarck didn't take to him at all. I was uncooperative. Told him next to nothing. Never mentioned your name. But I was foolish. I made out I'd had the document for years. Tucked away at the bottom of a shoe box. He said that was impossible. According to the embassy's experts, it had been composed within the last three years.'

'So how did all this finish with your Mr Rawlings? Did you send him packing?'

'More or less. But Maureen told me he wasn't the official who her friend had said might help throw light on the text. That was a fellow called Palmer. Rawlings said he had been dragged away on consular business. Some fuss up at the airport over an aggressive passenger holding up a flight.'

When the name Palmer coincided with a knock on her office door, Vanessa could scarcely have been more unequivocal in signalling 'not now' to a colleague poised on the threshold. 'Are you sure about that, Clare?' she asked, her mind making no sense of what she had just heard.

'Yes, he held up a KLM flight, I understand, to Amsterdam.'

'No, no, I mean about the name Palmer?'

'That was the name Maureen gave me originally. Why?'

'I know the man.'

'I hope he's more agreeable than James Rawlings.'

When Vanessa failed to respond, Clare's voice sounded back over the phone with renewed consternation. 'I truly hope I haven't got you into any trouble, Vanessa.'

'No, of course not. You didn't mention my name. If either Rawlings or Palmer comes poking his nose into your business any more, insist you've nothing more to tell them.'

'Well, I hope I won't have to.'

'Don't fret, Clare. If the embassy pressures you again, let me know, and I'll do something about it. After all, it was my fault for getting you into this.'

'Nonsense, I should never have …'

'We all make mistakes. I'm only sorry that this Rawlings fellow pestered you.'

'He had one of those nice Texan drawls. That is until he started being obnoxious.'

'Really?' For Vanessa this last piece of information nailed the lid on the coffin. 'Well, try to put him and this out of your mind. Perhaps I'll have a word with Mr Palmer. But not a word to him from you about me. Let me be the one to deal with this.'

'Of course, Vanessa.'

'Are we all right for this Wednesday's swim?

'Yes. I really need it.'

'Till Wednesday then. And, please, no more fretting. There's nothing for you to worry about. Leave me to clear up the whole misunderstanding.'

The call finished, Vanessa reached for her telephone directory and thumbed through the pages in search of the American embassy. After dialling the number and being put through a series of robotic language and information checks that meant pressing a succession of buttons until reaching someone actually sitting in front of the embassy's switchboard, she asked for James Rawlings and was put on hold.

'Legal Affairs,' said a helpful male voice.

'I'd like to speak to Mr Rawlings.'

'I'm afraid Mr Rawlings is away on business in Berlin. Perhaps I can help you.'

'Oh dear. I must just have missed him then. Did he fly out this afternoon?'

'Goodness, no. He's been attending a conference there since last Thursday.'

'I see. Well, thank you all the same, but I think my question can wait. When will Mr Rawlings be back?'

'Next Monday. Should I leave a message for him?'

'No, thank you. It's nothing that important.'

Vanessa took her time replacing the handset in its power slot. This called for another meeting of the Lenfindi Club, but yet again, damn it, without Justin. And had Rashid not rung her that morning only to say that he was about to leave on a further business trip to the Middle East? Tonight would have been the ideal time to get together after rehearsals, had everyone been present and she could rope in Tich. Now she would have to make do with two thirds of the membership.

⁂

By a quirk of synchronicity, at the same moment that Clara was put through to Vanessa, Georg Hoffarth picked up the phone in his office in Schönschlucht and dialled the number on London's South Bank given him by Bernard Faulkner.

'Yes,' answered the dry voice of a man sitting in the building overlooking the Thames which one design reviewer had slated as a botched compromise between a Mayan temple and an art deco factory.

Hoffarth ignored the crotchety tone behind the part questioning part condescending affirmative.

'Mr Clarence Swithinburn?'

'Who wants him?'

'This is a call from Luritania's police headquarters. I am Chief Inspector Georg Hoffarth charged with investigating recent murders on my patch. In the course of our enquiries, we ran up against a gentleman by the name of Bernard Faulkner. He claims to be in your employ.'

'He can claim that until the cows come home. We've never heard of him.'

'We', reflected Hoffarth, sounded injudicious compared to use of the first person singular pronoun.

'He gave me your business card.'

'Did he? Makes no difference, chief inspector, he's not one of ours.'

Despite recognising that Swithinburn was bound to disown all knowledge of

361

one of his field agents to a complete stranger, Georg Hoffarth was not prepared to leave it at that.

'I'm sure your people have any number of aliases and passports to protect them in the event of their falling into the wrong hands. Would it help if I were to describe the gentleman to you?'

'No.'

'Really?'

'Yes. Because we have nobody over there in Luritania at the moment. If we did, I'd be sure to know about it. My apologies, Inspector Hoffarth, but I think you've been had.'

Loath to be thought of as 'another of those gullible continentals', Georg Hoffarth refused to abandon the chase so quickly. 'If this fellow is an imposter, Mr Swithinburn, he's a polished one.'

'The best always are. Do you never have people wandering into your hospitals with all the accoutrements of a physician? You know the type I mean? They walk around wards taking patient's blood pressure and scratching nonsense on medical charts. The more ambitious set themselves up as certified GPs, doing untold damage before anyone latches on to them.'

'My man, who says he's your man, did not strike me as the type out to do untold damage. He seemed genuinely worried about the potential for damage on the part of other people.'

The inspector had to wait so long for any response from the other end that he began to wonder whether his listener had put the receiver down after being distracted by somebody closer to hand. But when Hoffarth, thinking that Swithinburn had ended the call with his SIS magic wand, was about to resign himself to calling it a day, the dry voice spoke up again.

'What fax number have you on that card?'

The inspector read the number out.

'Ask your man the name of the architect behind the design of the object on my wall overlooking the moat, and fax me his answer.'

After hanging up, Georg Hoffarth reflected that he was lucky not to have been treated as an imposter himself by the mandarin in Vauxhall. Until he acknowledged that someone with state-of-the-art intelligence technology at the tip of his fingers would have verified in no time at all that his caller was based in Schönschlucht's police HQ.

Something told the inspector that Bernard Faulkner was no imposter and that he knew the answer to Swithinburn's question.

❧

Memo from K to J

While our agents of influence are making good progress in stoking the fires of resurgent nationalism in the enemy's back yard, my people are elated to see IS and the Ottomans

siding with Veki against the League. Mind you, we would be the last to admit that
the Ottomans are adding lard to the caliphate's pork barrel by purchasing contraband
oil at knockdown prices.

Response from J

K, I don't think Muslims eat pork. And, as I understand it, certain elements of the
Vespuccian military are snapping up artefacts plundered by Islamic zealots in Syria.
You should keep a lid on that, seeing as how artefacts pay every bit as well as oil.

Response from K

Of course, if you were correct, something better not advertised. On the other hand,
think how O. Danger must squirm every time the media accuse his government of
subsidising the caliphate's war machine.

Given that Jean-Luc Meunier's view of the *entente cordiale* was as much of a dead
letter as Neville Chamberlain's piece of paper from Munich, it would be correct
to say that he knew on which side his *tartine* was buttered, and that was the dollar
side. For if the British Foreign Office gave the impression of watching every
penny, the U.S. Department of State's expense account boys were anything but
bean counters. It followed that, irrespective of the fact that the French diplomat's
information officer had borne out Jean-Luc's own memory of the American
embassy's latest cultural attaché with the succinct verdict, *c'est une ordure* (he's a
turd), France's *conseiller des affaires étrangères* knew that it could not be long before
Arnold Palmer gave him a call recommending a get-together to discuss business
of mutual interest.

'Here we are,' said Jean-Luc over a cell phone whose number his embassy
communicated to each new intel recruit, 'moving in the same circles and working
within spitting distance of one another, and we have rubbed shoulders only once.
And briefly at that.'

'Let's remedy that now,' replied Arnold. 'Are you booked up this afternoon or
can you make time for me?'

'I am hard put to remember, Arnold, when affairs of state weighed less heavily
upon me. Indeed, I have taken to counting the days until they ship me out of this
dead-end existence to somewhere with character.'

'Not the Middle East, I trust. That is one corner of the world overdosing on
character at the moment.'

'Exactly. I was thinking more of Martinique or Réunion.'

'Pending that happy day, would a reunion at three p.m. suit you?'

'It would. My diary is as empty as a whore's cleft on a day without customers.'

It was true that he U.S. embassy's new cultural attaché had been slow to take up the baton from a predecessor tasked with promoting his country's interests with a diplomat whose extra-marital liaisons required regular financial lubrication. But Arnold Palmer's hands had been tied by slightly more pressing matters than renewing collaborative links with France's *conseiller des affaires étrangères*, not to mention the fact that, as Dexter Nussbaum put it, 'When it comes to trustworthiness, nine out of ten French diplomats leave our Tour de France winner in the shade'.

Now that Arnold Palmer and Jean-Luc Meunier were actually sitting face to face over a tray of *coconut macaroons*, *cinnamon palmiers* and *financiers* (whose by no means adventitious presence the two men appreciated differently), the American with an espresso, his host with a *caffè macchiato*, Jean-Luc recalled their first meeting in Schönschlucht at the cocktail party thrown by the newly arrived Italian ambassadress to Luritania.

'What a happy occasion. A woman of supreme intelligence endowed with intoxicating sexual magnetism. For once, I thought that Luritania was perhaps no longer a *bled* (dump) but a *paradis terrestre* (earthly paradise) – until I was introduced to her young husband, a textile magnate with a yacht off Antibes and a villa outside Biarritz.'

Aware that three of the diplomat's lunch hours each week were a succession of amorous escapades, Arnold gave a slightly too knowing smile over the first half of his *palmier*. Were all Frenchmen cast in the same mould, he wondered, or did they feel obliged to simulate their largely undeserved reputation of perpetual philanderers?

'Still, you haven't come here to waste the afternoon in idle chatter, have you, *mon ami*?'

If Jean-Luc reflected that it called for a certain flair not to choke on one's own hypocrisy, Arnold, for his part, could not help thinking that, despite the other man's undoubted charm, the *mon ami* bit was a trifle premature to describe a relationship which had barely got off the ground. He could only imagine that Jean-Luc took it for granted that the hand which fed his expensive tastes remained bountiful irrespective of its owner.

'No, Jean-Luc, there has been an unfortunate intelligence leak.'

'Here of all places?'

'Of all places.'

'Unbelievable.'

Jean-Luc bit into a macaroon known as a *congolais* but which he invariably referred to as a *congolaise*. 'And how may I be of assistance?'

'I don't know whether your daughter has mentioned it, but she and I are taking part in the same amateur theatrical production.'

'No, that is news to me.'

If Palmer's pride was hurt, it was purely momentarily. The American had been disappointed but not surprised to see that young Isabelle Meunier should have fallen for Craig Roberts. 'You are most fortunate in having such a bright and attractive daughter. Hardly surprising that she and the talented director, Vanessa Curtis, should have become good friends.'

Unsure as to where Palmer was leading him, Jean-Luc drew sustenance from his *macchiato.*

'Vanessa Curtis,' Arnold continued, 'is also good friends with two characters key to my information leak. One, Justin Hendry, is, I am sure, already known to you. The other, Rashid Jabour, is a Lebanese banker with MEDRIMCOMB. I have every reason to believe that, by virtue of her proximity to these two men, Miss Curtis has become party to classified information. No, please don't ask me how we came by this intel. That's an entirely different and, as far as you and I are concerned, irrelevant ball game.'

Jean-Luc sensed where Palmer was heading. 'You want to use Isabelle to infiltrate … what a ghastly word … to eavesdrop on this group and feed what she learns back to me?'

'To be perfectly honest, no, Jean-Luc. I doubt she would agree. It's more likely that she would warn them off.'

'Then what?' asked the diplomat, beginning to feel that the sole coinage he was going to get his teeth into as a result of this conversation lay on the plate in the tray in front of him.

But at this moment the two men were obliged to interrupt their conversation as Lucie Picquet knocked on the door with correspondence for Jean-Luc's signature.

'Monsieur Meunier, the consul wants to see you about this letter before it goes off,' said Lucie, not unaware of the sudden shift of the visitor's appetite in her direction.

Jean-Luc took the letters across to his desk, signed the first four, handed them back to Lucie and, puzzled as to what could have caught the consul's attention with the fifth, armed himself with his reading glasses.

'What, now?'

'He said it should only take a moment.'

'Very good. Sorry about this, Monsieur Palmer. I'll be back in a minute.'

Time declining to vindicate either the consul's idea of a moment or Jean-Luc's of a minute, it was at least eight minutes later that the *conseiller* returned to join his visitor.

'A fuss about nothing,' he said. 'Sorry to keep you waiting.'

'No problem. Business first.'

'Speaking of business, where were we?' The question could not have been more redundant: Jean-Luc Meunier's recall of where they had left off was perfect.

As was Arnold Palmer's. 'How often do you see Isabelle?'

'She pays us a visit once a week. I know her mother's upset about her appearing onstage in the nearest thing to her birthday suit. I'm not enamoured of the idea either. Is your director out to shock the RCs in the audience taking photos on their cell phones?'

'Photography isn't permitted, and it won't be onstage, Jean-Luc. The play's being performed in the open air. In the courtyard of the Château de l'Aubaine.'

'Ah, yes, I seem to remember her telling me. Then her mother will worry that she'll catch a chill and contract pneumonia.' The *conseiller* cast a pensive look at the space on the desk cleared of the framed photograph taken in Afghanistan. 'Very well, now that we've dispensed with decency and health concerns, perhaps you could get to the point.'

'Has your daughter said anything to you about the discovery of a coded document?'

'I'm sorry for your sake, but no.'

'Has she given any indication of something on her mind she's reluctant to broach with you?'

'Frequently. Our political views have as much in common as the platforms of Marine Le Pen and Nicolas Sarkozy.'

'So if you were to broach a matter like this with her, you would get nowhere?'

'I could try,' said Jean-Luc with minimal deliberation, for he had no intention of implicating his daughter in Palmer's dirty business.

'When is she due to see you and your wife next?'

'On Wednesday.'

'I can't afford to wait that long. Can you not dream up an excuse for a meeting?'

'In the course of which, however delicately I go about things, I make it patently obvious that I'm prying on her and her friends?'

Arnold Palmer finished his espresso. 'I see your point.'

The subtext was unmistakable. Jean-Luc Meunier would continue to receive his monthly retainer, but there would be no top-up for zero feedback from the present intelligence request. The *conseiller* reached for the consolation prize of a financier.

In chewing on his first mouthful, he mulled over the thought that had occurred to him earlier. What if, as seemed likely, the classified intel of interest to Palmer was the same as that mentioned by J? That would put them at loggerheads, in which case Jean-Luc Meunier needed to decide where his loyalties lay.

As to his immediate loyalty to family, of that there could be no doubt. In other words, Jean-Luc would have to find a way of raising the contentious issue with his daughter, if only to protect her from the kind of retribution of which people of Palmer's ilk were capable.

But first *Géai*. No sooner had America's cultural attaché taken his leave than Jean-Luc picked up his iPhone to text the man staying in *L'Ambassadeur* the briefest of messages: *Stars and Stripes onto your leak with lead man Palmer.*

Before faxing Bernard Faulkner's two-word answer to Clarence Swithinburn, Georg Hoffarth looked up Friedrich Eisenlohr in his home encyclopaedia. It told him that the MI6 team leader had a cuckoo clock on his wall overlooking one of the Vauxhall building's moats and that it probably needed rewinding once every eight days. Clarence, he concluded, had to be one of the old school unable to shake off the world of Nigel Balchin's *The Small Back Room* or of Orson Welles's *The*

Third Man. The latter in particular, seeing that it was under Vienna's Ferris wheel that Harry Lime pointed up the productive difference between, on the one hand, the Italians with their Borgias and the Renaissance and, on the other, the Swiss with five hundred years of democracy and peace.

Rex Jericho's reply had come with the added comment: *Standard practice: deny all knowledge of your own kind to foreign parties.*

The inspector received a faxed response from the man on the South Bank roughly one hour after sending across the name of the German architect who in 1850 had won a clock case design competition launched in the Black Forest. Although he had to smile at the wording, it was a message that partially restored his bruised faith in human nature: *The Foreign Office requests and requires you to allow its agent Bernard Faulkner to pass freely without let or hindrance and to afford him such assistance and protection as may be necessary.*

<hr>

Once the evening's play reading and limited rehearsals were done and dusted, with a view to privacy and her own convenience Vanessa invited Isabelle and Craig back to her apartment. The trio found Tich waiting on the landing outside her door.

'There's onion soup I can warm up with slices of spelt loaf, if anyone's feeling hungry,' said Vanessa after her guests had settled down, Craig and Isabelle on a large sofa that had seen better days, Tich in a capacious armchair.

All three accepted. 'Make mine two slices,' said Tich. 'And if there's any cayenne, bring it on.'

'Right, Tich. Well, you can help set the bowls and soup spoons out, while I deal with the rest.'

'You called this a Lenfindi Club meeting,' said Craig from his side of the living area giving onto Vanessa's kitchen range. 'But we're missing Justin and Rashid. What's so important that it can't wait until they're back?'

'Let me serve the soup first, then we can get down to the nitty-gritty.'

'A bad sign,' commented Tich, who was relieving Vanessa of the job of slicing her loaf. 'Nitty-gritty spells indigestion.'

Five minutes later, with the onion soup ladled out and all four present sitting in front of a warm bowl, a full bread basket and a pot of cayenne pepper on a low-slung glass-topped coffee table – the central dining table being too cluttered – Vanessa, looking drained rather than energised after the evening's testing rehearsals, launched into her explanation for calling the meeting.

'The prince of Denmark complained that enterprises of great pith and moment go awry if we pussyfoot with them. But sometimes they go awry because they should never have been embarked upon in the first place. And I'm beginning to think that holds true of our decision to publish and be damned.

'I went to Justin's apartment yesterday to see how his ferret, Pliny, was doing, and got a couple of nasty surprises. First, it looked as if I hadn't fastened the latch on Pliny's cage properly when I left him the time before. I am either going to have to reupholster Justin's settee or buy him a new one. But that wasn't the worst of my surprises. There was blood on the floor. A trail of it leading to the bathroom. And I could hear breathing in there.'

Craig put down his soup bowl. 'If I'd been in your shoes, I'd have hightailed it. But Vanessa being Vanessa …'

Isabelle opened and closed her mouth in inarticulate incomprehension.

Tich was the most pragmatic. 'You had your Browning with you?'

'In my purse. But after I set that aside to deal with Pliny, it escaped my memory. Anyway, look, no harm came to me.'

Tich cast his eyes towards Vanessa's zodiac frieze on the ceiling. 'Thank your lucky stars.'

'You enjoy keeping people on tenterhooks?' said Craig. 'What next?'

'I found this respectable-looking, middle-aged gent sitting on Justin's laundry basket next to the loo with one trouser leg rolled up, hugging a blood-soaked calf out of which Pliny had taken a bite.'

'Well?' said Isabelle with a teasing grin that belied her worst fears, as Vanessa paused to drink her soup.

'I'm getting to that. Told me he was from MI6. Said his name was J, as in perhaps either Jay, the bird, or J the tenth letter of the alphabet – if you follow me. But you probably can't. Because it was also Chandler. Even Faulkner. In other words, no name at all. He must have broken into Justin's place by picking the lock. We didn't go into niceties. I helped dress his wound. Took him back into the living room, where he said that his people knew who had snaffled the Westminster MP's sensitive documents and that no one was happy about the thought of their going the rounds in Luritania, let alone further afield. They had to be irrevocably destroyed.'

Unable to hold back any longer, Isabelle pushed her soup bowl to one side. 'Vanessa, before you say any more, I have a confession to make. Concerned about Justin's well-being, I went to the police and suggested they keep an eye on his apartment and workplace. What you've just told us means that I was right but that they took no notice of me.'

'On the contrary. This was all caught on camera. Installed by the police. Their Chief Inspector Hoffarth paid me a call at the office. Wanted to know the full story. I told him what I knew.'

'Then things are looking up,' said Craig. 'It means the police will have put a tail on and probably cornered your man.'

Preferring to look at things from a different angle, Isabelle raised the same question that had been troubling Vanessa.

'What I fail to understand is what's bugging MI6? Their sensitive information is out in the open, and here they are getting into a flap about obliterating every last record of it. Unless …'

'Unless what?' Tich's stare suggested that he knew where Isabelle was heading.

Vanessa signalled understanding.

'Rashid was edgy when he returned from his last business trip to Beirut.

Clammed up on me when I asked if anything went wrong out there. Anyhow, that tense weekend coincided with his success in making sense of the second document. Remember what he told us about the rest of the text, the bigger part? That it wasn't worth wasting our time on a rambling report about the Afghan poppy harvest, which the encoders had interlarded with more controversial material?'

'Yes,' said Tich. 'You mean that perhaps Rashid was having you – us – on. Perhaps the bigger part was really juicy, and he decided that we'd all be better off if we knew nothing about it. So, thinking to save us from ourselves, he got out his censor's pencil.'

'Then again, perhaps there's more to the second document than meets the eye. Rashid mentioned that hummingbird logo in the second text. I don't think any of us paid much attention to the small print at the bottom of the last page: *Printed by Little Hermit Press.* There's no record of any such press that I can find. But the little hermit happens to be one of nature's smallest hummingbirds. In other words, Rashid was on the ball. An earlier idea of mine that MI6 feared we had discovered a secret department in their red briefcase was bunkum. It's more likely that the pixels composing our little hermit hold an eye-opener for those who know what they're looking for.'

'That would explain,' said Vanessa, 'why, it seems, MI6 will not rest happy until we destroy every hard copy and screen file in our possession.'

'And that's the other thing,' said Tich, spooning onion onto spelt bread. 'You bought his MI6 story?'

'What choice did I have?'

'Did he mention Klaus Radetzky?'

Vanessa went across to the kitchen area to fetch the tureen for those whose soup bowls looked in need of topping up. 'To be honest, Tich, I can't remember. Half the time we were sitting next to each other up close and cosy in Justin's living room my nerves were jangling with the thought that my respectable Jay might be Jekyll waiting to do a Hyde on me while my bag was out of reach. Because I didn't know what to believe. But the longer he kept talking the more I felt that there was more than a grain of truth to his warnings. As soon as Justin returns, he will tell him in no uncertain terms that unlawful possession of classified information is a criminal offence and that he risks imprisonment. I gather that, if we all cooperate, the F.O. won't turn this into a *cause célèbre'.*

Having discovered that her only taker for more soup was Tich, Vanessa returned the tureen to its place on the cooker and resumed her seat at the coffee table.

'That wasn't all, though. Mr Jay issued a blunt warning. MI6 is not the only party having kittens about our texts. There's someone else out there, and I hate to have to tell you this but we all know him. You see, I too have a confession to make.' Vanessa shook her head in a gesture of self-reproach. 'I felt that, if there was a genuine connection between Klaus Radetzky's death and our texts, perhaps our lives were also under threat. So I decided to make a hard copy of the full text of the second of Justin's documents taken by Rashid for decoding and to give this to someone for safekeeping. In the event that should anything happen to me, she

369

would twig the connection and alert the authorities. I chose my blind friend, Clara Bogen, but didn't tell her anything about the document. Just entrusted it to her in a sealed envelope. Unfortunately, inquisitiveness got the better of Clara. For all I know, she may even have sensed that I had something unhealthy to hide. Human nature has ways like that of compensating the bind.

'Anyway, she opened the envelope and had the contents converted to Braille. Of course, the Braille conversion only produced more claptrap. And that would probably have been the end of it, had not the secretary who carried out the Braille conversion made her own copy and passed this on to a boyfriend. A young man working in, of all places, the American embassy.

'The next day, she received a call from the embassy saying that their intelligence officers needed to know how she had come by the text. When the embassy learnt that the donor was a *Maison des Aveugles* resident, they pressed for an interview. A legal attaché, called James Rawlings, came knocking on the blind home's front door.

'And that's where things started to get nasty. Because Mr Rawlings explained that he was standing in for the intelligence officer called away on urgent embassy business. And that intelligence officer happened to be Arnold Palmer. After Clara rang to tell me about her interrogator, I phoned the American embassy. They informed me that Mr Rawlings was attending a conference in Berlin. Clara's description of the man posing as James Rawlings suggested that he was none other than Arnold. Since the interloper in Justin's apartment said we had every reason to fear the other party eager to get its hands on our texts, I needn't tell you what that means.'

'Wait a minute,' said Isabelle. "Did this Clara Bogen give Arnold your name?'

'No. I guess she was too frightened or guilt-ridden to do that.'

'So what have you or we to worry about?'

'Plenty,' said Tich. 'If Arnold's been given a mission, trust him to keep sniffing around until he roots something out.'

'In that case,' added Craig, 'we have the advantage over him. We have his number. He doesn't have ours.'

'For how long?' asked Vanessa.

Staring at the label on the pepper pot with its reminder of Devil's Island, Isabelle ventured a fragile note of optimism. 'Perhaps our best hope is for Vanessa's mystery man to get Justin to convince MI6 that we've followed their instructions to the letter.'

'All well and good,' said Tich, suppressing a rebellious bout of indigestion with a fist to his chest, 'but can we be sure that Mr Jay will keep to his word and not hit us with the full might of the Official Secrets Act? And if Arnold is in cahoots with the NSA, as I reckon he has to be, we're not out of the woods by a long stretch.'

'Unless,' said Craig, 'we convince Palmer he's wasting his time.'

Vanessa ceased nervously tapping her thigh to express unfeigned amazement. 'Craig, do you seriously think that somebody born to play Gutman will go along with that? And while we're at it, I think now would be a good time for each of us to say what we've done with our copies of Justin's documents. After hearing from Clara, I destroyed the paper versions of the binary text and its translation as well as Rashid's abridged version of the second document. The digital versions were stored by Rashid. How about the rest of you?'

'Scanned them onto the fitness centre's desktop,' said Craig. 'In a private folder, password-only accessible.'

'And the paper versions?'

'Sellotaped to the back of the inside of my locker.'

'For heaven's sake, why?'

'My idea of a joke. The side facing outwards – the blank side of Rashid's print-outs – carries the club's duplicated warning not to forget to lock your locker after leaving valuables in it.'

'Isabelle?'

'I didn't scan anything. As for the copies, they are in a safety deposit box in the bank where I work.'

Isabelle could not think why she had lied to Vanessa. Was it because she felt embarrassed by her choice of hiding place? Hardly. No, it was because she had already lied about the second document when persuading Vanessa to talk Rashid into making a full copy for her on the spurious grounds that it might help matters to sound out a cryptanalyst working in her father's embassy, an approachable person whom she had met at one of her parents' dinner parties. Spurious because Isabelle, who had never met any such person, nurtured the idea of showing the document one day to her father with a view to testing his reaction.

'Tich?'

'Lying as snug as pressed flowers between the pages of one of my *Tristram Shandy* tomes. Seems as if they belong to the belladonna and foxglove families.'

'So,' said Vanessa, 'nobody can accuse us of scattering them to the four winds.'

'Have you thought,' said Craig, 'of your friend Clara? Shouldn't you retrieve the original and get the secretary to delete her screen files, including the Braille versions?'

'We can forget the secretary, Craig. Her boyfriend will have beaten us to it. As for Clara, that's my responsibility. And if she's asked any further questions about provenance, I'll suggest she tell Arnold that she thinks she must have received the envelope in the post and stored it away absentmindedly.'

'Who oversees distribution of post to residents?'

'That would be the secretary, Maureen Prescott. PA to the manageress.'

'Too late to get her on our side?'

'I don't think so.' Vanessa turned to Tich. 'What's your advice, Tich? Where do you think we should go from here?'

'In the first place, wait until we're reunited with Justin and Rashid. In the meantime, do nothing to rock the boat. Did your Mr Jay tell you where he's staying?'

'*L'Ambassadeur* in town.'

'We need to contact him to find out what he knows about Arnold Palmer.'

'And if he's not and never has been staying at *L'Ambassadeur*?'

'Then we're in trouble.'

Memo from J to K

Are your people aware that a member of Urodina's parliament has set up a hate website listing the names and addresses of prominent domestic critics of Veki's war policy as well as of outspoken supporters of the rebels' cause? The lawyer and two journalists gunned down last week were on that list.

Response from K

I am more concerned about the fact that Veki's military is making money hand over fist out of selling our precious weaponry to Africa, which means it is augmenting IS's arsenal.

Isabelle Meunier tried to remember when her father had last invited her out for a relaxed one-on-one chat over lunch, and decided that it must have been a good year ago in this very restaurant on the banks of the Vaugruge. *La Toque blanche* served excellent poached turbot in a saffron cream sauce, which Jean-Luc was sorry to see his daughter washing down with *Genschen vert* mineral water as opposed to his choice of *Pinot Gris*. While appreciating the greater freedom she felt, in her mother's absence, to touch upon territory which Charlotte Meunier would have ruled off limits, Isabelle had only to observe her father's forced good humour to sense that he was the one likely sooner or later to step into alien territory.

For one heart-stopping moment she wondered whether the police had come up with evidence exonerating Eric Vandeweghe and incriminating a lowly *stagiaire* and her two helpers. Might Hoffarth have hesitated about making a direct arrest, before breaking the news to a prominent member of France's *corps diplomatique* that his daughter was suspected of masterminding Luritania's heist of the decade?

However, in the absence of any sign of bitterness, incredulity, disappointment or pent-up anger, she concluded that whatever was on her father's mind had nothing to do with the Mensdorf robbery.

Aware that diplomacy would never permit her father to approach sensitive matters head on, she sought distraction outside, where a barge was ploughing its way along the river. The owners had created a riot of colour at the vessel's houseboat end with an eye-catching display of geraniums and dahlias beneath a platform bearing a dinky Renault Twingo.

'The Americans never cease to amaze and amuse me in equal portions,' said Jean-Luc Meunier, breaking across his daughter's train of thought about a life of rootlessness. 'NASA's latest superb video posted on the Internet showed that, of all places on earth, Crimea boasts the best view of the night sky. This thirty-second clip closed with the words: "Crimea – it's Russia". By the time a NASA official cottoned on to the repercussions and had the clip withdrawn, it had been copied by hundreds of delighted partisans.'

Setting aside his knife, Jean-Claude used his fork to toy with some *gratin dauphinois* and sliced fennel. 'The trouble with the tribe the British call their transatlantic cousins,' he said at last, 'is that, like spoilt brats, they insist on having a finger in every pie. Yet more often than not it is pies of their own confection which give them the most indigestion.'

'You know my feelings about America and NATO, father. No need to preach to the converted.'

'Yes, Isabelle, but, you see, ever since 9/11 those arm's length cousins of the British have gone from one gradation of paranoia to the next, the NSA being a case in point.'

'One A short of NASA and hopelessly earthbound.'

'Not quite. Plenty of all-seeing space junk.'

'So they must know how that airliner was shot down over Ukraine?'

'I should think so.'

A puzzled Isabelle sensed that she was beginning to read the drift of her father's remarks.

Jean-Luc drew strength from his *Pinot Gris*. 'One of my contacts, an old acquaintance, paid me a visit yesterday. I gather his crowd was upset about *The Pulse* article. Not that they lost a dramatic amount of sleep over it. But, all the same, they seem to be sharpening their knives, because Hendry's reporting was come by illegally.'

Isabelle imitated mild surprise. 'More paranoia?'

Jean-Luc savoured a modest portion of turbot. 'Possibly, but, as he pointed out, it doesn't pay to cross today's transnational magnates.'

'Why are you telling me this?'

'Because Vanessa Curtis and you are friends. The British suspect her of playing the same game as Hendry.'

'What game might that be?'

'Baiting America. Look, Isabelle, I'm warning you not to get involved in any of this. Don't play with fire. The people Hendry and company are up against are vindictive. Not ones to forget a grudge.'

'In which case I should warn Vanessa.'

'Provided none of this rebounds on me.'

Vanessa impaled *gratin* and words with her fork. 'Your connections are too valuable.'

'There's no need to strike that tone.'

'I suppose it would be pointless to ask who your connections are in this affair?'

'Correct. Everything I've told you today is strictly between the two of us.' Eying what little was left in his glass, Jean-Luc wondered whether hemlock would have been more fitting than *Pinot Gris* by way of punishment for entertaining relations with foreign deities, one decidedly more pernicious than the other. The thought, dismissed as rapidly as it was conceived, was followed by a weary intake of breath. 'Isabelle, my dear, you should understand that I am concerned about your safety. Refuse to associate yourself with anything liable to upset Barack Hussein's not so merry men.'

Her appetite lost, Isabelle put down her knife and fork. She knew the answer to her next question before she put it. 'Why would your contact go to the trouble to tell you about this?'

'Because, because ...' Jean-Luc Meunier realised that whatever answer he gave could only be damning. 'He wanted me to persuade you to, as the Americans say, rat on Vanessa.'

'And has he relied on you before to rat for him?'

Failing to collect his thoughts in the haste to rectify his daughter's impression of him, Isabelle's father, who had confused himself in mixing Géai with Palmer, fell into a trap of his own making.

'The man has only been here a short time. He was barely known to me until yesterday.'

'Is that so?' she declared offhandedly, averting her gaze to the river which had long since borne away her carefree barge.

⁂

Memo from K to J

> *I have to admit that my gut still churns over about cover-up of that fire in Assedo's Trade Unions House two years ago. More than forty anti-government protesters died in that building, some beaten to death, others strangled by Urodina's pro-government fascists. And that's not counting the number of bodies carried outside the back door to be trucked away before the fire brigade and police arrived.*

Response from J

> *Yes, I saw the video images of people crying for help from the windows while the crowd below jeers at them. The way Vespuccia sided with the Veki leadership to sweep that crime under the carpet speaks volumes about its credibility as a moral force on the world stage.*

Response from K

> *Sad, but true.*

⁂

Recruiting Charlie Hathaway to Arnold Palmer's cause required no exceptional effort on the cultural attaché's part. Charlie was the high school student finally chosen by Vanessa, after much humming and hawing, to play the role of Kilroy, the all-American kid with a heart as big as the head of a baby, in her production of *Camino Real*. What Charlie lacked physically for the part in terms of cauliflower ears, a broken nose or stitched eyebrows, he more than made up for with his square-jawed good looks, thatch of blonde hair and shoulders broad enough to block the average receiver on an American football pitch. But the one essential characteristic that Charlie brought to the part in spades was ingenuousness. Hence, after Arnold quoted the Patriot Act at him, told Charlie that, whereas long before he was born America's bugbears were reds under the beds, nowadays his country's enemies were rats on prayer mats, and not all Arabic-speaking, Osama Bin Laden lookalikes, the testosterone-high adolescent was eating out of his hand – particularly with the promise of Arnold's slush fund loyalty rewards. In short, Palmer hauled his catch in by playing his fictional Gutman role to a T. Charlie agreed that next Saturday morning he would stand in for the temporarily indisposed clown, Macaroni, at the children's summer holiday closing party in *All The Right Moves*, on the understanding that the right move asked of him had nothing in common with aerobics.

'Put on that Patsy outfit Vanessa's wardrobe mistress found for you,' said Arnold, 'and, apart from wowing the kids, you and Craig might as well be brothers knocking at the door of the *Ritz Men Only*.'

⁂

With Isabelle Meunier now a regular participant in Craig's Saturday morning spin cycling routines, she and her instructor made a point of keeping their relationship sufficiently low-key to avoid complaints by other women cyclists of favouritism or unprofessionalism. If anything, Craig had become harder rather than softer on Isabelle by refusing to admit that she had reached her endurance plateau.

He had tried in vain, however, to persuade Vanessa of the benefits to be had from following his training regime. A committed semi-marathon participant, Vanessa scoffed at the idea of pedalling at a standstill together with 'a pack of maniacs reeking of sweat'. Instead of sitting indoors, gawping at posters of pin-ups in leotards with no sign of perspiration, and having her eardrums blasted by Destiny's Child, she had voted for the healthier solution, come rain, snow or shine, of filling her lungs with fresh air along woodland tracks alive with the sights and sounds of nature. As for the other members of the Lenfindi Club, while Vanessa had met with resistance from Justin to the suggestion that he share in her morning jogs, because, as a member of the *Luritanische Ruderer*, he worked out three times a week down on the Vaugruge, there had been no opposition from Rashid to the same idea. And finally Tich, the club's founder and doyen, had earned recognition among his peers as Craig's leading weightlifter. Thus each member of the Lenfindi Club enjoyed his or her own form of regular exercise.

On this particular Saturday – when Craig was exceptionally closing *All The Right Moves* at 2 p.m. to allow a team of housepainters to move in over the weekend – after showering and dressing, Isabelle and Craig decided to view the fun and games of the children's summer season ending party on the first-floor landing, where parents were already seated near the observation window sipping cool drinks and taking in their offspring's antics.

'Look at that,' exclaimed Craig, pulling up two free chairs. 'How come Macaroni's not here? That's Charlie Hathaway in his Kilroy clown get-up.'

Isabelle stared down at the young American School student, dressed in his *Camino Real* red fright wig, flashing lightbulb nose and flipper-sized shoes, standing on a box with *Ravioli* chalked in red on its front.

'He's giving a creditable performance compared to Macaroni. The kids seem to be enjoying things.'

Craig and Isabelle watched as Charlie held out two brass coins in either hand, one bearing a black disc, the other white. He then closed his grip over them and opened his hands to show that the black disc had turned white, the white disc black. One dark-skinned girl threw her hand up and shouted: 'That's cheating. Each coin is white on one side black on the other.'

'You think so, Louise?' said Charlie, before proceeding to rub the coins together and reveal one now with a disc coloured red, the other green. After which, he turned both over to show a blue and a yellow disc.

'Our talented Charlie,' remarked Isabelle.

Next, Ravioli the clown produced a miniature guillotine from his pocket and, after placing this on the table in front of him, inserted a forefinger, pushed down the blade, yelped, instantaneously covered the guillotine with his other hand and then held up what, after recovering from their initial shock, the children gleefully applauded for what it was: an imitation severed finger in a bloodstained bandage.

'Ravioli sauce,' he said, before showing five intact fingers. Then went on to use those fingers to create a number of well received dog and giraffe balloon animals.

The party concluded with some uncomplicated juggling, following which Charlie distributed gift bags of fruit, nuts, sweets, colouring books and a set of five stones provided courtesy of *All The Right Moves*.

Isabelle was waiting for Craig to finish closing down his workstation before turning off the fitness centre's lighting and air conditioning, when Charlie Hathaway appeared at the top of the stairs, his wig, red nose and outsize shoes tucked away in a canvas carry-all.

'How do you think it went?' he said, strolling up to Craig's desk, throwing himself down into the nearest chair, sticking his legs out in front of him and juggling three leftover tangerines.

'Never knew you were a magician, Charlie boy,' replied Craig with one eye on the last of the morning's e-mails.

'I'm not. But my dad is in his spare time. He lent me a few gimmicks, showed me how to use them. Nothing too demanding. Seemed to go down well with the kids.'

'What happened to Macaroni?'

'He and dad do the same party circuits. When Macaroni said he couldn't come today because of a doctor's appointment, Dad remembered my Patsy role and suggested I have a go at standing in for Macaroni.'

'Well, Charlie, we'll pay you the same we pay Macaroni, which is eighty euros. You okay with that?'

Charlie finished playing with his tangerines, lobbing the last of the fruit into the maw of his carrier bag. 'I certainly am. I would have done it for nothing. But since you're offering, perhaps Ravioli should think of going professional.'

'I'll have to give it you on the way out. We keep the petty cash downstairs.'

'Fine, but, look, I was wondering if you could help with something else, Craig. My smartphone has gone on the blink, and I wanted to research something on the Internet for a school project I need to hand in on Monday.'

'Well, strictly speaking, Charlie, I shouldn't let you use this desktop. It belongs to the fitness centre. But if you can assure me you'll confine yourself to googling or dogpiling, I can let you do a quick search.'

'That's good of you, Craig.'

'How long should it take?'

'No longer than ten … twelve minutes, if that's all right with you.'

'Be my guest. Give me a call when you're through. I still have other business to attend to, straightening up the equipment in the weights room, turning off the monitors, closing the blinds.'

Isabelle stood up to relieve the numbness in one foot caused by a pinched nerve. 'I think I'll wait for you two downstairs.'

'Okay,' said Craig, shutting down his e-mail box. 'If the painters turn up, tell them they can start right away. As for you, Charlie, be sure not to close this pc when you're finished. There are certain protocols I need to go through first.'

Charlie rose to his feet to occupy the swivel chair vacated by Craig. 'Sure, I'll stick to the search engine and leave you to sign off.'

The minute Isabelle disappeared downstairs and Craig into the weights room, Charlie Hathaway clicked on File Explorer and trawled through the computer's documents folders. It took him just short of three minutes to find what he was looking for. Checking to see whether the workstation's printer was loaded with paper, he activated the print command, all the while praying the soft whirring sound would not attract Craig's attention. His print-outs completed and their contents verified, Charlie double deleted the corresponding files.

After bringing back up the Google page thumb-nailed by him before starting his search, Charlie picked up his carry-all and went through to the weights room, where he found Craig racking dumbbells and barbells.

'That's it, thanks.'

'Glad to be of help. Found what you wanted?'

Charlie tapped his jacket pocket and unabashedly replied, 'Used your printer. Hope that was all right.'

'No problem. You coming to rehearsals tonight?'

'Yep, need to get my lines perfect for Blocks Four to Six.'

'See you later then.'

'Right.'

On his way out of the front door, seeing three men taking lightweight aluminium ladders, paint pots and rollers out of a van emblazoned with the lettering *Camille Renoir & Fils,* Charlie could not resist continuing to act the clown.

'Bonjour messieurs. Vous allez nous donner les grandes baigneuses?'

But his quip about the French impressionist's nude female bathers went down like a lead balloon. The men were not happy about having to work over the weekend.

Never mind, he thought. You can't win them all. And, if it comes to Windows, Kilroy definitely wasn't here.

'Bull's eye,' declared a satisfied Arnold Palmer on taking receipt of Charlie's print-outs.

'Any of that make sense to you then?' asked Charlie without being that interested in the answer, which he knew would be no answer at all.

'The fact that it has the letters GPWRO at the top and bottom of each page shows you've done me proud, Charlie. Now, you deleted the files, right?'

'All I could find. He'd stored them on the Cloud among other places. I think I got everything. But, of course, if he's saved them on a flash drive or some other medium. Or stored copies on a laptop at home …' The student puffed out his cheeks. 'Impossible to cover all the bases.'

'Never mind, Charlie, boy. You've done a good job. Worth every cent of your purse for this unequal contest.'

'Yep,' said Charlie Hathaway, accepting the two hundred euros capping eighty already in his wallet. 'Although I say so myself, it was like taking candy from a baby.'

Arnold Palmer gazed at the meaningless succession of letters, the cause of angst to Langley's Lester Kayser. The fact that they had been found on Craig's work computer meant that Jacques Casanova was not the only role being played by Mr All The Right Moves Roberts. He had to be part of a larger ring in need of dismantling by Arnold, but with only partial back-up from granite jaw. Could Arnold deliver? Demoralise, Kayser had said. That called for nous. The counterfeit cultural attaché felt a familiar raw cramping in the pit of his stomach.

'You all right, Arnold?" asked the student. 'You don't look too good.'

'Stomach problem. Crops up every so often. No hassle. I'll take something for it.'

'See you in rehearsals then.'

'Yes, Candy Man, see you in rehearsals.'

Scanning the morning's news headlines on the Internet, Vanessa suddenly turned a deathly white. There staring out at her was a photograph of her handsome lover,

Rashid Jabour, and above him the words: *MEDRIMCOMB employee victim of Beirut drive-by shooting*. Vanessa began shaking uncontrollably. It felt for a moment as if she might pass out, but then her head cleared and she clicked on the news item to bring up the details. According to the report filed by the BBC's man in Beirut, Rashid and another Lebanese had been cut down when exiting a café together. In claiming responsibility for the joint killings, Hezbollah expressed regret for the fact that Mr Jabour had suffered the same fate as their target, a paid Israeli informer. The young investment aid banker had been too close to the traitor to escape the hail of bullets.

Particularly crushing was the realisation that she would never see, touch or exchange another fond word with Rashid, that their parting had been so perfunctory, he in a hurry to get to work to collect his business papers before joining his colleagues in the taxi to the airport, she correcting her notes on the previous evening's play reading before stuffing them in her briefcase to drive to the office for a departmental restructuring meeting.

Now, Macbeth's cry of 'Out, out brief candle!' was ringing in her ears.

Dreading the working day in front of her, because she knew how easily she could flare up at the slightest misplaced remark or action, Vanessa turned away from the screen to bury her head in her hands. Coming as it did on the heels of her encounter with the man from MI6 and her phone conversation with Clara Bogen, Vanessa did not know what to think of this ghastly news. How could Arnold Palmer have had anything to do with a drive-by killing on the other side of the world? It was too ridiculous for words to think that the man playing Gutman was responsible for making her Lord Byron pay the price for something other than escaping his pitiable settlement. No, this had happened in the war-ravaged Middle East, and Hezbollah had claimed responsibility. She needed to get Tich to call a council of war to digest this terrible news and to prove her fantasising unfounded. With Justin back from Barcelona, the Lenfindi Club could meet after evening rehearsals.

Rehearsals? What was the fucking point of continuing with them? In looking back up at Rashid's smiling face on her monitor, Vanessa was struck by the irrational thought that she had been instrumental in her lover's death by casting him in the role of the doomed supporter of a lost cause. Her gloom deepened when she remembered that in the original Broadway production of *Camino Real* the same actor had played both Don Quixote and Lord Byron. She could hardly expect Justin, of all people, to take on Rashid's role. Vanessa hurled her battered, annotated copy of the play across the room.

❦

As the day wore on Vanessa was in two minds as to whether to call off that evening's rehearsals – until it occurred to her that bad news did not necessarily spread like wildfire around Schönschlucht. The last thing she wanted was to be the bearer of distressing tidings via her smartphone. It stood to reason that, after she broke the news with the members of her cast face to face, not one of them would feel like going ahead with the scheduled practice. On the other hand, everyone concerned needed to be given a say as to where to go from there: soldier on or pull the plug on her accursed production? If soldier on, how to find a stand-in at short notice to take on the role of Lord Byron? Should she argue in favour of pulling out all the stops in order to dedicate each performance to the memory of Rashid with a mention to this effect in the printed programme? No, thought Vanessa, she would never have the stomach for that. Better to consign her maiden production of *Camino Real* to the amateur theatrical dustbin.

An all but tangible pall hung over that evening's gathering following disclosure of Rashid's gratuitous murder. For, of those present, only Arnold Palmer had learnt of the attack in Beirut. And despite her conflicting emotions with respect to the cultural attaché and his employers' possible arm's length connivance with those it suited the State Department's contingent of Zionist sympathisers to label as terrorists, Vanessa conveyed no hint of her knowledge of the Clara Bogen episode or its impact on her opinion of him.

That was until Arnold advocated forging ahead with the production, and her composure was sorely tested.

'I think,' he said, 'that Rashid would have wanted to us to put our best foot forward. By all means, let's dedicate the production to his memory. But the best way to do that might be to omit Block Eight altogether. I doubt, Vanesssa, whether you can come up with as convincing a portrayer of Lord Byron as Rashid in the time left to us.'

'Unless,' said Isabelle, 'you manage to persuade Justin to take on the role. There's a precedent. The same actor played Don Quixote and Lord Byron when *Camino Real* premiered on Broadway.'

'I know,' said Vanessa. 'Hurd Hatfield.' She refrained from adding that, just as Hatfield felt poisoned by his earlier role in *The Picture of Dorian Gray,* how could Justin, for all his forgiving nature, be expected to jump at the idea of drinking from the chalice abandoned by his latest rival for her affection? 'But you're forgetting that I had to twist Justin's arm to play the Don.'

'Whatever some of you might think to the contrary,' said the doyen among Vanessa's performers, who had taken on the role of the Baron de Charlus, 'Byron's role is pivotal. Cut it out and – forgive me for speaking in character – but you castrate the play.'

Well, I go along with Arnold on this one,' said Charlie. 'All that the audience sees of Byron is confined to Block Eight.'

Despite jagged nerves, Vanessa stopped short of cutting Charlie down to size. As she saw it, Williams's Kilroy character served to point up the yawning gulf between American and European culture. Poe, reasoned Vanessa, would have been a better choice by far, although then the play would have taken on a darker colouring. But when Williams was dead set on the redeeming innocence of youth, how could you expect him to change horses in mid-stream?

Since Kilroy was, by Vanessa's standards, one of the least mature of Williams's characters, and the part fitted the young student as well as the gloves around his neck, Charley Hathaway's prejudiced opinion counted for nothing. Still, the boy needed correcting.

'You're forgetting that Byron makes his entrance at the play's midpoint. *Camino Real* would be immeasurably poorer without his tale of Shelley's funeral pyre on the beach at Viareggio. And in striking out from the police state into *Terra Incognita*, while all around remain caged and watched over by Gutman, Byron lays down a marker for Don Quixote's curtain-closing awakening to new horizons.'

'How about Kilroy's awakening?'

'Charley, have you not stopped to think that his very name dooms your character to a life of second-rate anonymity?'

The student took as an insult what was meant to be no more than sober reflection. 'I disagree. The Kilroys of this world are the lifeblood of America.'

'Yes, well, there's no getting away from the fact that Williams had a thing about salad days. But let's not kid ourselves he believed for one moment that Kilroy, a character wet behind the ears compared to the failed boxer played by Brando in *On The Waterfront*, would go on to become America's answer to Byron after escaping the Camino Real'.

The cast member playing Lord Mulligan voiced indirect agreement. 'Does Sancho Panza join Quixote in striking out into the wasteland at the end of the play? Or does Kilroy tag along as second best to the Don's long-suffering squire?'

'That's rubbish,' said a red-faced Charley.

Palmer raised a moderating hand. 'Arguing about the strong or weak points of Williams's characterisations is getting us nowhere. Shouldn't we be asking ourselves what Rashid would have wanted?'

'Or rather,' said Isabelle, 'whether we owe it to him to continue.'

'No need to delude yourselves on that score,' said Vanessa. 'I pressganged Rashid into playing the part of Byron. I'm sure he would have told us to forget all that nonsense about the show must go on.'

'But,' objected Isabelle, 'the tickets have already gone on sale.'

'Yes,' acknowledged Vanessa. 'And I've paid upfront for hire of the château courtyard, the costumes are well under way and …' Since thumping her brows with clenched fists did nothing to clear her head, she trailed off into a void of frustration.

'Perhaps,' said Arnold, revising his stance, 'you need to pressgang once more. Talk Justin into talking on the part.'

At pains not to advertise hostility to a suggestion she guessed to be prompted as much by an ego trip as by a private agenda, Vanessa turned the pages of her copy of the play to the scene dominated by Byron. 'It's a big part.'

'But nice and compact. Okay, some dense story-telling text, but easy to memorise. And instead of having to interact with other players during other scenes or blocks, Justin gets it over with in one.'

'You don't think we should pack it in?' said Vanessa, who was finding it increasingly difficult to master her emotions. If only, she thought, I could pinch myself and wake up to find Rashid's death and Palmer's shallow solicitude part of a bad dream.

'No. And I don't agree that Rashid could not have cared one way or the other whether we went ahead with the play or not.'

'All right, let me sleep on it. I'll put the proposal to Justin. But I'm not going to force his arm. Any other suggestions? No, then let's call it a night. I'll let you all know where we go from here by the weekend.'

⁓❦⁓

After clearing customs at Luritania's Lenfindi airport and seeing Gisela and Rosalie home to their front door, Justin returned to his apartment where he was met by the sight of torn sofa upholstery, traces of blood on his living room laminate and bathroom tiling, which Vanessa's sodium treatment had failed to remove completely, and a note left beside Pliny's cage with the message: *Justin, check your answerphone. Vanessa.*

Hers was the third message, telling him that: she had bad news she would rather not communicate over the phone; this had nothing to do with the meal Pliny had made of his Laura Ashley upholstery; if he had sufficient energy to drop everything and pop around to her apartment, she was holding a late-night emergency meeting with the rest of the Lenfindi club which would be incomplete without his presence.

Finding no signs of injury on Pliny but worried lest in his absence the ferret had savaged Vanessa, Justin checked the last of his messages, rang Vanessa, first, to enquire about her health and, second, to learn whether the meeting was still in progress, quickly printed out several copies of an unexpected message received on his iPad before boarding at Barcelona-El Prat airport and left his place to join her and his Sunday companions.

The moment she opened the door to him, it was obvious that Vanessa had been crying. The strained expression on the faces of those gathered around the living room table only confirmed his fears that something seriously bad had happened. After inviting him to sit down and offering a choice of single malt Scotch or cognac, which he declined, it being clear that he had heard nothing of the fate that had befallen Rashid, Vanessa broke the news of their friend's death.

After which she filled in the background as to why, following discussions with the rest of the cast of her sabotaged production, she had asked Tich to call this urgent club meeting. She explained how she had surprised the self-proclaimed MI6 intruder in Justin's apartment, reported his demands and warnings with respect to the stolen documents to police and friends, and finally related what had happened at *La Maison des Aveugles*, for which she accepted condign responsibility.

'MEDRIMCOMB's entire staff are stopping work at midday tomorrow,' added Vanessa. 'For two minutes' silence in memory of Rashid and as a token of respect by colleagues to whom he was unknown.'

'And,' said Tich, 'one of Rashid's workmates, an organist and director of music at the International School, has undertaken to conduct Mozart's *Requiem Mass* in Schönschlucht's *HeiligeGeistKirche* next Thursday evening.'

382

'Also,' said Isabelle, 'because Rashid's father is currently working as a field surgeon out in Lebanon for *Médecins Sans Frontières*, treating wounded Syrian war civilians and combatants, Craig has decided to name his cyclothon, *The Rashid Jabour MSF Memorial Appeal Cyclothon*.'

'Where is the poor guy being buried?' asked a bemused and saddened Justin.

'In one of Beirut's Christian cemeteries,' said Vanessa, 'alongside his grandfather. Rashid told me he had fond memories of Khalil Jabour, who used to take him fishing. Apparently, the old man wrote some fine poetry for which he is remembered to this day.

'Anyway, Rashid's mother and sister are already in Lebanon, having flown there from Paris. As for Rashid's father, the MSF surgeon working on the border with Syria, some oaf rushed into his tent to blurt out the news of his son's death while he was in mid-operation. The grief-stricken father handed everything over to a locum and rushed straight to Beirut.'

'Shouldn't we get together to send across a wreath?' said Isabelle, the lines across her forehead as much a sign of her fear of what the future might hold in store for her as of dejection at the sudden, inexplicable loss of a friend.

Tich nodded agreement. 'I was thinking the same. Better not to delay. I can order over the Internet. Flowers better than a wreath, perhaps.'

'Yes,' said Vanessa, snapping out of her contemplation of Rashid's coffin being lowered into the earth under a burning Lebanese sun. At the same time, she could not in all honesty say that she had been overwhelmingly in love with Rashid. They had known each other too briefly. Then again, had she ever truly loved anyone? Justin was probably more closely allied to her in nature than any other man she had slept with inasmuch as he was as scornful or afraid of commitment as she.

'Roses,' she remarked absently after a lengthy pause. 'Peace roses.'

'I'll see what I can do. And our message?'

'Well, there's a fitting quotation from Shelley's elegy on the death of Keats: *Peace, peace! he is not dead! he doth not sleep! He hath awaken'd from the dream of life.*'

Still reeling from the blow delivered by news of Rashid's death and gazing in disbelief from one face to the next, Justin leant forward in his seat, grabbed hold of the nearest bottle and poured himself a slug of Scotch. He grimaced as the amber liquid seared the back of his throat, then set his glass down and proceeded to recount his experience on the spiral staircase in the *Sagrada Família* tower and his, Gisela and Rosalie Radetzky's narrow escape on the pavement outside *El Corte Inglés*. In short, he did not believe that Rashid's death had been accidental.

Justin's sallow complexion and hollow eyes left those around the table in no doubt as to interpretation: their friend had been as stunned as the rest of them by the news of Rashid's death, but all the more so with attempts on his and his protégés' lives fresh in his memory.

'I repeat. In the light of what happened to me in Barcelona, I don't believe that Rashid was in the wrong place at the wrong time.'

Craig shook his head. 'It's natural enough that you should feel that way, but stop to think for a moment. You have to be the bogeyman as far as our enemies, whoever they may be, are concerned. You're the one who stuck his neck out and went public, not Rashid. What is there to connect Rashid with the papers in that red leather briefcase? Nothing.'

'Unless,' said Vanessa, 'the Arnold Palmers of this world have been burning the midnight oil trying to work out who else Justin may have told of his find. By which I mean us, the Lenfindi Club. In which case, if Palmer's done his homework, we're all under the microscope, all bacilli candidates for curative treatment.'

Isabelle felt the skin crawling on the back of her neck. 'That's preposterous, Vanessa. There's strength in numbers. Palmer's lot can't blithely set about bumping off a whole group of us off because they suspect we're accessories.'

'I've been thinking about that,' mused Tich, stroking his beard. 'First of all, I had this theory that we were sitting on today's answer to the microdot – steganography. But then a different idea came to me. What if there was a secret compartment in the briefcase that escaped our notice, but which contained something really damning? Names, say, plus amounts, donations, what have you. Maybe Justin photocopied these additional papers before returning every original to its rightful place. And these are seen by our enemies as a time bomb waiting to go off. Which means that Justin and the rest of us are too dangerous for their liking. We have to be stopped at all costs.'

'There's something I've yet to show you all,' said Justin, 'which bears out what Tich just said. I received an e-mail on the way out of Barcelona from Musgrave's widow. Here.' He opened a slim document case and passed round copies of two print-outs. The first read:

Mr Hendry,
Understand that it goes against the grain for me to address a stranger as 'Dear', especially one inhabiting a grey area kept secret from me over the years by my husband.

Would it comfort you to know that I have not bothered to get Google (that bastard offspring of goggle and ogle) to tell me who or what you might be? The 'who' factor, I am sure, would tell me nothing. And the 'what' factor is never for public consumption.

Whoever, whatever and wherever you may be, Mr Hendry, I fear that what I am passing on to you below may reach you too late. My deceased husband, Peregrine Musgrave, composed this warning message shortly before committing suicide. But never sent it. A case of second thoughts. I found it yesterday in his laptop's recycle bin.

Do not believe for one moment that I am forwarding Peregrine's message at this late stage out of the kindness of my heart. I am doing so in the fervent hope that you may hold the key to what pushed my husband to take his own life. Were this gesture on my part to be repaid with silence, I would have to conclude either that Peregrine's message arrived too late or that you are alive, well and despicable.

Widowed, childless and overtaken by darkness,
Margaret Musgrave

It was followed by:

Dear Mr Hendry,
You should know that I act as runner for powerful, vested interests. The man I prefer not to think of as my controller goes by the code name of the bird garrulus glandarius. In fact, he is anything but garrulous, though I cannot accuse him of being uncommunicative.

I should be emboldened by the knowledge that the creature from which he takes his name is hunted by owls during the night and by peregrines during the day, if it were not that I have the greater cause to feel hunted.

You see, Mr Hendry, this brightly plumed bird is only one half of the equation of concern to us, because he is in regular contact with a predatory character sitting in an eyrie in Virginia. Although that character takes his code name from a chemical element, I prefer to call him Josef. It is impossible to decide whether Josef is my bird's dupe or nemesis.

But be warned, Mr Hendry. Do not cross either individual. The first can bring you to justice, the second pursue you to the ends of the earth.

In short, disclosure of any material exchanged between these two would be the ultimate folly. I who have signed my own death warrant beg you not to be so unwise as to follow in my footsteps.
Peregrine Musgrave

Justin waited for his four companions to take in the contents of both messages, before adding his comments.

'For those of you like me unfamiliar with Linnaean taxonomy, *garrulous glandarius* is the Eurasian jay, a bird closely related to the Eurasian magpie considered a supremely intelligent bird. Not the way I'd care to describe the man caught in my bathroom by Vanessa nursing Pliny's calf bite. But whether or not a credible member of British intelligence, that jay is warbling the same song as the late peregrine, one we can't afford to ignore.

'Had I been found at the bottom of those steps with a broken neck, you can be sure that the coroner would have ruled the matter a case of accidental fatal injury. Similarly, had that car caught any of us outside *El Corte Inglés*, no doubt the verdict would have been involuntary manslaughter, after the driver's defence lawyer claimed that the man was either drunk or drugged when he lost control of his vehicle.'

'All right, how to cope with this?' said Vanessa. 'You're not suggesting, I hope, that we should pack up our bags and take the next *El Fugitivo* flight out of Luritania to the back of beyond?'

Justin helped himself to more Scotch. 'No, of course not. We need double insurance. Get your Georg Hoffarth and Mr Jay on our side. First, to clip Arnold's wings, second to ram the message home: we've learnt our lesson and can be counted on to hand over or destroy these people's coveted data.'

Tich's fingers performed a nervous, staccato beat on the tabletop. 'Sorry,

Justin, but I doubt whether Hoffarth is capable of clipping Arnold's wings. The diplomatic corps is beyond his reach. And as for Palmer, you don't seriously think that a cultural attaché is going to soil his hands, when the organisation behind him commands a network of drones ready to do its dirty work at a moment's notice? You didn't see hide nor hair of Palmer in Barcelona, did you? Then there's Jay. Straining at the leash to corner you. What's to say he's still around? And if he is, how can he hope to defuse things?'

Vanessa threw back her head in a gesture of despair. 'We don't have much fucking choice, do we, Tich? As Justin said, Hoffarth and Jay are our only life lines.'

'Ouch! Time, I see, for the devil's advocate to shut his sulphurous mouth.'

Isabelle returned to her copy of Justin's Musgrave print-outs. 'I think we have a lot to thank this poor woman for. I mean, she didn't have to forward Justin her husband's message. But she did. All right, it hasn't given us all the answers by far, but it has clarified a thing or two. Now she's asked a question, and someone owes her an answer.'

'You're right, Isabelle,' said Justin. 'But I don't see how we can supply it. Jay is the only person qualified to do that, and if he's chosen not to, why should he change his mind now?'

'Well, turn the screws on him,' suggested Vanessa. 'Get him to do the decent thing.'

Tich gave an exasperated grunt. 'What kind of fairy tale world are you living in, Van? If MI6 looked the other way after Peregrine Musgrave did himself in, why should it have a change of heart now?'

'The least I can do,' said Justin, 'is to tackle Jay on that. Isabelle's right. Margaret Musgrave deserves better.'

Given the mood of the meeting, Vanessa could not bring herself to propose that Justin take up the mantle of Lord Byron dropped by Rashid. The fact was that she had lost all interest in putting on *Camino Real*. Coleridge's albatross could not have called down a worse fate on her and her company than had Williams's play. Or so it seemed. As for the Lenfindi Club, it looked as if they had wandered blindly into a *Camino Irreal* with Perdition signposted at every turn.

Preparing food for the delectation of family and friends was one of the few sources of domestic satisfaction for Frank Welling. His father in his day having been a force to reckon with in the kitchen, Frank fancied that the old man had passed more than a soupçon of his culinary savoir-faire on to his son. It was a conclusion that neither his wife, whose cooking skills had been blunted by over-reliance on the pizzas and take-away curries of her undergraduate years, or his two daughters, one of whom had spent four years studying medicine in Montpellier, while the other had followed in the footsteps of Cartier Bresson by opening a photography gallery in Paris, would have gainsaid.

On the rear terrace of his villa on the outskirts of Schönschlucht, bent over a nine pound wild salmon to which he had added a handful of homegrown spring potatoes and courgettes and a sprinkling of herbs, Frank stood contentedly reprising Andrea Bocelli's lines from his *Pearl Fishers* duet with Placido Domingo. To his far right, the setting sun cast a mix of roseate and indigo brush strokes over the thin cloud banks in the skies above Lenfindi airport, whose air traffic controllers appeared to know better than to drown out celestial music.

The Welling villa was a modern, three-storey glass and steel construction, which at its rear overlooked a trout stream and golf course. Set in grounds of its own – twenty acres in all of well-kept gardens and woodland – this handsome property had cost Frank two and a half million euros. But the 1.5% MEDRIMCOMB mortgage loan repayable over fifteen years made scant impact on an already handsome salary. And Frank had his sights set on rising beyond his present station. You got nowhere, he told himself as he turned over the trout's head only to find the other eye glaring at him as balefully as its partner, sitting in the same career slot for too long. As soon as the opportunity arose, he would apply for a senior post in Credit Risk, Internal Audit, Project Oversight – one after the other, with a view to grooming himself for the role of Secretary-General.

Frank's attempts to do justice to Bizet and Bocelli, his thoughts of future advancement and of the more immediate rapturous reception guaranteed to be won by his barbecued salmon were interrupted by the ringing tone of the cell phone on the window ledge beside a full punch bowl. Setting down his tongs, Frank walked across to consult the monitor: *number withheld*. Offering a cheery wave through the living room window to a wife dutifully entertaining their guests within, he accepted the call.

'W,' came the rasping voice.

Frank Welling turned quickly away from the window and sidled back towards his grill. Eight o'clock in Schönschlucht meant two o'clock in Langley, Virginia. His American caller had got off to a bad start, using the puerile code to which Frank grudgingly subscribed. Here was K calling W. Kay was a woman's name. As in Kay Kendall. It was not as if Lester Kayser had gone through a sex change operation out of admiration for Rex Harrison's late wife. By the same token, Frank was averse to being called 'double u'. Not that, his mind still on air traffic, 'Kilo on the line for a chat with Whisky' would have been an improvement. Better Kong as in King Kong and Ton as in Wellington.

'Have I caught you at an awkward moment, W?'

'If Alexander Graham Bell's successors had got around to transmitting more than mere sound over the line, you would sense that I am barbequing something over a birch-wood grill.'

'Steak?'

'Salmon.'

'Caught fresh today?'

'Would it were so. We can fish trout at the bottom of our garden. But this remarkable specimen – excuse me while I dampen the flames – issues straight from the fish counter of our local supermarket.'

'You're on your own?'

'Yes.'

'I wish to offer my condolences about young Jabour.'

Welling decided it was time to think about removing some of his fare from the grill. 'Condolences or apologies?'

'Both. You're right. If our man had got to Mason before he got to you and Jabour, your loan officer would still be alive.'

It was certainly time to remove the head, otherwise Frank's wife, Sarah, would create a rumpus about her husband's serving up carcinogenic fish.

'What exactly happened?'

'Jabour must have made one trip too many out to Beirut for Hezbollah's liking. They had him down in their books as the man responsible for diverting that shipment of arms intended for their Syrian opposition movement to ISIL.'

'Mason engineered that?'

'Who else? Self-appointed leader of the anti-Zionist league.'

'Jabour was a bright young man.'

'Perhaps too bright for his own good.'

'What's that supposed to mean?'

'Bright but naïve. Allowed Mason to put one over on him.'

Frank tested a couple of spring potatoes. It looked as if they were ready. The longer this mock exculpatory telephone call went on the greater the chance that he would fail to live up to the standards advertised by the mustachioed chef depicted on his apron. 'Do you think I'm not continually kicking myself for introducing Jack to Jabour?'

'No, W, the blame is all mine.'

You're damn bloody right, thought Frank Welling, who would gladly have reserved the same fate for Lester Kayser as that meted out to Jeanne d'Arc minus canonisation. In mourning the loss of Rashid Jabour, the Mashreq Loan Operations Manager had been unable to suppress his rage faced with the knowledge that the chimps in America fed regular tidbits of MEDRIMCOMB policy decisions had ham-fistedly rewarded his services by setting in motion a chain of events costing him the life of one of his star recruits.

After ending the call with ill-concealed dudgeon – Lester's people might have paid well, but that didn't make Welling their door mat – Frank finished settling the fish and vegetables into two casserole dishes, wiped his hands on the whiskered linen face and helped himself to some punch. A triple-engined jumbo cargo jet chose that moment to assail his ear drums as it took off in the mid-distance above Lenfindi airport. He scowled. Sarah had overdone the gin.

Memo from K to J

When asked during yesterday's Casablanca press conference whether Vespuccia negotiates with terrorists, our spokesperson, something of a laughingstock on the Net, roundly rejected any such suggestion. I had expected her to reply: 'Negotiate with terrorists? Never. We only arm, train and finance them'.

Arnold Palmer sensed Dexter Nussbaum's half-hearted attempt at concealing his displeasure, when the ambassador informed him that he was wanted immediately in the bunker for a one-on-one with Lester Kayser now that the CIA man and Arnold's superior had finished their confidential chat. How much more would it take, if Nussbaum suspected him of covering up Chamberlain and Stenning's murders, for the ambassador to do the dirty on him with Kayser followed up by detailed written censure?

Brushing aside these misgivings as best he could, but unavoidably troubled as to what granite jaw might have in store for him, Arnold grabbed his tablet, made his way to the lift well, where he found an elevator conveniently waiting to take him to the basement, rode down three levels, stepped out into a no-expenses-spared, thickly carpeted corridor, whose walls were lined, on one side, with photographs of every president from Hoover to Obama, on the other, with pictures of four astronauts, eight sportsmen and athletes, one Jackson Pollock and two Mark Rothkos, and directed his steps along the twenty or so yards to the grey bunker room door, where he tapped the entry code into a small, green LCD box. A grim-faced (did he ever look any different?) Lester Kayser was sitting waiting for him on screen, a mug of coffee at his side, the blinds pulled down behind him against the early morning sun.

Things could hardly have got off to a worst start had it not, Arnold reflected, been for the saving grace of ambassador Nussbaum's absence.

'What's this,' barked Kayser, 'about Stenning and Chamberlain signing some crazy suicide pact? You knew them, Palmer, I take it?'

Surprised but grateful for the fact that the CIA emperor had not brought this matter up during the earlier videoconference when Arnold had the ambassador breathing down his neck, the cultural attaché had not come this time unprepared into the battleground but had armoured himself with a bullet-proof defence.

However, much depended on Arnold's opening gambit and whether Kayser fell for it. The cultural attaché chanced his arm, accompanying his question with a resigned sigh he thought worthy of plaudits from Vanessa Curtis and his fellow amateur thespians. 'What exactly did the ambassador tell you, sir?'

'That one of my best agents was found dead alongside his not so sharp companion in one of your safe houses.'

Arnold passed a weary hand over his forehead. 'I'm afraid the ambassador's got his wires crossed. A week ago, Luritania's diving club fished a body out of a local quarry. Called in to ID the corpse, I hesitated to confirm that what I was looking at was all that was left of Hugh Chamberlain. Water rats had eaten away a good part of the face. The body was bloated, but height, build and age suggested Chamberlain. I don't know whether news of the murder of a local cartoonist reached your ears over there in Langley. My guess was that Chamberlain and Stenning mistook the fellow on the staff of the *The Pulse* magazine for that editor who published the article with which you're familiar. After grilling him and recognising their blunder, one or both of them went ape and tossed him into the city gorge. Then they must have had a falling out. Stenning decided that Chamberlain was too much of a liability.'

'All guesswork on your part, Palmer. Perhaps you could explain why Dexter Nussbaum told me a totally different story.'

Succeeding in maintaining a straight face in the wake of a not unexpected blow to his credibility, Arnold Palmer managed a troubled frown.

'As I said, sir, the ambassador got his wires crossed. There have been increasing signs of late that he has not been his old self. The other morning, when his chauffeur, Eugene, stopped by his residence to drive him to the embassy, the boss told him he had business in Brussels. About halfway up the road outside Namur, the ambassador told Eugene to pull off into a roadside café for ham and eggs. After they had finished their breakfast, during which the ambassador apparently downed half a gallon of coffee, Dexter Nussbaum instructed his chauffeur to drive him back to the embassy.'

When Lester Kayser screwed his eyes up, it was evident that he was not protesting against sunlight. 'You trying to tell me that Dexter Nussbaum is losing the plot?'

'No sir, the ambassador has my utmost respect. It's just that …'

Arnold had to play his hand carefully. If he overdid the image of the sere ambassador losing his marbles with barely a year to go until retirement, Kayser would see through the subterfuge and Arnold's campaign would backfire on him. Under the circumstances, a sufficiently well-timed and well-judged hiatus came freighted with the right degree of innuendo.

'It's just what? I repeat, how is it that Dexter told me a completely different story?'

'You mean the story about the safe house suicide pact?' Arnold spread his hands in the manner of a mathematician trying to measure the compass of a theorem. 'Well, sir, he wasn't that wide of the mark. You see, after Warren Stenning rid himself of Hugh Chamberlain, instead of reporting immediately back to you, he must have decided to lie low for a few days to sort things out. But in letting himself into our safe house, he found the place taken over by two squatters. When it struck him that both these characters could be mistaken for him and Chamberlain, he decided to do away with them and make the whole thing look like a disastrous squabble between him and his associate. Instead of queering the CIA's pitch with the Luritanian authorities, he had handed the police the cartoonist's murderers on a plate. At the same time, relying heavily on us to go along with this fiction,

Stenning successfully quashed further probing into the dead men's backgrounds. I was quick to pick up on the notepad left by him beside the safe house's telephone. The top page bore the clear imprint of a number which I dialled straightaway on my cell. SAS's switchboard. Stenning had flown the coop to Scandinavia. Perhaps not alone. I could have been wrong about the body in the quarry. Maybe Stenning and Chamberlain flew off together to Copenhagen, Stockholm or Oslo. But I destroyed that note and played along with what I suspected was Warren Stenning's game.'

'Arnold,' (Palmer took it as an encouraging sign that Kayser chose this moment to adopt familiar first name terms.) 'Warren and Hugh may, as you say, have flown to somewhere south of the Arctic circle, but since then they've gone awol.'

Having foreseen this, Palmer paused to ponder the irrefutable for only so long before delivering his riposte. 'Difficult to say what people will do under stress, sir.'

'Warren Stenning was not made of the kind of stuff to fold up under stress.'

'I don't know what to say, sir. I did what I thought needed doing. To protect our interests.'

Kayser finished off a scribbled memo and, to Arnold Palmer's immense relief, switched subject.

'You must have heard about Beirut.'

Arnold Palmer made the error of taking this for a rhetorical question. Kayser drummed his fingers on the yellow legal pad in front of him.

'Well?'

'Yes, sir.' The bunker was beginning to feel too hot for comfort. Palmer would not have put it past the ambassador to have switched off the air-conditioning after finishing his business with the emperor. Arnold tentatively raised a hand towards easing a collar that had become too tight only to decide that such a move would telegraph weakness. 'Your people acted …' (Palmer was self-conscious of groping too long for the right adjective.) '… decisively.'

'Bullshit. Jabour was taken out by Daesh, those fucking jihadist towelheads.'

'But Hezbollah …'

'Arnold, Arnold. Haven't you learnt by now to take what you read in the press with a barrelful of salt?'

'It seemed to make sense.'

'Nothing makes sense out there.'

'So it really was bad luck on Jabour's part?'

'That's one way of putting it.' Lester Kayser sketched an R.I.P. on his pad. Why bother, he asked himself, to go over the same ground after shifting the onus, as he had with Frank Welling? 'Nasty, but simplifies matters for us.'

From the expression in Kayser's eyes when he looked up from his pad, Arnold could not make out whether the CIA man had simply tuned out or considered his remark to be in poor taste. Given Palmer's diffidence, Kayser's next words came like a kick in the stomach. 'Barcelona. Your baby. What did you hope to achieve with those scare tactics?'

'Just that, sir. Frighten Hendry enough for him to realise that if he put another foot wrong not only would he be imperilling his own life but the lives of those around him.'

'What makes you think it did the trick? What if his response is to retaliate?'

'He won't enjoy that opportunity. He and Roberts are due to get their comeuppance tomorrow. I've researched both their employers. Hendry's boss relies heavily on our subsidy. I told him that unless he took action against his editor-in-chief, we would pull the rug out from under him. As *The Pulse* is hardly his top-flight publication, he was quick to get the message.'

'You telling me he was a walkover? No gripes about interfering with the freedom of the press?'

'No, sir, the fellow is up to his ears in debt. I offered him one of our traditional sweeteners.'

'And Roberts?'

'Robert's boss, van der Meulen, was an easy nut to crack. I found out that Piet van der Meulen's father collaborated with the Germans after they invaded the Netherlands in 1942. He sold out three resistance fighters, tortured and shot by the Nazis. Piet saw eye to eye with me when I suggested that having that fact broadcast today would not help his reputation. He's on board.'

'Good, Arnold. I appreciate your bringing me up to speed on this. So where does that leave us with Miss Curtis?'

Drawing the line at giving the impression of a man faced with more labours than Hercules, Palmer heaved a sigh. 'I'm sorry, sir, I haven't got around yet to working out how to deal with her. She's a tough cookie.'

'Well, don't bother. I think I'll take a trip over to your neck of the woods and check out Miss Curtis myself.'

Uncertain that he fancied the idea of having the emperor treading on his turf, Arnold Palmer gave a nod of qualified comprehension. One problem less, if Kayser took on Vanessa alone. One problem more, if Dexter Nussbaum and Lester Kayser got their heads together.

Arnold disguised a nervous swallow with a cough. 'In that case, sir, I'd suggest going easy on her. Frankly, she's the least of our worries.'

'As I suspected, Arnold. You've a soft spot for this woman.'

The emperor or granite jaw, as Arnold liked to think of him interchangeably, was mistaken. That Arnold Palmer wanted to see no harm coming to Vanessa had less to do with dreams of bedding her than with reservations about meting out harsh treatment to the fair sex in general.

'No, sir. With all due respect, I think she can tell us nothing. She's too wrapped up in her amateur theatrical production.'

'I'll be the judge of that.'

Lester Kayser turned stern eyes on the framed presidential photograph on the wall behind Arnold. 'Are we forgetting anyone here, Arnold? Have you got all the bases covered?'

'Well, there's Roberts's girlfriend. He may have confided in her. But her father's our local contact in the French embassy. She strikes me as a chip off the old block. I doubt whether she'd kick over the traces. Anyway, shutting down her boyfriend should guarantee her cooperation.'

'On the contrary, Arnold. You might have to deal with the backlash.'

'Sir, excuse me, but the way I'm handling things …' Arnold put some drama into his hand gestures. '… It tells people there's nothing to be gained from flying solo.'

'I hope you're right, Arnold. Otherwise, I might have to make Miss …?'

'Mademoiselle, sir. Mademoiselle Meunier.'

'I might have to make Mademoiselle Meunier or her father's close acquaintance.'

'Of course.'

'That's it then. Don't fail to update me on the outcome of tomorrow's two singularities. The ambassador will give you my call-up details.

Not knowing what to make of hearing Kayser jazzing things up with a buzzword light years away from everyday CIA business and technospeak, the cultural attaché was gratified to be spared a response: the next second the screen went blank. Arnold's throat had rarely felt drier.

⁂

Memo from J to K

> *As you are aware, Urodina hopes to become a fully-fledged member of the Erubuan Union. Do you know what its most famous export is to that Union at present?*

Response from K

> *Arms?*

Response from J

> *And legs. Supplied by one hundred and fifty thousand tarts.*

⁂

A test, thought Vanessa, picking up the cordless telephone from her office handset, as to whether Jay (simpler to name him after Musgrave's feathered watcher than after the Compson family's or Philip Marlowe's creator) was a man of his word or a smooth-tongued confidence trickster. Was the Jay who had broken into another man's apartment, warned that she and her friends were in grave danger and announced that he would not leave Luritania until he had talked to Justin following his return from Barcelona, still in *L'Ambassadeur* or had he already spirited himself out of the country? The direct dial number Jay had given her was intercepted by

393

the switchboard. It caused Vanessa to hesitate. Had Jay booked in under the name of Faulkner, then changed rooms under the new name of Chandler? As that was the name he had given her, she went with it. The seconds that ticked soundlessly by made her wonder whether Jay had jumped ship. But moments later, Vanessa's first reassurance came when the girl on the switchboard said she was putting her through to Mr Chandler's room, her second when the familiar clipped, upper-class voice sounded in her ear: 'Chandler'.

'Vanessa Curtis,' she replied, relieved to learn that the man checked in to *L'Ambassadeur* under the name of Chandler was her man and not some robot vacuum cleaner salesman. 'I need to speak to you – urgently.'

'This is your lunch hour, I take it?'

'Yes, but I've lost my appetite. Need I explain?'

'No, I caught the news over the Internet. Come round now, if you can.'

'That was my idea.'

'You know the room number? If you do, don't say it over the phone.'

'I don't.'

'Ask at reception. I'll be waiting for you.'

Jay's room was on the seventh floor at the far end of a corridor a good sixty yards from the nearest elevator and facing, on the corridor side, the emergency staircase exit. Vanessa wondered whether this had been the best the booking-in clerk could offer or whether Jay suffered from the same phobia as Hans Christian Andersen. She gave the door a quick double rap. It took a minute or two before he opened up, during which time Vanessa stood well away from the door's fish eye viewer, partly reproaching herself for letting her imagination run wild, partly regretting not having asked Tich to accompany her.

But she was glad to find that there was nothing remotely menacing in Jay's mien. On the contrary, the tall Afghan veteran's expression, as the SIS man held out a welcoming hand, was one of affability tinged with concern.

Vanessa scarcely took in her surroundings as Jericho ushered her over to one of two armchairs drawn up with their backs to a writing desk on which stood an open laptop showing the familiar knowledge of evil logo. Apart from anything else, there was little to distinguish this room from a dozen other similar ones she had stayed in herself. She noted that the bed was already made and the curtains pulled back to offer a view of the road bridge spanning the city gorge and partly closed to traffic for construction work to accommodate the projected tram line. Jay was in shirtsleeves, his jacket and tie draped over the hotel's trouser press.

'Thank you, by the way, for your vaccination advice. I got that seen to.'

'Sensible. Beats running the risk of paralysis.'

'Can I offer you a drink? Tea or coffee?'

'Coffee. Black. No sugar.'

Seeing Vanessa's eyes fixed hypnotically on the cup and saucer placed in front of her on the room's chrome and glass-topped coffee table bearing a vase of artificial gerberas, Jericho gathered that his visitor's thoughts were elsewhere.

'Jabour was a close friend?'

The question brought Vanessa to her senses. She reached for the cup. 'Too young to die,' she said with feeling, after replacing the cup in its saucer.

'In every war I've known, it was never the old who laid down their lives in droves.'

Vanessa barely stopped her temper from flaring. 'Rashid wasn't a combatant in any war.'

'No, he was a victim of war.'

'An innocent civilian. He didn't lay down his life for a cause. He had his life snatched from him. And the worst of it is, I don't believe his death was an accident. And I'll tell you why.'

Vanessa related Justin's story of the twin attacks in Barcelona. Jericho's expression throughout remained impassive.

'So, you, he and your friends have cause to be worried,' said Rex at length, offering more coffee which she declined.

'Worried? We're running scared. This is totally unreal. Jabour did nothing to deserve this. Nor did Justin.'

'I fully understand your concern, and, although I can't promise to move mountains, I'll do my best to intervene in your defence. But first, I need to know precisely what and whom I'm dealing with. That means quickly arranging a meeting with Hendry and everyone else party to the contents of that briefcase. Remind me. How many people did you say were involved?'

Rex caught the hesitation. This young woman, he decided, was debating which of her and Hendry's associates to keep out of the equation. Indeed, wary of the seemingly artless invitation to jog Jay's memory, Vanessa was determined to protect Tich who, she hoped, had yet to cross Jay's or the other opponents' radar. Aware that she had given the game away, Vanessa compromised.

'Four or five.'

'Why the "or"?'

She shifted uncomfortably in her seat. 'The fifth is really a fringe participant.'

'Meaning?'

'A woman friend,' said Vanessa with exemplary composure, 'living in a home for the blind. I take her out swimming and for other recreation once a week.'

With Jay thrown off balance, she had no alternative other than to fill him in on the affair with Palmer.

'All right,' he said. 'Can you arrange for the four of you, that is to say excluding Fräulein Bogen, to meet me here at eight o'clock tonight?'

'If you intend visiting Justin … Mr Hendry … first, is there any …?'

'I don't. But there's every point in his being here tonight.'

'Very good. I'll have everyone here at eight o'clock.'

'Get them to come up one by one at intervals. That way it should go unnoticed by reception.'

'I'll come along first then to do the introductions.' Vanessa rose to her feet. 'Do you really think it's possible to put an end to this nightmare?'

Rex stood up in turn. 'Let me put it like this. I think I know who is behind your nightmare, and I would be most surprised if he had a hand in Rashid Jabour's death.'

'What about Barcelona?'

'Scare tactics.'

'Which included frightening the life out of a six-year-old. Well, I hope you're right. Co-operate, is that it, and we can turn the page on this ordeal?'

'Well, that's the general idea, Miss Curtis,' said Rex, of the opinion that his only hope of bringing influence to bear on K was to convince him of the need to safeguard the status quo without resorting to violence. 'But let's not count our chickens before they are hatched.'

'Till tonight then.'

After leaving *L'Ambassadeur* Vanessa decided to stop by a vegetarian restaurant in town for a soup, salad and quiche lunch in the course of which, ensconcing herself in a quiet corner of an upstairs room away from the babble of the ground floor and terrace, she rang up the rest of the Lenfindi Club and put each in the picture concerning her meeting with Jay. Her first and longest conversation was with Tich; the other calls she kept to a minimum, while explaining the need to meet up for the second evening in a row in her apartment, this time at seven p.m. in order to prepare the ground for their hotel appointment an hour later.

Memo from J to K

> *Have you noticed how the Invigilator has turned a blind eye to the fact that Urodina's extreme right party allied itself with a certain Reichskanzler in more ways than one during WWII, notably by taking the national anthem as a template for its own marching song in use to this day? What is 'Urodina ponad use!', if not cloned from 'Deutschland über alles'?*

Response from K

> *Understandable. Dogs don't eat the food people give them out of cans because they like it, but because it's forced on them. Generations of dumb dog owners have been given to believe this muck is the next best thing to canine tournedos Rossini. In the same way, if you want to get the masses on your side, prime them with a stirring rallying cry hallowed by custom. The more repetitive and mesmeric the better.*

Justin was the last to turn up at Vanessa's apartment that night on the heels of Craig and Isabelle, Tich having agreed to stay on the sidelines. Vanessa opened the meeting.

'When Jay told me he wanted to gather together everyone involved, I told him we were four in all, leaving aside Clara. Tich agreed it would be a mistake to lay all our cards on the table. Despite his repeated assurances, Jay is an unknown quantity. We know nothing about Jay's credentials. Peregrine Musgrave said nothing to indicate that the man works for MI6. And even if Jay is in the SIS's employ, are we better or worse off for that?'

'Whichever way you look at it, the man forced his way into my apartment,' protested Justin, 'and ransacked it.'

'Hang on, that's confusing Jay with Pliny.'

Justin was in no mood for frivolity. 'Serves the bugger right if he gets rabies.'

'I advised him to get a few shots, and he did.'

'More fool you. Look, Vanessa, as you said yourself, we don't know the first thing about your Jay.'

Vanessa paused in sketching a mock genealogical tree of stick characters identified by initial capitals – P for Palmer, H for Hoffarth, J for Jellicoe (a stab in the dark at someone less than admirable?), etc. – and tapped annoyance from her propelling pencil into her free hand. 'He's not my Jay.'

'He seems to have won you over.'

'I don't know where you get that idea from, Justin. We're between a rock and a hard place. It's a case of any port in a storm.'

'And what if tonight's meeting is a trap?'

'A repeat of Barcelona? Jay's not out to ambush us, Justin. He's trying to set things right.'

Craig scratched a dubious forehead. 'I don't know. Justin might have a point.'

An exasperated Vanessa threw down her pencil. 'Really, who got us into this fix in the first place, if it wasn't our pilfering news hound? Don't look at me like that, Justin. I know, this isn't a blame game. We agreed to play fucking follow my leader, and look where it's got us.' The deafening silence in the wake of this invective gave Vanessa time to catch her breath before returning to the fray. 'Come on, you two,' she said, in the face of querulous stares from Craig and Isabelle. 'It takes more than that to bruise his ego.'

Regretting the absence of Tich's moderating influence, Vanessa flung out disgruntled hands. 'All right, none of you is obliged to turn up tonight. But I, for one, am sure Jay doesn't intend to spring a trap on us. There'll be no members of the Met waiting with handcuffs behind his shower curtain. And, Tich has agreed to ring me every ten minutes. If I fail to answer, he'll call in Hoffarth.'

A scornful laugh issued from Justin. 'Fat use, if by the time Tich rings, Jay and his crowd have jammed plastic bags over our heads, dumped our lifeless bodies in the bathroom and checked out.'

'This is Luritania, Justin, not Caracas.'

'Try telling that to Gisela Radtezky.'

Unprepared for but resigned to opposition, Vanessa glanced at her watch. Time was running out.

'Where do you stand on this, Isabelle? If it helps at all, know that I'll be carrying my Browning.'

'Get Tich to tell Hoffarth what we're doing tonight and you can count me in.'

'Right, that's soon done. Craig? Justin?'

Craig nodded tacit agreement with Isabelle, before adding: 'All right. Benefit of the doubt. An opportunity better not left to let slip by.'

Outnumbered but unapologetic, Justin Hendry folded his arms in front of his chest and uttered a frustrated sigh. 'It would be churlish to refuse. A pity I can't charge sodding MI6 for the damage done to my sofa.'

If there was any relaxation in the taut lines around Vanessa's eyes, it was infinitesimal. 'Poor Justin. More sinned against than sinning.'

'Yes, well, before you recommend me for stoning, perhaps we could use this meeting to work in Margaret Musgrave's favour.'

'How, Justin?'

'By intimating she knows more than she does.'

Rex Jericho surveyed the faces of the quartet seated opposite him and told himself what he had guessed all along: this was not a full house. Lack of trust made his task none the easier, for without this emollient his enterprise would get off to a bad start.

Four individuals who risked burning quite a bit more than their fingers as a result of meddling in matters of state, although he could not deny that it would be stretching a point to dress the offence up in the garb of high treason. Well, no problem of gender inequality. In fact, had he not known otherwise, Rex would have said that Miss Curtis's strength of character marked her not Hendry out as ringleader. Not only had she taken the initiative in volunteering to introduce each of her companions as they came through the door, thereby allowing her to judge whether the man from MI6 had any tricks up his sleeve, but no doubt she had made the characters in this playlet of hers rehearse their lines – a suspicion borne out moments later when Hendry began mouthing Pericles at his host.

Whether Jericho liked it or not, the prime mover in this unfortunate affair which, with K's self-defence mechanisms working at high revs, risked spinning out of control, was Hendry. And despite the latter's insistence that it was preposterous to stigmatise the whistleblower for uncovering 'actions blacker than the night', Rex sensed that the editor, while shaken by two brushes with death in Barcelona, was riven with guilt over the Beirut slaying of their fifth – or was he their sixth? – fellow traveller. For Hendry would have nothing of assertions that Rashid Jabour's death was an unfortunate accident in no way connected with the botched Barcelona attacks.

But then the journalist had not impressed with his truculent drivel about the press's right to expose unsavoury plots hatched behind closed doors. Rex had no intention of letting Hendry and his acolytes in on how they had thrown a spanner in the works of an elaborate scheme, the fruit of months of patient toil on the part of those better placed than this amateurish foursome to appreciate what had been set in train. Nor could he afford to reveal that more interference stood to lose MI6 a fondly nurtured CIA insider.

These thoughts were interrupted by the ringing of Miss Curtis's cell phone. Rex noted that it was the second time that this had rang since the young woman's arrival. After giving the briefest of answers, Vanessa offered a token apology and switched incoming calls to voice mail.

Turning aside from his disapproval of Hendry, Rex considered the case of the attractive and self-contained Isabelle Meunier whom he judged to be as resourceful in her own way as Miss Curtis. How would Jean-Luc Meunier react were he to learn that his daughter had stumbled across secrets to which he was party but which he had kept hidden from his family for the past twelve years? More to the point, how would his daughter react were she to learn of her father's duplicity?

Of the four individuals assembled under his gaze, Rex fancied Roberts, the fitness expert, to be the weakest link in the chain: probably only in the game in order to curry favour with Isabelle Meunier.

'I apologise about the seating arrangements,' said Rex at last from the position he had taken up in front of the quartet on an upholstered bench no longer tacked on to the end of his queen-sized bed. From the apex of his triangle Rex looked down one side at Hendry and Roberts perched on the edge of that bed and down the other at Vanessa and Isabelle, who occupied the room's two armchairs. 'It would have been unwise to draw attention to ourselves by booking the hotel's conference room.'

'Your mattress could be firmer,' said Craig. 'Very bad for the back.'

'Yes. I might explain why they stock the cocktail cabinet with anaesthetics. Well, ladies and gentlemen, let me start by thanking you for accepting my invitation. Especially since, like it or not, my role tonight is that of examining magistrate. For your own as much as for my good. That being said, I don't think I need spell out the nature of your indictable offences. Nor need I stress how dangerous you have made things for yourselves. Witness recent events in Beirut and Barcelona. Mr Hendry explained how, when returning home from his aunt's funeral outside London, he, I regret to say misguidedly,' – Rex was not prepared to let the journalist off the hook – 'misappropriated a red leather briefcase containing classified documents belonging to a Westminster MP. I gather that all four of you then joined him in committing the error of succumbing to collective curiosity.

'Despite the fact that those papers clearly contained coded information, young Jabour – either under pressure from you or on his own initiative – was persuaded to try to break the code.' Rex paused to take a sip from a glass of water. 'Now, as I'm sure you will agree, in this day and age even more so than in the past, information is power. The real power brokers are those with access to jealously guarded inside information or with control over an efficient propaganda machine promoting their cause through sophisticated misinformation and disinformation tools. And in the race to outdistance the opposition, the power brokers with a head start over the rest of the field are those cracking a whip over the media. Past masters in the art of manipulation, they exploit attention spans, treating their audience like hospital patients reliant for their survival on drip feeding.

'This approach is particularly successful when leading a sustained but moderately dosed campaign designed to hide the fact that target audiences are being administered placebos. Similarly, in the event of adverse doses of information injurious to the campaigners' cause, the morphine of a constant stream of ever-changing news items not only distracts from the discomfort of conflicting information but ensures that memories are kept short.

'Excuse me for stating the obvious, but the whole point of bringing these verities home to you is to open your eyes to the fact that in a war as tooth and claw as this it was naïve on your part not to have stopped to think whether the texts decoded by you were framed with a purpose and message foreign to your superficial interpretation. You took the fact that the documents in question were found in Peregrine Musgrave's briefcase to imply that elements of Her Majesty's government, including MI5 and MI6, were in league with the devil. But the games which, Miss Curtis tells me, you are used to playing in your Sunday Club and the games you imagine the Secret Services indulging in are alike as blind man's buff and chess. You made the mistake of taking the decoded texts at face value.'

Justin raised his hand. 'Excuse me, but aren't you overdoing the *grave error of judgment* clause? Counting monthly website clicks, my review has a readership of between twenty and twenty-five thousand. And most of our subscribers live in the Greater Luritanian Region. The editorial wasn't properly syndicated. Yes, more than whispers of it reached Paris, New York, London, Frankfurt and Rome. But nothing front page. To quote your own argument, people's memories are short, especially when confronted with the umpteenth tired conspiracy theory.'

Rex let out the slightest of befuddled gasps. 'You didn't let me finish, Mr Hendry. What I was about to add by way of completeness was that a certain party who feels offended by your revelations suspects you of keeping a card or two up your sleeve. And he is prepared to move mountains to prevent you from laying one or more of these cards out in plain view on the table.'

'Well, then, your certain party is nothing short of paranoid. I, we, have no more cards tucked up our sleeves. If there was something else really mind-blowing in that briefcase, it was sufficiently well concealed to escape our attention.'

'That being so, let me ask each of you in turn whether you are still holding back hard or digital copies of the texts in question whether coded or decoded. I need honest answers, failing which you are slamming the cell door on yourselves. Miss Curtis?'

'There was little point in hanging on to the decoded version once it appeared modified in *The Pulse*, so I shredded it. The coded text is, as you already know, with Miss Clara Bogen.'

'Then reclaim and destroy it at the earliest opportunity. Miss Meunier?'

'Likewise for the decoded text. As for the coded version, I will comply with your instructions.'

'Mr Roberts?'

'I scanned and stored both the coded and decoded texts on my password-protected work pc. The paper versions I destroyed. It will take only a moment to delete the screen files from my hard disk.'

'Mr Hendry?'

'Ditto Craig's reply. In other words, that day you broke into my apartment you were wasting your time.'

'Right,' said Rex, ignoring the jibe, 'give me your guarantee that you will destroy all existing copies of these texts in paper and digital form, including any that you might prefer, for reasons best known to you, to keep secret from me, and I will use my best endeavours to clear your names with parties I fear likely to be after your blood.'

'Your best endeavours,' said Vanessa. 'How far do they extend?'

Rex spread his hands out wide. 'Since I can't rig the roulette wheel in your favour, I must convince the croupier that, if his casino disregards my guarantee of your goodwill, it will pay out substantially more than it rakes in.'

Justin raised a hand. 'Before we wind things up here, I'd like to say a word or two in support of Margaret Musgrave. She wrote to me while I was in Barcelona, asking about my connection with her husband. Whether I might have any idea about what pushed him over the edge.'

'How could she have known anything about you?'

'She didn't say. I suppose her husband must have left my business card lying around. The important point is that Margaret Musgrave has been left in the lurch. By your people. Don't you think that somebody inside that nebulous organisation of yours should set her mind at rest about her husband's ties with you – whether or not they advanced the cause of national security?'

Rex eased a stiff back. Yet again, less than the full story. Had Peregrine been careless with his private e-mails? Understandable perhaps in view of the stress which he and his wife had been under. But Hendry was right. The record needed setting straight, and the person who had been remiss about doing so was Rex Jericho.

'I agree,' he said. 'A sin of omission on my part that needs rectifying. Now then, one last not unimportant point. On the table by the window are forms requiring your signature under the Official Secrets Act. Take note of the wording before signing and keep a copy for yourselves on the way out.'

⁂

No sooner had the quartet led by Vanessa Curtis, left his room at *L'Ambassadeur* than Rex Jericho composed a short text for immediate e-mailing to Lester Kayser. Unscrambled, it read:

> *Given that our current headache occurred on my watch, I have, as promised, taken matters in hand. This entailed corralling four of five of the miscreants in my hotel room in Schönschlucht. As the fifth lives in a home for the blind, she can be rated as a dead letter drop rather than an active participant. To sum up: your man who has never worn the green jacket looks to have got Hendry running scared after a couple of narrow scrapes in Death In the Afternoon country. Combined with the Lebanon*

mishap (fortuitous?), these red alerts have undoubtedly sobered up the man from the press and his associates. Duly chastened, each has firmly pledged to destroy all digital and paper copies of the Westminster lost property in his or her possession, including that dead letter material, and to draw a line under the whole affair. Suggest instruct your Augusta Doppelgänger to stand down. Am considering some cross-border sightseeing before returning home.

The reply, brief and to the point, could hardly have been swifter in arriving:

Glad to learn you've got the bit between your teeth. But already reserved flight to Lenfindi, arriving Tuesday. Booked into Le Méridien. Stay put. Vital ensure no further fall-out. N.B. Your country's suffixless MEDRIMCOMB Duke to blame for Lebanon.

Rex gritted his teeth. Not that he had expected that Lester Kayser, faced with the prospect of both their covers being blown, would sit back and count the days till Christmas.

Resigning himself to the inevitable, Rex picked up the telephone and rang down to reception. Craig Roberts had nudged him from indecision. The hotel should either provide Mr Chandler with a firm mattress or find him a room with a bed from which he could awake refreshed not liverish. A good night's sleep would be essential if Rex was to forestall K's cloddish intervention.

But first of all, with Hendry's reprimand still fresh in his memory, Rex decided to correct a longstanding omission.

Seeking a meeting with Margaret Musgrave to explain face to face the nature of his relationship with her husband required courage of a different order to battlefield courage. Instead, he took a sheet of the hotel's cream letter paper and, after pausing to collect his thoughts, composed the following:

Dear Margaret,
Excuse me for taking the liberty of addressing you by your Christian name. Your husband was always Peregrine to me.

You should know that his contributions to the work of the Joint Committee on the National Security Strategy were highly regarded by his colleagues, who had many a cause to be grateful for the clarity of his judgment as for the importance he attached to informed decision-making in matters of risk assessment. I believe The Times made special mention of this in Peregrine's obituary.

Your husband's tireless support for the Joint Committee's work inevitably brought Peregrine into contact with the Secret Intelligence Service, which, in the light of his various roles, was happy to avail itself of his occasional assistance without, needless to say, taking him fully onboard.

The day of the tragic accident that befell your son, Stuart, coincided with a remit entrusted to Peregrine to convey SIS classified material to the Foreign Secretary. It was while travelling through the streets of London on his way to Whitehall that Peregrine first heard the news of Stuart's hospitalisation. Naturally enough, this appalling news left him distraught. So much so that, in his hurry to reach your son's bedside, Peregrine forgot all about the briefcase he was carrying with him in his minicab.

Unfortunately, one of the vehicle's later passengers took it into his head to misappropriate the briefcase and transport it to Europe, where he opened it – as a result of which sensitive documents fell into the wrong hands.

I feel sure that Peregrine kept this misadventure from you. Continually tormenting himself about the repercussions, he did everything in his power to recover the documents before anything was leaked. That proved impossible.

In view of the atrocious strain he was already under with respect to your son's condition, no doubt this reverse sapped Peregrine's already fragile morale, culminating in that most ill-starred of outcomes.

It is an outcome for which I cannot, in all truth, feel entirely irresponsible, since I was instrumental in urging him to regain those papers. But you should understand that any pressure which I exerted on Peregrine was intended to spare him the hostility of a third party desperate to keep the missing documents from being made public.

Nothing I can say can undo the wrongs already done. Nevertheless, permit me to offer my genuine appreciation of the services of a good and honest man devoted to his country's best interests, but on whom fate failed to smile.

Yours truly,

signed Rex Jericho

A feeble apologia, thought Rex, considering how rotten life had been to Peregrine and Margaret Musgrave. Had he done the right thing in refraining from expressing sympathy for the widow's dual loss? Rex thought so, given that Margaret Musgrave was unlikely to greet this long overdue message with anything other than contempt. Piling on the condolences would only make things worse.

Trusting that the widow had stayed on in the couple's Carlyle Square apartment, Rex sealed the envelope for handing to reception next morning. There was no problem with postage, since the room's previous occupant had conveniently left behind a stamp booklet. The € stamps all bore the same design, according pride of place to a dove of peace. After staring grimly at these for a few moments before affixing one, unable to rid himself of the thought, *après K , le déluge*, Rex decided on his next port of call: the cocktail cabinet

---

His working day got off to a bad start when Craig booted up his computer with a view to deleting all trace of the prohibited screen files only to ascertain that there was no sign of them. His first thought was that he must have been mistaken: perhaps he had stored the files on his home pc. Then he came to his senses. Had he not deliberately chosen to tuck this material out of sight on his workstation computer, because he alone had access to it, it was password protected and, deciding factor, the club's burglar alarm was connected to Schönschlucht's central police station? It took him a few moments to understand how the unimaginable could have occurred: a case of *Kilroy was here*.

But troubling enough as this discovery was, the day held worse in store for Craig Roberts foreshadowed by the unannounced arrival of the club's owner-manager.

Craig tried to remember the last time Piet van der Meulen had graced *All The Right Moves* with his presence. Constantly on the move from one European country to the next, indulging his passion for antiques, the Dutch manager had ended up renting out his little used pied-à-terre in Schönschlucht. Consequently, the owner's infrequent appearances left Craig pretty much of a free hand in the club's day-to-day running. When Piet did make a showing, it tended to be in connection with upkeep problems or, as Craig guessed on this occasion, event planning, namely the upcoming MSF cyclothon, which had attracted generous support from local business and institutional sponsors.

However, as the Dutchman invited his manager into the back office quickly vacated by the club's secretary, it was impossible to miss the fact that Piet's customary affability had deserted him. While Craig settled into his chair, the stooped fifty-year-old with a weak chin and sallow jowls preferred to avoid direct eye contact by concentrating on rubbing the red mark left on the bridge of his nose by a pair of ill-fitting bifocals.

'Just got back from Prague,' he said at last. 'Marvellous old city. Prague, Sofia, Bucharest. Never tire of them.' Van der Meulen was fond of attributing his *Wanderlust* to the fact that he had spent part of his student days rooming in the house in Delft (or was it The Hague?) where Vermeer painted *The Geographer.*

'Manage to snap up any bargains?'

'A couple of bronze statuettes.' Piet was about to elaborate – one statuette was of Narcissus, the other of a naiad – when the purpose of his visit brought him up short and he snatched a wary glance at Craig over the top of his glasses. 'Got the dealer to see things my way.'

Craig would not have expected otherwise. This was Piet's standard boast.

'So what's up? You plan on being here for the cyclothon?'

Van der Meulen averted his gaze from a holiday photograph of the club secretary and her two children taken under a palm tree. Somewhere far from Luritania.

'Craig, I'm sorry to say this but I have bad news for you.'

'There's a problem with the cyclothon?' From the unhealthy expression behind Piet's eyes Craig divined that the first thought to come to mind was the wrong one.

'No. a problem with you. I've had a written complaint from Toronto, maintaining that while in charge of one of Vancouver's health clubs you were accused of sexually assaulting an under-age female.'

Craig sat bolt upright in his chair. It took him a moment or two to come to his senses, but when he did, he bent forward, both hands firmly planted on his knees, and looked the Dutchman straight in the face.

'The whole thing was trumped up. The girl took it out on me for spurning her advances by claiming that I groped her. There was no foundation to anything she said. Nor were there any witnesses to bear her out. She failed to produce the slightest evidence to substantiate her accusations.'

'That may be, Craig, but, as you know, there's no statute of limitations on cases of this kind in Canada. And this female, a grown woman by now, has gone public on Facebook.'

Craig shook his head in speechless disbelief.

'Don't worry. Nobody's talking about extradition. Your accuser appears to be content to let off steam by calling you all the names under the sun. Sexual predator tops the list.'

Craig did not appreciate the voyeuristic glint in his boss's eyes. 'And you believe her story?'

'Frankly, I don't know what to think.' Piet pushed lopsided bifocals back up his nose.

'Jeez, Piet, this happened eight or nine years ago. I thought it was dead and buried. Why has she decided to rake the matter up now?'

'I've no idea, Craig. But whatever the rights or wrongs of the affair, I've received a number of heated e-mails suggesting that, before taking on new employees, I should be more careful in checking up on their background. A few of your spin cycling women are asking for their subscriptions back.'

'But this is absurd. The club found me innocent of this woman's allegations.'

'I'm sorry, Craig. I can't afford to keep you on. After you're finished with the cyclothon, I'm going to have to ask you to resign. The club can't afford this kind of bad publicity.'

'What? For heaven's sake, Piet, this is a storm in a teacup. My employers stood by my version of events. Miss Lescaut was a nympho, who took badly to rejection.'

'More than a storm in a teacup, Craig. A Super Bowl storm.' (This was one of Van der Meulen's ways of reminding people about the nation that had settled New Amsterdam.) 'According to the letter I have here …' The Dutchman produced an envelope from his pocket, extracted a sheet of paper and read from it. '… Mr Roberts was patrolling the changing rooms at the end of the morning, when he happened to see through an open door seventeen-year old Julia Lescaut, the last to leave, stepping out of one of the women's shower cubicles, accosted her and asked whether she would feel better for a friction rub.' The effort involved in quoting this last phrase caused Van der Meulen's face to turn crimson.

'And who wrote that letter?'

Piet handed the text over. 'Mrs Julia Gardner. Miss Lescaut has since married.'

Craig studied familiar words that he had hoped never to see or hear again. 'How did she track me down to here?' He tossed the letter demonstratively back onto the desk in front of his boss.

Unwilling or unable to answer this question, Piet decided to put a question of his own, proof of his inability to stifle lubricious curiosity. 'What actually happened, Craig?'

Craig passed a weary arm over his forehead. 'What happened is that she was the last club member to finish showering and dressing. She came out to me with a towel wrapped around her to say that her key wouldn't open her locker. I suggested that she might have tried the key in the wrong locker. She said no. The key was numbered. Which was correct. But this never stopped people from putting their key in the wrong lock. Anyway, I accompanied her into the changing room to check the key. It turned perfectly. But the moment I swung open the locker door she dropped her towel, climbed onto the nearest bench, grabbed hold of me, pushed her sex in my face and asked me to cure her saddle sores. To which I replied that she would do better to cover herself up, dress and leave as soon as possible, because I needed to close up shop. Which wasn't true, but I was alone and anxious to be rid of her and any further embarrassment.'

'Still, Vancouver believed her side of the story, didn't it Craig? You were shown the door.'

'Yes, the vindictive bitch did for me. Her parents sued the club, which stood by me throughout, until the authorities made a meal out of it. Christ, Piet, I can't believe that you're taking sides and making me pay a second time for an offence I never committed.'

'I'm truly sorry, Craig, but mud has a habit of sticking.'

It was then, in a flash, that everything became clear to Craig Roberts. Their MI6 saviour had been outgunned. 'Now I get it …'

As much unnerved as confused by this pronouncement, Piet van der Meulen stopped fussing with his bifocals. Yes, on the face of it, his action was inexcusable: turning a perfectly good employee into a sacrificial lamb for reasons which that self-satisfied, arm-twisting American had declined to explain. But in view of what the Dutchman stood to lose were he to renege on his pact with the man from Hades, the scintilla of remorse was short-lived.

'I'm afraid ..'

Piet's words might have been left hanging in the air, but there was no need to give substance to the unspoken.

'Can you at least write me a letter of recommendation?'

Piet van der Meulen twisted awkwardly in his seat. 'Eat my own words?'

'Come on, Piet, they're not yours, and you know it.'

'All the same … The social network is a bugger. Once something goes viral there, it's the devil's own job to set things straight.'

The Dutchman filed the discarded letter away in its envelope. 'Good luck with your cyclothon.'

The condescension underlying this last remark made Craig's bile rise. 'Are you telling me,' he said, after a strained pause, 'that you've already found a replacement?'

Losing patience with more than his bifocals, Piet folded these away into his pocket, cleared his throat and assumed the pose of an employer whose managerial acumen had been called into question. 'That's no concern of yours, Craig. I'd be grateful if, as soon as the cyclothon is over, you'd clear out all your things and put Betty into the picture about your software.'

Betty Hansen was the club secretary. Tempted though he was to clean *All The*

Right Moves' master computer of every piece of innovative software downloaded on it by him since he had taken over running of the club's training and diagnostics programmes, Craig realised not only that the programmes concerned were not his intellectual property but that, however much he despised Van der Meulen for abjectly caving in to outside pressure – what hold did Justin's and his enemies have over the Dutchman? – the last thing he wanted was to sabotage things for Betty and the rest of his colleagues.

'Understood.'

Piet pushed his chair back from the desk and cast a last look at three happy faces under a Mediterranean palm tree. 'As I said before, I'm sorry it had to come to this. You'll get two months' salary to tide you over until you find something better. Somewhere else.'

Refusing to fake appreciation of this last-minute gesture of appeasement cancelled out by Piet's 'Somewhere else', Craig rose to his feet, turned his back on the suborned owner and walked out, leaving wide open a door he refused to slam.

Craig Robert's summary dismissal preceded by discovery of deletion of all copies of Jay's sensitive files from the fitness centre's computer told Isabelle that the opposition had stolen a march on MI6.

'This means,' said Craig, looking at his girlfriend over a glass of *Pinot Gris* and the skeleton of a rainbow trout, 'that in five days from now I'm out of a job and unemployable.'

'We mustn't let these people beat us. Can't you set up on your own?'

'How, Isabelle? With no premises, no licence, no equipment.'

'You're forgetting the Chinese Reconstruction Bank kitty.'

'We never envisaged using it to our own advantage.'

'Come off it. Yes, we planned on acting the good Samaritan, but circumstances have changed.'

'There's something you're forgetting. My reputation as a fitness coach is finished here. Van der Meulen couldn't have made things plainer. And there's more to this. It didn't take me long to realise who got into the computer and deleted all that data. Charles Ravioli Hathaway. A young man of many parts, including that of American School student. He and Palmer are natural buddies.'

'Why not confront Palmer with this outright?'

'Where? On the shooting range?'

'No, Craig, this isn't Chicago.'

'Palmer is no more a full-time cultural attaché than I'm an Olympic gold medallist.'

'No, and he and the people behind him hold all the right cards. It would be suicidal to try playing them at their game.'

'I suggest cutting our losses and running.'

'Taking *El Fugitivo*? Out of the frying pan ...'

'No, not like that, Isabelle. Look, our original idea was to channel those BLR funds into deserving environmental and humanitarian charities. Why not offer our services and a slice of our finances, in addition to whatever we raise through the cyclothon, to *Médecins Sans Frontières,* the organisation that Rashid's father works for?'

'Our services? Neither of us has any medical qualifications. I doubt whether the first aid course I was sent on after signing up with BLR would count for much with MSF.'

'You're wrong. I've researched this. At the logistics end of things, MSF relies on back-up workers willing to help out with basic, non-surgical tasks, distributing food packs, mats, bedding. We wouldn't actually be employed by MSF so much as offering them our services through the local support infrastructure.'

'Burying the dead? Digging latrines? No bed of roses, Craig. I mean, are you thinking of Syria? Have you any idea what that would be like? Under constant threat of bombardment. Confined to a camp hospital site for weeks on end. Having to work alongside people from totally different backgrounds. Taking orders from doctors and nurses, who expect you to get a move on …'

'I'm prepared to give it a go.'

In two minds as to whether the offer of more *Pinot Gris* would aid clarity of thought, Isabelle stayed her hand.

'How about you? Don't tell me you've suddenly become wedded to the idea of a career in banking?'

Isabelle screwed up her face in distaste at the mere thought. 'You're saying we should put our principles where our mouth is?'

'That's about the size of it. Look, Isabelle, if Palmer has it in for me, you could be next in line. Do you think these people wouldn't dare, because of who your father is?'

'On the contrary,' said Isabelle, the paternal warning fresh in her memory.

Craig dragged his eyes away from a fish skeleton that reminded him of the time he had had to dissect a frog during one of his school biology classes. No, he would not be bringing any surgical skills to MSF field work.

'I think we should commit ourselves to something useful, if only for a year or two. MSF is a good cause.'

Reaching for the carafe, Isabelle poured *Pinot* into her empty glass, and surprised herself as much as Craig by saying, 'Perhaps not a bad idea. Let me think about it. But not Syria. That's definitely out.'

Stretched out on their sun loungers to one side of the swimming pool, Vanessa Curtis and Clara Bogen were engaging in one of their pastimes: identifying literary quotations. However, if Clara had just defeated Vanessa twice in a row as to the origin of 'All modern American literature comes from one book by Mark Twain' and 'Very well, I will marry you if you promise not to make me eat eggplant', it was not so much because of ignorance or memory lapses on Vanessa's part as because Vanessa was debating how best to advise Clara to deal with more importuning by American embassy staff.

But her astute friend was quick to break the ice. 'I'm sorry, Vanessa, but I get the impression your mind is elsewhere. Are you still worrying about that text of yours that Maureen should never have released to somebody outside the home?'

'Not the text, no. You've given it back to me, and I'll put it through the shredder at work. You haven't held back any copies, right?'

'You asked me that before and I told you. No, there are no more copies with me or Maureen. I saw to that. So what's upsetting you? I can feel that something is.'

'I'm worried in case I've paved the way for more grilling by those stuffed shirts waving their stars and stripes.'

'Set your mind at rest. I've told Maureen not to let them come anywhere near me.'

'She may not have a choice if they start hitting her with the official secrets act.'

'Is that what this is all about, Vanessa? So Miss Curtis has been leading a double life, has she? Knowing how fond you are of tiramisu, I should start looking for an apt quotation from Ian McEwan's *Sweet Tooth*.'

'It was wrong of me ever to have involved you in this miserable story.'

'Well, you didn't. I was the one who misbehaved in betraying your trust.'

'Nonsense. I'm the one at fault.'

'We won't get anywhere trying to outdo each other with *mea culpas*. And as for your worries about my being accused of aiding and abetting concealment of state secrets, let me tell you something I read in yesterday's press. A visually impaired supply teacher in Galicia, was invited to invigilate a set of secondary school exams. Naturally enough, she turned down the invitation on the grounds that she could not guarantee detecting whether students smuggled any cribs into the examination centre. The authorities' threatened to take her to court. Made out she was as good as refusing to do jury duty. But she wouldn't bow down. She went straight to the nearest human rights lawyer. In other words, let those Yankee clowns try the same on me and I'll give them as good as I get … in spades.'

Vanessa's taut features relaxed into a smile. 'Good on you, Clara. They need to know who's boss.'

⁓✻⁓

Memo from J to K

> *We should be grateful that, despite the rapprochement between Urodina and the Ottomans, next to no news of the extent to which Urodina is abusing human rights has reached the outside world. Following the outbreak of hostilities in the coal-rich eastern region, the authorities enacted legislation empowering them to arrest and emprison citizens suspected of sympathising with the rebel cause. I hesitate to hazard*

a guess as to the number of those languishing behind bars, but the list includes a prominent journalist judged guilty for speaking out against war in general. He had the hubris to denounce the coal region conflict as a senseless civilian war pitting fellow Urodinians against their own kind rather than against the Nevskian League. As a result of which he was thrown into solitary confinement, where he has been sitting with a weak heart condition, denied medical aid, for the past eighteen months.

Response from K

Yes, J, and not a word, if you please, about the fact that Vespuccia's military instructors have schooled Urodinians in appropriate interrogation techniques.

As for the scale of the Nevskian threat, it is unfortunate for us that this is now seen as bogus by not a few Urodinians distrustful of their leadership. Unnerved by the League's air campaign in Sennacheribia, these observers are questioning how the Veki army can have kept such a redoubtable force at bay for so long.

Justin Hendry was so used to learning about the Innova Press Corporation owner's work schedule via Skype that, on his first Monday back at work, he was surprised to find a blue Post-it stuck to the top of his workstation by Chantalle Boyer informing him that Dieter Wagener intended to drop by at 9 o'clock to 'have a word'.

With one and three quarter hours to go before Wagener's arrival, Justin had ample time to attend to current affairs and to wipe his office computer clean of all files created from the contents of the infamous red briefcase. Only since being shaken by Vanessa's news of Rashid's death under suspect circumstances had Justin developed a complex about the harm caused to others by his behaviour. Irreparable harm.

Despite the shock of Peregrine Musgrave's suicide, this had caused the young editor few twinges of conscience, believing as he did against the evidence of the GOSH letter that the MP's mind had been disturbed by an event of more tragic proportions than remiss loss of classified documents. But the advent of Margaret Musgrave's correspondence had forced him to face up to a truth which he had so far been unwilling to admit to, namely that his theft had precipitated the MP's mental breakdown. What plagued him now was the fear that he had exposed Vanessa to the merciless forces mooted by Jay. Hence, it was with no little satisfaction that he eradicated the wormwood of the incriminating files.

Ninety minutes later, knowing that Dieter Wagener was nothing if punctual, Justin cleared his desk of three problem files left over from the previous Friday and, in the quarter of an hour left to him, focused on four résumés, brought in by Chantalle with the rest of the morning's mail, submitted by candidates for the post of cartoonist left vacant by Klaus Radetzky. However, try as he might, Justin found it impossible to fight off the belief that the amateurs who had bungled both attempts on his life in Barcelona would not be so clumsy the third time around. And since the yob behind the wheel outside *El Corte Inglés* had been as much a threat to Gisela and Rosalie as to him, might not any person close to Justin risk becoming the victim of future reprisals?

Too preoccupied by these thoughts to give proper consideration to the respective merits of the four candidates, each of which had enclosed examples of their work, Justin allowed the minutes to slip by fruitlessly until a call from Chantalle over the intercom alerted him to Wagener's appearance caught on camera outside the front entrance. A few minutes later, she ushered the forty-year-old owner into Justin's office. Dieter Wagener was, in fact, the managing director of the European arm of *New Frontier Horizons*, a publishing house fielding an international portfolio of economic, political and thematic reviews and numbering the Innova Press Corporation among its subsidiaries.

Diminutive, white-haired before his time but conscious enough of his looks to dress smartly in line with Polonius's dictum 'the apparel oft proclaims the man', Dieter Wagener was a naturally jovial Austrian bursting with energy. So much so that Justin could not fail to detect the contrast between this morning's low-key demeanour and his employer's customary ebullience.

After a nonetheless convivial handshake, Justin, ever sensitive to his position within the company, followed his practice of uprooting himself from behind his desk and drawing up a chair for Wagener alongside him by the window.

The owner unbuttoned his jacket and stared admiringly at the triple gold towers of the InterEuropean Development Bank burnished by the morning sunlight. 'How are we getting on, Justin, finding a replacement for Klaus?'

'First batch of applications arrived with today's post. I haven't had time to weigh them up properly yet, but from the look of the artwork I should say that we probably won't need to look much further. Mind you, a lot depends on the salary they're expecting. We didn't put a figure on that, as you know.'

Wagener waved a dismissive, Rolex-braceleted hand. 'Money's no object. Within reason. But try to avoid anyone out to roast our trans-Atlantic sponsors.'

Justin kept his mirth as modest as possible. 'Best way to do that is to get those shortlisted to plough through the company's intelligence and psychological tests.'

'Fine.'

Wagener hesitated. Justin gathered that the man from Vienna was about to broach the real purpose of his visit, which took precedence over the matter of a new cartoonist for *The Pulse* whose appointment would nevertheless be subject to Wagener's approval.

Turning to face his editor-in-chief, Dieter Wagener forced a less than comfortable smile. 'The reason for my coming round today is about something more important than Klaus's replacement, compared to which Head Office has presented me with a bugger of a headache: finding a replacement for you.'

A benumbed Justin averted his eyes from dazzling architectural opulence to the fresh-shaven, rubicund man opposite him.

'No, wait, don't get me wrong. We're not raking over old coals. What's happened is that HQ have just lost one their best men in a road accident in Lagos. After sifting through all the possibilities, they came up with your name as the

411

ideal replacement. Young, unattached, upwardly mobile. It's a promotion not to be sniffed at, Justin. A remarkable opportunity, if I may say so.'

Having cleared the air at last, Wagener began to revert to his former laid-back self by clapping Justin on the shoulder. 'Congratulations, young man. Mind you, as I said, I'm going to have my work cut out finding someone to fill your shoes. Head Office has dropped a hot potato in my lap with that one.'

Uncertain as to whether to believe his ears, Justin was still grappling with the enormity of Wagener's proposal. On the one hand, to turn it down would appear to be pure folly. On the other, Justin did not need to read between the lines to grasp that this was no take-it-or-leave it affair.

'Wait a minute, Dieter. I'm trying to make sense of this. Head Office wants to take one of their European editor-in-chiefs with next to no knowledge of the world's second largest-continent and transfer him to the largest Anglophone state in Africa with a population of I don't know ...'

'One hundred and seventy-four million or thereabouts. Mind you, nowhere near that number subscribes to our publications in what will be your fiefdom, the Greater Lagos area.'

'All the same ...'

'In your position, Justin, I'd seize the opportunity. Let's face it, the longer you linger in this godforsaken European backwater, the more likely you are to be passed over on the company ladder.'

Wagener's enthusiasm was beginning to become infectious. The man who had entered his editor-in-chief's office somewhat mutedly was now bubbling over with goodwill. All the same, while chary of showing ingratitude, Justin could not help posing the obvious question.

'Why me, Dieter? There must be so many employees better qualified to fill this post.'

'Rubbish. My glowing reports on your performance have not gone unnoticed. It's as simple as that. I'm convinced you're the right man for the job. It's about time you spread your wings, my boy. Fresh fields and pastures new, and all that.'

Wagener made it sound as if he was half minded to renounce his directorship and blaze a new trail for the company in West Africa.

'Are you saying you want me to pack up here before you've found a successor?'

'I'm not the one who's calling the shots here, Justin. If it were up to me, yes, I'd prefer you stayed on to see in your replacement. But Lagos needs you as soon as possible. Of course, the company will fly you out there at its own expense, and you'll be given a handsome raise and a few welcome perks in view of the cost of living where you'll be working on Lagos Island. The area's bristling with banks and multinationals. Mind you, once you cross over to the mainland, things are not quite that ...' (Wagener rubbed an uplifted thumb and index finger in an attempt to conjure forth the least offensive qualifier.) '... advanced. But then you're unlikely to set foot outside the island while you're feeling your way. My goodness, I almost wish I could join you. But, for my sins, I can see myself having to slip on your shoes until we come up with Hendry Mark II.'

In the short time Justin had been given to mull the matter over it seemed on the face of it to be a godsend of an opportunity. On the one hand, he relished the prospect of a challenge of this magnitude. On the other, acceptance would mean waving goodbye to the Jays and Palmers of this world and their unholy cliques as well as sparing a recently widowed woman and her daughter further traumatic experiences.

It was only later that day when the import of Dietmar Wagener and his overlords' agenda was brought home to him by Craig and his news that it struck Justin as inconceivable that he could have been so blind. Compared to his friend's raw deal, had he really been gifted a trouble-free ticket out of his maze? From the little Justin understood of sectarian tensions in Nigeria, Lagos could be as much a hotbed of indiscriminate violence as Beirut.

꧁꧂

The weather on the morning of the Lenfindi Club's final meeting reflected the mood of the five participants. It rained continuously throughout the early hours and on into the late afternoon. In order to save on parking fees and petrol, Vanessa offered to pick up Craig and Isabelle. She drove to a suburban side street beside the Marriott Golf hotel a mere kilometer from the airport. All three struggled in against driving wind and rain to find Tich sitting in front of their customary twin tables with an espresso and an open weekend newspaper. In response to Vanessa's comment that he looked as if he had been lifted down from a rack at the dry cleaners, he explained that, since the spark plugs had given out that morning on his Renault Espace, he had cadged a lift with Justin, who was browsing the nearby newsagent's stand.

'We missed seeing his car out by the Marriott.'

'That's because he's parked it underground. One of his last expense account flings.'

'Wow, how profligate. What's taking him so long to buy a Sunday paper?'

'I think he's hoping to find a *Lonely Planet* travel guide to Nigeria.'

Tich folded his newspaper neatly and finished the last of his coffee. A waiter choosing that moment to arrive to take breakfast orders, Tich, his back to the newsagent's, added his own with the mention that a fifth member would be joining them shortly – only to give a start as Justin materialised next to him holding a copy of a German-language guide to Lagos and ready with his order.

'*Omelette aux fines herbes, frites, salade mixte et thé camomille.*'

'I see you have a healthy appetite this morning,' said Craig, as the waiter finished transmitting the group's orders to the kitchen and turned on his heel like a well-oiled automaton.

'You're speaking about a condemned man's last meal.'

Vanessa rocked back in her chair. 'Come off it, Justin. You're not headed for a war zone,'

'Oh no? What about Procul Harum?'

'I take it you mean Boko Haram.'

'No, I was right first time. Makes me turn a whiter shade of pale every time I think about them.'

'They operate out of north-eastern Nigeria, Justin. That's a long way from Lagos. Anyway, their speciality is kidnapping schoolgirls bred on McDonalds democracy, which promotes obesity and flatulence. They re-educate them to their cause by turning them into their mistresses or suicide bombers – sometimes both. I hardly think you need worry your head on that score.'

'Haram should be spelt harem?'

No, Justin. I thought you not only wrote the news but actually read other people's.'

Justin was flicking through the pages of his travel guide. 'Having you on, Vanessa. The more I think about this move, the more I like the sound of it. Especially since all augurs well on the Ebola front. No more cases in Nigeria, possibly due to the fact that the country's recent president went by the name of Goodluck Jonathan. But I do have a problem closer to home.'

'What's that?'

'Thought you'd never ask. Pliny.'

'You want me to adopt your ferret?'

'Not adopt. Be his B&B landlady. I shan't be out in Nigeria forever.'

'Oh dear, Justin, isn't it a bit facile to assume I'll be kicking my heels in Luritania until you return? What if next week I get chased out by Palmer in one of his tackier live theatre roles?'

'Right,' interposed Tich. 'Our nemeses seem to have hit upon a variant of Philip of Macedon's strategy. Divide and suppress.'

'Except for the fact,' said Craig,' that there's nothing to suppress. We've followed Jay's instructions to the letter. What else do they want from us?'

Tich's hand was ineffectual in rubbing exasperation from a creased forehead. 'They think we're holding out on them. That we've still got something to hide.'

'In other words,' said Isabelle, 'either Jay never interceded on our behalf or his intercession misfired.'

'Difficult to know what to believe. At worst, he's coxing for Palmer and his crew. At best, he's pulling for a rival team.'

'Well,' said Isabelle, 'if it's the latter, he's a good six lengths behind the competition'.

'There's another possibility …' said Vanessa, pausing to allow the waiter and waitress, who had floated up to their table, to set down the different breakfast orders. '… He can go only so far without compromising his own position.'

Craig finished cutting off a corner of *croque-monsieur*. 'One thing's as plain as a pikestaff. Palmer engineered my dismissal and Justin's transfer. He used Charlie Hathaway to talk me into letting him access my club pc so that the boy could hunt down Rashid's files and delete them while my back was turned. In short, we've got Uncle Sam's goat. As for Jay, I'm prepared to give him the benefit of the doubt. Hard to believe relations are that incestuous that the guys and girls in GCHQ are willing to risk crabs and worse by sleeping with the NSA.'

'Meaning,' said Tich, 'that MI6 is selective about how much and what data it relays to the NSA?'

'And vice versa.'

'None of which helps us playing piggy in the middle.'

Justin looked up from his triple-egg omelette. 'Although I originally had Jay down as a card sharp able to run rings around any lie detector test you threw at him, I'm beginning to think I might have been unfair. Perhaps he played a part in staying Palmer's hand against us. Because it looks as if this time around Arnold's people have substituted kid for boxing gloves. But with a wake-up call: *This a dose of what you get for rocking the boat – Capsize it and we'll feed you to the sharks.*'

'Well,' said Vanessa, 'why allow you, the instigator of all their woes, to come out of this so much better than Craig, a fringe participant?'

'Does there have to be rhyme or reason to it, Vanessa? These freaks take whatever remedies pop into their brain-dead heads.'

'There's no need to feel sorry for Craig,' said Isabelle. 'Although I must say that Justin's looking at this through rose-tinted spectacles if he thinks we view van der Meulen's behaviour as anything other than a blow below the belt.'

'I'm sorry,' said Justin, all too aware that Isabelle was awaiting an apology. 'It's me that's been given the kid glove treatment. Craig's is a lousy deal …' On the point of giving voice to the lurking fear that exile to West Africa might bring more in its wake than anodyne ostracism, Justin elected to seek comfort in protein.

'Well,' continued Isabelle, 'Craig and I put our heads together with a view to turning this body blow to our advantage. Tich already knows what I'm talking about. I think it better, Craig, if you go ahead and tell Justin and Vanessa about our decision.'

Craig set down his coffee cup. 'In fact, the idea was brewing in our minds long before van der Meulen gave me my cards. The fantastic success of yesterday's cyclothon at the end of which we had raised three quarters of a million euros for MSF, thanks largely to the MEDRIMCOMB's and BLR's generosity only served to reinforce our determination to chuck everything in here and offer our services to MSF.'

Justin held his knife in the manner of a surgeon manipulating a scalpel. 'Don't they require people with medical skills?'

'Of course. But backing up their professional teams of doctors, surgeons and nurses is a ground force of volunteers distributing food, water, sleeping-bags. All the basics needed by people injured in or fleeing war zones. And MSF's Paris office was quick to accept our offer of support when they got wind of that fat cyclothon cheque. We shall be packing up here next weekend and flying out to Afghanistan on Monday.'

Justin flashed a concerned look at his two friends. 'Afghanistan. How do your parents feel, Isabelle, about your knocking on the Taliban's back door?'

'Neither likes the idea. My father worked out there before I was born. He says the Russians and Americans should have thought better than to send so many of their young to die there for nothing. My mother. Well, you can imagine.'

415

'I think,' said Vanessa, 'that you're both incredibly plucky. Where are you off to, Kabul?'

'In the first place. In one of MSF's co-ordination offices. But after that we're due to help out in the field in a place called Kunduz.'

'Never heard of it.'

'Nor had we. But apparently it's a major MSF emergency trauma centre catering for the country's entire northeastern region. They've equipped it with three operating theatres and an intensive care unit.'

'Sounds a noble decision, Isabel,' said Tich. ' But a dangerous one. As good as in the thick of the fighting.'

'We think the Taliban have more sense than to target a facility treating their wounded alongside civilian casualties.'

'I can't believe this. Esmeralda and Casanova following in the footsteps of ...' Checking herself too late to salvage the situation, Vanessa cast around for a lifebuoy. '... What right have I to bemoan the death of a maiden theatrical production, when two of my leading lights are ready to brave the real world of operating and war theatres?'

'Come off it,' protested Craig, his embarrassment tinged with fear bred of doubt. 'Don't make us out to be something we're not, Vanessa. Isabelle and I see this as a form of absolution.'

'What? For that Mensdorf affair?'

'No. For standing by and doing nothing.'

'What you've chosen to do certainly doesn't qualify as taking *El Fugitivo* out of Luritania. Though it leaves me looking like a lemon. Where do I go from here?'

'Well,' said Tich, rolling his tongue around his gum to dislodge stubborn food remains. 'What's to say Palmer hasn't got plans for you? Nothing murky in your past that couldn't be used against you?'

Vanessa grimaced. 'Truancy? Shoplifting?'

'Wow, Van. *Harrods'* sheerest underwear?'

'Nothing that refined. Jelly babies pick and mix from Woolworths. Ten years old.'

'Pretty much of a clean slate compared to grand larceny,' said Tich, a sliver of uncertainty entering his mind after reading about how China was cracking down on corruption in ways that made Europe's lawmakers look as if they were playing puss in the corner. What if he became no less immune from Palmer's witch hunt than Vanessa or the rest of the group he preferred to think of as the Sunday Club?

'Right, they'll have a job raking up any mud against me. And if they try anything, they'll fucking regret it.'

'I suggest you get back to Jay and fill Hoffarth in on what's happened.'

'Fat lot of good that'll do, Tich. What if Jay has done a vanishing act? And how likely is Hoffarth to set his sniffer dogs on someone who has all the bases covered?'

'We don't have many options.'

Vanessa heaved a sigh. 'So this is our last Lenfindi Club meeting. We've gone from five to six, back to five and after today we're down to two. I can't see you and me exchanging views on Lawrence Sterne, Lewis Carroll and Samuel Becket with nobody else around to liven up the debate. In which connection, before we break up for good, are any of you ready to join me in taking a last few swings at mutual *divertimenti?*'

Justin added pepper to his omelette. 'Don't let the bastards get us down, is that it?'

Her attention caught by a figure in the mind-distance weaving its way through a gaggle of charter flight travellers, Vanessa appeared to be only half listening. For the briefest of moments, before realising that her mind was playing tricks on her, she could have sworn that she had spied Rashid hurrying towards the far passport check point. The same height, build and hair colouring, the same tasteful business suit a cut above his grey carbon-copy contemporaries. But no. He had not seen her. And had he, would he have paused to wave goodbye?

Chiding herself for maudlin vulnerability, Vanessa turned embittered eyes back to the solid world of the Lenfindi Club's two breakfast tables.

'Does anyone here apart from me know how Spike Milligan used to let off steam at the *Mermaid?* No, I thought not. Why should you? He kept a life-size dummy in one corner of the stage for something to kick the shit out of whenever he started to lose it. Know the feeling? Well, that's what I felt like on the back of Craig's news, coming, as it did, on top of … ' A floundering Vanessa cast around for safety from her demons. '… the difference being that my dummy of choice would be a dead ringer for Arnold Palmer.'

'With the emphasis on dead,' suggested Tich, already into his second *quiche.*

'That's it. But then I said, be realistic, put the blood lust on hold and make the most of our last communal here and now.'

Tich nodded approvingly. 'I'll second that. And, in fact, before you lot arrived, I came across one of the richest pieces of nonsense I'd read in a long time in this rag. So, to start the ball rolling, I give you the following.' Smudging newsprint with a greasy finger and thumb, Tich took up the folded newspaper in order to verify that his eyes and memory had not deceived him.

'You all know how paranoid the Baltic States have become about their Russian neighbour. One of them has now taken its detestation of the Russian Federation to a new level. Its Minister of Education has ruled that all geography classes in the country should be taught using new globes either omitting or leaving unnamed a certain nearby country which happens to account for one sixth of the planet's land area. Worthy of *Ripley's Believe It Or Not.*'

'I think I can go one better than that on much the same subject,' said Justin, bestowing a jaundiced eye on the amount of butter he had just spread on his bread roll. 'As you may or not know, Ukraine's president is a man with fingers in many pies, including his own television station. It's an effective tool for getting his message across to that largely uneducated chunk of the population yet to have gone online. So the latest piece of televised tomfoolery feeds off people's conviction that Crimea was annexed by force of arms and that an army of occupation is holding the peninsula's population in its thrall. How does it do this? By showing

417

footage of deserted beaches, streets empty of life, and shops with bare shelves – all because Crimeans are cowering in their cellars. But then, from the ridiculous to the sublime, this quasi-pastiche of Stanley Kramer's 1959 film *On The Beach* coincides with a televised documentary on a major French television channel showing Crimea's beaches packed with holidaymakers, people going about their life as normal on the streets of Sevastopol and Yalta, and shops in these cities with well-stocked window displays and interiors.'

Tich gave up trying to read the future from the dry bed of his coffee cup. 'And how, Justin, might I ask, did you come to clap eyes on that Ukrainian programme?'

'A good journalist never betrays his sources.'

'And fact, as we have learnt to our cost, is stranger than fiction. What about you, Isabelle? I suppose not. By the sound of things, you and Craig have had bigger fish to fry.'

'Yes, Tich. But I do have one language question. Why do you English call your James Bond Oh Oh Seven and not zero zero seven?'

Tich bestirred himself slowly. 'Yes, well, a bugger of a question, if you'll excuse my saying so, Isabelle. As any self-respecting Indian mathematician will tell you, O is not a number. It's a letter of the alphabet. But we pig-ignorant British whose telephone numbers include one or more zeroes persist in calling them Os. And international airport flight announcements in English invariably favour literacy rather than numeracy when stating boarding gate numbers including that figure resembling a squashed letter of the alphabet.'

'Come on, Tich,' objected Craig. 'It's a matter of economy. Why mouth two syllables when one will do just as well?'

'Goodness, Craig, that's throwing A.J. Ayer out of his Viennese tub along with the bathwater. Tell me, Isabelle, what do you call 007 in French?'

'*Agent double-zéro sept*. Which explains my question.'

'Well, my dear, this is a case of the *Académie française* going one better than Cubby Broccoli.'

'Do we think Jay has a number?' asked Vanessa, levity far from her thoughts.

'Licence to kill?' Tich gave a derogatory snort. 'Did this man who professes to be from MI6 strike you as someone taking his orders directly from Ralph Fiennes?'

'No, but that needn't mean a thing. I expect Her Majesty's Secret Services contract out their dirty work. Just as another agency did with Rashid.' Aware of the unintentionally deadening effect of her words on the rest of the club and struggling with her emotions, Vanessa finally failed to fight back nature: a solitary tear rolled down her cheek. 'I'm sorry. But, you know, a few minutes ago I could have sworn I saw Rashid hurrying to catch a flight. An illusion. It can't have been him. Whoever or whatever it was looked too substantial to have been a ghost.'

'I don't know,' said Isabelle. 'Our word *revenant* is perhaps more descriptive than your word ghost.'

'Yes,' added Justin, 'it being *sous-entendu* that we subjectify whoever returns to us.'

'And what fucking chokes me up,' continued Vanessa, glaring at a passer-by whose rucksack had dealt her shoulder a glancing blow, 'is that we can't pay these faceless bastards back in their own coin. I know it wouldn't bring Rashid back. Nothing can do that. But why should they be allowed to win hands-down?'

'Surely,' said Craig, 'it's all over now?'

'I'd like to believe you're right, but I can't.' Sorry, folk, I'm spoiling the party. *Illegitimi non carborundum*, shouldn't that be our motto?'

Tich scratched a stubbled jaw. 'Strictly speaking no, because, although meant to slate bastards, it is itself bastard Latin. But let's not quibble. Indeed, you should not let crap like Palmer get you down. And if I say you instead of we, it's because all four of you are entitled to begrudge my escaping victimisation. On the other hand, I suspect that could turn out to be wishful thinking on my part.'

'What an egotist,' said Vanessa, finally shaking free of dejection. 'They're leaving the best till last, is that it? What means do you think they'll use to unseat you? Break into your shop one night, fill a few shelves with pornography and have you blacklisted with the *Chambre de Commerce*?'

'Yes, that would do me no good, I suppose, although the same people thirsting to close me down for full frontals would never think of seeing whether I was making money out of *Justine* or *The 120 Days Of Sodom*. Of course, the sods unknown to the marquis would have to disable my burglar alarm. Not that that should be too difficult. Still, provided they left my late nineteenth century *Private Memoirs and Confessions of a Justified Sinner,* my first edition of *Three Men In A Boat* and my nine-volume *Tristram Shandy* untouched, I would consider myself a lucky man.'

Gratified to note that he had raised a smile or two, Tich returned to his *quiche,* Vanessa's mockery ringing uncomfortably in his ears.

Étienne Beauregard heaved his unwieldy frame out of a chair unsympathetic to his lumbar region and uttered a string of colourful expletives, culminating in: 'Ces enculés d'Américains, n'apprendront-ils jamais? These American arseholes, when will they ever learn?'

His second-in-command, Yannick Jouvet, an athletic-looking young man, who made a point of taking the occasional break from sitting in front of the French embassy's bank of security monitors to do burpees and chin-ups in the basement, bestowed an unsympathetic glance on Beauregard and his job lot chair.

'We have to let the ambassador see this,' said the junior security officer, pressing the open button on the room's digital video recorder in anticipation of what he knew to be his superior's only possible decision.

Beauregard belted the back of his chair with a meaty fist, wishing he could mete out punishment to something more responsive than an inanimate object.

'He's here all this morning as is Meunier. Hang on a minute while I call up Anglade's secretary.'

Some ten minutes later, Gérard Anglade, France's ambassador to Luritania, stepped through the open door into his head of security's office, a puzzled expression on his bronzed face. An accomplished downhill skier with two family chalets in Val d'Isère and Cortina d'Ampezzo, when told by the Italian ambassador to Luritania that it looked as if he brought the same energy to his diplomatic responsibilities as he did to his skiing, Anglade had replied: 'Were it so, my friend. You are forgetting that diplomacy is all uphill'.

He was quick to shake hands. In spite of the unwelcome news which they were about to impart, the two men felt relaxed in the ambassador's presence. Sanguine and pragmatic by nature, Gérard Anglade inspired confidence.

'You have something to show me, gentlemen?'

'Yes, sir,' replied Beauregard. 'Yannick was reviewing the latest set of internal surveillance videos when he latched on to something serious.'

Knowing better than to waste time with guessing games, Anglade gestured towards the large plasma display panel on the far wall. 'Well, put me in the picture.'

'Of course, sir. But before we play these images back, I ought first to explain what you'll be seeing. It's the office of Monsieur Meunier. And the person sitting there is the new cultural attaché at the American embassy down the road. He doesn't remain seated for very long.'

Beauregard pulled up a chair for his ambassador, but the latter preferred to stand. Jouvet sent the disk back into the DVR and fast forwarded to the precise point in time noted down by him, the hour, minute and unfolding seconds clearly indicated at the bottom of the screen. His superior thought fit to provide a basic explanatory commentary.

'Monsieur Meunier has just stepped out of the room to attend to some business with the consul. You'll see that he has kept the door between the two offices ajar. Insufficiently. Monsieur Palmer, the American cultural attaché left alone in Monsieur Meunier's office, is out of Mademoiselle Picquet's line of sight.'

Gérard Anglade watched as Arnold Palmer rose to his feet, extracted what the ambassador assumed to be a fountain pen from his pocket and pointed it towards the far ceiling.

'What's he doing there?'

'That's a laser directed at and blinding the camera lens. What Monsieur Palmer failed to realise was that there might be more than one camera in the room. The smaller one that recorded all this is concealed behind an overhead light.'

Yannick Youvet having temporarily halted the procession of images, the ambassador signalled for him to move on. Seconds later, he saw Palmer pocket the laser pointer, slip his Chopard from his wrist, prise open the rear cover, tap out a small device, replace the cover and watch, and cross the floor to the framed reproduction of a post-impressionist painting on the wall beneath the blinded camera. Whatever the cultural attaché had been holding in his hand before was no longer there when, after straightening the Cézanne, he returned to his seat. With a keen eye on the digits unrolling at the bottom of the screen, Gérard Anglade calculated that it had taken the man called Palmer less than seventy seconds to achieve his purpose. Several minutes later, Anglade's *conseiller des affaires étrangères* re-entered his office to find the American sitting where he had left him.

'A bug?'

'Yes, sir. Physically confirmed by Yannick here early this morning.'

'And this was Palmer's first visit to the embassy?'

'Yes, sir.'

'Like any other visitor, he was subjected to a full body scan?'

'Correct. He would have been asked to remove his watch, fountain pen, wallet, cell phone, car keys and loose change and place them in a basket outside the metal scanner before entering it. Car keys and cell phones are held back for collection on the way out. But once they've exited the scanner, visitors are allowed to retrieve smaller innocuous items.'

'What's your definition of innocuous, Étienne? No, it's all right, I'm not blaming you. We live and learn.' The ambassador turned to Beauregard's assistant. 'Did you remove the bug, Yannick?'

'No, sir. I, we both, felt it advisable to leave that decision to you.'

Instead of responding to this deferential suggestion, the ambassador asked Jouvet to replay the video.

After due rumination in the wake of the second showing, the ambassador indicated that he had seen enough. 'Leave the bug in place.'

'Right, sir.'

'Meunier knows it's there?'

'Not yet, sir. Once again, we thought …'

'You were right. Leave the Meunier side of things to me.'

'And what should our attitude be, sir, if this cultural attaché were to show his face here again?'

Gérard Anglade eyed both men impassively. 'That's not going to happen, Étienne.'

Beauregard nodded understanding. That pompous old fart Nussbaum was in for a bollicking, something confirmed by Jouvet seconds after the ambassador had strode out of the room.

'Did you recognise the painting?'

'Can't say I paid it much attention.'

Cézanne's father reading *L'Événement*. Ironic, no? Anglade's bound to rewrite the headlines with this one.'

※

Over Monday morning's breakfast, Jean-Luc Meunier was dealt the first of the day's two bad surprises. Having stayed up into the early hours working on her latest papier-mâché creation, Charlotte Meunier proudly showed off her fire-breathing dragon.

'What do you think, Jean-Luc? One of my best?'

Her husband had to admit that the dragon was quite a work of art.

'I intend offering it as one of the tombola prizes on the French stand at this year's Multinational Bazaar.'

'Wouldn't it be more appropriate to offer it to the Chinese?'

'No, Jean-Luc. As you well know, their New Year starts in February. And next year will be the year of the monkey.'

'What's this year?'

'The year of the horse.'

'Why not wait until the year of the dragon?'

Charlotte Meunier puffed out her cheeks. 'That's nine years away.'

'It's a beautiful dragon, Charlotte. A real fire-breathing beast. Let me have a closer look at it.'

Charlotte passed the lightweight model across the table. Jean-Luc took care not to bend the wire cage body overlaid with gold, red, orange and white-painted papier-mâché. However, despite the expert brush strokes or because of a wish not to let admirers lose sight of the fact that the medium used for this creation was printed paper some of the original lettering remained legible. Thus it was that the artist's husband sat so transfixed by the sight of a particular combination of letters that, instead of treating the dragon with the delicacy it merited, he all but crushed its ribs.

Charlotte Meunier attributed Jean-Luc's pained expression to dyspepsia. After all, some of the raspberries they were eating with their Greek yoghurt carried an acid aftertaste. 'What's wrong, Jean-Luc. Stomach upset? It wouldn't surprise me. I hate to think what chemicals they treated these berries with.'

The diplomat's eyes widened to take in their immediate surroundings beyond the narrow, mesmeric field of vision claimed by a paper dragon. 'Stomach? Why, no. Tell me, Sophie, where did you get the newsprint for this ...' Jean-Luc weighed his words. '... splendid dragon?'

'Goodness knows. Here, there and everywhere. From my usual stock of last week's newspapers on the pantry floor.'

'Are you sure? Think carefully.'

Charlotte Meunier turned questioning eyes on her husband. 'Are you sure you're feeling all right?'

'I'm feeling perfectly all right, Charlotte. Please try to remember which newspapers you used.'

'The ones you and I read each day of the week. *L'Humanité. Le Canard enchaîné. Le Mercredi.*'

Jean-Luc shook his head in what he considered to be a remarkable show of self-possession. If nothing else, the world of diplomacy had taught him the virtue of forbearance. 'Think again, Charlotte. Might you have used something else?'

Charlotte Meunier recovered the dragon and turned it around in her hands until part of the lettering seen by her husband came into view and prompted a memory. The *femme de ménage* had asked whether she could take some papers home for protecting her living room parquet from paint splashes, while her son was redecorating the walls. 'Wait a minute, now that I think of it, there wasn't enough paper in the pantry, because I had given some to Béatrix.'

This made eminent sense in Jean-Luc's eyes, for, although he might not have read every line of newsprint covered by those three newspapers, no one was better placed to understand that the series of coded letters used to identify the minutes of the Council of Twenty's meetings in north-western Europe could by no stretch of the imagination have appeared in the national press. For the simple reason that they were known solely to the Council members as such, a small circle of outsiders and the secretary responsible for minuting these meetings, Jean-Luc Meunier. All that remained now was for Charlotte to explain the seemingly inexplicable.

The diplomat commended himself on taking in his stride the hiatus which would have tested the patience of many a lesser husband as his wife set her creation down on the table and cast a dreamy-eyed look at the artistry of the blood-red tongue of fire issuing from its jaws.

'And after Béatrix had left you paperless?' said Jean-Luc, having imperceptibly counted off ten seconds on his fingers.

Charlotte Meunier jerked herself awake. 'Well, as soon as I realised that I needed only a little more paper to complete the task, I remembered chancing across some sheets the other day at the bottom of one of my dressing-table drawers. It looked like the kind of thing your computer spews out when it's looking for faults or viruses in the system. *Du galimatias* (Gibberish). So I concluded that Isabelle must have left it there as extra lining paper when we were sharing the same drawer before she set up in an apartment of her own.'

'Do you remember how many pages you used?'

'Really? Is it that important. Half a dozen. Perhaps more.'

'Did you use it all?'

'Yes, of that I am sure.' An exasperated Charlotte Meunier threw up her hands. 'Do you mind telling me what this is all about?'

Jean-Luc temporised. Things could not have been clearer. Why had it not struck him earlier? That mushroom cloud article in *The Pulse*. When he showed it to Isabelle, she had acted as if it was new to her. Yes. Acted, that was the word. His daughter had allowed herself to be sucked into something she only half understood. Something that had brought *Géai* scurrying across the channel, and that nasty piece of work, Palmer, suggesting he rat on his own flesh and blood. And now Isabelle and her boyfriend had decided to turn their backs on everything and to commit themselves to MSF's humanitarian aid programme in war-torn Afghanistan. How often had she told her father that the hollowness of diplomacy was exemplified by the board game of the same name, in which alliances and truces were established or broken under the impetus of power lust and avarice. In short, the be-all and end-all of diplomacy was land and natural resource acquisition compared to which people were chaff. And now to prove that people mattered, his daughter had thrown away a secure job in Luritania's banking sector to join her boyfriend, apparently a victim of unjust dismissal, in risking both their lives in an ungodly corner of the world. All this to his and his wife's distress. Small wonder that Charlotte sought solace in transmuting harsh news into more pleasurable forms.

Unable to banish these painful thoughts, Jean-Luc, nonetheless, sought to ease his wife's mind.

'It looks as if Isabelle must have found an old coded diplomatic print-out of mine which I should have shredded. In the event, Charlotte, no harm has been done, since you've converted my impenetrable text into a remarkable work of art.'

⁂

Jean-Luc Meunier's second bad surprise came later that same morning, when his ambassador walked into his office, shook hands, pulled up a chair in front of his desk and cast a pensive eye on a Cézanne that, in spite of Jean-Luc's attachment to this portrait of the artist's father, had not caught the *conseiller's* attention in a long time.

'How are things, Jean-Luc?'

Although the ambassador's manner was as polished as ever, his subordinate sensed an undercurrent of more serious matters to come.

'Nothing much on today, ambassador, apart from the monthly rotary club business lunch and a lecture by a visiting Palestinian journalist at the *Forum De Gaulle*.'

'What's he lecturing about?'

'Ostensibly, *Paths to peace resolution in the Middle East*. But to judge by some of his recent writings, I expect him to belittle Israel for trying to go one better than the Berlin Wall and apartheid.'

'Guaranteed to stir things up, but not half as much as I intend stirring things up with Nussbaum.'

The opening banter dispensed with, a bewildered Jean-Luc realised that Anglade had decided to cut to the quick.

'I see that the American embassy's new cultural attaché paid you a visit last week. Could you tell me what that was all about and your general impression of him?'

Jean-Luc Meunier felt the pulse begin to race in his wrist. Impossible to know where this line of questioning might be leading. Why jump to the wrong conclusion? Anglade's curiosity was perfectly natural.

'He called on me after meeting Philippe Morbier, our own cultural attaché, at a cocktail party. Philippe must have told him that I'd spent time out in Afghanistan and this new fellow, Palmer, who'd been out there as well, was interested in exchanging opinions on the direction in which that part of the world was headed.'

'He was interested in a great deal more than that,' said Anglade, both thumbs tucked under his chin, while he regarded his *conseiller* fixedly above interlaced fingers. 'Because in the short period while you were out of the room talking to the consul, he planted a bug in here.'

Jean-Luc Meunier found his tongue working dryly in his mouth. 'Caught on camera?'

'Right. Attaching a bug to the back of your Cézanne over there.'

Meunier's reaction could not have been more concise or heartfelt. '*Le salaud.* (The bastard).'

'You told him nothing of great importance?'

Jean-Luc rankled at the suggestion. 'Of course not, ambassador.'

'And at no stage did he strike you as someone out to cozen you?'

'He was a smooth character. But, no, he didn't strike me as … But then, I suppose his type wouldn't, would they?'

'Probably not. So Nussbaum's using a new kid on the block to pry on us. He might have gone about things more professionally, don't you think? Instead of using somebody wet behind the ears. What else do we know about this cultural character?'

'Outside sources tell me that he's a fitness addict and a first-class shot with a pistol.' By 'outside sources', Jean-Luc meant his daughter, but he was not about to drag her name into the proceedings. 'You heard about this weekend's cyclothon?'

'Yes, I believe we fielded a team. All for a good cause. MSF.'

'Yes, well, Palmer's team raised the most money, because its four cyclists chalked up one hundred and fourteen kilometres more than our men over a period of forty-eight hours with rest breaks.'

'America leading the field?'

'Apparently, wearing Italy's colours. But the day before the cyclothon this excrement called Palmer came second in an individual pistol competition at his shooting club. He scored seven hundred and fifty out of a possible eight hundred. The winner scored seven hundred and ninety.'

'An American beaten by a hot-shot Luritanian?'

'No, by an Englishwoman. Time-study engineer with the European Executive Committee.'

'I expect that took our cowboy down a peg or two.' Deciding that he had heard enough, Gérard Anglade rose to his feet. 'Well, now I intend to settle his hash properly. As for you, Jean-Luc, you will have nothing more to do with *ce connard* (this prick) outside our premises, where he will not be allowed to set foot again.'

'I'm glad to hear it, ambassador. I trust Beauregard has already removed the bug?'

The ambassador walked across to the far wall, lifted the picture off its hook, turned the frame around, grunted, hung Cézanne's news-hungry father back in place and returned to face his *conseiller des affaires étrangères*. 'No, I'll get him to remove it later. I was toying with the idea of giving our American friends something to chew over, but why descend to their level? Will they have heard anything from your end that might be cause for concern?'

Persuaded that he was not deceiving himself in thinking that the ambassador was hinting at sexual rather than political indiscretions, Jean-Luc gave a relaxed a smile. 'If anything, I fancy I may have ruffled a few feathers over the phone with my Italian opposite number. He missed last month's businessmen's lunch hosted by the *Association des constructeurs européens d'automobiles* (European Automobile Manufacturers' Association) and so didn't hear the American commercial attaché's blunder.'

'What was that?'

'He congratulated France on its latest *Citron* (Lemon) model unveiled at the Paris Motor Show.'

"Well, Jean-Luc, instead of ruffling feathers. I shall be putting a flea in the ear of somebody a sight weightier than a commercial attaché.'

⚜

Gérard Anglade was true to his word. The French ambassador's outspoken protestations ensured that Europe's media lost no time in rallying around the *tricolore* with Governments across the continent unanimous in supporting Anglade's, the Quai d'Orsay's and the Luritanian Chamber of Deputies' condemnation of bare-faced eavesdropping on *one of America's principal allies*. A member of France's far right party riposted that it was ludicrous to number his country among the United States' principal allies other than with reference to the war on terror. Should it come to power in the next presidential elections, Marine Le Penn's spokesman vowed to pull France out of NATO. The time had come, he declared, to reassert the nation's independence under leaders to whom patriotism meant sovereignty.

Dexter Nussbaum's contention that these base accusations of eavesdropping were fabricated by way of reprisal for the unjustified expulsion earlier the same year of two junior members of France's embassy in Washington thought to be spying on behalf of their government only served to get him into deeper water with his masters. Rather than rushing to Nussbaum's defence, they wilfully misconstrued the findings of the ambassador's annual medical examination to decide that, faced with incipient signs of dementia (the physician's report mentioned forgetfulness and loss of visual acuity: hardly sufficient indication of mental decline), the kindest solution for all concerned would be accelerated early retirement. After giving Palmer both barrels for his indefensible, lone wolf action, Nussbaum clawed back a modicum of satisfaction when those on high rubber-stamped his recommendation that Lester Kayser's flawed *Wunderkind* be repatriated post-haste.

⚜

After grinning and bearing two consecutive flight delays by an over-apologetic partnership dedicated to transporting its first-class passengers on schedule from Washington Dulles International Airport to Lenfindi via Amsterdam's Schiphol Airport, it was a worse for wear Lester Kayser who belatedly booked in to *Le Méridien* on Schönschlucht's busy Boulevard Impérial.

Experience having taught him that one of the surest methods of staying awake

426

and alert after a tiring trip was to engage in vigorous exercise, as soon as he had arranged his few belongings Kayser changed into T-shirt, shorts and sneakers, took a lift to the top floor and for the next fifty minutes made full use of the hotel's fitness room facilities. Not one to lose time, after showering and changing back into his everyday clothes, he telephoned *L'Ambassadeur* where Rex was waiting to receive his call.

'Le Méridien, eighth floor, panoramic bar,' said a nothing if not economical Kayser.

Some twenty minutes later, the two men were stretching their limbs in reclining chairs beside the hotel's rooftop swimming pool in company with a glass of Jack Daniel's.

'Surprised to find you here,' remarked Rex, an appreciative eye on the trim figure of a young woman performing athletic underwater lengths in an otherwise deserted pool. 'How's the Un-American Activities Committee going to react when you fail to put in accommodation expenses for the Holiday Inn or the Marriott?'

'When in Rome.'

'Except this isn't Rome. Luritania plays host to more nationalities than the flies on the combined corpses of the Greek and Ukrainian economies. Look for yourself. The barista's Italian. The lift attendants are French. The two women on reception have to be Indonesian. The only Luritanian I've come across this morning is your doorman.'

'Well, what about you, staying in *L'Ambassadeur*? Is there no *Hôtel Grande-Bretagne* in Schönschlucht?'

'Lester, you're forgetting that ever since Ted Heath's 1972 inking, we've gone European.'

'So much so that you'll soon be voting on whether Heath needed his head examining.'

'That's insularity for you. It's a long time since anyone talked about having Calais engraved upon their heart.'

'And tell me, how do you avoid showering people with spittle whenever you say Schönschlucht? What kind of a name is that anyway?'

'Ancient, Lester. With a pedigree more time-honoured than that scrap of paper signed in Philadelphia some two hundred and forty years ago.'

Equally alive, after his work-out, to the well-proportioned figure of the young woman now performing a leisurely backstroke across the pool's surface, Lester Kayser decided that they had indulged in enough small talk.

'How do you see our problem now?'

Rex Jericho rattled the ice in his glass reflectively. 'As I told you. Everything seems to be taken care of. After our miscreants acknowledged that it would be courting disaster to do other than to forget this whole sorry affair, they ate humble pie and destroyed every last scrap of intel. Your end engaged in overkill by banishing the ringleader to darkest Africa and turfing one of his inoffensive accomplices out of a job. Neutralising this coven was not enough for you. Not content to do things by halves, you hit them with a sledgehammer.'

'Would you have preferred me to sit back and allow both our covers to be blown?'

'There was never any danger of that, and you know it.'

'Do I?' Lester Kayser was pleased to see rewarded his hopes that, after showering and drying herself, the young woman would settle down on one of the beds warmed by a sun lamp beside the panoramic window. 'What about this Miss Curtis character and her blind friend?'

'Because Miss Curtis reproaches herself for ever having involved her friend in this business, she has taken the necessary steps to spare her further embarrassment. Of that I can assure you.'

'And Miss Curtis?'

'Give me one good reason why she should put her career on the line by marching further down Hendry or Jabour's road.'

'To hit back at us for Jabour – even if it means a Pyrhhic victory.'

'After she sees the man instrumental in ousting Hendry and Craig getting his comeuppance? Not one of your brightest, Arnold.'

Kayser switched his attention from the bathing beauty to the barista, agitating his cocktail mixer. It annoyed him that the dago and he shared similar thoughts. Lester transferred his discontent elsewhere. 'Little shithead. Overreached himself. Forgot an elementary lesson. Never go it alone without covering your ass.'

Sensing that the American remained unmoved by his arguments, Rex essayed a final pitch. 'Look, Lester, our opponents are a spent force. We'd do better to face up to the facts, bury the hatchet and get back to business as usual.'

Kayser interrupted his admiration of the contours of the beddable young woman who had just turned over on her stomach. Not an ounce of fat on that trim waist.

'I didn't come all the way out here to turn tail, Rex. I told you I need to be sure there are no loose ends. Miss Curtis sounds like a loose end. She may have won you over, but not me.'

'All right, let's stop pussyfooting around here, Lester. Supposing you're right and we have something to fear from this young woman …'

'She's into theatricals, isn't she? Drama's her stock in trade.'

'As is comedy.'

'In this case a comedy of errors.'

'What I was leading up to, Lester, was that if Miss Curtis has farmed our texts out to third parties, and I don't believe she has, would you expect her to confess as much?'

'If I touched on a raw nerve.'

'Come on, Lester. Be realistic. What do you propose doing? Threatening her? She's already pissed off. Pissing her off any more is only likely to make things worse.'

'Leave me to be the best judge of that, Rex. Remember, I stand to lose more than you, if our correspondence gets out.'

No longer knowing what to think – whether common sense would prevail over bloody-mindedness or whether his companion would bring MI6's delicately constructed house of cards down about their heads – Rex shook the last of his whisky around the bottom of its glass before righting what he saw as a listing vessel. 'It would take a Ramanujan to decode those messages.'

Lester Kayser narrowed his eyes. 'Precisely. What if Miss Curtis decides to get one over on us by shipping them across to one of your Cambridge colleges?'

Unsure how to interpret the look behind these words in eyes too questioning for his liking, Rex swallowed the whisky but not the half-sensed, half-feared bait. 'Believe me, that's not her style.'

'You're beginning to sound like Palmer. Bewitched.'

Coming as it did from a man unable to tear his eyes off a well-proportioned female, the irony of this last observation was not lost on Rex Jericho.

'Lester, you've inflicted enough wounds. Leave well alone.'

Prepared to vouchsafe only so much to Rex Jericho, Lester Kayser lifted his arm out straight and tested the steadiness of his hold on the glass of Jack Daniels. 'Relax, Rex. Don't confuse me with Palmer.'

Placing his own empty glass on the side table, Rex pulled himself to his feet and walked across to the window to look down on life in miniature in the boulevard below. The world, he thought, was the worse for people like Lester, who thought they sat on Olympus.

⚜

Memo from J to K

> With every passing day, the Urodinian Dara is growing more like the Royal Academy of Melodramatic Art than a parliament. Yesterday, one member directed his vituperation against the Gallic politician Nicolas Badinage for having the temerity to fly in the face of sanctions by escorting a group of his right-wing supporters on a fact-finding mission to the Tauric Peninsula. As if drawing inspiration from Samuel Butler's poem Hudibras (about a knight errant used to deciding 'all controversies by infallible artillery'), this dull-witted paragon of Urodinian parliamentary democracy recommended hitting Veki's Gallic embassy with an anti-tank missile.

Response from K

> And that was after Urodina's Minister of Culture declared Gaspard Depardiable persona non grata on the grounds that the actor supported the League's annexation of the Tauric peninsula.

⚜

On the day before they were due to fly off with Lufthansa to Kabul via Frankfurt and Istanbul, Craig and Isabelle paid Tich a visit in his shop.

429

'We've come to say goodbye, Tich,' said Craig. 'I think we're going to miss you out there in Afghanistan but not your Sunday homework.'

'Well, I'm certainly going to miss both of you. With only Van and yours truly left, our Sunday Club has bitten the dust.'

'You could always advertise for new members,' suggested Isabelle.

'No, my love, I doubt I'll do that. You're all prepared for this adventure of yours? No second thoughts?'

'Plenty,' replied Craig. 'But only from the point of view of wondering whether we have what it takes.'

'I shouldn't trouble yourselves about that. You're both made of stern stuff. Though it can't be easy on your parents, Isabelle. You said your father had worked out in Afghanistan. How does he feel about this?'

'Still unhappy. Made me swear I wouldn't stray outside the MSF compound.'

'Wouldn't it have been better for you two to test the lie of the land first in a less high-risk MSF theatre? I mean on one of the Greek islands, catering for refugees. Why this baptism of fire? What are you trying to prove?'

Isabelle shook her head. 'If we're trying to prove anything, it's to ourselves not to others. To prove we're made of that stern stuff. Don't think for one moment that we're trying to atone for the BLR theft. What's pushed us to this decision more than anything else has been the need to escape the suffocating environment here in Schönschlucht following on from Justin's small-time theft.'

'But,' said Craig, 'now that Isabelle's mentioned the BLR, there's something we want to talk to you about, Tich.'

'All right. But look, can I not offer you a coffee? Afraid that's all I've got. We could always drop across the road and have a proper farewell drink in the *bistrot*. Easy enough for me to shut up shop for half an hour or more.'

'No thanks, Tich. That's good of you, but we still have a few things to set straight before we fly off tomorrow. Apart from which, I think what we have to discuss is best kept within these four walls.'

'You guys have plans for that China Reconstruction Bank money?'

'Well,' said Isabelle, 'let's put it like this. We want you to know that if anything were to happen to us in that high-risk theatre, you should parcel the funds out to the charities we agreed upon. And if you think of anything that might improve your brother's health or living conditions, you shouldn't hesitate to use the money for that.'

'I see. But nothing is going to happen to you. Okay, if we're all worried for your safety, you should understand it's natural enough for friends and family to be concerned. On the other hand, let's be reasonable. As you said, the Taliban have more sense than to target field hospitals caring for their own kind.'

'All the same,' said Isabelle, 'we want you to know that the BLR money is not important to us. Put it to good use – if you have to.'

Tich scratched his beard. 'Well, Isabelle and Craig, I hope the day you're talking about never dawns.'

Vanessa rarely returned home during her lunchbreak, unless it was to check her mailbox for registered or express parcel delivery notes. But on this occasion she wanted to reassure herself that in her haste to avoid the morning rush hour she had not omitted to follow Justin's instructions about topping up Pliny's drinking water each time she added raw liver or chicken necks to his feeding bowl. Before leaving the office, she used her iPhone to bring up her apartment webcam. After learning about Inspector Hoffarth's installation in Justin's place and trawling the web for the best possible device, she had chanced upon the free offer of a webcam marketed by a Cambridge-based IT expert, who trusted that those downloading his software would be good enough to make a token donation to a charity of their choice. Vanessa decided in favour of *War on Want*.

She had downloaded this novel software, which offered scope for programming e-mail alerts of any movements detected by the camera, before taking on Pliny. Now that Justin's ferret was installed in her apartment, although Vanessa understood that placing his cage in another room would spare her unnecessary alerts, she had yet to get around to deciding whether to lodge Pliny in the kitchen or the utilities room. As it happened, when she viewed the webcam images of her living room before going down to her workplace's multi-level underground car park, she found Pliny asleep and nothing other than normal.

But upon arriving before her front door there was no mistaking that all was not well within in. Why else could she hear Pliny screaming and hurling himself against the side of his cage? Withholding her hand from the lock, Vanessa called up the webcam on her iPhone. There in plain sight was a stranger prowling around her living room. If it had been Jay, Hoffarth or his assistant, she would never have forgiven the man from MI6 or the Luritanian police for taking her for a fool. But whoever this intruder was, she doubted whether he belonged to Britain's Secret Service or Hoffarth's brigade. Her first thought was one of retreat: take the lift back downstairs, telephone the inspector and have his people teach this stranger a lesson. But the next moment, anger took over and Vanessa changed her mind. Why leave this to outsiders, when she could fend for herself? She called up the webcam images again, waiting to see whether the intruder was acting alone. One person, she could handle. More than one, she would have to think again.

And this, she felt sure, was no ordinary burglar in search of jewelry or ready cash, neither of which he would find in her apartment. She was up against the people Jay had warned her against. Not his own crowd. People cut from a different cloth. One of Palmer's tribe. But, by the look of it, only one man whom Pliny was straining to get his teeth into.

Vanessa inserted her key gently into the lock, found it already open and eased the door first ajar then wider onto an empty hallway. Stepping inside and pushing the door noiselessly to behind her, she took three steps towards the hat stand, placed her iPhone on the nearest shelf, bent down for her Browning, which she was relieved to find still concealed within one of her jogging shoes, extracted the pistol, released the safety catch and advanced gingerly towards the interior.

The disturbance created by Pliny, who was continuing to hiss, snarl and physically object to the injustice of his confinement in the face of this invader of his territory, meant that Lester Kayser was caught unawares by the dark-haired young woman suddenly facing him in the living room doorway. Seeing that her intruder was unarmed, Vanessa lowered the Browning to her side.

'Care to explain what you're doing here,' she said, her voice unwavering, her eyes and ears alert to the possibility of an accomplice or accomplices on the loose in other rooms.

Kayser held up placatory hands. 'I believe you and I have a mutual acquaintance – J. The difference between J and me is that, although we work on the same side, he's more trusting than I am when it comes to people who endanger my country's security.'

If the stranger's accent grated on her nerves, his temerity pushed Vanessa close to raising her gun hand. As it was, she managed to stay sorely tried anger.

'I might have guessed as much. Fucking CIA, is that it? Your type earns a living out of stirring up trouble worldwide in the name of pseudo-democracy. About time you got the message. Mind your own business. Sort out the Augean mess in your own stables.'

'The world's a global village, Miss Curtis. Any nation that closes its eyes to that fact is headed for history's trash can.'

The fact that she could hear nothing extraneous apart from the sound of Pliny's scurrying which, though still fretful, had diminished with her arrival, did not stop Vanessa from throwing the occasional glance towards her kitchen and bedroom doors. 'Does Jay know you're here?'

'Would that change anything?'

'Answer the fucking question.'

'You know how to use that thing? They're dangerous in the wrong hands.'

'I asked you a question,' said Vanessa unflinchingly. 'Does Jay know you're here?'

'No, I'm my own man.'

'You haven't found anything, have you? Because there's nothing to find. Not content to ruin lives, you bastards never know when to leave well alone. Can't you understand that neither I nor any of my friends give a toss about your fucking texts now that we've got rid of them? And still you refuse to let go. You have to grind us underfoot. Look at me, the sole fucking survivor. What kind of a threat do you think I am? I'm sick and tired of you and your coded bullshit.'

While on the receiving end of this tirade, Kayser was mulling over his chances of taking his adversary by surprise, all the more so since one thing Arnold Palmer had, out of injured pride, omitted to tell him was that Vanessa Curtis knew how to handle a sidearm. Consequently, given the distance separating the two of them, the CIA man doubted whether the young woman's reaction time and accuracy were remotely as sharp as his. And putting paid to her would wrap things up neatly.

Lester Kayser decided to exploit renewed agitation on the ferret's part. Pliny's fur was standing on end, the creature spitting out ferocious warnings as it sprang up and down from one end of its cage to the other.

'Quite an animal you've got there. Wouldn't he be better off out in the wild?'

'No, and believe me, you're a lot better off with him inside that cage. Like me, he gets hostile if you encroach on his space.'

'Seems a pity to keep a weasel cooped up. Whatever persuaded you to do that? Did he belong to another weasel? Jabour, is that it?'

Sensing that he had struck a weak spot, Kayser reached for the automatic in his shoulder holster. But excessive self-confidence went only so far. Since the CIA man's firearm skills had not been tested on a range in recent weeks, he was no match for a woman with lightning reflexes. Instantaneously raising the Browning to a firing position over which she had complete mastery, Vanessa took less than two seconds to secure her aim before despatching a single unerring shot into the centre of Kayser's forehead.

'That, motherfucker,' she said, slowly lowering her weapon arm, 'is what you asked for and what you got.'

Vanessa steadied herself against the possibility of somebody's bursting in from a neighbouring room. But dazed and with her ears blasted by the sound of the shot, she was unable to hear anything vaguely confirming her fear that the American might not be alone. Nor could she tell whether there was any clamour by the lift shaft or commotion in the outside passageway. If working couples occupied both apartments across from her, this was not to say that the shot had gone unheard by a tenant directly above or below. And, if they had heard anything, what would they do? Rush down or upstairs to see all was well? Hardly. They would dial one of the emergency services. And, that was what she ought to do now – without delay. Ring the police.

Staggering into the hallway, Vanessa dropped the Browning back into its shoe, retrieved her iPhone and searched for Hoffarth's number. She had forgotten that her call had to be routed through the switchboard. A series of voice recordings in Luritanian, French, German and English, interspersed with irritating strains of Beethoven's *Ode to Joy,* craved her indulgence only for the patience-begging cycle to start back on itself. Vanessa thumped the wall with her fist. Would it have been better to dial the three-figure emergency number? But the next moment the decision was taken out of her hands. After asking to be put through to Hoffarth's extension and limiting her restlessness to scratching at a join in wallpaper she had never liked, she was finally informed that the inspector was out on a mission.

'Well, this is urgent,' she barked hoarsely. 'Inspector Hoffarth instructed me to ring him after midday. Kindly give me his mobile number.'

Silence. An acid feeling eating away at the pit of her stomach, Vanessa wondered whether the police's switchboard operators were prohibited from disclosing officer's cell phone numbers.

'Hello, are you still there?'

'Yes, I have the number for you here,' came the reply from an operator who had come close to restoring Vanessa's faith in human nature.

With no writing instrument in easy reach, Vanessa asked her to repeat the number.

Compared to his headquarter's switchboard, the inspector was remarkably quick in answering her call.

'Inspector Hoffarth, this is Vanessa Curtis. I think you ought to come around to my apartment as soon as possible. I have just shot an intruder who pulled a gun on me.'

Vanessa heard the sharp intake of breath. 'Are you all right? Should I call an ambulance?' The touch of concern in Hoffarth's voice was a departure from the man's customary unflappable staidness.

'Me? I'm coping. Just about. But, inspector, I don't think I could bear up for long, if you were to send somebody else here. I need you. This is virtually a carbon copy of the incident in Justin Hendry's apartment.'

'The man you've shot, is he badly wounded?'

'Badly. He's dead. You'll need the meat wagon.'

'Remind me of your address, Miss Curtis.'

Vanessa explained how best to reach her at the end of a cul de sac.

'That's good. I'm only down the road. I'll be with you in ten minutes. In the meantime, sit down, give yourself a stiff drink and don't answer the door to anyone but me.'

Vanessa placed her iPhone back on the shelf of the hall cupboard next to the hat stand and started towards the kitchen. Steadying herself in front of the sink, she gulped water from the tap, then slumped to her knees, banging her forehead against the sink edge as she did so. All around seemed to be cloaked in silence, including Pliny. A stiff drink, the inspector had suggested. The only alcohol in the apartment was some leftover rotgut Chianti donated by the actor playing Lord Muilligan, and she could think of better sedatives. Vanessa gazed down at one of the crevices in the off-white rhomboid travertine tiling, where her weekend mopping had glided over a redcurrant stain. What a pity, she thought, not catching that American bastard in the kitchen. He had cost her a carpet.

Pulling herself to her feet, Vanessa returned to the living room only to give a gasp of disgust: the dead man had voided his bowels. Averting her gaze from the corpse, she fell to her knees again beside the nearest armchair and, wrapping her arms around herself, began rocking slowly forwards and backwards, a plaintive moan issuing from her lips.

'This doesn't bring you back, Rash, does it?' she cried helplessly.

At the mercy of one black thought after another, she rolled onto the floor moaning pathetically. Only when her head finally cleared did it occur to her that she should ring Jay. After all, was he not the person best placed to identify the intruder, especially since it was unlikely that any papers or cards found on that body bore the owner's real name? Better still, Jay could intercede for her in front of Hoffarth by endorsing her statement that she had been provoked. No, that was stupid. How could anyone expect a latecomer to corroborate her story? Surely playback of the webcam images would show the American to have made the first threatening move?

Vanessa struggled up again and back out to the hall. But, on the point of selecting the number stored in her iPhone for Jay's room in *L'Ambassadeur*, stayed her hand. What if, as opposed to working at cross purposes, MI6 and the CIA were operating on the same wavelength, the sole difference between the two lying in the methods employed to attain their ends? In other words, might not admission on her part to having killed the American not only alienate Jay but send him back into the woodwork from which he had emerged? No, she had to go about things differently.

Vanessa called up Jay's direct dial number. The phone rang and kept ringing, confirming her worst suspicion: Jay had returned to MI6's fold. 'Stupid bitch,' she muttered. 'Why should he stick around?' And then he picked up her call.

'Chandler.'

'Curtis. Thought I should let you know that I've found something disturbing in my apartment. Something you ought to know about. Not over the phone, you understand. Could you drop by now?'

'Give me your address.'

She waited while he took note of it.

'Not familiar with that area.'

'So feed it into your Garmin or TomTom. I'm not that far from your hotel.' She could not bring herself to add, 'in a dead end'.

Setting her iPhone aside, Vanessa retraced her steps to the kitchen, helped herself to a glass of filtered tap water and sat down at a bare teak table, thinking that it would be a long time before she ate another meal off it.

Hoffarth would have to jail her. Nobody walked free after committing manslaughter, however involuntary. Rather than chilling her to the marrow, the prospect of imprisonment seemed almost welcome. Temporary refuge from the madness with which she had been surrounded these plast weeks. And it had been involuntary, hadn't it? A clear-cut case of self-defence. What thought, if any, had flitted across her mind in the split second before reacting to the American's telltale move? Impossible to say. Hers had been the atavistic response of the hunter whose prey had turned on its pursuer. All the same, wasn't she supposed to feel devastated and conscience-ridden about taking a human life? Cardboard targets were one thing, live targets another. Vanessa was seized by a manic fit of laughter that had her choking over her drink. After drawing his arm, the man from the CIA, for such she guessed him to be, had paid the ultimate price by scrabbling to release the safety catch.

A few minutes later, feeling temporarily the better for a return to level-headedness, Vanessa gave a violent start as the front doorbell sounded shrilly in her ears. She sat frozen for several moments, fearing she knew not what. A look through the peep-hole revealed that Hoffarth, accompanied by his faithful amanuensis, had beaten Jay to her front door. Unsure whether this was such a good thing she opened up, ushering both men into the hallway. Two familiar faces. Vanessa hoped she would be spared the ignominy of handcuffs.

'Before I show you through to the living room, the handgun I used to defend myself, when he went for his weapon, is there.' She pointed to the Browning nestled inside her running shoe. 'The same .22 calibre that I use down on the shooting range and for which I have a licence.'

Hoffarth gave the briefest of nods, signifying that, as far as he was concerned, this piece of information was as valuable as his latest scratch card. 'Perhaps you could tell me, Mademoiselle, what the victim was doing in your apartment in the first place.'

Vanessa explained the course of events following on from her seeing images on her iPhone of a marauder prowling around her living room.

'I haven't touched anything,' she said in conclusion. 'He's there where he fell in a heap on my carpet. And he stinks to high heaven.'

'The ambulance should be here soon, Mademoiselle,' said Weiland, removing the lens cap from his camera.

The two men followed her through to the living room, where, confronted by two more unknown quantities, Pliny launched into a renewed series of frenzied protests.

It didn't call for qualified medical experience to tell that the man sprawled on the floor was dead. The neat bullet hole punched through the glabella (the bone above the eye sockets) said it all. Hoffarth motioned to his assistant to start photographing the body and adjacent areas.

It was after Weiland had finished photographing and while Hoffarth was going through the dead man's pockets that the doorbell rang again. In her haste to open the door, Vanessa forgot to look through the peep-hole. Her face fell when she saw three paramedics holding a stretcher. She felt certain that Jay would be frightened off the moment he saw their ambulance. Then it occurred to her that, had he arrived before the paramedics, the sight of Hoffarth's police car would have been enough to turn him away. Surely, now, his curiosity aroused, he would put in an appearance, rather than miss seeing with his own eyes who was bundled into the back of the meat wagon. On the other hand, if he delayed much longer, it would be a wasted journey. Not entirely wasted, she thought on reflection, because she could always play back the webcam.

But seconds later her anxiety was allayed. The inspector's cell phone chirped, and after a few unintelligible words, Hoffarth turned to explain that Jay was on his way up. Vanessa wondered whether the man from MI6 would have stayed away had the inspector not been at the scene. No, it was more likely that, if this had been the case, he would have asked Hoffarth to find out which of his people was on the spot and to tell them to stay put, because this case was the inspector's baby. As much as it galled her to think that she had become a criminal in the eyes of the law, Vanessa crossed her fingers that Hoffarth would back up her plea of extenuating circumstances.

And it was while pondering the legal upshot of her action and the damage to her career that she all but jumped out of her shoes hearing Jay's familiar voice over her shoulder. The paramedics had left the front door open for ease of exit with their stretcher.

Relieved though he was to learn that Vanessa was unhurt, despite being prepared for the worst Rex Jericho was unable to conceal his dismay at the sight of Lester Kayser's lifeless body, dismay which Hoffarth and Vanessa each interpreted erroneously in their own way. For the fact of the matter was that a single .22 calibre rimfire bullet had put paid to a relationship – baptised *Grandchild* – nourished by MI6 with all but blood, sweat and tears. It left Rex in something of a limbo.

'You know this man?' asked the inspector, who had moved to bend down over the body before it was bagged.

Rex looked from Hoffarth to his assistant. Weiland was holding a pocket dictaphone.

'Never seen him before.'

Hoffarth held up the wallet taken from Kayser's jacket. 'According to this business card, he's Robert Bruce Kingsmith, an oil refinery process engineer working for Conoco.'

Rex's eyes masked amused understanding. Lester Kayser seemed incapable of shaking off the stamp of superiority conferred on him by birth. Here he was virtually laying claim to Scottish antecedents.

Still trying to come to terms with the fact that the CIA maverick had effectively slammed the door in MI6's face, Rex watched the paramedics lift his body onto their stretcher. 'Before rushing to Interpol or the FBI with that ID, which is probably not worth the card it's printed on, I would advise you to consult the American embassy.'

Either forgetting or untroubled by the fact that he was being recorded, the inspector uttered a dry laugh. 'Not the best of house-warming presents for the new lady ambassador. I understand she's presenting her letters of credence to Grand Prince Philippe Étienne this afternoon.'

Rex nodded. Nussbaum had left under a cloud. As one Luritanian journalist had uncharitably put it: *Compared to the speed of Dexter Nussbaum's accelerated early retirement, the Large Hadron Collider down the road is positively sluggish.*

Hoffarth took pains to bag the dead man's automatic such that forensics would have nothing to quibble about. 'Safety catch engaged. The weapon hasn't been fired.'

'More fool him,' snapped Vanessa. 'And how was I to realise that?' She glanced unhappily at the man known to her as Jay. Perhaps the webcam would prove more of a curse than a blessing. For if playback was admissible in court, it might give to believe that she had brought her pistol up first: in other words, not in self-defence.

She turned to Hoffarth. 'Why don't I get the preachy warning about anything I might say being taken down and used as evidence against me?'

The inspector gave her the smile of an indulgent parent. 'You regret incriminating yourself, is that it? Don't worry, Mlle, you'll be able to give a full sworn statement down at the station.'

Her head swimming, Vanessa reached out for support from the back of the armchair beside which she had slumped down earlier. 'No, no, forget what I just said. All this is getting on top of me. It's difficult to think straight, inspector, when you've just killed someone. Whatever I admit to in your offices will not differ as to one iota from what I've said already. He pulled a gun on me and I responded.'

The inspector signalled Weiland to turn off his dictaphone. Both police officers, Rex and Vanessa stood aside to allow the paramedics to trundle their burden out to the lift.

'With commendable marksmanship,' said Rex. 'Against a moving target?'

Vanessa, who could have done without the implication behind Jay's praise, shrugged non-committally. 'Split-second judgment.'

Rex refrained from asking what she meant by judgment.

Inserting the last of the dead man's credit cards into his wallet, Hoffarth tapped it absently against the palm of his free hand. 'Since the prosecution will want to know why you didn't phone us instead of barging in and taking the law into your own hands, I would suggest not mentioning the iPhone. I take it you were able to open the door without Mr Kingsmith's hearing you because of the noise your ferret was creating. And it was only when inside that you realised something was badly amiss and had recourse to your firearm. Before I forget, bag it, Claude-Henri.'

'Of course,' said Rex, 'justice has to be done, inspector, but between you, me and the gatepost ...,' He paused as Weiland returned holding Vanessa's Browning in a taped Ziploc bag, after closing the front door behind the ambulance men.

Hoffarth answered the question behind the Englishman's eyes by ordering his assistant to continue to treat any further remarks as off the record.

'... I imagine the American embassy will want to see this dealt with discreetly.'

'What's your idea of discreet?'

'Portraying Kingsmith as a jewel thief with a record of assault and battery?'

'I'm sure they'll find the right rabbit to pull out of the hat,' said Georg Hoffarth, not only loath to give the impression of bending to a foreign will but suspicious of the other man's clandestine relationship with any one of a number of unsavoury American agencies.

But the next moment the situation assumed a different complexion as Claude-Henri Weiland, pointing at a brown leather attaché case on the carpet to the right of where Lester Kayser had fallen, said: 'Perhaps he was trying to steal that?'

'No,' replied Vanessa unthinkingly and to Rex's consternation, 'that's not mine.'

Hoffarth reasserted his authority. 'More grist to the mill. Perhaps Mr Kingsmith had already stolen a jewel or two before Mademoiselle surprised him.'

'Might I suggest again,' said Rex Jericho, hiding his annoyance that Vanessa had denied ownership, 'that you bring to the immediate notice of the American embassy anything found likely to be deemed sensitive material.'

The inspector's smile gave to believe that he was enjoying the Englishman's neatly disguised discomfort. 'I understood you thought that Monsieur Kingsmith was a common burglar.'

Vanessa and Rex exchanged glances. 'Hardly common,' remarked Vanessa with feeling.

'Well, I'm sure I'm right,' added Rex.

'That remains to be seen,' sighed an unconvinced and frustrated Georg Hoffarth.

'It's true,' replied Rex, refining certitude into conciliation. 'You never know.'

Having had his fill of disowned dead Americans, the inspector suspected there was, indeed, much behind this affair that he, for one, would never know.

⁂

After returning to police headquarters, Claude-Henri Weiland dutifully handed both handguns over to forensics. Cognisant of the prospect of outside pressure being brought to bear on the conduct of his investigations, the inspector refused to deviate from the rule book. The fingerprints on the weapon found by the body of the fictitious Kingsmith would, he trusted, enable the laboratory technicians to trace that gentleman's true identity.

While his assistant typed out Vanessa Curtis's statement for the young lady to verify, date and sign in the room next to his own, Georg Hoffarth pulled on a pair of the regulatory latex gloves and began examining the contents of Kingsmith's attaché case. The sole item of significance was a plastic folder holding print-outs of a document described by the wording on the label affixed to a small window in the transparent front cover as *Security Threat Material*. Having perused the two pages in question, the inspector came to the conclusion that had Weiland not seen the case either Vanessa or Jericho would have destroyed this evidence without so much as a second thought – each for his or her quite different reasons. With his sympathy inclining in favour of someone he saw as the victim of circumstances, for the briefest of moments the inspector was tempted to tear up both rule book and evidence. He threw an ironic glance at the framed axiom left hanging on the wall by his austere predecessor: *Fiat Justitia ruat caelum (Let justice be done, though the heavens fall)*. Would Bernard Faulkner have declared 'let justice be done', had he known the distressing surprise awaiting his protégé in Kingsmith's attaché case? Reluctant to assume the role of judge and jury, Georg Hoffarth decided to leave well alone.

A few minutes later, the door between the two offices opened and Claude-Henri Weiland walked in holding the signed statement, Vanessa Curtis following close behind. Inviting her to sit down, the inspector read the statement through.

'I think,' he said, when he had finished, 'that you need a lawyer to plead self-defence on your behalf. I'm sure the state prosecutor will allow you to post bail in what would appear to be a clear case of involuntary manslaughter under provocation.'

The strain began to show in Vanessa's faltering response. 'I don't have a lawyer.'

The inspector opened a drawer, pulled out a slim register and proffered this across his desk. 'Legal yellow pages. Every attorney in Luritania listed according to speciality and language. You might prefer somebody with a sound grasp of English.'

439

'Thank you,' she said, a careworn face indicative of how much the day's events had taken their toll. 'So I've well and truly reached the end of my *camino real*.'

'I beg your pardon?'

'Never mind, inspector. A warped metaphor for perdition.'

His forerunner's Latin hyperbole admonishing him from the wall, Hoffarth quelled fear of worse to come.

'No, mademoiselle. It's understandable that you should feel that way. But find the right lawyer and, I would say, you are assured of salvation.'

Those words would return to haunt him.

In fact, the first bad news for Georg Hoffarth to the effect that Kingsmith's latents showed up in none of the international fingerprint data bases searched by forensics – which meant either that the dead man had no connections with the CIA or FBI or that the NSA banned release of conclusive evidence to non-approved third parties – was soon eclipsed by the second revelation communicated to him by his Director-General, Helmut Schrottweiler.

'Madame l'Ambassadrice,' said Luritania's Chief of Police, an extremely tall man who tended to talk down to his staff in more senses than one, 'is not at all happy about the Curtis affair.'

Summoned to his boss's office by a male secretary with a voice that put him in mind of a castrated fishmonger, Georg Hoffarth sat facing Schrottweiler dressed in his finest livery fresh from a passing-out parade. It did not call for exceptional foresight on Hoffarth's part to understand that the contents of Kingsmith's attaché case had not gone down well with the recently appointed American ambassador, Marion Silverstein.

'Her people have identified the man shot by Mademoiselle Curtis,' continued Schrottweiler, careful not to preen himself on being party to for-your-ears-only information. 'For reasons of international security, I am unable to divulge his name. But what I can tell you is that he was charged with a particularly delicate anti-terrorist operation. More to the point, he was persuaded that Monsieur Jabour, who, as you know, had been cohabiting with Mademoiselle Curtis was working hand in glove with ISIL's representatives in Lebanon committed to the overthrow of Syria's Bashar al-Assad as part of the wider establishment of their caliphate.'

Hoffarth nodded sagely. Did Schrottweiler seriously believe that his inspector had not taken so much as a peek at what lay inside that attaché case or did he just like the sound of his own voice?

'I thoroughly appreciate Madame l'Ambassadrice's concern to put a lid on this information. It is essential that the outside world learn nothing of how near the man known as Kingsmith was to penetrating Islamic State's underground network in Lebanon.'

The inspector rightly sensed that his Director-General had kept the worst till last.

'But none of this alters the fact that Mademoiselle Curtis is suspected at the very least of being aware of Jabour's plans and intentions, if not complicit in them. In short, our American friends intend throwing the book at her for aiding and abetting a supporter of international terrorism. And in view of Luritania's shared interest in rooting out this evil wherever it's found, both Alex Henderscheid and Claudette Wolz have urged me to give this matter my undivided attention.'

For once Hoffarth was having to roll with the punches. Mention of the Minister for the Interior and the Minister for Internal Security meant that the outcome of this investigation would be as impartial as a trial by lynching. Unimpressed by Schrottweiler's reviewing officer posturing, the inspector seized on the end of the director-general's declaration to make his voice heard in what so far had been a one-way lecture.

'Does Madame l'Ambassadrice appreciate that we have been handling this affair from the word go? That we know these people better than anyone else?'

'Do we?'

'I fancy I do. I would suggest that whatever documentary proof was found within Mademoiselle Curtis's apartments was something she was sitting on unwittingly – probably printed out from Jabour's rather than her laptop.'

'No doubt that is the line she will take in mounting her defence. But I can tell you, Hoffarth, that Madame l'Ambassadrice considers an indictment for involuntary manslaughter small beer compared to one for complicity in international terrorism. In fact, her people are willing to bet their bottom dollar that Kingsmith's killing was no more involuntary than the attack on their twin towers. Guessing what Kingsmith was looking for, Mademoiselle Curtis murdered him in cold blood.'

'Then why didn't she destroy the evidence?'

'Too overwrought after murdering him to act quickly enough. Unless he fell on the attaché case. Did he?'

'No, it's clear from the webcam images that the case was already on the carpet to one side of him.'

'All the same, it escaped her notice. According to your report, that pet of hers was making a rumpus. Distraction enough, I would suggest.'

The inspector saw that he was getting nowhere against a fired-up chief of police bent on demonstrating allegiance to a higher cause.

It did nothing to salve Georg Hoffarth's conscience that, believing Vanessa Curtis to be innocent of any involvement in international terrorism, he had failed to act on his initial impulse and spurn his self-righteous precursor's aphorism. For in passing on those incriminating papers he had effectively sealed the poor woman's fate.

Memo from J to K

Fortunately for the Invigilator, media coverage of events in Urodina does not extend to the fact that taxpayers' money is funding construction of concentration camps for corralling ethinic Nevskian supporters of the breakaways republics once this conflict is over.

Response from K

I doubt whether you are correct, J, about the Invigilator. When the truth is unpalatable, how much more convenient to live with half-truths. On the other hand, by dint of pressing home our version of events, it looks as if we have won over a respectable portion of today's generation.

❦

Tich sat facing Vanessa in the visitors' room inside Luritania's infelicitously named Übelshof penitentiary. It was a drab, sparsely furnished room with the mandatory portrait of the Grand Prince on the off-white wall behind Vanessa and a rolling news television monitor near the ceiling behind Tich, who wondered whether the sole purpose of this anomaly was to keep the overweight warder sitting in the far corner from falling asleep on the job.

Vanessa was the first to pick up the phone in the booth on her side of the wooden partition separating prisoners from visitors. She used a handkerchief to wipe the instrument clean.

'I should do the same,' she advised. 'You never know who might have been dribbling or blubbering into it.'

Tich pulled out a packet of Kleenex tissues, spitting on the second of these to remove smudges left on the pane of glass between them by fingerprints and lipstick.

'When did this place last see a cleaning woman?'

'You're in a prison, Tich. No chambermaids here. We have to make our own beds.'

'Are these phones really necessary? This isn't America. So much for fraternity and equality. Not to mention the L word.'

'This isn't France, and I doubt whether prisons there treat visiting hours like teddy bears' picnic time any more than they do here.'

'I could understand it if this were a hospital. You're not HIV positive or radioactive, I hope?'

'Come on, Tich. They're worried you lot might try smuggling something in to us.'

'I went through a metal detector outside.'

'I don't think they pick up drugs. But they know people peddle them in here. You could always lob me a package, while the warder was looking elsewhere.'

'In which case, what's that Big Brother up there for?' Tich jabbed a finger towards the bulbous black glass eye mounted on the ceiling behind Vanessa.

'I guess the dumbos monitoring us might nod off or want to take a leak.'

'Well, the guy in the corner behind you, for one, is too busy playing games on his smart phone.'

The booths were constructed in such a way that Tich could see Vanessa but not the inmates on either side of her. However, he had only to lean backwards to take in each of their visitors. 'All right,' he said, grudgingly accepting that Übelshof appeared to respect its prisoners' privacy on occasions such as this, 'let's try to forget all this institutional crap. How's it going, Vanessa? How are they treating you?'

'Everything's fucking great. I'm sharing a cell with a junkie. A nineteen-year-old French girl called Géraldine, with the most godawful tattoo. A vulture perched on her shoulder with a snake in its mouth. She's got enough facial metal to set off a detector a mile down the road. Her nails are bitten to the raw, and I hate to think when she last had a bath. They limit us to one hour a day out in the fresh air. To judge by the racket overhead, we're right below Lenfindi's light path. My cellmate slept the sleep of the dead last night. I didn't drop off till around four a.m.'

'Sorry to hear that, Van. Easy for me to speak, I know, but look at it this way. You could be out of here before you know it. *Maître* Deleuze, the lawyer taking on your defence has one of the best acquittal track records in Luritania. It beats me why he hasn't already got you out on bail.'

'So you haven't heard?'

Tich shook his head. 'Heard what?'

'The prosecution barely gives a shit about my knocking off one of the CIA's special agents.'

'We don't know that's who Kingsmith was.'

'Jay knew who he was. Okay, I doubt he'd admit as much in court. Not that that's the point. Papers found in Kingsmith's briefcase mark Rashid and me out as terrorist sympathisers.'

'That's ludicrous.'

'Of course it is. Those papers are nothing other than a plant. The clever bastard somehow came up with a Word font identical to Rashid's, typed up the incriminating evidence, transferred it to a flash drive and printed the text out on my printer.'

'But surely that should be easy to shoot down once the screen file isn't found on Rashid's laptop, the one he presumably took with him to Beirut?'

'Wrong. Rashid took his work laptop to Beirut, and goodness knows where that is now. His private laptop he left with me. Kingsmith penetrated and downloaded his file onto that.'

'But this whole scenario is ridiculous. Anybody who knows you will speak up in your defence to maintain you're the last person on earth to cooperate with jihadists.'

'When you say anybody, Tich, who do you have in mind?'

'Me for one. Your colleagues at work. Your…' He hesitated to suggest Vanessa's father. '… sister.'

'You've run out of ideas, haven't you, Tich? Just stop to think how many people found guilty of conspiring with terrorists were up there with Mother Teresa or Nelson Mandela according to friends and next of kin before they learnt that their heroes had become radicalised.'

'Yes, but …' Tich spread his hands out wide as if to demonstrate the holes in a patently *ad hominem* argument.

'No buts, Tich. They're out for my scalp, and I doubt whether the gifted *Maître* Deleuze will manage to swing the magistrate in my favour.'

'You've got to get out of this negative rut, Van. We need to work out how to spike Marion Silverstein's guns. She's behind this, I suppose?'

'Of course. But **we** need to spike her guns? Meaning you, me and the *Maître*? Who else, for heaven's sake, can tell our side of the story? Wait a minute. Jay. We have to enlist his help. What's the matter? Why the long face?'

'I had that idea myself. Went and visited *L'Ambassadeur*. Your MI6 man checked out yesterday without, needless to say, leaving any forwarding address. He's probably back safe in the arms of MI6.'

'I should have guessed as much.'

'What, that he'd leave you in the lurch?'

'No, that he couldn't afford to queer his own pitch. To be fair to him, I believe he tried to intervene on our behalf. But he got overtaken by events. And his warning could not have been clearer: you've made your bed, now lie in it. Don't look so down in the mouth, Tich. Come what may, I'll cope.'

'Let me know what I can do to help. If it's a matter of money – I dare say that Deleuze charges a pretty penny – no need to worry your head on that score.' Tich paused. What if the prison authorities had bugged the room? No, that was paranoid. Luritania wasn't another banana republic, with Gutmans aka Palmers around every corner. If Human Rights Watch caught Übelshof eavesdropping on visiting-hour chats, it would come come down on the warden like a ton of bricks, before dragging Luritania through the mud at the European Court of Human Rights. All the same, Tich decided to rephrase his next thought.

'Your amateur theatrical and shooting club friends will rally round. I'll see to that.'

'Thanks, Tich. But there's something else that's worrying me more at present.' Vanessa lowered her voice against the welcome din created in the next cubicle, where an inmate hard of hearing was shouting back at her visitor. 'You had no problem visiting me today because we're at the pre-trial stage. But once we move on from that, I gather it's blood relatives only, unless I file an application on your behalf. That will mean coughing up a wealth of personal details. If you want my frank opinion, I think it was not only good but stupid of you to visit me here. You're the first to do so. Clara Bogen wants to follow in your footsteps. I told her to stay away. Why? Because the fucking Americans have watchdogs everywhere.'

'Come on, Van, what bone could they have to pick with me?'

'Anyone who visits me is automatically tarred with the same brush. No, listen, Tich. I'm sure I'm right. Now that it's come to this, there's something you should know. Before Justin left for Lagos, I had a long talk with him. I said we shouldn't let these buggers win hands down. That once the dust had settled, he ought to write up this story from beginning to end. He maintained he'd had enough of it, that the press would take one look at anything he put together and sling it on their crank file.

'I suggested a better but equally cathartic approach: turn the account into a faction novel. That really got Justin going. He ranted and raved, rejected the idea outright. Said he had caused enough heartache as it was and had no wish to make things worse for himself, me, you, or anyone else. I told him, if he was chicken, I'd be prepared to have a go. After which we had a good ding-dong up until the moment when he proposed you for the task.'

'Oh, thank you, Justin, my boy.'

'Well, thank me too, Tich, because I agreed and, when all is said and done, you have a way with words. I don't.'

'But, look, Van, you and Justin were always more on top of this than I was.'

'Rubbish. You've been kept abreast of just about every development along the way. And in many respects several of us, Isabelle in particular, have considered you a substitute father confessor ...'

'Try telling that to the Vatican. Look, let's be reasonable. There's so much behind the scenes ... The gift of the gab is one thing, seeing inside the heads of Palmer, Kingsmith, Jay and the people pulling their strings ... that's way out of my skill range.'

'Then invent. Use your imagination.'

'Justin and you really believe this could give those buggers the shivers?'

'The game's only over, Tich, if we let them have the last word.'

'Isn't that what they always have? The last nail-in-the-coffin word?'

'Now who's being defeatist? We make it our job to outwit them.'

Unable to ease his mind, Tich eased the stiffness in his back. 'I agree with Justin about one thing. Taking our story to the mainstream press would be a waste of time. We'd get the same unsympathetic reception as on Facebook, a social dustbin richer in nutcases than every insane asylum from Albania to Zimbabwe stood end to end. What's crazy about our situation is that, although neither Justin nor you is *Charlie* by a long chalk, Palmer and Kingsmith's people have pooled all their resources to ostracise him and to pursue you like a war criminal.'

'Then we must blaze a different trail.'

'There is no different trail, Van. We're up against a brick wall.'

'I never thought I'd hear that kind of language from you.'

'Well, tell me, please, what new trail your latter-day James Fennimore Cooper forward scout should blaze?'

'Take our story to one of the major publishing houses.'

'You're speaking to someone who knows more than a little about the book trade, Van. No publishers of any standing nowadays accept material from unknown quantities, unless it comes recommended by an agent. And agents are picky. They have to be. They can't afford to dent their reputation by promoting work that's not going to do the equivalent of a blockbuster at the box office. And what we have is puny compared to the kind of tale turned out by an SAS vet telling all about his fucking foxtrot heroics in the hills of Pakistan.'

'All right. Like I said, turn fact into the stuff of fiction. Tell our story in your own words. From the beginning.'

'Holiday leisure reading for the poolside tossed into the nearest rubbish bin as soon as people leave their hotel to return to nine-to-five reality, rush hours, family squabbling and the latest celebrity scandal?'

'At least it's aired and out there. Not everyone will forget after they've turned the last page. And it's something you could do, Tich. You know it. Of all of us, no one is better suited to the challenge than a fucking bibliophile, bibliopole or whatever dick biblio name you care to call yourself. After living with other people's words all these years, use your own inimitable prose to tell our story to the droves of slaves out there on the losing end of these bastards' machinations.'

No longer insensitive to persistent persuasiveness, Tich sat silently stroking his beard. Vanessa's proposition was beginning to crystallise into something not only feasible but appealing.

'Nothing smacking of autobiography,' he said at length. 'I refuse to turn this into a first person account when I'm only a small part of the story. Apart from which, any reader with a grain of commonsense avoids autobiographical narratives for what they are: self-indulgent The world would have been better off if that Greek poser, Narcissus, had fallen arse over tit and drowned in his pond. No, if I am going to do this, better to write in the third person.'

'Great. Let's not be losers. This may be my end station, but it mustn't be yours. You see what that means, don't you, Tich? You have to get the hell out of Luritania before Kingsmith's agents hunt you down.'

'That's a bugger in itself, Van. Okay, perhaps I should scarper. But to where? What's your idea of the heart of darkness? Don't suggest the Congo rain forest. I'd be sure to get bitten by a tsetse fly as soon as I set foot off the plane.'

'How about, Barrow? As in Barrow, Alaska.'

'Too frigging cold.'

'Ushuaia, Argentina?'

'Too frigging ...'

'Okay. Sub-equatorial is not at the top of your holiday wish list. Thule, Greenland?'

'What? That same Ultima Thule the ancients fantasised about, where your breathe freezes the moment you walk out of your Inuit igloo? Worse than Alaska, because the country's name fools the ignorant into thinking it's greener than a Welsh valley when it's whiter than a football fan's moon. No, thank you very much.'

'Tristan da Cunha?'

'Great. One of Lewis Carroll's brothers went out there for his sins as a missionary. Population around three hundred. Even if some warm-hearted farmer's wife were to take me in and shelter me under her bosom or haystack, Kingsmith's tribe would track me down in less time than it takes to say "Bejesus, Dedalus, my old son'. In other words, it would be asking for trouble to tuck myself away on a lump of rock famous solely for the fact that the nearest island is home to Boney's bones.'

'There's always that town in Tasmania called Hobart.'

'Very funny. The first place those geeks would coming looking for me.'

'Or the last place. Too obvious.'

'I'll think about it.'

Tich mused for a moment or two. 'Going back to your harebrained idea, we're always going to come up against the same barrier. Why should anyone risk publishing a first novel by an unknown quantity?'

'So make yourself known. Go the rounds of the agents. Invite them out to lunch. Tell them that there are influential people, who would not shed a tear if your brain had a close encounter with an ice pick. But if you are going to do this, do it now. In other words, light out of Luritania and tuck yourself away from prying eyes somewhere nobody will think of looking for you. Because the longer you stick around here, Tich, the greater the chance of your going down with me.'

'That graphic image of the ice pick helped concentrate my mind. I'm even beginning to warm to the idea. Of course, it would mean having to close up shop.'

'What about Horst Völkling. Couldn't he keep the home fires burning?'

Vanessa was referring to Tich's part-time assistant, a retired Latin and Classical Greek teacher, who helped out in *Bibliopole* on Saturdays as well as on Wednesday and Friday afternoons.

'Not the happiest of metaphors, Van. In the first place, I've installed the regulatory number of fire extinguishers and, in the second, I'm not going off to war.'

'Oh, but you are, Tich. You are. A war of words.'

Tich sat up to square shoulders that had become slouched. 'When you put it like that …'

'And you'd be leaving the business in capable hands.'

'I doubt Horst could run to a six-day week, but any cover's better than none.'

'The sooner the better. Tell Horst you're taking a sabbatical.' Vanessa paused meaningfully. 'That is, if you can afford one.'

Oh, yes, thought Tich, as Van well knew, he could afford one.

'Your suggestion,' he said, 'of soft-soaping literary agents has given me another idea. Because if I go it alone, I'm liable to end up sympathising with Laurence Sterne. The poor fellow was at his wits' end after being saddled with ten cartloads of unsold *Tristram Shandy* volumes five and six. So how about this? I approach an established author and talk him into publishing our story under his name without letting on that it was ghosted and on the understanding that the cream of the royalties accrue to him.'

'Sounds good, Tich. You're our man.'

Tich's enthusiasm, buoyed up by Sterne's injunction to *let people tell their stories their own way,* wilted under a sudden bout of inadequacy. 'On the other hand, what if I'm not the author's man? He can't be expected to give his name to something composed by a hack. It would harm his reputation.'

'You're forgetting something important. The reading public loves whistleblowers. Give your author the bare bones. Wait now, don't look all offended. Humility, Tich. Humility. You're not in contention for the Man Booker prize. On second thoughts, though, you'll have to flesh the story out to make things easier for him to … rework.'

Tich gave a wry smile compounded of injured pride and inescapable misgivings. 'It's no good, Van. I can't see this getting off the ground.'

'Rubbish. Prioritise. First, find your author. Second, win him over. Third, tell our … I mean your story. And while you're at it, change place names. We can't have rubberneckers beating a path to your shop.'

No, thought Tich – entertained rather than annoyed by Vanessa's belated correction of a slip of the tongue – or to Horatio's psychiatric hospital. Not that he was prepared to admit as much to Vanessa. Because even if he agreed to relate the Sunday Club's story in the third person, the tale would inevitably be told from his angle. And Horatio was very much a part of Tich's life. Humphrey Hobart had not shunted his brother into an asylum at the back of beyond to condemn him to anonymity. Out of sight was not out of mind. Others should be made to understand this, or so Tich reasoned.

Thoughts of Horatio reminded Tich of one of Seneca's tags that his Latin scholar brother liked quoting in the past: *Non quia difficilia sunt non audemus, sed quia non audemus difficilia sunt.* (It is not because things are difficult that we do not dare. It is because we do not dare that things are difficult.)

'I can't argue with that. Necessity is the mother of invention. Though that brings me back to my objection about failing to give people the facts. We're leaving too much to conjecture.'

'On the contrary, you know the essentials. The rest is window dressing.'

The more Tich chewed the matter over the more inclined he was to grasp the nettle.

'Very well,' he said at length. 'Time for me to climb down from my pedestal, roll up my sleeves and give these shits the works.'

'Right,' said Vanessa, before laying down the handset to sit back and take a breather. 'That's the spirit.'

And she was right about one thing, thought Tich, taking the opportunity to stretch aching limbs. There was no time to be lost, if he wanted to get this done before they wrote his epitaph.

Vanessa glanced at the prisoners on either side of her. Were pre-trial inmates spared the indignity of having to wear the drab orange uniform imposed on those in for the long haul? Or were the womenfolk, in general, free to dress in whatever they had worn when first brought in? Why not, since they were in the minority? Less than two dozen, she reckoned, to judge by the few she had seen so far in the dining area in her wing separate from the men's wings. She picked up the handset and turned again to Tich.

'There's something else I wanted to put to you, Tich. Pliny. Clara Bogen asked the manageress of her home whether she could care for him while I was detained. How I hate that word. *The Luritanische Bote reports that Miss Curtis risks being detained for the next eight years.*'

'Come on, Van, *Maître* Deleuze will never let it come to that.'

448

'Thanks for your vote of confidence. Anyway, what was I saying about Pliny? Clara Bogen. Of course, the manageress said no. Far too complicated, what with Clara's guide dog and the need to feed Justin's ferret a colony of live mice. So what's the solution? You can't release him out into the wild. He'd never cope there after months of domestication. All that's left is to give him to a pet shop.'

'No worry. I can take care of that, if you let me have your key.'

'Justin meant to give me his copy but forgot. He ended up leaving it with Chantalle Boyer. You really ought to go across to my place as soon as we're done here. Pliny needs his water topping up. And there's chopped liver in the fridge.'

'A shame I can't take him with me. He could serve as my inspiration. After all, his namesake provided Tacitus with an invaluable eyewitness account of the eruption of Vesuvius.'

'Our ferret's noble ancestor also penned a Greek tragedy in his youth. So, yes, the ideal Muse for you reincarnated in the form of a tiny, furry, male quadruped.'

'Pliny the Younger, lawyer and imperial magistrate. He'd be of greater use to you in court, if only he could speak, refuting those baseless charges.'

'I rather think, Tich, that Justin's Pliny would be more at home with me here transplanted from one caged environment to another – with the added attraction of a daily, sixty-minute constitutional around our walled exercise yard. But whoever framed Übelshof's regulations frowned as much on pets as they did on files and drills.'

Seeing Tich at an uncomfortable loss for words, Vanessa shifted her attention to the television monitor on the wall behind him showing scenes of artillery fire into a residential area where several buildings had already taken serious punishment. The rolling text read:

While most Europeans are preoccupied with the recent spate of attacks on their continent by homegrown jihadists or the influx of refugees, their governments seem to have forgotten the smouldering conflict in eastern Ukraine. Now that most volunteer rebel fighters, disheartened by the Kremlin's refusal to back their cause, have packed up and moved on, Kiev is profiting from this disaffection by moving heavy equipment across the ceasefire line and pounding any dwellings thought to shelter the remnants of the self-styled separatists or their supporters. Preoccupied with the aerial war in Syria and the war of words with Turkey's leadership, Putin is accused by his detractors of sacrificing patriotism on the altar of opportunism.

Annoyed by his lack of success with a game built around thirty-six largely unnumbered squares, which one colleague had disparagingly referred to as ninetendo, the warder took out his vexation on the television. Using the remote, he switched over to MTV and raised the volume. With Taylor Swift's *Shake It Off* assaulting her eardrums, the visitor in the booth next to Vanessa's was the first to give the warder a mouthful.

'Who asked you to turn that circus on? We can't hear ourselves speak.'

Tich rallied to the cause. 'Can it, will you? You're not at home here.'

Similar sentiments following in close succession down the line, the warder glowered, turned sound and picture off, returned to his smartphone and pecked through his games app in search of the less demanding stud poker.

'Would that I could shake it off,' said Vanessa, throwing her head back and gazing unseeingly at the ceiling.

'Van, you've got one of the best defence lawyers out there. He won't let them get away with murder.'

'You think not?' Lowering her eyes, she regarded Tich unwaveringly. 'They're out to blacken my name, cripple my career. Remember those imbecilic US online visa application questions about whether you intend to engage in espionage, sabotage or terrorist activities? Depend upon it, they've ticked all the yes boxes for me.'

'Agreed, this is a set-up. All the more reason to beat them at their own game.'

'Bright ideas welcome. I've been racking my brains and got nowhere.'

'Wait a minute. Maybe things aren't as hopeless as you make out.'

'Really? Well, keep your voice down, Archimedes.'

'Of course, the real bugger for Deleuze is how to convince the magistrate that Kingsmith planted the incriminating screenfile in Rashid's laptop. I reckon the only hope he has of doing that is to play your joker.'

'Which is?'

'The Jay card.'

'But only a moment ago, you said Jay had left us in the lurch to save his own skin.'

'That's certainly the way it looks. So get Deleuze to have Hoffarth hand over the webcam footage of that episode of yours with Jay in Justin's apartment.'

'Images only, Tich. No sound recording.'

'Yes, I know. You told me that before. Well, tell Deleuze to find a lip reader to interpret what was said.'

'Shit, Tich. That hinges on how much we faced the webcam and how much we turned away from it.'

'Think hard. Where were you standing or sitting in relation to the camera?'

'I never bothered to ask Hoffarth where his men concealed it. They obviously set it up on a computer out of sight of Justin's. On the other hand, your idea isn't a bad one. The webcam images must have picked up something useful for a lip reader to work on.'

'And – not that I have any sympathy for Jay now that he's run out on us – the only people to catch sight of the man from MI6 in the context of this case will be Deleuze, the prosecution and the magistrate handling this affair. Not the wider public. Meaning the magistrate could order that a copy of the video be sent across to the British Secret Service.'

'Queering Jay's pitch.'

'More fool him for asking for it.'

'A card worth playing?'

'You bet.'

'That's what I like to hear. Sounds more like the girl whose parents chose to christen her VC.'

'I think you have to be a member of the armed forces to qualify for the VC.'

'It doesn't alter the fact that we're at war.'

'Outnumbered and outgunned. Ants facing up to mammoths.'

'With guile. The one sure way to outwit mammoths.'

Vanessa's faraway expression suddenly changed to one of concern. 'How will your brother take to not seeing you for three months or more?'

'Difficult to understand Horatio's concept of time. As for me, I already feel churned up about the thought of walking out on him.'

'You could always Skype him.'

'True. Especially now that he has a room to himself and his own laptop. I'll ask the sanatorium to help Horatio set up a video chat account.'

'Yes, you really ought to do that.'

The next moment the strident clamour of a bell rent the air throughout the room, bringing all conversation to a grinding halt and visiting hours to an end.

Vanessa leant forward, inviting Tich to join her in pressing palms against the window in the partition between them.

'I appreciate your coming to see me today, Tich. But it's made you vulnerable. Get out while the going's good. And promise me our story will see the light of day?'

'I promise. But I'll try not to make a Greek tragedy of it.'

'Good. Just hit them where it hurts.'

''Twas ever my wont.' Tich paused as his eyes became creased in a look of undisguised concern. 'I don't like the idea of leaving you out on a limb, Van. I want to speak up for you in front of the magistrate.'

'Forget it, Tich. I've no shortage of well-wishers. But I tell you what, I'll give Clara Bogen your e-mail address. She can keep you updated.'

'Clara?'

'Yes, Clara. She's a touch typist in Braille. Once she's composed her messages to people like you and me, she uses the blind home's translation software to convert them to standard, readable texts and gets Margaret to forward them from her computer. Hey, before you go – don't forget Pliny. He's relying on you.'

'Not, I hope, for a volcanic eruption.'

⁂

Relieved to learn upon returning to 'the cage' that her cellmate, Géraldine, had left for the shower room, Vanessa collapsed onto an unforgiving bunk bed. In no time at all, the memory of the nightmare robbing her of sleep n the early morning hours returned to dog her.

Standing inside an art gallery before a painting of an ancient woodland scene, she had the unnerving impression that the benevolent greybeard in the lower left foreground was beckoning her to join him. Within seconds, without understanding how or why, she had stepped into the canvas. Only to find that her eyes had deceived her: either that or the old man had changed into a satyr, whose

451

expression was no longer kindly but sinister. Alarming enough to drive her to step back into the gallery. Impossible. At the sight of an observant museum attendant shaking a puzzled head, she tried to scream, gesticulate, pummel … against what? An intangible wall? All in vain when stricken with paralysis.

The end of the road, thought Vanessa, on coming to her senses. You've changed places with one of those characters trapped in the shabby terminal world of the *Camino Real* together with the rest of its burnouts and misfits.

Suddenly, meaninglessness shouted out at her on all sides from the mouth of that irrepressible jack-in-the-box Palmer in his seedy ringmaster role of Gutman.

'What a comedown this is, Señorita Curtis. Can it be that the creator of cardboard cut-outs obedient to her every whim, the director accomplished at ordering slices of other people's lives, has neglected her own direction?'

For several long moments, Vanessa lay stretched out, eyes screwed shut, hands clamped to her ears before shaking off the vision of that mocking face and the sound of that scoffing voice. Pulling herself together, she sat up, drew the rough linen blanket around her shoulders and gazed with bemused fixity at a pair of obscene blowflies copulating on top of Géraldine's iPhone.

Well, she thought at length, who in her life had been the exploiter and who the exploited? Easy to blame others, but it made no sense to hold that bastard of a father responsible for his daughter's lack of commitment to a stable relationship. Control freaks were hardly in the same category as child molesters, and Charles Curtis had never abused her.

Well then, perhaps she had inherited her father's domineering side, frightening off the likes of Rashid and Justin? No, she could not accept that there had been any exploitation there on either side. All of which tended to suggest that Vanessa Curtis was her own worst enemy.

Climbing down onto uncarpeted concrete, she walked across to the shelf containing her few belongings, where she gulped mineral water from a bottle marked with a deterrent skull and crossbones. 'Orderliness, Géraldine,' she muttered.

Except that there was a limit to orderliness. Because it was impossible to avoid the fact that, if to others Miss Clever Pants was the embodiment of efficiency and self-possession, in her own eyes Vanessa Curtis was a mess.

Hearing the sound of flip-flops slapping the corridor tiling on their way to 'the cage', Vanessa threw a despairing glance at the flickering ceiling light and concluded that its stroboscopic effect matched the vulture girl's brain wave frequencies.

Junkies, she thought. Two a penny. Géraldine, you pitiable specimen, get a reality check. Your kind are yesterday's news compared to the woman vilified as Luritania's Jihad Jane.

⁂

Warder Michel Petit, the same prison official who had fared no better with stud poker than he had with Sudoko, eased his bulky frame into a protesting lightweight metal chair and reached for his cell phone. The number selected by him was not a mobile phone number like his own but a landline number. Perhaps that was better in a way: it meant that his call would be routed through a switchboard, even recorded. In other words, he was on safe, official business. The person he needed to contact would live up to his promise.

'Andreotti,' said the voice at the end of the line recognisable to Petit as that of the American who, over a glass of *Pinot Noir premier cru* on the open-air terrace of a café-restaurant on Schönschlucht's Place de la Libération, had informed him that, although nominally the U.S. embassy's new *ad interim* cultural attaché, his main remit was regional security.

'Petit here. Übelshof.'

'You have news for me?'

'Yes, Mlle Curtis had her first visitor today. Aside from her lawyer, *capisce?*'

Less than captivated by the Belgian's familiarity, Adam Andreotti was dismissively curt. 'Who?'

'A middle-aged man signed in as Humphrey Hobart. Big. Strong as an ox. Mean anything to you?'

It did not, but even if it had meant anything Adam Andreotti would have been the last to admit as much to his informer.

'Runs a bookshop in town called *Bibliopole*. Looks like he lives on the premises.'

'What phone number did he give you?'

'The one for the bookshop.'

'Did he bring anything along for her?'

'No.'

'Good. You'll let me know as soon as anybody else turns up.'

'*Bien entendu.*'

'Right, your envelope will be ready for collection in the central post office as from tomorrow.'

If Petit hoped the conversation might have gone on a trifle longer to give him the opportunity to suggest that the cherry on the cake (Monsieur Hobart's address) merited more than the flat-rate five thousand euros, he was disappointed. On the other hand, five grand was not to be sniffed at. It would go towards that Toyota flatbed truck which he had his eye on for, among other things, conveying his wife's wares to the Saturday flea market across the border. Suzanne Petit had filled the spare room in their apartment to bursting with items retrieved from the local recycling centre. Michel's wife knew how to load up her trolley during the lunch break when the recycling centre staff's attention was on their bellies rather than on shelves from which visitors were limited to taking three items at a time. And since Luritanians thought nothing of discarding quality goods, which their average northern neighbour would have repaired, not everything Suzanne snapped up was junk.

Fleetingly, Michel Petit reproached himself for his cupidity. After all, repeat visitors were worth five hundred euros, and it would take only one more new visitor for him and his wife to be in clover.

It was a weight off Justin Hendry's mind to step free of the customs clearance area at Murtala Muhammed International airport after seeing the elderly couple in front of him asked to stand aside on their way through the green exit corridor. Justin could not imagine what contraband the customs officers thought the doddering pair might be trafficking, but watchful eyes scrutinising travellers from behind their one-way mirror glass had given him another clean bill of health.

The pockmarked man awaiting him with a card bearing his name offered a flabby handshake.

'Gerald Honeycut. Glad to see your flight made it on schedule, because I'm afraid all I have time for is to show you to a taxi for the Sheraton. My dentist won't appreciate my missing today's appointment nor will my two cavities. Sorry I can't hang around any longer. I'll try to drop by the hotel later. One piece of bad news, one piece of good. The bad, there's been a glitch with the fire sprinklers in the apartment we're renting for you. The good, this probably means you'll be staying in the Sheraton for three extra nights at the company's expense.'

'What went wrong? I was told the apartment had just been redecorated.'

'That's right. But when the fire inspector passed by, he discovered that the decorators had managed to disable three of the sprinklers by painting over the contacts. Although Lagos likes to make out it's ahead of the rest of the field in West Africa, words aren't always father to the deed.'

As it happened, the Sheraton was situated only a short distance from the airport. A travel weary Justin was glad to find a comfortable, spacious room booked for him on the third floor. Unable to summon up sufficient energy to perform his customary set of aerobic exercises for stretching and loosening muscles immobilised for long hours on a packed flight, Justin was torn between crashing out or taking his kit down to the hotel's fitness centre, which, according to the promotional material left in his room, was equipped to standards – gym, squash court, swimming pool – that would have met with Craig's unreserved approval. Two choices. One correct. One wrong. But there was no way that he could have known that.

Before checking out the fitness centre, Justin decided to call in at reception where, after booking in, he had been handed three communications, one of which he saw upon reaching his room was intended for a Mr Zimmermann, clearly either the room's previous occupant or a guest in a different room.

Exiting the lift on the ground-floor, he strolled through a tiled garden plaza equipped with a central fountain playing jets of water into a pool populated with brightly coloured koi. Hotel guests had tossed Nigerian small change into the pool, either to lighten their pockets or to invoke good luck. Justin failed to count a single silver disc among the rash of copper coins tossed into the fountain.

When he reached the lobby, he found it bustling with a large number of – to judge by skin colour, if not by baggage labels – international arrivals from the airport down the road. Counting no fewer than five queues fronting the reception desk, his first impulse was to stuff the envelope in his pocket and turn on his heels. But at that moment he caught sight of a particularly attractive young woman towards the back of one of the queues leading up to the reception desk. She had an air about her of the gypsy played by Isabelle in Vanessa's ill-fated *Camino Real*, so much so that, on closer inspection, Justin could have sworn he was looking at Isabelle's double. Consequently, instead of turning and stepping back towards the garden plaza, he took several paces forward to see whether his imagination was playing him tricks.

It is debatable whether the few yards gained by retracing his steps would have made any significant difference in relation to the distance between him and the woman standing in the far left queue two rows away from the centre of his attention. For, the next instant, Justin heard the raucous exclamation 'Allahu Akbar' followed by an ear-splitting explosion. Slammed to the floor under the force of shrapnel impacting his chest, he was one of many caught by the blast, when the male jihadist, with a compact Saudia bag at his feet and dressed from head to foot in the garb of a woman – an elegant blue abaya topped by a niqab of the same colour – detonated his suicide bomb.

But lying there on the lobby floor sufficiently conscious, as if in a heightened state of awareness as to his surroundings, to gather that others seemed to have fared worse – the mess of flesh, bone, blood and cartilage hurled on all sides from the spot where the woman had been standing proof enough that nothing remained of either her or the theatrical Isabelle's twin – Justin felt sublime gratitude for his good fortune. After all, could he not move his limbs? Had his sight not been spared? Others less fortunate than he had been dismembered, blinded, had their eardrums shattered. In fact, the noise of the explosion was still resounding in his ears, though surely not enough to spell deafness?

Yes, he should count himself fortunate. Except that then he remembered that some of that fanatic's explosive charge had hit him squarely in the chest. He needed to sit up in order to see the extent of the damage, because all of a sudden he sensed that his shirt front was sodden. It took considerable effort to pull himself upright on his elbows, after which he realised that not only was there nothing much left of his shirt but that two gaping wounds were pulsing blood.

An inner voice screaming at him not to be overcome by the apparent hopelessness of his situation, Justin started dragging himself back towards the garden area, thinking that once he arrived there he could rest against the fountain, even quench his first, but above all staunch the flow of blood by pressing on his wounds with both forearms. He had moved only a few inches, when his left hand came to rest on the blood-soaked stump of a severed leg, the shock of which caused him to keel over onto his stomach. To his right lay the decapitated head of Isabelle Meunier. He gave a stupid giggle. No, of her double. What, he asked himself feverishly, had she or he done to deserve this? Feeling increasingly weaker and coughing up spittle that was becoming redder by the minute, Justin uttered an insane laugh. *Jiggery-pokery*, he thought. *Harum-scarum, hugger-mugger jiggery-pokery.*

He made one last attempt to haul himself into a semi-upright position, before collapsing pathetically onto his ruined chest. So this was how it was going to end, was it? Where were the frigging emergency services? The lifesaving ambulance men? No, of course, this was Africa, where you had to wait three days to have your defective fire sprinklers repaired. At least it was easier, even comfortable lying stretched out like this on the floor. Perhaps the rescue services would get to him on time. He could already hear voices from people well and alive, who had just entered the hotel from outside. A series of unintelligible barked orders. If he turned slightly and waved an arm, somebody would come to his aid. With so many dead and wounded, the newcomers had to give priority to those between life and death. The only problem was how to raise his arm let alone how to power himself sufficiently upright. He resorted to croaking '*¡Socorro!*' (Help!), then laughed at the absurdity: Miguel Cervantes's don awaking from a bad dream at the foot of his fountain – except that he had not reached that far.

Suddenly, Rosalie Radetzky was standing in front of him, hugging her Tigger and crying, 'Get up, Justice. They won't notice you, if you don't move.'

Followed by more absurdity: the vision of Shrew, his grammar school biology master, pricking up his ears at the sound of church bells on the afternoon air.

'What class, does that make you think of?' Shrewsbury was asking, his head cocked sparrow-like to one side.

'Weddings, sir?'

'You're learning biology here, Jenkins, not anthropology.'

'Reproduction, sir.'

'Not bad, James, except that weddings traditionally take place on a Saturday. No, I would suggest rather that you recall what little you might have retained from Mr Henderson's readings to you during English literature of a certain poem by John Donne part of which Ernest Hemingway plundered for the title of one of his novels. No ideas, class? Dear me. The answer is not forty-two, my deep thinkers, but compost.'

Yes, thought an increasingly weary Justin: chirpy Aunt Clarissa, forever tending her vegetable patch, would have preferred to hear that story issuing from her nephew's lips as part of his farewell tribute rather than soppy lines taken from a lake poet. Although Bill Wordsworth had got it right for Lucy or his sister, Dotty: *Rolled round in earth's diurnal course, With rocks, and stones, and trees.*

He sensed the nearness of a helping hand, somebody bending over him. A harsh, negative voice. Damn it, all he had to do was to groan or twitch a limb. Quite ridiculous. Shrew would not have expected one of his pupils to end up enriching Nigeria's subsoil.

Rosalie's voice again. Weaker now. 'Get up, Justice.'

Had she forgotten they were on the Ferris wheel? Revolving slowly, admittedly. But unwise to stand up. Better to lie back and dream about opening your eyes to fresh wonders.

Memo from J to K

I don't expect your people to give a standing ovation to my suggestion that the Nevskian administration has pirated Vespuccia's dumming-down policy. But come on, don't pretend that the League hasn't cut back on education with a view to reducing literacy and the thirst for knowledge. Don't pretend that it hasn't supplanted education with aquavit, carbonated soft drinks, fast food and braindead television series. Don't pretend that it hasn't made it impossible for the gifted to gain access to the corridors of power, inhabited as they are by those least qualified to wield power.

Response from K

No argument from me, J. Who leads the world in the dissemination of ignorance? Who ushered in The Unenlightenment?

You forgot to mention how the League's ruling party puts the kibosh on solidarity by pitting its putative rival groups against one another.

⁂

Halfway down a quiet country road leading to Luritania's southern border with its large neighbour to the east, Tich pulled his Renault onto a deserted dirt track between immense swathes of sugarcane. When starting out on his journey he had kept an eye on the rearview mirror. But since the mid-afternoon traffic on the secondary road chosen by him out of the capital turned out to be light, it was not long before he sat back and relaxed in the knowledge that he had the road pretty much to himself. Only now, as he veered off the road onto the rutted packed earth track, did a solitary Hungarian logistics van pass him travelling in the opposite direction, its exhaust spewing pollution, its driver too involved in the music belted out from his dashboard radio to pay attention to someone probably in need of a pee.

Tich drove all the way to the top of the track, which ended in front of a dense wood where a metal plaque affixed to a hefty wooden pole strung between two posts barred entry to all traffic other than forestry service vehicles. Turning off the engine, he climbed out, opened up the boot and paused. Pliny looked up enquiringly from the back of his cage, where he had sat curled up contentedly for most of the journey, Tich being one of the three humans to whom the ferret was accustomed. But faced now with the look of trust in the creature's eyes, Tich began to wonder whether he had taken the right the decision. The truth of the matter was he knew next to nothing about mustelids, the family to which Pliny belonged, beyond what he had learnt from his two friends as to these creatures' sleeping, drinking and eating habits.

To start with, although ferrets were nocturnal by nature such that Pliny spent most of the daylight hours asleep, their waking hours could be irregular, particularly if they sensed a familiar or alien presence. It was also important that they be kept supplied with sufficient water to avoid dehydration. Consequently, before setting out on his journey, Tich had studied his relief map of southern Luritania to search out the ideal environmental conditions for a thirsty ferret. The woodland in front of him was flanked by a stream to his right overlying an aquifer from which farmers drew groundwater for irrigating their crops. Furthermore, each of the two farms at the bottom of the hill on the far side of the wood comprised a sprawling complex of barns and outhouses. If Justin had not been in the habit of feeding Pliny live field mice and the occasional young rabbit, Tich would have agreed with Van that the best home for Pliny was the temporary holding area of a pet shop. But in view of the spirited animal's tooth and claw instincts, he felt that if any unneutered, semi-domesticated ferret released into the wild stood a good chance of surviving – even mating and starting a family – that ferret was Pliny.

Tich liked to fancy there was something of Jack London's White Fang about Pliny. But now that reality was about to take over from fantasy, that comparison sparked worries about predators. In releasing Pliny here, Tich would be exposing him to owls, buzzards and foxes. On the other hand, on those bank holiday weekends when Tich had looked after Pliny for Justin, taking the creature for a romp on a long leash, he had been amazed at the furry creature's speed and agility. It had remained unchanged since the day when Justin first caught Pliny chasing a demented cat around the garden. Apart from which, what was life without risk? Actually, Pliny had been caged in Justin's apartment for less than five months. Did that really qualify as semi-domesticated?

Tich felt sure that Justin would have seen things his way. All right, he was going back on his word to Van, but she had too much on her plate to think this through properly. Pliny had been brought in from the wild, and now it was time for him to return there.

Tich lifted the cage gingerly out of the back of the Renault and set it on the ground with the door facing the wood. Pliny immediately pricked up his ears, scampering eagerly to the front of the cage and pawing at its matted floor. No reticence there, thought Tich.

'Pliny,' he said, 'I'm afraid we've come to the parting of the ways. Mind you, once I upon this door, that decision's yours. A life of fend-for-yourself freedom out there with the rest of Nature or a cosy existence with damn-all variety to it now that your master and mistress have left you in my hands and I too am having to flee the coop. I understand your namesake owned quite a few villas. Well, just over the hill down there, you'll find plenty of warm buildings with generous roofing to bed down in. There's no shortage of water. As for food, you'll have to go hunting for that. So what's it to be?'

Pliny was scratching away impatiently at the wire of his cage front.

'Yes, well, you won't have understood a word I've been blabbing on about. But your senses are what matters here. They should help you decide. So let's give it a try.'

Tich had half hoped that, after he opened the cage, Pliny might sniff around his hands and legs before tentatively exploring the immediate territory. But the creature bolted out of the back of the car into the nearest sugar cane thicket.

'Well,' sighed Tich, 'that's a creature who knows its own mind.'

Rather than replacing the cage straightaway in the boot, Tich left it open on the ground, locked up the Renault and headed into the woods for an afternoon stroll, all the time telling himself that, were Pliny to decide that he wanted to come back, he would be waiting for him.

But upon returning fifty minutes later after a refreshing walk through a wood rich in plant life, Tich found the cage as empty as he had left it. Uttering Pliny's name, he crouched down on all fours to look for the ferret under his vehicle. But came up red-faced, breathless and feeling foolish.

It was while he was returning the cage to the Renault's boot that he wondered whether he ought not to leave the few playthings hoarded by Pliny on the ground available for the ferret to pick up and take back to his new den. He removed them one by one: a badly chewed squash ball, a leather key chain toggle, a stale sock, two rusty keys on a ring and, something that had escaped his notice before because it was hidden under a pile of wood shavings: a silver tie clasp bearing a blue enamel badge with the numbers two and nine either side of a white, upraised sword. His first thought on seeing this was that he had never known Justin to wear a tie clip, his second that Pliny would be in serious trouble if he tried to swallow the object. In the event, concluding that this suggestion underrated Pliny's intelligence, Tich left the clasp together with the rest of the ferret's collectibles in a patch of grass beside two rows of sugarcane.

'Sorry about that, Van,' he said, climbing back into the driving seat. 'Strictly speaking, you're in greater need of releasing than Pliny, but this was the best I could manage.'

Tempted to return to the same spot in the early hours of the following morning, Tich finally allowed common sense to prevail over sentimentality. Pliny had been given a new lease of life. Now it was time for Humphrey Hobart to get on with his life and to ensure that the same murky characters who had visited ruination on his friends failed to muzzle the last of the Sunday Club.

⁂

Georg Hoffarth and Eugène Deleuze had been pals since the age of twelve, when they had first met seated side by side in their desks at the Collège Gaston Meyrich imbibing the wonders of mathematics dispensed by a teacher whose infectious enthusiasm for his subject inspired both boys to vie with each other in seeing who could turn in the best work.

Sitting together now in the more relaxed environment of *Beim Dickstufchen* at the bottom of Schönschlucht's valley gorge over a mug of the brasserie's unfermented beer and a crisp hock of ham nesting on a bed of sautée potatoes lent substance by a profusion of kidney beans in a rich brown sauce, both men were exchanging reminiscences triggered by the question 'Where in heavens did you go to school?' addressed by a middle-aged woman to an older man wrestling with the challenge of splitting the bill with another couple at the same table.

'You wait, *mon pote* (chum),' remarked Deleuze. 'Any minute now, he will pull out a pocket calculator. Enough to bring tears to the penguin's eyes.'

Georg Hoffarth raised his mug in a joint salute to Pythagoras and Bacchus. The teacher known affectionately by his class as Penguin – on account of his shape and monochrome sartorial preferences – had taught him and his friend shortcuts to solving problems of the kind that was tying the fellow opposite up in knots. 'What's the betting he can't cope with all those ninety-nine and forty-nine cents?'

'The wife holds the purse strings,' said Hoffarth. 'She just remarked, *"Wir haben kein Tropfen Sekt getrunken."* (We didn't drink a drop of champagne.)

'In which case,' said Deleuze, 'it wouldn't surprise me, if any minute now she came out with, *"Die schuffen fier dieren Secks bezwollen."* (They should pay for their sex. – A pun by the maître in Luritanian, Hoffarth's mother tongue.)

'Careful, Eugène, they might understand Luritanisch.'

'Well, so be it. I was simply explaining what France's prostitutes have to say about this new law which makes it illegal to pay for sex.'

With a smack of his lips the inspector set his Stein down and watched good-humouredly as his friend did battle with a piece of crackling. The two would never had met had Eugène's parents not taken the decision to put their son through the Luritanian school system. Given that Deleuze senior had come to Luritania as a Senior Advocate at the European Judicial Tribunal, and his Italian wife as Provost at the European Multidisciplinary Academy, they might have been expected to follow the standard practice of enrolling their sons in the European College. But the Deleuzes wanted to give their boys a true taste of Luritania, its people, culture and history. Hence, having learnt Luritanian at an early age, Eugène was as at home in that language as he was in the French and Italian spoken by his parents. The Collège Gaston Meyrich and student exchange holidays spent in Bonn and Oxford had also given him passable command of German and English. Consequently, it was not unusual for the two friends when chatting together to switch from one language to another, although Georg's limited Italian, characterised by bawdy cusswords taught him by his friend, meant that the inspector's forays into the language of Umberto Eco were rare.

The two friends were treating tonight as no different to any other occasion in the sense that while their jaws were seriously exercised by the hock of ham, their tongues still found time between mouthfuls to engage in linguistic gymnastics. Until Georg, aware that sooner rather than later the conversation would touch upon matters *sub judice* and that none of the brasserie's other diners was paying either man the slightest attention, broached the question uppermost in his mind, and the verbal gallivanting ceased.

'I'm afraid I've bad news for you and your client, Mademoiselle Curtis. Off the record, of course.'

'A case of forewarned meaning lay down your arms?'

'I should hope not.'

'*Alors, ne me tiens pas en haleine.* (Well, don't keep me in suspense.) But perhaps I can guess. *Un certain gros bonnet* (A certain prima donna) has put her oar in?'

'Yes and no. As you know, Eugène, Mlle Curtis has all my sympathy for the little it's worth. We, she and I, were hoping that the webcam images of what her intruder was up to before she came on the scene would play in her favour. And I, in particular, hoped that we could nail Kingsmith on the basis of two flash drives found in his pockets. But it seems that Kingsmith – let's call him that for want of anything better, all the more so since the American Embassy has twisted quite a few arms – knew what he was about. To start with, there was no need for him to disguise inserting a flash drive into Mlle Curtis's computer, if he was out to copy sensitive files. Neither of us, I suspect, believes that to have been the case. He was introducing not extracting data and had all the knowledge or software at his disposal to falsify his Word file's creation date. Furthermore, since he can hardly have known in advance what version of Word he would encounter in Mlle Curtis's apartment, he must have come equipped with different versions of the incriminating file.'

'And how, pray, did he get into her computer in the first place?'

'Mlle Curtis's laptop uses an old version of Windows, making it easy for an experienced hacker to crack her password.'

'All right, well, what about the key strokes on the print-out? Sizes, spaces between characters? How could Kingsmith's people be sure they matched those on her laptop?'

'They couldn't. You can try getting an expert to look into that, of course, but I doubt whether he'll have much luck. Not if Kingsmith was on the ball and input a number of additional files so harmless in content but in the same typeface as to present the prosecution with enough ammunition to maintain that not all of Mlle Curtis's document files originated in her laptop. The fact of the matter is that one of the two flash drives was empty. The other contained solely the incriminating file.'

'You think Kingsmith wiped both flash drives clean of the rest of his data?'

'Correct.

'What about Jabour's laptop? The prosecution is bound to view that as the source laptop.'

'Kingsmith doesn't seem to have touched it. I would have expected him to use the opportunity to make a damning case against Mlle Curtis. But the technical reports on the two computers lifted from the apartment show that the incriminating files are nowhere to be found on Jabour's pc. As for his work laptop, that has gone missing, presumably stolen from his Beirut hotel room. Perhaps Mlle Curtis caught Kingsmith before he had time to do anything with her boyfriend's computer.' Eugène Deleuze paused to slake his thirst. 'But that's not all.'

'You're beginning to give me indigestion, Georg.'

'I'll order you a Fernet-Branca.'

'Thanks for nothing. Go ahead. I'm listening.'

'When Mlle Curtis suggested hiring a lip reader to interpret the few words exchanged between her and Kingsmith, she forgot that he had his back to the camera. In other words, anyone hearing that version is likely to construe it one-sidedly.'

'Nothing to lose sleep over. I thought you were really going to give me gyp.'

'I've left the worst till last. What did you and she consider to be her ace in the hole?'

'Your people's webcam recording of her encounter with MI6's mystery man in Hendry's apartment – complete with lip reading, as most of the evidence in her favour would have been recorded with both participants face on to the camera.'

'Right. Would you believe me, if I told you that my boss passed that recording on to her majesty in the US embassy without thinking to make a copy?'

'I would.'

'And that her majesty then issued her sincerest apologies about said recording having gone missing?'

'When has sincerity ever been a diplomat's strong suit?'

'Frankly, you amaze me, Eugène. This has given your case for the defence a battering it could have done without.'

Deleuze's hitherto placid features broke into a scowl, before the lawyer shrugged philosophically and augmented his share of the kidney beans from a side dish.

'We both believe Mlle Curtis when she says she's been framed. I'll use her excellent professional and character references to show that she mistakenly befriended someone who came into wrongful possession of documents embarrassing to the American and British Secret Services, as a result of which one or the other or both of these services set out unashamedly to blacken her name.'

'You think you'll get anywhere with that line?'

'The minimum sentence for involuntary manslaughter plus a year or two for being an unwitting accessory after the fact. With early probationary release for good behaviour.'

'I feel as sick about this as you must do, Eugène.'

'What did that pompous oaf of a boss of yours have to say about *Madame l'Ambassadrice's* tall story?'

'Ours not to reason why. Ours but to do and die.'

'And what did you say?'

'That neither he nor I truly believed that anyone risked dying over this, but that there was more than one way of dying. You only had to see the blank expression on his face to understand that he had no idea what I was talking about.'

'Well, now that you've made my evening, Georg, let's both weep into a glass of Armagnac. Because as for your *maudit* (damn) Fernet-Branca, you know what you can do with that.'

'Ça ne plairait pas à mon proctologue. (My proctologist wouldn't approve.)'

'*Mon cher ami, tu m'as mal compris. Je visais soit ton chef soit madame l'ambassadrice.* (My dear friend, you misunderstood me. I was thinking either of your boss or the lady ambassador.)'

'A lawyer's idea of gender equality?'

'That's one way of putting it, though I side in this matter with Sir Henry

Wotton. Long before anyone entertained the idea of appointing women as ambassadors, this English diplomat's definition of an ambassador was "an honest gentleman sent to lie abroad for the good of his country".'

⁓✺⁓

It was ten o'clock on Tuesday morning, and Tich was poring over *Bibliopole's* accounts in his makeshift office at the back of the bookshop, leaving the front counter unoccupied, when the dissonant jangling of the doorbell alerted him to the fact that he had a customer, post or an express parcel delivery. This last possibility triggered memory of Vanessa's less than jocular warning that Tich should not make the mistake of thinking that he still enjoyed the same low profile as that obtaining up to the time of her incarceration. In future, he should treat every package supplied courtesy of TNT as if it emanated from a subsidiary operating under the more chilling acronym TNG. But one glance at the overhead CCTV monitor allayed any fears Tich might have nursed as to logistical entrapment: the newcomer looked to be a prospective customer, whom he had never seen before. Dressed as the stranger was in a business suit, Tich guessed that he was either passing by from the *Hotel Splendide* across the way or taking time out from an office in town rather than from one up on the Dombezirk plateau, home to Luritania's overcrowded European institutions on the fringe of Schönschlucht's city limits. Loath to tear himself away from the paperwork in hand, Tich decided to leave the new arrival to his own resources. With the labelled sides of each row of bookcases clearly identifying their contents by category, should the customer strike it lucky or need additional help, he had only to ring what Van called the virgin's tit bell on the front desk. In the meantime, Tich could keep an eye on the visitor's movements and behaviour – in his experience, few shoplifters in Schönschlucht wore hand-me-downs – while continuing with the more pressing matter of cross-checking his annual income tax declaration.

But to his annoyance, the respite was all too brief, because two minutes later the prospective buyer could be seen standing in the shop's Art section, smiling at a colour plate reproduction of Salvador Dali's *The Persistence of Memory* before walking back with his find to the counter. Anticipating the metallic ding, a somewhat crabby Tich placed a ruler under the last set of figures verified and went out into the shop.

'Quite a collection you've got here,' said the customer, as Tich settled himself behind the counter. The man spoke with a soft American accent. Although ages could be deceptive with stout people, Tich put this fair-haired stranger's age at no more than thirty-five. His podgy, large-knuckled hands reminded Tich of those of a butcher, though this fellow looked as if he would be more at ease pushing pens than sawing through racks of lamb.

'We try to cater for all tastes.'

'Your shop was recommended to me by a colleague. Unique, he said. There's an entire village dedicated to second-hand books across the border in King Leopold

463

land, but just one such shop in the principality. Allow me to introduce myself. Adam Andreotti.'

'No relation, I trust, to a prime minister thought to have been in league with the devil?'

Tich's customer gave a weak smile. 'No relation to Giulio. Nor even, I'm sad to say, to Aldo.'

'There you have me.'

'Aldo Andreotti, mathematican.'

'Capable of putting more than two and two together, I suppose? Anyway, Humphrey Hobart. Pleased to meet you.'

The firmness of Andreotti's handshake took Tich by surprise. Perhaps this fellow, who probably in his stockinged feet stood only one inch short of Tich, was capable of tearing Boston's telephone directory in half within twenty seconds. Not that Tich's own grip was any less firm.

'I understand you pump iron,' said Andreotti, pausing before adding: 'And that you are no slouch with a firearm.'

Tich needed no further prompting to realise to whom he was talking. 'Would you happen to be a colleague of Arnold Palmer's?'

'Right on the button. In fact, I've taken over from him.'

Doubting whether Andreotti had come to his shop on a goodwill let alone a fence-mending visit, Tich saw no point in dissembling. 'As I understand it, Arnold was sent home with his tail between his legs.'

'Whatever gave you that idea?' said the American embassy's new cultural attaché, disingenuously leafing through the Dali art book.

'Arnold's little trick got plastered all over the press. Next to impossible to keep secret something as newsworthy as the fact that your embassy was caught bugging the people who sold you Louisiana.'

'Without betraying any confidences, I can assure you there are always good reasons behind apparent diplomatic *faux pas*.'

Really? 'I thought the French were eating out of your hand. Whatever happened to "You're either with us or against us"?'

'Maybe instead of pointing the finger at Uncle Sam, Europeans should be wondering how many of their allies are wolves in sheep's clothing. We live in a surreal world.'

'You're an acolyte of Dali's?'

'Can't say I am. No, the MoMA is loaning out some of its Dali collection to Luritania's Prinz Felix Museum as part of a wider European exhibition circuit. Since the embassy is playing host to one of the MoMA's chief curators, I thought I ought to bone up on Salvador. Do these price tags on the inside front cover still mean anything?'

'Let me have a look.'

Andreotti handed over the book.

'No,' said Tich, who had the man summed up as a miser. 'They're out of date. Every now and then we offer readers the chance to buy certain books over two or three weeks at progressively favourable discounts. This publication never got sold, so the asking price is the original one pencilled in at the top of the first page. Twenty-one euros.'

'Well, that's above my budget.'

'Which is?'

'For a second-hand hardback – fifteen euros.'

'I seem to remember there's more than one Dali back there.'

'Yes, I looked. But this is the only one with colour plates.'

'I'm sorry then. I can't help you. I have a living to make.'

'I see it would be unwise for me to pick a fight with Mr Hobart.'

'You'd be the first person, Mr Andreotti, to pick a fight with me over a matter of six euros.'

'Yet certain parties might wonder whether some of this shop's sales were earning you money from the wrong type of literature.'

Tich, whose initial impression of the American had been quick to sour, was unable to contain a bark of laughter. 'What's that supposed to mean?'

'The kind of literature that incited people to public disorder.'

'And where, pray, would certain parties get that idea from?'

'Your association with a certain young lady behind bars awaiting trial for seditious behaviour.'

Tich worked hard to control his temper. 'Alleged seditious behavior. The charges levelled against Miss Curtis are bunkum.'

'Mr Hobart, who are we to argue against those who dispense justice in these nervous times?'

'*Je voudrais pouvoir aimer mon pays tout en aimant la justice.*'

'There you have me.'

'Albert Camus. I should like to be able to love my country and still love justice.'

'A noble sentiment. Do you take plastic?'

'Not an altar that I worship at personally, but, yes. For purchases over twenty-five euros.'

Simulating regret at having irked the shopkeeper, Adam Andreotti pulled out his wallet, withdrew one twenty euro banknote, fished around in his trouser pocket for the right coinage, laid the cash on the counter and took hold of his purchase.

'All in a good cause,' said Tich, glad to be rid of the man as soon as possible.

'If I could have a receipt, please, Mr Hobart.'

'I'll need the barcode.'

Andreotti surrendered his purchase. 'Of course.'

Tich swiped his reader over the code, leaving the American to tear off his proof of purchase from the counter's heavy-duty receipt printer. 'Good luck charging that to your expense account.'

'I can see we'll have to keep an eye on you, Mr Hobart. 'You're nobody's fool.'

Andreotti delivered these last words with a chortle, before pocketing a wallet bursting with credit cards, resecuring his purchase and turning on his heels. As the doorbell clanged discordantly in Andreotti's wake, Tich was reminded of Gwyneth's characterisation of Theodore Tartell, a local do-gooder: 'Get nobbled for long by Theo Tartuffe, and you won't need Molière or Shakespeare to tell you "one may smile, and smile, and be a villain".'

Memo from K to J

> *Some light relief in the form of a story going the rounds inside the League: The Wayfarer and the Bear are barbecuing Urodina's Mr Confectionery whose appetite extends to the eastern provinces' mining deposits. The Bear asks his boss why he is turning the spit so fast. The Wayfarer replies, 'To stop him from stealing the coal'.*

Response from J

> *When you see that the League's untouchables caught helping themselves to large slices of the budgetary pie pay for their peccadilloes with a show trial resulting in three months' house arrest followed by reinstatement, while hapless vagrants caught nabbing a sack of potatoes are put behind bars for a year, perhaps those barbecue roles should be reversed.*

Hooking up the 'temporarily closed' sign on the front door, Tich returned to the back room. The tax declaration could wait. Something else he had put off doing could not. Tich picked up his cell phone and rang his part-time assistant.

'Horst, how are things. Look, I'm sorry to lumber you with this but do you think you could take over in the shop here for the next three months, while I take a break? On the same basis as at present. Part time.'

'No problem,' came the gravelly reply – Horst was the bass lead in a prominent Schönschlucht choral group. 'Time on my hands at the moment, and I have no other commitments until January. Where are you off to? Fiji? Hawaii? World tour?'

'I'll explain later, Horst. The important thing to know is that the rent and all my utility bills are paid by standing order. I'll pop down to the bank for an *ordre de procuration* authorising you to pay in the monthly takings. TNT always leaves a delivery notice if I'm out when they call. Not that there's much expected from that end. I'll leave you a list. Oh, and I'll tell, Idalina, the *femme de ménage* that I've left you in charge. Otherwise, nothing for you to worry about. Just be sure to keep up to date with the accounts.'

'Don't forget to give me the keys. I'll also need to know how to operate that alarm. Best not to make us unpopular with the neighbours.'

'Thanks for reminding me. And, Horst, don't hesitate to go ahead with any bright theme ideas for the window.'

'The French are putting on *Antigone* here in October with Isabelle Huppert and Jean Reno. I could arrange a Greek literature and drama month.'

Tich, who had all but seen this coming, decided to leave well alone. Beggars could not be choosers. And it was not as if Horst was unfamiliar with sale or return orders. *Bibliopole* would not be landed with two dozen unsold copies of Sophocles's play.

No sooner had this thought crossed his mind than, for the first time, Tich was struck by naked fear. What if he were never to set foot in Luritania again, never to see Horatio again? Beelzebubs like Adam Andreotti could see to that.

'All very sudden then, Tich?'

Horst's words caught *Bibliopole's* owner by surprise, lost as he was in depressing thoughts.

'Afraid so. Wish I had more time to explain now, but I will later.'

'Good on you. No need to worry about *Bibliopole*. I'll take good care of her. Might even work a couple of extra days full-time. Not good for business if people get to see too many closed signs. If you're off to some place exotic, be sure to send me a decent postcard. I'll keep a rainfall record for when you return – reminder of how the other half lives.'

With Horst's parting words 'when you return' ringing ominously in his ears, Tich drew meagre satisfaction from the knowledge that he was leaving his premises in safe hands. The fact was that he might never see the inside of his bookshop again. End of an era, Gwyn, he thought. Now that Horst is left holding our baby, heaven help her if she's orphaned only to be fostered by a fast food artery choker.

His next problem: how to soften the blow to Horatio of absenting himself for the next three months, especially with the likes of Andreotti in the wings. Hatchet jobs, he had learnt, were anything but foreign to American cultural attachés, and the last thing Tich wanted was to expose his brother to intimidation. He would have to speak to Horatio over the phone, but if that only served to confuse his bro, he would find a way of putting Frans van Landewijk as little in the picture as he had Horst Völkling.

The tax return reclaimed his attention only briefly before he thought back to his previous evening's grim choice of DVD viewing: *The Seventh Seal*. Not that he shared much in common with Ingmar Bergman's existentially embittered knight home from the Crusades to a land in the grips of the plague. Except that he had been drawn into a game of chess, if not with Death, then with the devil. The thought that came to Tich as the credits faded from the screen, resurfaced now. The knight's one meaningful deed was what Vanessa and Justin were asking of him. Would he prove equal to the test?

❧

467

Memo from K to J

You win some, you lose some. We can rule out an early orange revolution in the League. A pity, because this promised not only to bring our liberal sycophants into power but also to satisfy Vespuccia's and its allies' hunger for that wealth of natural resources.

On the other hand, the more we shout from the rooftops that the League is preparing to swallow its Erebuan minnow neighbours, the easier it will be for us to lambaste the Nevskians in our Turtle Bay forum after baiting them into armed conflict in defence of repossession of the Tauric peninsula.

Response from J

We had not expected to see the League sitting for so long on the sidelines watching your people beef up Urodina. All the same, it would be prudent to trust those colonial administrators only so far. Best not to bite off more than you can chew by pushing Urodina into the folly of trying to reclaim that Tauric feather in The Wayfarer's cap. The League's response could be a direct, conventional attack against Vespuccia as prime instigator rather than against its arms' length puppets.

Clara Bogen was helped into her seat in front of the partition separating her from Vanessa by a warder with none of the curmudgeonly qualities of the prison officer who had presided over Tich's visit to Übelshof. Bismarck settled down tranquilly at her side.

'I find it indefensible,' said Clara, 'that people awaiting trial should be treated as if already convicted. Why, for heaven's sake, did you not apply for bail?'

'But I did, Clara. It was refused. The public prosecutor ruled that I should remain behind bars for my own good. Certain sections of the press are portraying me as Luritania's first female convert to jihadism.'

'Balderdash.'

'Of course, but, in taking this line, the public prosecutor has stirred up people's prejudices.'

'Didn't your lawyer protest?'

'He lodged a formal protest. But what happened in France and Belgium has given the law across Europe the jitters. I'm accused of manslaughter, remember. And the prosecution maintains that the person I killed worked for counter-terrorism.'

'The person you killed in self-defence. And the charges against you couldn't be flimsier.'

Vanessa laughed as Bismarck emitted a muted growl of endorsement. 'Yes. And my defence lawyer, *Maître* Deleuze, is building his case around the fact that I have no history identifying me with Muslim extremists, no visits to Schönschlucht's mosque where I might have been radicalised, no trips to Egypt, Libya or Pakistan, no crash courses in Arabic, not one publication at home or in the office smacking of anti-western propaganda. Deleuze will ridicule allegations of siding with the Islamic caliphate by waving my copies of *The Seven Pillars of Wisdom*, *The Rubáiyát of Omar Khayyam* and *The Prophet* under the magistrate's nose.'

'Deleuze's fees must be astronomical. Is anyone coordinating a support fund? If so, I want to contribute.'

'That's good of you, Clara, but I have savings to draw on. Apart from which, Marcello Ricoveri, my workplace's union leader, has persuaded the membership to meet fifty per cent of my legal expenses. After securing two and a half thousand signatures against the TTIP, Marcello needed no convincing as to who pressured the Luritanians into indicting me.'

Vanessa had added cause to be thankful for the union leader's efforts on her behalf: they had made it easier to turn down Tich's offer. The last thing she wanted was for her legal costs to be underwritten by stolen funds.

'Well, that's great news,' said Clara. 'So many people clubbing together to clear your name.'

'Under ordinary circumstances,' said Vanessa, unable to share her friend's confidence, 'the accusations against me would be laughable. But these are not ordinary circumstances. The moment people hear or smell rumours of jihadist terrorism, watch out for the knee-jerk, finger-pointing accusations hard to defend yourself against, especially with damning material on your laptop.'

'Put there to sully your name.'

'Well, Deleuze will argue the point that this character defamation is based on a misconception. Fearing that his client had it in her power to open up one of their cans of worms, two countries' Secret Services connived to silence her. In reality, had she been in possession of classified material discreditable to these services – which she had come to despise – she would have not sat upon it but broadcast it.'

'Do you know yet which examining magistrate is taking on your case?'

'Josephine Breidewinkel.'

'Don't know her. But the fact that she's a woman …'

'Means she can't afford to be predisposed in my favour. She's sifting through all the evidence before deciding whether the case should be taken to trial, which, according to *Maître* Deleuze, is a foregone conclusion. Because faced with a case as high profile as this and acting in her capacity as state prosecutor charged with uncovering all the relevant facts, Breidewinkel will have no alternative other than to refer the matter to trial by a panel of three judges. The real bummer with this way of proceeding, against which, by the way, the *Maître* has appealed, is that it loads the die against me. Once Breidewinkel decides to ratchet the case up to the next level, that trio of judges might as well be jackals circling carrion. None of your "innocent until proven guilty". And, apparently, the court hearings are certain to be held in closed session. I wasn't sure whether that's a good or a bad thing. But *Maître* Deleuze is convinced that Luritania's lawmakers have been forced into handling the case *sub rosa* to forestall leakage of anything remotely compromising to either Secret Service. His worst-case scenario is one in which the justice system makes me the scapegoat for these Services' sins. All very heartening.'

'What are the chances of *Maître* Deleuze's appeal succeeding?'

'Zero. But it gives us a breathing space. Time to plan how best to circumvent these insane accusations.'

'How much time?'

'Difficult to say. You know what they say about the law's delays. And the longer matters get dragged out, perhaps the better from the point of view of smothering public interest.'

'And all that time you'll be stuck here. Surely that's unconscionable. Your lawyer has to overturn …'

'No,' said Vanessa, anticipating Clara's train of thought. 'The stakes are too high. And like it or not, here on the continent I'm subject to the inquisitorial system. Unlike the adversarial system in common law countries such as England and the United States, where the judge or jury is expected to give a fair hearing to both sides, the inquisitorial system's examining magistrate and judges see the defendant through the state's eyes.'

'I think it's inhuman, keeping you here indefinitely, treating you as a common criminal.'

'Clara, I **have** killed someone.' Thinking back over a defining moment indelibly imprinted on her memory, Vanessa stopped short of owning to satisfaction at having rid the earth of the man she held responsible for Rashid's murder. 'And confinement here is not as bad as you make out. Breidewinkel has had the good grace to see that I will be moved to a cell of my own in the near future. The prison has a respectable library. I've said that if I'm likely to be here for any length of time, I'm willing to help run it the way it should be run, and the hierarchy has given me its blessing. The future book woman of Übelshof is even toying with the idea of encouraging some of the inmates to stage a small play or two. I thought Sartre's *Huis Clos* would do for starters in view of the prison's large francophone contingent.'

Clara clapped her hands to her face in mock disbelief. 'Not what you'd call a barrel of laughs.' Either this abrupt motion on his mistress's part or shared lack of sympathy with Vanessa's choice of theatrical production resulted in a further, this time disapproving, growl from an otherwise dormant Bismarck.

'Well, what would you suggest?'

'Something slightly more cheerful. A piece by Ayckbourn. Plenty of his work has been translated into French.'

'You see. You're coming around to my way of seeing things. I could make life here bearable.'

'For the short term only, Vanessa. How have your employers reacted to your imprisonment?'

'I'm glad to say they're giving me the benefit of the doubt. I conscripted a union arbitrator into pleading my case with the Personnel Department, as a result of which I'll be kept on the payroll until my case is decided. *Maître* Deleuze says that, should it come to the worst, he'll move mountains to secure minimum sentencing together with a recommendation that I not forfeit my career but be reinstated upon release…'

Vanessa broke off, a lump forming in her throat. What had upset her? Certainly not the prospect of being sidelined while others continued to plough their furrow along their chosen career path. No, the bitterest pill of all was the rape of her character, worse than physical defilement because harder to shake off in the minds of Sartre's *autrui*. Not for the first time was she overcome by the numbing thought of being treated as a leper on the grounds of contaminated digital DNA.

'That's good news,' said Clara, not insensitive to her friend's disquiet.

'Yes, but I don't see that washing with my employers. They might swallow a verdict of voluntary manslaughter, but not one, however tenuous, of complicity with terrorists.'

Vanessa darted a look at the overhead television screen behind Clara. A blurring succession of headlines raced across the monitor: *America strains relations with China by ramping up arms sales to Taiwan; Saudi Arabia to behead teenager accused of dissidence; On eve of entry into effect of Ukraine-EU free trade zone, Ukraine's far right threatens to blow up bridge under construction by China between mainland Russia and Crimea; Chelsea fans react angrily to Mourinho sacking; More votes for a horse than for Serena Williams; Star Wars: The Force Awakens fan beats man to death for slighting film …* A pepper spray of news bites, blinding the mind as much as the eyes of those addicted to the instantaneous and accustomed to mistaking packaging for content.

For a moment, Vanessa felt how much happier she would be to inhabit Bismarck's world.

'Enough of my woes, Clara. How are you and that faithful hound of yours?'

'Margaret had the devil's own job persuading the prison staff on the entrance door to relax their rules banning the admission of pets. It took a call to the warden for them to relent.'

'Poor docile old Bismarck. Wouldn't hurt a fly.'

Clara Bogen bent down to pat the German shepherd on the back. 'Mind you, he did get upset when Hoffarth's people came to search through my room.'

Vanessa's preoccupation with her own troubles was brought to a juddering halt with the realisation that her actions had visited fresh misfortune upon a friend ill-equipped to combat stratagems hatched by the Palmers and Kingsmiths of this world. 'When did they do this?'

'Yesterday. Arrived holding a warrant. Turned the place upside down. Impounded my laptop. That's when I had to restrain Bismarck. Then they impounded Margaret's workstation. She was hopping mad. Threatened them with legal action. Asked how they dared hamstring a charitable institution with Grand Prince Philippe Étienne as its patron.'

'And what did they say?'

'That her computer would be returned the next day. The home could survive without its workstation until then.'

'But you say they turned your room upside down?'

471

'And discovered nothing. How could they? You took back what we both know they were looking for.'

If Clara found renewed comfort in caressing her canine companion, it was because she was not about to admit that she had perversely hung on to a copy of Vanessa's texts. Hoffarth's men had not been sufficiently scrupulous to examine the opened box of dog biscuits on the floor beside Clara's fridge. Had they emptied this box of its plastic bag, their efforts would have been rewarded. And now Clara felt shamed at compounding the initial breach of Vanessa's trust by not surrendering her last printed copy of the original. At first, she had thought of using it as material to put her friend's persecutors in the dock. She would address it anonymously to a French embassy still reeling from the indignity of American eavesdropping. But she soon reasoned that such a move could rebound adversely on the Meuniers by virtue of their daughter's association with Vanessa. Her next idea had been to hold the text in reserve for Vanessa's lawyer as a last ditch weapon to confound the enemy – except that there was no guarantee that its contents once decrypted would not backfire on the user. In two minds as to whether to confess as much to Vanessa, Clara clammed up. Matters were not helped by the awareness that what she was masquerading as supportiveness was nothing other than a vendetta against the American embassy.

For her part, Vanessa found it hard to believe that, notwithstanding the lengths to which it had gone to silence her and her friends, the enemy was still running scared. The extent of this paranoia could mean only one thing: certain anonymous individuals, aware that they could no more count on mercy than could that young Saudi, were feverishly pulling out all the stops to deafen the public to everything other than their tune. She began to regret going along with Jay's advice. Instead of destroying every scrap of Musgrave's classified shit, they should have plastered it over the Internet.

'What's the matter, Vanessa?' Deprived of sight did not mean deprived of hearing. Clara was alive to the slightest variations in her friend's breathing.

Vanessa shook her head. 'Didn't someone say that facts don't cease to exist because they are ignored? Perhaps the truth will come out before they write our obituaries.'

※

'Andreotti.'

If anything was calculated to get up Michel Petit's nose, it was the imperious ring to those four syllables yapped at him by the American. Of course, the cultural attaché's cell phone had identified its caller. The Übelshof employee doubted whether Andreotti adopted the same tone on his internal line at the embassy when taking a call from his supremo. Yes, both were newcomers to Luritania, but Andreotti hardly carried the same clout as the lady ambassador.

'A couple more visits for you,' said Petit, deciding, irrespective of pecuniary reward, to make the American wait for what he had to tell him.

'Why are you using my cell phone? I thought we agreed that was for emergencies only.'

Petit gave a self-satisfied grin. 'Your office line was engaged,' he said, pleased to have riled someone used to calling all the shots.

'Well, what have you got for me?'

'Deleuze spent a full hour with his client this morning.'

'Did he? Nothing surprising in that.'

No, thought Petit. Not that, to be honest, he had expected this piece of information to herald untold riches. 'Then there was this blind woman, Miss Bogen, with her guide dog. Came during normal visiting hours.'

'We already know about Bogen. You can count her out.'

Michel Petit swallowed hard. This was not playing the game. 'You never told me that.'

'Well, I'm telling you now.'

'Anyone else of zero interest to you that I should know about. I'd hate to be wasting your time.'

'No one else,' replied Andreotti on whom Petit's sarcasm seemed to be lost, although the Übelshof informer was not to know that the cultural attaché had been distracted by another incoming call.

'Do I still get paid for repeats?' Faced with lack of gratitude, Petit practically ground the question out.

'What's that supposed to mean?'

'If Hobart reappears, you want to know? Or am I wasting my time writing it down?' Not wishing to pander to Andreotti twice in a row, Petit pointedly used the first person singular form of the possessive pronoun.

'No. If he does pop up again, be sure to let me know. The bookshop owner is worth ten yellow ones. For anybody else who's a first-timer, you get the agreed mazuma.'

'The what?'

It had not occurred to Andreotti that this piece of Yiddish slang might be unfamiliar to French ears.

'The needful.'

Silence signalling lack of comprehension, the American came to Petit's rescue. '*Fric – pognon.* Dough.'

Not that this explanation improved the Übelshof's man's mood. To Petit's mind, there were only two reasons why pretrial inmates such as the one in which Andreotti took so much interest – and who looked as if she had turned down bail despite qualifying for and being able to afford it – would not have people queuing up to visit them: either these people thought the person concerned innocent and bound to walk free sooner rather than later; or they believed the contrary and, because of the level of media interest, preferred to keep their distance in order to avoid being tainted with the same brush. In the latter case, which Petit feared to be the more likely, the deal struck with the American was beginning to turn to ashes in his mouth. Unless, of course, Hobart, who, to judge by his build, looked the type to brazen his way past the media, if not to rubbish a camera pushed in his face, came back for more.

But even then, thought the Frenchman, as Andreotti signed off with his ' Stay on the ball, Michel', it looked as if his wife and he would need to sign a *contrat de location-vente* (hire-purchase agreement) before they could hope to lay hands on that Toyota truck.

⁂

Tich decided that itt made no sense to leave the remainder of Isabelle and Craig's bank haul mouldering in the China Reconstruction Bank's branch across the border in northeastern France. He reasoned that neither would have begrudged him his decision, all the more so since he intended to remain true to their wishes and put the lion's share of the funds to good use.

After ordering a sizeable renminbi wire transfer to an account opened with one of the China Reconstruction Bank's Beijing branches, he made three airline bookings: the first with Cathay Pacific to Guangzhou via Frankfurt and Hong Kong; the second with Qantas to Hobart (Australia) via Frankfurt, Singapore and Melbourne; and the third, his sole one-way reservation, with Icelandair to Akureryi (Greenland) via Paris Charles De Gaulle and Reykjavik. A waste of money that wasn't his, Craig's or Isabelle to squander, and an attempt as desperate as it was ill-conceived at throwing sand in his pursuers' eyes. But Tich was in a hurry, and with only one legitimate passport there was little he could do to disguise his moves from hide-and-seek experts. Alive to the amateurishness of these diversionary tactics compared to the means at the disposal of his adversaries, Tich threw himself on fortune's mercy.

After arriving in Guangzhou, he checked into the nearest tourist hotel, spent the night and morning of the next day knocked out in a room with a bed designed to Chinese Procrustean standards and a plunger which Tich was obliged to employ each time he used the washbasin.

Despite the fact that his destination was situated to the southeast, in order to cover his tracks he adopted a variant of the isosceles triangle approach more familiar to him with a Browning in his hands: instead of travelling as the crow flies along the southern base of his Beijing-Guangzhou, Beijing-Shanghai triangle, the day following his arrival in Guangzhou, he boarded the bullet train to Beijing, where this time he booked into a hotel for three nights, did some sightseeing, checked out of his room and then took up his sleeping car reservation on the bullet train back south to Shanghai. More sand throwing courtesy of BLR.

Sitting in front of his laptop on the twenty-second floor of the Jumeirah Himalayas hotel, his end station, Tich was finally beginning to feel something like his old self. A relaxing massage in the hotel's spa had eased out the physical kinks. All that remained was to smooth out the cerebral kinks.

The bitch was knowing where to start. Not that he hadn't been mulling things over before arriving in mainland China. Nor was he lacking in notes, including the belladonna pages removed from *Tristram Shandy* before closing up *Bibliopole*.

After an hour's agonising with nothing to show for repeated deletions of a synopsis thrown together on his Toshiba, Tich stormed out of his chair, walked across to the window and scowled down at the ugly, squat structure of the international expo centre across the way. Faced with the city's nighttime firefly display of residential and industrial lighting, the absence of inner illumination was all the more jarring.

But after a few minutes of standing rooted to the spot immersed in his thoughts and no longer taking in the nightscape beneath his window, Tich suddenly heard Gwyneth's calm, measured voice behind him.

'Come on, boyo, stop dithering. You know this chess board. Every move made by your Sunday Club and most of the moves made by its opponents. So set to it and finish the match off.'

Tich turned to see his beloved Gwyneth standing in front of him in her cream, brown and red Indian cotton dress, the one decorated with elephants decked with howdahs. His first thought was that it made no sense for her to look the picture of health. Then the painful realisation hit home that this miraculous phantom could dissolve at any moment.

'The Gladiator,' she said, reminding him of that time with Craig in the tea house overlooking Schönschlucht's Place de la Libération, where the brass band was practising in the rotunda.

Yearning to reach out and embrace his Gwyn, Tich was held back by the fear that this would snuff out the illusion of her presence. The effort it cost him to summon a reply risked his seeing Gwyneth evaporate before he could get the words out.

'You want me to march to Lloyd George's music, Gwyn, is that it?'

'It would be an improvement on Boy George.'

'Where should I start?'

'Not once upon a time in Luritania. You can do better than that.'

'Well then, where?'

'According to Holy Scripture, *he rested on the seventh day from all his work*. You can't afford to do that, Humphrey. Time is at a premium. Take Sunday as your starting point. That creation which gave you the company you craved. Unlike Him. He didn't need company. He was playing games. Don't play games, Humphrey. No time for games. Horatio would say the same. Get on with it, Bob.'

Humphrey Hobart fancied later that if Gwyn had appeared less substantial, less electrifyingly real, he would never have reached out to her. But he could not resist stepping forward. And she was gone in a flash.

Leaving him shaking from head to foot. How could someone stone cold sober, he asked himself, dream up a vision as seemingly flesh and blood as that – a vision which had spoken to him like the ghost of Hamlet's father? Tottering into the bathroom, he took a damp face cloth, wet it more thoroughly under the cold water tap and clamped it to his forehead.

Time, as Gwyn had said, was at a premium. The fact that she had chosen this moment to appear to him after all these years could mean only one thing: Humphrey was destined to join her in the near future. In which case, yes, he had to get cracking.

Tich made his way slowly back into the bedroom and dropped down into the seat in front of his laptop.

'Gwyn's spot on,' he muttered. 'Forget airport frivolities. This is elbow grease time.'

So it was that, spurred to action by the thought of Gwyneth craning over his shoulder, Humphrey Robert Hobart embarked on his narrative:

Events would have taken a different turn, had Justin not hailed that London minicab. But let's not get ahead of things, because, despite the fashion for shuttling the reader in and out between past, present and future corridors, it makes more sense to begin at the beginning in a corner of north-western Europe familiarly known as Luritania.

They started out as a quartet: three men (Tich – the group's founder and doyen – Justin and Craig) and one woman (Vanessa).

Editor's Note

When Humphrey Hobart entrusted this work to the VanGuard Press, he described it as a blend of fact and fiction known in the trade as faction. Unfortunately, the author's unaccounted for disappearance on the heels of submission of this work leaves more questions unanswered than that of where to draw the line between fact and fiction. One such question occurring to readers might be why, if Humphrey Hobart is alive and well, has he not, at the very least, tried to contact his brother?

Particularly in view of recent events, which call for explanation of the umbilical link between the main and subsidiary texts comprising this novel.

At the beginning of May of this year, a Netherlands sanatorium found itself at the centre of a short-lived media storm after a blog posted on the Internet by one of its inpatients, under the pseudonym *Hornblower*, went viral. This news item unveiled covert plans aimed at reducing sub-Saharan population levels, promoting weapons' sales to terrorist groups and muscling in on the Russian Federation's territorial resources. It gave rise to a flood of tweets, the most catching of which bore the hashtag #burythe1%beforetheyburyyou.

In a BBC *Hard Talk* interview, Frans van Landewijk, the director of the Baalbek *Holistische Welzijn Sanatorium (HWS)*, revealed that the blog's originator was the inmate of one of his psychiatric wards where those under treatment were subject to minimum intrusive observation. While this patient had, for many years since his admission following a serious road accident, suffered from distressing identity and memory disorders, medical staff had noticed marked changes for the better in recent months, albeit of variable duration. Though rare in occurrence, it was not unknown for the right brain activity of victims of cerebral concussion to come to be affected in such a way that new creative faculties came to the fore long after the trauma necessitating isolation from the social mainstream. Van Landewijk explained that creative rehabilitation could take the form of exceptional musical skills or, as in the present case, the 'literary fantasies of a particularly-fertile imagination'.

An event which failed to make the same headlines a month later was the photo opportunity privileging the *Krant van Baalbek* with its scoop about the surprise visit paid to van Landewijk from The Hague by the American Ambassador to the Kingdom of the Netherlands for the express purpose of presenting a handsome cheque towards investment in leading-edge HWS mental care facilities catering specifically for OSCE civilian and NATO military personnel.

However, in the week following the televised interview, after first approaching the sanatorium by phone, I had a video chat with its director about what, for want of a better description, I took to be Humphrey Hobart's literary legacy. Frans van Landewijk was open to my suggestion that we send our chief investigative reporter across from Singapore to apprise Horatio Hobart of the publication commissioned from us by his brother. As to my further proposal that our fact finder discuss with Horatio points of possible interest to Humphrey's readers in the context of the brothers' relationship and the genesis of the proposed novel, van Landewijk was more circumspect. He made his agreement conditional upon having any such discussion handled with due tact and discretion in his presence.

It helped matters that our representative was a charming, thirty-five-year-old female journalist adept at handling the more delicate interviews with compassion. The day after my video chat with van Landewijk, she flew out from Shanghai to visit the HWS sanatorium near the Netherlands' border with Luritania.

Unfortunately, Horatio Hobart did not appear to be enjoying one of his better days, and our reporter gleaned little information of use for present purposes concerning the brothers' history or their literary ties. There was, I am sorry to say, nothing to indicate that the sanatorium had set up a Skype account for Horatio or that Humphrey had been in touch with his younger brother prior to his departure from Luritania.

But after this conversation of sorts with Horatio Hobart came to an end, and the director left the room to allow our representative to pay her farewells, delving beneath his bedside table, Horatio swiftly freed an envelope taped to the underside of the bottom drawer and thrust this, with a cautioning gesture, into the hands of our reporter, who packed this away with her notes. Horatio's parting words to our journalist, 'Nectar for Bob. Bob *necatur*', combined with an expression that had changed from vacant to woeful, gave to believe that the younger brother sensed that his sibling had been murdered.

Readers will now understand the origin of the italicised paragraphs in this novel recording a series of classified memos between J and K which the editorial team at VanGuard Press decided would, together with the full text of the decrypted binary code document, make fitting adjuncts to Humphrey Hobart's manuscript. Though readers may quibble about the arbitrary distribution of the italicised entries, we thought it appropriate to keep them in the same order as that in which they were presented to us by Horatio.

Those of you inclined to look down your nose at J and K's *Boys' Own* use of country and personality code names would do well to remember that this is common practice in military and clandestine planning circles. As it happens, many of the cryptonyms are transparent.

Finally, VanGuard Press firmly rejects the accusations of unethical behaviour levelled against it by HWS's management. The document entrusted to our reporter was handed over to her entirely of Horatio Hobart's free will. Moreover, in response to Frans van Landewijk's assertion that it was the product of a hyperactive imagination, I would suggest that it is inconceivable that Humphrey could have mentioned this or any other element of the present novel to his brother before its seeds had germinated in Vanessa Curtis's, Justin Hendry's or his own mind.

David Waterford
Editor-in-Chief
VanGuard Press
118a Yongshou Road
Shanghai

Afterword

VanGuard Press deeply regrets the part unwittingly played by it in the assassination announced today of Philippe Farid Jabour, the renowned French surgeon.

Jabour was held in considerable esteem *by Médecins Sans Frontières* (MSF) for the willingness with which, whenever the Salpêtrière-la-Neuve's demands so permitted, he responded to *MSF's* calls for his aid in war or natural disaster zones. Following release of this appalling news, MSF has been unstinting in its praise of Jabour's 'tireless and selfless dedication to the saving of battlefront lives both civilian and military'.

According to the statement issued by Agence France-Presse (AFP) a matter of hours before the first edition of *The Milan Briefcase* was due to go to press, a hooded individual, caught on camera, stepped up behind the surgeon as he was entering the lift to his Paris apartment in the rue de Rivoli around seven o'clock this morning, fired two bullets into the back of his head and dashed out of the apartment building onto the pillion of a waiting motorcycle. In a phone call made to AFP ten minutes later, a man claiming to be a jihadist took responsibility for the murder in the name of Islamic State, saying that it was 'the judgment of Allah enforced by one of his humble servants, and a lesson to all MSF surgeons withholding field hospital succour from IS combatants, victims of the USA's, Russia's and their infidel allies' air strikes against Syria'.

Contacted by AFP, MSF strongly denied that its field surgeons engaged in any form of discrimination in the treatment of war-wounded, whether civilians, serving soldiers or members of armed militias.

In the wake of Jabour's assassination, MSF immediately called upon the authorities worldwide to provide its volunteer workforce with robust protection against similar despicable acts.

Much as VanGuard Press bitterly regrets the taking of Philippe Farid Jabour's life, it cannot accept responsibility for every deranged act committed with reference to its publications. Nor does it understand, despite ongoing internal investigations, what might have motivated any of its employees or proofreaders to leak *The Milan Briefcase* in whole or in part prior to publication. We extend our heartfelt sympathy to the surgeon's surviving wife and daughter for the loss of a devoted husband and father, whom his peers knew to be the personification of selflessness.

David Waterford
Editor-in-Chief
VanGuard Press

Author's Postscript

Readers should note that a number of events in this faction novel have been conflated or reordered. They include two which must have been brought to the notice of Humphrey Hobart last autumn during his stay in China Leaving aside Humphrey's camouflage and invention, the bedrock of this tale constitutes an alarming commentary on the times we are living through.

However, just as in life we are faced with many loose ends, so with *The Milan Briefcase*. Its unfinished nature means that we can only guess as to the shattering effect of the airstrike against MSF's Kunduz trauma centre on the lives of Charlotte and Jean-Luc Meunier. The novel also leaves us in the dark as to whether Maître Deleuze's plea for leniency in the case of Vanessa Curtis was successful or whether she was found guilty of complicity in terrorism and sentenced correspondingly. Might Clara Bogen have finally interceded on her behalf? And did Humphrey and Clara exchange e-mails after he left for China? We shall never know. Similarly shrouded in mystery is the ultimate apportionment or fate of the stolen BLR euros converted by Humphrey into yuan. And, last but not least, a question mark hangs over the fate of the man who initialled this work HRH.

If my own contributions to *The Milan Briefcase* are few in number and limited in volume, this is largely because I was won over by Humphrey Hobart's text. But, as sponsor of this work, I accept responsibility for all errors and omissions.

Much as I regret never having met Humphrey, I feel that, despite his avowed intention of taking a back seat in relating this story, *The Milan Briefcase* provides us with no small insight into the character of the man known to his friends as Tich.

Graham Fulbright

November 2016